THE DEADLY SUNRISE

What was that? A brilliant flash of light, infinitely brighter than any of the stars, had suddenly exploded overhead. Miles above him, a huge mirror was sailing across the sky, reflecting the sunlight as it slowly turned through space. Such a thing was utterly impossible; he was beginning to suffer from hallucinations, and it was time he took his leave. Already the sweat was pouring from his body, and in a few seconds the capsule would be a furnace.

He waited no longer, but pulled on the Emergency Release with all his waning strength, bracing himself at the same moment to face the end.

Nothing happened; the lever would not move. He tugged it again and again before he realized it was hopelessly jammed. There was no easy way out for him, no merciful death as the air gushed from his lungs.

It was then—as the true terror of the situation struck home to him—that his nerve finally broke and Sherrard began to scream like a trapped animal. . . .

Books by Arthur C. Clarke

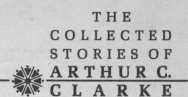

THE
COLLECTED
STORIES OF
ARTHUR C.
CLARKE

MORE
THAN
ONE
UNIVERSE

SPECTRA™

BANTAM BOOKS
NEW YORK • TORONTO • LONDON • SYDNEY • AUCKLAND

This edition contains the complete text
of the original hardcover edition.
Not one word has been omitted.

MORE THAN ONE UNIVERSE

A Bantam Spectra Book / published by arrangement
with Harcourt Brace Jovanovich

PRINTING HISTORY

Harcourt Brace Jovanovich edition of *Tales of Ten Worlds* published April 1973
Harcourt Brace Jovanovich edition of *The Other Side of the Sky* published
November 1959
Harcourt Brace Jovanovich edition of *The Nine Billion Names of God* published
June 1974
Harcourt Brace Jovanovich edition of *The Wind from the Sun* published July 1973

Bantam edition / September 1991

Pages v and vi constitute an extension of the copyright page.

THE NINE BILLION NAMES OF GOD

CONTENTS

viii

MORE THAN
ONE UNIVERSE

I REMEMBER
BABYLON

MY NAME IS Arthur C. Clarke, and I wish I had no connection with this whole sordid business. But as the moral—repeat, moral—integrity of the United States is involved, I must first establish my credentials. Only thus will you understand how, with the aid of the late Dr. Alfred Kinsey, I have unwittingly triggered an avalanche that may sweep away much of Western civilization.

Back in 1945, while a radar officer in the Royal Air Force, I had the only original idea of my life. Twelve years before the first Sputnik started beeping, it occurred to me that an artificial satellite would be a wonderful place for a television transmitter, since a station several thousand miles high could broadcast to half the globe. I wrote up the idea the week after Hiroshima, proposing a network of relay satellites twenty-two thousand miles above the Equator; at this height, they'd take exactly one day to complete a revolution, and so would remain fixed over the same spot on the Earth.

The piece appeared in the October 1945 issue of *Wireless*

World; not expecting that celestial mechanics would be commercialized in my lifetime, I made no attempt to patent the idea, and doubt if I could have done so anyway. (If I'm wrong, I'd prefer not to know.) But I kept plugging it in my books, and today the idea of communications satellites is so commonplace that no one knows its origin.

I did make a plaintive attempt to put the record straight when approached by the House of Representatives Committee on Astronautics and Space Exploration; you'll find my evidence on page thirty-two of its report, *The Next Ten Years in Space.* And as you'll see in a moment, my concluding words had an irony I never appreciated at the time: "Living as I do in the Far East, I am constantly reminded of the struggle between the Western World and the USSR for the uncommitted millions of Asia . . . When line-of-sight TV transmissions become possible from satellites directly overhead, the propaganda effect may be decisive. . . ."

I still stand by those words, but there were angles I hadn't thought of—and which, unfortunately, other people have.

It all began during one of those official receptions which are such a feature of social life in Eastern capitals. They're even more common in the West, of course, but in Colombo there's little competing entertainment. At least once a week, if you are anybody, you get an invitation to cocktails at an embassy or legation, the British Council, the U.S. Operations Mission, L'Alliance Française, or one of the countless alphabetical agencies the United Nations has begotten.

At first, being more at hóme beneath the Indian Ocean than in diplomatic circles, my partner and I were nobodies and were left alone. But after Mike *compéred* Dave Brubeck's tour of Ceylon, people started to take notice of us—still more so when he married one of the island's best-known beauties. So now our consumption of cocktails and canapés is limited chiefly by reluctance to abandon our comfortable sarongs for such Western absurdities as trousers, dinner jackets, and ties.

It was the first time we'd been to the Soviet Embassy, which was throwing a party for a group of Russian oceanographers who'd just come into port. Beneath the inevitable paintings of Lenin and Marx, a couple of hundred guests of all colors, religions, and languages were milling around, chatting with friends, or single-mindedly demolishing the vodka and caviar. I'd been separated from Mike and Elizabeth, but could see them at the other side of the room. Mike was doing his "There was I at fifty fathoms" act to a fascinated audience, while Elizabeth watched him quizzically—and rather more people watched Elizabeth.

Ever since I lost an eardrum while pearl-diving on the Great Barrier Reef, I've been at a considerable disadvantage at functions of this kind; the surface noise is about twelve decibels too much for me to cope with. And this is no small handicap when being introduced to people with names like Dharmasiriwardene, Tissaveerasinghe, Goonetilleke, and Jayawickrema. When I'm not raiding the buffet, therefore, I usually look for a pool of relative quiet where there's a chance of following more than fifty per cent of any conversation in which I may get involved. I was standing in the acoustic shadow of a large ornamental pillar, surveying the scene in my detached or Somerset Maugham manner, when I noticed that someone was looking at me with that "Haven't we met before?" expression.

I'll describe him with some care, because there must be many people who can identify him. He was in his mid-thirties, and I guessed he was American; he had that well-scrubbed, crew-cut, man-about-Rockefeller-Center look that used to be a hallmark until the younger Russian diplomats and technical advisers started imitating it so successfully. He was about six feet in height, with shrewd brown eyes and black hair, prematurely gray at the sides. Though I was fairly certain we'd never met before, his face reminded me of someone. It took me a couple of days to work it out: remember the late John Garfield? That's who it was, as near as makes no difference.

When a stranger catches my eye at a party, my standard operating procedure goes into action automatically. If he seems a pleasant-enough person but I don't feel like introductions at the moment, I give him the Neutral Scan, letting my eyes sweep past him without a flicker of recognition, yet without positive unfriendliness. If he looks like a creep, he receives the *Coup d'oeil,* which consists of a long, disbelieving stare followed by an unhurried view of the back of my neck. In extreme cases, an expression of revulsion may be switched on for a few milliseconds. The message usually gets across.

But this character seemed interesting, and I was getting bored, so I gave him the Affable Nod. A few minutes later he drifted through the crowd, and I aimed my good ear toward him.

"Hello," he said (yes, he *was* American), "my name's Gene Hartford. I'm sure we've met somewhere."

"Quite likely," I answered, "I've spent a good deal of time in the States. I'm Arthur Clarke."

Usually that produces a blank stare, but sometimes it doesn't. I could almost see the IBM cards flickering behind those hard brown eyes, and was flattered by the brevity of his access time.

"The science writer?"

"Correct."

"Well, this is fantastic." He seemed genuinely astonished. *"Now* I know where I've seen you. I was in the studio once when you were on the Dave Garroway show."

(This lead may be worth following up, though I doubt it; and I'm sure that "Gene Hartford" was phony—it was too smoothly synthetic.)

"So you're in TV?" I said. "What are you doing here—collecting material, or just on vacation?"

He gave me the frank, friendly smile of a man who has plenty to hide.

"Oh, I'm keeping my eyes open. But this really is amazing; I read your *Exploration of Space* when it came out back in, ah—"

"Nineteen fifty-two; the Book-of-the-Month Club's never been quite the same since."

All this time I had been sizing him up, and though there was something about him I didn't like, I was unable to pin it down. In any case, I was prepared to make substantial allowances for someone who had read my books and was also in TV; Mike and I are always on the lookout for markets for our underwater movies. But that, to put it mildly, was not Hartford's line of business.

"Look," he said eagerly, "I've a big network deal cooking that will interest you—in fact, *you* helped to give me the idea."

This sounded promising, and my coefficient of cupidity jumped several points.

"I'm glad to hear it. What's the general theme?"

"I can't talk about it here, but could we meet at my hotel, around three tomorrow?"

"Let me check my diary; yes, that's O.K."

There are only two hotels in Colombo patronized by Americans, and I guessed right the first time. He was at the Mount Lavinia, and though you may not know it, you've seen the place where we had our private chat. Around the middle of *Bridge on the River Kwai*, there's a brief scene at a military hospital, where Jack Hawkins meets a nurse and asks her where he can find Bill Holden. We have a soft spot for this episode, because Mike was one of the convalescent naval officers in the background. If you look smartly you'll see him on the extreme right, beard in full profile, signing Sam Spiegel's name to his sixth round of bar chits. As the picture turned out, Sam could afford it.

It was here, on this diminutive plateau high above the miles of palm-fringed beach, that Gene Hartford started to unload—and my simple hopes of financial advantage started to evaporate. What his exact motives were, if indeed he knew them himself, I'm still uncertain. Surprise at meeting me, and a twisted feeling of gratitude (which I would gladly have done without) undoubtedly played a part, and for all his air of confidence he must have been a bitter, lonely man who desperately needed approval and friendship.

He got neither from me. I have always had a sneaking sympathy for Benedict Arnold, as must anyone who knows the full facts of the case. But Arnold merely betrayed his country; no one before Hartford ever tried to seduce it.

What dissolved my dream of dollars was the news that Hartford's connection with American TV had been severed, somewhat violently, in the early fifties. It was clear that he'd been bounced out of Madison Avenue for Party-lining, and it was equally clear that his was one case where no grave injustice had been done. Though he talked with a certain controlled fury of his fight against asinine censorship, and wept for a brilliant—but unnamed—cultural series he'd started before being kicked off the air, by this time I was beginning to smell so many rats that my replies were distinctly guarded. Yet as my pecuniary interest in Mr. Hartford diminished, so my personal curiosity increased. Who *was* behind him? Surely not the BBC . . .

He got round to it at last, when he'd worked the self-pity out of his system.

"I've some news that will make you sit up," he said smugly. "The American networks are soon going to have some real competition. And it will be done just the way you predicted; the people who sent a TV transmitter to the Moon can put a much bigger one in orbit round the Earth."

"Good for them," I said cautiously. "I'm all in favor of healthy competition. When's the launching date?"

"Any moment now. The first transmitter will be parked due south of New Orleans—on the equator, of course. That puts it way out in the open Pacific; it won't be over anyone's territory, so there'll be no political complications on that score. Yet it will be sitting up there in the sky in full view of everybody from Seattle to Key West. Think of it—the only TV station the whole United States can tune in to! Yes, even Hawaii! There won't be any way of jamming it; for the first time, there'll be a clear channel into every American home. And J. Edgar's Boy Scouts can't do a thing to block it."

So that's your little racket, I thought; at least you're being frank. Long ago I learned not to argue with Marxists and Flat-Earthers, but if Hartford was telling the truth, I wanted to pump him for all he was worth.

"Before you get too enthusiastic," I said, "there are a few points you may have overlooked."

"Such as?"

"This will work both ways. Everyone knows that the Air Force, NASA, Bell Labs, I. T. & T., Hughes, and a few dozen other agencies are working on the same project. Whatever Russia does to the States in the propaganda line, she'll get back with compound interest."

Hartford grinned mirthlessly.

"Really, Clarke!" he said. (I was glad he hadn't first-named me.) "I'm a little disappointed. Surely you know that the United States is years behind in payload capacity! And do you imagine that the old T.3 is Russia's last word?"

It was at this moment that I began to take him very seriously. He was perfectly right. The T.3 could inject at least five times the payload of any American missile into that critical twenty-two-thousand-mile orbit—the only one that would allow a satellite to remain fixed above the Earth. And by the time the U.S. could match that performance, heaven knows where the Russians would be. Yes, heaven certainly *would* know. . . .

"All right," I conceded. "But why should fifty million American homes start switching channels just as soon as they can tune in to Moscow? I admire the Russians, but their entertainment is worse than their politics. After the Bolshoi, what have you? And for me, a little ballet goes a long, long way."

Once again I was treated to that peculiarly humorless smile. Hartford had been saving up his Sunday punch, and now he let me have it.

"You were the one who brought in the Russians," he said. "They're involved, sure—but only as contractors. The independent agency I'm working for is hiring their services."

"That," I remarked dryly, "must be some agency."

"It is; just about the biggest. Even though the United States tries to pretend it doesn't exist."

"Oh," I said, rather stupidly. "So *that's* your sponsor."

I'd heard those rumors that the USSR was going to launch satellites for the Chinese; now it began to look as if the rumors fell far short of the truth. But how far short, I'd still no conception.

"You are so right," continued Hartford, obviously enjoying himself, "about Russian entertainment. After the initial novelty, the Nielson rating would drop to zero. But not with the program *I'm* planning. My job is to find material that will put everyone else out of business when it goes on the air. You think it can't be done? Finish that drink and come up to my room. I've a highbrow movie about ecclesiastical art that I'd like to show you."

Well, he wasn't crazy, though for a few minutes I wondered. I could think of few titles more carefully calculated to make the viewer reach for the channel switch than the one that flashed on the screen: ASPECTS OF THIRTEENTH-CENTURY TANTRIC SCULPTURE.

"Don't be alarmed," Hartford chuckled, above the whirr of the projector. "That title saves me having trouble with inquisitive Customs inspectors. It's perfectly accurate, but we'll change it to something with a bigger box-office appeal when the time comes."

A couple of hundred feet later, after some innocuous architectural long shots, I saw what he meant.

You may know that there are certain temples in India covered with superbly executed carvings of a kind that we in the West scarcely associate with religion. To say that they are frank is a laughable understatement; they leave nothing to the imagination—*any* imagination. Yet at the same time they are genuine works of art. And so was Hartford's movie.

It had been shot, in case you're interested, at the Temple of the Sun, Konarak. I've since looked it up; it's on the Orissa coast, about twenty-five miles northeast of Puri. The reference books are pretty mealymouthed; some apologize for the "obvious" impossibility of providing illustrations, but Percy Brown's *Indian Architecture* minces no words. The carvings, it says primly, are of "a shamelessly erotic character that have no parallel in any known building." A sweeping claim, but I can believe it after seeing that movie.

Camera work and editing were brilliant, the ancient stones coming to life beneath the roving lens. There were breath-taking time-lapse shots as the rising sun chased the shadows from bodies intertwined in ecstasy; sudden startling close-ups of scenes which at first the mind refused to recognize; soft-focus studies of stone shaped by a master's hand in all the fantasies and aberrations of love; restless zooms and pans whose meaning eluded the eye until they froze into patterns of timeless desire, eternal fulfillment. The music—mostly percussion, with a thin, high thread of sound from some stringed instrument that I could not identify—perfectly fitted the tempo of the cutting. At one moment it would be languorously slow, like the opening bars of Debussy's "L'Après-midi"; then the drums would swiftly work themselves up to a frenzied, almost unendurable climax. The art of the ancient sculptors and the skill of the modern cameraman had combined across the centuries to create a poem of rapture, an orgasm of celluloid which I would defy any man to watch unmoved.

There was a long silence when the screen flooded with light and the lascivious music ebbed into exhaustion.

"My God!" I said, when I had recovered some of my composure. "Are you going to telecast *that*?"

Hartford laughed.

"Believe me," he answered, "that's nothing; it just happens to be the only reel I can carry around safely. We're prepared to defend it any day on grounds of genuine art, historic interest, religious tolerance—oh, we've thought of all the angles. But it doesn't really matter; no one can stop us. For the first time in history, any form of censorship's become utterly impossible. There's simply no way of enforcing it; the customer can get what he wants, right in his own home. Lock the door, switch on the TV set—friends and family will never know."

"Very clever," I said, "but don't you think such a diet will soon pall?"

"Of course; variety is the spice of life. We'll have plenty of conventional entertainment; let *me* worry about that. And every so often we'll have information programs—I hate that word 'propaganda'—to tell the cloistered American public what's really happening in the world. Our special features will just be the bait."

"Mind if I have some fresh air?" I said. "It's getting stuffy in here."

Hartford drew the curtains and let daylight back into the room. Below us lay that long curve of beach, with the outrigger fishing boats drawn up beneath the palms, and the little waves falling in foam at the end of their weary march from Africa. One of the loveliest sights in the world, but I couldn't focus on it now. I was still seeing those writhing stone limbs, those faces frozen with passions which the centuries could not slake.

That lickerish voice continued behind my back.

"You'd be astonished if you knew just how much material there is. Remember, we've absolutely no taboos. If you can film it, we can telecast it."

He walked over to his bureau and picked up a heavy, dog-eared volume.

"This has been my Bible," he said, "or my Sears, Roebuck, if you prefer. Without it, I'd never have sold the series to my sponsors. They're great believers in science, and they swallowed the whole thing, down to the last decimal point. Recognize it?"

I nodded; whenever I enter a room, I always monitor my host's literary tastes.

"Dr. Kinsey, I presume."

"I guess I'm the only man who's read it from cover to cover, and not just looked up his own vital statistics. You see, it's the only piece of market research in its field. Until something better comes along, we're making the most of it. It tells us what the customer wants, and we're going to supply it."

"*All* of it?"

"If the audience is big enough, yes. We won't bother about feeble-minded farm boys who get too attached to the stock. But the four main sexes will get the full treatment. That's the beauty of the movie you just saw—it appeals to them all."

"You can say that again," I muttered.

"We've had a lot of fun planning the feature I've christened 'Queer Corner.' Don't laugh—no go-ahead agency can afford to ignore *that* audience. At least ten million, if you count the ladies—bless their clogs and tweeds. If you think I'm exaggerating, look at all the male art mags on the newsstands. It was no trick, blackmailing some of the daintier musclemen to perform for us."

He saw that I was beginning to get bored; there are some kinds of single-mindedness that I find depressing. But I had done Hartford an injustice, as he hastened to prove.

"Please don't think," he said anxiously, "that sex is our only weapon. Sensation is almost as good. Ever see the job Ed Murrow did on the late sainted Joe McCarthy? That was milk and water compared with the profiles we're planning in 'Washington Confidential.'

"And there's our 'Can You Take It?' series, designed to separate the men from the milksops. We'll issue so many advance warnings that every red-blooded American will feel he has to watch the show. It will start innocently enough, on ground nicely prepared by Hemingway. You'll see some bull-fighting sequences that will really lift you out of your seat—or send you running to the bathroom—because they show all the little details you never get in those cleaned-up Hollywood movies.

"We'll follow that with some really unique material that cost us exactly nothing. Do you remember the photographic evidence the Nuremburg war trials turned up? You've never seen it, because it wasn't publishable. There were quite a few amateur photographers in the concentration camps, who made the most of opportunities they'd never get again. Some of them were hanged on the testimony of their own cameras, but their work wasn't wasted. It will lead nicely into our series 'Torture Through the Ages'—very scholarly and thorough, yet with a remarkably wide appeal. . . .

"And there are dozens of other angles, but by now you'll have the general picture. The Avenue thinks it knows all about Hidden Persuasion—believe me, it doesn't. The world's best *practical* psychologists are in the East these days. Remember Korea, and brainwashing? We've learned a lot since then. There's no need for violence any more; people enjoy being brainwashed, if you set about it the right way."

"And you," I said, "are going to brainwash the United States. Quite an order."

"Exactly—and the country will love it, despite all the screams from Congress and the churches. Not to mention the networks, of course. They'll make the biggest fuss of all, when they find they can't compete with us."

Hartford glanced at his watch, and gave a whistle of alarm.

"Time to start packing," he said, "I've got to be at that unpronounceable airport of yours by six. There's no chance, I suppose, that you can fly over to Macao and see us sometime?"

"Not a hope; but I've got a pretty good idea of the picture now. And incidentally, aren't you afraid that I'll spill the beans?"

"Why should I be? The more publicity you can give us, the better. Although our advertising campaign doesn't go into top gear for a few months yet, I feel you've earned this advance notice. As I said, your books helped to give me the idea."

His gratitude was quite genuine, by God; it left me completely speechless.

"Nothing can stop us," he declared—and for the first time the fanaticism that lurked behind that smooth, cynical façade was not altogether under control. "History is on our side. We'll be using America's own decadence as a weapon against her, and it's a weapon for which there's no defense. The Air Force won't attempt space piracy by shooting down a satellite nowhere near American territory. The FCC can't even protest to a country that doesn't exist in the eyes of the State Department. If you've any other suggestions, I'd be most interested to hear them."

I had none then, and I have none now. Perhaps these words may give some brief warning before the first teasing advertisements appear in the trade papers, and may start stirrings of elephantine alarm among the networks. But will it make any difference? Hartford did not think so, and he may be right.

"History is on our side." I cannot get those words out of my head. Land of Lincoln and Franklin and Melville, I love you and I wish you well. But into my heart blows a cold wind from the past; for I remember Babylon.

SUMMERTIME ON ICARUS

WHEN COLIN SHERRARD opened his eyes after the crash, he could not imagine where he was. He seemed to be lying, trapped in some kind of vehicle, on the summit of a rounded hill, which sloped steeply away in all directions. Its surface was seared and blackened, as if a great fire had swept over it. Above him was a jet-black sky, crowded with stars; one of them hung like a tiny, brilliant sun low down on the horizon.

Could it be the sun? Was he so far from Earth? No—that was impossible. Some nagging memory told him that the sun was very close—hideously close—not so distant that it had shrunk to a star. And with that thought, full consciousness returned. Sherrard knew exactly where he was, and the knowledge was so terrible that he almost fainted again.

He was nearer to the sun than any man had ever been. His damaged space-pod was lying on no hill, but on the steeply curving surface of a world only two miles in diameter. That brilliant star sinking swiftly in the west was the light of *Prometheus*, the ship that had brought him here across so many millions of miles of space. She was hanging up there among the stars, wondering why his pod had not returned like a homing pigeon to its roost. In a few minutes she would have passed from sight, dropping below the horizon in her perpetual game of hide-and-seek with the sun.

That was a game that he had lost. He was still on the night side of the asteroid, in the cool safety of its shadow, but the short night would be ending soon. The four-hour day of Icarus was spinning him swiftly toward that dreaded dawn, when a sun thirty times larger than ever shone upon Earth would blast these rocks with fire. Sherrard knew all too well why everything around him was burned and blackened. Icarus was still a week from perihelion but the temperature at noon had already reached a thousand degrees Fahrenheit.

Though this was no time for humor, he suddenly remembered Captain McClellan's description of Icarus: "The hottest piece of real estate in the solar system." The truth of that jest had been proved, only a few days before, by one of those simple and unscientific experiments that are so much more impressive than any number of graphs and instrument readings.

Just before daybreak, someone had propped a piece of wood on the summit of one of the tiny hills. Sherrard had been watching, from the safety of the night side, when the first rays of the rising sun had touched the hilltop. When his eyes had adjusted to the sudden detonation of light, he saw that the wood was already beginning to blacken and char. Had there been an atmosphere here, the stick would have burst into flames; such was dawn, upon Icarus. . . .

Yet it had not been impossibly hot at the time of their first landing, when they were passing the orbit of Venus five weeks ago. *Prometheus* had overtaken the asteroid as it was beginning its plunge toward the sun, had matched speed with the little world and had touched down upon its surface as lightly as a snowflake. (A snowflake on Icarus—*that* was quite a thought. . . .) Then the scientists had fanned out across the fifteen square miles of jagged nickle-iron that covered most of the asteroid's surface, setting up their instruments and check-points, collecting samples and making endless observations.

Everything had been carefully planned, years in advance,

as part of the International Astrophysical Decade. Here was a unique opportunity for a research ship to get within a mere seventeen million miles of the sun, protected from its fury by a two-mile-thick shield of rock and iron. In the shadow of Icarus, the ship could ride safely round the central fire which warmed all the planets, and upon which the existence of all life depended. As the Prometheus of legend had brought the gift of fire to mankind, so the ship that bore his name would return to Earth with other unimagined secrets from the heavens.

There had been plenty of time to set up the instruments and make the surveys before *Prometheus* had to take off and seek the permanent shade of night. Even then, it was still possible for men in the tiny self-propelled space-pods—miniature spaceships, only ten feet long—to work on the night side for an hour or so, as long as they were not overtaken by the advancing line of sunrise. That had seemed a simple-enough condition to meet, on a world where dawn marched forward at only a mile an hour; but Sherrard had failed to meet it, and the penalty was death.

He was still not quite sure what had happened. He had been replacing a seismograph transmitter at Station 145, unofficially known as Mount Everest because it was a full ninety feet above the surrounding territory. The job had been a perfectly straightforward one, even though he had to do it by remote control through the mechanical arms of his pod. Sherrard was an expert at manipulating these; he could tie knots with his metal fingers almost as quickly as with his flesh-and-bone ones. The task had taken little more than twenty minutes, and then the radioseismograph was on the air again, monitoring the tiny quakes and shudders that racked Icarus in ever-increasing numbers as the asteroid approached the sun. It was small satisfaction to know that he had now made a king-sized addition to the record.

After he had checked the signals, he had carefully replaced the sun screens around the instrument. It was hard to believe that two flimsy sheets of polished metal foil, no thicker than paper, could turn aside a flood of radiation that would melt lead or tin within seconds. But the first screen reflected more than ninety per cent of the sunlight falling upon its mirror surface and the second turned back most of the rest, so that only a harmless fraction of the heat passed through.

He had reported completion of the job, received an acknowledgment from the ship, and prepared to head for home. The brilliant floodlights hanging from *Prometheus*—without which the night side of the asteroid would have been in utter darkness—had been an unmistakable target in the sky. The ship was only two miles up, and in this feeble gravity he could have jumped that distance had he been wearing a planetary-type space suit with flexible legs. As it was, the low-powered micro-rockets of his pod would get him there in a leisurely five minutes.

He had aimed the pod with its gyros, set the rear jets at Strength Two, and pressed the firing button. There had been a violent explosion somewhere in the vicinity of his feet and he had soared away from Icarus—but not toward the ship. Something was horribly wrong; he was tossed to one side of the vehicle, unable to reach the controls. Only one of the jets was firing, and he was pinwheeling across the sky, spinning faster and faster under the off-balanced drive. He tried to find the cutoff, but the spin had completely disorientated him. When he was able to locate the controls, his first reaction made matters worse—he pushed the throttle over to full, like a nervous driver stepping on the accelerator instead of the brake. It took only a second to correct the mistake and kill the jet, but by then he was spinning so rapidly that the stars were wheeling round in circles.

Everything had happened so quickly that there was no time for fear, no time even to call the ship and report what was happening. He took his hands away from the controls; to touch them now would only make matters worse. It would take two or three minutes of cautious jockeying to unravel his spin, and from the flickering glimpses of the approaching rocks it was obvious that he did not have as many seconds. Sherrard remembered a piece of advice at the front of the *Spaceman's Manual* "When you don't know what to do, *do nothing.*" He was still doing it when Icarus fell upon him, and the stars went out.

It had been a miracle that the pod was unbroken, and that he was not breathing space. (Thirty minutes from now he might be glad to do so, when the capsule's heat insulation began to fail. . . .) There had been some damage, of course.

The rear-view mirrors, just outside the dome of transparent plastic that enclosed his head, were both snapped off, so that he could no longer see what lay behind him without twisting his neck. This was a trivial mishap; far more serious was the fact that his radio antennas had been torn away by the impact. He could not call the ship, and the ship could not call him. All that came over the radio was a faint crackling, probably produced inside the set itself. He was absolutely alone, cut off from the rest of the human race.

It was a desperate situation, but there was one faint ray of hope. He was not, after all, completely helpless. Even if he could not use the pod's rockets—he guessed that the starboard motor had blown back and ruptured a fuel line, something the designers said was impossible—he was still able to move. He had his arms.

But which way should he crawl? He had lost all sense of location, for though he had taken off from Mount Everest, he might now be thousands of feet away from it. There were no recognizable landmarks in his tiny world; the rapidly sinking star of *Prometheus* was his best guide, and if he could keep the ship in view he would be safe. It would only be a matter of minutes before his absence was noted, if indeed it had not been discovered already. Yet without radio, it might take his colleagues a long time to find him; small though Icarus was, its fifteen square miles of fantastically rugged no man's land could provide an effective hiding place for a ten-foot cylinder. It might take an hour to locate him —which meant that he would have to keep ahead of the murderous sunrise.

He slipped his fingers into the controls that worked his mechanical limbs. Outside the pod, in the hostile vacuum that surrounded him, his substitute arms came to life. They reached down, thrust against the iron surface of the asteroid, and levered the pod from the ground. Sherrard flexed them, and the capsule jerked forward, like some weird, two-legged insect . . . first the right arm, then the left, then the right. . . .

It was less difficult than he had feared, and for the first time he felt his confidence return. Though his mechanical arms had been designed for light precision work, it needed very little pull to set the capsule moving in this weightless environment. The gravity of Icarus was ten thousand times weaker than Earth's: Sherrard and his space-pod weighed less than an ounce here, and once he had set himself in motion he floated forward with an effortless, dreamlike ease.

Yet that very effortlessness had its dangers. He had traveled several hundred yards, and was rapidly overhauling the sinking star of the *Prometheus,* when overconfidence betrayed him. (Strange how quickly the mind could switch from one extreme to the other; a few minutes ago he had been steeling himself to face death—now he was wondering if he would be late for dinner.) Perhaps the novelty of the movement, so unlike anything he had ever attempted before, was responsible for the catastrophe; or perhaps he was still suffering from the after-effects of the crash.

Like all astronauts, Sherrard had learned to orientate himself in space, and had grown accustomed to living and working when the Earthly conceptions of up and down were meaningless. On a world such as Icarus, it was necessary to pretend that there was a real, honest-to-goodness planet "beneath" your feet, and that when you moved you were traveling over a horizontal plain. If this innocent self-deception failed, you were heading for space vertigo.

The attack came without warning, as it usually did. Quite suddenly, Icarus no longer seemed to be beneath him, the stars no longer above. The universe tilted through a right angle; he was moving straight *up* a vertical cliff, like a mountaineer scaling a rock face, and though Sherrard's reason told him that this was pure illusion, all his senses screamed that it was true. In a moment gravity must drag him off this sheer wall, and he would drop down mile upon endless mile until he smashed into oblivion.

Worse was to come; the false vertical was still swinging like a compass needle that had lost the pole. Now he was on the *underside* of an immense rocky roof, like a fly clinging to a ceiling; in another moment it would have become a wall again—but this time he would be moving straight down it, instead of up. . . .

He had lost all control over the pod, and the clammy sweat that had begun to dew his brow warned him that he would soon lose control of his body. There was only one thing to do; he clenched his eyes tightly shut, squeezed as far back as possible into the tiny closed world of the capsule, and pretended with all his might that the universe outside did not exist. He did not even allow the slow, gentle crunch of his second crash to interfere with his self-hypnosis.

When he again dared to look outside, he found that the pod had come to rest against a large boulder. Its mechanical arms had broken the force of the impact, but at a cost that was more than he could afford to pay. Though the capsule was virtually weightless here, it still possessed its normal five hundred pounds of inertia, and it had been moving at perhaps four miles an hour. The momentum had been too much for the metal arms to absorb; one had snapped, and the other was hopelessly bent.

When he saw what had happened, Sherrard's first reaction was not despair, but anger. He had been so certain of success when the pod had started its glide across the barren face of Icarus. And now this, all through a moment of physical weakness! But space made no allowance for human frailties or emotions, and a man who did not accept that fact had no right to be here.

At least he had gained precious time in his pursuit of the ship; he had put an extra ten minutes, if not more, between himself and dawn. Whether that ten minutes would merely prolong the agony or whether it would give his shipmates the extra time they needed to find him, he would soon know.

Where were they? Surely they had started the search by now! He strained his eyes toward the brilliant star of the ship, hoping to pick out the fainter lights of space-pods moving toward him—but nothing else was visible against the slowly turning vault of heaven.

He had better look to his own resources, slender though they were. Only a few minutes were left before the *Prometheus* and her trailing lights would sink below the edge of the asteroid and leave him in darkness. It was true that the darkness would be all too brief, but before it fell upon him he might find some shelter against the coming day. This rock into which he had crashed, for example. . . .

Yes, it would give some shade, until the sun was halfway up the sky. Nothing could protect him if it passed right overhead, but it was just possible that he might be in a latitude where the sun never rose far above the horizon at this season of Icarus' four-hundred-and-nine-day year. Then he might survive the brief period of daylight; that was his only hope, if the rescuers did not find him before dawn.

There went *Prometheus* and her lights, below the edge of the world. With her going, the now-unchallenged stars blazed forth with redoubled brilliance. More glorious than any of them—so lovely that even to look upon it almost brought tears to his eyes—was the blazing beacon of Earth, with its companion moon beside it. He had been born on one, and had walked on the other; would he see either again?

Strange that until now he had given no thought to his wife and children, and to all that he loved in the life that now seemed so far away. He felt a spasm of guilt, but it passed swiftly. The ties of affection were not weakened, even across the hundred million miles of space that now sundered him from his family. At this moment, they were simply irrelevant. He was now a primitive, self-centered animal fighting for his life, and his only weapon was his brain. In this conflict, there was no place for the heart; it would merely be a hindrance, spoiling his judgment and weakening his resolution.

And then he saw something that banished all thoughts of his distant home. Reaching up above the horizon behind him, speading across the stars like a milky mist, was a faint and ghostly cone of phosphorescence. It was the herald of the sun—the beautiful, pearly phantom of the corona, visible on Earth only during the rare moments of a total eclipse. When the corona was rising, the sun would not be far behind, to smite this little land with fury.

Sherrard made good use of the warning. Now he could judge, with some accuracy, the exact point where the sun would rise. Crawling slowly and clumsily on the broken stumps of his metal arms, he dragged the capsule round to the side of the boulder that should give the greatest shade. He had barely reached it when the sun was upon him like a beast of prey, and his tiny world exploded into light.

He raised the dark filters inside his helmet, one thickness after another, until he could endure the glare. Except where the broad shadow of the boulder lay across the asteroid, it was like looking into a furnace. Every detail of the desolate land around him was revealed by that merciless light; there were no greys, only blinding whites and impenetrable blacks. All the shadowed cracks and hollows were pools of ink, while the higher ground already seemed to be on fire, as it caught the sun. Yet it was only a minute after dawn.

Now Sherrard could understand how the scorching heat of a billion summers had turned Icarus into a cosmic cinder, baking the rocks until the last traces of gas had bubbled out of them. Why should men travel, he asked himself bitterly, across the gulf of stars at such expense and risk—merely to land on a spinning slag heap? For the same reason, he knew, that they had once struggled to reach Everest and the Poles and the far places of the Earth—for the excitement of the body that was adventure, and the more enduring excitement of the mind that was discovery. It was an answer that gave him little consolation, now that he was about to be grilled like a joint on the turning spit of Icarus.

Already he could feel the first breath of heat upon his face. The boulder against which he was lying gave him protection from direct sunlight, but the glare reflected back at him from those blazing rocks only a few yards away was striking through the transparent plastic of the dome. It would grow swiftly more intense as the sun rose higher; he had even less time than he had thought, and with the knowledge came a kind of numb resignation that was beyond fear. He would wait—if he could—until the sunrise engulfed him and the capsule's cooling unit gave up the unequal struggle; then he would crack the pod and let the air gush out into the vacuum of space.

Nothing to do but to sit and think in the minutes that were left to him before his pool of shadow contracted. He did not try to direct his thoughts, but let them wander where they willed. How strange that he should be dying now, because back in the nineteen-forties—years before he was born —a man at Palomar had spotted a streak of light on a photographic plate, and had named it so appropriately after the boy who flew too near the sun.

One day, he supposed, they would build a monument here for him on this blistered plain. What would they inscribe upon it? "Here died Colin Sherrard, astronics engineer, in the cause of Science." That would be funny, for he had never understood half the things that the scientists were trying to do.

Yet some of the excitement of their discoveries had communicated itself to him. He remembered how the geologists had scraped away the charred skin of the asteroid, and had polished the metallic surface that lay beneath. It had been covered with a curious pattern of lines and scratches, like one of the abstract paintings of the Post-Picasso Decadents. But these lines had some meaning; they wrote the history of Icarus, though only a geologist could read it. They revealed, so Sherrard had been told, that this lump of iron and rock had not always floated alone in space. At some remote time in the past, it had been under enormous pressure—and that could mean only one thing. Billions of years ago it had been part of a much larger body, perhaps a planet like Earth. For some reason that planet had blown up, and Icarus and all the thousands of other asteroids were the fragments of that cosmic explosion.

Even at this moment, as the incandescent line of sunlight came closer, this was a thought that stirred his mind. What Sherrard was lying upon was the core of a world—perhaps a world that had once known life. In a strange, irrational way it comforted him to know that his might not be the only ghost to haunt Icarus until the end of time.

The helmet was misting up; that could only mean that the cooling unit was about to fail. It had done its work well; even now, though the rocks only a few yards away must be glowing a sullen red, the heat inside the capsule was not unendurable. When failure came, it would be sudden and catastrophic.

He reached for the red lever that would rob the sun of its prey—but before he pulled it, he would look for the last time upon Earth. Cautiously, he lowered the dark filters, adjusting them so that they still cut out the glare from the rocks, but no longer blocked his view of space.

The stars were faint now, dimmed by the advancing glow of the corona. And just visible over the boulder whose shield would soon fail him was a stub of crimson flame, a crooked finger of fire jutting from the edge of the sun itself. He had only seconds left.

There was the Earth, there was the moon. Good-by to them both, and to his friends and loved ones on each of them. While he was looking at the sky, the sunlight had begun to lick the base of the capsule, and he felt the first touch of fire. In a reflex as automatic as it was useless, he drew up his legs, trying to escape the advancing wave of heat.

What was that? A brilliant flash of light, infinitely

brighter than any of the stars, had suddenly exploded over-head. Miles above him, a huge mirror was sailing across the sky, reflecting the sunlight as it slowly turned through space. Such a thing was utterly impossible; he was beginning to suffer from hallucinations, and it was time he took his leave. Already the sweat was pouring from his body, and in a few seconds the capsule would be a furnace.

He waited no longer, but pulled on the Emergency Re-lease with all his waning strength, bracing himself at the same moment to face the end.

Nothing happened; the lever would not move. He tugged it again and again before he realized that it was hopelessly jammed. There was no easy way out for him, no merciful death as the air gushed from his lungs. It was then, as the true terror of his situation struck home to him, that his nerve finally broke and he began to scream like a trapped animal.

When he heard Captain McClellan's voice speaking to him, thin but clear, he knew that it must be another hallucination. Yet some last remnant of discipline and self-control checked his screaming; he clenched his teeth and listened to that familiar, commanding voice.

"Sherrard! Hold on, man! We've got a fix on you—but keep shouting!"

"Here I am!" he cried, "but hurry, for God's sake! I'm burning!"

Deep down in what was left of his rational mind he real-ized what had happened. Some feeble ghost of a signal was leaking through the broken stubs of his antennas, and the searchers had heard his screams—as he was hearing their voices. That meant they must be very close indeed, and the knowledge gave him sudden strength.

He stared through the steaming plastic of the dome, look-ing once more for that impossible mirror in the sky. There it was again—and now he realized that the baffling perspec-tives of space had tricked his senses. The mirror was not miles away, nor was it huge. It was almost on top of him, and it was moving fast.

He was still shouting when it slid across the face of the rising sun, and its blessed shadow fell upon him like a cool wind that had blown out of the heart of winter, over leagues of snow and ice. Now that it was so close, he recognized it at once; it was merely a large metal-foil radiation screen, no doubt hastily snatched from one of the instrument sites. In the safety of its shadow, his friends had been searching for him.

A heavy-duty, two-man capsule was hovering overhead, holding the glittering shield in one set of arms and reaching for him with the other. Even through the misty dome and the haze of heat that still sapped his senses, he recognized Captain McClellan's anxious face, looking down at him from the other pod.

So this was what birth was like, for truly he had been reborn. He was too exhausted for gratitude—that would come later—but as he rose from the burning rocks his eyes sought and found the bright star of Earth. "Here I am," he said silently. "I'm coming back."

Back to enjoy and cherish all the beauties of the world he had thought was lost forever. No—not all of them.

He would never enjoy summer again.

OUT OF THE CRADLE, ENDLESSLY ORBITING . . .

BEFORE WE START, I'd like to point out something that a good many people seem to have overlooked. The twenty-first century does *not* begin tomorrow; it begins a year later, on January 1, 2001. Even though the calendar reads 2000 from midnight, the old century still has twelve months to run. Every hundred years we astronomers have to explain this all over again, but it makes no difference. The celebrations start just as soon as the two zeros go up. . . .

So you want to know my most memorable moment in fifty years of space exploration . . . I suppose you've already interviewed von Braun? How is he? Good; I've not seen him since that symposium we arranged in Astrograd on his eightieth birthday, the last time he came down from the Moon.

Yes—I've been present at some of the biggest moments in the history of space flight, right back to the launching of the first satellite. I was only twenty-five then, and a very junior mathematician at Kapustin Yar—not important enough to be in the control center during the countdown. But I heard the take-off: it was the second most awe-inspiring sound I've heard in my entire life. (The first? I'll come to that later.) When we knew we'd hit orbit, one of the senior scientists called for his Zis, and we drove into Stalingrad for a real party. Only the very top people had cars in the Worker's Paradise, you know; we made the hundred-kilometer drive in just about the same time the Sputnik took for one circuit of Earth, and *that* was pretty good going. Someone calculated that the amount of vodka consumed the next day could have launched the satellite the Americans were building, but I don't think that was quite true.

Most of the history books say that the Space Age began then, on October 4, 1957; I'm not going to argue with them, but I think the really exciting times came later. For sheer drama you can't beat the U.S. Navy's race to fish Dimitri Kalinin out of the South Atlantic before his capsule sank. Then there was Jerry Wingate's radio commentary, with all the adjectives which no network dared to censor, as he rounded the Moon and became the first man to see its hidden face. And, of course, only five years later, that TV broadcast from the cabin of the *Hermann Oberth* as she touched down on the plateau in the Bay of Rainbows, where she still stands, an eternal monument to the men buried beside her.

Those were the great landmarks on the road to space, but you're wrong if you think I'm going to talk about them; for what made the greatest impact on me was something very, very different. I'm not even sure if I can share the experience, and if I succeed you won't be able to make a story out of it. Not a new one, anyway, for the papers were full of it at the time. But most of them missed the point completely; to them it was just good human-interest material, nothing more.

The time was twenty years after the launching of Sputnik I, and by then, with a good many other people, I was on the Moon . . . and too important, alas, to be a real scientist any more. It had been a dozen years since I'd programmed an electronic computer; now I had the slightly more difficult task of programming human beings, since I was Chief Coordinator of Project Ares, the first manned expedition to Mars.

We were starting from the Moon, of course, because of

the low gravity; it's about fifty times easier, in terms of fuel, to take off from there than from the Earth. We'd thought of constructing the ships in a satellite orbit, which would have cut fuel requirements even further, but when we looked into it, the idea wasn't as good as it seemed. It's not easy to set up factories and machine shops in space; the absence of gravity is a nuisance rather than an advantage when you want things to stay put. By that time, at the end of the seventies, the First Lunar Base was getting well organized, with chemical processing plants and all kinds of small-scale industrial operations to turn out the things the colony needed. So we decided to use the existing facilities rather than set up new ones, at great difficulty and expense, out in space.

Alpha, Beta, and *Gamma,* the three ships of the expedition, were being built inside the ramparts of Plato, perhaps the most perfect of all the walled plains on this side of the Moon. It's so large that if you stand in the middle you could never guess that you were inside a crater; the ring of mountains around you is hidden far below the horizon. The pressure domes of the base were about ten kilometers from the launching site, connected to it by one of those overhead cable systems that the tourists love to ride on, but which have ruined so much of the lunar scenery.

It was a rugged sort of life, in those pioneering days, for we had none of the luxuries everyone now takes for granted. Central Dome, with its parks and lakes, was still a dream on the architects' drawing boards; even if it had existed, we would have been too busy to enjoy it, for Project Ares devoured all our waking moments. It would be Man's first great leap into space; by that time we already looked on the Moon as no more than a suburb of Earth, a steppingstone on the way to places that really mattered. Our beliefs were neatly expressed by that famous remark of Tsiolkovsky's, which I'd hung up for everyone to see as they entered my office:

EARTH IS THE CRADLE OF THE MIND—BUT YOU CANNOT LIVE IN THE CRADLE FOREVER

(What was that? No—of *course* I never knew Tsiolkovsky! I was only four years old when he died in 1936!)

After half a lifetime of secrecy, it was good to be able to work freely with men of all nations, on a project that was backed by the entire world. Of my four chief assistants, one was American, one Indian, one Chinese, and one Russian. We often congratulated ourselves on escaping from Security and the worst excesses of nationalism, and though there was plenty of good-natured rivalry between scientists from different countries, it gave a stimulus to our work. I sometimes boasted to visitors who remembered the bad old days, "There are no secrets on the Moon."

Well, I was wrong; there *was* a secret, and it was under my very nose—in my own office. Perhaps I might have suspected something if I hadn't been so immersed in the multitudinous details of Project Ares that I'd no opportunity of taking the wider view. Looking back on it afterward, of course, I knew there were all sorts of hints and warnings, but I never noticed any of them at the time.

True, I was vaguely aware that Jim Hutchins, my young American assistant, was becoming increasingly abstracted, as if he had something on his mind. Once or twice I had to pull him up for some minor inefficiency; each time he looked hurt and promised it wouldn't happen again. He was one of those typical, clean-cut college boys the United States produces in such quantities—usually very reliable, but not exceptionally brilliant. He'd been on the Moon for three years, and was one of the first to bring his wife up from Earth when the ban on nonessential personnel was lifted. I'd never quite understood how he'd managed that; he must have been able to pull some strings, but certainly he was the last person you'd expect to find at the center of a world-wide conspiracy. World-wide, did I say? No—it was bigger than that, for it extended all the way back to Earth. Dozens of people were involved, right up to the top brass of the Astronautics Authority. It still seems a miracle that they were able to keep the plot from leaking out.

The slow sunrise had been under way for two days, Earth time, and though the needle-sharp shadows were shortening, it was still five days to noon. We were ready to make the first static tests of *Alpha*'s motors, for the power plant had been installed and the framework of the ship was complete. It stood out there on the plain looking more like a half-built oil refinery than a space ship, but to us it was beautiful, with its

promise of the future. It was a tense moment; never before
had a thermonuclear engine of such size been operated, and
despite all the safety precautions that had been taken, one
could never be sure. . . . If anything went wrong now, it
could delay Project Ares by years.

The countdown had already begun when Hutchins, looking rather pale, came hurrying up to me. "I have to report to
Base at once," he said. "It's very important." "More important than *this*?" I retorted sarcastically, for I was mighty
annoyed. He hesitated for a moment, as if wanting to tell me
something; then he replied, "I think so." "O.K.," I said, and
he was gone in a flash. I could have questioned him, but one
has to trust one's subordinates. As I went back to the central
control panel, in rather a bad temper, I decided that I'd had
enough of my temperamental young American and would
ask for him to be transferred. It was odd, though—he'd been
as keen as anybody on this test, and now he was racing back
to Base on the cable car. The blunt cylinder of the shuttle
was already halfway to the nearest suspension tower, sliding
along its almost invisible wires like some strange bird skimming across the lunar surface.

Five minutes later, my temper was even worse. A group
of vital recording instruments had suddenly packed up, and
the whole test would have to be postponed for at least three
hours. I stormed around the blockhouse telling everyone
who would listen (and of course everyone had to) that we
used to manage things much better at Kapustin Yar. I'd
quieted down a bit and we were on our second round of
coffee when the General Attention signal sounded from the
speakers. There's only one call with a higher priority than
that—the wail of the emergency alarms, which I've heard
just twice in all my years in the Lunar Colony, and hope
never to hear again.

The voice that echoed through every enclosed space on
the Moon, and over the radios of every worker out on the
soundless plains, was that of General Moshe Stein, Chairman of the Astronautics Authority. (There were still lots of
courtesy titles around in those days, though they didn't
mean anything any more.)

"I'm speaking from Geneva," he said, "and I have an
important announcement to make. For the last nine months,
a great experiment has been in progress. We have kept it

secret for the sake of those directly involved, and because we did not wish to raise false hopes or fears. Not long ago, you will remember, many experts refused to believe that men could survive in space; this time, also, there were pessimists who doubted if we could take the next step in the conquest of the universe. We have proved that they were wrong; for now I would like to introduce you to George Jonathan Hutchins—first Citizen of Space."

There was a click as the circuit was rerouted, followed by a pause full of indeterminate shufflings and whisperings. And then, over all the Moon and half the Earth, came the noise I promised to tell you about—the most awe-inspiring sound I've ever heard in my life.

It was the thin cry of a newborn baby—the first child in all the history of mankind to be brought forth on another world than Earth. We looked at each other, in the suddenly silenced blockhouse, and then at the ships we were building out there on the blazing lunar plain. They had seemed so important, a few minutes ago. They still were—but not as important as what had happened over in Medical Center, and would happen again billions of times on countless worlds down all the ages to come.

For that was the moment, gentlemen, when I knew that Man had *really* conquered space.

WHO'S THERE?

WHEN SATELLITE CONTROL called me, I was writing up the day's progress report in the Observation Bubble—the glass-domed office that juts out from the axis of the Space Station like the hubcap of a wheel. It was not really a good place to work, for the view was too overwhelming. Only a few yards away I could see the construction teams performing their slow-motion ballet as they put the station together like a giant jigsaw puzzle. And beyond them, twenty thousand miles below, was the blue-green glory of the full Earth, floating against the raveled star clouds of the Milky Way.

"Station Supervisor here," I answered. "What's the trouble?"

"Our radar's showing a small echo two miles away, almost stationary, about five degrees west of Sirius. Can you give us a visual report on it?"

Anything matching our orbit so precisely could hardly be a meteor; it would have to be something we'd dropped—perhaps an inadequately secured piece of equipment that had drifted away from the station. So I assumed; but when I pulled out my binoculars and searched the sky around Orion, I soon found my mistake. Though this space traveler was man-made, it had nothing to do with us.

"I've found it," I told Control. "It's someone's test satellite—cone-shaped, four antennas, and what looks like a lens system in its base. Probably U.S. Air Force, early nineteen-sixties, judging by the design. I know they lost track of several when their transmitters failed. There were quite a few attempts to hit this orbit before they finally made it."

After a brief search through the files, Control was able to confirm my guess. It took a little longer to find out that Washington wasn't in the least bit interested in our discovery of a twenty-year-old stray satellite, and would be just as happy if we lost it again.

"Well, we can't do *that*," said Control. "Even if nobody wants it, the thing's a menace to navigation. Someone had better go out and haul it aboard."

That someone, I realized, would have to be me. I dared not detach a man from the closely knit construction teams, for we were already behind schedule—and a single day's delay on this job cost a million dollars. All the radio and TV networks on Earth were waiting impatiently for the moment when they could route their programs through us, and thus provide the first truly global service, spanning the world from Pole to Pole.

"I'll go out and get it," I answered, snapping an elastic band over my papers so that the air currents from the ventilators wouldn't set them wandering around the room. Though I tried to sound as if I was doing everyone a great favor, I was secretly not at all displeased. It had been at least two weeks since I'd been outside; I was getting a little tired of stores schedules, maintenance reports, and all the glamorous ingredients of a Space Station Supervisor's life.

The only member of the staff I passed on my way to the air lock was Tommy, our recently acquired cat. Pets mean a great deal to men thousands of miles from Earth, but there are not many animals that can adapt themselves to a weightless environment. Tommy mewed plaintively at me as I clambered into my spacesuit, but I was in too much of a hurry to play with him.

At this point, perhaps I should remind you that the suits we use on the station are completely different from the flexible affairs men wear when they want to walk around on the moon. Ours are really baby spaceships, just big enough to hold one man. They are stubby cylinders, about seven feet long, fitted with low-powered propulsion jets, and have a pair of accordion-like sleeves at the upper end for the operator's arms. Normally, however, you keep your hands drawn inside the suit, working the manual controls in front of your chest.

As soon as I'd settled down inside my very exclusive spacecraft, I switched on power and checked the gauges on the tiny instrument panel. There's a magic word, "FORB," that you'll often hear spacemen mutter as they climb into their suits; it reminds them to test fuel, oxygen, radio, batteries. All my needles were well in the safety zone, so I lowered the transparent hemisphere over my head and sealed myself in. For a short trip like this, I did not bother to check the suit's internal lockers, which were used to carry food and special equipment for extended missions.

As the conveyor belt decanted me into the air lock, I felt like an Indian papoose being carried along on its mother's back. Then the pumps brought the pressure down to zero, the outer door opened, and the last traces of air swept me out into the stars, turning very slowly head over heels.

The station was only a dozen feet away, yet I was now an independent planet—a little world of my own. I was sealed up in a tiny, mobile cylinder, with a superb view of the entire universe, but I had practically no freedom of movement inside the suit. The padded seat and safety belts prevented me from turning around, though I could reach all the controls and lockers with my hands or feet.

In space, the great enemy is the sun, which can blast you to blindness in seconds. Very cautiously, I opened up the dark filters on the "night" side of my suit, and turned my head to look out at the stars. At the same time I switched the helmet's external sunshade to automatic, so that whichever way the suit gyrated my eyes would be shielded from that intolerable glare.

Presently, I found my target—a bright fleck of silver whose metallic glint distinguished it clearly from the surrounding stars. I stamped on the jet-control pedal, and felt the mild surge of acceleration as the low-powered rockets set me moving away from the station. After ten seconds of steady thrust, I estimated that my speed was great enough, and cut off the drive. It would take me five minutes to coast the rest of the way, and not much longer to return with my salvage.

And it was at that moment, as I launched myself out into the abyss, that I knew that something was horribly wrong.

It is never completely silent inside a spacesuit; you can always hear the gentle hiss of oxygen, the faint whirr of fans and motors, the susurration of your own breathing—even, if you listen carefully enough, the rhythmic thump that is the pounding of your heart. These sounds reverberate through the suit, unable to escape into the surrounding void; they are the unnoticed background of life in space, for you are aware of them only when they change.

They had changed now; to them had been added a sound which I could not identify. It was an intermittent, muffled thudding, sometimes accompanied by a scraping noise, as of metal upon metal.

I froze instantly, holding my breath and trying to locate the alien sound in my ears. The meters on the control board gave no clues; all the needles were rock-steady on their scales, and there were none of the flickering red lights that would warn of impending disaster. That was some comfort, but not much. I had long ago learned to trust my instincts in such matters; their alarm signals were flashing now, telling me to return to the station before it was too late. . . .

Even now, I do not like to recall those next few minutes, as panic slowly flooded into my mind like a rising tide, overwhelming the dams of reason and logic which every man must erect against the mystery of the universe. I knew then what it was like to face insanity; no other explanation fitted the facts.

For it was no longer possible to pretend that the noise disturbing me was that of some faulty mechanism. Though I was in utter isolation, far from any other human being or indeed any material object, I was not alone. The soundless void was bringing to my ears the faint but unmistakable stirrings of life.

In that first, heart-freezing moment it seemed that something was trying to get into my suit—something invisible, seeking shelter from the cruel and pitiless vacuum of space. I whirled madly in my harness, scanning the entire sphere of

vision around me except for the blazing, forbidden cone toward the sun. There was nothing there, of course. There
could not be—yet that purposeful scrabbling was clearer
than ever.

Despite the nonsense that has been written about us, it is
not true that spacemen are superstitious. But can you blame
me if, as I came to the end of logic's resources, I suddenly
remembered how Bernie Summers had died, no farther from
the station than I was at this very moment?

It was one of those "impossible" accidents; it always is.
Three things had gone wrong at once. Bernie's oxygen regu-
lator had run wild and sent the pressure soaring, the safety
valve had failed to blow—and a faulty joint had given way
instead. In a fraction of a second, his suit was open to space.

I had never known Bernie, but suddenly his fate became
of overwhelming importance to me—for a horrible idea had
come into my mind. One does not talk about these things,
but a damaged spacesuit is too valuable to be thrown away,
even if it has killed its wearer. It is repaired, renumbered—
and issued to someone else. . . .

*What happens to the soul of a man who dies between the
stars, far from his native world? Are you still here, Bernie,
clinging to the last object that linked you to your lost and
distant home?*

As I fought the nightmares that were swirling around me
—for now it seemed that the scratchings and soft fumblings
were coming from all directions—there was one last hope to
which I clung. For the sake of my sanity, I had to prove that
this wasn't Bernie's suit—that the metal walls so closely
wrapped around me had never been another man's coffin.

It took me several tries before I could press the right
button and switch my transmitter to the emergency wave
length. "Station!" I gasped. "I'm in trouble! Get records to
check my suit history and—"

I never finished; they say my yell wrecked the microphone. But what man alone in the absolute isolation of a
spacesuit would *not* have yelled when something patted him
softly on the back of the neck?

I must have lunged forward, despite the safety harness,
and smashed against the upper edge of the control panel.
When the rescue squad reached me a few minutes later, I

was still unconscious, with an angry bruise across my fore-head.

And so I was the last person in the whole satellite relay system to know what had happened. When I came to my senses an hour later, all our medical staff was gathered around my bed, but it was quite a while before the doctors bothered to look at me. They were much too busy playing with the three cute little kittens our badly misnamed Tommy had been rearing in the seclusion of my spacesuit's Number Five Storage Locker.

INTO THE COMET

"I DON'T KNOW why I'm recording this," said George Takeo Pickett slowly into the hovering microphone. "There's no chance that anyone will ever hear it. They say the comet will bring us back to the neighborhood of Earth in about two million years, when it makes its next turn around the sun. I wonder if mankind will still be in existence then, and whether the comet will put on as good a display for our descendants as it did for us? Maybe they'll launch an expedition, just as we have done, to see what they can find. And they'll find us. . . .

"For the ship will still be in perfect condition, even after all those ages. There'll be fuel in the tanks, maybe even plenty of air, for our food will give out first, and we'll starve before we suffocate. But I guess we won't wait for that; it will be quicker to open the air lock and get it all over.

"When I was a kid, I read a book on polar exploration called *Winter Amid the Ice*. Well, that's what we're facing now. There's ice all around us, floating in great porous bergs. *Challenger*'s in the middle of a cluster, orbiting round one another so slowly that you have to wait several minutes before you're certain they've moved. But no expedition to Earth's poles ever faced *our* winter. During most of that two million years, the temperature will be four hundred and fifty below zero. We'll be so far away from the sun that it'll give about as much heat as the stars. And who ever tried to warm his hands by Sirius on a cold winter night?"

That absurd image, coming suddenly into his mind, broke him up completely. He could not speak because of memories of moonlight upon snowfields, of Christmas chimes ringing across a land already fifty million miles away. Suddenly he was weeping like a child, his self-control dissolved by the remembrance of all the familiar, disregarded beauties of the Earth he had forever lost.

And everything had begun so well, in such a blaze of excitement and adventure. He could recall (was it only six months ago?) the very first time he had gone out to look for the comet, soon after eighteen-year-old Jimmy Randall had found it in his homemade telescope and sent his famous telegram to Mount Stromlo Observatory. In those early days, it had been only a faint polliwog of mist, moving slowly through the constellation of Eridanus, just south of the Equator. It was still far beyond Mars, sweeping sunward along its immensely elongated orbit. When it had last shone in the skies of Earth, there were no men to see it, and there might be none when it appeared again. The human race was seeing Randall's comet for the first and perhaps the only time.

As it approached the sun, it grew, blasting out plumes and jets, the smallest of which was larger than a hundred Earths. Like a great pennant streaming down some cosmic breeze, the comet's tail was already forty million miles long when it raced past the orbit of Mars. It was then that the astronomers realized that this might be the most spectacular sight ever to appear in the heavens; the display put on by Halley's comet, back in 1986, would be nothing in comparison. And it was then that the administrators of the International Astrophysical Decade decided to send the research ship *Challenger* chasing after it, if she could be fitted out in time; for here was a chance that might not come again in a thousand years.

For weeks on end, in the hours before dawn, the comet

sprawled across the sky like a second but far brighter Milky Way. As it approached the sun, and felt again the fires it had not known since the mammoths shook the Earth, it became steadily more active. Gouts of luminous gas erupted from its core, forming great fans which turned like slowly swinging searchlights across the stars. The tail, now a hundred million miles long, divided into intricate bands and streamers which changed their patterns completely in the course of a single night. Always they pointed away from the sun, as if driven starward by a great wind blowing forever outward from the heart of the solar system.

When the *Challenger* assignment had been given to him, George Pickett could hardly believe his luck. Nothing like this had happened to any reporter since William Laurence and the atom bomb. The facts that he had a science degree, was unmarried, in good health, weighed less than one hundred and twenty pounds, and had no appendix undoubtedly helped. But there must have been many others equally qualified; well, their envy would soon turn to relief.

Because the skimpy pay load of *Challenger* could not accommodate a mere reporter, Pickett had had to double up in his spare time as executive officer. This meant, in practice, that he had to write up the log, act as Captain's secretary, keep track of stores, and balance the accounts. It was very fortunate, he often thought, that one needed only three hours' sleep in every twenty-four, in the weightless world of space.

Keeping his two duties separate had required a great deal of tact. When he was not writing in his closet-sized office, or checking the thousands of items stacked away in stores, he would go on the prowl with his recorder. He had been careful, at one time or another, to interview every one of the twenty scientists and engineers who manned *Challenger*. Not all the recordings had been radioed back to Earth; some had been too technical, some too inarticulate, and others too much the reverse. But at least he had played no favorites and, as far as he knew, had trodden on no toes. Not that it mattered now.

He wondered how Dr. Martens was taking it; the astronomer had been one of his most difficult subjects, yet the one who could give the most information. On a sudden impulse, Pickett located the earliest of the Martens tapes, and inserted it in the recorder. He knew that he was trying to escape from the present by retreating into the past, but the only effect of that self-knowledge was to make him hope the experiment would succeed.

He still had vivid memories of that first interview, for the weightless microphone, wavering only slightly in the draft of air from the ventilators, had almost hypnotized him into incoherence. Yet no one would have guessed: his voice had its normal, professional smoothness.

They had been twenty million miles behind the comet, but swiftly overtaking it, when he had trapped Martens in the observatory and thrown that opening question at him.

"Dr. Martens," he began, "just what *is* Randall's comet made of?"

"Quite a mixture," the astronomer had answered, "and it's changing all the time as we move away from the sun. But the tail's mostly ammonia, methane, carbon dioxide, water vapor, cyanogen—"

"Cyanogen? Isn't that a poison gas? What would happen if the Earth ran into it?"

"Not a thing. Though it looks so spectacular, by our normal standards a comet's tail is a pretty good vacuum. A volume as big as Earth contains about as much gas as a matchbox full of air."

"And yet this thin stuff puts on such a wonderful display!"

"So does the equally thin gas in an electric sign, and for the same reason. A comet's tail glows because the sun bombards it with electrically charged particles. It's a cosmic skysign; one day, I'm afraid, the advertising people will wake up to this, and find a way of writing slogans across the solar system."

"That's a depressing thought—though I suppose someone will claim it's a triumph of applied science. But let's leave the tail; how soon will we get into the heart of the comet—the nucleus, I believe you call it?"

"Since a stern chase always takes a long time, it will be another two weeks before we enter the nucleus. We'll be plowing deeper and deeper into the tail, taking a cross section through the comet as we catch up with it. But though the nucleus is still twenty million miles ahead, we've already learned a good deal about it. For one thing, it's extremely small—less than fifty miles across. And even that's not solid, but probably consists of thousands of smaller bodies, all milling round in a cloud."

"Will we be able to go into the nucleus?"

"We'll know when we get there. Maybe we'll play safe and study it through our telescopes from a few thousand miles away. But personally, I'll be disappointed unless we go right inside. Won't you?"

Pickett switched off the recorder. Yes, Martens had been right. He *would* have been disappointed, especially since there had seemed no possible source of danger. Nor was there, as far as the comet was concerned. The danger had come from within.

They had sailed through one after another of the huge but unimaginably tenuous curtains of gas that Randall's comet was still ejecting as it raced away from the sun. Yet even now, though they were approaching the densest regions of the nucleus, they were for all practical purposes in a perfect vacuum. The luminous fog that stretched around *Challenger* for so many millions of miles scarcely dimmed the stars; but directly ahead, where lay the comet's core, was a brilliant patch of hazy light, luring them onward like a will-o'-the-wisp.

The electrical disturbances now taking place around them with ever-increasing violence had almost completely cut their link with Earth. The ship's main radio transmitter could just get a signal through, but for the last few days they had been reduced to sending "O.K." messages in Morse. When they broke away from the comet and headed for home, normal communication would be resumed; but now they were almost as isolated as explorers had been in the days before radio. It was inconvenient, but that was all. Indeed, Pickett rather welcomed this state of affairs; it gave him more time to get on with his clerical duties. Though *Challenger* was sailing into the heart of a comet, on a course that no captain could have dreamed of before the twentieth century, someone still had to check the provisions and count the stores.

Very slowly and cautiously, her radar probing the whole sphere of space around her, *Challenger* crept into the nucleus of the comet. And there she came to rest—amid the ice.

Back in the nineteen-forties, Fred Whipple, of Harvard, had guessed the truth, but it was hard to believe it even when the evidence was before one's eyes. The comet's relatively tiny core was a loose cluster of icebergs, drifting and turning round one another as they moved along their orbit. But unlike the bergs that floated in polar seas, they were not a dazzling white, nor were they made of water. They were a dirty gray, and very porous, like partly thawed snow. And they were riddled with pockets of methane and frozen ammonia, which erupted from time to time in gigantic gas jets as they absorbed the heat of the sun. It was a wonderful display, but Pickett had little time to admire it. Now he had far too much.

He had been doing his routine check of the ship's stores when he came face to face with disaster—though it was some time before he realized it. For the supply situation had been perfectly satisfactory; they had ample stocks for the return to Earth. He had checked that with his own eyes, and now had merely to confirm the balances recorded in the pinhead-sized section of the ship's electronic memory which stored all the accounts.

When the first crazy figures flashed on the screen, Pickett assumed that he had pressed the wrong key. He cleared the totals, and fed the information into the computer once more.

Sixty cases of pressed meat to start with; 17 consumed so far; quantity left: 99999943.

He tried again, and again, with no better result. Then, feeling annoyed but not particularly alarmed, he went in search of Dr. Martens.

He found the astronomer in the Torture Chamber—the tiny gym, squeezed between the technical stores and the bulkhead of the main propellant tank. Each member of the crew had to exercise here for an hour a day, lest his muscles waste away in this gravityless environment. Martens was wrestling with a set of powerful springs, an expression of grim determination on his face. It became much grimmer when Pickett gave his report.

A few tests on the main input board quickly told them the worst. "The computer's insane," said Martens. "It can't even add or subtract."

"But surely we can fix it!"

Martens shook his head. He had lost all his usual cocky

self-confidence; he looked, Pickett told himself, like an inflated rubber doll that had started to leak.

"Not even the builders could do that. It's a solid mass of microcircuits, packed as tightly as the human brain. The memory units are still operating, but the computing section's utterly useless. It just scrambles the figures you feed into it."

"And where does that leave us?" Pickett asked.

"It means that we're all dead," Martens answered flatly. "Without the computer, we're done for. It's impossible to calculate an orbit back to Earth. It would take an army of mathematicians weeks to work it out on paper."

"That's ridiculous! The ship's in perfect condition, we've plenty of food and fuel—and you tell me we're all going to die just because we can't do a few sums."

"A *few* sums!" retorted Martens, with a trace of his old spirit. "A major navigational change, like the one needed to break away from the comet and put us on an orbit to Earth, involves about a hundred thousand separate calculations. Even the computer needs several minutes for the job."

Pickett was no mathematician, but he knew enough of astronautics to understand the situation. A ship coasting through space was under the influence of many bodies. The main force controlling it was the gravity of the sun, which kept all the planets firmly chained in their orbits. But the planets themselves also tugged it this way and that, though with much feebler strength. To allow for all these conflicting tugs and pulls—above all, to take advantage of them to reach a desired goal scores of millions of miles away—was a problem of fantastic complexity. He could appreciate Martens' despair; no man could work without the tools of his trade, and no trade needed more elaborate tools than this one.

Even after the captain's announcement, and that first emergency conference when the entire crew had gathered to discuss the situation, it had taken hours for the facts to sink home. The end was still so many months away that the mind could not grasp it; they were under the sentence of death, but there was no hurry about the execution. And the view was still superb. . . .

Beyond the glowing mists that enveloped them—and which would be their celestial monument to the end of time

—they could see the great beacon of Jupiter, brighter than all the stars. Some of them might still be alive, if the others were willing to sacrifice themselves, when the ship went past the mightiest of the sun's children. Would the extra weeks of life be worth it, Pickett asked himself, to see with your own eyes the sight that Galileo had first glimpsed through his crude telescope four centuries ago—the satellites of Jupiter, shuttling back and forth like beads upon an invisible wire?

Beads upon a wire. With that thought, an all-but-forgotten childhood memory exploded out of his subconscious. It must have been there for days, struggling upward into the light. Now at last it had forced itself upon his waiting mind.

"No!" he cried aloud. "It's ridiculous! They'll laugh at me!"

So what? said the other half of his mind. You've nothing to lose; if it does no more, it will keep everyone busy while the food and the oxygen dwindle away. Even the faintest hope is better than none at all. . . .

He stopped fidgeting with the recorder; the mood of maudlin self-pity was over. Releasing the elastic webbing that held him to his seat, he set off for the technical stores in search of the material he needed.

"This," said Dr. Martens three days later, "isn't my idea of a joke." He gave a contemptuous glance at the flimsy structure of wire and wood that Pickett was holding in his hand.

"I guessed you'd say that," Pickett replied, keeping his temper under control. "But please listen to me for a minute. My grandmother was Japanese, and when I was a kid she told me a story that I'd completely forgotten until this week. I think it may save our lives.

"Sometime after the Second World War, there was a contest between an American with an electric desk calculator and a Japanese using an abacus like this. The abacus won."

"Then it must have been a poor desk machine, or an incompetent operator."

"They used the best in the U.S. Army. But let's stop arguing. Give me a test—say a couple of three-figure numbers to multiply."

"Oh—856 times 437."

Pickett's fingers danced over the beads, sliding them up and down the wires with lightning speed. There were twelve wires in all, so that the abacus could handle numbers up to 999,999,999,999—or could be divided into separate sections where several independent calculations could be carried out simultaneously.

"374072," said Pickett, after an incredibly brief interval of time. "Now see how long *you* take to do it, with pencil and paper."

There was a much longer delay before Martens, who like most mathematicians was poor at arithmetic, called out "375072." A hasty check soon confirmed that Martens had taken at least three times as long as Pickett to arrive at the wrong answer.

The astronomer's face was a study in mingled chagrin, astonishment, and curiosity.

"Where did you learn that trick?" he asked. "I thought those things could only add and subtract."

"Well—multiplication's only repeated addition, isn't it? All I did was to add 856 seven times in the unit column, three times in the tens column, and four times in the hundreds column. You do the same thing when you use pencil and paper. Of course, there are some short cuts, but if you think *I'm* fast, you should have seen my granduncle. He used to work in a Yokohama bank, and you couldn't see his fingers when he was going at speed. He taught me some of the tricks, but I've forgotten most of them in the last twenty years. I've only been practicing for a couple of days, so I'm still pretty slow. All the same, I hope I've convinced you that there's something in my argument."

"You certainly have: I'm quite impressed. Can you divide just as quickly?"

"Very nearly, when you've had enough experience."

Martens picked up the abacus, and started flicking the beads back and forth. Then he sighed.

"Ingenious—but it doesn't really help us. Even if it's ten times as fast as a man with pencil and paper—which it isn't —the computer was a million times faster."

"I've thought of that," answered Pickett, a little impatiently.

(Martens had no guts—he gave up too easily. How did he think astronomers managed a hundred years ago before there were any computers?)

"This is what I propose—tell me if you can see any flaws in it. . . ."

Carefully and earnestly he detailed his plan. As he did so, Martens slowly relaxed, and presently he gave the first laugh that Pickett had heard about *Challenger* for days.

"I want to see the skipper's face," said the astronomer, "when you tell him that we're all going back to the nursery to start playing with beads."

There was skepticism at first, but it vanished swiftly when Pickett gave a few demonstrations. To men who had grown up in a world of electronics, the fact that a simple structure of wire and beads could perform such apparent miracles was a revelation. It was also a challenge, and because their lives depended upon it, they responded eagerly.

As soon as the engineering staff had built enough smoothly operating copies of Pickett's crude prototype, the classes began. It took only a few minutes to explain the basic principles; what required time was practice—hour after hour of it, until the fingers flew automatically across the wires and flicked the beads into the right positions without any need for conscious thought. There were some members of the crew who never acquired both accuracy and speed, even after a week of constant practice: but there were others who quickly outdistanced Pickett himself.

They dreamed counters and columns, and flicked beads in their sleep. As soon as they had passed beyond the elementary stage they were divided into teams, which then competed fiercely against each other, until they had reached still higher standards of proficiency. In the end, there were men aboard *Challenger* who could multiply four-figure numbers on the abacus in fifteen seconds, and keep it up hour after hour.

Such work was purely mechanical; it required skill, but no intelligence. The really difficult job was Martens', and there was little that anyone could do to help him. He had to forget all the machine-based techniques he had taken for granted, and rearrange his calculations so that they could be carried out automatically by men who had no idea of the meaning of the figures they were manipulating. He would feed them the basic data, and then they would follow the program he had laid down. After a few hours of patient routine work, the answer would emerge from the end of the mathematical production line—provided that no mistakes had been made. And the way to guard against that was to have two independent teams working, cross-checking results at regular intervals.

"What we've done," said Pickett into his recorder, when at last he had time to think of the audience he had never expected to speak to again, "is to build a computer out of human beings instead of electronic circuits. It's a few thousand times slower, can't handle many digits, and gets tired easily—but it's doing the job. Not the whole job of navigating to Earth—that's far too complicated—but the simpler one of giving us an orbit that will bring us back into radio range. Once we've escaped from the electrical interference around us, we can radio our position and the big computers on Earth can tell us what to do next.

"We've already broken away from the comet and are no longer heading out of the solar system. Our new orbit checks with the calculations, to the accuracy that can be expected. We're still inside the comet's tail, but the nucleus is a million miles away and we won't see those ammonia icebergs again. They're racing on toward the stars into the freezing night between the suns, while we are coming home. . . .

"Hello, Earth . . . hello, Earth! This is *Challenger* calling, *Challenger* calling. Signal back as soon as you receive us —we'd like you to check our arithmetic—before we work our fingers to the bone!"

AN APE ABOUT
THE HOUSE

GRANNY THOUGHT IT a perfectly horrible idea; but then, she could remember the days when there were *human* servants.

"If you imagine," she snorted, "that I'll share the house with a monkey, you're very much mistaken."

"Don't be so old-fashioned," I answered. "Anyway, Dorcas isn't a monkey."

"Then what is she—it?"

I flipped through the pages of the Biological Engineering Corporation's guide. "Listen to this, Gran," I said. " 'The Superchimp (Registered Trade-mark) *Pan Sapiens* is an intelligent anthropoid, derived by breeding and genetic modification from basic chimpanzee stock—' "

"Just what I said! A monkey!"

" '—and with a large-enough vocabulary to understand simple orders. It can be trained to perform all types of domestic work or routine manual labor and is docile, affectionate, housebroken, and particularly good with children—' "

"Children! Would you trust Johnnie and Susan with a—a *gorilla*?"

I put the handbook down with a sigh.

"You've got a point there. Dorcas *is* expensive, and if I find the little monsters knocking her about—"

At this moment, fortunately, the door buzzer sounded. "Sign, please," said the delivery man. I signed, and Dorcas entered our lives.

"Hello, Dorcas," I said. "I hope you'll be happy here."

Her big, mournful eyes peered out at me from beneath their heavy ridges. I'd met much uglier humans, though she was rather an odd shape, being only about four feet tall and very nearly as wide. In her neat, plain uniform she looked just like a maid from one of those early twentieth-century movies; her feet, however, were bare and covered an astonishing amount of floor space.

"Morning, Ma'am," she answered, in slurred but perfectly intelligible accents.

"She can speak!" squawked Granny.

"Of course," I answered. "She can pronounce over fifty words, and can understand two hundred. She'll learn more as she grows used to us, but for the moment we must stick to the vocabulary on pages forty-two and forty-three of the handbook." I passed the instruction manual over to Granny; for once, she couldn't find a single word to express *her* feelings.

Dorcas settled down very quickly. Her basic training—Class A Domestic, plus Nursery Duties—had been excellent, and by the end of the first month there were very few jobs around the house that she couldn't do, from laying the table to changing the children's clothes. At first she had an annoying habit of picking up things with her feet; it seemed as natural to her as using her hands, and it took a long time to break her of it. One of Granny's cigarette butts finally did the trick.

She was good-natured, conscientious, and didn't answer back. Of course, she was not terribly bright, and some jobs had to be explained to her at great length before she got the point. It took several weeks before I discovered her limitations and allowed for them; at first it was quite hard to remember that she was not exactly human, and that it was no good engaging her in the sort of conversations we women occupy ourselves with when we get together. Or not many of them; she did have an interest in clothes, and was fascinated by colors. If I'd let her dress the way she wanted, she'd have looked like a refugee from Mardi Gras.

The children, I was relieved to find, adored her. I know what people say about Johnnie and Sue, and admit that it contains some truth. It's so hard to bring up children when their father's away most of the time, and to make matters worse, Granny spoils them when I'm not looking. So indeed does Eric, whenever his ship's on Earth, and I'm left to cope with the resulting tantrums. Never marry a spaceman if you can possibly avoid it; the pay may be good, but the glamour soon wears off.

By the time Eric got back from the Venus run, with three weeks' accumulated leave, our new maid had settled down as one of the family. Eric took her in his stride; after all, he'd met much odder creatures on the planets. He grumbled about the expense, of course, but I pointed out that now that so much of the housework was taken off my hands, we'd be able to spend more time together and do some of the visiting that had proved impossible in the past. I looked forward to having a little social life again, now that Dorcas could take care of the children.

For there was plenty of social life at Port Goddard, even though we were stuck in the middle of the Pacific. (Ever since what happened to Miami, of course, all major launching sites have been a long, long way from civilization.) There was a constant flow of distinguished visitors and travelers from all parts of the Earth—not to mention remoter points.

Every community has its arbiter of fashion and culture, its *grande dame* who is resented yet copied by all her unsuccessful rivals. At Port Goddard it was Christine Swanson; her husband was Commodore of the Space Service, and she never let us forget it. Whenever a liner touched down, she would invite all the officers on Base to a reception at her stylishly antique nineteenth-century mansion. It was advisable to go, unless you had a very good excuse, even though that meant looking at Christine's paintings. She fancied herself as an artist, and the walls were hung with multicolored daubs. Thinking of polite remarks to make about them was one of the major hazards of Christine's parties; another was her meter-long cigarette holder.

There was a new batch of paintings since Eric had been away: Christine had entered her "square" period. "You see, my dears," she explained to us, "the old-fashioned oblong pictures are terribly dated—they just don't go with the Space Age. There's no such thing as up or down, horizontal or vertical out *there*, so no really modern picture should have one side longer than another. And ideally, it should look *exactly* the same whichever way you hang it—I'm working on that right now."

"That seems very logical," said Eric tactfully. (After all, the Commodore was his boss.) But when our hostess was out of earshot, he added, "I don't know if Christine's pictures are hung the right way up, but I'm sure they're hung the wrong side to the wall."

I agreed; before I got married I spent several years at the art school and considered I knew something about the subject. Given as much cheek as Christine, I could have made quite a hit with my own canvases, which were now gathering dust in the garage.

"You know, Eric," I said a little cattily, "I could teach Dorcas to paint better than this."

He laughed and answered, "It might be fun to try it some day, if Christine gets out of hand." Then I forgot all about the matter—until a month later, when Eric was back in space.

The exact cause of the fight isn't important; it arose over a community development scheme on which Christine and I took opposing viewpoints. She won, as usual, and I left the meeting breathing fire and brimstone. When I got home, the first thing I saw was Dorcas, looking at the colored pictures in one of the weeklies—and I remembered Eric's words.

I put down my handbag, took off my hat, and said firmly: "Dorcas—come out to the garage."

It took some time to dig out my oils and easel from under the pile of discarded toys, old Christmas decorations, skin-diving gear, empty packing cases, and broken tools (it seemed that Eric never had time to tidy up before he shot off into space again). There were several unfinished canvases buried among the debris, which would do for a start. I set up

a landscape which had got as far as one skinny tree, and
said: "Now, Dorcas—I'm going to teach you to paint."

My plan was simple and not altogether honest. Although
apes had, of course, splashed paint on canvas often enough
in the past, none of them had created a genuine, properly
composed work of art. I was sure that Dorcas couldn't either, but no one need know that mine was the guiding hand.
She could get all the credit.

I was not actually going to lie to anyone, however.
Though I would create the design, mix the pigments, and do
most of the execution, I would let Dorcas tackle just as
much of the work as she could handle. I hoped that she
could fill in the areas of solid color, and perhaps develop a
characteristic style of brushwork in the process. With any
luck, I estimated, she might be able to do perhaps a quarter
of the actual work. Then I could claim it was all hers with a
reasonably clear conscience—for hadn't Michelangelo and
Leonardo signed paintings that were largely done by their
assistants? I'd be Dorcas' "assistant."

I must confess that I was a little disappointed. Though
Dorcas quickly got the general idea, and soon understood
the use of brush and palette, her execution was very clumsy.
She seemed unable to make up her mind which hand to use,
but kept transferring the brush from one to the other. In the
end I had to do almost all the work, and she merely contrib-
uted a few dabs of paint.

Still, I could hardly expect her to become a master in a
couple of lessons, and it was really of no importance. If
Dorcas was an artistic flop, I would just have to stretch the
truth a little farther when I claimed that it was all her own
work.

I was in no hurry; this was not the sort of thing that
could be rushed. At the end of a couple of months, the
School of Dorcas had produced a dozen paintings, all of
them on carefully chosen themes that would be familiar to a
Superchimp at Port Goddard. There was a study of the lagoon, a view of our house, an impression of a night launching (all glare and explosions of light), a fishing scene, a palm
grove—clichés, of course, but anything else would rouse suspicion. Before she came to us, I don't suppose Dorcas had
seen much of the world outside the labs where she had been
reared and trained.

The best of these paintings (and some of them *were* good —after all, I should know) I hung around the house in places where my friends could hardly fail to notice them. Everything worked perfectly; admiring queries were followed by astonished cries of "You don't say!" when I modestly disclaimed responsibility. There was some skepticism, but I soon demolished that by letting a few privileged friends see Dorcas at work. I chose the viewers for their ignorance of art, and the picture was an abstraction in red, gold, and black which no one dared to criticize. By this time, Dorcas could fake it quite well, like a movie actor pretending to play a musical instrument.

Just to spread the news around, I gave away some of the best paintings, pretending that I considered them no more than amusing novelties—yet at the same time giving just the barest hint of jealousy. "I've hired Dorcas," I said testily, "to work for me—not for the Museum of Modern Art." And I was *very* careful not to draw any comparisons between her paintings and those of Christine: our mutual friends could be relied upon to do that.

When Christine came to see me, ostensibly to discuss our quarrel "like two sensible people," I knew that she was on the run. So I capitulated gracefully as we took tea in the drawing room, beneath one of Dorcas' most impressive productions. (Full moon rising over the lagoon—very cold, blue, and mysterious. I was really quite proud of it.) There was not a word about the picture, or about Dorcas; but Christine's eyes told me all I wanted to know. The next week, an exhibition she had been planning was quietly canceled.

Gamblers say that you should quit when you're ahead of the game. If I had stopped to think, I should have known that Christine would not let the matter rest there. Sooner or later, she was bound to counterattack.

She chose her time well, waiting until the kids were at school, Granny was away visiting, and I was at the shopping center on the other side of the island. Probably she phoned first to check that no one was at home—no one human, that is. We had told Dorcas not to answer calls; though she'd done so in the early days, it had not been a success. A Superchimp on the phone sounds exactly like a drunk, and this can lead to all sorts of complications.

I can reconstruct the whole sequence of events: Christine must have driven up to the house, expressed acute disappointment at my absence, and invited herself in. She would have wasted no time in getting to work on Dorcas, but luckily I'd taken the precaution of briefing my anthropoid colleague. "Dorcas make," I'd said, over and over again, each time one of our productions was finished. "Not Missy make —*Dorcas* make." And, in the end, I'm sure she believed this herself.

If my brainwashing, and the limitations of a fifty-word vocabulary, baffled Christine, she did not stay baffled for long. She was a lady of direct action, and Dorcas was a docile and obedient soul. Christine, determined to expose fraud and collusion, must have been gratified by the promptness with which she was led into the garage studio; she must also have been just a little surprised.

I arrived home about half an hour later, and knew that there was trouble afoot as soon as I saw Christine's car parked at the curb. I could only hope I was in time, but as soon as I stepped into the uncannily silent house, I realized that it was too late. *Something* had happened; Christine would surely be talking, even if she had only an ape as audience. To her, any silence was as great a challenge as a blank canvas; it had to be filled with the sound of her own voice.

The house was utterly still; there was no sign of life. With a sense of mounting apprehension, I tiptoed through the drawing room, the dining room, the kitchen, and out into the back. The garage door was open, and I peered cautiously through.

It was a bitter moment of truth. Finally freed from my influence, Dorcas had at last developed a style of her own. She was swiftly and confidently painting—but not in the way *I* had so carefully taught her. And as for her subject . . .

I was deeply hurt when I saw the caricature that was giving Christine so much obvious enjoyment. After all that I had done for Dorcas, this seemed sheer ingratitude. Of course, I know now that no malice was involved, and that she was merely expressing herself. The psychologists, and the critics who wrote those absurd program notes for her exhibition at the Guggenheim, say that her portraits cast a vivid light on man-animal relationships, and allow us to look for the first time at the human race from outside. But I did not see it *that* way when I ordered Dorcas back into the kitchen.

For the subject was not the only thing that upset me: what really rankled was the thought of all the time I had wasted improving her technique—and her manners. She was ignoring everything I had ever told her, as she sat in front of the easel with her arms folded motionless on her chest.

Even then, at the very beginning of her career as an independent artist, it was painfully obvious that Dorcas had more talent in either of her swiftly moving feet than I had in both my hands.

LET THERE
BE LIGHT

THE CONVERSATION HAD come around to death rays
again, and some carping critic was poking fun at the old
science-fiction magazines whose covers so often displayed
multicolored beams creating havoc in all directions. "Such
an elementary scientific blunder," he snorted. "All the visible radiations are harmless—we wouldn't be alive if they
weren't. So anybody should have known that the green rays
and purple rays and scots-tartan rays were a lot of nonsense.
You might even make a rule—if you could see a ray, it
couldn't hurt you."

"An interesting theory," said Harry Purvis, "but not in
accordance with the facts. The only death ray that I, personally, have ever come across was perfectly visible."

"Indeed? What color was it?"

"I'll come round to that in a minute—if you want me to.
But talking of rounds . . ."

We caught Charlie Willis before he could sneak out of the
bar, and practiced a little jujitsu on him until all the glasses
were filled again. Then that curious, suspenseful silence de-

scended over the White Hart that all the regulars recognize as the prelude to one of Harry Purvis' improbable stories.

Edgar and Mary Burton were a somewhat ill-assorted pair, and none of their friends could explain why they had married. Perhaps the cynical explanation was the correct one; Edgar was almost twenty years older than his wife, and had made a quarter of a million on the stock exchange before retiring at an unusually early age. He had set himself this financial target, had worked hard to attain it—and when his bank balance had reached the desired figure had instantly lost all ambition. From now on he intended to live the life of a country gentleman, and to devote his declining years to his one absorbing hobby—astronomy.

For some reason, it seems to surprise many people that an interest in astronomy is compatible with business acumen or even with common sense. This is a complete delusion, said Harry with much feeling; I was once practically skinned alive at a poker game by a professor of astrophysics from the California Institute of Technology. But in Edgar's case, shrewdness seemed to have been combined with a vague impracticality in one and the same person; once he had made his money, he took no further interest in it, or indeed in anything else except the construction of progressively larger reflecting telescopes.

On his retirement, Edgar had purchased a fine old house high up on the Yorkshire moors. It was not as bleak and Wuthering-Heightsish as it may sound; there was a splendid view, and the Bentley would get you into town in fifteen minutes. Even so, the change did not altogether suit Mary, and it is hard not to feel rather sorry for her. There was no work for her to do, since the servants ran the house, and she had few intellectual resources to fall back on. She took up riding, joined all the book clubs, read the *Tatler* and *Country Life* from cover to cover, but still felt that there was something missing.

It took her about four months to find what she wanted; and then she met it at an otherwise dismal village fete. It was six foot three, ex-Coldstream Guards, with a family that looked on the Norman Conquest as a recent and regrettable piece of impertinence. It was called Rupert de Vere Courtenay (we'll forget about the other six Christian names) and it was generally regarded as the most eligible bachelor in the district.

Two full weeks passed before Rupert, who was a high-principled English gentleman, brought up in the best traditions of the aristocracy, succumbed to Mary's blandishments. His downfall was accelerated by the fact that his family was trying to arrange a match for him with the Honorable Felicity Fauntleroy, who was generally admitted to be no great beauty. Indeed, she looked so much like a horse that it was risky for her to go near her father's famous stables when the stallions were exercising.

Mary's boredom, and Rupert's determination to have a last desperate fling, had the inevitable result. Edgar saw less and less of his wife, who found an amazing number of reasons for driving into town during the week. At first he was quite glad that the circle of her acquaintances was widening so rapidly, and it was several months before he realized that it was doing nothing of the sort.

It is quite impossible to keep any liaison secret for long in a small country town like Stocksborough, though this is a fact that every generation has to learn afresh, usually the hard way. Edgar discovered the truth by accident, but some kind friend would have told him sooner or later. He had driven into town for a meeting of the local astronomical society—taking the Rolls, since his wife had already gone with the Bentley—and was momentarily held up on the way home by the crowds emerging from the last performance at the local cinema. In the heart of the crowd was Mary, accompanied by a handsome young man whom Edgar had seen before but couldn't identify at the moment. He would have thought no more of the matter had not Mary gone out of her way the next morning to mention that she'd been unable to get a seat in the cinema and had spent a quiet evening with one of her women friends.

Even Edgar, engrossed though he now was in the study of variable stars, began to put two and two together when he realized that his wife was gratuitously lying. He gave no hint of his vague suspicions, which ceased to be vague after the local Hunt Ball. Though he hated such functions (and this one, by bad luck, occurred just when U Orionis was going through its minimum and he had to miss some vital observations), he realized that this would give him a chance of identifying his wife's companion, since everyone in the district would be there.

It proved absurdly easy to locate Rupert and to get into conversation with him. Although the young man seemed a little ill at ease, he was pleasant company, and Edgar was surprised to find himself taking quite a fancy to him. If his wife had to have a lover, on the whole he approved her choice.

And there matters rested for some months, largely because Edgar was too busy grinding and figuring a fifteen-inch mirror to do anything about it. Twice a week Mary drove into town, ostensibly to meet her friends or to go to the cinema, and arrived back at the lodge just before midnight. Edgar could see the lights of the car for miles away across the moor, the beams twisting and turning as his wife drove homeward with what always seemed to him excessive speed. That had been one of the reasons why they seldom went out together; Edgar was a sound but cautious driver, and his comfortable cruising speed was ten miles an hour below Mary's.

About three miles from the house the lights of the car would disappear for several minutes as the road was hidden by a hill. There was a dangerous hairpin bend here; in a piece of highway construction more reminiscent of the Alps than of rural England, the road hugged the edge of a cliff and skirted an unpleasant hundred-foot drop before it straightened out on the homeward stretch. As the car rounded this bend, its headlights would shine full on the house, and there were many evenings when Edgar was dazzled by the sudden glare as he sat at the eyepiece of his telescope. Luckily, this stretch of road was very little used at night; if it had been, observations would have been well-nigh impossible, since it took Edgar's eyes ten or twenty minutes to recover fully from the direct blast of the headlights. This was no more than a minor annoyance, but when Mary started to stay out four or five evenings a week it became a confounded nuisance. Something, Edgar decided, Would Have To Be Done.

It will not have escaped your notice, continued Harry Purvis, that throughout all this affair Edgar Burton's behavior was hardly that of a normal person. Indeed, anyone who could have switched his mode of life so completely from that of a busy London stockbroker to that of a near-recluse on the Yorkshire moors must have been a little odd in the first place. I would hesitate, however, to say that he was more than eccentric until the time when Mary's midnight arrivals started to interfere with the serious business of observation. And even thereafter, one must admit that there was a certain crazy logic in his actions.

He had ceased to love his wife some years earlier, but he did object to her making a fool of him. And Rupert de Vere Courtenay seemed a pleasant young chap; it would be an act of kindness to rescue him. Well, there was a beautifully simple solution, which had come to Edgar in a literally blinding flash. And I literally mean literally, for it was while he was blinking in the glare of Mary's headlights that Edgar conceived the only really perfect murder I've ever encountered. It is strange how apparently irrelevant factors can determine a man's life; though I hate to say anything against the oldest and noblest of the sciences, it cannot be denied that if Edgar had never become an astronomer, he would never have become a murderer. For his hobby provided part of the motive, and a good deal of the means. . . .

He could have made the mirror he needed—he was quite an expert by this time—but astronomical accuracy was unnecessary in this case, and it was simpler to pick up a secondhand searchlight reflector at one of those war-surplus shops off Leicester Square. The mirror was about three feet across, and it was only a few hours' work to fix up a mounting for it and to arrange a crude but effective arc light at its focus. Getting the beam lined up was equally straightforward, and no one took the slightest notice of his activities, since his experimenting was now taken for granted by wife and servants alike.

He made the final brief test on a clear, dark night and settled down to await Mary's return. He did not waste the time, of course, but continued his routine observations of a group of selected stars. By midnight, there was still no sign of Mary, but Edgar did not mind, because he was getting a nicely consistent series of stellar magnitudes which were lying smoothly on his curves. Everything was going well, though he did not stop to wonder just why Mary was so unusually late.

At last he saw the headlights of the car flickering on the

horizon, and rather reluctantly broke off his observations. When the car had disappeared behind the hill, he was waiting with his hand on the switch. His timing was perfect; the instant the car came around the curve and the headlights shone on him, he closed the arc.

Meeting another car at night can be unpleasant enough even when you are prepared for it and are driving on a straight road. But if you are rounding a hairpin bend, and *know* that there is no other car coming, yet suddenly find yourself staring directly into a beam fifty times as powerful as any headlight—well, the results are more than unpleasant.

They were exactly what Edgar had calculated. He switched off his beam almost at once, but the car's own lights showed him all that he wanted to see. He watched them swing out over the valley and then curve down, ever more and more swiftly, until they disappeared below the crest of the hill. A red glow flared for a few seconds, but the explosion was barely audible, which was just as well, since Edgar did not want to disturb the servants.

He dismantled his little searchlight and returned to the telescope; he had not quite completed his observations. Then, satisfied that he had done a good night's work, he went to bed.

His sleep was sound but short, for about an hour later the telephone started to ring. No doubt someone had found the wreckage, but Edgar wished they could have left it until morning, for an astronomer needed all the sleep he could get. With some irritation he picked up the phone, and it was several seconds before he realized that his wife was at the other end of the line. She was calling from Courtenay Place, and wanted to know what had happened to Rupert.

It seemed that they had decided to make a clean breast of the whole affair, and Rupert (not unfortified by strong liquor) had agreed to be a man and break the news to Edgar. He was going to call back as soon as he had done this, and tell Mary how her husband had received it. She had waited with mounting impatience and alarm as long as she could, until at last anxiety had got the better of discretion.

I need hardly say that the shock to Edgar's already somewhat unbalanced nervous system was considerable. After Mary had been talking to her husband for several minutes, she realized that he had gone completely round the bend. It was not until the next morning that she discovered that this was precisely what Rupert had failed to do, unfortunately for him.

In the long run, I think Mary came out of it rather well. Rupert wasn't really very bright, and it would never have been a satisfactory match. As it was, when Edgar was duly certified, Mary received power of attorney for the estate and promptly moved to Dartmouth, where she took a charming flat near the Royal Naval College and seldom had to drive the new Bentley for herself.

But all that is by the way, concluded Harry, and before some of you skeptics ask me how I know all this, I got it from the dealer who purchased Edgar's telescopes when they locked him up. It's a sad fact that no one would believe his confession; the general opinion was that Rupert had had too much to drink and had been driving too fast on a dangerous road. That may be true, but I prefer to think it isn't. After all, that is such a humdrum way to die. To be killed by a death ray would be a fate much more fitting for a de Vere Courtenay—and in the circumstances I don't see how anyone can deny that it *was* a death ray that Edgar had used. It was a ray, and it killed someone. What more do you want?

DEATH AND
THE SENATOR

WASHINGTON HAD NEVER looked lovelier in the spring; and this was the last spring, thought Senator Steelman bleakly, that he would ever see. Even now, despite all that Dr. Jordan had told him, he could not fully accept the truth. In the past there had always been a way of escape; no defeat had been final. When men had betrayed him, he had discarded them—even ruined them, as a warning to others. But now the betrayal was within himself; already, it seemed, he could feel the labored beating of the heart that would soon be stilled. No point in planning now for the Presidential election of 1976; he might not even live to see the nominations. . . .

It was an end of dreams and ambition, and he could not console himself with the knowledge that for all men these must end someday. For him it was too soon; he thought of Cecil Rhodes, who had always been one of his heroes, crying "So much to do—so little time to do it in!" as he died before his fiftieth birthday. He was already older than Rhodes, and had done far less.

The car was taking him away from the Capitol; there was symbolism in that, and he tried not to dwell upon it. Now he was abreast of the New Smithsonian—that vast complex of museums he had never had time to visit, though he had watched it spread along the Mall throughout the years he had been in Washington. How much he had missed, he told himself bitterly, in his relentless pursuit of power. The whole universe of art and culture had remained almost closed to him, and that was only part of the price that he had paid. He had become a stranger to his family and to those who were once his friends. Love had been sacrificed on the altar of ambition, and the sacrifice had been in vain. Was there anyone in all the world who would weep at his departure?

Yes, there was. The feeling of utter desolation relaxed its grip upon his soul. As he reached for the phone, he felt ashamed that he had to call the office to get this number, when his mind was cluttered with memories of so many less important things.

(There was the White House, almost dazzling in the spring sunshine. For the first time in his life he did not give it a second glance. Already it belonged to another world—a world that would never concern him again.)

The car circuit had no vision, but he did not need it to sense Irene's mild surprise—and her still milder pleasure.

"Hello, Renee—how are you all?"

"Fine, Dad. When are we going to see you?"

It was the polite formula his daughter always used on the rare occasions when he called. And invariably, except at Christmas or birthdays, his answer was a vague promise to drop around at some indefinite future date.

"I was wondering," he said slowly, almost apologetically, "if I could borrow the children for an afternoon. It's a long time since I've taken them out, and I felt like getting away from the office."

"But of course," Irene answered, her voice warming with pleasure. "They'll love it. When would you like them?"

"Tomorrow would be fine. I could call around twelve, and take them to the Zoo or the Smithsonian, or anywhere else they felt like visiting."

Now she was really startled, for she knew well enough that he was one of the busiest men in Washington, with a schedule planned weeks in advance. She would be wondering what had happened; he hoped she would not guess the truth. No reason why she should, for not even his secretary knew of the stabbing pains that had driven him to seek this long-overdue medical checkup.

"That would be wonderful. They were talking about you only yesterday, asking when they'd see you again."

His eyes misted, and he was glad that Renee could not see him.

"I'll be there at noon," he said hastily, trying to keep the emotion out of his voice. "My love to you all." He switched off before she could answer, and relaxed against the upholstery with a sigh of relief. Almost upon impulse, without conscious planning, he had taken the first step in the reshaping of his life. Though his own children were lost to him, a bridge across the generations remained intact. If he did nothing else, he must guard and strengthen it in the months that were left.

Taking two lively and inquisitive children through the natural-history building was not what the doctor would have ordered, but it was what he wanted to do. Joey and Susan had grown so much since their last meeting, and it required both physical and mental alertness to keep up with them. No sooner had they entered the rotunda than they broke away from him, and scampered toward the enormous elephant dominating the marble hall.

"What's that?" cried Joey.

"It's an elephant, stupid," answered Susan with all the crushing superiority of her seven years.

"I know it's an effelant," retorted Joey. "But what's its name?"

Senator Steelman scanned the label, but found no assistance there. This was one occasion when the risky adage "Sometimes wrong, never uncertain" was a safe guide to conduct.

"He was called—er—Jumbo," he said hastily. "Just look at those tusks!"

"Did he ever get toothache?"

"Oh no."

"Then how did he clean his teeth? Ma says that if I don't clean mine . . ."

Steelman saw where the logic of this was leading, and thought it best to change the subject.

"There's a lot more to see inside. Where do you want to start—birds, snakes, fish, mammals?"

"Snakes!" clamored Susan. "I wanted to keep one in a box, but Daddy said no. Do you think he'd change his mind if you asked him?"

"What's a mammal?" asked Joey, before Steelman could work out an answer to that.

"Come along," he said firmly. "I'll show you."

As they moved through the halls and galleries, the children darting from one exhibit to another, he felt at peace with the world. There was nothing like a museum for calming the mind, for putting the problems of everyday life in their true perspective. Here, surrounded by the infinite variety and wonder of Nature, he was reminded of truths he had forgotten. He was only one of a million million creatures that shared this planet Earth. The entire human race, with its hopes and fears, its triumphs and its follies, might be no more than an incident in the history of the world. As he stood before the monstrous bones of Diplodocus (the children for once awed and silent), he felt the winds of Eternity blowing through his soul. He could no longer take so seriously the gnawing of ambition, the belief that he was the man the nation needed. *What* nation, if it came to that? A mere two centuries ago this summer, the Declaration of Independence had been signed; but this old American had lain in the Utah rocks for a hundred million years. . . .

He was tired when they reached the Hall of Oceanic Life, with its dramatic reminder that Earth still possessed animals greater than any that the past could show. The ninety-foot blue whale plunging into the ocean, and all the other swift hunters of the sea, brought back memories of hours he had once spent on a tiny, glistening deck with a white sail billowing above him. That was another time when he had known contentment, listening to the swish of water past the prow, and the sighing of the wind through the rigging. He had not sailed for thirty years; this was another of the world's pleasures he had put aside.

"I don't like fish," complained Susan. "When do we get to the snakes?"

"Presently," he said. "But what's the hurry? There's plenty of time."

The words slipped out before he realized it. He checked his step, while the children ran on ahead. Then he smiled, without bitterness. For in a sense, it was true enough. There *was* plenty of time. Each day, each hour could be a universe of experience, if one used it properly. In the last weeks of his life, he would begin to live.

As yet, no one at the office suspected anything. Even his outing with the children had not caused much surprise; he had done such things before, suddenly canceling his appointments and leaving his staff to pick up the pieces. The pattern of his behavior had not yet changed, but in a few days it would be obvious to all his associates that something had happened. He owed it to them—and to the party—to break the news as soon as possible; there were, however, many personal decisions he had to make first, which he wished to settle in his own mind before he began the vast unwinding of his affairs.

There was another reason for his hesitancy. During his career, he had seldom lost a fight, and in the cut and thrust of political life he had given quarter to none. Now, facing his ultimate defeat, he dreaded the sympathy and the condolences that his many enemies would hasten to shower upon him. The attitude, he knew, was a foolish one—a remnant of his stubborn pride which was too much a part of his personality to vanish even under the shadow of death.

He carried his secret from committee room to White House to Capitol, and through all the labyrinths of Washington society, for more than two weeks. It was the finest performance of his career, but there was no one to appreciate it. At the end of that time he had completed his plan of action; it remained only to dispatch a few letters he had written in his own hand, and to call his wife.

The office located her, not without difficulty, in Rome. She was still beautiful, he thought, as her features swam on to the screen; she would have made a fine First Lady, and that would have been some compensation for the lost years. As far as he knew, she had looked forward to the prospect; but had he ever really understood what she wanted?

"Hello, Martin," she said, "I was expecting to hear from you. I suppose you want me to come back."

"Are you willing to?" he asked quietly. The gentleness of his voice obviously surprised her.

"I'd be a fool to say no, wouldn't I? But if they don't elect you, I want to go my own way again. You must agree to that."

"They won't elect me. They won't even nominate me. You're the first to know this, Diana. In six months, I shall be dead."

The directness was brutal, but it had a purpose. That fraction-of-a-second delay while the radio waves flashed up to the communication satellites and back again to Earth had never seemed so long. For once, he had broken through the beautiful mask. Her eyes widened with disbelief, her hand flew to her lips.

"You're joking!"

"About *this*? It's true enough. My heart's worn out. Dr. Jordan told me, a couple of weeks ago. It's my own fault, of course, but let's not go into that."

"So that's why you've been taking out the children: I wondered what had happened."

He might have guessed that Irene would have talked with her mother. It was a sad reflection on Martin Steelman, if so commonplace a fact as showing an interest in his own grandchildren could cause curiosity.

"Yes," he admitted frankly. "I'm afraid I left it a little late. Now I'm trying to make up for lost time. Nothing else seems very important."

In silence, they looked into each other's eyes across the curve of the Earth, and across the empty desert of the dividing years. Then Diana answered, a little unsteadily, "I'll start packing right away."

Now that the news was out, he felt a great sense of relief. Even the sympathy of his enemies was not as hard to accept as he had feared. For overnight, indeed, he had no enemies. Men who had not spoken to him in years, except with invective, sent messages whose sincerity could not be doubted. Ancient quarrels evaporated, or turned out to be founded on misunderstandings. It was a pity that one had to die to learn these things. . . .

He also learned that, for a man of affairs, dying was a

full-time job. There were successors to appoint, legal and
financial mazes to untangle, committee and state business to
wind up. The work of an energetic lifetime could not be
terminated suddenly, as one switches off an electric light. It
was astonishing how many responsibilities he had acquired,
and how difficult it was to divest himself of them. He had
never found it easy to delegate power (a fatal flaw, many
critics had said, in a man who hoped to be Chief Executive),
but now he must do so, before it slipped forever from his
hands.

It was as if a great clock was running down, and there
was no one to rewind it. As he gave away his books, read
and destroyed old letters, closed useless accounts and files,
dictated final instructions, and wrote farewell notes, he
sometimes felt a sense of complete unreality. There was no
pain; he could never have guessed that he did not have years
of active life ahead of him. Only a few lines on a cardiogram
lay like a roadblock across his future—or like a curse, written in some strange language the doctors alone could read.

Almost every day now Diana, Irene, or her husband
brought the children to see him. In the past he had never felt
at ease with Bill, but that, he knew, had been his own fault.
You could not expect a son-in-law to replace a son, and it
was unfair to blame Bill because he had not been cast in the
image of Martin Steelman, Jr. Bill was a person in his own
right; he had looked after Irene, made her happy, and fa-
thered her children. That he lacked ambition was a flaw—if
flaw indeed it was—that the Senator could at last forgive.

He could even think, without pain or bitterness, of his
own son, who had traveled this road before him and now
lay, one cross among many, in the United Nations cemetery
at Capetown. He had never visited Martin's grave; in the
days when he had the time, white men were not popular in
what was left of South Africa. Now he could go if he wished,
but he was uncertain if it would be fair to harrow Diana
with such a mission. His own memories would not trouble
him much longer, but she would be left with hers.

Yet he would like to go, and felt it was his duty. Moreover, it would be a last treat for the children. To them it
would be only a holiday in a strange land, without any tinge
of sorrow for an uncle they had never known. He had

started to make the arrangements when, for the second time within a month, his whole world was turned upside down.

Even now, a dozen or more visitors would be waiting for him each morning when he arrived at his office. Not as many as in the old days, but still a sizable crowd. He had never imagined, however, that Dr. Harkness would be among them.

The sight of that thin, gangling figure made him momentarily break his stride. He felt his cheeks flush, his pulse quicken at the memory of ancient battles across committee-room tables, of angry exchanges that had reverberated along the myriad channels of the ether. Then he relaxed; as far as he was concerned, all that was over.

Harkness rose to his feet, a little awkwardly, as he approached. Senator Steelman knew that initial embarrassment—he had seen it so often in the last few weeks. Everyone he now met was automatically at a disadvantage, always on the alert to avoid the one subject that was taboo.

"Well, Doctor," he said. "This is a surprise—I never expected to see *you* here."

He could not resist the little jab, and derived some satisfaction at watching it go home. But it was free from bitterness, as the other's smile acknowledged.

"Senator," replied Harkness, in a voice that was pitched so low that he had to lean forward to hear it, "I've some extremely important information for you. Can we speak alone for a few minutes? It won't take long."

Steelman nodded; he had his own ideas of what was important now, and felt only a mild curiosity as to why the scientist had come to see him. The man seemed to have changed a good deal since their last encounter, seven years ago. He was much more assured and self-confident, and had lost the nervous mannerisms that had helped to make him such an unconvincing witness.

"Senator," he began, when they were alone in the private office, "I've some news that may be quite a shock to you. I believe that you can be cured."

Steelman slumped heavily in his chair. This was the one thing he had never expected; from the first, he had not encumbered himself with the burden of vain hopes. Only a fool fought against the inevitable, and he had accepted his fate.

For a moment he could not speak; then he looked up at

his old adversary and gasped: "Who told you that? All my doctors—"

"Never mind them; it's not their fault they're ten years behind the times. Look at this."

"What does it mean? I can't read Russian."

"It's the latest issue of the USSR *Journal of Space Medicine.* It arrived a few days ago, and we did the usual routine translation. This note here—the one I've marked—refers to some recent work at the Mechnikov Station."

"What's that?"

"You don't *know*? Why, that's their Satellite Hospital, the one they've built just below the Great Radiation Belt."

"Go on," said Steelman, in a voice that was suddenly dry and constricted. "I'd forgotten they'd called it that." He had hoped to end his life in peace, but now the past had come back to haunt him.

"Well, the note itself doesn't say much, but you can read a lot between the lines. It's one of those advance hints that scientists put out before they have time to write a full-fledged paper, so they can claim priority later. The title is: 'Therapeutic Effects of Zero Gravity on Circulatory Diseases.' What they've done is to induce heart disease artificially in rabbits and hamsters, and then take them up to the space station. In orbit, of course, nothing has any weight; the heart and muscles have practically no work to do. And the result is exactly what I tried to tell you, years ago. Even extreme cases can be arrested, and many can be cured."

The tiny, paneled office that had been the center of his world, the scene of so many conferences, the birthplace of so many plans, became suddenly unreal. Memory was much more vivid: he was back again at those hearings, in the fall of 1969, when the National Aeronautics and Space Administration's first decade of activity had been under review—and, frequently, under fire.

He had never been chairman of the Senate Committee on Astronautics, but he had been its most vocal and effective member. It was here that he had made his reputation as a guardian of the public purse, as a hardheaded man who could not be bamboozled by utopian scientific dreamers. He had done a good job; from that moment, he had never been far from the headlines. It was not that he had any particular feeling for space and science, but he knew a live issue when

he saw one. Like a tape-recorder unrolling in his mind, it all
came back. . . .

"Dr. Harkness, you are Technical Director of the National
Aeronautics and Space Administration?"

"That is correct."

"I have here the figures for NASA's expenditure over the
period 1959–69; they are quite impressive. At the moment
the total is $82,547,450,000, and the estimate for fiscal 69–
70 is well over ten billions. Perhaps you could give us some
indication of the return we can expect from all this."

"I'll be glad to do so, Senator."

That was how it had started, on a firm but not unfriendly
note. The hostility had crept in later. That it was unjustified,
he had known at the time; any big organization had weaknesses and failures, and one which literally aimed at the
stars could never hope for more than partial success. From
the beginning, it had been realized that the conquest of space
would be at least as costly in lives and treasure as the conquest of the air. In ten years, almost a hundred men had
died—on Earth, in space, and upon the barren surface of the
Moon. Now that the urgency of the early sixties was over,
the public was asking "Why?" Steelman was shrewd enough
to see himself as mouthpiece for those questioning voices.
His performance had been cold and calculated; it was convenient to have a scapegoat, and Dr. Harkness was unlucky
enough to be cast for the role.

"Yes, Doctor, I understand all the benefits we've received
from space research in the way of improved communications and weather forecasting, and I'm sure everyone appre-
ciates them. But almost all this work has been done with
automatic, unmanned vehicles. What I'm worried about—
what many people are worried about—is the mounting expense of the Man-in-Space program, and its very marginal
utility. Since the original Dyna-Soar and Apollo projects,
almost a decade ago, we've shot billions of dollars into
space. And with what result? So that a mere handful of men
can spend a few uncomfortable hours outside the atmosphere, achieving nothing that television cameras and automatic equipment couldn't do—much better and cheaper.
And the lives that have been lost! None of us will forget
those screams we heard coming over the radio when the

X-21 burned up on re-entry. What right have we to send men to such deaths?"

He could still remember the hushed silence in the committee chamber when he had finished. His questions were very reasonable ones, and deserved to be answered. What was unfair was the rhetorical manner in which he had framed them and, above all, the fact that they were aimed at a man who could not answer them effectively. Steelman would not have tried such tactics on a von Braun or a Rickover; they would have given him at least as good as they received. But Harkness was no orator; if he had deep personal feelings, he kept them to himself. He was a good scientist, an able administrator—and a poor witness. It had been like shooting fish in a barrel. The reporters had loved it; he never knew which of them coined the nickname "Hapless Harkness."

"Now this plan of yours, Doctor, for a fifty-man space laboratory—*how* much did you say it would cost?"

"I've already told you—just under one and a half billions."

"And the annual maintenance?"

"Not more than $250,000,000."

"When we consider what's happened to previous estimates, you will forgive us if we look upon these figures with some skepticism. But even assuming that they are right, what will we get for the money?"

"We will be able to establish our first large-scale research station in space. So far, we have had to do our experimenting in cramped quarters aboard unsuitable vehicles, usually when they were engaged on some other mission. A permanent, manned satellite laboratory is essential. Without it, further progress is out of the question. Astrobiology can hardly get started—"

"Astro what?"

"Astrobiology—the study of living organisms in space. The Russians really started it when they sent up the dog Laika in Sputnik II and they're still ahead of us in this field. But no one's done any serious work on insects or invertebrates—in fact, on any animals except dogs, mice, and monkeys."

"I see. Would I be correct in saying that you would like funds for building a zoo in space?"

The laughter in the committee room had helped to kill the project. And it had helped, Senator Steelman now realized, to kill him.

He had only himself to blame, for Dr. Harkness had tried, in his ineffectual way, to outline the benefits that a space laboratory might bring. He had particularly stressed the medical aspects, promising nothing but pointing out the possibilities. Surgeons, he had suggested, would be able to develop new techniques in an environment where the organs had no weight; men might live longer, freed from the wear and tear of gravity, for the strain on heart and muscles would be enormously reduced. Yes, he had mentioned the heart; but that had been of no interest to Senator Steelman —healthy, and ambitious, and anxious to make good copy. . . .

"Why have you come to tell me this?" he said dully. "Couldn't you let me die in peace?"

"That's the point," said Harkness impatiently. "There's no need to give up hope."

"Because the Russians have cured some hamsters and rabbits?"

"They've done much more than that. The paper I showed you only quoted the preliminary results; its already a year out of date. They don't want to raise false hopes, so they are keeping as quiet as possible."

"How do you know this?"

Harkness looked surprised.

"Why, I called Professor Stanyukovitch, my opposite number. It turned out that he was up on the Mechnikov Station, which proves how important they consider this work. He's an old friend of mine, and I took the liberty of mentioning your case."

The dawn of hope, after its long absence, can be as painful as its departure. Steelman found it hard to breathe and for a dreadful moment he wondered if the final attack had come. But it was only excitement; the constriction in his chest relaxed, the ringing in his ears faded away, and he heard Dr. Harkness' voice saying: "He wanted to know if you could come to Astrograd right away, so I said I'd ask you. If you can make it, there's a flight from New York at ten-thirty tomorrow morning."

Tomorrow he had promised to take the children to the Zoo; it would be the first time he had let them down. The thought gave him a sharp stab of guilt, and it required almost an effort of will to answer: "I can make it."

He saw nothing of Moscow during the few minutes that the big intercontinental ramjet fell down from the stratosphere. The view-screens were switched off during the descent, for the sight of the ground coming straight up as a ship fell vertically on its sustaining jets was highly disconcerting to passengers.

At Moscow he changed to a comfortable but old-fashioned turboprop, and as he flew eastward into the night he had his first real opportunity for reflection. It was a very strange question to ask himself, but was he altogether glad that the future was no longer wholly certain? His life, which a few hours ago had seemed so simple, had suddenly become complex again, as it opened out once more into possibilities he had learned to put aside. Dr. Johnson had been right when he said that nothing settles a man's mind more wonderfully than the knowledge that he will be hanged in the morning. For the converse was certainly true—nothing unsettled it so much as the thought of a reprieve.

He was asleep when they touched down at Astrograd, the space capital of the USSR. When the gentle impact of the landing shook him awake, for a moment he could not imagine where he was. Had he dreamed that he was flying halfway around the world in search of life? No; it was not a dream, but it might well be a wild-goose chase.

Twelve hours later, he was still waiting for the answer. The last instrument reading had been taken; the spots of light on the cardiograph display had ceased their fateful dance. The familiar routine of the medical examination and the gentle, competent voices of the doctors and nurses had done much to relax his mind. And it was very restful in the softly lit reception room, where the specialists had asked him to wait while they conferred together. Only the Russian magazines, and a few portraits of somewhat hirsute pioneers of Soviet medicine, reminded him that he was no longer in his own country.

He was not the only patient. About a dozen men and women, of all ages, were sitting around the wall, reading magazines and trying to appear at ease. There was no conversation, no attempt to catch anyone's eye. Every soul in this room was in his private limbo, suspended between life and death. Though they were linked together by a common misfortune, the link did not extend to communication. Each seemed as cut off from the rest of the human race as if he was already speeding through the cosmic gulfs where lay his only hope.

But in the far corner of the room, there was an exception. A young couple—neither could have been more than twenty-five—were huddling together in such desperate misery that at first Steelman found the spectacle annoying. No matter how bad their own problems, he told himself severely, people should be more considerate. They should hide their emotions—especially in a place like this, where they might upset others.

His annoyance quickly turned to pity, for no heart can remain untouched for long at the sight of simple, unselfish love in deep distress. As the minutes dripped away in a silence broken only by the rustling of papers and the scraping of chairs, his pity grew almost to an obsession.

What was their story, he wondered? The boy had sensitive, intelligent features; he might have been an artist, a scientist, a musician—there was no way of telling. The girl was pregnant; she had one of those homely peasant faces so common among Russian women. She was far from beautiful, but sorrow and love had given her features a luminous sweetness. Steelman found it hard to take his eyes from her—for somehow, though there was not the slightest physical resemblance, she reminded him of Diana. Thirty years ago, as they had walked from the church together, he had seen that same glow in the eyes of his wife. He had almost forgotten it; was the fault his, or hers, that it had faded so soon?

Without any warning, his chair vibrated beneath him. A swift, sudden tremor had swept through the building, as if a giant hammer had smashed against the ground, many miles away. An earthquake? Steelman wondered; then he remembered where he was, and started counting seconds.

He gave up when he reached sixty; presumably the sound-proofing was so good that the slower, air-borne noise had not reached him, and only the shock wave through the ground recorded the fact that a thousand tons had just leapt into the sky. Another minute passed before he heard, distant but clear, a sound as of a thunderstorm raging below the edge of the world. It was even more miles away than he had dreamed; what the noise must be like at the launching site was beyond imagination.

Yet that thunder would not trouble him, he knew, when he also rose into the sky; the speeding rocket would leave it far behind. Nor would the thrust of acceleration be able to touch his body, as it rested in its bath of warm water—more comfortable even than this deeply padded chair.

That distant rumble was still rolling back from the edge of space when the door of the waiting room opened and the nurse beckoned to him. Though he felt many eyes following him, he did not look back as he walked out to receive his sentence.

The news services tried to get in contact with him all the way back from Moscow, but he refused to accept the calls. "Say I'm sleeping and mustn't be disturbed," he told the stewardess. He wondered who had tipped them off, and felt annoyed at this invasion of his privacy. Yet privacy was something he had avoided for years, and had learned to appreciate only in the last few weeks. He could not blame the reporters and commentators if they assumed that he had reverted to type.

They were waiting for him when the ramjet touched down at Washington. He knew most of them by name, and some were old friends, genuinely glad to hear the news that had raced ahead of him.

"What does it feel like, Senator," said Macauley, of the *Times*, "to know you're back in harness? I take it that it's true—the Russians can cure you?"

"They *think* they can," he answered cautiously. "This is a new field of medicine, and no one can promise anything."

"When do you leave for space?"

"Within the week, as soon as I've settled some affairs here."

"And when will you be back—if it works?"

"That's hard to say. Even if everything goes smoothly, I'll be up there at least six months."

Involuntarily, he glanced at the sky. At dawn or sunset— even during the daytime, if one knew where to look—the

Mechnikov Station was a spectacular sight, more brilliant than any of the stars. But there were now so many satellites of which this was true that only an expert could tell one from another.

"Six months," said a newsman thoughtfully. "That means you'll be out of the picture for seventy-six."

"But nicely in it for 1980," said another.

"And 1984," added a third. There was a general laugh; people were already making jokes about 1984, which had once seemed so far in the future, but would soon be a date no different from any other . . . it was hoped.

The ears and the microphones were waiting for his reply. As he stood at the foot of the ramp, once more the focus of attention and curiosity, he felt the old excitement stirring in his veins. What a comeback it would be, to return from space a new man! It would give him a glamour that no other candidate could match; there was something Olympian, almost godlike, about the prospect. Already he found himself trying to work it into his election slogans. . . .

"Give me time to make my plans," he said. "It's going to take me a while to get used to this. But I promise you a statement before I leave Earth."

Before I leave Earth. Now, there was a fine, dramatic phrase. He was still savoring its rhythm with his mind when he saw Diana coming toward him from the airport buildings.

Already she had changed, as he himself was changing; in her eyes was a wariness and reserve that had not been there two days ago. It said, as clearly as any words: "Is it going to happen, all over again?" Though the day was warm, he felt suddenly cold, as if he had caught a chill on those far Siberian plains.

But Joey and Susan were unchanged, as they ran to greet him. He caught them up in his arms, and buried his face in their hair, so that the cameras would not see the tears that had started from his eyes. As they clung to him in the innocent, unself-conscious love of childhood, he knew what his choice would have to be.

They alone had known him when he was free from the itch for power; that was the way they must remember him, if they remembered him at all.

     •   •   •

"Your conference call, Mr. Steelman," said his secretary. "I'm routing it on to your private screen."

He swiveled round in his chair and faced the gray panel on the wall. As he did so, it split into two vertical sections. On the right half was a view of an office much like his own, and only a few miles away. But on the left—

Professor Stanyukovitch, lightly dressed in shorts and singlet, was floating in mid-air a good foot above his seat. He grabbed it when he saw that he had company, pulled himself down, and fastened a webbed belt around his waist. Behind him were ranged banks of communications equipment; and behind those, Steelman knew, was space.

Dr. Harkness spoke first, from the right-hand screen.

"We were expecting to hear from you, Senator. Professor Stanyukovitch tells me that everything is ready."

"The next supply ship," said the Russian, "comes up in two days. It will be taking me back to Earth, but I hope to see you before I leave the station."

His voice was curiously high-pitched, owing to the thin oxyhelium atmosphere he was breathing. Apart from that, there was no sense of distance, no background of interference. Though Stanyukovitch was thousands of miles away, and racing through space at four miles a second, he might have been in the same office. Steelman could even hear the faint whirring of electric motors from the equipment racks behind him.

"Professor," answered Steelman, "there are a few things I'd like to ask before I go."

"Certainly."

Now he could tell that Stanyukovitch was a long way off. There was an appreciable time lag before his reply arrived; the station must be above the far side of the Earth.

"When I was at Astrograd, I noticed many other patients at the clinic. I was wondering—on what basis do you select those for treatment?"

This time the pause was much greater than the delay due to the sluggish speed of radio waves. Then Stanyukovitch answered: "Why, those with the best chance of responding."

"But your accommodations must be very limited. You must have many other candidates besides myself."

"I don't quite see the point—" interrupted Dr. Harkness, a little too anxiously.

Steelman swung his eyes to the right-hand screen. It was quite difficult to recognize, in the man staring back at him, the witness who had squirmed beneath his needling only a few years ago. That experience had tempered Harkness, had given him his baptism in the art of politics. Steelman had taught him much, and he had applied his hard-won knowledge.

His motives had been obvious from the first. Harkness would have been less than human if he did not relish this sweetest of revenges, this triumphant vindication of his faith. And as Space Administration Director, he was well aware that half his budget battles would be over when all the world knew that a potential President of the United States was in a Russian space hospital . . . because his own country did not possess one.

"Dr. Harkness," said Steelman gently, "this is *my* affair. I'm still waiting for your answer, Professor."

Despite the issues involved, he was quite enjoying this. The two scientists, of course, were playing for identical stakes. Stanyukovitch had his problems too; Steelman could guess the discussions that had taken place at Astrograd and Moscow, and the eagerness with which the Soviet astronauts had grasped this opportunity—which, it must be admitted, they had richly earned.

It was an ironic situation, unimaginable only a dozen years before. Here were NASA and the USSR Commission of Astronautics working hand in hand, using him as a pawn for their mutual advantage. He did not resent this, for in their place he would have done the same. But he had no wish to be a pawn: he was an individual who still had some control of his own destiny.

"It's quite true," said Stanyukovitch, very reluctantly, "that we can only take a limited number of patients here in Mechnikov. In any case, the station's a research laboratory, not a hospital."

"How many?" asked Steelman relentlessly.

"Well—fewer than ten," admitted Stanyukovitch, still more unwillingly.

It was an old problem, of course, though he had never imagined that it would apply to him. From the depths of memory there flashed a newspaper item he had come across long ago. When penicillin had been first discovered, it was so rare that if both Churchill and Roosevelt had been dying for lack of it, only one could have been treated. . . .

Fewer than ten. He had seen a dozen waiting at Astrograd, and how many were there in the whole world? Once again, as it had done so often in the last few days, the memory of those desolate lovers in the reception room came back to haunt him. Perhaps they were beyond his aid; he would never know.

But one thing he did know. He bore a responsibility that he could not escape. It was true that no man could foresee the future, and the endless consequences of his actions. Yet if it had not been for him, by this time his own country might have had a space hospital circling beyond the atmosphere. How many American lives were upon his conscience? Could he accept the help he had denied to others? Once he might have done so—but not now.

"Gentlemen," he said, "I can speak frankly with you both, for I know your interests are identical." (His mild irony, he saw, did not escape them.) "I appreciate your help and the trouble you have taken; I am sorry it has been wasted. No—don't protest; this isn't a sudden, quixotic decision on my part. If I was ten years younger, it might be different. Now I feel that this opportunity should be given to someone else—especially in view of my record." He glanced at Dr. Harkness, who gave an embarrassed smile. "I also have other, personal reasons, and there's no chance that I will change my mind. Please don't think me rude or ungrateful, but I don't wish to discuss the matter any further. Thank you again, and good-by."

He broke the circuit; and as the image of the two astonished scientists faded, peace came flooding back into his soul.

Imperceptibly, spring merged into summer. The eagerly awaited Bicentenary celebrations came and went; for the first time in years, he was able to enjoy Independence Day as a private citizen. Now he could sit back and watch the others perform—or he could ignore them if he wished.

Because the ties of a lifetime were too strong to break, and it would be his last opportunity to see many old friends, he spent hours looking in on both conventions and listening to the commentators. Now that he saw the whole world beneath the light of Eternity, his emotions were no longer involved; he understood the issues, and appreciated the arguments, but already he was as detached as an observer from another planet. The tiny, shouting figures on the screen were amusing marionettes, acting out roles in a play that was entertaining, but no longer important—at least, to him.

But it was important to his grandchildren, who would one day move out onto this same stage. He had not forgotten that; they were his share of the future, whatever strange form it might take. And to understand the future, it was necessary to know the past.

He was taking them into that past, as the car swept along Memorial Drive. Diana was at the wheel, with Irene beside her, while he sat with the children, pointing out the familiar sights along the highway. Familiar to him, but not to them; even if they were not old enough to understand all that they were seeing, he hoped they would remember.

Past the marble stillness of Arlington (the thought again of Martin, sleeping on the other side of the world) and up into the hills the car wound its effortless way. Behind them, like a city seen through a mirage, Washington danced and trembled in the summer haze, until the curve of the road hid it from view.

It was quiet at Mount Vernon; there were few visitors so early in the week. As they left the car and walked toward the house, Steelman wondered what the first President of the United States would have thought could he have seen his home as it was today. He could never have dreamed that it would enter its second century still perfectly preserved, a changeless island in the hurrying river of time.

They walked slowly through the beautifully proportioned rooms, doing their best to answer the children's endless questions, trying to assimilate the flavor of an infinitely simpler, infinitely more leisurely mode of life. (But had it seemed simple or leisurely to those who lived it?) It was so hard to imagine a world without electricity, without radio, without any power save that of muscle, wind, and water. A world where nothing moved faster than a running horse, and most men died within a few miles of the place where they were born.

The heat, the walking, and the incessant questions proved more tiring than Steelman had expected. When they had reached the Music Room, he decided to rest. There were some attractive benches out on the porch, where he could sit in the fresh air and feast his eyes upon the green grass of the lawn.

"Meet me outside," he explained to Diana, "when you've done the kitchen and the stables. I'd like to sit down for a while."

"You're sure you're quite all right?" she said anxiously.

"I never felt better, but I don't want to overdo it. Besides, the kids have drained me dry—I can't think of any more answers. You'll have to invent some; the kitchen's your department, anyway."

Diana smiled.

"I was never much good in it, was I? But I'll do my best —I don't suppose we'll be more than thirty minutes."

When they had left him, he walked slowly out onto the lawn. Here Washington must have stood, two centuries ago, watching the Potomac wind its way to the sea, thinking of past wars and future problems. And here Martin Steelman, thirty-eighth President of the United States, might have stood a few months hence, had the fates ruled otherwise.

He could not pretend that he had no regrets, but they were very few. Some men could achieve both power and happiness, but that gift was not for him. Sooner or later, his ambition would have consumed him. In the last few weeks he had known contentment, and for that no price was too great.

He was still marveling at the narrowness of his escape when his time ran out and Death fell softly from the summer sky.

TROUBLE WITH
TIME

"WE DON'T HAVE much crime on Mars," said Detective
Inspector Rawlings, a little sadly. "In fact, that's the chief
reason I'm going back to the Yard. If I stayed here much
longer, I'd get completely out of practice."

We were sitting in the main observation lounge of the
Phobos Spaceport, looking out across the jagged, sun-
drenched crags of the tiny moon. The ferry rocket that had
brought us up from Mars had left ten minutes ago, and was
now beginning the long fall back to the ocher-tinted globe
hanging there against the stars. In half an hour we would be
boarding the liner for Earth—a world upon which most of
the passengers had never set foot, but which they still called
"home."

"At the same time," continued the Inspector, "now and
then there's a case that makes life interesting. You're an art
dealer, Mr. Maccar; I'm sure you heard about that spot of
bother at Meridian City a couple of months ago."

"I don't think so," replied the plump, olive-skinned little
man I'd taken for just another returning tourist. Presumably

the Inspector had already checked through the passenger list; I wondered how much he knew about me, and tried to reassure myself that my conscience was—well—reasonably clear. After all, everybody took *something* out through Martian Customs—

"It's been rather well hushed up," said the Inspector, "but you can't keep these things quiet for long. Anyway, a jewel thief from Earth tried to steal Meridian Museum's greatest treasure—the Siren Goddess."

"But that's absurd!" I objected. "It's priceless, of course —but it's only a lump of sandstone. You couldn't sell it to anyone—you might just as well steal the Mona Lisa."

The Inspector grinned, rather mirthlessly. "*That's* happened once," he said. "Maybe the motive was the same. There are collectors who would give a fortune for such an object, even if they could only look at it themselves. Don't you agree, Mr. Maccar?"

"That's perfectly true. In my business, you meet all sorts of crazy people."

"Well, this chappie—name's Danny Weaver—had been well paid by one of them. And if it hadn't been for a piece of fantastically bad luck, he might have brought it off."

The Spaceport P.A. system apologized for a further slight delay owing to final fuel checks, and asked a number of passengers to report to Information. While we were waiting for the announcement to finish, I recalled what little I knew about the Siren Goddess. Though I'd never seen the original, like most other departing tourists I had a replica in my baggage. It bore the certificate of the Mars Bureau of Antiquities, guaranteeing that "this full-scale reproduction is an exact copy of the so-called Siren Goddess, discovered in the Mare Sirenium by the Third Expedition, A.D. 2012 (A.M. 23)."

It's quite a tiny thing to have caused so much controversy. Only eight or nine inches high—you wouldn't look at it twice if you saw it in a museum on Earth. The head of a young woman, with slightly oriental features, elongated earlobes, hair curled in tight ringlets close to the scalp, lips half parted in an expression of pleasure or surprise—that's all. But it's an enigma so baffling that it's inspired a hundred religious sects, and driven quite a few archaeologists round the bend. For a perfectly human head has no right whatsoever to be found on Mars, whose only intelligent inhabitants were crustaceans—"educated lobsters," as the newspapers are fond of calling them. The aboriginal Martians never came near to achieving space flight, and in any event their civilization died before men existed on Earth. No wonder the Goddess is the solar system's number-one mystery; I don't suppose we'll find the answer in my lifetime—if we ever do.

"Danny's plan was beautifully simple," continued the Inspector. "You know how absolutely dead a Martian city gets on Sunday, when everything closes down and the colonists stay home to watch the TV from Earth. Danny was counting on this, when he checked into the hotel in Meridian West, late Friday afternoon. He'd have Saturday for reconnoitering the Museum, an undisturbed Sunday for the job itself, and on Monday morning he'd be just another tourist leaving town. . . .

"Early Saturday he strolled through the little park and crossed over into Meridian East, where the Museum stands. In case you don't know, the city gets its name because it's exactly on longitude one hundred and eighty degrees; there's a big stone slab in the park with the prime meridian engraved on it, so that visitors can get themselves photographed standing in two hemispheres at once. Amazing what simple things amuse some people.

"Danny spent the day going over the Museum, exactly like any other tourist determined to get his money's worth. But at closing time he didn't leave; he'd holed up in one of the galleries not open to the public, where the Museum had been arranging a Late Canal Period reconstruction but had run out of money before the job could be finished. He stayed there until about midnight, just in case there were any enthusiastic researchers still in the building. Then he emerged and got to work."

"Just a minute," I interrupted. "What about the night watchman?"

The Inspector laughed.

"My dear chap! They don't have such luxuries on Mars. There weren't even any alarms, for who would bother to steal lumps of stone? True, the Goddess was sealed up neatly in a strong glass-and-metal cabinet, just in case some souvenir hunter took a fancy to her. But even if she were stolen, there was nowhere the thief could hide, and of course all outgoing traffic would be searched as soon as the statue was missed."

That was true enough. I'd been thinking in terms of Earth, forgetting that every city on Mars is a closed little world of its own beneath the force-field that protects it from the freezing near-vacuum. Beyond those electronic shields is the utterly hostile emptiness of the Martian Outback, where a man will die in seconds without protection. That makes law enforcement very easy; no wonder there's so little crime on Mars. . . .

"Danny had a beautiful set of tools, as specialized as a watchmaker's. The main item was a microsaw no bigger than a soldering iron; it had a wafer-thin blade, driven at a million cycles a second by an ultrasonic power pack. It would go through glass or metal like butter—and left a cut only about as thick as a hair. Which was very important for Danny, since he had to leave no traces of his handiwork.

"I suppose you've guessed how he intended to operate. He was going to cut through the base of the cabinet, and substitute one of those souvenir replicas for the real Goddess. It might be a couple of years before some inquisitive expert discovered the awful truth; long before then the original would have traveled back to Earth, perfectly disguised as a copy of itself, with a genuine certificate of authenticity. Pretty neat, eh?

"It must have been a weird business, working in that darkened gallery with all those million-year-old carvings and unexplainable artifacts around him. A museum on Earth is bad enough at night, but at least it's—well—*human*. And Gallery Three, which houses the Goddess, is particularly unsettling. It's full of bas-reliefs showing quite incredible animals fighting each other; they look rather like giant beetles, and most paleontologists flatly deny that they could ever have existed. But imaginary or not, they belonged to this world, and they didn't disturb Danny as much as the Goddess, staring at him across the ages and defying him to explain her presence here. She gave him the creeps. How do I know? He told me.

"Danny set to work on that cabinet as carefully as any diamond cutter preparing to cleave a gem. It took most of the night to slice out the trap door, and it was nearly dawn when he relaxed and put down the saw. There was still a lot of work to do, but the hardest part was over. Putting the replica into the case, checking its appearance against the photos he'd thoughtfully brought with him, and covering up his traces might take most of Sunday, but that didn't worry him in the least. He had another twenty-four hours, and would positively welcome Monday's first visitors so that he could mingle with them and make his inconspicuous exit.

It was a perfectly horrible shock to his nervous system, therefore, when the main doors were noisily unbarred at eight thirty and the museum staff—all six of them—started to open up for the day. Danny bolted for the emergency exit, leaving everything behind—tools, Goddesses, the lot. He had another big surprise when he found himself in the street; it should have been completely deserted at this time of day, with everyone at home reading the Sunday papers. But here were the citizens of Meridian East, as large as life, heading for plant or office on what was obviously a normal working day.

"By the time poor Danny got back to his hotel, we were waiting for him. We couldn't claim much credit for deducing that only a visitor from Earth—and a very recent one at that—could have overlooked Meridian City's chief claim to fame. And I presume you know what *that* is."

"Frankly, I don't," I answered. "You can't see much of Mars in six weeks, and I never went east of the Syrtis Major."

"Well, it's absurdly simple, but we shouldn't be too hard on Danny; even the locals occasionally fall into the same trap. It's something that doesn't bother us on Earth, where we've been able to dump the problem in the Pacific Ocean. But Mars, of course, is all dry land; and that means that *somebody* has to live with the International Date Line. . . .

"Danny, you see, had worked from Meridian West. It was Sunday over there all right—and it was still Sunday when we picked him up back at the hotel. But over in Meridian East, half a mile away, it was only Saturday. That little trip across the park had made all the difference; I told you it was rotten luck."

There was a long moment of silent sympathy; then I asked, "What did he get?"

"Three years," said Inspector Rawlings.

"That doesn't seem very much."

"Mars years; that makes it almost six of ours. And a whacking fine which, by an odd coincidence, came to just the refund value of his return ticket to Earth. He isn't in jail, of course; Mars can't afford that kind of nonproductive luxury. Danny has to work for a living, under discreet surveillance. I told you that the Meridian Museum couldn't afford a night watchman. Well, it has one now. Guess who."

"All passengers prepare to board in ten minutes! Please collect your hand baggage!" ordered the loudspeakers.

As we started to move toward the air lock, I couldn't help asking one more question.

"What about the people who put Danny up to it? There must have been a lot of money behind him. Did you get them?"

"Not yet; they'd covered their tracks pretty thoroughly, and I believe Danny was telling the truth when he said he couldn't give us any leads. Still, it's not my case; as I told you, I'm going back to my old job at the Yard. But a policeman always keeps his eyes open—like an art dealer, eh, Mr. Maccar? Why, you look a bit green about the gills. Have one of my space-sickness tablets."

"No, thank you," answered Mr. Maccar, "I'm quite all right."

His tone was distinctly unfriendly; the social temperature seemed to have dropped below zero in the last few minutes. I looked at Mr. Maccar, and I looked at the Inspector. And suddenly I realized that we were going to have a very interesting trip.

BEFORE EDEN

"I GUESS," SAID Jerry Garfield, cutting the engines, "that this is the end of the line." With a gentle sigh, the underjets faded out; deprived of its air cushion, the scout car *Rambling Wreck* settled down upon the twisted rocks of the Hesperian Plateau.

There was no way forward; neither on its jets nor its tractors could S.5—to give the *Wreck* its official name—scale the escarpment that lay ahead. The South Pole of Venus was only thirty miles away, but it might have been on another planet. They would have to turn back, and retrace their four-hundred-mile journey through this nightmare landscape.

The weather was fantastically clear, with visibility of almost a thousand yards. There was no need of radar to show the cliffs ahead; for once, the naked eye was good enough. The green auroral light, filtering down through clouds that had rolled unbroken for a million years, gave the scene an underwater appearance, and the way in which all distant objects blurred into the haze added to the impression. Sometimes it was easy to believe that they were driving across a shallow sea bed, and more than once Jerry had imagined that he had seen fish floating overhead.

"Shall I call the ship, and say we're turning back?" he asked.

"Not yet," said Dr. Hutchins. "I want to think."

Jerry shot an appealing glance at the third member of the crew, but found no moral support there. Coleman was just as bad; although the two men argued furiously half the time, they were both scientists and therefore, in the opinion of a hardheaded engineer-navigator, not wholly responsible citizens. If Cole and Hutch had bright ideas about going forward, there was nothing he could do except register a protest.

Hutchins was pacing back and forth in the tiny cabin, studying charts and instruments. Presently he swung the car's searchlight toward the cliffs, and began to examine them carefully with binoculars. Surely, thought Jerry, he doesn't expect me to drive up there! S.5 was a hovertrack, not a mountain goat. . . .

Abruptly, Hutchins found something. He released his breath in a sudden explosive gasp, then turned to Coleman.

"Look!" he said, his voice full of excitement. "Just to the left of that black mark! Tell me what you see."

He handed over the glasses, and it was Coleman's turn to stare.

"Well I'm damned," he said at length. "You were right. There *are* rivers on Venus. That's a dried-up waterfall."

"So you owe me one dinner at the Bel Gourmet when we get back to Cambridge. With champagne."

"No need to remind me. Anyway, it's cheap at the price. But this still leaves your other theories strictly on the crackpot level."

"Just a minute," interjected Jerry. "What's all this about rivers and waterfalls? Everyone knows they can't exist on Venus. It never gets cold enough on this steam bath of a planet for the clouds to condense."

"Have you looked at the thermometer lately?" asked Hutchins with deceptive mildness.

"I've been slightly too busy driving."

"Then I've news for you. It's down to two hundred and thirty, and still falling. Don't forget—we're almost at the

Pole, it's wintertime, and we're sixty thousand feet above the lowlands. All this adds up to a distinct nip in the air. If the temperature drops a few more degrees, we'll have rain. The water will be boiling, of course—but it will be water. And though George won't admit it yet, this puts Venus in a completely different light."

"Why?" asked Jerry, though he had already guessed.

"Where there's water, there may be life. We've been in too much of a hurry to assume that Venus is sterile, merely because the average temperature's over five hundred degrees. It's a lot colder here, and that's why I've been so anxious to get to the Pole. There are lakes up here in the highlands, and I want to look at them."

"But *boiling* water!" protested Coleman. "Nothing could live in that!"

"There are algae that manage it on Earth. And if we've learned one thing since we started exploring the planets, it's this: wherever life has the slightest chance of surviving, you'll find it. This is the only chance it's ever had on Venus."

"I wish we could test your theory. But you can see for yourself—we can't go up that cliff."

"Perhaps not in the car. But it won't be too difficult to climb those rocks, even wearing thermosuits. All we need do is walk a few miles toward the Pole; according to the radar maps, it's fairly level once you're over the rim. We could manage in—oh, twelve hours at the most. Each of us has been out for longer than that, in much worse conditions."

That was perfectly true. Protective clothing that had been designed to keep men alive in the Venusian lowlands would have an easy job here, where it was only a hundred degrees hotter than Death Valley in midsummer.

"Well," said Coleman, "you know the regulations. You can't go by yourself, and someone has to stay here to keep contact with the ship. How do we settle it this time—chess or cards?"

"Chess takes too long," said Hutchins, "especially when you two play it." He reached into the chart table and produced a well-worn pack. "Cut them, Jerry."

"Ten of spades. Hope you can beat it, George."

"So do I. Damn—only five of clubs. Well, give my regards to the Venusians."

Despite Hutchins' assurance, it was hard work climbing

the escarpment. The slope was not too steep, but the weight of oxygen gear, refrigerated thermosuit, and scientific equipment came to more than a hundred pounds per man. The lower gravity—thirteen per cent weaker than Earth's—gave a little help, but not much, as they toiled up screes, rested on ledges to regain breath, and then clambered on again through the submarine twilight. The emerald glow that washed around them was brighter than that of the full moon on Earth. A moon would have been wasted on Venus, Jerry told himself; it could never have been seen from the surface, there were no oceans for it to rule—and the incessant aurora was a far more constant source of light.

They had climbed more than two thousand feet before the ground leveled out into a gentle slope, scarred here and there by channels that had clearly been cut by running water. After a little searching, they came across a gulley wide and deep enough to merit the name of river bed, and started to walk along it.

"I've just thought of something," said Jerry after they had traveled a few hundred yards. "Suppose there's a storm up ahead of us? I don't feel like facing a tidal wave of boiling water."

"If there's a storm," replied Hutchins a little impatiently, "we'll hear it. There'll be plenty of time to reach high ground."

He was undoubtedly right, but Jerry felt no happier as they continued to climb the gently shelving watercourse. His uneasiness had been growing ever since they had passed over the brow of the cliff and had lost radio contact with the scout car. In this day and age, to be out of touch with one's fellow men was a unique and unsettling experience. It had never happened to Jerry before in all his life; even aboard the *Morning Star*, when they were a hundred million miles from Earth, he could always send a message to his family and get a reply back within minutes. But now, a few yards of rock had cut him off from the rest of mankind; if anything happened to them here, no one would ever know, unless some later expedition found their bodies. George would wait for the agreed number of hours; then he would head back to the ship—alone. I guess I'm not really the pioneering type, Jerry told himself. I like running complicated machines, and that's how I got involved in space flight. But I never stopped to think where it would lead, and now it's too late to change my mind. . . .

They had traveled perhaps three miles toward the Pole, following the meanders of the river bed, when Hutchins stopped to make observations and collect specimens. "Still getting colder!" he said. "The temperature's down to one hundred and ninety-nine. That's far and away the lowest ever recorded on Venus. I wish we could call George and let him know."

Jerry tried all the wave bands; he even attempted to raise the ship—the unpredictable ups and downs of the planet's ionosphere sometimes made such long-distance reception possible—but there was not a whisper of a carrier wave above the roar and crackle of the Venusian thunderstorms.

"This is even better," said Hutchins, and now there was real excitement in his voice. "The oxygen concentration's way up—fifteen parts in a million. It was only five back at the car, and down in the lowlands you can scarcely detect it."

"But fifteen in a *million*!" protested Jerry. "Nothing could breathe that!"

"You've got hold of the wrong end of the stick," Hutchins explained. "Nothing does breathe it. Something *makes* it. Where do you think Earth's oxygen comes from? It's all produced by life—by growing plants. Before there were plants on Earth, our atmosphere was just like this one—a mess of carbon dioxide and ammonia and methane. Then vegetation evolved, and slowly converted the atmosphere into something that animals could breathe."

"I see," said Jerry, "and you think that the same process has just started here?"

"It looks like it. *Something* not far from here is producing oxygen—and plant life is the simplest explanation."

"And where there are plants," mused Jerry, "I suppose you'll have animals, sooner or later."

"Yes," said Hutchins, packing his gear and starting up the gulley, "though it takes a few hundred million years. We may be too soon—but I hope not."

"That's all very well," Jerry answered. "But suppose we meet something that doesn't like us? We've no weapons."

Hutchins gave a snort of disgust.

"And we don't need them. Have you stopped to think

what we look like? Any animal would run a mile at the sight of us."

There was some truth in that. The reflecting metal foil of their thermosuits covered them from head to foot like flexible, glittering armor. No insects had more elaborate antennas than those mounted on their helmets and back packs, and the wide lenses through which they stared out at the world looked like blank yet monstrous eyes. Yes, there were few animals on Earth that would stop to argue with such apparitions; but any Venusians might have different ideas.

Jerry was still mulling this over when they came upon the lake. Even at that first glimpse, it made him think not of the life they were seeking, but of death. Like a black mirror, it lay amid a fold of the hills; its far edge was hidden in the eternal mist, and ghostly columns of vapor swirled and danced upon its surface. All it needed, Jerry told himself, was Charon's ferry waiting to take them to the other side—or the Swan of Tuonela swimming majestically back and forth as it guarded the entrance to the Underworld. . . .

Yet for all this, it was a miracle—the first free water that men had ever found on Venus. Hutchins was already on his knees, almost in an attitude of prayer. But he was only collecting drops of the precious liquid to examine through his pocket microscope.

"Anything there?" asked Jerry anxiously.

Hutchins shook his head.

"If there is, it's too small to see with this instrument. I'll tell you more when we're back at the ship." He sealed a test tube and placed it in his collecting bag, as tenderly as any prospector who had just found a nugget laced with gold. It might be—it probably was—nothing more than plain water. But it might also be a universe of unknown, living creatures on the first stage of their billion-year journey to intelligence.

Hutchins had walked no more than a dozen yards along the edge of the lake when he stopped again, so suddenly that Garfield nearly collided with him.

"What's the matter?" Jerry asked. "Seen something?"

"That dark patch of rock over there. I noticed it before we stopped at the lake."

"What about it? It looks ordinary enough to me."

"I think it's grown bigger."

All his life, Jerry was to remember this moment. Somehow he never doubted Hutchins' statement; by this time he could believe anything, even that rocks could grow. The sense of isolation and mystery, the presence of that dark and brooding lake, the never-ceasing rumble of distant storms and the green flickering of the aurora—all these had done something to his mind, had prepared it to face the incredible. Yet he felt no fear; that would come later.

He looked at the rock. It was about five hundred feet away, as far as he could estimate. In this dim, emerald light it was hard to judge distances or dimensions. The rock—or whatever it was—seemed to be a horizontal slab of almost black material, lying near the crest of a low ridge. There was a second, much smaller, patch of similar material near it; Jerry tried to measure and memorize the gap between them, so that he would have some yardstick to detect any change.

Even when he saw that the gap was slowly shrinking, he still felt no alarm—only a puzzled excitement. Not until it had vanished completely, and he realized how his eyes had tricked him, did that awful feeling of helpless terror strike into his heart.

Here were no growing or moving rocks. What they were watching was a dark tide, a crawling carpet, sweeping slowly but inexorably toward them over the top of the ridge.

The moment of sheer, unreasoning panic lasted, mercifully, no more than a few seconds. Garfield's first terror began to fade as soon as he recognized its cause. For that advancing tide had reminded him, all too vividly, of a story he had read many years ago about the army ants of the Amazon, and the way in which they destroyed everything in their path. . . .

But whatever this tide might be, it was moving too slowly to be a real danger, unless it cut off their line of retreat. Hutchins was staring at it intently through their only pair of binoculars; he was the biologist, and he was holding his ground. No point in making a fool of myself, thought Jerry, by running like a scalded cat, if it isn't necessary.

"For heaven's sake," he said at last, when the moving carpet was only a hundred yards away and Hutchins had not uttered a word or stirred a muscle. "What *is* it?"

Hutchins slowly unfroze, like a statue coming to life.

"Sorry," he said. "I'd forgotten all about you. It's a plant, of course. At least, I suppose we'd better call it that."

"But it's *moving!*"

"Why should that surprise you? So do terrestrial plants. Ever seen speeded-up movies of ivy in action?"

"That still stays in one place—it doesn't crawl all over the landscape."

"Then what about the plankton plants of the sea? *They* can swim when they have to."

Jerry gave up; in any case, the approaching wonder had robbed him of words.

He still thought of the thing as a carpet—a deep-pile one, raveled into tassels at the edges. It varied in thickness as it moved; in some parts it was a mere film; in others, it heaped up to a depth of a foot or more. As it came closer and he could see its texture, Jerry was reminded of black velvet. He wondered what it felt like to the touch, then remembered that it would burn his fingers even if it did nothing else to them. He found himself thinking, in the lightheaded nervous reaction that often follows a sudden shock: "If there *are* any Venusians, we'll never be able to shake hands with them. They'd burn us, and we'd give them frostbite."

So far, the thing had shown no signs that it was aware of their presence. It had merely flowed forward like the mindless tide that it almost certainly was. Apart from the fact that it climbed over small obstacles, it might have been an advancing flood of water.

And then, when it was only ten feet away, the velvet tide checked itself. On the right and the left, it still flowed forward; but dead ahead it slowed to a halt.

"We're being encircled," said Jerry anxiously. "Better fall back, until we're sure it's harmless."

To his relief, Hutchins stepped back at once. After a brief hesitation, the creature resumed its slow advance and the dent in its front line straightened out.

Then Hutchins stepped forward again—and the thing slowly withdrew. Half a dozen times the biologist advanced, only to retreat again, and each time the living tide ebbed and flowed in synchronism with his movements. I never imagined, Jerry told himself, that I'd live to see a man waltzing with a plant. . . .

"Thermophobia," said Hutchins. "Purely automatic reaction. It doesn't like our heat."

"Our heat!" protested Jerry. "Why, we're living icicles by comparison."

"Of course—but our suits aren't, and that's all it knows about."

Stupid of me, thought Jerry. When you were snug and cool inside your thermosuit, it was easy to forget that the refrigeration unit on your back was pumping a blast of heat out into the surrounding air. No wonder the Venusian plant had shied away. . . .

"Let's see how it reacts to light," said Hutchins. He switched on his chest lamp, and the green auroral glow was instantly banished by the flood of pure white radiance. Until Man had come to this planet, no white light had ever shone upon the surface of Venus, even by day. As in the seas of Earth, there was only a green twilight, deepening slowly to utter darkness.

The transformation was so stunning that neither man could check a cry of astonishment. Gone in a flash was the deep, somber black of the thick-piled velvet carpet at their feet. Instead, as far as their lights carried, lay a blazing pattern of glorious, vivid reds, laced with streaks of gold. No Persian prince could ever have commanded so opulent a tapestry from his weavers, yet this was the accidental product of biological forces. Indeed, until they had switched on their floods, these superb colors had not even existed, and they would vanish once more when the alien light of Earth ceased to conjure them into being.

"Tikov was right," murmured Hutchins. "I wish he could have known."

"Right about what?" asked Jerry, though it seemed almost a sacrilege to speak in the presence of such loveliness.

"Back in Russia, fifty years ago, he found that plants living in very cold climates tended to be blue and violet, while those from hot ones were red or orange. He predicted that the Martian vegetation would be violet, and said that if there were plants on Venus they'd be red. Well, he was right on both counts. But we can't stand here all day—we've work to do."

"You're sure it's quite safe?" asked Jerry, some of his caution reasserting itself.

"Absolutely—it can't touch our suits even if it wants to. Anyway, it's moving past us."

That was true. They could see now that the entire creature—if it was a single plant, and not a colony—covered a roughly circular area about a hundred yards across. It was sweeping over the ground, as the shadow of a cloud moves before the wind—and where it had rested, the rocks were pitted with innumerable tiny holes that might have been etched by acid.

"Yes," said Hutchins, when Jerry remarked about this. "That's how some lichens feed; they secrete acids that dissolve rock. But no questions, please —not till we get back to the ship. I've several lifetimes' work here, and a couple of hours to do it in."

This was botany on the run. . . . The sensitive edge of the huge plant-thing could move with surprising speed when it tried to evade them. It was as if they were dealing with an animated flapjack, an acre in extent. There was no reaction —apart from the automatic avoidance of their exhaust heat —when Hutchins snipped samples or took probes. The creature flowed steadily onward over hills and valleys, guided by some strange vegetable instinct. Perhaps it was following some vein of mineral; the geologists could decide that, when they analyzed the rock samples that Hutchins had collected both before and after the passage of the living tapestry.

There was scarcely time to think or even to frame the countless questions that their discovery had raised. Presumably these creatures must be fairly common, for them to have found one so quickly. How did they reproduce? By shoots, spores, fission, or some other means? Where did they get their energy? What relatives, rivals, or parasites did they have? This could not be the only form of life on Venus—the very idea was absurd, for if you had one species, you must have thousands. . . .

Sheer hunger and fatigue forced them to a halt at last. The creature they were studying could eat its way around Venus—though Hutchins believed that it never went very far from the lake, as from time to time it approached the water and inserted a long, tubelike tendril into it—but the animals from Earth had to rest.

It was a great relief to inflate the pressurized tent, climb in through the air lock, and strip off their thermosuits. For the first time, as they relaxed inside their tiny plastic hemisphere, the true wonder and importance of the discovery forced itself upon their minds. This world around them was no longer the same; Venus was no longer dead—it had joined Earth and Mars.

For life called to life, across the gulfs of space. Everything that grew or moved upon the face of any planet was a portent, a promise that Man was not alone in this universe of blazing suns and swirling nebulae. If as yet he had found no companions with whom he could speak, that was only to be expected, for the light-years and the ages still stretched before him, waiting to be explored. Meanwhile, he must guard and cherish the life he found, whether it be upon Earth or Mars or Venus.

So Graham Hutchins, the happiest biologist in the solar system, told himself as he helped Garfield collect their refuse and seal it into a plastic disposal bag. When they deflated the tent and started on the homeward journey, there was no sign of the creature they had been examining. That was just as well; they might have been tempted to linger for more experiments, and already it was getting uncomfortably close to their deadline.

No matter; in a few months they would be back with a team of assistants, far more adequately equipped and with the eyes of the world upon them. Evolution had labored for a billion years to make this meeting possible; it could wait a little longer.

For a while nothing moved in the greenly glimmering, fog-bound landscape; it was deserted by man and crimson carpet alike. Then, flowing over the wind-carved hills, the creature reappeared. Or perhaps it was another of the same strange species; no one would ever know.

It flowed past the little cairn of stones where Hutchins and Garfield had buried their wastes. And then it stopped.

It was not puzzled, for it had no mind. But the chemical urges that drove it relentlessly over the polar plateau were crying: Here, here! Somewhere close at hand was the most precious of all the foods it needed—phosphorous, the element without which the spark of life could never ignite. It began to nuzzle the rocks, to ooze into the cracks and crannies, to scratch and scrabble with probing tendrils. Nothing that it did was beyond the capacity of any plant or tree on Earth—but it moved a thousand times more quickly, requiring only minutes to reach its goal and pierce through the plastic film.

And then it feasted, on food more concentrated than any it had ever known. It absorbed the carbohydrates and the proteins and the phosphates, the nicotine from the cigarette ends, the cellulose from the paper cups and spoons. All these it broke down and assimilated into its strange body, without difficulty and without harm.

Likewise it absorbed a whole microcosmos of living creatures—the bacteria and viruses which, upon an older planet, had evolved into a thousand deadly strains. Though only a very few could survive in this heat and this atmosphere, they were sufficient. As the carpet crawled back to the lake, it carried contagion to all its world.

Even as the Morning Star set course for her distant home, Venus was dying. The films and photographs and specimens that Hutchins was carrying in triumph were more precious even than he knew. They were the only record that would ever exist of life's third attempt to gain a foothold in the solar system.

Beneath the clouds of Venus, the story of Creation was ended.

A SLIGHT CASE
OF SUNSTROKE

SOMEONE ELSE SHOULD be telling this story—someone who understands the funny kind of football they play down in South America. Back in Moscow, Idaho, we grab the ball and run with it. In the small but prosperous republic which I'll call Perivia, they kick it around with their feet. And that is nothing to what they do to the referee.

Hasta la Vista, the capital of Perivia, is a fine, modern town up in the Andes, almost two miles above sea level. It is very proud of its magnificent football stadium, which can hold a hundred thousand people. Even so, it's hardly big enough to pack in all the fans who turn up when there's a really important game—such as the annual one with the neighboring republic of Panagura.

One of the first things I learned when I got to Perivia, after various distressing adventures in the less democratic parts of South America, was that last year's game had been lost because of the knavish dishonesty of the ref. He had, it seemed, penalized most of the players on the team, disallowed a goal, and generally made sure that the best side wouldn't win. This diatribe made me quite homesick, but remembering where I was, I merely commented, "You should have paid him more money." "We did," was the bitter reply, "but the Panagurans got at him later." "Too bad," I answered. "It's hard nowadays to find an honest man who stays bought." The Customs Inspector who'd just taken my last hundred-dollar bill had the grace to blush beneath his stubble as he waved me across the border.

The next few weeks were tough, which isn't the only reason why I'd rather not talk about them. But presently I was back in the agricultural-machinery business—though none of the machines I imported ever went near a farm, and it now cost a good deal more than a hundred dollars a time to get them over the frontier without some busybody looking into the packing cases. The last thing I had time to bother about was football; I knew that my expensive imports were going to be used at any moment, and wanted to make sure that *this* time my profits went with me when I left the country.

Even so, I could hardly ignore the excitement as the day for the return game drew nearer. For one thing, it interfered with business. I'd go to a conference, arranged with great difficulty and expense at a safe hotel or in the house of some reliable sympathizer, and half the time everyone would be talking about football. It was maddening, and I began to wonder if the Perivians took their politics as seriously as their sports. "Gentlemen!" I'd protest. "Our next consignment of rotary drills is being unloaded tomorrow, and unless we get that permit from the Minister of Agriculture, someone may open the cases and then . . ."

"Don't worry, my boy," General Sierra or Colonel Pedro would answer airily, "that's already taken care of. Leave it to the Army."

I knew better than to retort "Which army?", and for the next ten minutes I'd have to listen while an argument raged about football tactics and the best way of dealing with recalcitrant referees. I never dreamed—and I'm sure that no one else did—that this topic was intimately bound up with our particular problem.

Since then, I've had the leisure to work out what really happened, though it was very confusing at the time. The central figure in the whole improbable drama was undoubtedly Don Hernando Días—millionaire playboy, football fan, scientific dilettante, and, I am sure, future President of Perivia. Owing to his fondness for racing cars and Hollywood beauties, which has made him one of his country's best-known exports, most people assume that the "playboy" label describes Don Hernando completely. Nothing, but nothing, could be farther from the truth.

I knew that Don Hernando was one of us, but at the same time he was a considerable favorite of President Ruiz, which placed him in a powerful yet delicate position. Naturally, I'd never met him; he had to be very particular about his friends, and there were few people who cared to meet *me,* unless they had to. His interest in science I didn't discover until much later; it seems that he has a private observatory which is in frequent use on clear nights, though rumor has it that its functions are not entirely astronomical.

It must have taken all Don Hernando's charm and powers of persuasion to talk the President into it; if the old boy hadn't been a football fan too, and smarting under last year's defeat like every other patriotic Perivian, he would never have agreed. But the sheer originality of the scheme must have appealed to him even though he may not have been too happy about having half his troops out of action for the best part of an afternoon. Still, as Don Hernando undoubtedly reminded him, what better way of ensuring the loyalty of the Army than by giving it fifty thousand seats for the game of the year?

I knew nothing about all this when I took my place in the stadium on that memorable day. If you think I had no wish to be there, you are quite correct. But Colonel Pedro had given me a ticket, and it was unhealthy to hurt his feelings by not using it. So there I was, under the sweltering sun, fanning myself with the program and listening to the commentary over my portable radio while we waited for the game to begin.

The stadium was packed, its great oval bowl a solid sea of faces. There had been a slight delay in admitting the spectators; the police had done their best, but it takes time to search a hundred thousand people for concealed firearms. The visiting team had insisted on this, to the great indignation of the locals. The protests faded swiftly enough, however, as the artillery accumulated at the check points.

It was easy to tell the exact moment the referee drove up in his armor-plated Cadillac; you could follow his progress by the booing of the crowd. "Surely," I said to my neighbor —a young lieutenant so junior that it was safe for him to be seen out with me—"you could change the ref if you feel that way about him?"

He shrugged resignedly. "The visitors have the right to choose. There's nothing we can do about it."

"Then at least you ought to win the games you play in Panagura."

"True," he agreed. "But last time we were overconfident. We played so badly that even our ref couldn't save us."

I found it hard to feel much sympathy for either side, and settled down to a couple of hours of noisy boredom. Seldom have I been more mistaken.

Admittedly, the game took some time to get started. First a sweating band played the two national anthems, then the teams were presented to El Presidente and his lady, then the Cardinal blessed everybody, then there was a pause while the two captains had some obscure argument over the size or shape of the ball. I spent the waiting period reading my program, an expensive and beautifully produced affair that had been given to me by the lieutenant. It was tabloid size, printed on art paper, lavishly illustrated, and looked as if it had been bound in silver. It seemed unlikely that the publishers would get their money back, but this was obviously a matter of prestige rather than economics. In any event there was an impressive list of subscribers, headed by the President, to this "Special Victory Souvenir Issue." Most of my friends were on it, and I noted with amusement that the bill for presenting fifty thousand free copies to our gallant fighting men had been met by Don Hernando. It seemed a somewhat naïve bid for popularity, and I doubted if the good will was worth the considerable cost. The "Victory" also struck me as a trifle premature, not to say tactless.

These reflections were interrupted by the roar of the enormous crowd as play started. The ball slammed into action, but had barely zigzagged halfway down the field when a blue-jerseyed Perivian tripped a black-striped Panaguran. They don't waste much time, I told myself; what's the ref going to do? To my surprise, he did nothing, and I wondered if this match we'd got him to accept C.O.D. terms.

"Wasn't that a foul, or whatever you call it?" I said to my companion.

"Pfui!" he answered, not taking his eyes off the game. "Nobody bothers about *that* sort of thing. Besides, the coyote never saw it."

That was true. The referee was a long way down the field, and seemed to be finding it hard to keep up with the game. His movements were distinctly labored, and that puzzled me until I guessed the reason. Have you ever seen a man trying to run in a bulletproof vest? Poor devil, I thought, with the detached sympathy of one crook for another; you're earning your bribe. *I* was finding it hot enough merely sitting still.

For the first ten minutes, it was a pretty open game, and I don't think there were more than three fights. The Perivians just missed one goal; the ball was headed out so neatly that the frantic applause from the Panaguran supporters (who had a special police guard and a fortified section of the stadium all to themselves) went quite unbooed. I began to feel disappointed. Why, if you changed the shape of the ball this might be a good-natured game back home.

Indeed, there was no real work for the Red Cross until nearly half time, when three Perivians and two Panagurans (or it may have been the other way around) fused together in a magnificent melee from which only one survivor emerged under his own power. The casualties were carted off the field of battle amid much pandemonium, and there was a short break while replacements were brought up. This started the first major incident: the Perivians complained that the other side's wounded were shamming so that fresh reserves could be poured in. But the ref was adamant, the new men came on, and the background noise dropped to just below the threshold of pain as the game resumed.

The Panagurans promptly scored, and though none of my neighbors actually committed suicide, several seemed close to it. The transfusion of new blood had apparently pepped up the visitors, and things looked bad for the home team. Their opponents were passing the ball with such skill that the Perivian defenses were as porous as a sieve. At this rate, I told myself, the ref can afford to be honest; his side will win anyway. And to give him his due, I'd seen no sign of any obvious bias so far.

I didn't have long to wait. A last-minute rally by the

home team blocked a threatened attack on their goal, and a mighty kick by one of the defenders sent the ball rocketing toward the other end of the field. Before it had reached the apex of its flight, the piercing shriek of the referee's whistle brought the game to a halt. There was a brief consultation between ref and captains, which almost at once broke up in disorder. Down there on the field everyone was gesticulating violently, and the crowd was roaring its disapproval. "What's happening now?" I asked plaintively.

"The ref says our man was off side."

"But how can he be? He's on top of his own goal!"

"Shush!" said the lieutenant, unwilling to waste time enlightening my ignorance. I don't shush easily, but this time I let it go, and tried to work things out for myself. It seemed that the ref had awarded the Panagurans a free kick at our goal, and I could understand the way everybody felt about it.

The ball soared through the air in a beautiful parabola, nicked the post—and cannoned in despite a flying leap by the goalie. A mighty roar of anguish rose from the crowd, then died abruptly to a silence that was even more impressive. It was as if a great animal had been wounded—and was biding the time for its revenge. Despite the heat pouring down from the not-far-from-vertical sun, I felt a sudden chill, as if a cold wind had swept past me. Not for all the wealth of the Incas would I have changed places with the man sweating out there on the field in his bulletproof vest.

We were two down, but there was still hope—it was not yet half time and a lot could happen before the end of the game. The Perivians were on their mettle now, playing with almost demonic intensity, like men who had accepted a challenge and were going to show that they could meet it.

The new spirit paid off promptly. The home team scored one impeccable goal within a couple of minutes, and the crowd went wild with joy. By this time I was shouting like everyone else, and telling that referee things I didn't know I could say in Spanish. One to two now, and a hundred thousand people praying and cursing for the goal that would bring us level again.

It came just before half time. In a matter that had such grave consequences, I want to be perfectly fair. The ball had been passed to one of our forwards, he ran about fifty feet with it, evaded a couple of the defenders with some neat footwork, and kicked it cleanly into the goal. It had scarcely dropped down from the net when that whistle went again.

Now what? I wondered. He can't disallow *that*.

But he did. The ball, it seemed, had been handled. I've got pretty good eyes, and I never saw it. So I cannot honestly say that I blame the Perivians for what happened next.

The police managed to keep the crowd off the field, though it was touch and go for a minute. The two teams drew apart, leaving the center of the field bare except for the stubbornly defiant figure of the referee. He was probably wondering how he could make his escape from the stadium, and was consoling himself with the thought that when this game was over he could retire for good.

The thin, high bugle call took everyone completely by surprise—everyone, that is, except the fifty thousand well-trained men who had been waiting for it with mounting impatience. The whole arena became instantly silent, so silent that I could hear the noise of the traffic outside the stadium. A second time that bugle sounded—and all the vast acreage of faces opposite me vanished in a blinding sea of fire.

I cried out and covered my eyes; for one horrified moment I thought of atomic bombs and braced myself uselessly for the blast. But there was no concussion—only that flickering veil of flame that beat even through my closed eyelids for long seconds, then vanished as swiftly as it had come when the bugle blared out for the third and last time.

Everything was just as it had been before, except for one minor item. Where the referee had been standing there was a small, smoldering heap, from which a thin column of smoke curled up into the still air.

What in heaven's name had happened? I turned to my companion, who was as shaken as I was. *"Madre de Dios,"* I heard him mutter, "I never knew it would do *that.*" He was staring, not at the small funeral pyre down there on the field, but at the handsome souvenir program spread across his knees. And then, in a flash of incredulous comprehension, I understood.

Yet even now, when it's all been explained to me, I still find it hard to credit what I saw with my own eyes. It was so simple, so logical—so unbelievable.

Have you ever annoyed anyone by flicking a pocket mirror across his eyes? I guess every kid has; I remember doing it to a teacher once, and getting duly paddled. But I'd never imagined what would happen if fifty thousand well-trained men did the same trick, each using a tin-foil reflector a couple of feet square.

A mathematically minded friend of mine has worked it out—not that I needed any further proof, but I always like to get to the bottom of things. I never knew, until then, just how much energy there is in sunlight; it's well over a horsepower on every square yard facing the sun. Most of the heat falling on one side of that enormous stadium had been diverted into the single small area occupied by the late ref. Even allowing for all the programs that weren't aimed in the right direction, he must have intercepted at least a thousand horsepower of raw heat. He couldn't have felt much; it was as if he had been dropped into a blast furnace.

I'm sure that no one except Don Hernando realized what was likely to happen; his well-drilled fans had been told that the ref would merely be blinded and put out of action for the rest of the game. But I'm also equally sure that no one had any regrets. They play football for keeps in Perivia.

Likewise politics. While the game was continuing to its now-predictable end, beneath the benign gaze of a new and understandably docile referee, my friends were hard at work. When our victorious team had marched off the field (the final score was fourteen to two), everything had been settled. There had been practically no shooting, and as the President emerged from the stadium he was politely informed that a seat had been reserved for him on the morning flight to Mexico City.

As General Sierra remarked to me when I boarded the same plane as his late chief, "We let the Army win the football match, and while it was busy we won the country. So everybody's happy."

Though I was too polite to voice any doubts, I could not help thinking that this was a rather shortsighted attitude. Several million Panagurans were very unhappy indeed, and sooner or later there would be a day of reckoning.

I suspect that it's not far away. Last week a friend of mine, who is one of the world's top experts in his specialized field but prefers to work on a free-lance basis under an assumed name, indiscreetly blurted out one of his problems to me.

"Joe," he said, "why the devil should anyone want me to build a guided rocket that can fit inside a football?"

DOG STAR

WHEN I HEARD Laika's frantic barking, my first reaction was one of annoyance. I turned over in my bunk and murmured sleepily, "Shut up, you silly bitch." That dreamy interlude lasted only a fraction of a second; then consciousness returned—and, with it, fear. Fear of loneliness, and fear of madness.

For a moment I dared not open my eyes; I was afraid of what I might see. Reason told me that no dog had ever set foot upon this world, that Laika was separated from me by a quarter of a million miles of space—and, far more irrevocably, five years of time.

"You've been dreaming," I told myself angrily. "Stop being a fool—open your eyes! You won't see anything except the glow of the wall paint."

That was right, of course. The tiny cabin was empty, the door tightly closed. I was alone with my memories, overwhelmed by the transcendental sadness that often comes when some bright dream fades into drab reality. The sense of loss was so desolating that I longed to return to sleep. It was well that I failed to do so, for at that moment sleep would have been death. But I did not know this for another five seconds, and during that eternity I was back on Earth, seeking what comfort I could from the past.

No one ever discovered Laika's origin, though the Observatory staff made a few enquiries and I inserted several advertisements in the Pasadena newspapers. I found her, a lost and lonely ball of fluff, huddled by the roadside one summer evening when I was driving up to Palomar. Though I have never liked dogs, or indeed any animals, it was impossible to leave this helpless little creature to the mercy of the passing cars. With some qualms, wishing that I had a pair of gloves, I picked her up and dumped her in the baggage compartment. I was not going to hazard the upholstery of my new '92 Vik, and felt that she could do little damage there. In this, I was not altogether correct.

When I had parked the car at the Monastery—the astronomers' residential quarters, where I'd be living for the next week—I inspected my find without much enthusiasm. At that stage, I had intended to hand the puppy over to the janitor; but then it whimpered and opened its eyes. There was such an expression of helpless trust in them that—well, I changed my mind.

Sometimes I regretted that decision, though never for long. I had no idea how much trouble a growing dog could cause, deliberately and otherwise. My cleaning and repair bills soared; I could never be sure of finding an unravaged pair of socks or an unchewed copy of the *Astrophysical Journal*. But eventually Laika was both house-trained and Observatory-trained: she must have been the only dog ever to be allowed inside the two-hundred-inch dome. She would lie there quietly in the shadows for hours, while I was up in the cage making adjustments, quite content if she could hear my voice from time to time. The other astronomers became equally fond of her (it was old Dr. Anderson who suggested her name), but from the beginning she was my dog, and would obey no one else. Not that she would always obey me.

She was a beautiful animal, about ninety-five percent Alsatian. It was that missing five percent, I imagine, that led to her being abandoned. (I still feel a surge of anger when I think of it, but since I shall never know the facts, I may be jumping to false conclusions.) Apart from two dark patches over the eyes, most of her body was a smoky gray, and her coat was soft as silk. When her ears were pricked up, she looked incredibly intelligent and alert; sometimes I would be discussing spectral types of stellar evolution with my colleagues, and it would be hard to believe that she was not following the conversation.

Even now, I cannot understand why she became so attached to me, for I have made very few friends among human beings. Yet when I returned to the Observatory after an absence, she would go almost frantic with delight, bouncing around on her hind legs and putting her paws on my shoulders—which she could reach quite easily—all the while uttering small squeaks of joy which seemed highly inappropriate from so large a dog. I hated to leave her for more than a few days at a time, and though I could not take her with me on overseas trips, she accompanied me on most of my shorter journeys. She was with me when I drove north to attend that ill-fated seminar at Berkeley.

We were staying with university acquaintances; they had been polite about it, but obviously did not look forward to having a monster in the house. However, I assured them that Laika never gave the slightest trouble, and rather reluctantly they let her sleep in the living room. "You needn't worry about burglars tonight," I said. "We don't have any in Berkeley," they answered, rather coldly.

In the middle of the night, it seemed that they were wrong. I was awakened by a hysterical, high-pitched barking from Laika which I had heard only once before—when she had first seen a cow, and did not know what on earth to make of it. Cursing, I threw off the sheets and stumbled out into the darkness of the unfamiliar house. My main thought was to silence Laika before she roused my hosts—assuming that this was not already far too late. If there had been an intruder, he would certainly have taken flight by now. Indeed, I rather hoped that he had.

For a moment I stood beside the switch at the top of the stairs, wondering whether to throw it. Then I growled, "Shut up, Laika!" and flooded the place with light.

She was scratching frantically at the door, pausing from time to time to give that hysterical yelp. "If you want out," I said angrily, "there's no need for all that fuss." I went down, shot the bolt, and she took off into the night like a rocket.

It was very calm and still, with a waning Moon struggling to pierce the San Francisco fog. I stood in the luminous haze, looking out across the water to the lights of the city, waiting for Laika to come back so that I could chastise her suitably. I was still waiting when, for the second time in the twentieth century, the San Andreas Fault woke from its sleep.

Oddly enough, I was not frightened—at first. I can remember that two thoughts passed through my mind, in the moment before I realized the danger. Surely, I told myself, the geophysicists could have given us *some* warning. And then I found myself thinking, with great surprise, "I'd no idea that earthquakes make so much noise!"

It was about then that I knew that this was no ordinary quake; what happened afterward, I would prefer to forget. The Red Cross did not take me away until quite late the next morning, because I refused to leave Laika. As I looked at the shattered house containing the bodies of my friends, I knew that I owed my life to her; but the helicopter pilots could not be expected to understand that, and I cannot blame them for thinking that I was crazy, like so many of the others they had found wandering among the fires and the debris.

After that, I do not suppose we were ever apart for more than a few hours. I have been told—and I can well believe it —that I became less and less interested in human company, without being actively unsocial or misanthropic. Between them, the stars and Laika filled all my needs. We used to go for long walks together over the mountains; it was the happiest time I have ever known. There was only one flaw; I knew, though Laika could not, how soon it must end.

We had been planning the move for more than a decade. As far back as the nineteen-sixties it was realized that Earth was no place for an astronomical observatory. Even the small pilot instruments on the Moon had far outperformed all the telescopes peering through the murk and haze of the terrestrial atmosphere. The story of Mount Wilson, Palomar, Greenwich, and the other great names was coming to an end; they would still be used for training purposes, but the research frontier must move out into space.

I had to move with it; indeed, I had already been offered the post of Deputy Director, Farside Observatory. In a few months, I could hope to solve problems I had been working on for years. Beyond the atmosphere, I would be like a blind man who had suddenly been given sight.

It was utterly impossible, of course, to take Laika with me. The only animals on the Moon were those needed for experimental purposes; it might be another generation before pets were allowed, and even then it would cost a fortune to carry them there—and to keep them alive. Providing Laika with her usual two pounds of meat a day would, I calculated, take several times my quite comfortable salary.

The choice was simple and straightforward. I could stay on Earth and abandon my career. Or I could go to the Moon —and abandon Laika.

After all, she was only a dog. In a dozen years, she would be dead, while I should be reaching the peak of my profession. No sane man would have hesitated over the matter; yet I did hesitate, and if by now you do not understand why, no further words of mine can help.

In the end, I let matters go by default. Up to the very week I was due to leave, I had still made no plans for Laika. When Dr. Anderson volunteered to look after her, I accepted numbly, with scarcely a word of thanks. The old physicist and his wife had always been fond of her, and I am afraid that they considered me indifferent and heartless— when the truth was just the opposite. We went for one more walk together over the hills; then I delivered her silently to the Andersons, and did not see her again.

Take-off was delayed almost twenty-four hours, until a major flare storm had cleared the Earth's orbit; even so, the Van Allen belts were still so active that we had to make our exit through the North Polar Gap. It was a miserable flight; apart from the usual trouble with weightlessness, we were all groggy with antiradiation drugs. The ship was already over Farside before I took much interest in the proceedings, so I missed the sight of Earth dropping below the horizon. Nor was I really sorry; I wanted no reminders, and intended to think only of the future. Yet I could not shake off that feeling of guilt; I had deserted someone who loved and trusted me, and was no better than those who had abandoned Laika when she was a puppy, beside the dusty road to Palomar.

The news that she was dead reached me a month later. There was no reason that anyone knew; the Andersons had done their best, and were very upset. She had just lost interest in living, it seemed. For a while, I think I did the same; but work is a wonderful anodyne, and my program was just getting under way. Though I never forgot Laika, in a little while the memory ceased to hurt.

Then why had it come back to haunt me, five years later, on the far side of the Moon? I was searching my mind for the reason when the metal building around me quivered as if under the impact of a heavy blow. I reacted without thinking, and was already closing the helmet of my emergency suit when the foundations slipped and the wall tore open with a short-lived scream of escaping air. Because I had automatically pressed the General Alarm button, we lost only two men, despite the fact that the tremor—the worst ever recorded on Farside—cracked all three of the Observatory's pressure domes.

It is hardly necessary for me to say that I do not believe in the supernatural; everything that happened has a perfectly rational explanation, obvious to any man with the slightest knowledge of psychology. In the second San Francisco earthquake, Laika was not the only dog to sense approaching disaster; many such cases were reported. And on Farside, my own memories must have given me that heightened awareness, when my never-sleeping subconscious detected the first faint vibrations from within the Moon.

The human mind has strange and labyrinthine ways of going about its business; it knew the signal that would most swiftly rouse me to the knowledge of danger. There is nothing more to it than that; though in a sense one could say that Laika woke me on both occasions, there is no mystery about it, no miraculous warning across the gulf that neither man nor dog can ever bridge.

Of that I am sure, if I am sure of anything. Yet sometimes I wake now, in the silence of the Moon, and wish that the dream could have lasted a few seconds longer—so that I could have looked just once more into those luminous brown eyes, brimming with an unselfish, undemanding love I have found nowhere else on this or on any other world.

THE NINE BILLION NAMES OF GOD

"THIS IS A slightly unusual request," said Dr. Wagner, with what he hoped was commendable restraint. "As far as I know, it's the first time anyone's been asked to supply a Tibetan monastery with an Automatic Sequence Computer. I don't wish to be inquisitive, but I should hardly have thought that your—ah—establishment had much use for such a machine. Could you explain just what you intend to do with it?"

"Gladly," replied the lama, readjusting his silk robes and carefully putting away the slide rule he had been using for currency conversions. "Your Mark V Computer can carry out any routine mathematical operation involving up to ten digits. However, for our work we are interested in *letters*, not numbers. As we wish you to modify the output circuits, the machine will be printing words, not columns of figures."

"I don't quite understand. . . ."

"This is a project on which we have been working for the last three centuries—since the lamasery was founded, in fact. It is somewhat alien to your way of thought, so I hope you will listen with an open mind while I explain it."

"Naturally."

"It is really quite simple. We have been compiling a list which shall contain all the possible names of God."

"I beg your pardon?"

"We have reason to believe," continued the lama imperturbably, "that all such names can be written with not more than nine letters in an alphabet we have devised."

"And you have been doing this for three centuries?"

"Yes: we expected it would take us about fifteen thousand years to complete the task."

"Oh," Dr. Wagner looked a little dazed. "Now I see why you wanted to hire one of our machines. But exactly what is the *purpose* of this project?"

The lama hesitated for a fraction of a second, and Wagner wondered if he had offended him. If so, there was no trace of annoyance in the reply.

"Call it ritual, if you like, but it's a fundamental part of our belief. All the many names of the Supreme Being—God, Jehovah, Allah, and so on—they are only man-made labels. There is a philosophical problem of some difficulty here, which I do not propose to discuss, but somewhere among all the possible combinations of letters that can occur are what one may call the *real* names of God. By systematic permutation of letters, we have been trying to list them all."

"I see. You've been starting at AAAAAAA . . . and working up to ZZZZZZZZ. . . ."

"Exactly—though we use a special alphabet of our own. Modifying the electromatic typewriters to deal with this is, of course, trivial. A rather more interesting problem is that of devising suitable circuits to eliminate ridiculous combinations. For example, no letter must occur more than three times in succession."

"Three? Surely you mean two."

"Three is correct: I am afraid it would take too long to explain why, even if you understood our language."

"I'm sure it would," said Wagner hastily. "Go on."

"Luckily, it will be a simple matter to adapt your Automatic Sequence Computer for this work, since once it has been programed properly it will permute each letter in turn and print the result. What would have taken us fifteen thousand years it will be able to do in a hundred days."

Dr. Wagner was scarcely conscious of the faint sounds from the Manhattan streets far below. He was in a different world, a world of natural, not man-made, mountains. High up in their remote aeries these monks had been patiently at work, generation after generation, compiling their lists of meaningless words. Was there any limit to the follies of mankind? Still, he must give no hint of his inner thoughts. The customer was always right. . . .

"There's no doubt," replied the doctor, "that we can modify the Mark V to print lists of this nature. I'm much more worried about the problem of installation and maintenance. Getting out to Tibet, in these days, is not going to be easy."

"We can arrange that. The components are small enough to travel by air—that is one reason why we chose your machine. If you can get them to India, we will provide transport from there."

"And you want to hire two of our engineers?"

"Yes, for the three months that the project should occupy."

"I've no doubt that Personnel can manage that." Dr. Wagner scribbled a note on his desk pad. "There are just two other points—"

Before he could finish the sentence the lama had produced a small slip of paper.

"This is my certified credit balance at the Asiatic Bank."

"Thank you. It appears to be—ah—adequate. The second matter is so trivial that I hesitate to mention it—but it's surprising how often the obvious gets overlooked. What source of electrical energy have you?"

"A diesel generator providing fifty kilowatts at a hundred and ten volts. It was installed about five years ago and is quite reliable. It's made life at the lamasery much more comfortable, but of course it was really installed to provide power for the motors driving the prayer wheels."

"Of course," echoed Dr. Wagner. "I should have thought of that."

The view from the parapet was vertiginous, but in time one gets used to anything. After three months, George Hanley was not impressed by the two-thousand-foot swoop into the abyss or the remote checkerboard of fields in the valley below. He was leaning against the wind-smoothed stones and staring morosely at the distant mountains whose names he had never bothered to discover.

This, thought George, was the craziest thing that had ever happened to him. "Project Shangri-la," some wit back at the labs had christened it. For weeks now the Mark V had been churning out acres of sheets covered with gibberish. Patiently, inexorably, the computer had been rearranging letters in all their possible combinations, exhausting each class before going on to the next. As the sheets had emerged from the electromatic typewriters, the monks had carefully cut them up and pasted them into enormous books. In another week, heaven be praised, they would have finished. Just what obscure calculations had convinced the monks that they needn't bother to go on to words of ten, twenty, or a hundred letters, George didn't know. One of his recurring nightmares was that there would be some change of plan, and that the high lama (whom they'd naturally called Sam Jaffe, though he didn't look a bit like him) would suddenly announce that the project would be extended to approximately A.D. 2060. They were quite capable of it.

George heard the heavy wooden door slam in the wind as Chuck came out onto the parapet beside him. As usual, Chuck was smoking one of the cigars that made him so popular with the monks—who, it seemed, were quite willing to embrace all the minor and most of the major pleasures of life. That was one thing in their favor: they might be crazy, but they weren't bluenoses. Those frequent trips they took down to the village, for instance . . .

"Listen, George," said Chuck urgently. "I've learned something that means trouble."

"What's wrong? Isn't the machine behaving?" That was the worst contingency George could imagine. It might delay his return, and nothing could be more horrible. The way he felt now, even the sight of a TV commercial would seem like manna from heaven. At least it would be some link with home.

"No—it's nothing like that." Chuck settled himself on the parapet, which was unusual because normally he was scared of the drop. "I've just found what all this is about."

"What d'ya mean? I thought we knew."

"Sure—we know what the monks are trying to do. But we didn't know *why*. It's the craziest thing—"

"Tell me something new," growled George.

"—but old Sam's just come clean with me. You know the way he drops in every afternoon to watch the sheets roll out. Well, this time he seemed rather excited, or at least as near as he'll ever get to it. When I told him that we were on the last cycle he asked me, in that cute English accent of his, if I'd ever wondered what they were trying to do. I said, 'Sure' —and he told me."

"Go on: I'll buy it."

"Well, they believe that when they have listed all His names—and they reckon that there are about nine billion of them—God's purpose will be achieved. The human race will have finished what it was created to do, and there won't be any point in carrying on. Indeed, the very idea is something like blasphemy."

"Then what do they expect us to do? Commit suicide?"

"There's no need for that. When the list's completed, God steps in and simply winds things up . . . bingo!"

"Oh, I get it. When we finish our job, it will be the end of the world."

Chuck gave a nervous little laugh.

"That's just what I said to Sam. And do you know what happened? He looked at me in a very queer way, like I'd been stupid in class, and said, 'It's nothing as trivial as *that.*'"

George thought this over for a moment.

"That's what I call taking the Wide View," he said presently. "But what d'you suppose we should do about it? I don't see that it makes the slightest difference to us. After all, we already knew that they were crazy."

"Yes—but don't you see what may happen? When the list's complete and the Last Trump doesn't blow—or whatever it is they expect—*we* may get the blame. It's our machine they've been using. I don't like the situation one little bit."

"I see," said George slowly. "You've got a point there. But this sort of thing's happened before, you know. When I was a kid down in Louisiana we had a crackpot preacher who once said the world was going to end next Sunday.

Hundreds of people believed him—even sold their homes. Yet when nothing happened, they didn't turn nasty, as you'd expect. They just decided that he'd made a mistake in his calculations and went right on believing. I guess some of them still do."

"Well, this isn't Louisiana, in case you hadn't noticed. There are just two of us and hundreds of these monks. I like them, and I'll be sorry for old Sam when his lifework backfires on him. But all the same, I wish I was somewhere else."

"I've been wishing that for weeks. But there's nothing we can do until the contract's finished and the transport arrives to fly us out."

"Of course," said Chuck thoughtfully, "we could always try a bit of sabotage."

"Like hell we could! That would make things worse."

"Not the way I meant. Look at it like this. The machine will finish its run four days from now, on the present twenty-hours-a-day basis. The transport calls in a week. O.K.—then all we need to do is to find something that needs replacing during one of the overhaul periods—something that will hold up the works for a couple of days. We'll fix it, of course, but not too quickly. If we time matters properly, we can be down at the airfield when the last name pops out of the register. They won't be able to catch us then."

"I don't like it," said George. "It will be the first time I ever walked out on a job. Besides, it would make them suspicious. No, I'll sit tight and take what comes."

"I *still* don't like. it," he said, seven days later, as the tough little mountain ponies carried them down the winding road. "And don't you think I'm running away because I'm afraid. I'm just sorry for those poor old guys up there, and I don't want to be around when they find what suckers they've been. Wonder how Sam will take it?"

"It's funny," replied Chuck, "but when I said good-by I got the idea he knew we were walking out on him—and that he didn't care because he knew the machine was running smoothly and that the job would soon be finished. After that —well, of course, for him there just isn't any After That. . . ."

George turned in his saddle and stared back up the mountain road. This was the last place from which one could get a clear view of the lamasery. The squat, angular buildings were silhouetted against the afterglow of the sunset: here and there, lights gleamed like portholes in the side of an ocean liner. Electric lights, of course, sharing the same circuit as the Mark V. How much longer would they share it? wondered George. Would the monks smash up the computer in their rage and disappointment? Or would they just sit down quietly and begin their calculations all over again?

He knew exactly what was happening up on the mountain at this very moment. The high lama and his assistants would be sitting in their silk robes, inspecting the sheets as the junior monks carried them away from the typewriters and pasted them into the great volumes. No one would be saying anything. The only sound would be the incessant patter, the never-ending rainstorm of the keys hitting the paper, for the Mark V itself was utterly silent as it flashed through its thousands of calculations a second. Three months of this, thought George, was enough to start anyone climbing up the wall.

"There she is!" called Chuck, pointing down into the valley. "Ain't she beautiful!"

She certainly was, thought George. The battered old DC3 lay at the end of the runway like a tiny silver cross. In two hours she would be bearing them away to freedom and sanity. It was a thought worth savoring like a fine liqueur. George let it roll round his mind as the pony trudged patiently down the slope.

The swift night of the high Himalayas was now almost upon them. Fortunately, the road was very good, as roads went in that region, and they were both carrying torches. There was not the slightest danger, only a certain discomfort from the bitter cold. The sky overhead was perfectly clear, and ablaze with the familiar, friendly stars. At least there would be no risk, thought George, of the pilot being unable to take off because of weather conditions. That had been his only remaining worry.

He began to sing, but gave it up after a while. This vast arena of mountains, gleaming like whitely hooded ghosts on every side, did not encourage such ebullience. Presently George glanced at his watch.

"Should be there in an hour," he called back over his shoulder to Chuck. Then he added, in an afterthought:

"Wonder if the computer's finished its run. It was due about now."

Chuck didn't reply, so George swung round in his saddle. He could just see Chuck's face, a white oval turned toward the sky.

"Look," whispered Chuck, and George lifted his eyes to heaven. (There is always a last time for everything.)

Overhead, without any fuss, the stars were going out.

REFUGEE

"WHEN HE COMES aboard," said Captain Saunders, as he waited for the landing ramp to extrude itself, "what the devil shall I call him?"

There was a thoughtful silence while the navigation officer and the assistant pilot considered this problem in etiquette. Then Mitchell locked the main control panel, and the ship's multitudinous mechanisms lapsed into unconsciousness as power was withdrawn from them.

"The correct address," he drawled slowly, "is 'Your Royal Highness.' "

"Huh!" snorted the captain. "I'll be damned if I'll call anyone *that* !"

"In these progressive days," put in Chambers helpfully, "I believe that 'Sir' is quite sufficient. But there's no need to worry if you forget: it's been a long time since anyone went to the Tower. Besides, this Henry isn't as tough a proposition as the one who had all the wives."

"From all accounts," added Mitchell, "he's a very pleasant young man. Quite intelligent, too. He's often been known to ask people technical questions that they couldn't answer."

Captain Saunders ignored the implications of this remark, beyond resolving that if Prince Henry wanted to know how a Field Compensation Drive Generator worked, then Mitchell could do the explaining. He got gingerly to his feet—they'd been operating on half a gravity during flight, and now they were on Earth, he felt like a ton of bricks—and started to make his way along the corridors that led to the lower air lock. With an oily purring, the great curving door side-stepped out of his way. Adjusting his smile, he walked out to meet the television cameras and the heir to the British throne.

The man who would, presumably, one day be Henry IX of England was still in his early twenties. He was slightly below average height, and had fine-drawn, regular features that really lived up to all the genealogical clichés. Captain Saunders, who came from Dallas and had no intention of being impressed by any prince, found himself unexpectedly moved by the wide, sad eyes. They were eyes that had seen too many receptions and parades, that had had to watch countless totally uninteresting things, that had never been allowed to stray far from the carefully planned official routes. Looking at that proud but weary face, Captain Saunders glimpsed for the first time the ultimate loneliness of royalty. All his dislike of that institution became suddenly trivial against its real defect: what was wrong with the Crown was the unfairness of inflicting such a burden on any human being. . . .

The passageways of the *Centaurus* were too narrow to allow for general sight-seeing, and it was soon clear that it suited Prince Henry very well to leave his entourage behind. Once they had begun moving through the ship, Saunders lost all his stiffness and reserve, and within a few minutes was treating the prince exactly like any other visitor. He did not realize that one of the earliest lessons royalty has to learn is that of putting people at their ease.

"You know, Captain," said the prince wistfully, "this is a big day for us. I've always hoped that one day it would be possible for spaceships to operate from England. But it still seems strange to have a port of our own here, after all these years. Tell me—did you ever have much to do with rockets?"

"Well, I had some training on them, but they were already on the way out before I graduated. I was lucky: some older men had to go back to school and start all over again —or else abandon space completely if they couldn't convert to the new ships."

"It made as much difference as that?"

"Oh yes—when the rocket went, it was as big as the change from sail to steam. That's an analogy you'll often hear, by the way. There was a glamour about the old rockets, just as there was about the old windjammers, which these modern ships haven't got. When the *Centaurus* takes off, she goes up as quietly as a balloon—and as slowly, if she wants to. But a rocket blast-off shook the ground for miles, and you'd be deaf for days if you were too near the launching apron. Still, you'll know all that from the old news recordings."

The prince smiled.

"Yes," he said. "I've often run through them at the Palace. I think I've watched every incident in all the pioneering expeditions. I was sorry to see the end of the rockets, too. But we could never have had a spaceport here on Salisbury plain—the vibration would have shaken down Stonehenge!"

"Stonehenge?" queried Saunders as he held open a hatch and let the prince through into Hold Number 3.

"Ancient monument—one of the most famous stone circles in the world. It's really impressive, and about three thousand years old. See it if you can—it's only ten miles from here."

Captain Saunders had some difficulty in suppressing a smile. What an odd country this was: where else, he wondered, would you find contrasts like this? It made him feel very young and raw when he remembered that back home Billy the Kid was ancient history, and there was hardly anything in the whole of Texas as much as five hundred years old. For the first time he began to realize what tradition meant: it gave Prince Henry something that he could never possess. Poise—self-confidence, yes, that was it. And a pride that was somehow free from arrogance because it took itself so much for granted that it never had to be asserted.

It was surprising how many questions Prince Henry

managed to ask in the thirty minutes that had been allotted for his tour of the freighter. They were not the routine questions that people asked out of politeness, quite uninterested in the answers. H.R.H. Prince Henry knew a lot about spaceships, and Captain Saunders felt completely exhausted when he handed his distinguished guest back to the reception committee, which had been waiting outside the *Centaurus* with well-simulated patience.

"Thank you very much, Captain," said the prince as they shook hands in the air lock. "I've not enjoyed myself so much for ages. I hope you have a pleasant stay in England, and a successful voyage." Then his retinue whisked him away, and the port officials, frustrated until now, came aboard to check the ship's papers.

"Well," said Mitchell when it was all over, "what did you think of our Prince of Wales?"

"He surprised me," answered Saunders frankly. "I'd never have guessed he was a prince. I always thought they were rather dumb. But heck, he *knew* the principles of the Field Drive! Has he ever been up in space?"

"Once, I think. Just a hop above the atmosphere in a Space Force ship. It didn't even reach orbit before it came back again—but the Prime Minister nearly had a fit. There were questions in the House and editorials in the *Times*. Everyone decided that the heir to the throne was too valuable to risk in these newfangled inventions. So, though he has the rank of commodore in the Royal Space Force, he's never even been to the moon."

"The poor guy," said Captain Saunders.

He had three days to burn, since it was not the captain's job to supervise the loading of the ship or the preflight maintenance. Saunders knew skippers who hung around breathing heavily on the necks of the servicing engineers, but he wasn't that type. Besides, he wanted to see London. He had been to Mars and Venus and the moon, but this was his first visit to England. Mitchell and Chambers filled him with useful information and put him on the monorail to London before dashing off to see their own families. They would be returning to the spaceport a day before he did, to see that everything was in order. It was a great relief having officers one could rely on so implicitly: they were unimaginative and cautious, but thoroughgoing almost to a fault. If *they* said that everything was shipshape, Saunders knew he could take off without qualms.

The sleek, streamlined cylinder whistled across the carefully tailored landscape. It was so close to the ground, and traveling so swiftly, that one could only gather fleeting impressions of the towns and fields that flashed by. Everything, thought Saunders, was so incredibly compact, and on such a Lilliputian scale. There were no open spaces, no fields more than a mile long in any direction. It was enough to give a Texan claustrophobia—particularly a Texan who also happened to be a space pilot.

The sharply defined edge of London appeared like the bulwark of some walled city on the horizon. With few exceptions, the buildings were quite low—perhaps fifteen or twenty stories in height. The monorail shot through a narrow canyon, over a very attractive park, across a river that was presumably the Thames, and then came to rest with a steady, powerful surge of deceleration. A loudspeaker announced, in a modest voice that seemed afraid of being overheard: "This is Paddington. Passengers for the North please remain seated." Saunders pulled his baggage down from the rack and headed out into the station.

As he made for the entrance to the Underground, he passed a bookstall and glanced at the magazines on display. About half of them, it seemed, carried photographs of Prince Henry or other members of the royal family. This, thought Saunders, was altogether too much of a good thing. He also noticed that all the evening papers showed the prince entering or leaving the *Centaurus,* and bought copies to read in the subway—he begged its pardon, the "Tube."

The editorial comments had a monotonous similarity. At last, they rejoiced, England need no longer take a back seat among the space-going nations. Now it was possible to operate a space fleet without having a million square miles of desert: the silent, gravity-defying ships of today could land, if need be, in Hyde Park, without even disturbing the ducks on the Serpentine. Saunders found it odd that this sort of patriotism had managed to survive into the age of space, but he guessed that the British had felt it pretty badly when they'd had to borrow launching sites from the Australians, the Americans, and the Russians.

The London Underground was still, after a century and a half, the best transport system in the world, and it deposited Saunders safely at his destination less than ten minutes after he had left Paddington. In ten minutes the *Centaurus* could have covered fifty thousand miles; but space, after all, was not quite so crowded as this. Nor were the orbits of space craft so tortuous as the streets Saunders had to negotiate to reach his hotel. All attempts to straighten out London had failed dismally, and it was fifteen minutes before he completed the last hundred yards of his journey.

He stripped off his jacket and collapsed thankfully on his bed. Three quiet, carefree days all to himself: it seemed too good to be true.

It was. He had barely taken a deep breath when the phone rang.

"Captain Saunders? I'm so glad we found you. This is the B.B.C. We have a program called 'In Town Tonight' and we were wondering . . ."

The thud of the air-lock door was the sweetest sound Saunders had heard for days. Now he was safe; nobody could get at him here in his armored fortress, which would soon be far out in the freedom of space. It was not that he had been treated badly: on the contrary, he had been treated altogether too well. He had made four (or was it five?) appearances on various TV programs; he had been to more parties than he could remember; he had acquired several hundred new friends and (the way his head felt now) forgotten all his old ones.

"Who started the rumor," he said to Mitchell as they met at the port, "that the British were reserved and standoffish? Heaven help me if I ever meet a *demonstrative* Englishman."

"I take it," replied Mitchell, "that you had a good time."

"Ask me tomorrow," Saunders replied. "I may have reintegrated my psyche by then."

"I saw you on that quiz program last night," remarked Chambers. "You looked pretty ghastly."

"Thank you: that's just the sort of sympathetic encouragement I need at the moment. I'd like to see you think of a synonym for 'jejune' after you'd been up until three in the morning."

"Vapid," replied Chambers promptly.

"Insipid," said Mitchell, not to be outdone.

"You win. Let's have those overhaul schedules and see what the engineers have been up to."

Once seated at the control desk, Captain Saunders quickly became his usual efficient self. He was home again, and his training took over. He knew exactly what to do, and would do it with automatic precision. To right and left of him, Mitchell and Chambers were checking their instruments and calling the control tower.

It took them an hour to carry out the elaborate preflight routine. When the last signature had been attached to the last sheet of instructions, and the last red light on the monitor panel had turned to green, Saunders flopped back in his seat and lit a cigarette. They had ten minutes to spare before take-off.

"One day," he said, "I'm going to come to England incognito to find what makes the place tick. I don't understand how you can crowd so many people onto one little island without it sinking."

"Huh," snorted Chambers. "You should see Holland. That makes England look as wide open as Texas."

"And then there's this royal family business. Do you know, wherever I went everybody kept asking me how I got on with Prince Henry—what we'd talked about—didn't I think he was a fine guy, and so on. Frankly, I got fed up with it. I can't imagine how you've managed to stand it for a thousand years."

"Don't think that the royal family's been popular all the time," replied Mitchell. "Remember what happened to Charles the First? And some of the things we said about the early Georges were quite as rude as the remarks your people made later."

"We just happen to like tradition," said Chambers. "We're not afraid to change when the time comes, but as far as the royal family is concerned—well, it's unique and we're rather fond of it. Just the way you feel about the Statue of Liberty."

"Not a fair example. I don't think it's right to put human beings up on a pedestal and treat them as if they're—well, minor deities. Look at Prince Henry, for instance. Do you think he'll ever have a chance of doing the things he really wants to do? I saw him three times on TV when I was in

London. The first time he was opening a new school some-where; then he was giving a speech to the Worshipful Company of Fishmongers at the Guildhall (I swear I'm not making *that* up), and finally he was receiving an address of welcome from the mayor of Podunk, or whatever your equivalent is." ("Wigan," interjected Mitchell.) "I think I'd rather be in jail than live that sort of life. Why can't you leave the poor guy alone?"

For once, neither Mitchell nor Chambers rose to the challenge. Indeed, they maintained a somewhat frigid silence. That's torn it, thought Saunders. I should have kept my big mouth shut; now I've hurt their feelings. I should have remembered that advice I read somewhere: "The British have two religions—cricket and the royal family. Never attempt to criticize either."

The awkward pause was broken by the radio and the voice of the spaceport controller.

"Control to *Centaurus*. Your flight lane clear. O.K. to lift."

"Take-off program starting—*now*!" replied Saunders, throwing the master switch. Then he leaned back, his eyes taking in the entire control panel, his hands clear of the board but ready for instant action.

He was tense but completely confident. Better brains than his—brains of metal and crystal and flashing electron streams—were in charge of the *Centaurus* now. If necessary, he could take command, but he had never yet lifted a ship manually and never expected to do so. If the automatics failed, he would cancel the take-off and sit here on Earth until the fault had been cleared up.

The main field went on, and weight ebbed from the *Centaurus*. There were protesting groans from the ship's hull and structure as the strains redistributed themselves. The curved arms of the landing cradle were carrying no load now; the slightest breath of wind would carry the freighter away into the sky.

Control called from the tower: "Your weight now zero: check calibration."

Saunders looked at his meters. The upthrust of the field would now exactly equal the weight of the ship, and the meter readings should agree with the totals on the loading schedules. In at least one instance this check had revealed the presence of a stowaway on board a spaceship—the gauges were as sensitive as that.

"One million, five hundred and sixty thousand, four hundred and twenty kilograms," Saunders read off from the thrust indicators. "Pretty good—it checks to within fifteen kilos. The first time I've been underweight, though. You could have taken on some more candy for that plump girl friend of yours in Port Lowell, Mitch."

The assistant pilot gave a rather sickly grin. He had never quite lived down a blind date on Mars which had given him a completely unwarranted reputation for preferring statuesque blondes.

There was no sense of motion, but the *Centaurus* was now falling up into the summer sky as her weight was not only neutralized but reversed. To the watchers below, she would be a swiftly mounting star, a silver globule climbing through and beyond the clouds. Around her, the blue of the atmosphere was deepening into the eternal darkness of space. Like a bead moving along an invisible wire, the freighter was following the pattern of radio waves that would lead her from world to world.

This, thought Captain Saunders, was his twenty-sixth take-off from Earth. But the wonder would never die, nor would he ever outgrow the feeling of power it gave him to sit here at the control panel, the master of forces beyond even the dreams of mankind's ancient gods. No two departures were ever the same; some were into the dawn, some toward the sunset, some above a cloud-veiled Earth, some through clear and sparkling skies. Space itself might be unchanging, but on Earth the same pattern never recurred, and no man ever looked twice at the same landscape or the same sky. Down there the Atlantic waves were marching eternally toward Europe, and high above them—but so far below the *Centaurus!*—the glittering bands of cloud were advancing before the same winds. England began to merge into the continent, and the European coast line became foreshortened and misty as it sank hull down beyond the curve of the world. At the frontier of the west, a fugitive stain on the horizon was the first hint of America. With a single glance, Captain Saunders could span all the leagues across which Columbus had labored half a thousand years ago.

With the silence of limitless power, the ship shook itself

free from the last bonds of Earth. To an outside observer, the only sign of the energies it was expending would have been the dull red glow from the radiation fins around the vessel's equator, as the heat loss from the mass-converters was dissipated into space.

"14:03:45," wrote Captain Saunders neatly in the log. "Escape velocity attained. Course deviation negligible."

There was little point in making the entry. The modest 25,000 miles an hour that had been the almost unattainable goal of the first astronauts had no practical significance now, since the *Centaurus* was still accelerating and would continue to gain speed for hours. But it had a profound psychological meaning. Until this moment, if power had failed, they would have fallen back to Earth. But now gravity could never recapture them: they had achieved the freedom of space, and could take their pick of the planets. In practice, of course, there would be several kinds of hell to pay if they did not pick Mars and deliver their cargo according to plan. But Captain Saunders, like all spacemen, was fundamentally a romantic. Even on a milk run like this he would sometimes dream of the ringed glory of Saturn or the somber Neptunian wastes, lit by the distant fires of the shrunken sun.

An hour after take-off, according to the hallowed ritual, Chambers left the course computer to its own devices and produced the three glasses that lived beneath the chart table. As he drank the traditional toast to Newton, Oberth, and Einstein, Saunders wondered how this little ceremony had originated. Space crews had certainly been doing it for at least sixty years: perhaps it could be traced back to the legendary rocket engineer who made the remark, "I've burned more alcohol in sixty seconds than you've ever sold across this lousy bar."

Two hours later, the last course correction that the tracking stations on Earth could give them had been fed into the computer. From now on, until Mars came sweeping up ahead they were on their own. It was a lonely thought, yet a curiously exhilarating one. Saunders savored it in his mind. There were just the three of them here—and no one else within a million miles.

In the circumstances, the detonation of an atomic bomb could hardly have been more shattering than the modest knock on the cabin door. . . .

Captain Saunders had never been so startled in his life. With a yelp that had already left him before he had a chance to suppress it, he shot out of his seat and rose a full yard before the ship's residual gravity field dragged him back. Chambers and Mitchell, on the other hand, behaved with traditional British phlegm. They swiveled in their bucket seats, stared at the door, and then waited for their captain to take action.

It took Saunders several seconds to recover. Had he been confronted with what might be called a normal emergency, he would already have been halfway into a space suit. But a diffident knock on the door of the control cabin, when everybody else in the ship was sitting beside him, was not a fair test.

A stowaway was simply impossible. The danger had been so obvious, right from the beginning of commercial space flight, that the most stringent precautions had been taken against it. One of his officers, Saunders knew, would always have been on duty during loading; no one could possibly have crept in unobserved. Then there had been the detailed preflight inspection, carried out by both Mitchell and Chambers. Finally, there was the weight check at the moment before take-off; *that* was conclusive. No, a stowaway was totally . . .

The knock on the door sounded again. Captain Saunders clenched his fists and squared his jaw. In a few minutes, he thought, some romantic idiot was going to be very, very sorry.

"Open the door, Mr. Mitchell," Saunders growled. In a single long stride, the assistant pilot crossed the cabin and jerked open the hatch.

For an age, it seemed, no one spoke. Then the stowaway, wavering slightly in the low gravity, came into the cabin. He was completely self-possessed, and looked very pleased with himself.

"Good afternoon, Captain Saunders," he said, "I must apologize for this sudden intrusion."

Saunders swallowed hard. Then, as the pieces of the jigsaw fell into place, he looked first at Mitchell, then at Chambers. Both of his officers stared guilelessly back at him with expressions of ineffable innocence. "So *that's* it," he said bitterly. There was no need for any explanations: everything was perfectly clear. It was easy to picture the complicated negotiations, the midnight meetings, the falsification of records, the off-loading of nonessential cargoes that his trusted colleagues had been conducting behind his back. He was sure it was a most interesting story, but he didn't want to hear about it now. He was too busy wondering what the *Manual of Space Law* would have to say about a situation like this, though he was already gloomily certain that it would be of no use to him at all.

It was too late to turn back, of course: the conspirators wouldn't have made an elementary miscalculation like that. He would just have to make the best of what looked to be the trickiest voyage in his career.

He was still trying to think of something to say when the PRIORITY signal started flashing on the radio board. The stowaway looked at his watch.

"I was expecting that," he said. "It's probably the Prime Minister. I think I'd better speak to the poor man."

Saunders thought so too.

"Very well, Your Royal Highness," he said sulkily, and with such emphasis that the title sounded almost like an insult. Then, feeling much put upon, he retired into a corner.

It was the Prime Minister all right, and he sounded very upset. Several times he used the phrase "your duty to your people" and once there was a distinct catch in his throat as he said something about "devotion of your subjects to the Crown." Saunders realized, with some surprise, that he really meant it.

While this emotional harangue was in progress, Mitchell leaned over to Saunders and whispered in his ear:

"The old boy's in a sticky wicket, and he knows it. The people will be behind the prince when they hear what's happened. Everybody knows he's been trying to get into space for years."

"I wish he hadn't chosen *my* ship," said Saunders. "And I'm not sure that this doesn't count as mutiny."

"The heck it does. Mark my words—when this is all over you'll be the only Texan to have the Order of the Garter. Won't that be nice for you?"

"Shush!" said Chambers. The prince was speaking, his

words winging back across the abyss that now sundered him from the island he would one day rule.

"I am sorry, Mr. Prime Minister," he said, "if I've caused you any alarm. I will return as soon as it is convenient. Someone has to do everything for the first time, and I felt the moment had come for a member of my family to leave Earth. It will be a valuable part of my education, and will make me more fitted to carry out my duty. Good-by."

He dropped the microphone and walked over to the observation window—the only spaceward-looking port on the entire ship. Saunders watched him standing there, proud and lonely but contented now. And as he saw the prince staring out at the stars which he had at last attained, all his annoyance and indignation slowly evaporated.

No one spoke for a long time. Then Prince Henry tore his gaze away from the blinding splendor beyond the port, looked at Captain Saunders, and smiled.

"Where's the galley, Captain?" he asked. "I may be out of practice, but when I used to go scouting I was the best cook in my patrol."

Saunders slowly relaxed, then smiled back. The tension seemed to lift from the control room. Mars was still a long way off, but he knew now that this wasn't going to be such a bad trip after all. . . .

THE OTHER SIDE
OF THE SKY

Special Delivery

I CAN STILL remember the excitement, back in 1957, when Russia launched the first artificial satellites and managed to hang a few pounds of instruments up here above the atmosphere. Of course, I was only a kid at the time, but I went out in the evening like everyone else, trying to spot those little magnesium spheres as they zipped through the twilight sky hundreds of miles above my head. It's strange to think that some of them are still there—but that now they're *below* me, and I'd have to look down toward Earth if I wanted to see them. . . .

Yes, a lot has happened in the last forty years, and sometimes I'm afraid that you people down on Earth take the space stations for granted, forgetting the skill and science and courage that went to make them. How often do you stop to think that all your long-distance phone calls, and most of your TV programs, are routed through one or the other of the satellites? And how often do you give any credit to the meteorologists up here for the fact that weather forecasts are no longer the joke they were to our grandfathers, but are dead accurate ninety-nine per cent of the time?

It was a rugged life, back in the seventies, when I went up to work on the outer stations. They were being rushed into operation to open up the millions of new TV and radio circuits which would be available as soon as we had transmitters out in space that could beam programs to anywhere on the globe.

The first artificial satellites had been very close to Earth but the three stations forming the great triangle of the Relay Chain had to be twenty-two thousand miles up, spaced equally around the equator. At this altitude—and at no other—they would take exactly a day to go around their orbit, and so would stay poised forever over the same spot on the turning Earth.

In my time I've worked on all three of the stations, but my first tour of duty was aboard Relay Two. That's almost exactly over Entebbe, Uganda, and provides service for Europe, Africa, and most of Asia. Today it's a huge structure hundreds of yards across, beaming thousands of simultaneous programs down to the hemisphere beneath it as it carries the radio traffic of half the world. But when I saw it for the first time from the port of the ferry rocket that carried me up to orbit, it looked like a junk pile adrift in space. Prefabricated parts were floating around in hopeless confusion, and it seemed impossible that any order could ever emerge from this chaos.

Accommodation for the technical staff and assembling crews was primitive, consisting of a few unserviceable ferry rockets that had been stripped of everything except air purifiers. "The Hulks," we christened them; each man had just enough room for himself and a couple of cubic feet of personal belongings. There was a fine irony in the fact that we were living in the midst of infinite space—and hadn't room to swing a cat.

It was a great day when we heard that the first pressurized living quarters were on their way up to us—complete with needle-jet shower baths that would operate even here, where water—like everything else—had no weight. Unless you've lived aboard an overcrowded spaceship, you won't appreciate what that meant. We could throw away our damp sponges and feel really clean at last. . . .

Nor were the showers the only luxury promised us. On the way up from Earth was an inflatable lounge spacious enough to hold no fewer than eight people, a microfilm library, a magnetic billiard table, lightweight chess sets, and similar novelties for bored spacemen. The very thought of all these comforts made our cramped life in the Hulks seem quite unendurable, even though we were being paid about a thousand dollars a week to endure it.

Starting from the Second Refueling Zone, two thousand miles above Earth, the eagerly awaited ferry rocket would take about six hours to climb up to us with its precious cargo. I was off duty at the time, and stationed myself at the telescope where I'd spent most of my scanty leisure. It was impossible to grow tired of exploring the great world hanging there in space beside us; with the highest power of the telescope, one seemed to be only a few miles above the surface. When there were no clouds and the seeing was good, objects the size of a small house were easily visible. I had never been to Africa, but I grew to know it well while I was off duty in Station Two. You may not believe this, but I've often spotted elephants moving across the plains, and the immense herds of zebras and antelopes were easy to see as they flowed back and forth like living tides on the great reservations.

But my favorite spectacle was the dawn coming up over the mountains in the heart of the continent. The line of sunlight would come sweeping across the Indian Ocean, and the new day would extinguish the tiny, twinkling galaxies of the cities shining in the darkness below me. Long before the sun had reached the lowlands around them, the peaks of Kilimanjaro and Mount Kenya would be blazing in the dawn, brilliant stars still surrounded by the night. As the sun rose higher, the day would march swiftly down their slopes and the valleys would fill with light. Earth would then be at its first quarter, waxing toward full.

Twelve hours later, I would see the reverse process as the same mountains caught the last rays of the setting sun. They would blaze for a little while in the narrow belt of twilight; then Earth would spin into darkness, and night would fall upon Africa.

It was not the beauty of the terrestrial globe I was concerned with now. Indeed, I was not even looking at Earth, but at the fierce blue-white star high above the western edge of the planet's disk. The automatic freighter was eclipsed in Earth's shadow; what I was seeing was the incandescent flare of its rockets as they drove it up on its twenty-thousand-mile climb.

I had watched ships ascending to us so often that I knew every stage of their maneuver by heart. So when the rockets didn't wink out, but continued to burn steadily, I knew within seconds that something was wrong. In sick, helpless fury I watched all our longed-for comforts—and, worse still, our mail!—moving faster and faster along the unintended orbit. The freighter's autopilot had jammed; had there been a human pilot aboard, he could have overridden the controls and cut the motor, but now all the fuel that should have driven the ferry on its two-way trip was being burned in one continuous blast of power.

By the time the fuel tanks had emptied, and that distant star had flickered and died in the field of my telescope, the tracking stations had confirmed what I already knew. The freighter was moving far too fast for Earth's gravity to recapture it—indeed, it was heading into the cosmic wilderness beyond Pluto. . . .

It took a long time for morale to recover, and it only made matters worse when someone in the computing section worked out the future history of our errant freighter. You see, nothing is ever really lost in space. Once you've calculated its orbit, you know where it is until the end of eternity. As we watched our lounge, our library, our games, our mail receding to the far horizons of the solar system, we knew that it would all come back one day in perfect condition. If we have a ship standing by it will be easy to intercept it the second time it comes around the sun—quite early in the spring of the year A.D. 15,862.

Feathered Friend

To the best of my knowledge, there's never been a regulation that forbids one to keep pets in a space station. No one ever thought it was necessary—and even had such a rule existed, I am quite certain that Sven Olsen would have ignored it.

With a name like that, you will picture Sven at once as a six-foot-six Nordic giant, built like a bull and with a voice to match. Had this been so, his chances of getting a job in space would have been very slim; actually he was a wiry little fellow, like most of the early spacers, and managed to qualify easily for the 150-pound bonus that kept so many of us on a reducing diet.

Sven was one of our best construction men, and excelled at the tricky and specialized work of collecting assorted girders as they floated around in free fall, making them do the slow-motion, three-dimensional ballet that would get them into their right positions, and fusing the pieces together when they were precisely dovetailed into the intended pattern. I never tired of watching him and his gang as the station grew under their hands like a giant jigsaw puzzle; it was a skilled and difficult job, for a space suit is not the most convenient of garbs in which to work. However, Sven's team had one great advantage over the construction gangs you see putting up skyscrapers down on Earth. They could step back and admire their handiwork without being abruptly parted from it by gravity. . . .

Don't ask me why Sven wanted a pet, or why he chose the one he did. I'm not a psychologist, but I must admit that his selection was very sensible. Claribel weighed practically nothing, her food requirements were infinitesimal—and she was not worried, as most animals would have been, by the absence of gravity.

I first became aware that Claribel was aboard when I was sitting in the little cubbyhole laughingly called my office, checking through my lists of technical stores to decide what items we'd be running out of next. When I heard the musical whistle beside my ear, I assumed that it had come over the station intercom, and waited for an announcement to follow. It didn't; instead, there was a long and involved pattern of melody that made me look up with such a start that I forgot all about the angle beam just behind my head. When the stars had ceased to explode before my eyes, I had my first view of Claribel.

She was a small yellow canary, hanging in the air as motionless as a hummingbird—and with much less effort, for her wings were quietly folded along her sides. We stared at each other for a minute; then, before I had quite recovered my wits, she did a curious kind of backward loop I'm sure no earthbound canary had ever managed, and departed with a few leisurely flicks. It was quite obvious that she'd already learned how to operate in the absence of gravity, and did not believe in doing unnecessary work.

Sven didn't confess to her ownership for several days, and by that time it no longer mattered, because Claribel was a general pet. He had smuggled her up on the last ferry from Earth, when he came back from leave—partly, he claimed, out of sheer scientific curiosity. He wanted to see just how a bird would operate when it had no weight but could still use its wings.

Claribel thrived and grew fat. On the whole, we had little trouble concealing our unauthorized guest when VIP's from Earth came visiting. A space station has more hiding places than you can count; the only problem was that Claribel got rather noisy when she was upset, and we sometimes had to think fast to explain the curious peeps and whistles that came from ventilating shafts and storage bulkheads. There were a couple of narrow escapes—but then who would dream of looking for a canary in a space station?

We were now on twelve-hour watches, which was not as bad as it sounds, since you need little sleep in space. Though of course there is no "day" and "night" when you are floating in permanent sunlight, it was still convenient to stick to the terms. Certainly when I woke up that "morning" it felt like 6:00 A.M. on Earth. I had a nagging headache, and vague memories of fitful, disturbed dreams. It took me ages to undo my bunk straps, and I was still only half awake when I joined the remainder of the duty crew in the mess. Breakfast was unusually quiet, and there was one seat vacant.

"Where's Sven?" I asked, not very much caring.

"He's looking for Claribel," someone answered. "Says he can't find her anywhere. She usually wakes him up."

Before I could retort that she usually woke me up, too, Sven came in through the doorway, and we could see at once that something was wrong. He slowly opened his hand, and there lay a tiny bundle of yellow feathers, with two clenched claws sticking pathetically up into the air.

"What happened?" we asked, all equally distressed.

"I don't know," said Sven mournfully. "I just found her like this."

"Let's have a look at her," said Jock Duncan, our cook-doctor-dietitian. We all waited in hushed silence while he held Claribel against his ear in an attempt to detect any heartbeat.

Presently he shook his head. "I can't hear anything, but that doesn't prove she's dead. I've never listened to a canary's heart," he added rather apologetically.

"Give her a shot of oxygen," suggested somebody, pointing to the green-banded emergency cylinder in its recess beside the door. Everyone agreed that this was an excellent idea, and Claribel was tucked snugly into a face mask that was large enough to serve as a complete oxygen tent for her.

To our delighted surprise, she revived at once. Beaming broadly, Sven removed the mask, and she hopped onto his fingers. She gave her series of "Come to the cookhouse, boys" trills—then promptly keeled over again.

"I don't get it," lamented Sven. "What's wrong with her? She's never done this before."

For the last few minutes, something had been tugging at my memory. My mind seemed to be very sluggish that morning, as if I was still unable to cast off the burden of sleep. I felt that I could do with some of that oxygen—but before I could reach the mask, understanding exploded in my brain. I whirled on the duty engineer and said urgently:

"Jim! There's something wrong with the air! That's why Claribel's passed out. I've just remembered that miners used to carry canaries down to warn them of gas."

"Nonsense!" said Jim. "The alarms would have gone off. We've got duplicate circuits, operating independently."

"Er—the second alarm circuit isn't connected up yet," his assistant reminded him. That shook Jim; he left without a word, while we stood arguing and passing the oxygen bottle around like a pipe of peace.

He came back ten minutes later with a sheepish expression. It was one of those accidents that couldn't possibly happen; we'd had one of our rare eclipses by Earth's shadow that night; part of the air purifier had frozen up, and the single alarm in the circuit had failed to go off. Half a million dollars' worth of chemical and electronic engineering had let us down completely. Without Claribel, we should soon have been slightly dead.

So now, if you visit any space station, don't be surprised if you hear an inexplicable snatch of bird song. There's no need to be alarmed: on the contrary, in fact. It will mean that you're being doubly safeguarded, at practically no extra expense.

Take a Deep Breath

A long time ago I discovered that people who've never left Earth have certain fixed ideas about conditions in space. Everyone "knows," for example, that a man dies instantly and horribly when exposed to the vacuum that exists beyond the atmosphere. You'll find numerous gory descriptions of exploded space travelers in the popular literature, and I won't spoil your appetite by repeating them here. Many of those tales, indeed, are basically true. I've pulled men back through the air lock who were very poor advertisements for space flight.

Yet, at the same time, there are exceptions to every rule— even this one. I should know, for I learned the hard way.

We were on the last stages of building Communications Satellite Two; all the main units had been joined together, the living quarters had been pressurized, and the station had been given the slow spin around its axis that had restored the unfamiliar sensation of weight. I say "slow," but at its rim our two-hundred-foot-diameter wheel was turning at thirty miles an hour. We had, of course, no sense of motion, but the centrifugal force caused by this spin gave us about half the weight we would have possessed on Earth. That was enough to stop things from drifting around, yet not enough to make us feel uncomfortably sluggish after our weeks with no weight at all.

Four of us were sleeping in the small cylindrical cabin known as Bunkhouse Number 6 on the night that it happened. The bunkhouse was at the very rim of the station; if you imagine a bicycle wheel, with a string of sausages replacing the tire, you have a good idea of the layout.

Bunkhouse Number 6 was one of these sausages, and we were slumbering peacefully inside it.

I was awakened by a sudden jolt that was not violent enough to cause me alarm, but which did make me sit up and wonder what had happened. Anything unusual in a space station demands instant attention, so I reached for the intercom switch by my bed. "Hello, Central," I called. "What was that?"

There was no reply; the line was dead.

Now thoroughly alarmed, I jumped out of bed—and had an even bigger shock. *There was no gravity.* I shot up to the ceiling before I was able to grab a stanchion and bring myself to a halt, at the cost of a sprained wrist.

It was impossible for the entire station to have suddenly stopped rotating. There was only one answer; the failure of the intercom and, as I quickly discovered, of the lighting circuit as well forced us to face the appalling truth. We were no longer part of the station; our little cabin had somehow come adrift, and had been slung off into space like a raindrop falling off a spinning flywheel.

There were no windows through which we could look out, but we were not in complete darkness, for the battery-powered emergency lights had come on. All the main air vents had closed automatically when the pressure dropped. For the time being, we could live in our own private atmosphere, even though it was not being renewed. Unfortunately, a steady whistling told us that the air we did have was escaping through a leak somewhere in the cabin.

There was no way of telling what had happened to the rest of the station. For all we knew, the whole structure might have come to pieces, and all our colleagues might be dead or in the same predicament as we—drifting through space in leaking cans of air. Our one slim hope was the possibility that we were the only castaways, that the rest of the station was intact and had been able to send a rescue team to find us. After all, we were receding at no more than thirty miles an hour, and one of the rocket scooters could catch up to us in minutes.

It actually took an hour, though without the evidence of my watch I should never have believed that it was so short a time. We were now gasping for breath—and the gauge on our single emergency oxygen tank had dropped to one division above zero.

The banging on the wall seemed like a signal from another world. We banged back vigorously, and a moment later a muffled voice called to us through the wall. Someone outside was lying with his space-suit helmet pressed against the metal, and his shouted words were reaching us by direct conduction. Not as clear as radio—but it worked.

The oxygen gauge crept slowly down to zero while we had our council of war. We would be dead before we could be towed back to the station; yet the rescue ship was only a few feet away from us, with its air lock already open. Our little problem was to cross that few feet—*without* space suits.

We made our plans carefully, rehearsing our actions in the full knowledge that there could be no repeat performance. Then we each took a deep, final swig of oxygen, flushing out our lungs. When we were all ready, I banged on the wall to give the signal to our friends waiting outside.

There was a series of short, staccato raps as the power tools got to work on the thin hull. We clung tightly to the stanchions, as far away as possible from the point of entry, knowing just what would happen. When it came, it was so sudden that the mind couldn't record the sequence of events. The cabin seemed to explode, and a great wind tugged at me. The last trace of air gushed from my lungs, through my already-opened mouth. And then—utter silence, and the stars shining through the gaping hole that led to life.

Believe me, I didn't stop to analyze my sensations. I think—though I can never be sure that it wasn't imagination —that my eyes were smarting and there was a tingling feeling all over my body. And I felt very cold, perhaps because evaporation was already starting from my skin.

The only thing I can be certain of is that uncanny silence. It is never completely quiet in a space station, for there is always the sound of machinery or air pumps. But this was the absolute silence of the empty void, where there is no trace of air to carry sound.

Almost at once we launched ourselves out through the shattered wall, into the full blast of the sun. I was instantly blinded—but that didn't matter, because the men waiting in space suits grabbed me as soon as I emerged and hustled me into the air lock. And there, sound slowly returned as the air rushed in, and we remembered we could breathe again. The entire rescue, they told us later, had lasted just twenty seconds. . . .

Well, we were the founding members of the Vacuum-Breathers' Club. Since then, at least a dozen other men have done the same thing, in similar emergencies. The record time in space is now two minutes; after that, the blood begins to form bubbles as it boils at body temperature, and those bubbles soon get to the heart.

In my case, there was only one aftereffect. For maybe a quarter of a minute I had been exposed to *real* sunlight, not the feeble stuff that filters down through the atmosphere of Earth. Breathing space didn't hurt me at all—but I got the worst dose of sunburn I've ever had in my life.

Freedom of Space

Not many of you, I suppose, can imagine the time before the satellite relays gave us our present world communications system. When I was a boy, it was impossible to send TV programs across the ocean, or even to establish reliable radio contact around the curve of the Earth without picking up a fine assortment of crackles and bangs on the way. Yet now we take interference-free circuits for granted, and think nothing of seeing our friends on the other side of the globe as clearly as if we were standing face to face. Indeed, it's a simple fact that without the satellite relays, the whole structure of world commerce and industry would collapse. Unless we were up here on the space stations to bounce their messages around the globe, how do you think any of the world's big business organizations could keep their widely scattered electronic brains in touch with each other?

But all this was still in the future, back in the late seventies, when we were finishing work on the Relay Chain. I've already told you about some of our problems and near disasters; they were serious enough at the time, but in the end we overcame them all. The three stations spaced around Earth were no longer piles of girders, air cylinders, and plastic pressure chambers. Their assembly had been completed, we had moved aboard, and could now work in comfort, unhampered by space suits. And we had gravity again, now that the stations had been set slowly spinning. Not real gravity, of course; but centrifugal force feels exactly the same when you're out in space. It was pleasant being able to pour drinks and to sit down without drifting away on the first air current.

Once the three stations had been built, there was still a year's solid work to be done installing all the radio and TV equipment that would lift the world's communications networks into space. It was a great day when we established the first TV link between England and Australia. The signal was beamed up to us in Relay Two, as we sat above the center of Africa, we flashed it across to Three—poised over New Guinea—and they shot it down to Earth again, clear and clean after its ninety-thousand-mile journey.

These, however, were the engineers' private tests. The official opening of the system would be the biggest event in the history of world communication—an elaborate global telecast, in which every nation would take part. It would be a three-hour show, as for the first time the live TV camera roamed around the world, proclaiming to mankind that the last barrier of distance was down.

The program planning, it was cynically believed, had taken as much effort as the building of the space stations in the first place, and of all the problems the planners had to solve, the most difficult was that of choosing a *compère* or master of ceremonies to introduce the items in the elaborate global show that would be watched by half the human race.

Heaven knows how much conniving, blackmail, and downright character assassination went on behind the scenes. All we knew was that a week before the great day, a nonscheduled rocket came up to orbit with Gregory Wendell aboard. This was quite a surprise, since Gregory wasn't as big a TV personality as, say, Jeffers Jackson in the U.S. or Vince Clifford in Britain. However, it seemed that the big boys had canceled each other out, and Gregg had got the coveted job through one of those compromises so well known to politicians.

Gregg had started his career as a disc jockey on a university radio station in the American Midwest, and had worked his way up through the Hollywood and Manhattan nightclub circuits until he had a daily, nation-wide program of his own. Apart from his cynical yet relaxed personality, his biggest asset was his deep velvet voice, for which he could probably thank his Negro blood. Even when you flatly disagreed with what he was saying—even, indeed, when he was tearing you to pieces in an interview—it was still a pleasure to listen to him.

We gave him the grand tour of the space station, and even (strictly against regulations) took him out through the air lock in a space suit. He loved it all, but there were two things he liked in particular. "This air you make," he said, "it beats the stuff we have to breathe down in New York. This is the first time my sinus trouble has gone since I went into TV." He also relished the low gravity; at the station's rim, a man had half his normal, Earth weight—and at the axis he had no weight at all.

However, the novelty of his surroundings didn't distract Gregg from his job. He spent hours at Communications Central, polishing his script and getting his cues right, and studying the dozens of monitor screens that would be his windows on the world. I came across him once while he was running through his introduction of Queen Elizabeth, who would be speaking from Buckingham Palace at the very end of the program. He was so intent on his rehearsal that he never even noticed I was standing beside him.

Well, that telecast is now part of history. For the first time a billion human beings watched a single program that came "live" from every corner of the Earth, and was a roll call of the world's greatest citizens. Hundreds of cameras on land and sea and air looked inquiringly at the turning globe; and at the end there was that wonderful shot of the Earth through a zoom lens on the space station, making the whole planet recede until it was lost among the stars. . . .

There were a few hitches, of course. One camera on the bed of the Atlantic wasn't ready on cue, and we had to spend some extra time looking at the Taj Mahal. And owing to a switching error Russian subtitles were superimposed on the South American transmissions, while half the U.S.S.R. found itself trying to read Spanish. But this was nothing to what *might* have happened.

Through the entire three hours, introducing the famous and the unknown with equal ease, came the mellow yet never orotund flow of Gregg's voice. He did a magnificent job; the congratulations came pouring up the beam the moment the broadcast finished. But he didn't hear them; he made one short, private call to his agent, and then went to bed.

Next morning, the Earth-bound ferry was waiting to take him back to any job he cared to accept. But it left without Gregg Wendell, now junior station announcer of Relay Two.

"They'll think I'm crazy," he said, beaming happily, "but why should I go back to that rat race down there? I've all the universe to look at, I can breathe smog-free air, the low gravity makes me feel a Hercules, and my three darling ex-wives can't get at me." He kissed his hand to the departing rocket. "So long, Earth," he called. "I'll be back when I start pining for Broadway traffic jams and bleary penthouse dawns. And if I get homesick, I can look at anywhere on the planet just by turning a switch. Why, I'm more in the middle of things here than I could ever be on Earth, yet I can cut myself off from the human race whenever I want to."

He was still smiling as he watched the ferry begin the long fall back to Earth, toward the fame and fortune that could have been his. And then, whistling cheerfully, he left the observation lounge in eight-foot strides to read the weather forecast for Lower Patagonia.

Passer-by

It's only fair to warn you, right at the start, that this is a story with no ending. But it has a definite beginning, for it was while we were both students at Astrotech that I met Julie. She was in her final year of solar physics when I was graduating, and during our last year at college we saw a good deal of each other. I've still got the woolen tam-o'shanter she knitted so that I wouldn't bump my head against my space helmet. (No, I never had the nerve to wear it.)

Unfortunately, when I was assigned to Satellite Two Julie went to the Solar Observatory—at the same distance from Earth, but a couple of degrees eastward along the orbit. So there we were, sitting twenty-two thousand miles above the middle of Africa—but with nine hundred miles of empty, hostile space between us.

At first we were both so busy that the pang of separation was somewhat lessened. But when the novelty of life in space had worn off, our thoughts began to bridge the gulf that divided us. And not only our thoughts, for I'd made friends with the communications people, and we used to have little chats over the intersection TV circuit. In some ways it made matters worse seeing each other face to face and never knowing just how many other people were looking in at the same time. There's not much privacy in a space station. . . .

Sometimes I'd focus one of our telescopes onto the distant, brilliant star of the observatory. In the crystal clarity of space, I could use enormous magnifications, and could see every detail of our neighbors' equipment—the solar telescopes, the pressurized spheres of the living quarters that housed the staff, the slim pencils of visiting ferry rockets that had climbed up from Earth. Very often there would be space-suited figures moving among the maze of apparatus, and I would strain my eyes in a hopeless attempt at identification. It's hard enough to recognize anyone in a space suit when you're only a few feet apart—but that didn't stop me from trying.

We'd resigned ourselves to waiting, with what patience we could muster, until our Earth leave was due in six months' time, when we had an unexpected stroke of luck. Less than half our tour of duty had passed when the head of the transport section suddenly announced that he was going outside with a butterfly net to catch meteors. He didn't become violent, but had to be shipped hastily back to Earth. I took over his job on a temporary basis and now had—in theory at least—the freedom of space.

There were ten of the little low-powered rocket scooters under my proud command, as well as four of the larger interstation shuttles used to ferry stores and personnel from orbit to orbit. I couldn't hope to borrow one of *those,* but after several weeks of careful organizing I was able to carry out the plan I'd conceived some two microseconds after being told I was now head of transport.

There's no need to tell how I juggled duty lists, cooked logs and fuel registers, and persuaded my colleagues to cover up for me. All that matters is that, about once a week, I would climb into my personal space suit, strap myself to the spidery framework of a Mark III Scooter, and drift away from the station at minimum power. When I was well clear, I'd go over to full throttle, and the tiny rocket motor would hustle me across the nine-hundred-mile gap to the observatory.

The trip took about thirty minutes, and the navigational requirements were elementary. I could see where I was going and where I'd come from, yet I don't mind admitting that I often felt—well, a trifle lonely—around the mid-point of the journey. There was no other solid matter within almost five hundred miles—and it looked an awfully long way down to Earth. It was a great help, at such moments, to tune the suit radio to the general service band, and to listen to all the back-chat between ships and stations.

At mid-flight I'd have to spin the scooter around and start braking, and ten minutes later the observatory would be close enough for its details to be visible to the unaided eye. Very shortly after that I'd drift up to a small, plastic pressure bubble that was in the process of being fitted out as a spectroscopic laboratory—and there would be Julie, waiting on the other side of the air lock. . . .

I won't pretend that we confined our discussions to the latest results in astrophysics, or the progress of the satellite construction schedule. Few things, indeed, were further from our thoughts; and the journey home always seemed to flash by at a quite astonishing speed.

It was around mid-orbit on one of those homeward trips that the radar started to flash on my little control panel. There was something large at extreme range, and it was coming in fast. A meteor, I told myself—maybe even a small asteroid. Anything giving such a signal should be visible to the eye: I read off the bearings and searched the star fields in the indicated direction. The thought of a collision never even crossed my mind; space is so inconceivably vast that I was thousands of times safer than a man crossing a busy street on Earth.

There it was—a bright and steadily growing star near the foot of Orion. It already outshone Rigel, and seconds later it was not merely a star, but had begun to show a visible disk. Now it was moving as fast as I could turn my head; it grew to a tiny, misshaped moon, then dwindled and shrank with the same silent, inexorable speed.

I suppose I had a clear view of it for perhaps half a second, and that half-second has haunted me all my life. The —object—had already vanished by the time I thought of checking the radar again, so I had no way of gauging how close it came, and hence how large it really was. It could have been a small object a hundred feet away—or a very large one, ten miles off. There is no sense of perspective in space, and unless you know what you are looking at, you cannot judge its distance.

Of course, it *could* have been a very large and oddly shaped meteor; I can never be sure that my eyes, straining to grasp the details of so swiftly moving an object, were not hopelessly deceived. I may have imagined that I saw that broken, crumpled prow, and the cluster of dark ports like the sightless sockets of a skull. Of one thing only was I certain, even in that brief and fragmentary vision. If it *was* a ship, it was not one of ours. Its shape was utterly alien, and it was very, very old.

It may be that the greatest discovery of all time slipped from my grasp as I struggled with my thoughts midway between the two space stations. But I had no measurements of speed or direction; whatever it was that I had glimpsed was now lost beyond recapture in the wastes of the solar system.

What should I have done? No one would ever have believed me, for I would have had no proof. Had I made a report, there would have been endless trouble. I should have become the laughingstock of the Space Service, would have been reprimanded for misuse of equipment—and would certainly not have been able to see Julie again. And to me, at that age, nothing else was as important. If you've been in love yourself, you'll understand; if not, then no explanation is any use.

So I said nothing. To some other man (how many centuries hence?) will go the fame for proving that we were not the first-born of the children of the sun. Whatever it may be that is circling out there on its eternal orbit can wait, as it has waited ages already.

Yet I sometimes wonder. Would I have made a report,

after all—had I known that Julie was going to marry someone else?

The Call of the Stars

Down there on Earth the twentieth century is dying. As I look across at the shadowed globe blocking the stars, I can see the lights of a hundred sleepless cities, and there are moments when I wish that I could be among the crowds now surging and singing in the streets of London, Capetown, Rome, Paris, Berlin, Madrid. . . . Yes, I can see them all at a single glance, burning like fireflies against the darkened planet. The line of midnight is now bisecting Europe: in the eastern Mediterranean a tiny, brilliant star is pulsing as some exuberant pleasure ship waves her searchlights to the sky. I think she is deliberately aiming at us; for the past few minutes the flashes have been quite regular and startlingly bright. Presently I'll call the communications center and find out who she is, so that I can radio back our own greetings.

Passing into history now, receding forever down the stream of time, is the most incredible hundred years the world has ever seen. It opened with the conquest of the air, saw at its mid-point the unlocking of the atom—and now ends with the bridging of space.

(For the past five minutes I've been wondering what's happening to Nairobi; now I realize that they are putting on a mammoth fireworks display. Chemically fueled rockets may be obsolete out here—but they're still using lots of them down on Earth tonight.)

The end of a century—and the end of a millennium. What will the hundred years that begin with two and zero bring? The planets, of course; floating there in space, only a mile away, are the ships of the first Martian expedition. For two years I have watched them grow, assembled piece by piece, as the space station itself was built by the men I worked with a generation ago.

Those ten ships are ready now, with all their crews aboard, waiting for the final instrument check and the signal for departure. Before the first day of the new century has passed its noon, they will be tearing free from the reins of Earth, to head out toward the strange world that may one day be man's second home.

As I look at the brave little fleet that is now preparing to challenge infinity, my mind goes back forty years, to the days when the first satellites were launched and the moon still seemed very far away. And I remember—indeed, I have never forgotten—my father's fight to keep me down on Earth.

There were not many weapons he had failed to use. Ridicule had been the first: "Of course they can do it," he had sneered, "but what's the point? Who wants to go out into space while there's so much to be done here on Earth? There's not a single planet in the solar system where men can live. The moon's a burnt-out slag heap, and everywhere else is even worse. *This* is where we were meant to live."

Even then (I must have been eighteen or so at the time) I could tangle him up in points of logic. I can remember answering, "How do you know where we were meant to live, Dad? After all, we were in the sea for about a billion years before we decided to tackle the land. Now we're making the next big jump: I don't know where it will lead—nor did that first fish when it crawled up on the beach, and started to sniff the air."

So when he couldn't outargue me, he had tried subtler pressures. He was always talking about the dangers of space travel, and the short working life of anyone foolish enough to get involved in rocketry. At that time, people were still scared of meteors and cosmic rays; like the "Here Be Dragons" of the old map makers, they were the mythical monsters on the still-blank celestial charts. But they didn't worry me; if anything, they added the spice of danger to my dreams.

While I was going through college, Father was comparatively quiet. My training would be valuable whatever profession I took up in later life, so he could not complain—though he occasionally grumbled about the money I wasted buying all the books and magazines on astronautics that I could find. My college record was good, which naturally pleased him; perhaps he did not realize that it would also help me to get my way.

All through my final year I had avoided talking of my

plans. I had even given the impression (though I am sorry for that now) that I had abandoned my dream of going into space. Without saying anything to him, I put in my application to Astrotech, and was accepted as soon as I had graduated.

The storm broke when that long blue envelope with the embossed heading "Institute of Astronautical Technology" dropped into the mailbox. I was accused of deceit and ingratitude, and I do not think I ever forgave my father for destroying the pleasure I should have felt at being chosen for the most exclusive—and most glamorous—apprenticeship the world has ever known.

The vacations were an ordeal; had it not been for Mother's sake, I do not think I would have gone home more than once a year, and I always left again as quickly as I could. I had hoped that Father would mellow as my training progressed and as he accepted the inevitable, but he never did.

Then had come that stiff and awkward parting at the spaceport, with the rain streaming down from leaden skies and beating against the smooth walls of the ship that seemed so eagerly waiting to climb into the eternal sunlight beyond the reach of storms. I know now what it cost my father to watch the machine he hated swallow up his only son: for I understand many things today that were hidden from me then.

He knew, even as we parted at the ship, that he would never see me again. Yet his old, stubborn pride kept him from saying the only words that might have held me back. I knew that he was ill, but how ill, he had told no one. That was the only weapon he had not used against me, and I respect him for it.

Would I have stayed had I known? It is even more futile to speculate about the unchangeable past than the unforeseeable future; all I can say now is that I am glad I never had to make the choice. At the end he let me go; he gave up his fight against my ambition, and a little while later his fight with Death.

So I said good-by to Earth, and to the father who loved me but knew no way to say it. He lies down there on the planet I can cover with my hand; how strange it is to think that of the countless billion human beings whose blood runs in my veins, I was the very first to leave his native world. . . .

The new day is breaking over Asia; a hairline of fire is rimming the eastern edge of Earth. Soon it will grow into a burning crescent as the sun comes up out of the Pacific—yet Europe is preparing for sleep, except for those revelers who will stay up to greet the dawn.

And now, over there by the flagship, the ferry rocket is coming back for the last visitors from the station. Here comes the message I have been waiting for: CAPTAIN STEVENS PRESENTS HIS COMPLIMENTS TO THE STATION COMMANDER. BLAST-OFF WILL BE IN NINETY MINUTES; HE WILL BE GLAD TO SEE YOU ABOARD NOW.

Well, Father, now I know how you felt: time has gone full circle. Yet I hope that I have learned from the mistakes we both made, long ago. I shall remember you when I go over there to the flagship *Starfire* and say good-by to the grandson you never knew.

SECURITY CHECK

IT IS OFTEN said that in our age of assembly lines and mass production there's no room for the individual craftsman, the artist in wood or metal who made so many of the treasures of the past. Like most generalizations, this simply isn't true. He's rarer now, of course, but he's certainly not extinct. He has often had to change his vocation, but in his modest way he still flourishes. Even on the island of Manhattan he may be found, if you know where to look for him. Where rents are low and fire regulations unheard of, his minute, cluttered workshops may be discovered in the basements of apartment houses or in the upper stories of derelict shops. He may no longer make violins or cuckoo clocks or music boxes, but the skills he uses are the same as they always were, and no two objects he creates are ever identical. He is not contemptuous of mechanization: you will find several electric hand tools under the debris on his bench. He has moved with the times: he will always be around, the universal odd-job man who is never aware of it when he makes an immortal work of art.

Hans Muller's workshop consisted of a large room at the

back of a deserted warehouse, no more than a vigorous stone's throw from the Queensborough Bridge. Most of the building had been boarded up awaiting demolition, and sooner or later Hans would have to move. The only entrance was across a weed-covered yard used as a parking place during the day, and much frequented by the local juvenile delinquents at night. They had never given Hans any trouble, for he knew better than to co-operate with the police when they made their periodic inquiries. The police fully appreciated his delicate position and did not press matters, so Hans was on good terms with everybody. Being a peaceable citizen, that suited him very well.

The work on which Hans was now engaged would have deeply puzzled his Bavarian ancestors. Indeed, ten years ago it would have puzzled Hans himself. And it had all started because a bankrupt client had given him a TV set in payment for services rendered. . . .

Hans had accepted the offer reluctantly, not because he was old-fashioned and disapproved of TV, but simply because he couldn't imagine where he would find time to look at the darned thing. Still, he thought, at least I can always sell it for fifty dollars. But before I do that, let's see what the programs are like. . . .

His hand had gone out to the switch: the screen had filled with moving shapes—and, like millions of men before him, Hans was lost. He entered a world he had not known existed —a world of battling spaceships, of exotic planets and strange races—the world, in fact, of Captain Zipp, Commander of the Space Legion.

Only when the tedious recital of the virtues of Crunche, the Wonder Cereal, had given way to an almost equally tedious boxing match between two muscle-bound characters who seemed to have signed a nonaggression pact, did the magic fade. Hans was a simple man. He had always been fond of fairy tales—and *this* was the modern fairy tale, with trimmings of which the Grimm Brothers had never dreamed. So Hans did not sell his TV set.

It was some weeks before the initial naïve, uncritical enjoyment wore off. The first thing that began to annoy Hans was the furniture and general décor in the world of the future. He was, as has been indicated, an artist—and he refused to believe that in a hundred years taste would have deteriorated as badly as the Crunche sponsors seemed to imagine.

He also thought very little of the weapons that Captain Zipp and his opponents used. It was true that Hans did not pretend to understand the principles upon which the portable proton disintegrator was based, but however it worked, there was certainly no reason why it should be *that* clumsy. The clothes, the spaceship interiors—they just weren't convincing. How did he know? He had always possessed a highly developed sense of the fitness of things, and it could still operate even in this novel field.

We have said that Hans was a simple man. He was also a shrewd one, and he had heard that there was money in TV. So he sat down and began to draw.

Even if the producer of Captain Zipp had not lost patience with his set designer, Hans Muller's ideas would certainly have made him sit up and take notice. There was an authenticity and realism about them that made them quite outstanding. They were completely free from the element of phonyness that had begun to upset even Captain Zipp's most juvenile followers. Hans was hired on the spot.

He made his own conditions, however. What he was doing he did largely for love, not withstanding the fact that it was earning him more money than anything he had ever done before in his life. He would take no assistants, and would remain in his little workshop. All that he wanted to do was to produce the prototypes, the basic designs. The mass production could be done somewhere else—he was a craftsman, not a factory.

The arrangement had worked well. Over the last six months Captain Zipp had been transformed and was now the despair of all the rival space operas. This, his viewers thought, was not just a serial about the future. It *was* the future—there was no argument about it. Even the actors seemed to have been inspired by their new surroundings: off the set, they sometimes behaved like twentieth-century time travelers stranded in the Victorian Age, indignant because they no longer had access to the gadgets that had always been part of their lives.

But Hans knew nothing about this. He toiled happily away, refusing to see anyone except the producer, doing all his business over the telephone—and watching the final result to ensure that his ideas had not been mutilated. The only sign of his connection with the slightly fantastic world of commercial TV was a crate of Crunche in one corner of the workshop. He had sampled one mouthful of this present from the grateful sponsor and had then remembered thankfully that, after all, he was not paid to eat the stuff.

He was working late one Sunday evening, putting the final touches to a new design for a space helmet, when he suddenly realized that he was no longer alone. Slowly he turned from the workbench and faced the door. It had been locked—how could it have been opened so silently? There were two men standing beside it, motionless, watching him. Hans felt his heart trying to climb into his gullet, and summoned up what courage he could to challenge them. At least, he felt thankfully, he had little money here. Then he wondered if, after all, this was a good thing. They might be annoyed. . . .

"Who are you?" he asked. "What are you doing here?"

One of the men moved toward him while the other remained watching alertly from the door. They were both wearing very new overcoats, with hats low down on their heads so that Hans could not see their faces. They were too well dressed, he decided, to be ordinary holdup men.

"There's no need to be alarmed, Mr. Muller," replied the nearer man, reading his thoughts without difficulty. "This isn't a holdup. It's official. We're from—Security."

"I don't understand."

The other reached into a portfolio he had been carrying beneath his coat, and pulled out a sheaf of photographs. He riffled through them until he had found the one he wanted.

"You've given us quite a headache, Mr. Muller. It's taken us two weeks to find you—your employers were so secretive. No doubt they were anxious to hide you from their rivals. However, here we are and I'd like you to answer some questions."

"I'm not a spy!" answered Hans indignantly as the meaning of the words penetrated. "You can't do this! I'm a loyal American citizen!"

The other ignored the outburst. He handed over the photograph.

"Do you recognize this?" he said.

"Yes. It's the inside of Captain Zipp's spaceship."

"And you designed it?"

"Yes."

Another photograph came out of the file.

"And what about this?"

"That's the Martian city of Paldar, as seen from the air."

"Your own idea?"

"Certainly," Hans replied, now too indignant to be cautious.

"And *this*?"

"Oh, the proton gun. I was quite proud of that."

"Tell me, Mr. Muller—are these all your own ideas?"

"Yes, *I* don't steal from other people."

His questioner turned to his companion and spoke for a few minutes in a voice too low for Hans to hear. They seemed to reach agreement on some point, and the conference was over before Hans could make his intended grab at the telephone.

"I'm sorry," continued the intruder. "But there has been a serious leak. It may be—uh—accidental, even unconscious, but that does not affect the issue. We will have to investigate you. Please come with us."

There was such power and authority in the stranger's voice that Hans began to climb into his overcoat without a murmur. Somehow, he no longer doubted his visitors' credentials and never thought of asking for any proof. He was worried, but not yet seriously alarmed. Of course, it was obvious what had happened. He remembered hearing about a science-fiction writer during the war who had described the atom bomb with disconcerting accuracy. When so much secret research was going on, such accidents were bound to occur. He wondered just what it was he had given away.

At the doorway, he looked back into his workshop and at the men who were following him.

"It's all a ridiculous mistake," he said. "If I *did* show anything secret in the program, it was just a coincidence. I've never done anything to annoy the FBI."

It was then that the second man spoke at last, in very bad English and with a most peculiar accent.

"What is the FBI?" he asked.

But Hans didn't hear him. He had just seen the spaceship.

NO MORNING AFTER

"BUT THIS IS terrible!" said the Supreme Scientist. "Surely there is *something* we can do!"

"Yes, Your Cognizance, but it will be extremely difficult. The planet is more than five hundred light-years away, and it is very hard to maintain contact. However, we believe we can establish a bridgehead. Unfortunately, that is not the only problem. So far, we have been quite unable to communicate with these beings. Their telepathic powers are exceedingly rudimentary—perhaps even nonexistent. And if we cannot talk to them, there is no way in which we can help."

There was a long mental silence while the Supreme Scientist analyzed the situation and arrived, as he always did, at the correct answer.

"Any intelligent race must have *some* telepathic individuals," he mused. "We must send out hundreds of observers, tuned to catch the first hint of stray thought. When you find a single responsive mind, concentrate all your efforts upon it. We *must* get our message through."

"Very good, Your Cognizance. It shall be done."

Across the abyss, across the gulf which light itself took half a thousand years to span, the questing intellects of the planet Thaar sent out their tendrils of thought, searching desperately for a single human being whose mind could perceive their presence. And as luck would have it, they encountered William Cross.

At least, they thought it was luck at the time, though later they were not so sure. In any case, they had little choice. The combination of circumstances that opened Bill's mind to them lasted only for seconds, and was not likely to occur again this side of eternity.

There were three ingredients in the miracle; it is hard to say if one was more important than another. The first was the accident of position. A flask of water, when sunlight falls upon it, can act as a crude lens, concentrating the light into a small area. On an immeasurably larger scale, the dense core of the Earth was converging the waves that came from Thaar. In the ordinary way, the radiations of thought are unaffected by matter—they pass through it as effortlessly as light through glass. But there is rather a lot of matter in a planet, and the whole Earth was acting as a gigantic lens. As it turned, it was carrying Bill through its focus, where the feeble thought impulses from Thaar were concentrated a hundredfold.

Yet millions of other men were equally well placed: they received no message. But they were not rocket engineers: they had not spent years thinking and dreaming of space until it had become part of their very being.

And they were not, as Bill was, blind drunk, teetering on the last knife-edge of consciousness, trying to escape from reality into the world of dreams, where there were no disappointments and setbacks.

Of course, he could see the Army's point of view. "You are paid, Dr. Cross," General Potter had pointed out with unnecessary emphasis, "to design missiles, *not*—ah—spaceships. What you do in your spare time is your own concern, but I must ask you not to use the facilities of the establishment for your hobby. From now on, all projects for the computing section will have to be cleared by me. That is all."

They couldn't sack him, of course: he was too important. But he was not sure that he wanted to stay. He was not really sure of anything except that the job had backfired on him, and that Brenda had finally gone off with Johnny Gardner—putting events in their order of importance.

Wavering slightly, Bill cupped his chin in his hands and stared at the whitewashed brick wall on the other side of the table. The only attempt at ornamentation was a calendar from Lockheed and a glossy six-by-eight from Aerojet showing L'il Abner Mark I making a boosted take-off. Bill gazed morosely at a spot midway between the two pictures, and emptied his mind of thought. The barriers went down. . . .

At that moment, the massed intellects of Thaar gave a soundless cry of triumph, and the wall in front of Bill slowly dissolved into a swirling mist. He appeared to be looking down a tunnel that stretched to infinity. As a matter of fact, he was.

Bill studied the phenomenon with mild interest. It had a certain novelty, but was not up to the standard of previous hallucinations. And when the voice started to speak in his mind, he let it ramble on for some time before he did anything about it. Even when drunk, he had an old-fashioned prejudice against starting conversations with himself.

"Bill," the voice began, "listen carefully. We have had great difficulty in contacting you, and this is extremely important."

Bill doubted this on general principles. *Nothing* was important any more.

"We are speaking to you from a very distant planet," continued the voice in a tone of urgent friendliness. "You are the only human being we have been able to contact, so you *must* understand what we are saying."

Bill felt mildly worried, though in an impersonal sort of way, since it was now rather hard to focus on his own problems. How serious was it, he wondered, when you started to hear voices? Well, it was best not to get excited. You can take it or leave it, Dr. Cross, he told himself. Let's take it until it gets to be a nuisance.

"O.K.," he answered with bored indifference. "Go right ahead and talk to me. I won't mind as long as it's interesting."

There was a pause. Then the voice continued, in a slightly worried fashion.

"We don't quite understand. Our message isn't merely

interesting. It's vital to your entire race, and you must notify your government immediately."

"I'm waiting," said Bill. "It helps to pass the time."

Five hundred light-years away, the Thaarns conferred hastily among themselves. Something seemed to be wrong, but they could not decide precisely what. There was no doubt that they had established contact, yet this was not the sort of reaction they had expected. Well, they could only proceed and hope for the best.

"Listen, Bill," they continued. "Our scientists have just discovered that your sun is about to explode. It will happen three days from now—seventy-four hours, to be exact. Nothing can stop it. But there's no need to be alarmed. We can save you, if you'll do what we say."

"Go on," said Bill. This hallucination was ingenious.

"We can create what we call a bridge—it's a kind of tunnel through space, like the one you're looking into now. The theory is far too complicated to explain, even to one of your mathematicians."

"Hold on a minute!" protested Bill. "I *am* a mathematician, and a damn good one, even when I'm sober. And I've read all about this kind of thing in the science-fiction magazines. I presume you're talking about some kind of short cut through a higher dimension of space. That's old stuff—pre-Einstein."

A sensation of distinct surprise seeped into Bill's mind.

"We had no idea you were so advanced scientifically," said the Thaarns. "But we haven't time to talk about the theory. All that matters is this—if you were to step into that opening in front of you, you'd find yourself instantly on another planet. It's a short cut, as you said—in this case through the thirty-seventh dimension."

"And it leads to your world?"

"Oh no—you couldn't live here. But there are plenty of planets like Earth in the universe, and we've found one that will suit you. We'll establish bridgeheads like this all over Earth, so your people will only have to walk through them to be saved. Of course, they'll have to start building up civilization again when they reach their new homes, but it's their only hope. You have to pass on this message, and tell them what to do."

"I can just see them listening to me," said Bill. "Why don't you go and talk to the president?"

"Because yours was the only mind we were able to contact. Others seemed closed to us: we don't understand why."

"I could tell you," said Bill, looking at the nearly empty bottle in front of him. He was certainly getting his money's worth. What a remarkable thing the human mind was! Of course, there was nothing at all original in this dialogue: it was easy to see where the ideas came from. Only last week he'd been reading a story about the end of the world, and all this wishful thinking about bridges and tunnels through space was pretty obvious compensation for anyone who'd spent five years wrestling with recalcitrant rockets.

"If the sun does blow up," Bill asked abruptly—trying to catch his hallucination unawares—"what would happen?"

"Why, your planet would be melted instantly. All the planets, in fact, right out to Jupiter."

Bill had to admit that this was quite a grandiose conception. He let his mind play with the thought, and the more he considered it, the more he liked it.

"My dear hallucination," he remarked pityingly, "if I believed you, d'you know what I'd say?"

"But you *must* believe us!" came the despairing cry across the light-years.

Bill ignored it. He was warming to his theme.

"I'd tell you this. *It would be the best thing that could possibly happen.* Yes, it would save a whole lot of misery. No one would have to worry about the Russians and the atom bomb and the high cost of living. Oh, it would be wonderful! It's just what everybody really wants. Nice of you to come along and tell us, but just you go back home and pull your old bridge after you."

There was consternation on Thaar. The Supreme Scientist's brain, floating like a great mass of coral in its tank of nutrient solution, turned slightly yellow about the edges— something it had not done since the Xantil invasion, five thousand years ago. At least fifteen psychologists had nervous breakdowns and were never the same again. The main computer in the College of Cosmophysics started dividing every number in its memory circuits by zero, and promptly blew all its fuses.

And on Earth, Bill Cross was really hitting his stride.

"Look at *me*," he said, pointing a wavering finger at his chest. "I've spent years trying to make rockets do something useful, and they tell me I'm only allowed to build guided missiles, so that we can all blow each other up. The sun will make a neater job of it, and if you did give us another planet we'd only start the whole damn thing all over again."

He paused sadly, marshaling his morbid thoughts.

"And now Brenda heads out of town without even leaving a note. So you'll pardon my lack of enthusiasm for your Boy Scout act."

He couldn't have said "enthusiasm" aloud, Bill realized. But he could still think it, which was an interesting scientific discovery. As he got drunker and drunker, would his cogitation—whoops, *that* nearly threw him!—finally drop down to words of one syllable?

In a final despairing exertion, the Thaarns sent their thoughts along the tunnel between the stars.

"You can't really mean it, Bill! Are *all* human beings like you?"

Now that was an interesting philosophical question! Bill considered it carefully—or as carefully as he could in view of the warm, rosy glow that was now beginning to envelop him. After all, things might be worse. He could get another job, if only for the pleasure of telling General Potter what he could do with his three stars. And as for Brenda—well, women were like streetcars: there'd always be another along in a minute.

Best of all, there was a second bottle of whisky in the Top Secret file. Oh, frabjous day! He rose unsteadily to his feet and wavered across the room.

For the last time, Thaar spoke to Earth.

"Bill!" it repeated desperately. "Surely all human beings can't be like you!"

Bill turned and looked into the swirling tunnel. Strange—it seemed to be lighted with flecks of starlight, and was really rather pretty. He felt proud of himself: not many people could imagine *that*.

"Like me?" he said. "No, they're not." He smiled smugly across the light-years, as the rising tide of euphoria lifted him out of his despondency. "Come to think of it," he added, "there are a lot of people much worse off than me. Yes, I guess I must be one of the lucky ones, after all."

He blinked in mild surprise, for the tunnel had suddenly collapsed upon itself and the whitewashed wall was there again, exactly as it had always been. Thaar knew when it was beaten.

"So much for *that* hallucination," thought Bill. "I was getting tired of it, anyway. Let's see what the next one's like."

As it happened, there wasn't a next one, for five seconds later he passed out cold, just as he was setting the combination of the file cabinet.

The next two days were rather vague and bloodshot, and he forgot all about the interview.

On the third day something was nagging at the back of his mind: he might have remembered if Brenda hadn't turned up again and kept him busy being forgiving.

And there wasn't a fourth day, of course.

VENTURE TO THE MOON

The Starting Line

THE STORY OF the first lunar expedition has been written so many times that some people will doubt if there is anything fresh to be said about it. Yet all the official reports and eyewitness accounts, the on-the-spot recordings and broadcasts never, in my opinion, gave the full picture. They said a great deal about the discoveries that were made—but very little about the men who made them.

As captain of the *Endeavour* and thus commander of the British party, I was able to observe a good many things you will not find in the history books, and some—though not all —of them can now be told. One day, I hope, my opposite numbers on the *Goddard* and the *Ziolkovski* will give their points of view. But as Commander Vandenburg is still on Mars and Commander Krasnin is somewhere inside the orbit of Venus, it looks as if we will have to wait a few more years for *their* memoirs.

Confession, it is said, is good for the soul. I shall certainly feel much happier when I have told the true story behind the timing of the first lunar flight, about which there has always been a good deal of mystery.

As everyone knows, the American, Russian, and British ships were assembled in the orbit of Space Station Three, five hundred miles above the Earth, from components flown up by relays of freight rockets. Though all the parts had been prefabricated, the assembly and testing of the ships took over two years, by which time a great many people— who did not realize the complexity of the task—were beginning to get slightly impatient. They had seen dozens of photos and telecasts of the three ships floating there in space beside Station Three, apparently quite complete and ready to pull away from Earth at a moment's notice. What the pictures didn't show was the careful and tedious work still in progress as thousands of pipes, wires, motors, and instruments were fitted and subjected to every conceivable test.

There was no definite target date for departure; since the moon is always at approximately the same distance, you can leave for it at almost any time you like—once you are ready. It makes practically no difference, from the point of view of fuel consumption, if you blast off at full moon or new moon or at any time in between. We were very careful to make no predictions about blast-off, though everyone was always trying to get us to fix the time. So many things can go wrong in a spaceship, and we were not going to say good-by to Earth until we were ready down to the last detail.

I shall always remember the last commanders' conference, aboard the space station, when we all announced that we were ready. Since it was a co-operative venture, each party specializing in some particular task, it had been agreed that we should all make our landings within the same twenty-four-hour period, on the preselected site in the Mare Imbrium. The details of the journey, however, had been left to the individual commanders, presumably in the hope that we would not copy each other's mistakes.

"I'll be ready," said Commander Vandenburg, "to make my first dummy take-off at 0900 tomorrow. What about you, gentlemen? Shall we ask Earth Control to stand by for all three of us?"

"That's O.K. by me," said Krasnin, who could never be

convinced that his American slang was twenty years out of date.

I nodded my agreement. It was true that one bank of fuel gauges was still misbehaving, but that didn't really matter; they would be fixed by the time the tanks were filled.

The dummy run consisted of an exact replica of a real blast-off, with everyone carrying out the job he would do when the time came for the genuine thing. We had practiced, of course, in mock-ups down on Earth, but this was a perfect imitation of what would happen to us when we finally took off for the moon. All that was missing was the roar of the motors that would tell us that the voyage had begun.

We did six complete imitations of blast-off, took the ships to pieces to eliminate anything that hadn't behaved perfectly, then did six more. The *Endeavour,* the *Goddard,* and the *Ziolkovski* were all in the same state of serviceability. There now only remained the job of fueling up, and we would be ready to leave.

The suspense of those last few hours is not something I would care to go through again. The eyes of the world were upon us; departure time had now been set, with an uncertainty of only a few hours. All the final tests had been made, and we were convinced that our ships were as ready as humanly possible.

It was then that I had an urgent and secret personal radio call from a very high official indeed, and a suggestion was made which had so much authority behind it that there was little point in pretending that it wasn't an order. The first flight to the moon, I was reminded, was a co-operative venture—but think of the prestige if *we* got there first. It need only be by a couple of hours. . . .

I was shocked at the suggestion, and said so. By this time Vandenburg and Krasnin were good friends of mine, and we were all in this together. I made every excuse I could and said that since our flight paths had already been computed there wasn't anything that could be done about it. Each ship was making the journey by the most economical route, to conserve fuel. If we started together, we should arrive together—within seconds.

Unfortunately, someone had thought of the answer to that. Our three ships, fueled up and with their crews standing by, would be circling Earth in a state of complete readiness for several hours before they actually pulled away from their satellite orbits and headed out to the moon. At our five-hundred-mile altitude, we took ninety-five minutes to make one circuit of the Earth, and only once every revolution would the moment be ripe to begin the voyage. If we could jump the gun by one revolution, the others would have to wait that ninety-five minutes before they could follow. And so they would land on the moon ninety-five minutes behind us. . . .

I won't go into the arguments, and I'm still a little ashamed that I yielded and agreed to deceive my two colleagues. We were in the shadow of Earth, in momentary eclipse, when the carefully calculated moment came. Vandenburg and Krasnin, honest fellows, thought I was going to make one more round trip with them before we all set off together. I have seldom felt a bigger heel in my life than when I pressed the firing key and felt the sudden thrust of the motors as they swept me away from my mother world.

For the next ten minutes we had no time for anything but our instruments, as we checked to see that the *Endeavour* was forging ahead along her precomputed orbit. Almost at the moment that we finally escaped from Earth and could cut the motors, we burst out of shadow into the full blaze of the sun. There would be no more night until we reached the moon, after five days of effortless and silent coasting through space.

Already Space Station Three and the two other ships must be a thousand miles behind. In eighty-five more minutes Vandenburg and Krasnin would be back at the correct starting point and could take off after me, as we had all planned. But they could never overcome my lead, and I hoped they wouldn't be too mad at me when we met again on the moon.

I switched on the rear camera and looked back at the distant gleam of the space station, just emerging from the shadow of Earth. It was some moments before I realized that the *Goddard* and the *Ziolkovski* weren't still floating beside it where I'd left them. . . .

No; they were just half a mile away, neatly matching my velocity. I stared at them in utter disbelief for a second, before I realized that every one of us had had the same idea. "Why, you pair of double-crossers!" I gasped. Then I began to laugh so much that it was several minutes before I dared call up a very worried Earth Control and tell them that everything had gone according to plan—though in no case was it the plan that had been originally announced. . . .

We were all very sheepish when we radioed each other to exchange mutual congratulations. Yet at the same time, I think everyone was secretly pleased that it had turned out this way. For the rest of the trip, we were never more than a few miles apart, and the actual landing maneuvers were so well synchronized that our three braking jets hit the moon simultaneously.

Well, almost simultaneously. I might make something of the fact that the recorder tape shows I touched down two-fifths of a second ahead of Krasnin. But I'd better not, for Vandenburg was precisely the same amount ahead of me.

On a quarter-of-a-million-mile trip, I think you could call that a photo finish. . . .

Robin Hood, F R S

We had landed early in the dawn of the long lunar day, and the slanting shadows lay all around us, extending for miles across the plain. They would slowly shorten as the sun rose higher in the sky, until at noon they would almost vanish— but noon was still five days away, as we measured time on Earth, and nightfall was seven days later still. We had almost two weeks of daylight ahead of us before the sun set and the bluely gleaming Earth became the mistress of the sky.

There was little time for exploration during those first hectic days. We had to unload the ships, grow accustomed to the alien conditions surrounding us, learn to handle our electrically powered tractors and scooters, and erect the igloos that would serve as homes, offices, and labs until the time came to leave. At a pinch, we could live in the spaceships, but it would be excessively uncomfortable and cramped. The igloos were not exactly commodious, but they were luxury after five days in space. Made of tough, flexible plastic, they were blown up like balloons, and their interiors were then partitioned into separate rooms. Air locks allowed access to the outer world, and a good deal of plumbing linked to the ships' air-purification plants kept the atmosphere breathable. Needless to say, the American igloo was the biggest one, and had come complete with everything, *including* the kitchen sink—not to mention a washing machine, which we and the Russians were always borrowing.

It was late in the "afternoon"—about ten days after we had landed—before we were properly organized and could think about serious scientific work. The first parties made nervous little forays out into the wilderness around the base, familiarizing themselves with the territory. Of course, we already possessed minutely detailed maps and photographs of the region in which we had landed, but it was surprising how misleading they could sometimes be. What had been marked as a small hill on a chart often looked like a mountain to a man toiling along in a space suit, and apparently smooth plains were often covered knee-deep with dust, which made progress extremely slow and tedious.

These were minor difficulties, however, and the low gravity—which gave all objects only a sixth of their terrestrial weight—compensated for much. As the scientists began to accumulate their results and specimens, the radio and TV circuits with Earth became busier and busier, until they were in continuous operation. We were taking no chances; even if *we* didn't get home, the knowledge we were gathering would do so.

The first of the automatic supply rockets landed two days before sunset, precisely according to plan. We saw its braking jets flame briefly against the stars, then blast again a few seconds before touchdown. The actual landing was hidden from us, since for safety reasons the dropping ground was three miles from the base. And on the moon, three miles is well over the curve of the horizon.

When we got to the robot, it was standing slightly askew on its tripod shock absorbers, but in perfect condition. So was everything aboard it, from instruments to food. We carried the stores back to base in triumph, and had a celebration that was really rather overdue. The men had been working too hard, and could do with some relaxation.

It was quite a party; the high light, I think, was Commander Krasnin trying to do a Cossack dance in a space suit. Then we turned our minds to competitive sports, but found that, for obvious reasons, outdoor activities were somewhat restricted. Games like croquet or bowls would have been practical had we had the equipment; but cricket and football were definitely out. In that gravity, even a football would go half a mile if it were given a good kick—and a cricket ball would never be seen again.

Professor Trevor Williams was the first person to think of a practical lunar sport. He was our astronomer, and also one of the youngest men ever to be made a Fellow of the Royal Society, being only thirty when this ultimate accolade was conferred upon him. His work on methods of interplanetary navigation had made him world famous; less well known, however, was his skill as a toxophilite. For two years in succession he had been archery champion for Wales. I was not surprised, therefore, when I discovered him shooting at a target propped up on a pile of lunar slag.

The bow was a curious one, strung with steel control wire and shaped from a laminated plastic bar. I wondered where Trevor had got hold of it, then remembered that the robot freight rocket had now been cannibalized and bits of it were appearing in all sorts of unexpected places. The arrows, however, were the really interesting feature. To give them stability on the airless moon, where, of course, feathers would be useless, Trevor had managed to rifle them. There was a little gadget on the bow that set them spinning, like bullets, when they were fired, so that they kept on course when they left the bow.

Even with this rather makeshift equipment, it was possible to shoot a mile if one wished to. However, Trevor didn't want to waste arrows, which were not easy to make; he was more interested in seeing the sort of accuracy he could get. It was uncanny to watch the almost flat trajectory of the arrows: they seemed to be traveling parallel with the ground. If he wasn't careful, someone warned Trevor, his arrows might become lunar satellites and would hit him in the back when they completed their orbit.

The second supply rocket arrived the next day, but this time things didn't go according to plan. It made a perfect touchdown, but unfortunately the radar-controlled automatic pilot made one of those mistakes that such simple-minded machines delight in doing. It spotted the only really unclimbable hill in the neighborhood, locked its beam onto the summit of it, and settled down there like an eagle descending upon its mountain aerie.

Our badly needed supplies were five hundred feet above our heads, and in a few hours night would be falling. What was to be done?

About fifteen people made the same suggestion at once, and for the next few minutes there was a great scurrying about as we rounded up all the nylon line on the base. Soon there was more than a thousand yards of it coiled in neat loops at Trevor's feet while we all waited expectantly. He tied one end to his arrow, drew the bow, and aimed it experimentally straight toward the stars. The arrow rose a little more than half the height of the cliff; then the weight of the line pulled it back.

"Sorry," said Trevor. "I just can't make it. And don't forget—we'd have to send up some kind of grapnel as well, if we want the end to stay up there."

There was much gloom for the next few minutes, as we watched the coils of line fall slowly back from the sky. The situation was really somewhat absurd. In our ships we had enough energy to carry us a quarter of a million miles from the moon—yet we were baffled by a puny little cliff. If we had time, we could probably find a way up to the top from the other side of the hill, but that would mean traveling several miles. It would be dangerous, and might well be impossible, during the few hours of daylight that were left.

Scientists were never baffled for long, and too many ingenious (sometimes overingenious) minds were working on the problem for it to remain unresolved. But this time it was a little more difficult, and only three people got the answer simultaneously. Trevor thought it over, then said noncommittally, "Well, it's worth trying."

The preparations took a little while, and we were all watching anxiously as the rays of the sinking sun crept higher and higher up the sheer cliff looming above us. Even if Trevor could get a line and grapnel up there, I thought to myself, it would not be easy making the ascent while encumbered with a space suit. I have no head for heights, and was glad that several mountaineering enthusiasts had already volunteered for the job.

At last everything was ready. The line had been carefully arranged so that it would lift from the ground with the minimum of hindrance. A light grapnel had been attached to the line a few feet behind the arrow; we hoped that it would catch in the rocks up there and wouldn't let us down—all too literally—when we put our trust in it.

This time, however, Trevor was not using a single arrow. He attached four to the line, at two-hundred-yard intervals. And I shall never forget that incongruous spectacle of the space-suited figure, gleaming in the last rays of the setting sun, as it drew its bow against the sky.

The arrow sped toward the stars, and before it had lifted more than fifty feet Trevor was already fitting the second one to his improvised bow. It raced after its predecessor, carrying the other end of the long loop that was now being hoisted into space. Almost at once the third followed, lifting its section of line—and I swear that the fourth arrow, with its section, was on the way before the first had noticeably slackened its momentum.

Now that there was no question of a single arrow lifting the entire length of line, it was not hard to reach the required altitude. The first two times the grapnel fell back; then it caught firmly somewhere up on the hidden plateau—and the first volunteer began to haul himself up the line. It was true that he weighed only about thirty pounds in this low gravity, but it was still a long way to fall.

He didn't. The stores in the freight rocket started coming down the cliff within the next hour, and everything essential had been lowered before nightfall. I must confess, however, that my satisfaction was considerably abated when one of the engineers proudly showed me the mouth organ he had sent from Earth. Even then I felt certain that we would all be very tired of that instrument before the long lunar night had ended. . . .

But that, of course, was hardly Trevor's fault. As we walked back to the ship together, through the great pools of shadow that were flowing swiftly over the plain, he made a proposal that, I am sure, has puzzled thousands of people ever since the detailed maps of the first lunar expedition were published.

After all, it does seem a little odd that a flat and lifeless plain, broken by a single small mountain, should now be labeled on all the charts of the moon as Sherwood Forest.

Green Fingers

I am very sorry, now that it's too late, that I never got to know Vladimir Surov. As I remember him, he was a quiet little man who could understand English but couldn't speak it well enough to make conversation. Even to his colleagues, I suspect he was a bit of an enigma. Whenever I went aboard the *Ziolkovski,* he would be sitting in a corner working on his notes or peering through a microscope, a man who clung to his privacy even in the tight and tiny world of a spaceship. The rest of the crew did not seem to mind his aloofness; when they spoke to him, it was clear that they regarded him with tolerant affection, as well as with respect. That was hardly surprising; the work he had done developing plants and trees that could flourish far inside the Arctic Circle had already made him the most famous botanist in Russia.

The fact that the Russian expedition had taken a botanist to the moon had caused a good deal of amusement, though it was really no odder than the fact that there were biologists on both the British and American ships. During the years before the first lunar landing, a good deal of evidence had accumulated hinting that some form of vegetation might exist on the moon, despite its airlessness and lack of water. The president of the U.S.S.R. Academy of Science was one of the leading proponents of this theory, and being too old to make the trip himself had done the next best thing by sending Surov.

The complete absence of any such vegetation, living or fossil, in the thousand or so square miles explored by our various parties was the first big disappointment the moon had reserved for us. Even those skeptics who were quite certain that no form of life could exist on the moon would have been very glad to have been proved wrong—as of course they were, five years later, when Richards and Shannon made their astonishing discovery inside the great walled plain of Eratosthenes. But *that* revelation still lay in the future; at the time of the first landing, it seemed that Surov had come to the moon in vain.

He did not appear unduly depressed, but kept himself as busy as the rest of the crew studying soil samples and looking after the little hydroponic farm whose pressurized, transparent tubes formed a gleaming network around the *Ziolkovski*. Neither we nor the Americans had gone in for this sort of thing, having calculated that it was better to ship food from Earth than to grow it on the spot—at least until the time came to set up a permanent base. We were right in terms of economics, but wrong in terms of morale. The tiny airtight greenhouses inside which Surov grew his vegetables and dwarf fruit trees were an oasis upon which we often feasted our eyes when we had grown tired of the immense desolation surrounding us.

One of the many disadvantages of being commander was that I seldom had much chance to do any active exploring; I was too busy preparing reports for Earth, checking stores, arranging programs and duty rosters, conferring with my opposite numbers in the American and Russian ships, and trying—not always successfully—to guess what would go wrong next. As a result, I sometimes did not go outside the base for two or three days at a time, and it was a standing joke that my space suit was a haven for moths.

Perhaps it is because of this that I can remember all my trips outside so vividly; certainly I can recall my only encounter with Surov. It was near noon, with the sun high above the southern mountains and the new Earth a barely visible thread of silver a few degrees away from it. Henderson, our geophysicist, wanted to take some magnetic readings at a series of check points a couple of miles to the east of the base. Everyone else was busy, and I was momentarily on top of my work, so we set off together on foot.

The journey was not long enough to merit taking one of the scooters, especially because the charges in the batteries were getting low. In any case, I always enjoyed walking out in the open on the moon. It was not merely the scenery, which even at its most awe-inspiring one can grow accustomed to after a while. No—what I never tired of was the effortless, slow-motion way in which every step took me bounding over the landscape, giving me the freedom that before the coming of space flight men only knew in dreams.

We had done the job and were halfway home when I noticed a figure moving across the plain about a mile to the south of us—not far, in fact, from the Russian base. I snapped my field glasses down inside my helmet and took a careful look at the other explorer. Even at close range, of course, you can't identify a man in a space suit, but because the suits are always coded by color and number that makes no practical difference.

"Who is it?" asked Henderson over the short-range radio channel to which we were both tuned.

"Blue suit, Number 3—that would be Surov. But I don't understand. *He's by himself.*"

It is one of the most fundamental rules of lunar exploration that no one goes anywhere alone on the surface of the moon. So many accidents can happen, which would be trivial if you were with a companion—but fatal if you were by yourself. How would you manage, for example, if your space suit developed a slow leak in the small of the back and you couldn't put on a repair patch? That may sound funny; but it's happened.

"Perhaps his buddy has had an accident and he's going to fetch help," suggested Henderson. "Maybe we had better call him."

I shook my head. Surov was obviously in no hurry. He had been out on a trip of his own, and was making his leisurely way back to the *Ziolkovski.* It was no concern of mine if Commander Krasnin let his people go out on solo trips, though it seemed a deplorable practice. And if Surov was breaking regulations, it was equally no concern of mine to report him.

During the next two months, my men often spotted Surov making his lone way over the landscape, but he always avoided them if they got too near. I made some discreet inquiries, and found that Commander Krasnin had been forced, owing to shortage of men, to relax some of his safety rules. But I couldn't find out what Surov was up to, though I never dreamed that his commander was equally in the dark.

It was with an "I told you so" feeling that I got Krasnin's emergency call. We had all had men in trouble before and had had to send out help, but this was the first time anyone had been lost and had not replied when his ship had sent out the recall signal. There was a hasty radio conference, a line of action was drawn up, and search parties fanned out from each of the three ships.

Once again I was with Henderson, and it was only common sense for us to backtrack along the route that we had seen Surov following. It was in what we regarded as "our" territory, quite some distance away from Surov's own ship, and as we scrambled up the low foothills it occurred to me for the first time that the Russian might have been doing something he wanted to keep from his colleagues. What it might be, I could not imagine.

Henderson found him, and yelled for help over his suit radio. But it was much too late; Surov was lying, face down, his deflated suit crumpled around him. He had been kneeling when something had smashed the plastic globe of his helmet; you could see how he had pitched forward and died instantaneously.

When Commander Krasnin reached us, we were still staring at the unbelievable object that Surov had been examining when he died. It was about three feet high, a leathery, greenish oval rooted to the rocks with a widespread network of tendrils. Yes—rooted; for it was a plant. A few yards away were two others, much smaller and apparently dead, since they were blackened and withered.

My first reaction was: "So there *is* life on the moon, after all!" It was not until Krasnin's voice spoke in my ears that I realized how much more marvelous was the truth.

"Poor Vladimir!" he said. "We knew he was a genius, yet we laughed at him when he told us of his dream. So he kept his greatest work a secret. He conquered the Arctic with his hybrid wheat, but *that* was only a beginning. He has brought life to the moon—and death as well."

As I stood there, in that first moment of astonished revelation, it still seemed a miracle. Today, all the world knows the history of "Surov's cactus," as it was inevitably if quite inaccurately christened, and it has lost much of its wonder. His notes have told the full story, and have described the years of experimentation that finally led him to a plant whose leathery skin would enable it to survive in vacuum, and whose far-ranging, acid-secreting roots would enable it to grow upon rocks where even lichens would be hard put to thrive. And we have seen the realization of the second stage of Surov's dream, for the cactus which will forever bear his name has already broken up vast areas of the lunar rock and so prepared a way for the more specialized plants that now feed every human being upon the moon.

Krasnin bent down beside the body of his colleague and lifted it effortlessly against the low gravity. He fingered the shattered fragments of the plastic helmet, and shook his head in perplexity.

"What could have happened to him?" he said. "It almost looks as if the plant did it, but that's ridiculous."

The green enigma stood there on the no-longer barren plain, tantalizing us with its promise and its mystery. Then Henderson said slowly, as if thinking aloud:

"I believe I've got the answer; I've just remembered some of the botany I did at school. If Surov designed this plant for lunar conditions, how would he arrange for it to propagate itself? The seeds would have to be scattered over a very wide area in the hope of finding a few suitable places to grow. There are no birds or animals here to carry them, in the way that happens on Earth. I can only think of one solution— and some of our terrestrial plants have already used it."

He was interrupted by my yell. Something had hit with a resounding clang against the metal waistband of my suit. It did no damage, but it was so sudden and unexpected that it took me utterly by surprise.

A seed lay at my feet, about the size and shape of a plum stone. A few yards away, we found the one that had shattered Surov's helmet as he bent down. He must have known that the plant was ripe, but in his eagerness to examine it he had forgotten what that implied. I have seen a cactus throw its seed a quarter of a mile under the low lunar gravity. Surov had been shot at point-blank range by his own creation.

All That Glitters

This is really Commander Vandenburg's story, but he is too many millions of miles away to tell it. It concerns his geophysicist, Dr. Paynter, who was generally believed to have gone to the moon to get away from his wife.

At one time or other, we were all supposed (often by our wives) to have done just that. However, in Paynter's case, there was just enough truth to make it stick.

It was not that he disliked his wife; one could almost say

the contrary. He would do anything for her, but unfortunately the things that she wanted him to do cost rather too much. She was a lady of extravagant tastes, and such ladies are advised not to marry scientists—even scientists who go to the moon.

Mrs. Paynter's weakness was for jewelry, particularly diamonds. As might be expected, this was a weakness that caused her husband a good deal of worry. Being a conscientious as well as an affectionate husband, he did not merely worry about it—he did something about it. He became one of the world's leading experts on diamonds, from the scientific rather than the commercial point of view, and probably knew more about their composition, origin, and properties than any other man alive. Unfortunately, you may know a lot about diamonds without ever possessing any, and her husband's erudition was not something that Mrs. Paynter could wear around her neck when she went to a party.

Geophysics, as I have mentioned, was Dr. Paynter's real business; diamonds were merely a sideline. He had developed many remarkable surveying instruments which could probe the interior of the Earth by means of electric impulses and magnetic waves, so giving a kind of X-ray picture of the hidden strata far below. It was hardly surprising, therefore, that he was one of the men chosen to pry into the mysterious interior of the moon.

He was quite eager to go, but it seemed to Commander Vandenburg that he was reluctant to leave Earth at this particular moment. A number of men had shown such symptoms; sometimes they were due to fears that could not be eradicated, and an otherwise promising man had to be left behind. In Paynter's case, however, the reluctance was quite impersonal. He was in the middle of a big experiment—something he had been working on all his life—and he didn't want to leave Earth until it was finished. However, the first lunar expedition could not wait for him, so he had to leave his project in the hands of his assistants. He was continually exchanging cryptic radio messages with them, to the great annoyance of the signals section of Space Station Three.

In the wonder of a new world waiting to be explored, Paynter soon forgot his earthly preoccupations. He would dash hither and yon over the lunar landscape on one of the neat little electric scooters the Americans had brought with them, carrying seismographs, magnetometers, gravity meters, and all the other esoteric tools of the geophysicist's trade. He was trying to learn, in a few weeks, what it had taken men hundreds of years to discover about their own planet. It was true that he had only a small sample of the moon's fourteen million square miles of territory to explore, but he intended to make a thorough job of it.

From time to time he continued to get messages from his colleagues back on Earth, as well as brief but affectionate signals from Mrs. P. Neither seemed to interest him very much; even when you are not so busy that you hardly have time to sleep, a quarter of a million miles puts most of your personal affairs in a different perspective. I think that on the moon Dr. Paynter was really happy for the first time in his life; if so, he was not the only one.

Not far from our base there was a rather fine crater pit, a great blowhole in the lunar surface almost two miles from rim to rim. Though it was fairly close at hand, it was outside the normal area of our joint operations, and we had been on the moon for six weeks before Paynter led a party of three men off in one of the baby tractors to have a look at it. They disappeared from radio range over the edge of the moon, but we weren't worried about that because if they ran into trouble they could always call Earth and get any message relayed back to us.

Paynter and his men were gone forty-eight hours, which is about the maximum for continuous working on the moon, even with booster drugs. At first their little expedition was quite uneventful and therefore quite unexciting; everything went according to plan. They reached the crater, inflated their pressurized igloo and unpacked their stores, took their instrument readings, and then set up a portable drill to get core samples. It was while he was waiting for the drill to bring him up a nice section of the moon that Paynter made his second great discovery. He had made his first about ten hours before, but he didn't know it yet.

Around the lip of the crater, lying where they had been thrown up by the great explosions that had convulsed the lunar landscape three hundred million years before, were immense piles of rock which must have come from many miles down in the moon's interior. Anything he could do

with his little drill, thought Paynter, could hardly compare
with *this*. Unfortunately, the mountain-sized geological
specimens that lay all around him were not neatly arranged
in their correct order; they had been scattered over the landscape, much farther than the eye could see, according to the
arbitrary violence of the eruptions that had blasted them
into space.

Paynter climbed over these immense slag heaps, taking a
swing at likely samples with his little hammer. Presently his
colleagues heard him yell, and saw him come running back
to them carrying what appeared to be a lump of rather poor
quality glass. It was some time before he was sufficiently
coherent to explain what all the fuss was about—and some
time later still before the expedition remembered its real job
and got back to work.

Vandenburg watched the returning party as it headed
back to the ship. The four men didn't seem as tired as one
would have expected, considering the fact that they had
been on their feet for two days. Indeed, there was a certain
jauntiness about their movements which even the space suits
couldn't wholly conceal. You could see that the expedition
had been a success. In that case, Paynter would have two
causes for congratulation. The priority message that had just
come from Earth was very cryptic, but it was clear that
Paynter's work there—whatever it was—had finally reached
a triumphant conclusion.

Commander Vandenburg almost forgot the message
when he saw what Paynter was holding in his hand. He
knew what a raw diamond looked like, and this was the
second largest that anyone had ever seen. Only the Cullinan,
tipping the scales at 3,026 carats, beat it by a slender margin. "We ought to have expected it," he heard Paynter bab-
ble happily. "Diamonds are always found associated with
volcanic vents. But somehow I never thought the analogy
would hold here."

Vandenburg suddenly remembered the signal, and
handed it over to Paynter. He read it quickly, and his jaw
dropped. Never in his life, Vandenburg told me, had he seen
a man so instantly deflated by a message of congratulation.
The signal read: WE'VE DONE IT. TEST 541 WITH MODIFIED
PRESSURE CONTAINER COMPLETE SUCCESS. NO PRACTICAL
LIMIT TO SIZE. COSTS NEGLIGIBLE.

"What's the matter?" said Vandenburg, when he saw the stricken look on Paynter's face. "It doesn't seem bad news to me, whatever it means."

Paynter gulped two or three times like a stranded fish, then stared helplessly at the great crystal that almost filled the palm of his hand. He tossed it into the air, and it floated back in that slow-motion way everything has under lunar gravity.

Finally he found his voice.

"My lab's been working for years," he said, "trying to synthesize diamonds. Yesterday this thing was worth a million dollars. Today it's worth a couple of hundred. I'm not sure I'll bother to carry it back to Earth."

Well, he *did* carry it back; it seemed a pity not to. For about three months, Mrs. P. had the finest diamond necklace in the world, worth every bit of a thousand dollars— mostly the cost of cutting and polishing. Then the Paynter Process went into commercial production, and a month later she got her divorce. The grounds were extreme mental cruelty; and I suppose you could say it was justified.

Watch This Space

It was quite a surprise to discover, when I looked it up, that the most famous experiment we carried out while we were on the moon had its beginnings way back in 1955. At that time, high-altitude rocket research had been going for only about ten years, mostly at White Sands, New Mexico. Nineteen fifty-five was the date of one of the most spectacular of those early experiments, one that involved the ejection of sodium into the upper atmosphere.

On Earth, even on the clearest night, the sky between the stars isn't completely dark. There's a very faint background glow, and part of it is caused by the fluorescence of sodium atoms a hundred miles up. Since it would take the sodium in a good many cubic miles of the upper atmosphere to fill a single matchbox, it seemed to the early investigators that they could make quite a fireworks display if they used a rocket to dump a few pounds of the stuff into the ionosphere.

They were right. The sodium squirted out of a rocket above White Sands early in 1955 produced a great yellow glow in the sky which was visible, like a kind of artificial moonlight, for over an hour, before the atoms dispersed. This experiment wasn't done for fun (though it *was* fun) but for a serious scientific purpose. Instruments trained on this glow were able to gather new knowledge about the upper air —knowledge that went into the stockpile of information without which space flight would never have been possible.

When they got to the moon, the Americans decided that it would be a good idea to repeat the experiment there, on a much larger scale. A few hundred kilograms of sodium fired up from the surface would produce a display that would be visible from Earth, with a good pair of field glasses, as it fluoresced its way up through the lunar atmosphere.

(Some people, by the way, still don't realize that the moon *has* an atmosphere. It's about a million times too thin to be breathable, but if you have the right instruments you can detect it. As a meteor shield, it's first-rate, for though it may be tenuous it's hundreds of miles deep.)

Everyone had been talking about the experiment for days. The sodium bomb had arrived from Earth in the last supply rocket, and a very impressive piece of equipment it looked. Its operation was extremely simple; when ignited, an incendiary charge vaporized the sodium until a high pressure was built up, then a diaphragm burst and the stuff was squirted up into the sky through a specially shaped nozzle. It would be shot off soon after nightfall, and when the cloud of sodium rose out of the moon's shadow into direct sunlight it would start to glow with tremendous brilliance.

Nightfall, on the moon, is one of the most awe-inspiring sights in the whole of nature, made doubly so because as you watch the sun's flaming disk creep so slowly below the mountains you know that it will be fourteen days before you see it again. But it does not bring darkness—at least, not on this side of the moon. There is always the Earth, hanging motionless in the sky, the one heavenly body that neither rises nor sets. The light pouring back from her clouds and seas floods the lunar landscape with a soft, blue-green radiance, so that it is often easier to find your way around at night than under the fierce glare of the sun.

Even those who were not supposed to be on duty had

come out to watch the experiment. The sodium bomb had been placed at the middle of the big triangle formed by the three ships, and stood upright with its nozzles pointing at the stars. Dr. Anderson, the astronomer of the American team, was testing the firing circuits, but everyone else was at a respectful distance. The bomb looked perfectly capable of living up to its name, though it was really about as dangerous as a soda-water siphon.

All the optical equipment of the three expeditions seemed to have been gathered together to record the performance. Telescopes, spectroscopes, motion-picture cameras, and everything else one could think of were lined up ready for action. And this, I knew, was nothing compared with the battery that must be zeroed on us from Earth. Every amateur astronomer who could see the moon tonight would be standing by in his back garden, listening to the radio commentary that told him of the progress of the experiment. I glanced up at the gleaming planet that dominated the sky above me; the land areas seemed to be fairly free from cloud, so the folks at home should have a good view. That seemed only fair; after all, they were footing the bill.

There were still fifteen minutes to go. Not for the first time, I wished there was a reliable way of smoking a cigarette inside a space suit without getting the helmet so badly fogged that you couldn't see. Our scientists had solved so many much more difficult problems; it seemed a pity that they couldn't do something about *that* one.

To pass the time—for this was an experiment where I had nothing to do—I switched on my suit radio and listened to Dave Bolton, who was making a very good job of the commentary. Dave was our chief navigator, and a brilliant mathematician. He also had a glib tongue and a picturesque turn of speech, and sometimes his recordings had to be censored by the B.B.C. There was nothing they could do about this one, however, for it was going out live from the relay stations on Earth.

Dave had finished a brief and lucid explanation of the purpose of the experiment, describing how the cloud of glowing sodium would enable us to analyze the lunar atmosphere as it rose through it at approximately a thousand miles an hour. "However," he went on to tell the waiting millions on Earth, "let's make one point clear. Even when the bomb has gone off, you won't see a darn thing for ten minutes—and neither will we. The sodium cloud will be completely invisible while it's rising up through the darkness of the moon's shadow. Then, quite suddenly, it will flash into brilliance as it enters the sun's rays, which are streaming past over our heads right now as we stare up into space. No one is quite sure how bright it will be, but it's a pretty safe guess that you'll be able to see it in any telescope bigger than a two-inch. So it should just be within the range of a good pair of binoculars."

He had to keep this sort of thing up for another ten minutes, and it was a marvel to me how he managed to do it. Then the great moment came, and Anderson closed the firing circuit. The bomb started to cook, building up pressure inside as the sodium volatilized. After thirty seconds, there was a sudden puff of smoke from the long, slender nozzle pointing up at the sky. And then we had to wait for another ten minutes while the invisible cloud rose to the stars. After all this build-up, I told myself, the result had better be good.

The seconds and minutes ebbed away. Then a sudden yellow glow began to spread across the sky, like a vast and unwavering aurora that became brighter even as we watched. It was as if an artist was sprawling strokes across the stars with a flame-filled brush. And as I stared at those strokes, I suddenly realized that someone had brought off the greatest advertising coup in history. For the strokes formed letters, and the letters formed two words—the name of a certain soft drink too well known to need any further publicity from me.

How had it been done? The first answer was obvious. Someone had placed a suitably cut stencil in the nozzle of the sodium bomb, so that the stream of escaping vapor had shaped itself to the words. Since there was nothing to distort it, the pattern had kept its shape during its invisible ascent to the stars. I had seen skywriting on Earth, but this was something on a far larger scale. Whatever I thought of them, I couldn't help admiring the ingenuity of the men who had perpetrated the scheme. The O's and A's had given them a bit of trouble, but the C's and L's were perfect.

After the initial shock, I am glad to say that the scientific program proceeded as planned. I wish I could remember how Dave Bolton rose to the occasion in his commentary; it must have been a strain even for his quick wits. By this time, of course, half the Earth could see what he was describing. The next morning, every newspaper on the planet carried that famous photo of the crescent moon with the luminous slogan painted across its darkened sector.

The letters were visible, before they finally dispersed into space, for over an hour. By that time the words were almost a thousand miles long, and were beginning to get blurred. But they were still readable until they at last faded from sight in the ultimate vacuum between the planets.

Then the real fireworks began. Commander Vandenburg was absolutely furious, and promptly started to grill all his men. However, it was soon clear that the saboteur—if you could call him that—had been back on Earth. The bomb had been prepared there and shipped ready for immediate use. It did not take long to find, and fire, the engineer who had carried out the substitution. He couldn't have cared less, since his financial needs had been taken care of for a good many years to come.

As for the experiment itself, it was completely successful from the scientific point of view; all the recording instruments worked perfectly as they analyzed the light from the unexpectedly shaped cloud. But we never let the Americans live it down, and I am afraid poor Captain Vandenburg was the one who suffered most. Before he came to the moon he was a confirmed teetotaler, and much of his refreshment came from a certain wasp-waisted bottle. But now, as a matter of principle, he can only drink beer—and he hates the stuff.

A Question of Residence

I have already described the—shall we say—jockeying for position before take-off on the first flight to the moon. As it turned out, the American, Russian, and British ships landed just about simultaneously. No one has ever explained, however, why the British ship came back nearly two weeks after the others.

Oh, I know the official story; I ought to, for I helped to

concoct it. It is true as far as it goes, but it scarcely goes far enough.

On all counts, the joint expedition had been a triumphant success. There had been only one casualty, and in the manner of his death Vladimir Surov had made himself immortal. We had gathered knowledge that would keep the scientists of Earth busy for generations, and that would revolutionize almost all our ideas concerning the nature of the universe around us. Yes, our five months on the moon had been well spent, and we could go home to such welcomes as few heroes had ever had before.

However, there was still a good deal of tidying up to be done. The instruments that had been scattered all over the lunar landscape were still busily recording, and much of the information they gathered could not be automatically radioed back to Earth. There was no point in all three of the expeditions staying on the moon to the last minute; the personnel of one would be sufficient to finish the job. But who would volunteer to be caretaker while the others went back to gain the glory? It was a difficult problem, but one that would have to be solved very soon.

As far as supplies were concerned, we had little to worry about. The automatic freight rockets could keep us provided with air, food, and water for as long as we wished to stay on the moon. We were all in good health, though a little tired. None of the anticipated psychological troubles had cropped up, perhaps because we had all been so busy on tasks of absorbing interest that we had had no time to worry about going crazy. But, of course, we all looked forward to getting back to Earth and seeing our families again.

The first change of plans was forced upon us by the *Ziolkovski* being put out of commission when the ground beneath one of her landing legs suddenly gave way. The ship managed to stay upright, but the hull was badly twisted and the pressure cabin sprang dozens of leaks. There was much debate about on-the-spot repairs, but it was decided that it would be far too risky for her to take off in this condition. The Russians had no alternative but to thumb lifts back in the *Goddard* and the *Endeavour;* by using the *Ziolkovski's* unwanted fuel, our ships would be able to manage the extra load. However, the return flight would be extremely cramped and uncomfortable for all concerned because everyone would have to eat and sleep in shifts.

Either the American or the British ship, therefore, would be the first back to Earth. During those final weeks, as the work of the expedition was brought to its close, relations between Commander Vandenburg and myself were somewhat strained. I even wondered if we ought to settle the matter by tossing for it. . . .

Another problem was also engaging my attention—that of crew discipline. Perhaps this is too strong a phrase; I would not like it to be thought that a mutiny ever seemed probable. But all my men were now a little abstracted and liable to be found, if off duty, scribbling furiously in corners. I knew exactly what was going on, for I was involved in it myself. There wasn't a human being on the moon who had not sold exclusive rights to some newspaper or magazine, and we were all haunted by approaching deadlines. The radio-teletype to Earth was in continuous operation, sending tens of thousands of words being dictated over the speech circuits.

It was Professor Williams, our very practical-minded astronomer, who came to me one day with the answer to my main problem.

"Skipper," he said, balancing himself precariously on the all-too-collapsible table I used as my working desk inside the igloo, "there's no technical reason, is there, why we should get back to Earth first?"

"No," I said, "merely a matter of fame, fortune, and seeing our families again. But I admit those aren't technical reasons. We could stay here another year if Earth kept sending supplies. If you want to suggest that, however, I shall take great pleasure in strangling you."

"It's not as bad as that. Once the main body has gone back, whichever party is left can follow in two or three weeks at the latest. They'll get a lot of credit, in fact, for self-sacrifice, modesty, and similar virtues."

"Which will be very poor compensation for being second home."

"Right—we need something else to make it worthwhile. Some more material reward."

"Agreed. What do you suggest?"

Williams pointed to the calendar hanging on the wall in

front of me, between the two pin-ups we had stolen from the
Goddard. The length of our stay was indicated by the days
that had been crossed off in red ink; a big question mark in
two weeks' time showed when the first ship would be heading back to Earth.

"There's your answer," he said. "If we go back then, do
you realize what will happen? I'll tell you."

He did, and I kicked myself for not having thought of it
first.

The next day, I explained my decision to Vandenburg and
Krasnin.

"We'll stay behind and do the mopping up," I said. "It's
a matter of common sense. The *Goddard*'s a much bigger
ship than ours and can carry an extra four people, while we
can manage only two more, and even then it will be a
squeeze. If you go first, Van, it will save a lot of people from
eating their hearts out here for longer than necessary."

"That's very big of you," replied Vandenburg. "I won't
hide the fact that we'll be happy to get home. And it's logical, I admit, now that the *Ziolkovski*'s out of action. Still, it
means quite a sacrifice on your part, and I don't really like
to take advantage of it."

I gave an expansive wave.

"Think nothing of it," I answered. "As long as you boys
don't grab all the credit, we'll take our turn. After all, we'll
have the show here to ourselves when you've gone back to
Earth."

Krasnin was looking at me with a rather calculating expression, and I found it singularly difficult to return his
gaze.

"I hate to sound cynical," he said, "but I've learned to be
a little suspicious when people start doing big favors without
very good reasons. And frankly, I don't think the reason
you've given is good enough. You wouldn't have anything
else up your sleeve, would you?"

"Oh, very well," I sighed. "I'd hoped to get a *little* credit,
but I see it's no use trying to convince anyone of the purity
of my motives. I've got a reason, and you might as well
know it. But please don't spread it around; I'd hate the folks
back on Earth to be disillusioned. They still think of us as
noble and heroic seekers after knowledge; let's keep it that
way, for all our sakes."

Then I pulled out the calendar, and explained to Vandenburg and Krasnin what Williams had already explained to me. They listened with skepticism, then with growing sympathy.

"I had no idea it was *that* bad," said Vandenburg at last.

"Americans never have," I said sadly. "Anyway, that's the way it's been for half a century, and it doesn't seem to get any better. So you agree with my suggestion?"

"Of course. It suits us fine, anyhow. Until the next expedition's ready, the moon's all yours."

I remembered that phrase, two weeks later, as I watched the *Goddard* blast up into the sky toward the distant, beckoning Earth. It was lonely, then, when the Americans and all but two of the Russians had gone. We envied them the reception they got, and watched jealously on the TV screens their triumphant processions through Moscow and New York. Then we went back to work, and bided our time. Whenever we felt depressed, we would do little sums on bits of paper and would be instantly restored to cheerfulness.

The red crosses marched across the calendar as the short terrestrial days went by—days that seemed to have very little connection with the slow cycle of lunar time. At last we were ready; all the instrument readings were taken, all the specimens and samples safely packed away aboard the ship. The motors roared into life, giving us for a moment the weight we would feel again when we were back in Earth's gravity. Below us the rugged lunar landscape, which we had grown to know so well, fell swiftly away; within seconds we could see no sign at all of the buildings and instruments we had so laboriously erected and which future explorers would one day use.

The homeward voyage had begun. We returned to Earth in uneventful discomfort, joined the already half-dismantled *Goddard* beside Space Station Three, and were quickly ferried down to the world we had left seven months before.

Seven months: that, as Williams had pointed out, was the all-important figure. We had been on the moon for more than half a financial year—and for all of us, it had been the most profitable year of our lives.

Sooner or later, I suppose, this interplanetary loophole will be plugged; the Department of Inland Revenue is still fighting a gallant rear-guard action, but we seem neatly covered under Section 57, paragraph 8 of the Capital Gains Act of 1972. We wrote our books and articles on the moon—and until there's a lunar government to impose income tax, we're hanging on to every penny.

And if the ruling finally goes against us—well, there's always Mars. . . .

ALL THE TIME IN THE WORLD

WHEN THE QUIET knock came on the door, Robert Ashton surveyed the room in one swift, automatic movement. Its dull respectability satisfied him and should reassure any visitor. Not that he had any reason to expect the police, but there was no point in taking chances.

"Come in," he said, pausing only to grab Plato's *Dialogues* from the shelf beside him. Perhaps this gesture was a little too ostentatious, but it always impressed his clients.

The door opened slowly. At first, Ashton continued his intent reading, not bothering to glance up. There was the slightest acceleration of his heart, a mild and even exhilarating constriction of the chest. Of course, it couldn't possibly be a flatfoot: someone would have tipped him off. Still, any unheralded visitor was unusual and thus potentially dangerous.

Ashton laid down the book, glanced toward the door and remarked in a noncommittal voice: "What can I do for you?" He did not get up; such courtesies belonged to a past he had buried long ago. Besides, it was a woman. In the circles he now frequented, women were accustomed to receive jewels and clothes and money but never respect.

Yet there was something about this visitor that drew him slowly to his feet. It was not merely that she was beautiful but she had a poised and effortless authority that moved her into a different world from the flamboyant doxies he met in the normal course of business. There was a brain and a purpose behind those calm, appraising eyes—a brain, Ashton suspected, the equal of his own.

He did not know how grossly he had underestimated her.

"Mr. Ashton," she began, "let us not waste time. I know who you are and I have work for you. Here are my credentials."

She opened a large, stylish handbag and extracted a thick bundle of notes.

"You may regard this," she said, "as a sample."

Ashton caught the bundle as she tossed it carelessly toward him. It was the largest sum of money he had ever held in his life—at least a hundred fivers, all new and serially numbered. He felt them between his fingers. If they were not genuine, they were so good that the difference was of no practical importance.

He ran his thumb to and fro along the edge of the wad as if feeling a pack for a marked card, and said thoughtfully, "I'd like to know where you got these. If they aren't forgeries, they must be hot and will take some passing."

"They are genuine. A very short time ago they were in the Bank of England. But if they are of no use to you throw them in the fire. I merely let you have them to show that I mean business."

"Go on." He gestured to the only seat and balanced himself on the edge of the table.

She drew a sheaf of papers from the capacious handbag and handed it across to him.

"I am prepared to pay you any sum you wish if you will secure these items and bring them to me, at a time and place to be arranged. What is more, I will guarantee that you can make the thefts with no personal danger."

Ashton looked at the list, and sighed. The woman was mad. Still, she had better be humored. There might be more money where this came from.

"I notice," he said mildly, "that all these items are in the

British Museum, and that most of them are, quite literally, priceless. By that I mean that you could neither buy nor sell them."

"I do not wish to sell them. I am a collector."

"So it seems. What are you prepared to pay for these acquisitions?"

"Name a figure."

There was a short silence. Ashton weighed the possibilities. He took a certain professional pride in his work, but there were some things that no amount of money could accomplish. Still, it would be amusing to see how high the bidding would go.

He looked at the list again.

"I think a round million would be a very reasonable figure for this lot," he said ironically.

"I fear you are not taking me very seriously. With your contacts, you should be able to dispose of these."

There was a flash of light and something sparkled through the air. Ashton caught the necklace before it hit the ground, and despite himself was unable to suppress a gasp of amazement. A fortune glittered through his fingers. The central diamond was the largest he had ever seen—it must be one of the world's most famous jewels.

His visitor seemed completely indifferent as he slipped the necklace into his pocket. Ashton was badly shaken; he knew she was not acting. To her, that fabulous gem was of no more value than a lump of sugar. This was madness on an unimaginable scale.

"Assuming that you can deliver the money," he said, "how do you imagine that it's physically possible to do what you ask? One might steal a single item from this list, but within a few hours the Museum would be solid with police."

With a fortune already in his pocket, he could afford to be frank. Besides, he was curious to learn more about his fantastic visitor.

She smiled, rather sadly, as if humoring a backward child.

"If I show you the way," she said softly, "will you do it?"

"Yes—for a million."

"Have you noticed anything strange since I came in? Is it not—very quiet?"

Ashton listened. My God, she was right! This room was

never completely silent, even at night. There had been a wind blowing over the roof tops; where had it gone now? The distant rumble of traffic had ceased; five minutes ago he had been cursing the engines shunting in the marshaling yard at the end of the road. What had happened to them?

"Go to the window."

He obeyed the order and drew aside the grimy lace curtains with fingers that shook slightly despite all attempt at control. Then he relaxed. The street was quite empty, as it often was at this time in the midmorning. There was no traffic, and hence no reason for sound. Then he glanced down the row of dingy houses toward the shunting yard.

His visitor smiled as he stiffened with the shock.

"Tell me what you see, Mr. Ashton."

He turned slowly, face pale and throat muscles working. "What are you?" he gasped. "A witch?"

"Don't be foolish. There is a simple explanation. It is not the world that has changed—but you."

Ashton stared again at that unbelievable shunting engine, the plume of steam frozen motionless above it as if made from cotton wool. He realized now that the clouds were equally immobile; they should have been scudding across the sky. All around him was the unnatural stillness of the high-speed photograph, the vivid unreality of a scene glimpsed in a flash of lighting.

"You are intelligent enough to realize what is happening, even if you cannot understand how it is done. Your time scale has been altered: a minute in the outer world would be a year in this room."

Again she opened the handbag, and this time brought forth what appeared to be a bracelet of some silvery metal, with a series of dials and switches molded into it.

"You can call this a personal generator," she said. "With it strapped about your arm, you are invincible. You can come and go without hindrance—you can steal everything on that list and bring it to me before one of the guards in the Museum has blinked an eyelid. When you have finished, you can be miles away before you switch off the field and step back into the normal world.

"Now listen carefully, and do exactly what I say. The field has a radius of about seven feet, so you must keep at least that distance from any other person. Secondly, you must not switch it off again until you have completed your task and I have given you your payment. *This is most important.* Now, the plan I have worked out is this. . . ."

No criminal in the history of the world had ever possessed such power. It was intoxication—yet Ashton wondered if he would ever get used to it. He had ceased to worry about explanations, at least until the job was done and he had collected his reward. Then, perhaps, he would get away from England and enjoy a well-earned retirement.

His visitor had left a few minutes ahead of him, but when he stepped out into the street the scene was completely unchanged. Though he had prepared for it, the sensation was still unnerving. Ashton felt an impulse to hurry, as if this condition couldn't possibly last and he had to get the job done before the gadget ran out of juice. But that, he had been assured, was impossible.

In the High Street he slowed down to look at the frozen traffic, the paralyzed pedestrians. He was careful, as he had been warned, not to approach so close to anyone that they came within his field. How ridiculous people looked when one saw them like this, robbed of such grace as movement could give, their mouths half open in foolish grimaces!

Having to seek assistance went against the grain, but some parts of the job were too big for him to handle by himself. Besides, he could pay liberally and never notice it. The main difficulty, Ashton realized, would be to find someone who was intelligent enough not to be scared—or so stupid that he would take everything for granted. He decided to try the first possibility.

Tony Marchetti's place was down a side street so close to the police station that one felt it was really carrying camouflage too far. As he walked past the entrance, Ashton caught a glimpse of the duty sergeant at his desk and resisted a temptation to go inside to combine a little pleasure with business. But that sort of thing could wait until later.

The door of Tony's opened in his face as he approached. It was such a natural occurrence in a world where nothing was normal that it was a moment before Ashton realized its implications. Had his generator failed? He glanced hastily down the street and was reassured by the frozen tableau behind him.

"Well, if it isn't Bob Ashton!" said a familiar voice. "Fancy meeting you as early in the morning as this. That's an odd bracelet you're wearing. I thought I had the only one."

"Hello, Aram," replied Ashton. "It looks as if there's a lot going on that neither of us knows about. Have you signed up Tony, or is he still free?"

"Sorry. We've a little job which will keep him busy for a while."

"Don't tell me. It's at the National Gallery or the Tate."

Aram Albenkian fingered his neat goatee. "Who told you that?" he asked.

"No one. But, after all, you *are* the crookedest art dealer in the trade, and I'm beginning to guess what's going on. Did a tall, very good-looking brunette give you that bracelet and a shopping list?"

"I don't see why I should tell you, but the answer's no. It was a man."

Ashton felt a momentary surprise. Then he shrugged his shoulders. "I might have guessed that there would be more than one of them. I'd like to know who's behind it."

"Have you any theories?" said Albenkian guardedly.

Ashton decided that it would be worth risking some loss of information to test the other's reactions. "It's obvious they're not interested in money—they have all they want and can get more with this gadget. The woman who saw me said she was a collector. I took it as a joke, but I see now that she meant it seriously."

"Why do we come into the picture? What's to stop them doing the whole job themselves?" Albenkian asked.

"Maybe they're frightened. Or perhaps they want our— er—specialized knowledge. Some of the items on my list are rather well cased in. My theory is that they're agents for a mad millionaire."

It didn't hold water, and Ashton knew it. But he wanted to see which leaks Albenkian would try to plug.

"My dear Ashton," said the other impatiently, holding up his wrist. "How do you explain this little thing? I know nothing about science, but even I can tell that it's beyond the wildest dreams of our technologies. There's only one conclusion to be drawn from that."

"Go on."

"These people are from—somewhere else. Our world is being systematically looted of its treasures. You know all this stuff you read about rockets and spaceships? Well, someone else has done it first."

Ashton didn't laugh. The theory was no more fantastic than the facts.

"Whoever they are," he said, "they seem to know their way around pretty well. I wonder how many teams they've got? Perhaps the Louvre and the Prado are being reconnoitered at this very minute. The world is going to have a shock before the day's out."

They parted amicably enough, neither confiding any details of real importance about his business. For a fleeting moment Ashton thought of trying to buy over Tony, but there was no point in antagonizing Albenkian. Steve Regan would have to do. That meant walking about a mile, since of course any form of transport was impossible. He would die of old age before a bus completed the journey. Ashton was not clear what would happen if he attempted to drive a car when the field was operating, and he had been warned not to try any experiments.

It astonished Ashton that even such a nearly certified moron as Steve could take the accelerator so calmly; there was something to be said, after all, for the comic strips which were probably his only reading. After a few words of grossly simplified explanation, Steve buckled on the spare wristlet which, rather to Ashton's surprise, his visitor had handed over without comment. Then they set out on their long walk to the Museum.

Ashton, or his client, had thought of everything. They stopped once at a park bench to rest and enjoy some sandwiches and regain their breath. When at last they reached the Museum, neither felt any the worse for the unaccustomed exercise.

They walked together through the gates of the Museum —unable, despite logic, to avoid speaking in whispers—and up the wide stone steps into the entrance hall. Ashton knew his way perfectly. With whimsical humor he displayed his

Reading Room ticket as they walked, at a respectful distance, past the statuesque attendants. It occurred to him that the occupants of the great chamber, for the most part, looked just the same as they normally did, even without the benefit of the accelerator.

It was a straightforward but tedious job collecting the books that had been listed. They had been chosen, it seemed, for their beauty as works of art as much as for their literary content. The selection had been done by someone who knew his job. Had *they* done it themselves, Ashton wondered, or had they bribed other experts as they were bribing him? He wondered if he would ever glimpse the full ramifications of their plot.

There was a considerable amount of panel-smashing to be done, but Ashton was careful not to damage any books, even the unwanted ones. Whenever he had collected enough volumes to make a comfortable load, Steve carried them out into the courtyard and dumped them on the paving stones until a small pyramid had accumulated.

It would not matter if they were left for short periods outside the field of the accelerator. No one would notice their momentary flicker of existence in the normal world.

They were in the library for two hours of their time, and paused for another snack before passing to the next job. On the way Ashton stopped for a little private business. There was a tinkle of glass as the tiny case, standing in solitary splendor, yielded up its treasure: then the manuscript of *Alice* was safely tucked into Ashton's pocket.

Among the antiquities, he was not quite so much at home. There were a few examples to be taken from every gallery, and sometimes it was hard to see the reasons for the choice. It was as if—and again he remembered Albenkian's words—these works of art had been selected by someone with totally alien standards. This time, with a few exceptions, *they* had obviously not been guided by the experts.

For the second time in history the case of the Portland Vase was shattered. In five seconds, thought Ashton, the alarms would be going all over the Museum and the whole building would be in an uproar. And in five seconds he could be miles away. It was an intoxicating thought, and as he worked swiftly to complete his contract he began to regret the price he had asked. Even now, it was not too late.

He felt the quiet satisfaction of the good workman as he watched Steve carry the great silver tray of the Mildenhall Treasure out into the courtyard and place it beside the now impressive pile. "That's the lot," he said. "I'll settle up at my place this evening. Now let's get this gadget off you."

They walked out into High Holborn and chose a secluded side street that had no pedestrians near it. Ashton unfastened the peculiar buckle and stepped back from his cohort, watching him freeze into immobility as he did so. Steve was vulnerable again, moving once more with all other men in the stream of time. But before the alarm had gone out he would have lost himself in the London crowds.

When he re-entered the Museum yard, the treasure had already gone. Standing where it had been was his visitor of how long ago? She was still poised and graceful, but, Ashton thought, looking a little tired. He approached until their fields merged and they were no longer separated by an impassable gulf of silence. "I hope you're satisfied," he said. "How did you move the stuff so quickly?"

She touched the bracelet around her own wrist and gave a wan smile. "We have many other powers besides this."

"Then why did you need my help?"

"There were technical reasons. It was necessary to remove the objects we required from the presence of other matter. In this way, we could gather only what we needed and not waste our limited—what shall I call them?—transporting facilities. Now may I have the bracelet back?"

Ashton slowly handed over the one he was carrying, but made no effort to unfasten his own. There might be danger in what he was doing, but he intended to retreat at the first sign of it.

"I'm prepared to reduce my fee," he said. "In fact I'll waive all payment—in exchange for this." He touched his wrist, where the intricate metal band gleamed in the sunlight.

She was watching him with an expression as fathomless as the Gioconda smile. (Had *that*, Ashton wondered, gone to join the treasure he had gathered? How much had they taken from the Louvre?)

"I would not call that reducing your fee. All the money in the world could not purchase one of those bracelets."

"Or the things I have given you."

"You are greedy, Mr. Ashton. You know that with an accelerator the entire world would be yours."

"What of that? Do you have any farther interest in our planet, now you have taken what you need?"

There was a pause. Then, unexpectedly, she smiled. "So you have guessed I do not belong to your world."

"Yes. And I know that you have other agents besides myself. Do you come from Mars, or won't you tell me?"

"I am quite willing to tell you. But you may not thank me if I do."

Ashton looked at her warily. What did she mean by that? Unconscious of his action, he put his wrist behind his back, protecting the bracelet.

"No, I am not from Mars, or any planet of which you have ever heard. You would not understand *what* I am. Yet I will tell you this. I am from the Future."

"The Future! That's ridiculous!"

"Indeed? I should be interested to know why."

"If that sort of thing were possible, our past history would be full of time travelers. Besides, it would involve a *reductio ad absurdum.* Going into the past could change the present and produce all sorts of paradoxes."

"Those are good points, though not perhaps as original as you suppose. But they only refute the possibility of time travel in general, not in the very special case which concerns us now."

"What is peculiar about it?" he asked.

"On very rare occasions, and by the release of an enormous amount of energy, it is possible to produce a—*singularity*—in time. During the fraction of a second when that singularity occurs, the past becomes accessible to the future, though only in a restricted way. We can send our minds back to you, but not our bodies."

"You mean," said Ashton, "that you are *borrowing* the body I see?"

"Oh, I have paid for it, as I am paying you. The owner has agreed to the terms. We are very conscientious in these matters."

Ashton was thinking swiftly. If this story was true, it gave him a definite advantage.

"You mean," he continued, "that you have no direct control over matter, and must work through human agents?"

"Yes. Even those bracelets were made here, under our mental control."

She was explaining too much too readily, revealing all her weaknesses. A warning signal was flashing in the back of Ashton's mind, but he had committed himself too deeply to retreat.

"Then it seems to me," he said slowly, "that you cannot force me to hand this bracelet back."

"That is perfectly true."

"That's all I want to know."

She was smiling at him now, and there was something in that smile that chilled him to the marrow.

"We are not vindictive or unkind, Mr. Ashton," she said quietly. "What I am going to do now appeals to my sense of justice. You have asked for that bracelet; you can keep it. Now I shall tell you just how useful it will be."

For a moment Ashton had a wild impulse to hand back the accelerator. She must have guessed his thoughts.

"No, it's too late. I insist that you keep it. And I can reassure you on one point. It won't wear out. It will last you"—again that enigmatic smile—"the rest of your life.

"Do you mind if we go for a walk, Mr. Ashton? I have done my work here, and would like to have a last glimpse of your world before I leave it forever."

She turned toward the iron gates, and did not wait for a reply. Consumed by curiosity, Ashton followed.

They walked in silence until they were standing among the frozen traffic of Tottenham Court Road. For a while she stood staring at the busy yet motionless crowds; then she sighed.

"I cannot help feeling sorry for them, and for you. I wonder what you would have made of yourselves."

"What do you mean by that?"

"Just now, Mr. Ashton, you implied that the future cannot reach back into the past, because that would alter history. A shrewd remark, but, I am afraid, irrelevant. You see, *your* world has no more history to alter."

She pointed across the road, and Ashton turned swiftly on his heels. There was nothing there except a newsboy crouching over his pile of papers. A placard formed an impossible curve in the breeze that was blowing through this motionless world. Ashton read the crudely lettered words with difficulty:

SUPER—BOMB TEST TODAY

The voice in his ears seemed to come from a very long way off.

"I told you that time travel, even in this restricted form, requires an enormous release of energy—far more than a single bomb can liberate, Mr. Ashton. But that bomb is only a trigger—"

She pointed to the solid ground beneath their feet. "Do you know anything about your own planet? Probably not; your race has learned so little. But even your scientists have discovered that, two thousand miles down, the Earth has a dense, liquid core. That core is made of compressed matter, and it can exist in either of two stable states. Given a certain stimulus, it can change from one of those states to another, just as a seesaw can tip over at the touch of a finger. But that change, Mr. Ashton, will liberate as much energy as all the earthquakes since the beginning of your world. The oceans and continents will fly into space; the sun will have a second asteroid belt.

"That cataclysm will send its echoes down the ages, and will open up to us a fraction of a second in your time. During that instant, we are trying to save what we can of your world's treasures. It is all that we can do; even if your motives were purely selfish and completely dishonest, you have done your race a service you never intended.

"And now I must return to our ship, where it waits by the ruins of Earth almost a hundred thousand years from now. You can keep the bracelet."

The withdrawal was instantaneous. The woman suddenly froze and became one with the other statues in the silent street. He was alone.

Alone! Ashton held the gleaming bracelet before his eyes, hypnotized by its intricate workmanship and by the powers it concealed. He had made a bargain, and he must keep it. He could live out the full span of his life—at the cost of an isolation no other man had ever known. If he switched off the field, the last seconds of history would tick inexorably away.

Seconds? Indeed, there was less time than that. For he knew that the bomb must already have exploded.

He sat down on the edge of the pavement and began to think. There was no need to panic; he must take things calmly, without hysteria. After all, he had plenty of time.

All the time in the world.

COSMIC CASANOVA

THIS TIME I was five weeks out from Base Planet before the symptoms became acute. On the last trip it had taken only a month; I was not certain whether the difference was due to advancing age or to something the dietitians had put into my food capsules. Or it could merely have been that I was busier; the arm of the galaxy I was scouting was heavily populated, with stars only a couple of light-years apart, so I had little time to brood over the girls I'd left behind me. As soon as one star had been classified, and the automatic search for planets had been completed, it was time to head for the next sun. And when, as happened in about one case out of ten, planets *did* turn up, I'd be furiously busy for several days seeing that Max, the ship's electronic computer, got all the information down on his tapes.

Now, however, I was through this densely packed region of space, and it sometimes took as much as three days to get from sun to sun. That was time enough for Sex to come tiptoeing aboard the ship, and for the memories of my last leave to make the months ahead look very empty indeed.

Perhaps I had overdone it, back on Diadne V, while my ship was being reprovisioned and I was supposed to be resting between missions. But a survey scout spends eighty per cent of his time alone in space, and human nature being what it is, he must be expected to make up for lost time. I had not merely done that; I'd built up considerable credit for the future—though not, it seemed, enough to last me through this trip.

First, I recalled wistfully, there had been Helene. She was blonde, cuddly, and compliant, though rather unimaginative. We had a fine time together until her husband came back from *his* mission; he was extremely decent about it but pointed out, reasonably enough, that Helene would now have very little time for other engagements. Fortunately, I had already made contact with Iris, so the hiatus was negligible.

Now Iris was really something. Even now, it makes me squirm to think of her. When that affair broke up—for the simple reason that a man has to get a little sleep sometime—I swore off women for a whole week. Then I came across a touching poem by an old Earth writer named John Donne—he's worth looking up, if you can read Primitive English—which reminded me that time lost could never be regained.

How true, I thought, so I put on my spaceman's uniform and wandered down to the beach of Diadne V's only sea. There was need to walk no more than a few hundred meters before I'd spotted a dozen possibilities, brushed off several volunteers, and signed up Natalie.

That worked out pretty well at first, until Natalie started objecting to Ruth (or was it Kay?). I can't *stand* girls who think they own a man, so I blasted off after a rather difficult scene that was quite expensive in crockery. This left me at loose ends for a couple of days; then Cynthia came to the rescue and—but by now you'll have gotten the general idea, so I won't bore you with details.

These, then, were the fond memories I started to work back through while one star dwindled behind me and the next flared up ahead. On this trip I'd deliberately left my pin-ups behind, having decided that they only made matters worse. This was a mistake; being quite a good artist in a rather specialized way, I started to draw my own, and it wasn't long before I had a collection it would be hard to match on any respectable planet.

I would hate you to think that this preoccupation affected my efficiency as a unit of the Galactic Survey. It was only on the long, dull runs between the stars, when I had no one to talk to but the computer, that I found my glands getting the better of me. Max, my electronic colleague, was good enough company in the ordinary course of events, but there are some things that a machine can't be expected to understand. I often hurt his feelings when I was in one of my irritable moods and lost my temper for no apparent reason. "What's the matter, Joe?" Max would say plaintively. "Surely you're not mad at me because I beat you at chess again? Remember, I warned you I would."

"Oh, go to hell!" I'd snarl back—and then I'd have an anxious five minutes while I straightened things out with the rather literal-minded Navigation Robot.

Two months out from Base, with thirty suns and four solar systems logged, something happened that wiped all my personal problems from my mind. The long-range monitor began to beep; a faint signal was coming from somewhere in the section of space ahead of me. I got the most accurate bearing that I could; the transmission was unmodulated, very narrow band—clearly a beacon of some kind. Yet no ship of ours, to the best of my knowledge, had ever entered this remote neck of the universe; I was supposed to be scouting completely unexplored territory.

This, I told myself, is IT—my big moment, the payoff for all the lonely years I'd spent in space. At some unknown distance ahead of me was another civilization—a race sufficiently advanced to possess hyper-radio.

I knew exactly what I had to do. As soon as Max had confirmed my readings and made his analysis, I launched a message carrier back to Base. If anything happened to me, the Survey would know where and could guess why. It was some consolation to think that if I didn't come home on schedule, my friends would be out here in force to pick up the pieces.

Soon there was no doubt where the signal was coming from, and I changed course for the small yellow star that was dead in line with the beacon. No one, I told myself, would put out a wave this strong unless they had space travel themselves; I might be running into a culture as advanced as my own—with all that that implied.

I was still a long way off when I started calling, not very hopefully, with my own transmitter. To my surprise, there was a prompt reaction. The continuous wave immediately broke up into a string of pulses, repeated over and over again. Even Max couldn't make anything of the message; it probably meant "Who the heck are you?"—which was not a big enough sample for even the most intelligent of translating machines to get its teeth into.

Hour by hour the signal grew in strength; just to let them know I was still around and was reading them loud and clear, I occasionally shot the same message back along the way it had come. And then I had my second big surprise.

I had expected them—whoever or whatever they might be—to switch to speech transmission as soon as I was near enough for good reception. This was precisely what they did; what I had not expected was that their voices would be human, the language they spoke an unmistakable but to me unintelligible brand of English. I could identify about one word in ten; the others were either quite unknown or else distorted so badly that I could not recognize them.

When the first words came over the loudspeaker, I guessed the truth. This was no alien, nonhuman race, but something almost as exciting and perhaps a good deal safer as far as a solitary scout was concerned. I had established contact with one of the lost colonies of the First Empire— the pioneers who had set out from Earth in the early days of interstellar exploration, five thousand years ago. When the empire collapsed, most of these isolated groups had perished or had sunk back to barbarism. Here, it seemed, was one that had survived.

I talked back to them in the slowest and simplest English I could muster, but five thousand years is a long time in the life of any language and no real communication was possible. They were clearly excited at the contact—pleasurably, as far as I could judge. This is not always the case; some of the isolated cultures left over from the First Empire have become violently xenophobic and react almost with hysteria to the knowledge that they are not alone in space.

Our attempts to communicate were not making much progress, when a new factor appeared—one that changed my outlook abruptly. A woman's voice started to come from the speaker.

It was the most beautiful voice I'd ever heard, and even without the lonely weeks in space that lay behind me I think I would have fallen in love with it at once. Very deep, yet still completely feminine, it had a warm, caressing quality that seemed to ravish all my senses. I was so stunned, in fact, that it was several minutes before I realized that I could understand what my invisible enchantress was saying. She was speaking English that was almost fifty per cent comprehensible.

To cut a short story shorter, it did not take me very long to learn that her name was Liala, and that she was the only philologist on her planet to specialize in Primitive English. As soon as contact had been made with my ship, she had been called in to do the translating. Luck, it seemed, was very much on my side; the interpreter could so easily have been some ancient, white-bearded fossil.

As the hours ticked away and her sun grew ever larger in the sky ahead of me, Liala and I became the best of friends. Because time was short, I had to operate faster than I'd ever done before. The fact that no one else could understand exactly what we were saying to each other insured our privacy. Indeed, Liala's own knowledge of English was sufficiently imperfect for me to get away with some outrageous remarks; there's no danger of going too far with a girl who'll give you the benefit of the doubt by deciding you couldn't possibly have meant what she thought you said. . . .

Need I say that I felt very, very happy? It looked as if my official and personal interests were neatly coinciding. There was, however, just one slight worry. So far, I had not seen Liala. What if she turned out to be absolutely hideous?

My first chance of settling that important question came six hours from planet-fall. Now I was near enough to pick up video transmissions, and it took Max only a few seconds to analyze the incoming signals and adjust the ship's receiver accordingly. At last I could have my first close-ups of the approaching planet—and of Liala.

She was almost as beautiful as her voice. I stared at the screen, unable to speak, for timeless seconds. Presently she broke the silence. "What's the matter?" she asked. "Haven't you ever seen a girl before?"

I had to admit that I'd seen two or even three, but never one like her. It was a great relief to find that her reaction to me was quite favorable, so it seemed that nothing stood in the way of our future happiness—if we could evade the army of scientists and politicians who would surround me as soon as I landed. Our hopes of privacy were very slender; so much so, in fact, that I felt tempted to break one of my most ironclad rules. I'd even consider *marrying* Liala if that was the only way we could arrange matters. (Yes, that two months in space had really put a strain on my system. . . .)

Five thousand years of history—ten thousand, if you count mine as well—can't be condensed easily into a few hours. But with such a delightful tutor, I absorbed knowledge fast, and everything I missed, Max got down in his infallible memory circuits.

Arcady, as their planet was charmingly called, had been at the very frontier of interstellar colonization; when the tide of empire had retreated, it had been left high and dry. In the struggle to survive, the Arcadians had lost much of their original scientific knowledge, including the secret of the Star Drive. They could not escape from their own solar system, but they had little incentive to do so. Arcady was a fertile world and the low gravity—only a quarter of Earth's—had given the colonists the physical strength they needed to make it live up to its name. Even allowing for any natural bias on Liala's part, it sounded a very attractive place.

Arcady's little yellow sun was already showing a visible disk when I had my brilliant idea. That reception committee had been worrying me, and I suddenly realized how I could keep it at bay. The plan would need Liala's co-operation, but by this time that was assured. If I may say so without sounding too immodest, I have always had a way with women, and this was not my first courtship by TV.

So the Arcadians learned, about two hours before I was due to land, that survey scouts were very shy and suspicious creatures. Owing to previous sad experiences with unfriendly cultures, I politely refused to walk like a fly into their parlor. As there was only one of me, I preferred to meet only one of them, in some isolated spot to be mutually selected. If that meeting went well, I would then fly to the capital city; if not—I'd head back the way I came. I hoped that they would not think this behavior discourteous, but I was a lonely traveler a long way from home, and as reasonable people, I was sure they'd see my point of view. . . .

They did. The choice of the emissary was obvious, and Liala promptly became a world heroine by bravely volunteering to meet the monster from space. She'd radio back, she told her anxious friends, within an hour of coming aboard my ship. I tried to make it two hours, but she said that might be overdoing it, and nasty-minded people might start to talk.

The ship was coming down through the Arcadian atmosphere when I suddenly remembered my compromising pin ups, and had to make a rapid spring-cleaning. (Even so, one rather explicit masterpiece slipped down behind a chart rack and caused me acute embarrassment when it was discovered by the maintenance crew months later.) When I got back to the control room, the vision screen showed the empty, open plain at the very center of which Liala was waiting for me; in two minutes, I would hold her in my arms, be able to drink the fragrance of her hair, feel her body yield in all the right places—

I didn't bother to watch the landing, for I could rely on Max to do his usual flawless job. Instead, I hurried down to the air lock and waited with what patience I could muster for the opening of the doors that barred me from Liala.

It seemed an age before Max completed the routine air check and gave the "Outer Door Opening" signal. I was through the exit before the metal disk had finished moving, and stood at last on the rich soil of Arcady.

I remembered that I weighed only forty pounds here, so I moved with caution despite my eagerness. Yet I'd forgotten, living in my fool's paradise, what a fractional gravity could do to the human body in the course of two hundred generations. On a small planet, evolution can do a lot in five thousand years.

Liala was waiting for me, and she was as lovely as her picture. There was, however, one trifling matter that the TV screen hadn't told me.

I've never liked big girls, and I like them even less now. If I'd still wanted to, I suppose I could have embraced Liala. But I'd have looked like such a fool, standing there on tiptoe with my arms wrapped around her knees.

THE STAR

IT IS THREE thousand light-years to the Vatican. Once, I believed that space could have no power over faith, just as I believed that the heavens declared the glory of God's handiwork. Now I have seen that handiwork, and my faith is sorely troubled. I stare at the crucifix that hangs on the cabin wall above the Mark VI Computer, and for the first time in my life I wonder if it is no more than an empty symbol.

I have told no one yet, but the truth cannot be concealed. The facts are there for all to read, recorded on the countless miles of magnetic tape and the thousands of photographs we are carrying back to Earth. Other scientists can interpret them as easily as I can, and I am not one who would condone that tampering with the truth which often gave my order a bad name in the olden days.

The crew is already sufficiently depressed: I wonder how they will take this ultimate irony. Few of them have any religious faith, yet they will not relish using this final weapon in their campaign against me—that private, good-natured, but fundamentally serious, war which lasted all the way from Earth. It amused them to have a Jesuit as chief astrophysicist: Dr. Chandler, for instance, could never get over it (why are medical men such notorious atheists?). Sometimes he would meet me on the observation deck, where the lights are always low so that the stars shine with undiminished glory. He would come up to me in the gloom and stand staring out of the great oval port, while the heavens crawled slowly around us as the ship turned end over end with the residual spin we had never bothered to correct.

"Well, Father," he would say at last, "it goes on forever and forever, and perhaps *Something* made it. But how you can believe that Something has a special interest in us and our miserable little world—that just beats me." Then the argument would start, while the stars and nebulae would swing around us in silent, endless arcs beyond the flawlessly clear plastic of the observation port.

It was, I think, the apparent incongruity of my position that caused most amusement to the crew. In vain I would point to my three papers in the *Astrophysical Journal,* my five in the *Monthly Notices of the Royal Astronomical Society.* I would remind them that my order has long been famous for its scientific works. We may be few now, but ever since the eighteenth century we have made contributions to astronomy and geophysics out of all proportion to our numbers. Will my report on the Phoenix Nebula end our thousand years of history? It will end, I fear, much more than that.

I do not know who gave the nebula its name, which seems to me a very bad one. If it contains a prophecy, it is one that cannot be verified for several billion years. Even the word nebula is misleading: this is a far smaller object than those stupendous clouds of mist—the stuff of unborn stars— that are scattered throughout the length of the Milky Way. On the cosmic scale, indeed, the Phoenix Nebula is a tiny thing—a tenuous shell of gas surrounding a single star.

Or what is left of a star . . .

The Rubens engraving of Loyola seems to mock me as it hangs there above the spectrophotometer tracings. What would *you,* Father, have made of this knowledge that has come into my keeping, so far from the little world that was all the universe you knew? Would your faith have risen to the challenge, as mine has failed to do?

You gaze into the distance, Father, but I have traveled a distance beyond any that you could have imagined when you founded our order a thousand years ago. No other survey ship has been so far from Earth: we are at the very frontiers of the explored universe. We set out to reach the Phoenix Nebula, we succeeded, and we are homeward bound with our burden of knowledge. I wish I could lift that burden from my shoulders, but I call to you in vain across the centuries and the light-years that lie between us.

On the book you are holding the words are plain to read. AD MAIOREM DEI GLORIAM, the message runs, but it is a message I can no longer believe. Would you still believe it, if you could see what we have found?

We knew, of course, what the Phoenix Nebula was. Every year, in our galaxy alone, more than a hundred stars explode, blazing for a few hours or days with thousands of times their normal brilliance before they sink back into death and obscurity. Such are the ordinary nova—the commonplace disasters of the universe. I have recorded the spectrograms and light curves of dozens since I started working at the Lunar Observatory.

But three or four times in every thousand years occurs something beside which even a nova pales into total insignificance.

When a star becomes a *supernova*, it may for a little while outshine all the massed suns of the galaxy. The Chinese astronomers watched this happen in A.D. 1054, not knowing what it was they saw. Five centuries later, in 1572, a supernova blazed in Cassiopeia so brilliantly that it was visible in the daylight sky. There have been three more in the thousand years that have passed since then.

Our mission was to visit the remnants of such a catastrophe, to reconstruct the events that led up to it, and, if possible, to learn its cause. We came slowly in through the concentric shells of gas that had been blasted out six thousand years before, yet were expanding still. They were immensely hot, radiating even now with a fierce violet light, but were far too tenuous to do us any damage. When the star had exploded, its outer layers had been driven upward with such speed that they had escaped completely from its

gravitational field. Now they formed a hollow shell large
enough to engulf a thousand solar systems, and at its center
burned the tiny, fantastic object which the star had now
become—a White Dwarf, smaller than the Earth, yet weighing a million times as much.

The glowing gas shells were all around us, banishing the
normal night of interstellar space. We were flying into the
center of a cosmic bomb that had detonated millennia ago
and whose incandescent fragments were still hurtling apart.
The immense scale of the explosion, and the fact that the
debris already covered a volume of space many billions of
miles across, robbed the scene of any visible movement. It
would take decades before the unaided eye could detect any
motion in these tortured wisps and eddies of gas, yet the
sense of turbulent expansion was overwhelming.

We had checked our primary drive hours before, and
were drifting slowly toward the fierce little star ahead. Once
it had been a sun like our own, but it had squandered in a
few hours the energy that should have kept it shining for a
million years. Now it was a shrunken miser, hoarding its
resources as if trying to make amends for its prodigal youth.

No one seriously expected to find planets. If there had
been any before the explosion, they would have been boiled
into puffs of vapor, and their substance lost in the greater
wreckage of the star itself. But we made the automatic
search, as we always do when approaching an unknown sun,
and presently we found a single small world circling the star
at an immense distance. It must have been the Pluto of this
vanished solar system, orbiting on the frontiers of the night.
Too far from the central sun ever to have known life, its
remoteness had saved it from the fate of all its lost companions.

The passing fires had seared its rocks and burned away
the mantle of frozen gas that must have covered it in the
days before the disaster. We landed, and we found the Vault.

Its builders had made sure that we should. The mono-
lithic marker that stood above the entrance was now a fused
stump, but even the first long-range photographs told us
that here was the work of intelligence. A little later we detected the continent-wide pattern of radioactivity that had
been buried in the rock. Even if the pylon above the Vault
had been destroyed, this would have remained, an immov-

able and all but eternal beacon calling to the stars. Our ship fell toward this gigantic bull's-eye like an arrow into its target.

The pylon must have been a mile high when it was built, but now it looked like a candle that had melted down into a puddle of wax. It took us a week to drill through the fused rock, since we did not have the proper tools for a task like this. We were astronomers, not archeologists, but we could improvise. Our original purpose was forgotten: this lonely monument, reared with such labor at the greatest possible distance from the doomed sun, could have only one meaning. A civilization that knew it was about to die had made its last bid for immortality.

It will take us generations to examine all the treasures that were placed in the Vault. They had plenty of time to prepare, for their sun must have given its first warnings many years before the final detonation. Everything that they wished to preserve, all the fruit of their genius, they brought here to this distant world in the days before the end, hoping that some other race would find it and that they would not be utterly forgotten. Would we have done as well, or would we have been too lost in our own misery to give thought to a future we could never see or share?

If only they had had a little more time! They could travel freely enough between the planets of their own sun, but they had not yet learned to cross the interstellar gulfs, and the nearest solar system was a hundred light-years away. Yet even had they possessed the secret of the Transfinite Drive, no more than a few millions could have been saved. Perhaps it was better thus.

Even if they had not been so disturbingly human as their sculpture shows, we could not have helped admiring them and grieving for their fate. They left thousands of visual records and the machines for projecting them, together with elaborate pictorial instructions from which it will not be difficult to learn their written language. We have examined many of these records, and brought to life for the first time in six thousand years the warmth and beauty of a civilization that in many ways must have been superior to our own. Perhaps they only showed us the best, and one can hardly blame them. But their worlds were very lovely, and their cities were built with a grace that matches anything of man's. We have watched them at work and play, and listened to their musical speech sounding across the centuries. One scene is still before my eyes—a group of children on a beach of strange blue sand, playing in the waves as children play on Earth. Curious whiplike trees line the shore, and some very large animal is wading in the shadows yet attracting no attention at all.

And sinking into the sea, still warm and friendly and life-giving, is the sun that will soon turn traitor and obliterate all this innocent happiness.

Perhaps if we had not been so far from home and so vulnerable to loneliness, we should not have been so deeply moved. Many of us had seen the ruins of ancient civilizations on other worlds, but they had never affected us so profoundly. This tragedy was unique. It is one thing for a race to fail and die, as nations and cultures have done on Earth. But to be destroyed so completely in the full flower of its achievement, leaving no survivors—how could that be reconciled with the mercy of God?

My colleagues have asked me that, and I have given what answers I can. Perhaps you could have done better, Father Loyola, but I have found nothing in the *Exercitia Spiritualia* that helps me here. They were not an evil people: I do not know what gods they worshiped, if indeed they worshiped any. But I have looked back at them across the centuries, and have watched while the loveliness they used their last strength to preserve was brought forth again into the light of their shrunken sun. They could have taught us much: why were they destroyed?

I know the answers that my colleagues will give when they get back to Earth. They'll say that the universe has no purpose and no plan, that since a hundred suns explode every year in our galaxy, at this very moment some race is dying in the depths of space. Whether that race has done good or evil during its lifetime will make no difference in the end: there is no divine justice, for there is no God.

Yet, of course, what we have seen proves nothing of the sort. Anyone who argues thus is being swayed by emotion, not logic. God has no need to justify His actions to man. He who built the universe can destroy it when He chooses. It is arrogance—it is perilously near blasphemy—for us to say what He may or may not do.

This I could have accepted, hard though it is to look upon whole worlds and peoples thrown into the furnace. But there comes a point when even the deepest faith must falter, and now, as I look at the calculations lying before me, I know I have reached that point at last.

We could not tell, before we reached the nebula, how long ago the explosion took place. Now, from the astronomical evidence and the record in the rocks of that one surviving planet, I have been able to date it very exactly. I know in what year the light of this colossal conflagration reached our Earth. I know how brilliantly the supernova whose corpse now dwindles behind our speeding ship once shone in terrestrial skies. I know how it must have blazed low in the east before sunrise, like a beacon in that oriental dawn.

There can be no reasonable doubt: the ancient mystery is solved at last. Yet, oh God, there were so many stars you could have used. What was the need to give these people to the fire, that the symbol of their passing might shine above Bethlehem?

OUT OF THE SUN

IF YOU HAVE only lived on Earth, you have never seen the sun. Of course, we could not look at it directly, but only through dense filters that cut its rays down to endurable brilliance. It hung there forever above the low, jagged hills to the west of the Observatory, neither rising nor setting, yet moving around a small circle in the sky during the eighty-eight-day year of our little world. For it is not quite true to say that Mercury keeps the same face always turned toward the sun; it wobbles slightly on its axis, and there is a narrow twilight belt which knows such terrestrial commonplaces as dawn and sunset.

We were on the edge of the twilight zone, so that we could take advantage of the cool shadows yet could keep the sun under continuous surveillance as it hovered there above the hills. It was a full-time job for fifty astronomers and other assorted scientists; when we've kept it up for a hundred years or so, we may know something about the small star that brought life to Earth.

There wasn't a single band of solar radiation that someone at the Observatory had not made a life's study and was watching like a hawk. From the far X rays to the longest of radio waves, we had set our traps and snares; as soon as the sun thought of something new, we were ready for it. So we imagined. . . .

The sun's flaming heart beats in a slow, eleven-year rhythm, and we were near the peak of the cycle. Two of the greatest spots ever recorded—each of them large enough to swallow a hundred Earths—had drifted across the disk like great black funnels piercing deeply into the turbulent outer layers of the sun. They were black, of course, only by contrast with the brilliance all around them; even their dark, cool cores were hotter and brighter than an electric arc. We had just watched the second of them disappear around the edge of the disk, wondering if it would survive to reappear two weeks later, when something blew up on the equator.

It was not too spectacular at first, partly because it was almost exactly beneath us—at the precise center of the sun's disk—and so was merged into all the activity around it. If it had been near the edge of the sun, and thus projected against the background of space, it would have been truly awe-inspiring.

Imagine the simultaneous explosion of a million H-bombs. You can't? Nor can anyone else—but that was the sort of thing we were watching climb up toward us at hundreds of miles a second, straight out of the sun's spinning equator. At first it formed a narrow jet, but it was quickly frayed around the edges by the magnetic and gravitational forces that were fighting against it. The central core kept right on, and it was soon obvious that it had escaped from the sun completely and was headed out into space—with us as its first target.

Though this had happened half a dozen times before, it was always exciting. It meant that we could capture some of the very substance of the sun as it went hurtling past in a great cloud of electrified gas. There was no danger; by the time it reached us it would be far too tenuous to do any damage, and, indeed, it would take sensitive instruments to detect it at all.

One of those instruments was the Observatory's radar, which was in continual use to map the invisible ionized layers that surround the sun for millions of miles. This was my department; as soon as there was any hope of picking up the oncoming cloud against the solar background, I aimed my giant radio mirror toward it.

It came in sharp and clear on the long-range screen—a vast, luminous island still moving outward from the sun at hundreds of miles a second. At this distance it was impossible to see its finer details, for my radar waves were taking minutes to make the round trip and to bring me back the information they were presenting on the screen. Even at its speed of not far short of a million miles an hour, it would be almost two days before the escaping prominence reached the orbit of Mercury and swept past us toward the outer planets. But neither Venus nor Earth would record its passing, for they were nowhere near its line of flight.

The hours drifted by; the sun had settled down after the immense convulsion that had shot so many millions of tons of its substance into space, never to return. The aftermath of that eruption was now a slowly twisting and turning cloud a hundred times the size of Earth, and soon it would be close enough for the short-range radar to reveal its finer structure.

Despite all the years I have been in the business, it still gives me a thrill to watch that line of light paint its picture on the screen as it spins in synchronism with the narrow beam of radio waves from the transmitter. I sometimes think of myself as a blind man exploring the space around him with a stick that may be a hundred million miles in length. For man is truly blind to the things I study; these great clouds of ionized gas moving far out from the sun are completely invisible to the eye and even to the most sensitive of photographic plates. They are ghosts that briefly haunt the solar system during the few hours of their existence; if they did not reflect our radar waves or disturb our magnetometers, we should never know that they were there.

The picture on the screen looked not unlike a photograph of a spiral nebula, for as the cloud slowly rotated it trailed ragged arms of gas for ten thousand miles around it. Or it might have been a terrestrial hurricane that I was watching from above as it spun through the atmosphere of Earth. The internal structure was extremely complicated, and was changing minute by minute beneath the action of forces which we have never fully understood. Rivers of fire were flowing in curious paths under what could only be the influence of electric fields; but why were they appearing from nowhere and disappearing again as if matter was being created and destroyed? And what were those gleaming nodules, larger than the moon, that were being swept along like boulders before a flood?

Now it was less than a million miles away; it would be upon us in little more than an hour. The automatic cameras were recording every complete sweep of the radar scan, storing up evidence which was to keep us arguing for years. The magnetic disturbance riding ahead of the cloud had already reached us; indeed, there was hardly an instrument in the Observatory that was not reacting in some way to the onrushing apparition.

I switched to the short-range scanner, and the image of the cloud expanded so enormously that only its central portion was on the screen. At the same time I began to change frequency, tuning across the spectrum to differentiate among the various levels. The shorter the wave length, the farther you can penetrate into a layer of ionized gas; by this technique I hoped to get a kind of X-ray picture of the cloud's interior.

It seemed to change before my eyes as I sliced down through the tenuous outer envelope with its trailing arms, and approached the denser core. "Denser," of course, was a purely relative word; by terrestrial standards even its most closely packed regions were still a fairly good vacuum. I had almost reached the limit of my frequency band, and could shorten the wave length no farther, when I noticed the curious, tight little echo not far from the center of the screen.

It was oval, and much more sharp-edged than the knots of gas we had watched adrift in the cloud's fiery streams. Even in that first glimpse, I knew that here was something very strange and outside all previous records of solar phenomena. I watched it for a dozen scans of the radar beam, then called my assistant away from the radiospectrograph, with which he was analyzing the velocities of the swirling gas as it spun toward us.

"Look, Don," I asked him, "have you ever seen anything like that?"

"No," he answered after a careful examination. "What holds it together? It hasn't changed its shape for the last two minutes."

"That's what puzzles me. Whatever it is, it should have started to break up by now, with all that disturbance going on around it. But it seems as stable as ever."

"How big would you say it is?"

I switched on the calibration grid and took a quick reading.

"It's about five hundred miles long, and half that in width."

"Is this the largest picture you can get?"

"I'm afraid so. We'll have to wait until it's closer before we can see what makes it tick."

Don gave a nervous little laugh.

"This is crazy," he said, "but do you know something? I feel as if I'm looking at an amoeba under a microscope."

I did not answer; for, with what I can only describe as a sensation of intellectual vertigo, exactly the same thought had entered my mind.

We forgot about the rest of the cloud, but luckily the automatic cameras kept up their work and no important observations were lost. From now on we had eyes only for that sharp-edged lens of gas that was growing minute by minute as it raced toward us. When it was no farther away than is the moon from Earth, it began to show the first signs of its internal structure, revealing a curious mottled appearance that was never quite the same on two successive sweeps of the scanner.

By now, half the Observatory staff had joined us in the radar room, yet there was complete silence as the oncoming enigma grew swiftly across the screen. It was coming straight toward us; in a few minutes it would hit Mercury somewhere in the center of the daylight side, and that would be the end of it—whatever it was. From the moment we obtained our first really detailed view until the screen became blank again could not have been more than five minutes; for every one of us, that five minutes will haunt us all our lives.

We were looking at what seemed to be a translucent oval, its interior laced with a network of almost invisible lines. Where the lines crossed there appeared to be tiny, pulsing nodes of light; we could never be quite sure of their existence because the radar took almost a minute to paint the complete picture on the screen—and between each sweep the object moved several thousand miles. There was no doubt, however, that the network itself existed; the cameras settled any arguments about that.

So strong was the impression that we were looking at a solid object that I took a few moments off from the radar screen and hastily focused one of the optical telescopes on the sky. Of course, there was nothing to be seen—no sign of anything silhouetted against the sun's pock-marked disk. This was a case where vision failed completely and only the electrical senses of the radar were of any use. The thing that was coming toward us out of the sun was as transparent as air—and far more tenuous.

As those last moments ebbed away, I am quite sure that every one of us had reached the same conclusion—and was waiting for someone to say it first. What we were seeing was impossible, yet the evidence was there before our eyes. We were looking at life, where no life could exist. . . .

The eruption had hurled the thing out of its normal environment, deep down in the flaming atmosphere of the sun. It was a miracle that it had survived its journey through space; already it must be dying, as the forces that controlled its huge, invisible body lost their hold over the electrified gas which was the only substance it possessed.

Today, now that I have run through those films a hundred times, the idea no longer seems so strange to me. For what is life but organized energy? Does it matter *what* form that energy takes—whether it is chemical, as we know it on Earth, or purely electrical, as it seemed to be here? Only the pattern is important; the substance itself is of no significance. But at the time I did not think of this; I was conscious only of a vast and overwhelming wonder as I watched this creature of the sun live out the final moments of its existence.

Was it intelligent? Could it understand the strange doom that had befallen it? There are a thousand such questions that may never be answered. It is hard to see how a creature born in the fires of the sun itself could know anything of the external universe, or could even sense the existence of something as unutterably cold as rigid nongaseous matter. The living island that was falling upon us from space could never have conceived, however intelligent it might be, of the world it was so swiftly approaching.

Now it filled our sky—and perhaps, in those last few seconds, it knew that something strange was ahead of it. It may have sensed the far-flung magnetic field of Mercury, or felt the tug of our little world's gravitational pull. For it had begun to change; the luminous lines that must have been what passed for its nervous system were clumping together in new patterns, and I would have given much to know their meaning. It may be that I was looking into the brain of a mindless beast in its last convulsion of fear—or of a godlike being making its peace with the universe.

Then the radar screen was empty, wiped clean during a single scan of the beam. The creature had fallen below our horizon, and was hidden from us now by the curve of the planet. Far out in the burning dayside of Mercury, in the inferno where only a dozen men have ever ventured and fewer still come back alive, it smashed silently and invisibly against the seas of molten metal, the hills of slowly moving lava. The mere impact could have meant nothing to such an entity; what it could not endure was its first contact with the inconceivable cold of solid matter.

Yes, *cold*. It had descended upon the hottest spot in the solar system, where the temperature never falls below seven hundred degrees Fahrenheit and sometimes approaches a thousand. And that was far, far colder to it than the antarctic winter would be to a naked man.

We did not see it die, out there in the freezing fire; it was beyond the reach of our instruments now, and none of them recorded its end. Yet every one of us knew when that moment came, and that is why we are not interested when those who have seen only the films and tapes tell us that we were watching some purely natural phenomenon.

How can one explain what we felt, in that last moment when half our little world was enmeshed in the dissolving tendrils of that huge but immaterial brain? I can only say that it was a soundless cry of anguish, a death pang that seeped into our minds without passing through the gateways of the senses. Not one of us doubted then, or has ever doubted since, that he had witnessed the passing of a giant.

We may have been both the first and the last of all men to see so mighty a fall. Whatever *they* may be, in their unimaginable world within the sun, our paths and theirs may never cross again. It is hard to see how we can ever make contact with them, even if their intelligence matches ours.

And does it? It may be well for us if we never know the answer. Perhaps they have been living there inside the sun since the universe was born, and have climbed to peaks of wisdom that we shall never scale. The future may be theirs, not ours; already they may be talking across the light-years to their cousins in other stars.

One day they may discover us, by whatever strange senses they possess, as we circle around their mighty, ancient home, proud of our knowledge and thinking ourselves lords of creation. They may not like what they find, for to them we should be no more than maggots, crawling upon the skins of worlds too cold to cleanse themselves from the corruption of organic life.

And then, if they have the power, they will do what they consider necessary. The sun will put forth its strength and lick the faces of its children; and thereafter the planets will go their way once more as they were in the beginning—clean and bright. . . . and sterile.

TRANSIENCE

THE FOREST, WHICH came almost to the edge of the beach, climbed away into the distance up the flanks of the low, misty hills. Underfoot, the sand was coarse and mixed with myriads of broken shells. Here and there the retreating tide had left long streamers of weed trailed across the beach. The rain, which seldom ceased, had for the moment passed inland, but ever and again large, angry drops would beat tiny craters in the sand.

It was hot and sultry, for the war between sun and rain was never-ending. Sometimes the mists would lift for a while and the hills would stand out clearly above the land they guarded. These hills arced in a semicircle along the bay, following the line of the beach, and beyond them could sometimes be seen, at an immense distance, a wall of mountains lying beneath perpetual clouds. The trees grew everywhere, softening the contours of the land so that the hills blended smoothly into each other. Only in one place could the bare, uncovered rock be seen, where long ago some fault had weakened the foundations of the hills, so that for a mile or more the sky line fell sharply away, dropping down to the sea like a broken wing.

Moving with the cautious alertness of a wild animal, the child came through the stunted trees at the forest's edge. For a moment he hesitated; then, since there seemed to be no danger, walked slowly out onto the beach.

He was naked, heavily built, and had coarse black hair tangled over his shoulders. His face, brutish though it was, might almost have passed in human society, but the eyes would have betrayed him. They were not the eyes of an animal, for there was something in their depths that no animal had ever known. But it was no more than a promise. For this child, as for all his race, the light of reason had yet to dawn. Only a hairsbreadth still separated him from the beasts among whom he dwelt.

The tribe had not long since come into this land, and he was the first ever to set foot upon that lonely beach. What had lured him from the known dangers of the forest into the unknown and therefore more terrible dangers of this new element, he could not have told even had he possessed the power of speech. Slowly he walked out to the water's edge, always with backward glances at the forest behind him; and as he did so, for the first time in all history, the level sand bore upon its face the footprints it would one day know so well.

He had met water before, but it had always been bounded and confined by land. Now it stretched endlessly before him, and the sound of its laboring beat ceaselessly upon his ears.

With the timeless patience of the savage, he stood on the moist sand that the water had just relinquished, and as the tide line moved out he followed it slowly, pace by pace. When the waves reached toward his feet with a sudden access of energy, he would retreat a little way toward the land. But something held him here at the water's edge, while his shadow lengthened along the sands and the cold evening wind began to rise around him.

Perhaps into his mind had come something of the wonder of the sea, and a hint of all that it would one day mean to man. Though the first gods of his people still lay far in the future, he felt a dim sense of worship stir within him. He knew that he was now in the presence of something greater than all the powers and forces he had ever met.

The tide was turning. Far away in the forest, a wolf howled once and was suddenly silent. The noises of the night were rising around him, and it was time to go.

Under the low moon, the two lines of footprints interlaced across the sand. Swiftly the oncoming tide was smoothing them away. But they would return in their thousands and millions, in the centuries yet to be.

The child playing among the rock pools knew nothing of the forest that had once ruled all the land around him. It had left no trace of its existence. As ephemeral as the mists that had so often rolled down from the hills, it, too, had veiled them for a little while and now was gone. In its place had come a checkerboard of fields, the legacy of a thousand years of patient toil. And so the illusion of permanence remained, though everything had altered save the line of the hills against the sky. On the beach, the sand was finer now, and the land had lifted so that the old tide line was far beyond the reach of the questing waves.

Beyond the sea wall and the promenade, the little town was sleeping through the golden summer day. Here and there along the beach, people lay at rest, drowsy with heat and lulled by the murmur of the waves.

Out across the bay, white and gold against the water, a great ship was moving slowly to sea. The boy could hear, faint and far away, the beat of its screws and could still see the tiny figures moving upon its decks and superstructure. To the child—and not to him alone—it was a thing of wonder and beauty. He knew its name and the land to which it was steaming; but he did not know that the splendid ship was both the last and greatest of its kind. He scarcely noticed, almost lost against the glare of the sun, the thin white vapor trails that spelled the doom of the proud and lovely giant.

Soon the great liner was no more than a dark smudge on the horizon and the boy turned again to his interrupted play, to the tireless building of his battlements of sand. In the west the sun was beginning its long decline, but the evening was still far away.

Yet it came at last, when the tide was returning to the land. At his mother's words, the child gathered up his playthings and, wearily contented, began to follow his parents back to the shore. He glanced once only at the sand castles he had built with such labor and would not see again. Without regret he left them to the advancing waves, for tomorrow he would return and the future stretched endlessly before him.

That tomorrow would not always come, either for himself or for the world, he was still too young to know.

And now even the hills had changed, worn away by the weight of years. Not all the change was the work of nature, for one night in the long-forgotten past something had come sliding down from the stars, and the little town had vanished in a spinning tower of flame. But that was so long ago that it was beyond sorrow or regret. Like the fall of fabled Troy or the overwhelming of Pompeii, it was part of the irremediable past and could rouse no pity now.

On the broken sky line lay a long metal building supporting a maze of mirrors that turned and glittered in the sun. No one from an earlier age could have guessed its purpose. It was as meaningless as an observatory or a radio station would have been to ancient man. But it was neither of these things.

Since noon, Bran had been playing among the shallow pools left by the retreating tide. He was quite alone, though the machine that guarded him was watching unobtrusively from the shore. Only a few days ago, there had been other children playing beside the blue waters of this lovely bay. Bran sometimes wondered where they had vanished, but he was a solitary child and did not greatly care. Lost in his own dreams, he was content to be left alone.

In the last few hours he had linked the tiny pools with an intricate network of waterways. His thoughts were very far from Earth, both in space and time. Around him now were the dull, red sands of another world. He was Cardenis, prince of engineers, fighting to save his people from the encroaching deserts. For Bran had looked upon the ravaged face of Mars; he knew the story of its long tragedy and the help from Earth that had come too late.

Out to the horizon the sea was empty, untroubled by ships, as it had been for ages. For a little while, near the beginning of time, man had fought his brief war against the oceans of the world. Now it seemed that only a moment lay between the coming of the first canoes and the passing of the last great Megatheria of the seas.

Bran did not even glance at the sky when the monstrous shadow swept along the beach. For days past, those silver giants had been rising over the hills in an unending stream, and now he gave them little thought. All his life he had watched the great ships climbing through the skies of Earth on their way to distant worlds. Often he had seen them return from those long journeys, dropping down through the clouds with cargoes beyond imagination.

He wondered sometimes why they came no more, those returning voyagers. All the ships he saw now were outward bound; never one drove down from the skies to berth at the great port beyond the hills. Why this should be, no one would tell him. He had learned not to speak of it now, having seen the sadness that his questions brought.

Across the sands the robot was calling to him softly. "Bran," came the words, echoing the tones of his mother's voice, "Bran—it's time to go."

The child looked up, his face full of indignant denial. He could not believe it. The sun was still high and the tide was far away. Yet along the shore his mother and father were already coming toward him.

They walked swiftly, as though the time were short. Now and again his father would glance for an instant at the sky, then turn his head quickly away as if he knew well that there was nothing he could hope to see. But a moment later he would look again.

Stubborn and angry, Bran stood at bay among his canals and lakes. His mother was strangely silent, but presently his father took him by the hand and said quietly, "You must come with us, Bran. It's time we went."

The child pointed sullenly at the beach. "But it's too early. I haven't finished."

His father's reply held no trace of anger, only a great sadness. "There are many things, Bran, that will not be finished now."

Still uncomprehending, the boy turned to his mother.

"Then can I come again tomorrow?"

With a sense of desolating wonder, Bran saw his mother's eyes fill with sudden tears. And he knew at last that never again would he play upon the sands by the azure waters;

never again would he feel the tug of the tiny waves about his feet. He had found the sea too late, and now must leave it forever. Out of the future, chilling his soul, came the first faint intimation of the long ages of exile that lay ahead.

He never looked back as they walked silently together across the clinging sand. This moment would be with him all his life, but he was still too stunned to do more than walk blindly into a future he could not understand.

The three figures dwindled into the distance and were gone. A long while later, a silver cloud seemed to lift above the hills and move slowly out to sea. In a shallow arc, as though reluctant to leave its world, the last of the great ships climbed toward the horizon and shrank to nothingness over the edge of the Earth.

The tide was returning with the dying day. As though its makers still walked within its walls, the low metal building upon the hills had begun to blaze with light. Near the zenith, one star had not waited for the sun to set, but already burned with a fierce white glare against the darkening sky. Soon its companions, no longer in the scant thousands that man had once known, began to fill the heavens. The Earth was now near the center of the universe, and whole areas of the sky were an unbroken blaze of light.

But rising beyond the sea in two long curving arms, something black and monstrous eclipsed the stars and seemed to cast its shadow over all the world. The tentacles of the Dark Nebula were already brushing against the frontiers of the solar system. . . .

In the east, a great yellow moon was climbing through the waves. Though man had torn down its mountains and brought it air and water, its face was the one that had looked upon Earth since history began, and it was still the ruler of the tides. Across the sand the line of foam moved steadily onward, overwhelming the little canals and planing down the tangled footprints.

On the sky line, the lights in the strange metal building suddenly died, and the spinning mirrors ceased their moonlight glittering. From far inland came the blinding flash of a great explosion, then another, and another fainter yet.

Presently the ground trembled a little, but no sound disturbed the solitude of the deserted shore.

Under the level light of the sagging moon, beneath the myriad stars, the beach lay waiting for the end. It was alone now, as it had been at the beginning. Only the waves would move, and but for a little while, upon its golden sands.

For Man had come and gone.

THE SONGS OF
DISTANT EARTH

BENEATH THE PALM trees Lora waited, watching the sea.
Clyde's boat was already visible as a tiny notch on the far
horizon—the only flaw in the perfect mating of sea and sky.
Minute by minute it grew in size, until it had detached itself
from the featureless blue globe that encompassed the world.
Now she could see Clyde standing at the prow, one hand
twined around the rigging, statue-still as his eyes sought her
among the shadows.

"Where are you, Lora?" his voice asked plaintively from
the radio bracelet he had given her when they became engaged. "Come and help me—we've got a big catch to bring
home."

So! Lora told herself; *that's* why you asked me to hurry
down to the beach. Just to punish Clyde and to reduce him
to the right state of anxiety, she ignored his call until he had
repeated it half a dozen times. Even then she did not press
the beautiful golden pearl set in the "Transmit" button, but
slowly emerged from the shade of the great trees and walked
down the sloping beach.

Clyde looked at her reproachfully, but gave her a satisfactory kiss as soon as he had bounded ashore and secured the boat. Then they started unloading the catch together, scooping fish large and small from both hulls of the catamaran. Lora screwed up her nose but assisted gamely, until the waiting sand sled was piled high with the victims of Clyde's skill.

It was a good catch; when she married Clyde, Lora told herself proudly, she'd never starve. The clumsy, armored creatures of this young planet's sea were not true fish; it would be a hundred million years before nature invented scales here. But they were good enough eating, and the first colonists had labeled them with names they had brought, with so many other traditions, from unforgotten Earth.

"That's the lot!" grunted Clyde, tossing a fair imitation of a salmon onto the glistening heap. "I'll fix the nets later—let's go!"

Finding a foothold with some difficulty, Lora jumped onto the sled behind him. The flexible rollers spun for a moment against the sand, then got a grip. Clyde, Lora, and a hundred pounds of assorted fish started racing up the wave-scalloped beach. They had made half the brief journey when the simple, carefree world they had known all their young lives came suddenly to its end.

The sign of its passing was written there upon the sky, as if a giant hand had drawn a piece of chalk across the blue vault of heaven. Even as Clyde and Lora watched, the gleaming vapor trail began to fray at its edges, breaking up into wisps of cloud.

And now they could hear, falling down through the miles above their heads, a sound their world had not known for generations. Instinctively they grasped each other's hands, as they stared at that snow-white furrow across the sky and listened to the thin scream from the borders of space. The descending ship had already vanished beyond the horizon before they turned to each other and breathed, almost with reverence, the same magic word: "Earth!"

After three hundred years of silence, the mother world had reached out once more to touch Thalassa. . . .

Why? Lora asked herself, when the long moment of revelation had passed and the scream of torn air ceased to echo from the sky. What had happened, after all these years, to bring a ship from mighty Earth to this quiet and contented world? There was no room for more colonists here on this one island in a watery planet, and Earth knew that well enough. Its robot survey ships had mapped and probed Thalassa from space five centuries ago, in the early days of interstellar exploration. Long before man himself had ventured out into the gulfs between the stars, his electronic servants had gone ahead of him, circling the worlds of alien suns and heading homeward with their store of knowledge, as bees bring honey back to the parent hive.

Such a scout had found Thalassa, a freak among worlds with its single large island in a shoreless sea. One day continents would be born here, but this was a new planet, its history still waiting to be written.

The robot had taken a hundred years to make its homeward journey, and for a hundred more its garnered knowledge had slept in the electronic memories of the great computers which stored the wisdom of Earth. The first waves of colonization had not touched Thalassa; there were more profitable worlds to be developed—worlds that were not nine-tenths water. Yet at last the pioneers had come; only a dozen miles from where she was standing now, Lora's ancestors had first set foot upon this planet and claimed it for mankind.

They had leveled hills, planted crops, moved rivers, built towns and factories, and multiplied until they reached the natural limits of their land. With its fertile soil, abundant seas, and mild, wholly predictable weather, Thalassa was not a world that demanded much of its adopted children. The pioneering spirit had lasted perhaps two generations; thereafter the colonists were content to work as much as necessary (but no more), to dream nostalgically of Earth, and to let the future look after itself.

The village was seething with speculation when Clyde and Lora arrived. News had already come from the northern end of the island that the ship had spent its furious speed and was heading back at a low altitude, obviously looking for a place to land. "They'll still have the old maps," someone said. "Ten to one they'll ground where the first expedition landed, up in the hills."

It was a shrewd guess, and within minutes all available transport was moving out of the village, along the seldom used road to the west. As befitted the mayor of so important a cultural center as Palm Bay (population: 572; occupations: fishing, hydroponics; industries: none), Lora's father led the way in his official car. The fact that its annual coat of paint was just about due was perhaps a little unfortunate; one could only hope that the visitors would overlook the occasional patches of bare metal. After all, the car itself was quite new; Lora could distinctly remember the excitement its arrival had caused, only thirteen years ago.

The little caravan of assorted cars, trucks, and even a couple of straining sand sleds rolled over the crest of the hill and ground to a halt beside the weathered sign with its simple but impressive words:

LANDING SITE OF THE FIRST EXPEDITION
TO THALASSA
JANUARY, YEAR ZERO
(28 MAY A.D. 2626)

The *first* expedition, Lora repeated silently. There had never been a second one—*but here it was. . . .*

The ship came in so low, and so silently, that it was almost upon them before they were aware of it. There was no sound of engines—only a brief rustling of leaves as the displaced air stirred among the trees. Then all was still once more, but it seemed to Lora that the shining ovoid resting on the turf was a great silver egg, waiting to hatch and to bring something new and strange into the peaceful world of Thalassa.

"It's so small," someone whispered behind her. "They couldn't have come from Earth in *that* thing!"

"Of course not," the inevitable self-appointed expert replied at once. "That's only a lifeboat—the real ship's up there in space. Don't you remember that the first expedition—"

"Sshh!" someone else remonstrated. "They're coming out!"

It happened in the space of a single heartbeat. One second the seamless hull was so smooth and unbroken that the eye looked in vain for any sign of an opening. And then, an instant later, there was an oval doorway with a short ramp leading to the ground. Nothing had moved, but something had *happened.* How it had been done, Lora could not imagine, but she accepted the miracle without surprise. Such things were only to be expected of a ship that came from Earth.

There were figures moving inside the shadowed entrance; not a sound came from the waiting crowd as the visitors slowly emerged and stood blinking in the fierce light of an unfamiliar sun. There were seven of them—all men—and they did not look in the least like the super-beings she had expected. It was true that they were all somewhat above the average in height and had thin, clear-cut features; but they were so pale that their skins were almost white. They seemed, moreover, worried and uncertain, which was something that puzzled Lora very much. For the first time it occurred to her that this landing on Thalassa might be unintentional, and that the visitors were as surprised to be here as the islanders were to greet them.

The mayor of Palm Bay, confronted with the supreme moment of his career, stepped forward to deliver the speech on which he had been frantically working ever since the car left the village. A second before he opened his mouth, a sudden doubt struck him and sponged his memory clean. Everyone had automatically assumed that this ship came from Earth—but that was pure guesswork. It might just as easily have been sent here from one of the other colonies, of which there were at least a dozen much closer than the parent world. In his panic over protocol, all that Lora's father could manage was: "We welcome you to Thalassa. You're from Earth—I presume?" That "I presume?" was to make Mayor Fordyce immortal; it would be a century before anyone discovered that the phrase was not quite original.

In all that waiting crowd, Lora was the only one who never heard the confirming answer, spoken in English that seemed to have speeded up a trifle during the centuries of separation. For in that moment, she saw Leon for the first time.

He came out of the ship, moving as unobtrusively as possible to join his companions at the foot of the ramp. Perhaps he had remained behind to make some adjustment to the controls; perhaps—and this seemed more likely—he had been reporting the progress of the meeting to the great mother ship, which must be hanging up there in space, far beyond the uttermost fringes of the atmosphere. Whatever the reason, from then onward Lora had eyes for no one else.

Even in that first instant, she knew that her life could never again be the same. This was something new and beyond all her experience, filling her at the same moment with wonder and fear. Her fear was for the love she felt for Clyde; her wonder for the new and unknown thing that had come into her life.

Leon was not as tall as his companions, but was much more stockily built, giving an impression of power and competence. His eyes, very dark and full of animation, were deep-set in rough-hewn features which no one could have called handsome, yet which Lora found disturbingly attractive. Here was a man who had looked upon sights she could not imagine—a man who, perhaps, had walked the streets of Earth and seen its fabled cities. What was he doing here on lonely Thalassa, and why were those lines of strain and worry about his ceaselessly searching eyes?

He had looked at her once already, but his gaze had swept on without faltering. Now it came back, as if prompted by memory, and for the first time he became conscious of Lora, as all along she had been aware of him. Their eyes locked, bridging gulfs of time and space and experience. The anxious furrows faded from Leon's brow, the tense lines slowly relaxed; and presently he smiled.

It was dusk when the speeches, the banquets, the receptions, the interviews were over. Leon was very tired, but his mind was far too active to allow him to sleep. After the strain of the last few weeks, when he had awakened to the shrill clamor of alarms and fought with his colleagues to save the wounded ship, it was hard to realize that they had reached safety at last. What incredible good fortune that this inhabited planet had been so close! Even if they could not repair the ship and complete the two centuries of flight that still lay before them, here at least they could remain among friends. No shipwrecked mariners, of sea or space, could hope for more than that.

The night was cool and calm, and ablaze with unfamiliar stars. Yet there were still some old friends, even though the ancient patterns of the constellations were hopelessly lost. There was mighty Rigel, no fainter for all the added light-years that its rays must now cross before they reached his eyes. And that must be giant Canopus, almost in line with their destination, but so much more remote that even when they reached their new home, it would seem no brighter than in the skies of Earth.

Leon shook his head, as if to clear the stupefying, hypnotic image of immensity from his mind. Forget the stars, he told himself; you will face them again soon enough. Cling to this little world while you are upon it, even though it may be a grain of dust on the road between the Earth you will never see again and the goal that waits for you at journey's end, two hundred years from now.

His friends were already sleeping, tired and content, as they had a right to be. Soon he would join them—when his restless spirit would allow him to. But first he would see something of this world to which chance had brought him, this oasis peopled by his own kinsmen in the deserts of space.

He left the long, single-storied guesthouse that had been prepared for them in such obvious haste, and walked out into the single street of Palm Bay. There was no one about, though sleepy music came from a few houses. It seemed that the villagers believed in going to bed early—or perhaps they, too, were exhausted by the excitement and hospitality of the day. That suited Leon, who wanted only to be left alone until his racing thoughts had slowed to rest.

Out of the quiet night around him he became aware of the murmuring sea, and the sound drew his footsteps away from the empty street. It was dark among the palms, when the lights of the village had faded behind him, but the smaller of Thalassa's two moons was high in the south and its curious yellow glow gave him all the guidance he required. Presently he was through the narrow belt of trees, and there at the end of the steeply shelving beach lay the ocean that covered almost all of this world.

A line of fishing boats was drawn up at the water's edge, and Leon walked slowly toward them, curious to see how the craftsmen of Thalassa had solved one of man's oldest problems. He looked approvingly at the trim plastic hulls, the narrow outrigger float, the power-operated winch for raising the nets, the compact little motor, the radio with its direction-finding loop. This almost primitive, yet completely adequate, simplicity had a profound appeal to him; it was hard to think of a greater contrast with the labyrinthine complexities of the mighty ship hanging up there above his head. For a moment he amused himself with fantasy; how pleasant to jettison all his years of training and study, and to exchange the life of a starship propulsion engineer for the peaceful, undemanding existence of a fisherman! They must need someone to keep their boats in order, and perhaps he could think of a few improvements. . . .

He shrugged away the rosy dream, without bothering to marshal all its obvious fallacies, and began to walk along the shifting line of foam where the waves had spent their last strength against the land. Underfoot was the debris of this young ocean's newborn life—empty shells and carapaces that might have littered the coasts of Earth a billion years ago. Here, for instance, was a tightly wound spiral of lime-stone which he had surely seen before in some museum. It might well be; any design that had once served her purpose, Nature repeated endlessly on world after world.

A faint yellow glow was spreading swiftly across the eastern sky; even as Leon watched, Selene, the inner moon, edged itself above the horizon. With astonishing speed, the entire gibbous disk climbed out of the sea, flooding the beach with sudden light.

And in that burst of brilliance, Leon saw that he was not alone.

The girl was sitting on one of the boats, about fifty yards farther along the beach. Her back was turned toward him and she was staring out to sea, apparently unaware of his presence. Leon hesitated, not wishing to invade her solitude, and also being uncertain of the local mores in these matters. It seemed highly likely, at such a time and place, that she was waiting for someone; it might be safest, and most tact-ful, to turn quietly back to the village.

He had decided too late. As if startled by the flood of new light along the beach, the girl looked up and at once caught sight of him. She rose to her feet with an unhurried grace, showing no signs of alarm or annoyance. Indeed, if Leon could have seen her face clearly in the moonlight, he would have been surprised at the quiet satisfaction it expressed.

Only twelve hours ago, Lora would have been indignant had anyone suggested that she would meet a complete stranger here on this lonely beach when the rest of her world was slumbering. Even now, she might have tried to rationalize her behavior, to argue that she felt restless and could not sleep, and had therefore decided to go for a walk. But she knew in her heart that this was not the truth; all day long she had been haunted by the image of that young engineer, whose name and position she had managed to discover without, she hoped, arousing too much curiosity among her friends.

It was not even luck that she had seen him leave the guesthouse; she had been watching most of the evening from the porch of her father's residence, on the other side of the street. And it was certainly not luck, but deliberate and careful planning, that had taken her to this point on the beach as soon as she was sure of the direction Leon was heading.

He came to a halt a dozen feet away. (Did he recognize her? Did he guess that this was no accident? For a moment her courage almost failed her, but it was too late now to retreat.) Then he gave a curious, twisted smile that seemed to light up his whole face and made him look even younger than he was.

"Hello," he said. "I never expected to meet anyone at this time of night. I hope I haven't disturbed you."

"Of course not," Lora answered, trying to keep her voice as steady and emotionless as she could.

"I'm from the ship, you know. I thought I'd have a look at Thalassa while I'm here."

At those last words, a sudden change of expression crossed Lora's face; the sadness he saw there puzzled Leon, for it could have no cause. And then, with an instantaneous shock of recognition, he knew that he had seen this girl before, and understood what she was doing here. This was the girl who had smiled at him when he came out of the ship —no, that was not right; *he* had been the one who smiled. . . .

There seemed nothing to say. They stared at each other across the wrinkled sand, each wondering at the miracle that had brought them together out of the immensity of time and space. Then, as if in unconscious agreement, they sat facing each other on the gunwale of the boat, still without a word.

This is folly, Leon told himself. What am I doing here? What right have I, a wanderer passing through this world, to touch the lives of its people? I should make my apologies and leave this girl to the beach and the sea that are her birthright, not mine.

Yet he did not leave. The bright disk of Selene had risen a full hand's breadth above the sea when he said at last: "What's your name?"

"I'm Lora," she answered, in the soft, lilting accent of the islanders, which was so attractive, but not always easy to understand.

"And I'm Leon Carrell, Assistant Propulsion Engineer, Starship *Magellan.*"

She gave a little smile as he introduced himself, and at that moment Leon was certain that she already knew his name. At the same time a completely irrelevant and whimsical thought struck him; until a few minutes ago he had been dead-tired, just about to turn back for his overdue sleep. Yet now he was fully awake and alert—poised, as it were, on the brink of a new and unpredictable adventure.

But Lora's next remark was predictable enough: "How do you like Thalassa?"

"Give me time," Leon countered. "I've only seen Palm Bay, and not much of that."

"Will you be here—very long?"

The pause was barely perceptible, but his ear detected it. *This* was the question that really mattered.

"I'm not sure," he replied, truthfully enough. "It depends on how long the repairs take."

"What went wrong?"

"Oh, we ran into something too big for our meteor screen to absorb. And—bang!—that was the end of the screen. So we've got to make a new one."

"And you think you can do that here?"

"We hope so. The main problem will be lifting about a million tons of water up to the *Magellan.* Luckily, I think Thalassa can spare it."

"Water? I don't understand."

"Well, you know that a starship travels at almost the speed of light; even then it takes years to get anywhere, so that we have to go into suspended animation and let the automatic controls run the ship."

Lora nodded. "Of course—that's how our ancestors got here."

"Well, the speed would be no problem if space was really empty—but it isn't. A starship sweeps up thousands of atoms of hydrogen, particles of dust, and sometimes larger fragments, every second of its flight. At nearly the speed of light, these bits of cosmic junk have enormous energy, and could soon burn up the ship. So we carry a shield about a mile ahead of us, and let *that* get burned up instead. Do you have umbrellas on this world?"

"Why—yes," Lora replied, obviously baffled by the incongruous question.

"Then you can compare a starship to a man moving head down through a rainstorm behind the cover of an umbrella. The rain is the cosmic dust between the stars, and our ship was unlucky enough to lose its umbrella."

"And you can make a new one of *water*?"

"Yes; it's the cheapest building material in the universe. We freeze it into an iceberg which travels ahead of us. What could be simpler than that?"

Lora did not answer; her thoughts seemed to have veered onto a new track. Presently she said, her voice so low and wistful that Leon had to bend forward to hear it against the rolling of the surf: "And you left Earth a hundred years ago."

"A hundred and four. Of course, it seems only a few weeks, since we were deep-sleeping until the autopilot revived us. All the colonists are still in suspended animation; they don't know that anything's happened."

"And presently you'll join them again, and sleep your way on to the stars."

Leon nodded, avoiding her eye. "That's right. Planetfall will be a few months late, but what does that matter on a trip that takes three hundred years?"

Lora pointed to the island behind them, and then to the shoreless sea at whose edge they stood.

"It's strange to think that your sleeping friends up there will never know anything of all this. I feel sorry for them."

"Yes, only we fifty or so engineers will have any memories of Thalassa. To everyone else in the ship, our stop here will be nothing more than a hundred-year-old entry in the logbook."

He glanced at Lora's face, and saw again that sadness in her eyes.

"Why does that make you unhappy?"

She shook her head, unable to answer. How could one express the sense of loneliness that Leon's words had brought to her? The lives of men, and all their hopes and fears, were so little against the inconceivable immensities that they had dared to challenge. The thought of that three-hundred-year journey, not yet half completed, was something from which her mind recoiled in horror. And yet—in her own veins was the blood of those earlier pioneers who had followed the same path to Thalassa, centuries ago.

The night was no longer friendly; she felt a sudden longing for her home and family, for the little room that held everything she owned and that was all the world she knew or wanted. The cold of space was freezing her heart; she wished now that she had never come on this mad adventure. It was time—more than time—to leave.

As she rose to her feet, she noticed that they had been sitting on Clyde's boat, and wondered what unconscious prompting of her mind had brought her here to this one vessel out of all the little fleet lined up along the beach. At the thought of Clyde, a spasm of uncertainty, even of guilt, swept over her. Never in her life, except for the most fleeting moments, had she thought of any other man but him. Now she could no longer pretend that this was true.

"What's the matter?" asked Leon. "Are you cold?" He held out his hand to her, and for the first time their fingers touched as she automatically responded. But at the instant of contact, she shied like a startled animal and jerked away.

"I'm all right," she answered, almost angrily. "It's late—I must go home. Good-by."

Her reaction was so abrupt that it took Leon by surprise. Had he said anything to offend her? he wondered. She was already walking quickly away when he called after her: "Will I see you again?"

If she answered, the sound of the waves carried away her voice. He watched her go, puzzled and a little hurt, while not for the first time in his life he reflected how hard it was to understand the mind of a woman.

For a moment he thought of following her and repeating the question, but in his heart he knew there was no need. As surely as the sun would rise tomorrow, they would meet again.

.   .   .

And now the life of the island was dominated by the crippled giant a thousand miles out in space. Before dawn and after sunset, when the world was in darkness but the light of the sun still streamed overhead, the *Magellan* was visible as a brilliant star, the brightest object in all the sky except the two moons themselves. But even when it could not be seen —when it was lost in the glare of day or eclipsed by the shadow of Thalassa—it was never far from men's thoughts.

It was hard to believe that only fifty of the starship's crew had been awakened, and that not even half of those were on Thalassa at any one time. They seemed to be everywhere, usually in little groups of two or three, walking swiftly on mysterious errands or riding small antigravity scooters which floated a few feet from the ground and moved so silently that they made life in the village rather hazardous. Despite the most pressing invitations, the visitors had still taken no part in the cultural and social activities of the island. They had explained, politely but firmly, that until the safety of their ship was secured, they would have no time for any other interests. Later, certainly, but not now . . .

So Thalassa had to wait with what patience it could muster while the Earthmen set up their instruments, made their surveys, drilled deep into the rocks of the island, and carried out scores of experiments which seemed to have no possible connection with their problem. Sometimes they consulted briefly with Thalassa's own scientists, but on the whole they kept to themselves. It was not that they were unfriendly or aloof; they were working with such a fierce and dedicated intensity that they were scarcely aware of anyone around them.

After their first meeting, it was two days before Lora spoke to Leon again. She saw him from time to time as he hurried about the village, usually with a bulging briefcase and an abstracted expression, but they were able to exchange only the briefest of smiles. Yet even this was enough to keep her emotions in turmoil, to banish her peace of mind, and to poison her relationship with Clyde.

As long as she could remember, he had been part of her life; they had had their quarrels and disagreements, but no one else had ever challenged his place in her heart. In a few months they would be married—yet now she was not even sure of that, or indeed of anything.

"Infatuation" was an ugly word, which one applied only to other people. But how else could she explain this yearning to be with a man who had come suddenly into her life from nowhere, and who must leave again in a few days or weeks? No doubt the glamour and romance of his origin was partly responsible, but that alone was not enough to account for it. There were other Earthmen better looking than Leon, yet she had eyes for him alone, and her life now was empty unless she was in his presence.

By the end of the first day, only her family knew about her feelings; by the end of the second, everyone she passed gave her a knowing smile. It was impossible to keep a secret in such a tight and talkative community as Palm Bay, and she knew better than to attempt it.

Her second meeting with Leon was accidental—as far as such things can ever be accidents. She was helping her father deal with some of the correspondence and inquiries that had flooded upon the village since the Earthmen's arrival, and was trying to make some sense out of her notes when the door of the office opened. It had opened so often in the last few days that she had ceased to look up; her younger sister was acting as receptionist and dealt with all the visitors. Then she heard Leon's voice; and the paper blurred before her eyes, the notes might have been in an unknown language.

"Can I see the mayor, please?"

"Of course, Mr.—?"

"Assistant Engineer Carrell."

"I'll go and fetch him. Won't you sit down?"

Leon slumped wearily in the ancient armchair that was the best the reception room could offer its infrequent visitors, and not until then did he notice that Lora was watching him silently from the other side of the room. At once he sloughed off his tiredness and shot to his feet.

"Hello—I didn't know you worked here."

"I live here; my father's the mayor."

This portentous news did not seem to impress Leon unduly. He walked over to the desk and picked up the fat volume through which Lora had been browsing between her secretarial duties.

"A Concise History of Earth," he read, *"from the Dawn of Civilization to the Beginning of Interstellar Flight.* And all in a thousand pages! It's a pity it ends three hundred years ago."

"We hope that you'll soon bring us up to date. Has much happened since that was written?"

"Enough to fill about fifty libraries, I suppose. But before we go we'll leave you copies of all our records, so that your history books will only be a hundred years out of date."

They were circling around each other, avoiding the only thing that was important. *When can we meet again?* Lora's thoughts kept hammering silently, unable to break through the barrier of speech. *And does he really like me or is he merely making polite conversation?*

The inner door opened, and the mayor emerged apologetically from his office.

"Sorry to keep you waiting, Mr. Carrell, but the president was on the line—he's coming over this afternoon. And what can I do for you?"

Lora pretended to work, but she typed the same sentence eight times while Leon delivered his message from the captain of the *Magellan.* She was not a great deal wiser when he had finished; it seemed that the starship's engineers wished to build some equipment on a headland a mile from the village, and wanted to make sure there would be no objection.

"Of course!" said Mayor Fordyce expansively, in his nothing's-too-good-for-our-guests tone of voice. "Go right ahead—the land doesn't belong to anybody, and no one lives there. What do you want to do with it?"

"We're building a gravity inverter, and the generator has to be anchored in solid bedrock. It may be a little noisy when it starts to run, but I don't think it will disturb you here in the village. And of course we'll dismantle the equipment when we've finished."

Lora had to admire her father. She knew perfectly well that Leon's request was as meaningless to him as it was to her, but one would never have guessed it.

"That's perfectly all right—glad to be of any help we can. And will you tell Captain Gold that the president's coming at five this afternoon? I'll send my car to collect him; the reception's at five thirty in the village hall."

When Leon had given his thanks and departed, Mayor Fordyce walked over to his daughter and picked up the slim pile of correspondence she had none-too-accurately typed.

"He seems a pleasant young man," he said, "but is it a good idea to get too fond of him?"

"I don't know what you mean."

"Now, Lora! After all, I *am* your father, and I'm not *completely* unobservant."

"He's not"—sniff—"a bit interested in me."

"Are you interested in him?"

"I don't know. Oh, Daddy, I'm so unhappy!"

Mayor Fordyce was not a brave man, so there was only one thing he could do. He donated his handkerchief, and fled back into his office.

It was the most difficult problem that Clyde had ever faced in his life, and there were no precedents that gave any help at all. Lora belonged to him—everyone knew that. If his rival had been another villager, or someone from any other part of Thalassa, he knew exactly what he would have done. But the laws of hospitality, and, above all, his natural awe for anything of Earth, prevented him from politely asking Leon to take his attentions elsewhere. It would not be the first time *that* had happened, and there had never been the slightest trouble on those earlier occasions. That could have been because Clyde was over six feet tall, proportionally broad, and had no excess fat on his one hundred and ninety pound frame.

During the long hours at sea, when he had nothing else to do but to brood, Clyde toyed with the idea of a short, sharp bout with Leon. It would be very short; though Leon was not as skinny as most of the Earthmen, he shared their pale, washed-out look and was obviously no match for anyone who led a life of physical activity. That was the trouble—it wouldn't be fair. Clyde knew that public opinion would be outraged if he had a fight with Leon, however justified he might be.

And how justified was he? That was the big problem that worried Clyde, as it had worried a good many billion men before him. It seemed that Leon was now practically one of the family; every time he called at the mayor's house, the Earthman seemed to be there on some pretext or other. Jealousy was an emotion that had never afflicted Clyde before, and he did not enjoy the symptoms.

He was still furious about the dance. It had been the biggest social event for years; indeed, it was not likely that Palm Bay would ever match it again in the whole of its history. To have the president of Thalassa, half the council, and fifty visitors from Earth in the village at the same moment was not something that could happen again this side of eternity.

For all his size and strength, Clyde was a good dancer—especially with Lora. But that night he had had little chance of proving it; Leon had been too busy demonstrating the latest steps from Earth (latest, that is, if you overlooked the fact that they must have passed out of fashion a hundred years ago—unless they had come back and were now the latest thing). In Clyde's opinion Leon's technique was very poor and the dances were ugly; the interest that Lora showed in them was perfectly ridiculous.

He had been foolish enough to tell her so when his opportunity came; and that had been the last dance he had had with Lora that evening. From then onward, he might not have been there, as far as she was concerned. Clyde had endured the boycott as long as he could, then had left for the bar with one objective in mind. He had quickly attained it, and not until he had come reluctantly to his senses the next morning did he discover what he had missed.

The dancing had ended early; there had been a short speech from the president—his third that evening—introducing the commander of the starship and promising a little surprise. Captain Gold had been equally brief; he was obviously a man more accustomed to orders than orations.

"Friends," he began, "you know why we're here, and I've no need to say how much we appreciate your hospitality and kindness. We shall never forget you, and we're only sorry that we have had so little time to see more of your beautiful island and its people. I hope you will forgive us for any seeming discourtesy, but the repair of our ship, and the safety of our companions, has had to take priority in our minds.

"In the long run, the accident that brought us here may be fortunate for us both. It has given us happy memories, and also inspiration. What we have seen here is a lesson to us. May we make the world that is waiting at the end of our journey as fair a home for mankind as you have made Thalassa.

"And before we resume our voyage, it is both a duty and a pleasure to leave with you all the records we can that will bridge the gap since you last had contact with Earth. Tomorrow we shall invite your scientists and historians up to our ship so that they can copy any of our information tapes they desire. Thus we hope to leave you a legacy which will enrich your world for generations to come. That is the very least we can do.

"But tonight, science and history can wait, for we have other treasures aboard. Earth has not been idle in the centuries since your forefathers left. Listen, now, to some of the heritage we share together, and which we will leave upon Thalassa before we go our way."

The lights had dimmed; the music had begun. No one who was present would ever forget that moment; in a trance of wonder, Lora had listened to what men had wrought in sound during the centuries of separation. Time had meant nothing; she had not even been conscious of Leon standing by her side, holding her hand, as the music ebbed and flowed around them.

These were the things that she had never known, the things that belonged to Earth, and to Earth alone. The slow beat of mighty bells, climbing like invisible smoke from old cathedral spires; the chant of patient boatmen, in a thousand tongues now lost forever, rowing home against the tide in the last light of day; the songs of armies marching into battles that time had robbed of all their pain and evil; the merged murmur of ten million voices as man's greatest cities woke to meet the dawn; the cold dance of the Aurora over endless seas of ice; the roar of mighty engines climbing upward on the highway to the stars. All these she had heard in the music and the songs that had come out of the night—the songs of distant Earth, carried to her across the light-years. . . .

A clear soprano voice, swooping and soaring like a bird at the very edge of hearing, sang a wordless lament that tore at the heart. It was a dirge for all loves lost in the loneliness of space, for friends and homes that could never again be seen and must fade at last from memory. It was a song for all exiles, and it spoke as clearly to those who were sundered from Earth by a dozen generations as to the voyagers to whom its fields and cities still seemed only weeks away.

The music had died into the darkness; misty-eyed, avoiding words, the people of Thalassa had gone slowly to their homes. But Lora had not gone to hers; against the loneliness that had pierced her very soul, there was only one defense. And presently she had found it, in the warm night of the forest, as Leon's arms tightened around her and their souls and bodies merged. Like wayfarers lost in a hostile wilderness, they had sought warmth and comfort beside the fire of love. While that fire burned, they were safe from the shadows that prowled in the night; and all the universe of stars and planets shrank to a toy that they could hold within their hands.

To Leon, it was never wholly real. Despite all the urgency and peril that had brought them here, he sometimes fancied that at journey's end it would be hard to convince himself that Thalassa was not a dream that had come in his long sleep. This fierce and foredoomed love, for example; he had not asked for it—it had been thrust upon him. Yet there were few men, he told himself, who would not have taken it, had they, too, landed, after weeks of grinding anxiety, on this peaceful, pleasant world.

When he could escape from work, he took long walks with Lora in the fields far from the village, where men seldom came and only the robot cultivators disturbed the solitude. For hours Lora would question him about Earth—but she would never speak of the planet that was the *Magellan*'s goal. He understood her reasons well enough, and did his best to satisfy her endless curiosity about the world that was already "home" to more men than had ever seen it with their own eyes.

She was bitterly disappointed to hear that the age of cities had passed. Despite all that Leon could tell her about the completely decentralized culture that now covered the planet from pole to pole, she still thought of Earth in terms of such vanished giants as Chandrigar, London, Astrograd, New York, and it was hard for her to realize that they had gone forever, and with them the way of life they represented.

"When we left Earth," Leon explained, "the largest centers of population were university towns like Oxford or Ann Arbor or Canberra; some of them had fifty thousand students and professors. There are no other cities left of even half that size."

"But what happened to them?"

"Oh, there was no single cause, but the development of communications started it. As soon as anyone on Earth could see and talk to anyone else by pressing a button, most of the need for cities vanished. Then antigravity was invented, and you could move goods or houses or anything else through the sky without bothering about geography. That completed the job of wiping out distance, which the airplane had begun a couple of centuries earlier. After that, men started to live where they liked, and the cities dwindled away."

For a moment Lora did not answer; she was lying on a bank of grass, watching the behavior of a bee whose ancestors, like hers, had been citizens of Earth. It was trying vainly to extract nectar from one of Thalassa's native flowers; insect life had not yet arisen on this world, and the few indigenous flowers had not yet invented lures for air-borne visitors.

The frustrated bee gave up the hopeless task and buzzed angrily away; Lora hoped that it would have enough sense to head back to the orchards, where it would find more cooperative flowers. When she spoke again, it was to voice a dream that had now haunted mankind for almost a thousand years.

"Do you suppose," she said wistfully, "that we'll ever break through the speed of light?"

Leon smiled, knowing where her thoughts were leading. To travel faster than light—to go home to Earth, yet to return to your native world while your friends were still alive—every colonist must, at some time or other, have dreamed of this. There was no problem, in the whole history of the human race, that had called forth so much effort and that still remained so utterly intractable.

"I don't believe so," he said. "If it could be done, someone would have discovered how by this time. No—we have to do it the slow way, because there isn't any other. That's how the universe is built, and there's nothing we can do about it."

"But surely we could still keep in touch!"

Leon nodded. "That's true," he said, "and we try to. I don't know what's gone wrong, but you should have heard from Earth long before now. We've been sending out robot message carriers to all the colonies, carrying a full history of everything that's happened up to the time of departure, and asking for a report back. As the news returns to Earth, it's all transcribed and sent out again by the next messenger. So we have a kind of interstellar news service, with the Earth as the central clearinghouse. It's slow, of course, but there's no other way of doing it. If the last messenger to Thalassa has been lost, there must be another on the way—maybe several, twenty or thirty years apart."

Lora tried to envisage the vast, star-spanning network of message carriers, shuttling back and forth between Earth and its scattered children, and wondered why Thalassa had been overlooked. But with Leon beside her, it did not seem important. He was here; Earth and the stars were very far away. And so also, with whatever unhappiness it might bring, was tomorrow. . . .

By the end of the week, the visitors had built a squat and heavily braced pyramid of metal girders, housing some obscure mechanism, on a rocky headland overlooking the sea. Lora, in common with the 571 other inhabitants of Palm Bay and the several thousand sight-seers who had descended upon the village, was watching when the first test was made. No one was allowed to go within a quarter of a mile of the machine—a precaution that aroused a good deal of alarm among the more nervous islanders. Did the Earthmen know what they were doing? Suppose that something went wrong. And *what* were they doing, anyway?

Leon was there with his friends inside that metal pyramid, making the final adjustments—the "coarse focusing," he had told Lora, leaving her none the wiser. She watched with the same anxious incomprehension as all her fellow islanders until the distant figures emerged from the machine and walked to the edge of the flat-topped rock on which it was built. There they stood, a tiny group of figures silhouetted against the ocean, staring out to sea.

A mile from the shore, something strange was happening to the water. It seemed that a storm was brewing—but a storm that kept within an area only a few hundred yards across. Mountainous waves were building up, smashing against each other and then swiftly subsiding again. Within a few minutes the ripples of the disturbance had reached the shore, but the center of the tiny storm showed no sign of movement. It was as if, Lora told herself, an invisible finger had reached down from the sky and was stirring the sea.

Quite abruptly, the entire pattern changed. Now the waves were no longer battering against each other; they were marching in step, moving more and more swiftly in a light circle. A cone of water was rising from the sea, becoming taller and thinner with every second. Already it was a hundred feet high, and the sound of its birth was an angry roaring that filled the air and struck terror into the hearts of all who heard it. All, that is, except the little band of men who had summoned this monster from the deep, and who still stood watching it with calm assurance, ignoring the waves that were breaking almost against their feet.

Now the spinning tower of water was climbing swiftly up the sky, piercing the clouds like an arrow as it headed toward space. Its foam-capped summit was already lost beyond sight, and from the sky there began to fall a steady shower of rain, the drops abnormally large, like those which prelude a thunderstorm. Not all the water that was being lifted from Thalassa's single ocean was reaching its distant goal; some was escaping from the power that controlled it and was falling back from the edge of space.

Slowly the watching crowd drifted away, astonishment and fright already yielding to a calm acceptance. Man had been able to control gravity for half a thousand years, and this trick—spectacular though it was—could not be compared with the miracle of hurling a great starship from sun to sun at little short of the speed of light.

The Earthmen were now walking back toward their machine, clearly satisfied with what they had done. Even at this distance, one could see that they were happy and relaxed—perhaps for the first time since they had reached Thalassa. The water to rebuild the *Magellan*'s shield was on its way out into space, to be shaped and frozen by the other strange forces that these men had made their servants. In a few days, they would be ready to leave, their great interstellar ark as good as new.

Even until this minute, Lora had hoped that they might

fail. There was nothing left of that hope now, as she watched the man-made waterspout lift its burden from the sea. Sometimes it wavered slightly, its base shifting back and forth as if at the balance point between immense and invisible forces. But it was fully under control, and it would do the task that had been set for it. That meant only one thing to her; soon she must say good-by to Leon.

She walked slowly toward the distant group of Earthmen, marshaling her thoughts and trying to subdue her emotions. Presently Leon broke away from his friends and came to meet her; relief and happiness were written across his face, but they faded swiftly when he saw Lora's expression.

"Well," he said lamely, almost like a schoolboy caught in some crime, "we've done it."

"And now—how long will you be here?"

He scuffed nervously at the sand, unable to meet her eye.

"Oh, about three days—perhaps four."

She tried to assimilate the words calmly; after all, she had expected them—this was nothing new. But she failed completely, and it was as well that there was no one near them.

"You can't leave!" she cried desperately. "Stay here on Thalassa!"

Leon took her hands gently, then murmured: "No, Lora —this isn't my world; I would never fit into it. Half my life's been spent training for the work I'm doing now; I could never be happy here, where there aren't any more frontiers. In a month I should die of boredom."

"Then take me with you!"

"You don't really mean that."

"But I do!"

"You only think so; you'd be more out of place in my world than I would be in yours."

"I could learn—there would be plenty of things I could do. As long as we could stay together!"

He held her at arm's length, looking into her eyes. They mirrored sorrow, and also sincerity. She really believed what she was saying, Leon told himself. For the first time, his conscience smote him. He had forgotten—or chosen not to remember—how much more serious these things could be to a woman than to a man.

He had never intended to hurt Lora; he was very fond of her, and would remember her with affection all his life. Now he was discovering, as so many men before him had done, that it was not always easy to say good-by.

There was only one thing to do. Better a short, sharp pain than a long bitterness.

"Come with me, Lora," he said. "I have something to show you."

They did not speak as Leon led the way to the clearing that the Earthmen used as a landing ground. It was littered with pieces of enigmatic equipment, some of them being repacked while others were being left behind for the islanders to use as they pleased. Several of the antigravity scooters were parked in the shade beneath the palms; even when not in use they spurned contact with the ground, and hovered a couple of feet above the grass.

But it was not these that Leon was interested in; he walked purposefully toward the gleaming oval that dominated the clearing, and spoke a few words to the engineer who was standing beside it. There was a short argument; then the other capitulated with fairly good grace.

"It's not fully loaded," Leon explained as he helped Lora up the ramp. "But we're going just the same. The other shuttle will be down in half an hour, anyway."

Already Lora was in a world she had never known before —a world of technology in which the most brilliant engineer or scientist of Thalassa would be lost. The island possessed all the machines it needed for its life and happiness; this was something utterly beyond its ken. Lora had once seen the great computer that was the virtual ruler of her people and with whose decisions they disagreed not once in a generation. That giant brain was huge and complex, but there was an awesome simplicity about this machine that impressed even her nontechnical mind. When Leon sat down at the absurdly small control board, his hands seemed to do nothing except rest lightly upon it.

Yet the walls were suddenly transparent—and there was Thalassa, already shrinking below them. There had been no sense of movement, no whisper of sound, yet the island was dwindling even as she watched. The misty edge of the world, a great bow dividing the blue of the sea from the velvet blackness of space, was becoming more curved with every passing second.

"Look," said Leon, pointing to the stars.

The ship was already visible, and Lora felt a sudden sense of disappointment that it was so small. She could see a cluster of portholes around the center section, but there appeared to be no other breaks anywhere on the vessel's squat and angular hull.

The illusion lasted only for a second. Then, with a shock of incredulity that made her senses reel and brought her to the edge of vertigo, she saw how hopelessly her eyes had been deceived. Those were not portholes; the ship was still miles away. What she was seeing were the gaping hatches through which the ferries could shuttle on their journeys between the starship and Thalassa.

There is no sense of perspective in space, where all objects are still clear and sharp whatever their distance. Even when the hull of the ship was looming up beside them, an endless curving wall of metal eclipsing the stars, there was still no real way of judging its size. She could only guess that it must be at least two miles in length.

The ferry berthed itself, as far as Lora could judge, without any intervention from Leon. She followed him out of the little control room, and when the air lock opened she was surprised to discover that they could step directly into one of the starship's passageways.

They were standing in a long tubular corridor that stretched in each direction as far as the eye could see. The floor was moving beneath their feet, carrying them along swiftly and effortlessly—yet strangely enough Lora had felt no sudden jerk as she stepped onto the conveyer that was now sweeping her through the ship. One more mystery she would never explain; there would be many others before Leon had finished showing her the *Magellan*.

It was an hour before they met another human being. In that time they must have traveled miles, sometimes being carried along by the moving corridors, sometimes being lifted up long tubes within which gravity had been abolished. It was obvious what Leon was trying to do; he was attempting to give her some faint impression of the size and complexity of this artificial world that had been built to carry the seeds of a new civilization to the stars.

The engine room alone, with its sleeping, shrouded monsters of metal and crystal, must have been half a mile in length. As they stood on the balcony high above that vast arena of latent power, Leon said proudly, and perhaps not altogether accurately: "These are mine." Lora looked down on the huge and meaningless shapes that had carried Leon to her across the light-years, and did not know whether to bless them for what they had brought or to curse them for what they might soon take away.

They sped swiftly through cavernous holds, packed with all the machines and instruments and stores needed to mold a virgin planet and to make it a fit home for humanity. There were miles upon miles of storage racks, holding in tape or microfilm or still more compact form the cultural heritage of mankind. Here they met a group of experts from Thalassa, looking rather dazed, trying to decide how much of all this wealth they could loot in the few hours left to them.

Had her own ancestors, Lora wondered, been so well equipped when they crossed space? She doubted it; their ship had been far smaller, and Earth must have learned much about the techniques of interstellar colonization in the centuries since Thalassa was opened up. When the *Magellan*'s sleeping travelers reached their new home, their success was assured if their spirit matched their material resources.

Now they had come to a great white door which slid silently open as they approached, to reveal—of all incongruous things to find inside a spaceship—a cloakroom in which lines of heavy furs hung from pegs. Leon helped Lora to climb into one of these, then selected another for himself. She followed him uncomprehendingly as he walked toward a circle of frosted glass set in the floor; then he turned to her and said: "There's no gravity where we're going now, so keep close to me and do exactly as I say."

The crystal trap door swung upward like an opening watch glass, and out of the depths swirled a blast of cold such as Lora had never imagined, still less experienced. Thin wisps of moisture condensed in the freezing air, dancing around her like ghosts. She looked at Leon as if to say, "Surely you don't expect me to go down *there*!"

He took her arm reassuringly and said, "Don't worry— you won't notice the cold after a few minutes. I'll go first."

The trap door swallowed him; Lora hesitated for a moment, then lowered herself after him. *Lowered?* No; that was the wrong word; up and down no longer existed here. Gravity had been abolished—she was floating without weight in this frigid, snow-white universe. All around her were glittering honeycombs of glass, forming thousands and tens of thousands of hexagonal cells. They were laced together with clusters of pipes and bundles of wiring, and each cell was large enough to hold a human being.

And each cell did. There they were, sleeping all around her, the thousands of colonists to whom Earth was still, in literal truth, a memory of yesterday. What were they dreaming, less than halfway through their three-hundred-year sleep? Did the brain dream at all in this dim no man's land between life and death?

Narrow, endless belts, fitted with handholds every few feet, were strung across the face of the honeycomb. Leon grabbed one of these, and let it tow them swiftly past the great mosaic of hexagons. Twice they changed direction, switching from one belt to another, until at last they must have been a full quarter of a mile from the point where they had started.

Leon released his grip, and they drifted to rest beside one cell no different from all the myriads of others. But as Lora saw the expression on Leon's face, she knew why he had brought her here, and knew that her battle was already lost.

The girl floating in her crystal coffin had a face that was not beautiful, but was full of character and intelligence. Even in this centuries-long repose, it showed determination and resourcefulness. It was the face of a pioneer, of a frontiers-woman who could stand beside her mate and help him wield whatever fabulous tools of science might be needed to build a new Earth beyond the stars.

For a long time, unconscious of the cold, Lora stared down at the sleeping rival who would never know of her existence. Had any love, she wondered, in the whole history of the world, ever ended in so strange a place?

At last she spoke, her voice hushed as if she feared to wake these slumbering legions.

"Is she your wife?"

Leon nodded.

"I'm sorry, Lora. I never intended to hurt you. . . ."

"It doesn't matter now. It was my fault, too." She

paused, and looked more closely at the sleeping woman. "And your child as well?"

"Yes; it will be born three months after we land."

How strange to think of a gestation that would last nine months and three hundred years! Yet it was all part of the same pattern; and that, she knew now, was a pattern that had no place for her.

These patient multitudes would haunt her dreams for the rest of her life; as the crystal trap door closed behind her, and warmth crept back into her body, she wished that the cold that had entered her heart could be so easily dispelled. One day, perhaps, it would be; but many days and many lonely nights must pass ere that time came.

She remembered nothing of the journey back through the labyrinth of corridors and echoing chambers; it took her by surprise when she found herself once more in the cabin of the little ferry ship that had brought them up from Thalassa. Leon walked over to the controls, made a few adjustments, but did not sit down.

"Good-by, Lora," he said. "My work is done. It would be better if I stayed here." He took her hands in his; and now, in the last moment they would ever have together, there were no words that she could say. She could not even see his face for the tears that blurred her vision.

His hands tightened once, then relaxed. He gave a strangled sob, and when she could see clearly again, the cabin was empty.

A long time later a smooth, synthetic voice announced from the control board, "We have landed; please leave by the forward air lock." The pattern of opening doors guided her steps, and presently she was looking out into the busy clearing she had left a lifetime ago.

A small crowd was watching the ship with attentive interest, as if it had not landed a hundred times before. For a moment she did not understand the reason; then Clyde's voice roared, "Where is he? I've had enough of this!"

In a couple of bounds he was up the ramp and had gripped her roughly by the arm. "Tell him to come out like a man!"

Lora shook her head listlessly.

"He's not here," she answered. "I've said good-by to him. I'll never see him again."

Clyde stared at her disbelievingly, then saw that she spoke the truth. In the same moment she crumbled into his arms, sobbing as if her heart would break. As she collapsed, his anger, too, collapsed within him, and all that he had intended to say to her vanished from his mind. She belonged to him again; there was nothing else that mattered now.

For almost fifty hours the geyser roared off the coast of Thalassa, until its work was done. All the island watched, through the lenses of the television cameras, the shaping of the iceberg that would ride ahead of the *Magellan* on her way to the stars. May the new shield serve her better, prayed all who watched, than the one she had brought from Earth. The great cone of ice was itself protected, during these few hours while it was close to Thalassa's sun, by a paper-thin screen of polished metal that kept it always in shadow. The sunshade would be left behind as soon as the journey began; it would not be needed in the interstellar wastes.

The last day came and went; Lora's heart was not the only one to feel sadness now as the sun went down and the men from Earth made their final farewells to the world they would never forget—and which their sleeping friends would never remember. In the same swift silence with which it had first landed, the gleaming egg lifted from the clearing, dipped for a moment in salutation above the village, and climbed back into its natural element. Then Thalassa waited.

The night was shattered by a soundless detonation of light. A point of pulsing brilliance no larger than a single star had banished all the hosts of heaven and now dominated the sky, far outshining the pale disk of Selene and casting sharp-edged shadows on the ground—shadows that moved even as one watched. Up there on the borders of space the fires that powered the suns themselves were burning now, preparing to drive the starship out into immensity on the last leg of her interrupted journey.

Dry-eyed, Lora watched the silent glory on which half her heart was riding out toward the stars. She was drained of emotion now; if she had tears, they would come later.

Was Leon already sleeping or was he looking back upon Thalassa, thinking of what might have been? Asleep or waking, what did it matter now . . . ?

She felt Clyde's arms close around her, and welcomed their comfort against the loneliness of space. This was where she belonged; her heart would not stray again. *Good-by, Leon—may you be happy on that far world which you and your children will conquer for mankind. But think of me sometimes, two hundred years behind you on the road to Earth.*

She turned her back upon the blazing sky and buried her face in the shelter of Clyde's arms. He stroked her hair with clumsy gentleness, wishing that he had words to comfort her yet knowing that silence was best. He felt no sense of victory; though Lora was his once more, their old and innocent companionship was gone beyond recall. Leon's memory would fade, but it would never wholly die. All the days of his life, Clyde knew, the ghost of Leon would come between him and Lora—the ghost of a man who would be not one day older when they lay in their graves.

The light was fading from the sky as the fury of the star drive dwindled along its lonely and unreturning road. Only once did Lora turn away from Clyde to look again at the departing ship. Its journey had scarcely begun, yet already it was moving across the heavens more swiftly than any meteor; in a few moments it would have fallen below the edge of the horizon as it plunged past the orbit of Thalassa, beyond the barren outer planets, and on into the abyss.

She clung fiercely to the strong arms that enfolded her, and felt against her cheek the beating of Clyde's heart—the heart that belonged to her and which she would never spurn again. Out of the silence of the night there came a sudden, long-drawn sigh from the watching thousands, and she knew that the *Magellan* had sunk out of sight below the edge of the world. It was all over.

She looked up at the empty sky to which the stars were now returning—the stars which she could never see again without remembering Leon. But he had been right; that way was not for her. She knew now, with a wisdom beyond her years, that the starship *Magellan* was outward bound into history; and that was something of which Thalassa had no further part. Her world's story had begun and ended with the pioneers three hundred years ago, but the colonists of the *Magellan* would go on to victories and achievements as great as any yet written in the sagas of mankind. Leon and his companions would be moving seas, leveling mountains, and conquering unknown perils when her descendants eight generations hence would still be dreaming beneath the sun-soaked palms.

And which was better, who could say?

THE FOOD OF
THE GODS

IT'S ONLY FAIR to warn you, Mr. Chairman, that much of my evidence will be highly nauseating; it involves aspects of human nature that are very seldom discussed in public, and certainly not before a congressional committee. But I am afraid that they have to be faced; there are times when the veil of hypocrisy has to be ripped away, and this is one of them.

You and I, gentlemen, have descended from a long line of carnivores. I see from your expressions that most of you don't recognize the term. Well, that's not surprising—it comes from a language that has been obsolete for two thousand years. Perhaps I had better avoid euphemisms and be brutally frank, even if I have to use words that are never heard in polite society. I apologize in advance to anyone I may offend.

Until a few centuries ago, the favorite food of almost all men was *meat*—the *flesh* of once living animals. I'm not trying to turn your stomachs; this is a simple statement of fact, which you can check in any history book. . . .

Why, certainly, Mr. Chairman. I'm quite prepared to wait until Senator Irving feels better. We professionals sometimes forget how laymen may react to statements like that. At the same time, I must warn the committee that there is very much worse to come. If any of you gentlemen are at all squeamish, I suggest you follow the Senator before it's too late. . . .

Well, if I may continue. Until modern times, all food fell into two categories. Most of it was produced from plants—cereals, fruits, plankton, algae, and other forms of vegetation. It's hard for us to realize that the vast majority of our ancestors were farmers, winning food from land or sea by primitive and often backbreaking techniques; but that is the truth.

The second type of food, if I may return to this unpleasant subject, was meat, produced from a relatively small number of animals. You may be familiar with some of them —cows, pigs, sheep, whales. Most people—I am sorry to stress this, but the fact is beyond dispute—preferred meat to any other food, though only the wealthiest were able to indulge this appetite. To most of mankind, meat was a rare and occasional delicacy in a diet that was more than ninety percent vegetable.

If we look at the matter calmly and dispassionately—as I hope Senator Irving is now in a position to do—we can see that meat was bound to be rare and expensive, for its production is an extremely inefficient process. To make a kilo of meat, the animal concerned had to eat at least ten kilos of vegetable food—very often food that could have been consumed directly by human beings. Quite apart from any consideration of aesthetics, this state of affairs could not be tolerated after the population explosion of the twentieth century. Every man who ate meat was condemning ten or more of his fellow humans to starvation. . . .

Luckily for all of us, the biochemists solved the problem; as you may know, the answer was one of the countless by-products of space research. All food—animal or vegetable—is built up from a very few common elements. Carbon, hydrogen, oxygen, nitrogen, traces of sulphur and phosphorus —these half-dozen elements, and a few others, combine in an almost infinite variety of ways to make up every food that man has ever eaten or ever will eat. Faced with the problem of colonizing the Moon and planets, the biochemists of the twenty-first century discovered how to synthesize any desired food from the basic raw materials of water, air, and rock. It was the greatest, and perhaps the most important, achievement in the history of science. But we should not feel too proud of it. The vegetable kingdom had beaten us by a billion years.

The chemists could now synthesize any conceivable food, whether it had a counterpart in nature or not. Needless to say, there were mistakes—even disasters. Industrial empires rose and crashed; the switch from agriculture and animal husbandry to the giant automatic processing plants and omniverters of today was often a painful one. But it had to be made, and we are the better for it. The danger of starvation has been banished forever, and we have a richness and variety of food that no other age has ever known.

In addition, of course, there was a moral gain. We no longer murder millions of living creatures, and such revolting institutions as the slaughterhouse and the butcher shop have vanished from the face of the Earth. It seems incredible to us that even our ancestors, coarse and brutal though they were, could ever have tolerated such obscenities.

And yet—it is impossible to make a clean break with the past. As I have already remarked, we are carnivores; we inherit tastes and appetites that have been acquired over a million years of time. Whether we like it or not, only a few years ago some of our great-grandparents were enjoying the flesh of cattle and sheep and pigs—when they could get it. *And we still enjoy it today. . . .*

Oh dear, maybe Senator Irving had better stay outside from now on. Perhaps I should not have been quite so blunt. What I meant, of course, was that many of the synthetic foods we now eat have the same formula as the old natural products; some of them, indeed, are such exact replicas that no chemical or other test could reveal any difference. This situation is logical and inevitable; we manufacturers simply took the most popular presynthetic foods as our models, and reproduced their taste and texture.

Of course, we also created new names that didn't hint of an anatomical or zoological origin, so that no one would be reminded of the facts of life. When you go into a restaurant, most of the words you'll find on the menu have been invented since the beginning of the twenty-first century, or else adapted from French originals that few people would recognize. If you ever want to find your threshold of tolerance, you can try an interesting but highly unpleasant experiment. The classified section of the Library of Congress has a large number of menus from famous restaurants—yes, and White House banquets—going back for five hundred years. They have a crude, dissecting-room frankness that makes them almost unreadable. I cannot think of anything that reveals more vividly the gulf between us and our ancestors of only a few generations ago. . . .

Yes, Mr. Chairman—I *am* coming to the point; all this is highly relevant, however disagreeable it may be. I am not trying to spoil your appetites; I am merely laying the groundwork for the charge I wish to bring against my competitor, Triplanetary Food Corporation. Unless you understand this background, you may think that this is a frivolous complaint inspired by the admittedly serious losses my firm has sustained since Ambrosia Plus came on the market.

New foods, gentlemen, are invented every week. It is hard to keep track of them. They come and go like women's fashions, and only one in a thousand becomes a permanent addition to the menu. It is *extremely* rare for one to hit the public fancy overnight, and I freely admit that the Ambrosia Plus line of dishes has been the greatest success in the entire history of food manufacture. All you know the position: everything else has been swept off the market.

Naturally, we were forced to accept the challenge. The biochemists of my organization are as good as any in the solar system, and they promptly got to work on Ambrosia Plus. I am not giving away any trade secrets when I tell you that we have tapes of practically every food, natural or synthetic, that has ever been eaten by mankind—right back to exotic items that you've never heard of, like fried squid, locusts in honey, peacocks' tongues, Venusian polypod. . . . Our enormous library of flavors and textures is our basic stock in trade, and it is with all firms in the business. From it we can select and mix items in any conceivable combination; and usually we can duplicate, without too much trouble, any product that our competitors put out.

But Ambrosia Plus had us baffled for quite some time. Its protein-fat breakdown classified it as a straightforward meat, without too many complications—yet we couldn't match it exactly. It was the first time my chemists had failed; not one of them could explain just what gave the stuff its extraordinary appeal—which, as we all know, makes every other food seem insipid by comparison. As well it might . . . but I am getting ahead of myself.

Very shortly, Mr. Chairman, the president of Triplanetary Foods will be appearing before you—rather reluctantly, I'm sure. He will tell you that Ambrosia Plus is synthesized from air, water, limestone, sulphur, phosphorus, and the rest. That will be perfectly true, but it will be the least important part of the story. For we have now discovered his secret—which, like most secrets, is very simple once you know it.

I really must congratulate my competitor. He has at last made available unlimited quantities of what is, from the nature of things, the ideal food for mankind. Until now, it has been in extremely short supply, and therefore all the more relished by the few connoisseurs who could obtain it. Without exception, they have sworn that nothing else can remotely compare with it.

Yes, Triplanetary's chemists have done a superb technical job. Now *you* have to resolve the moral and philosophical issues. When I began my evidence, I used the archaic word "carnivore." Now I must introduce you to another: I'll spell it out the first time: C-A-N-N-I-B-A-L. . . .

May 1961

MAELSTROM II

HE WAS NOT the first man, Cliff Leyland told himself bitterly, to know the exact second and the precise manner of his death. Times beyond number, condemned criminals had waited for their last dawn. Yet until the very end they could hope for a reprieve; human judges can show mercy. But against the laws of nature, there is no appeal.

And only six hours ago, he had been whistling happily while he packed his ten kilos of personal baggage for the long fall home. He could still remember (even now, after all that had happened) how he had dreamed that Myra was already in his arms, that he was taking Brian and Sue on that promised cruise down the Nile. In a few minutes, as Earth rose above the horizon, he might see the Nile again; but memory alone could bring back the faces of his wife and children. And all because he had tried to save nine hundred and fifty sterling dollars by riding home on the freight catapult, instead of the rocket shuttle.

He had expected the first twelve seconds of the trip to be rough, as the electric launcher whipped the capsule along its

ten-mile track and shot him off the Moon. Even with the
protection of the water-bath in which he would float during
countdown, he had not looked forward to the twenty g's of
take-off. Yet when the acceleration had gripped the capsule,
he had been hardly aware of the immense forces acting upon
him. The only sound was a faint creaking from the metal
walls; to anyone who had experienced the thunder of a
rocket launch the silence was uncanny. When the cabin
speaker had announced "T plus five seconds; speed two
thousand miles an hour," he could scarcely believe it.

Two thousand miles an hour in five seconds from a stand
ing start with seven seconds still to go as the generators
smashed their thunderbolts of power into the launcher. He
was riding the lightning across the face of the Moon. And at
T plus seven seconds, the lightning failed.

Even in the womblike shelter of the tank, Cliff could
sense that something had gone wrong. The water around
him, until now frozen almost rigid by its weight, seemed
suddenly to become alive. Though the capsule was still hurtling along the track, all acceleration had ceased, and it was
merely coasting under its own momentum.

He had no time to feel fear, or to wonder what had happened for the power failure lasted little more than a second.
Then with a jolt that shook the capsule from end to end and
set off a series of ominous, tinkling crashes, the field came on
again.

When the acceleration faded for the last time, all weight
vanished with it. Cliff needed no instrument but his stomach
to tell that the capsule had left the end of the track and was
rising away from the surface of the Moon. He waited impatiently until the automatic pumps had drained the tank and
the hot-air driers had done their work; then he drifted across
the control panel, and pulled himself down into the bucket
seat.

"Launch Control," he called urgently, as he drew the
restraining straps around his waist, "what the devil happened?"

A brisk but worried voice answered at once.

"We're still checking—call you back in thirty seconds."
Then it added belatedly. "Glad you're O.K."

While he was waiting, Cliff switched to forward vision.
There was nothing ahead except stars—which was as it

should be. At least he had taken off with most of his planned speed, and there was no danger that he would crash back to the Moon's surface immediately. But he would crash back sooner or later, for he could not possibly have reached escape velocity. He must be rising out into space along a great ellipse—and, in a few hours, he would be back at his starting point.

"Hello Cliff," said Launch Control suddenly. "We've found what happened. The circuit breakers tripped when you went through section five of the track. So your take-off speed was seven hundred miles an hour low. That will bring you back in just over five hours—but don't worry; your course-correction jets can boost you into a stable orbit. We'll tell you when to fire them. Then all you have to do is to sit tight until we can send someone to haul you down."

Slowly, Cliff allowed himself to relax. He had forgotten the capsule's vernier rockets. Low-powered though they were, they could kick him into an orbit that would clear the Moon. Though he might fall back to within a few miles of the lunar surface, skimming over mountains and plains at a breath-taking speed, he would be perfectly safe.

Then he remembered those tinkling crashes from the control compartment, and his hopes dimmed again, for there were not many things that could break in a space vehicle without most unpleasant consequences.

He was facing those consequences, now that the final checks of the ignition circuits had been completed. Neither on MANUAL nor on AUTO would the navigation rockets fire. The capsule's modest fuel reserves, which could have taken him to safety, were utterly useless. In five hours he would complete his orbit—and return to his launching point.

I wonder if they'll name the new crater after me, thought Cliff. "Crater Leyland: diameter . . ." What diameter? Better not exaggerate—I don't suppose it will be more than a couple of hundred yards across. Hardly worth putting on the map.

Launch Control was still silent, but that was not surprising. There was little that one could say to a man already as good as dead. And yet, though he knew that nothing could alter his trajectory, even now he could not believe that he would soon be scattered over most of Farside. He was still soaring away from the Moon, snug and comfortable in his little cabin. The idea of death was utterly incongruous—as it is to all men until the final second.

And then, for a moment, Cliff forgot his own problem. The horizon ahead was no longer flat. Something more brilliant even than the blazing lunar landscape was lifting against the stars. As the capsule curved round the edge of the Moon, it was creating the only kind of earthrise that was possible—a man-made one. In a minute it was all over, such was his speed in orbit. By that time the Earth had leaped clear of the horizon, and was climbing swiftly up the sky.

It was three-quarters full, and almost too bright to look upon. Here was a cosmic mirror made not of dull rocks and dusty plains, but of snow and cloud and sea. Indeed, it was almost all sea, for the Pacific was turned toward him, and the blinding reflection of the sun covered the Hawaiian Islands. The haze of the atmosphere—that soft blanket that should have cushioned his descent in a few hours' time—obliterated all geographical details; perhaps that darker patch emerging from night was New Guinea, but he could not be sure.

There was a bitter irony in the knowledge that he was heading straight toward that lovely, gleaming apparition. Another seven hundred miles an hour and he would have made it. Seven hundred miles an hour—that was all. He might as well ask for seven million.

The sight of the rising Earth brought home to him, with irresistible force, the duty he feared but could postpone no longer.

"Launch Control," he said, holding his voice steady with a great effort, "please give me a circuit to Earth."

This was one of the strangest things he had ever done in his life: to sit here above the Moon and listen to the telephone ring in his own home, a quarter of a million miles away. It must be near midnight down there in Africa, and it would be some time before there would be any answer. Myra would stir sleepily; then, because she was a spaceman's wife, always alert for disaster, she would be instantly awake. But they had both hated to have a phone in the bedroom, and it would be at least fifteen seconds before she could switch on the light, close the nursery door to avoid disturbing the baby, get down the stairs, and . . .

Her voice came clear and sweet across the emptiness of

space. He would recognize it anywhere in the universe, and he detected at once the undertone of anxiety.

"Mrs. Leyland?" said the Earthside operator. "I have a call from your husband. Please remember the two-second time lag."

Cliff wondered how many people were listening to this call, on either the Moon, the Earth, or the relay satellites. It was hard to talk for the last time to your loved ones when you didn't know how many eavesdroppers there might be. But as soon as he began to speak, no one else existed but Myra and himself.

"Darling," he began, "this is Cliff. I'm afraid I won't be coming home, as I promised. There's been a . . . a technical slip. I'm quite all right at the moment, but I'm in big trouble."

He swallowed, trying to overcome the dryness in his mouth, then went on quickly before she could interrupt. As briefly as he could, he explained the situation. For his own sake as well as hers, he did not abandon all hope.

"Everyone's doing their best," he said. "Maybe they can get a ship up to me in time. But in case they can't . . . well, I wanted to speak to you and the children."

She took it well, as he had known that she would. He felt pride as well as love when her answer came back from the dark side of Earth.

"Don't worry, Cliff. I'm sure they'll get you out, and we'll have our holiday after all, exactly the way we planned."

"I think so, too," he lied. "But just in case, would you wake the children? Don't tell them that anything's wrong."

It was an endless half-minute before he heard their sleepy, yet excited, voices. Cliff would willingly have given these last few hours of his life to have seen their faces once again, but the capsule was not equipped with such luxuries as vision. Perhaps it was just as well, for he could not have hidden the truth had he looked into their eyes. They would know it soon enough, but not from him. He wanted to give them only happiness in these last moments together.

Yet it was hard to answer their questions, to tell them that he would soon be seeing them, to make promises that he could not keep. It needed all his self-control when Brian

reminded him of the moondust he had forgotten once before
—but had remembered this time.

"I've got it, Brian; it's in a jar right beside me. Soon
you'll be able to show it to your friends." (No: soon it will be
back on the world from which it came.) "And Susie—be a
good girl and do everything that Mummy tells you. Your
last school report wasn't too good, you know, especially
those remarks about behavior. . . . Yes, Brian, I have those
photographs, and the piece of rock from Aristarchus. . . ."

It was hard to die at thirty-five; but it was hard, too, for a
boy to lose his father at ten. How would Brian remember
him in the years ahead? Perhaps as no more than a fading
voice from space, for he had spent so little time on Earth. In
the last few minutes, as he swung outward and then back to
the Moon, there was little enough that he could do except
project his love and his hopes across the emptiness that he
would never span again. The rest was up to Myra.

When the children had gone, happy but puzzled, there
was work to do. Now was the time to keep one's head, to be
businesslike and practical. Myra must face the future without him, but at least he could make the transition easier.
Whatever happens to the individual, life goes on; and to
modern man life involves mortgages and installments due,
insurance policies and joint bank accounts. Almost imper-
sonally, as if they concerned someone else—which would
soon be true enough—Cliff began to talk about these things.
There was a time for the heart and a time for the brain. The
heart would have its final say three hours from now, when
he began his last approach to the surface of the Moon.

No one interrupted them. There must have been silent
monitors maintaining the link between two worlds, but the
two of them might have been the only people alive. Sometimes while he was speaking Cliff's eyes would stray to the
periscope, and be dazzled by the glare of Earth—now more
than halfway up the sky. It was impossible to believe that it
was home for seven billion souls. Only three mattered to
him now.

It should have been four, but with the best will in the
world he could not put the baby on the same footing as the
others. He had never seen his younger son; and now he
never would.

At last he could think of no more to say. For some things,

a lifetime was not enough—but an hour could be too much. He felt physically and emotionally exhausted, and the strain on Myra must have been equally great. He wanted to be alone with his thoughts and with the stars, to compose his mind and to make his peace with the universe.

"I'd like to sign off for an hour or so, darling," he said. There was no need for explanations; they understood each other too well. "I'll call you back—in plenty of time. Good-by for now."

He waited the two and a half seconds for the answering good-by from Earth; then he cut the circuit and stared blankly at the tiny control desk. Quite unexpectedly, without desire or volition, tears sprang from his eyes, and suddenly he was weeping like a child.

He wept for his family, and for himself. He wept for the future that might have been, and the hopes that would soon be incandescent vapor, drifting between the stars. And he wept because there was nothing else to do.

After a while he felt much better. Indeed, he realized that he was extremely hungry. There was no point in dying on an empty stomach, and he began to rummage among the space rations in the closet-sized galley. While he was squeezing a tube of chicken-and-ham paste into his mouth, Launch Control called.

There was a new voice at the end of the line—a slow, steady, and immensely competent voice that sounded as if it would brook no nonsense from inanimate machinery.

"This is Van Kessel, Chief of Maintenance, Space Vehicles Division. Listen carefully, Leyland. We think we've found a way out. It's a long shot—but it's the only chance you have."

Alternations of hope and despair are hard on the nervous system. Cliff felt a sudden dizziness; he might have fallen had there been any direction in which to fall.

"Go ahead," he said faintly, when he had recovered. Then he listened to Van Kessel with an eagerness that slowly changed to incredulity.

"I don't believe it!" he said at last. "It just doesn't make sense!"

"You can't argue with the computers," answered Van Kessel. "They've checked the figures about twenty different ways. And it makes sense, all right. You won't be moving so fast as apogee, and it doesn't need much of a kick then to change your orbit. I suppose you've never been in a deep-space rig before?"

"No, of course not."

"Pity—but never mind. If you follow instructions, you can't go wrong. You'll find the suit in the locker at the end of the cabin. Break the seals and haul it out."

Cliff floated the full six feet from the control desk to the rear of the cabin and pulled on the lever marked EMER-GENCY ONLY—TYPE 17 DEEP-SPACE SUIT. The door opened, and the shining silver fabric hung flaccid before him.

"Strip down to your underclothes and wriggle into it," said Van Kessel. "Don't bother about the biopack—you clamp that on later."

"I'm in," said Cliff presently. "What do I do now?"

"You wait twenty minutes—and then we'll give you the signal to open the air lock and jump."

The implications of that word "jump" suddenly pene-trated. Cliff looked around the now familiar, comforting lit-tle cabin, and then thought of the lonely emptiness between the stars—the unreverberant abyss through which a man could fall until the end of time.

He had never been in free space; there was no reason why he should. He was just a farmer's boy with a master's degree in agronomy, seconded from the Sahara Reclamation Proj-ect and trying to grow crops on the Moon. Space was not for him; he belonged to the worlds of soil and rock, of moon-dust and vacuum-formed pumice.

"I can't do it," he whispered. "Isn't there any other way?"

"There's not," snapped Van Kessel. "We're doing our damnedest to save you, and this is no time to get neurotic. Dozens of men have been in far worse situations—badly injured, trapped in wreckage a million miles from help. But you're not even scratched, and already you're squealing! Pull yourself together—or we'll sign off and leave you to stew in your own juice."

Cliff turned slowly red, and it was several seconds before he answered.

"I'm all right," he said at last. "Let's go through those instructions again."

"That's better," said Van Kessel approvingly. "Twenty minutes from now, when you're at apogee, you'll go into the air lock. From that point, we'll lose communication; your suit radio has only a ten-mile range. But we'll be tracking you on radar and we'll be able to speak to you when you pass over us again. Now, about the controls on your suit . . ."

The twenty minutes went quickly enough. At the end of that time, Cliff knew exactly what he had to do. He had even come to believe that it might work.

"Time to bail out," said Van Kessel. "The capsule's correctly oriented —the air lock points the way you want to go. But direction isn't critical. *Speed* is what matters. Put everything you've got into that jump—and good luck!"

"Thanks," said Cliff inadequately. "Sorry that I . . ."

"Forget it," interrupted Van Kessel. "Now get moving!"

For the last time, Cliff looked around the tiny cabin, wondering if there was anything that he had forgotten. All his personal belongings would have to be abandoned, but they could be replaced easily enough. Then he remembered the little jar of moondust he had promised Brian; this time he would not let the boy down. The minute mass of the sample —only a few ounces—would make no difference to his fate. He tied a piece of string around the neck of the jar and attached it to the harness of his suit.

The air lock was so small that there was literally no room to move; he stood sandwiched between inner and outer doors until the automatic pumping sequence was finished. Then the wall slowly opened away from him, and he was facing the stars.

With his clumsy gloved fingers, he hauled himself out of the air lock and stood upright on the steeply curving hull, bracing himself tightly against it with the safety line. The splendor of the scene held him almost paralyzed. He forgot all his fears of vertigo and insecurity as he gazed around him, no longer constrained by the narrow field of vision of the periscope.

The Moon was a gigantic crescent, the dividing line between night and day a jagged arch sweeping across a quarter of the sky. Down there the sun was setting, at the beginning of the long lunar night, but the summits of isolated peaks were still blazing with the last light of day, defying the darkness that had already encircled them.

That darkness was not complete. Though the sun had gone from the land below, the almost full Earth flooded it with glory. Cliff could see, faint but clear in the glimmering earthlight, the outlines of seas and highlands, the dim stars of mountain peaks, the dark circles of craters. He was flying above a ghostly, sleeping land—a land that was trying to drag him to his death. For now he was poised at the highest point of his orbit, exactly on the line between Moon and Earth. It was time to go.

He bent his legs, crouching against the hull. Then, with all his force, he launched himself toward the stars, letting the safety line run out behind him.

The capsule receded with surprising speed, and as it did so, he felt a most unexpected sensation. He had anticipated terror or vertigo, but not this unmistakable, haunting sense of familiarity. All this had happened before; not to him, of course, but to someone else. He could not pinpoint the memory, and there was no time to hunt for it now.

He flashed a quick glance at Earth, Moon, and receding spacecraft, and made his decision without conscious thought. The line whipped away as he snapped the quick-release. Now he was alone, two thousand miles above the Moon, a quarter of a million miles from Earth. He could do nothing but wait; it would be two and a half hours before he would know if he could live—and if his own muscles had performed the task that the rockets had failed to do.

And as the stars slowly revolved around him, he suddenly knew the origin of that haunting memory. It was many years since he had read Poe's short stories, but who could ever forget them?

He, too, was trapped in a maelstrom, being whirled down to his doom; he, too, hoped to escape by abandoning his vessel. Though the forces involved were totally different, the parallel was striking. Poe's fisherman had lashed himself to a barrel because stubby, cylindrical objects were being sucked down into the great whirlpool more slowly than his ship. It was a brilliant application of the laws of hydrodynamics. Cliff could only hope that his use of celestial mechanics would be equally inspired.

How fast had he jumped away from the capsule? At a

good five miles an hour, surely. Trivial though that speed was by astronomical standards, it should be enough to inject him into a new orbit—one that, Van Kessel had promised him, would clear the Moon by several miles. That was not much of a margin, but it would be enough on this airless world, where there was no atmosphere to claw him down.

With a sudden spasm of guilt, Cliff realized that he had never made that second call to Myra. It was Van Kessel's fault; the engineer had kept him on the move, given him no time to brood over his own affairs. And Van Kessel was right: in a situation like this, a man could think only of himself. All his resources, mental and physical, must be concentrated on survival. This was no time or place for the distracting and weakening ties of love.

He was racing now toward the night side of the Moon, and the daylit crescent was shrinking as he watched. The intolerable disc of the Sun, at which he dared not look, was falling swiftly toward the curved horizon. The crescent moonscape dwindled to a burning line of light, a bow of fire set against the stars. Then the bow fragmented into a dozen shining beads, which one by one winked out as he shot into the shadow of the Moon.

With the going of the Sun, the earthlight seemed more brilliant than ever, frosting his suit with silver as he rotated slowly along his orbit. It took him about ten seconds to make each revolution; there was nothing he could do to check his spin, and indeed he welcomed the constantly changing view. Now that his eyes were no longer distracted by occasional glimpses of the Sun, he could see the stars in thousands, where there had been only hundreds before. The familiar constellations were drowned, and even the brightest of the planets were hard to find in that blaze of light.

The dark disc of the lunar night land lay across the star field like an eclipsing shadow, and it was slowly growing as he fell toward it. At every instant some star, bright or faint, would pass behind its edge and wink out of existence. It was almost as if a hole were growing in space, eating up the heavens.

There was no other indication of his movement, or of the passage of time—except for his regular ten-second spin. When he looked at his watch, he was astonished to see that he had left the capsule half an hour ago. He searched for it among the stars, without success. By now, it would be several miles behind. But presently it would draw ahead of him, as it moved on its lower orbit, and would be the first to reach the Moon.

Cliff was still puzzling over this paradox when the strain of the last few hours, combined with the euphoria of weightlessness, produced a result he would hardly have believed possible. Lulled by the gentle susurration of the air inlets, floating lighter than any feather as he turned beneath the stars, he fell into a dreamless sleep.

When he awoke at some prompting of his subconscious, the Earth was nearing the edge of the Moon. The sight almost brought on another wave of self-pity, and for a moment he had to fight for control of his emotions. This was the very last he might ever see of Earth, as his orbit took him back over Farside, into the land where the earthlight never shone. The brilliant antarctic icecaps, the equatorial cloud belts, the scintillation of the Sun upon the Pacific—all were sinking swiftly behind the lunar mountains. Then they were gone; he had neither Sun nor Earth to light him now, and the invisible land below was so black that it hurt his eyes.

Unbelievably, a cluster of stars had appeared *inside* the darkened disc, where no stars could possibly be. Cliff stared at them in astonishment for a few seconds, then realized he was passing above one of the Farside settlements. Down there beneath the pressure domes of their city, men were waiting out the lunar night—sleeping, working, loving, resting, quarreling. Did they know that he was speeding like an invisible meteor through their sky, racing above their heads at four thousand miles an hour? Almost certainly; for by now the whole Moon, and the whole Earth, must know of his predicament. Perhaps they were searching for him with radar and telescope, but they would have little time to find him. Within seconds, the unknown city had dropped out of sight, and he was once more alone above Farside.

It was impossible to judge his altitude above the blank emptiness speeding below, for there was no sense of scale or perspective. Sometimes it seemed that he could reach out and touch the darkness across which he was racing; yet he knew that in reality it must still be many miles beneath him. But he also knew that he was still descending, and that at any moment one of the crater walls or mountain peaks that strained invisibly toward him might claw him from the sky.

In the darkness somewhere ahead was the final obstacle —the hazard he feared most of all. Across the heart of Farside, spanning the equator from north to south in a wall more than a thousand miles long, lay the Soviet Range. He had been a boy when it was discovered, back in 1959, and could still remember his excitement when he had seen the first smudged photographs from Lunik III. He could never have dreamed that one day he would be flying toward those same mountains, waiting for them to decide his fate.

The first eruption of dawn took him completely by surprise. Light exploded ahead of him, leaping from peak to peak until the whole arc of the horizon was lined with flame. He was hurtling out of the lunar night, directly into the face of the Sun. At least he would not die in darkness, but the greatest danger was yet to come. For now he was almost back where he had started, nearing the lowest point of his orbit. He glanced at the suit chronometer, and saw that five full hours had now passed. Within moments, he would hit the Moon—or skim it and pass safely out into space.

As far as he could judge, he was less than twenty miles above the surface, and he was still descending, though very slowly now. Beneath him, the long shadows of the lunar dawn were daggers of darkness, stabbing toward the night land. The steeply slanting sunlight exaggerated every rise in the ground, making even the smallest hills appear to be mountains. And now, unmistakably, the land ahead was rising, wrinkling into the foothills of the Soviet Range. More than a hundred miles away, but approaching at a mile a second, a wave of rock was climbing from the face of the Moon. There was nothing he could do to avoid it; his path was fixed and unalterable. All that could be done had already been done, two and a half hours ago.

It was not enough. He was not going to rise above these mountains; they were rising above him.

Now he regretted his failure to make that second call to the woman who was still waiting, a quarter of a million miles away. Yet perhaps it was just as well, for there had been nothing more to say.

Other voices were calling in the space around him, as he came once more within range of Launch Control. They waxed and waned as he flashed through the radio shadow of the mountains; they were talking about him, but the fact scarcely registered on him. He listened with an impersonal interest, as if to messages from some remote point of space or time, of no concern to him. Once he heard Van Kessel's voice say, quite distinctly: "Tell *Callisto*'s skipper we'll give him an intercept orbit as soon as we know that Leyland's past perigee. Rendezvous time should be one hour five minutes from now." I hate to disappoint you, thought Cliff, but that's one appointment I'll never keep.

Now the wall of rock was only fifty miles away, and each time he spun helplessly in space it came ten miles closer. There was no room for optimism now, and he sped more swiftly than a rifle bullet toward that implacable barrier. This was the end, and suddenly it became of great importance to know whether he would meet it face first, with open eyes, or with his back turned, like a coward.

No memories of his past life flashed through Cliff's mind as he counted the seconds that remained. The swiftly unrolling moonscape rotated beneath him, every detail sharp and clear in the harsh light of dawn. Now he was turned away from the onrushing mountains, looking back on the path he had traveled, the path that should have led to Earth. No more than three of his ten-second days were left to him.

And then the moonscape exploded into silent flame. A light as fierce as that of the sun banished the long shadows, struck fire from the peaks and craters spread below. It lasted for only a fraction of a second, and had faded completely before he had turned toward its source.

Directly ahead of him, only twenty miles away, a vast cloud of dust was expanding toward the stars. It was as if a volcano had erupted in the Soviet Range—but that, of course, was impossible. Equally absurd was Cliff's second thought—that by some fantastic feat of organization and logistics the Farside Engineering Division had blasted away the obstacle in his path.

For it was gone. A huge, crescent-shaped bite had been taken out of the approaching skyline; rocks and debris were still rising from a crater that had not existed five seconds ago. Only the energy of an atomic bomb, exploded at precisely the right moment in his path, could have wrought such a miracle. And Cliff did not believe in miracles.

He had made another complete revolution, and was almost upon the mountains, when he remembered that, all this while, there had been a cosmic bulldozer moving invisibly ahead of him. The kinetic energy of the abandoned capsule—a thousand tons, traveling at over a mile a second—was quite sufficient to have blasted the gap through which he was now racing. The impact of the man-made meteor must have jolted the whole of Farside.

His luck held to the end. There was a brief pitter-patter of dust particles against his suit, and he caught a blurred glimpse of glowing rocks and swiftly dispersing smoke clouds flashing beneath him. (How strange to see a cloud upon the Moon!) Then he was through the mountains, with nothing ahead but blessed empty sky.

Somewhere up there, an hour in the future along his second orbit, *Callisto* would be moving to meet him. But there was no hurry now; he had escaped from the maelstrom. For better or for worse, he had been granted the gift of life.

There was the launching track, a few miles to the right of his path; it looked like a hairline scribed across the face of the Moon. In a few moments he would be within radio range. Now, with thankfulness and joy, he could make that second call to Earth, to the woman who was still waiting in the African night.

May 1962

THE SHINING ONES

WHEN THE SWITCHBOARD said that the Soviet Embassy was on the line, my first reaction was: "Good—another job!" But the moment I heard Goncharov's voice, I knew there was trouble.

"Klaus? This is Mikhail. Can you come over at once? It's very urgent, and I can't talk on the phone."

I worried all the way to the Embassy, marshaling my defenses in case anything had gone wrong at our end. But I could think of nothing; at the moment, we had no outstanding contracts with the Russians. The last job had been completed six months ago, on time, and to their entire satisfaction.

Well, they were not satisfied with it now, as I discovered quickly enough. Mikhail Goncharov, the Commercial Attaché, was an old friend of mine; he told me all he knew, but it was not much.

"We've just had an urgent cable from Ceylon," he said. "They want you out there immediately. There's serious trouble at the hydrothermal project."

"What sort of trouble?" I asked. I knew at once, of course, that it would be the deep end, for that was the only part of the installation that had concerned us. The Russians themselves had done all the work on land, but they had had to call on us to fix those grids three thousand feet down in the Indian Ocean. There is no other firm in the world that can live up to our motto: ANY JOB, ANY DEPTH.

"All I know," said Mikhail, "is that the site engineers report a complete breakdown, that the Prime Minister of Ceylon is opening the plant three weeks from now, and that Moscow will be very, very unhappy if it's not working then."

My mind went rapidly through the penalty clauses in our contract. The firm seemed to be covered, because the client had signed the takeover certificate, thereby admitting that the job was up to specification. However, it was not as simple as that; if negligence on our part was proved, we might be safe from legal action—but it would be very bad for business. And it would be even worse for me, personally; for I had been project supervisor in Trinco Deep.

Don't call me a diver, please; I hate the name. I'm a deep-sea engineer, and I use diving gear about as often as an airman uses a parachute. Most of my work is done with TV and remote-controlled robots. When I do have to go down myself, I'm inside a minisub with external manipulators. We call it a lobster, because of its claws; the standard model works down to five thousand feet, but there are special versions that will operate at the bottom of the Marianas Trench. I've never been there myself, but will be glad to quote terms if you're interested. At a rough estimate, it will cost you a dollar a foot plus a thousand an hour on the job itself.

I realized that the Russians meant business when Mikhail said that a jet was waiting at Zurich, and could I be at the airport within two hours?

"Look," I said, "I can't do a thing without equipment—and the gear needed even for an inspection weighs tons. Besides, it's all at Spezia."

"I know," Mikhail answered implacably. "We'll have another jet transport there. Cable from Ceylon as soon as you know what you want: it will be on the site within twelve hours. But please don't talk to anyone about this; we prefer to keep our problems to ourselves."

I agreed with this, for it was my problem, too. As I left the office, Mikhail pointed to the wall calendar, said "Three weeks," and ran his finger around his throat. And I knew he wasn't thinking of *his* neck.

Two hours later I was climbing over the Alps, saying good-by to the family by radio, and wondering why, like every other sensible Swiss, I hadn't become a banker or gone into the watch business. It was all the fault of the Picards and Hannes Keller, I told myself moodily: why did they have to start this deep-sea tradition, in Switzerland of all countries? Then I settled down to sleep, knowing that I would have little enough in the days to come.

We landed at Trincomalee just after dawn, and the huge, complex harbor—whose geography I've never quite mastered—was a maze of capes, islands, interconnecting waterways, and basins large enough to hold all the navies of the world. I could see the big white control building, in a somewhat flamboyant architectural style, on a headland overlooking the Indian Ocean. The site was pure propaganda—though of course if I'd been Russian I'd have called it "public relations."

Not that I really blamed my clients; they had good reason to be proud of this, the most ambitious attempt yet made to harness the thermal energy of the sea. It was not the first attempt. There had been an unsuccessful one by the French scientist Georges Claude in the 1930's, and a much bigger one at Abidjan, on the west coast of Africa, in the 1950's.

All these projects depended on the same surprising fact: even in the tropics the sea a mile down is almost at freezing point. When billions of tons of water are concerned, this temperature difference represents a colossal amount of energy—and a fine challenge to the engineers of power-starved countries.

Claude and his successors had tried to tap this energy with low-pressure steam engines; the Russians had used a much simpler and more direct method. For over a hundred years it had been known that electric currents flow in many materials if one end is heated and the other cooled, and ever since the 1940s Russian scientists had been working to put this "thermoelectric" effect to practical use. Their earliest devices had not been very efficient—though good enough to power thousands of radios by the heat of kerosene lamps. But in 1974 they had made a big, and still-secret, breakthrough. Though I fixed the power elements at the cold end of the system, I never really saw them; they were completely hidden in anticorrosive paint. All I know is that they formed a big grid, like lots of old-fashioned steam radiators bolted together.

I recognized most of the faces in the little crowd waiting on the Trinco airstrip; friends or enemies, they all seemed glad to see me—especially Chief Engineer Shapiro.

"Well, Lev," I said, as we drove off in the station wagon, "what's the trouble?"

"We don't know," he said frankly. "It's your job to find out—and to put it right."

"Well, what *happened*?"

"Everything worked perfectly up to the full-power tests," he answered. "Output was within five per cent of estimate until 0134 Tuesday morning." He grimaced; obviously that time was engraved on his heart. "Then the voltage started to fluctuate violently, so we cut the load and watched the meters. I thought that some idiot of a skipper had hooked the cables—you know the trouble we've taken to avoid *that* happening—so we switched on the searchlights and looked out to sea. There wasn't a ship in sight. Anyway, who would have tried to anchor just *outside* the harbor on a clear, calm night?

"There was nothing we could do except watch the instruments and keep testing; I'll show you all the graphs when we get to the office. After four minutes everything went open circuit. We can locate the break exactly, of course—and it's in the deepest part, right at the grid. It *would* be there, and not at *this* end of the system," he added gloomily, pointing out the window.

We were just driving past the Solar Pond—the equivalent of the boiler in a conventional heat engine. This was an idea that the Russians had borrowed from the Israelis. It was simply a shallow lake, blackened at the bottom, holding a concentrated solution of brine. It acts as a very efficient heat trap, and the sun's rays bring the liquid up to almost two hundred degrees Fahrenheit. Submerged in it were the "hot" grids of the thermoelectric system, every inch of two fathoms down. Massive cables connected them to my department, a hundred and fifty degrees colder and three thousand feet lower, in the undersea canyon that comes to the very entrance of Trinco harbor.

"I suppose you checked for earthquakes?" I asked, not very hopefully.

"Of course. There was nothing on the seismograph."

"What about whales? I warned you that they might give trouble."

More than a year ago, when the main conductors were being run out to sea, I'd told the engineers about the drowned sperm whale found entangled in a telegraph cable half a mile down off South America. About a dozen similar cases are known—but ours, it seemed, was not one of them.

"That was the second thing we thought of," answered Shapiro. "We got onto the Fisheries Department, the Navy, and the Air Force. No whales anywhere along the coast."

It was at that point that I stopped theorizing, because I overheard something that made me a little uncomfortable. Like all Swiss, I'm good at languages, and have picked up a fair amount of Russian. There was no need to be much of a linguist, however, to recognize the word *sabotash*.

It was spoken by Dimitri Karpukhin, the political adviser on the project. I didn't like him; nor did the engineers, who sometimes went out of their way to be rude to him. One of the old-style Communists who had never quite escaped from the shadow of Stalin, he was suspicious of everything outside the Soviet Union, and most of the things inside it. Sabotage was just the explanation that would appeal to him.

There were, of course, a great many people who would not exactly be brokenhearted if the Trinco Power Project failed. Politically, the prestige of the USSR was committed; economically, billions were involved, for if hydrothermal plants proved a success, they might compete with oil, coal, water power, and, especially, nuclear energy.

Yet I could not really believe in sabotage; after all, the Cold War was over. It was just possible that someone had made a clumsy attempt to grab a sample of the grid, but even this seemed unlikely. I could count on my fingers the number of people in the world who could tackle such a job —and half of them were on my payroll.

The underwater TV camera arrived that same evening, and by working all through the night we had cameras, monitors, and over a mile of coaxial cable loaded aboard a launch. As we pulled out of the harbor, I thought I saw a familiar figure standing on the jetty, but it was too far to be certain and I had other things on my mind. If you must know, I am not a good sailor; I am only really happy *underneath* the sea.

We took a careful fix on the Round Island lighthouse and stationed ourselves directly above the grid. The self-propelled camera, looking like a midget bathyscape, went over the side; as we watched the monitors, we went with it in spirit.

The water was extremely clear, and extremely empty, but as we neared the bottom there were a few signs of life. A small shark came and stared at us. Then a pulsating blob of jelly went drifting by, followed by a thing like a big spider, with hundreds of hairy legs tangling and twisting together. At last the sloping canyon wall swam into view. We were right on target, for there were the thick cables running down into the depths, just as I had seen them when I made the final check of the installation six months ago.

I turned on the low-powered jets and let the camera drift down the power cables. They seemed in perfect condition, still firmly anchored by the pitons we had driven into the rock. It was not until I came to the grid itself that there was any sign of trouble.

Have you ever seen the radiator grille of a car after it's run into a lamppost? Well, one section of the grid looked very much like that. Something had battered it in, as if a madman had gone to work on it with a sledgehammer.

There were gasps of astonishment and anger from the people looking over my shoulder. I heard *sabotash* muttered again, and for the first time began to take it seriously. The only other explanation that made sense was a falling boulder, but the slopes of the canyon had been carefully checked against this very possibility.

Whatever the cause, the damaged grid had to be replaced. That could not be done until my lobster—all twenty tons of it—had been flown out from the Spezia dockyard where it was kept between jobs.

"Well," said Shapiro, when I had finished my visual inspection and photographed the sorry spectacle on the screen. "How long will it take?"

I refused to commit myself. The first thing I ever learned in the underwater business is that no job turns out as you expect. Cost and time estimates can never be firm because it's not until you're halfway through a contract that you know exactly what you're up against.

My private guess was three days. So I said: "If everything goes well, it shouldn't take more than a week."

Shapiro groaned. "Can't you do it quicker?"

"I won't tempt fate by making rash promises. Anyway, that still gives you two weeks before your deadline."

He had to be content with that, though he kept nagging at me all the way back into the harbor. When we got there, he had something else to think about.

"Morning, Joe," I said to the man who was still waiting patiently on the jetty. "I thought I recognized you on the way out. What are *you* doing here?"

"I was going to ask you the same question."

"You'd better speak to my boss. Chief Engineer Shapiro, meet Joe Watkins, science correspondent of *Time*."

Lev's response was not exactly cordial. Normally, there was nothing he liked better than talking to newsmen, who arrived at the rate of about one a week. Now, as the target date approached, they would be flying in from all directions. Including, of course, Russia. And at the present moment Tass would be just as unwelcome as *Time*.

It was amusing to see how Karpukhin took charge of the situation. From that moment, Joe had permanently attached to him as guide, philosopher, and drinking companion, a smooth young public-relations type named Sergei Markov. Despite all Joe's efforts, the two were inseparable. In the middle of the afternoon, weary after a long conference in Shapiro's office, I caught up with them for a belated lunch at the government resthouse.

"What's going on here, Klaus?" Joe asked pathetically. "I smell trouble, but no one will admit anything."

I toyed with my curry, trying to separate the bits that were safe from those that would take off the top of my head.

"You can't expect me to discuss a client's affairs," I answered.

"You were talkative enough," Joe reminded me, "when you were doing the survey for the Gibraltar Dam."

"Well, yes," I admitted. "And I appreciate the write-up you gave me. But this time there are trade secrets involved. I'm—ah—making some last-minute adjustments to improve the efficiency of the system."

And that, of course, was the truth; for I was indeed hoping to raise the efficiency of the system from its present value of exactly zero.

"Hmm," said Joe sarcastically. "Thank you very much."

"Anyway," I said, trying to head him off, "what's *your* latest crackbrained theory?"

For a highly competent science writer, Joe has an odd liking for the bizarre and the improbable. Perhaps it's a form of escapism; I happen to know that he also writes science fiction, though this is a well-kept secret from his employers. He has a sneaking fondness for poltergeists and ESP and flying saucers, but lost continents are his real specialty.

"I *am* working on a couple of ideas," he admitted. "They cropped up when I was doing the research on this story."

"Go on," I said, not daring to look up from the analysis of my curry.

"The other day I came across a very old map—Ptolemy's, if you're interested—of Ceylon. It reminded me of another old map in my collection, and I turned it up. There was the same central mountain, the same arrangement of rivers flowing to the sea. But *this* was a map of Atlantis."

"Oh, no!" I groaned. "Last time we met, you convinced me that Atlantis was in the western Mediterranean basin."

Joe gave his engaging grin.

"I could be wrong, couldn't I? Anyway, I've a much more striking piece of evidence. What's the old national name for Ceylon—and the modern Sinhalese one, for that matter?"

I thought for a second, then exclaimed: "Good Lord! Why, Lanka, of course. Lanka—Atlantis." I rolled the names off my tongue.

"Precisely," said Joe. "But two clues, however striking, don't make a full-fledged theory; and that's as far as I've got at the moment."

"Too bad," I said, genuinely disappointed. "And your other project?"

"This will really make you sit up," Joe answered smugly. He reached into the battered briefcase he always carried and pulled out a bundle of papers.

"This happened only one hundred and eighty miles from here, and just over a century ago. The source of my information, you'll note, is about the best there is."

He handed me a photostat, and I saw that it was a page of the London *Times* for July 4, 1874. I started to read without much enthusiasm, for Joe was always producing bits of ancient newspapers, but my apathy did not last for long.

Briefly—I'd like to give the whole thing, but if you want more details your local library can dial you a facsimile in ten seconds—the clipping described how the one-hundred-and-fifty-ton schooner *Pearl* left Ceylon in early May 1874 and then fell becalmed in the Bay of Bengal. On May 10, just before nightfall, an enormous squid surfaced half a mile from the schooner, whose captain foolishly opened fire on it with his rifle.

The squid swam straight for the *Pearl*, grabbed the masts with its arms, and pulled the vessel over on her side. She sank within seconds, taking two of her crew with her. The others were rescued only by the lucky chance that the P. and O. steamer *Strathowen* was in sight and had witnessed the incident herself.

"Well," said Joe, when I'd read through it for the second time, "what do you think?"

"I don't believe in sea monsters."

"The London *Times*," Joe answered, "is not prone to sensational journalism. And giant squids exist, though the biggest *we* know about are feeble, flabby beasts and don't weigh more than a ton, even when they have arms forty feet long."

"So? An animal like that couldn't capsize a hundred-and-fifty-ton schooner."

"True—but there's a lot of evidence that the so-called

giant squid is merely a large squid. There may be decapods in the sea that really are giants. Why, only a year after the *Pearl* incident, a sperm whale off the coast of Brazil was seen struggling inside gigantic coils which finally *dragged it down into the sea.* You'll find the incident described in the *Illustrated London News* for November 20, 1875. And then, of course, there's that chapter in *Moby Dick. . . ."*

"What chapter?"

"Why, the one called 'Squid.' We know that Melville was a very careful observer—but here he really lets himself go. He describes a calm day when a great white mass rose out of the sea 'like a snow-slide, new slid from the hills.' And this happened here in the Indian Ocean, perhaps a thousand miles south of the *Pearl* incident. Weather conditions were identical, please note.

"What the men of the *Pequod* saw floating on the water —I know this passage by heart, I've studied it so carefully— was a 'vast pulpy mass, furlongs in length and breadth, of a glancing cream-color, innumerable long arms radiating from its center, curling and twisting like a nest of anacondas.' "

"Just a minute," said Sergei, who had been listening to all this with rapt attention. "What's a furlong?"

Joe looked slightly embarrassed.

"Actually, it's an eighth of a mile—six hundred and sixty feet." He raised his hand to stop our incredulous laughter. "Oh, I'm sure Melville didn't mean that *literally.* But here was a man who met sperm whales every day, groping for a unit of length to describe something a lot bigger. So he automatically jumped from fathoms to furlongs. That's my theory, anyway."

I pushed away the remaining untouchable portions of my curry.

"If you think you've scared me out of my job," I said, "you've failed miserably. But I promise you this—when I do meet a giant squid, I'll snip off a tentacle and bring it back as a souvenir."

Twenty-four hours later I was out there in the lobster, sinking slowly down toward the damaged grid. There was no way in which the operation could be kept secret, and Joe was an interested spectator from a nearby launch. That was the Russians' problem, not mine; I had suggested to Shapiro that they take him into their confidence, but this, of course, was vetoed by Karpukhin's suspicious Slavic mind. One could almost see him thinking: Just *why* should an American reporter turn up at this moment? And ignoring the obvious answer that Trincomalee was now big news.

There is nothing in the least exciting or glamorous about deep-water operations—if they're done properly. Excitement means lack of foresight, and that means incompetence. The incompetent do not last long in my business, nor do those who crave excitement. I went about my job with all the pent-up emotion of a plumber dealing with a leaking faucet.

The grids had been designed for easy maintenance, since sooner or later they would have to be replaced. Luckily, none of the threads had been damaged, and the securing nuts came off easily when gripped with the power wrench. Then I switched control to the heavy-duty claws, and lifted out the damaged grid without the slightest difficulty.

It's bad tactics to hurry an underwater operation. If you try to do too much at once, you are liable to make mistakes. And if things go smoothly and you finish in a day a job you said would take a week, the client feels he hasn't had his money's worth. Though I was sure I could replace the grid that same afternoon, I followed the damaged unit up to the surface and closed shop for the day.

The thermoelement was rushed off for an autopsy, and I spent the rest of the evening hiding from Joe. Trinco is a small town, but I managed to keep out of his way by visiting the local cinema, where I sat through several hours of an interminable Tamil movie in which three successive generations suffered identical domestic crises of mistaken identity, drunkenness, desertion, death, and insanity, all in Technicolor and with the sound track turned full up.

The next morning, despite a mild headache, I was at the site soon after dawn. (So was Joe, and so was Sergei, all set for a quiet day's fishing.) I cheerfully waved to them as I climbed into the lobster, and the tender's crane lowered me over the side. Over the other side, where Joe couldn't see it, went the replacement grid. A few fathoms down I lifted it out of the hoist and carried it to the bottom of Trinco Deep, where, without any trouble, it was installed by the middle of the afternoon. Before I surfaced again, the lock nuts had been secured, the conductors spot-welded, and the engineers on shore had completed their continuity tests. By the time I was back on deck, the system was under load once more, everything was back to normal, and even Karpukhin was smiling—except when he stopped to ask himself the question that no one had yet been able to answer.

I still clung to the falling-boulder theory—for want of a better. And I hoped that the Russians would accept it, so that we could stop this silly cloak-and-dagger business with Joe.

No such luck, I realized, when both Shapiro and Karpukhin came to see me with very long faces.

"Klaus," said Lev, "we want you to go down again."

"It's your money," I replied. "But what do you want me to do?"

"We've examined the damaged grid, and there's a section of the thermoelement missing. Dimitri thinks that—someone—has deliberately broken it off and carried it away."

"Then they did a damn clumsy job," I answered. "I can promise you it wasn't one of *my* men."

It was risky to make such jokes around Karpukhin, and no one was at all amused. Not even me; for by this time I was beginning to think that he had something.

The sun was setting when I began my last dive into Trinco Deep, but the end of day has no meaning down there. I fell for two thousand feet with no lights, because I like to watch the luminous creatures of the sea, as they flash and flicker in the darkness, sometimes exploding like rockets just outside the observation window. In this open water, there was no danger of a collision; in any case, I had the panoramic sonar scan running, and that gave far better warning than my eyes.

At four hundred fathoms, I knew that something was wrong. The bottom was coming into view on the vertical sounder—but it was approaching much too slowly. My rate of descent was far too slow. I could increase it easily enough by flooding another buoyancy tank—but I hesitated to do so. In my business, anything out of the ordinary needs an explanation; three times I have saved my life by waiting until I had one.

The thermometer gave me the answer. The temperature outside was five degrees higher than it should have been, and I am sorry to say that it took me several seconds to realize why.

Only a few hundred feet below me, the repaired grid was now running at full power, pouring out megawatts of heat as it tried to equalize the temperature difference between Trinco Deep and the Solar Pond up there on land. It wouldn't succeed, of course; but in the attempt it was generating electricity—and I was being swept upward in the geyser of warm water that was an incidental by-product.

When I finally reached the grid, it was quite difficult to keep the lobster in position against the upwelling current, and I began to sweat uncomfortably as the heat penetrated into the cabin. Being too hot on the sea bed was a novel experience; so also was the miragelike vision caused by the ascending water, which made my searchlights dance and tremble over the rock face I was exploring.

You must picture me, lights ablaze in that five-hundred-fathom darkness, moving slowly down the slope of the canyon, which at this spot was about as steep as the roof of a house. The missing element—*if* it was still round—could not have fallen very far before coming to rest. I would find it in ten minutes, or not at all.

After an hour's searching, I had turned up several broken light bulbs (it's astonishing how many get thrown overboard from ships—the sea beds of the world are covered with them), an empty beer bottle (same comment), and a brand-new boot. That was the last thing I found, for then I discovered that I was no longer alone.

I never switch off the sonar scan, and even when I'm not moving I always glance at the screen about once a minute to check the general situation. The situation now was that a large object—at least the size of the lobster—was approaching from the north. When I spotted it, the range was about five hundred feet and closing slowly. I switched off my lights, cut the jets I had been running at low power to hold me in the turbulent water, and drifted with the current.

Though I was tempted to call Shapiro and report that I had company, I decided to wait for more information. There were only three nations with depth ships that could operate at this level, and I was on excellent terms with all of them. It would never do to be too hasty, and to get myself involved in unnecessary political complications.

Though I felt blind without the sonar, I did not wish to advertise my presence, so I reluctantly switched it off and relied on my eyes. Anyone working at this depth would have to use lights, and I'd see them coming long before they could see me. So I waited in the hot, silent little cabin, straining my eyes into the darkness, tense and alert but not particularly worried.

First there was a dim glow, at an indefinite distance. It grew bigger and brighter, yet refused to shape itself into any pattern that my mind could recognize. The diffuse glow concentrated into myriad spots, until it seemed that a constellation was sailing toward me. Thus might the rising star clouds of the galaxy appear, from some world close to the heart of the Milky Way.

It is not true that men are frightened of the unknown; they can be frightened only of the known, the already experienced. I could not imagine what was approaching, but no creature of the sea could touch me inside six inches of good Swiss armor plate.

The thing was almost upon me, glowing with the light of its own creation, when it split into two separate clouds. Slowly they came into focus—not of my eyes, but of my understanding—and I knew that beauty and terror were rising toward me out of the abyss.

The terror came first, when I saw that the approaching beasts were squids, and all Joe's tales reverberated in my brain. Then, with a considerable sense of letdown, I realized that they were only about twenty feet long—little larger than the lobster, and a mere fraction of its weight. They could do me no harm. And quite apart from that, their indescribable beauty robbed them of all menace.

This sounds ridiculous, but it is true. In my travels I have seen most of the animals of this world, but none to match the luminous apparitions floating before me now. The colored lights that pulsed and danced along their bodies made them seem clothed with jewels, never the same for two seconds at a time. There were patches that glowed a brilliant blue, like flickering mercury arcs, then changed almost instantly to burning neon red. The tentacles seemed strings of luminous beads, trailing through the water—or the lamps along a super-highway, when you look down upon it from the air at night. Barely visible against this background glow were the enormous eyes, uncannily human and intelligent, each surrounded by a diadem of shining pearls.

I am sorry, but that is the best I can do. Only the movie camera could do justice to these living kaleidoscopes. I do not know how long I watched them, so entranced by their luminous beauty that I had almost forgotten my mission. That those delicate, whiplash tentacles could not possibly have broken the grid was already obvious. Yet the presence of these creatures here was, to say the least, very curious. Karpukhin would have called it suspicious.

I was about to call the surface when I saw something incredible. It had been before my eyes all the time, but I had not realized it until now.

The squids were talking to each other.

Those glowing, evanescent patterns were not coming and going at random. They were as meaningful, I was suddenly sure, as the illuminated signs of Broadway or Piccadilly. Every few seconds there was an image that almost made sense, but it vanished before I could interpret it. I knew, of course, that even the common octopus shows its emotions with lightning-fast color changes—but this was something of a much brighter order. It was real communication: here were two living electric signs, flashing messages to one another.

When I saw an unmistakable picture of the lobster, my last doubts vanished. Though I am no scientist, at that moment I shared the feelings of a Newton or an Einstein at some moment of revelation. *This* would make me famous. . . .

Then the picture changed—in a most curious manner. There was the lobster again, but rather smaller. And there beside it, much smaller still, were two peculiar objects. Each consisted of a pair of black dots surrounded by a pattern of ten radiating lines.

Just now I said that we Swiss are good at languages. However, it required little intelligence to deduce that this was a formalized squid's-eye-view of itself, and that what I was seeing was a crude sketch of the situation. But why the absurdly small size of the squids?

I had no time to puzzle that out before there was another change. A third squid symbol appeared on the living screen —and this one was enormous, completely dwarfing the others. The message shone there in the eternal night for a few seconds. Then the creature bearing it shot off at incredible speed, and left me alone with its companion.

Now the meaning was all too obvious. "My God!" I said to myself. "They feel they can't handle me. They've gone to fetch Big Brother."

And of Big Brother's capabilities, I already had better evidence than Joe Watkins, for all his research and newspaper clippings.

That was the point—you won't be surprised to hear— when I decided not to linger. But before I went, I thought I would try some talking myself.

After hanging here in darkness for so long, I had forgotten the power of my lights. They hurt my eyes, and must have been agonizing to the unfortunate squid. Transfixed by that intolerable glare, its own illumination utterly quenched, it lost all its beauty, becoming no more than a pallid bag of jelly with two black buttons for eyes. For a moment it seemed paralyzed by the shock; then it darted after its companion, while I soared upward to a world that would never be the same again.

"I've found your saboteur," I told Karpukhin, when they opened the hatch of the lobster. "If you want to know all about him, ask Joe Watkins."

I let Dimitri sweat over that for a few seconds while I enjoyed his expression. Then I gave my sightly edited report. I implied—without actually saying so—that the squids I'd met were powerful enough to have done all the damage; and I said nothing about the conversation I'd overseen. That would only cause incredulity. Besides, I wanted time to think matters over, and to tidy up the loose ends—if I could.

Joe has been a great help, though he still knows no more than the Russians. He's told me what wonderfully developed nervous systems squids possess, and has explained how some of them can change their appearance in a flash through instantaneous three-color printing, thanks to the extraordinary network of "chromophores" covering their bodies.

Presumably this evolved for camouflage; but it seems natural—even inevitable—that it should develop into a communication system.

But there's one thing that worries Joe.

"What were they *doing* around the grid?" he keeps asking me plaintively. "They're cold-blooded invertebrates. You'd expect them to dislike heat as much as they object to light."

That puzzles Joe; but it doesn't puzzle me. Indeed, I think it's the key to the whole mystery.

Those squids, I'm now certain, are in Trinco Deep for the same reason that there are men at the South Pole—or on the Moon. Pure scientific curiosity has drawn them from their icy home, to investigate the geyser of hot water welling from the sides of the canyon. Here is a strange and inexplicable phenomenon—possibly one that menaces their way of life. So they have summoned their giant cousin (servant? slave!) to bring them a sample for study. I cannot believe that they have a hope of understanding it; after all, no scientist on earth could have done so as little as a century ago. But they are trying; and that is what matters.

Tomorrow, we begin our countermeasures. I go back into Trinco Deep to fix the great lights that Shapiro hopes will keep the squids at bay. But how long will that ruse work, if intelligence is dawning in the deep?

As I dictate this, I'm sitting here below the ancient battlements of Fort Frederick, watching the Moon come up over the Indian Ocean. If everything goes well, this will serve as the opening of the book that Joe has been badgering me to write. If it doesn't—then hello, Joe, I'm talking to you now. Please edit this for publication, in any way you think fit, and my apologies to you and Lev for not giving you all the facts before. Now you'll understand why.

Whatever happens, please remember this: they are beautiful, wonderful creatures; try to come to terms with them if you can.

TO: Ministry of Power, Moscow
FROM: Lev Shapiro, Chief Engineer, Trincomalee Thermoelectric Power Project

Herewith the complete transcript of the tape recording found among Herr Klaus Muller's effects after his last dive. We are much indebted to Mr. Joe Watkins, of *Time,* for assistance on several points.

You will recall that Herr Muller's last intelligible message was directed to Mr. Watkins and ran as follows: "Joe! You were right about Melville! The thing is absolutely gigan—"

December 1962

THE WIND FROM THE SUN

THE ENORMOUS DISC of sail strained at its rigging, already filled with the wind that blew between the worlds. In three minutes the race would begin, yet now John Merton felt more relaxed, more at peace, than at any time for the past year. Whatever happened when the Commodore gave the starting signal, whether *Diana* carried him to victory or defeat, he had achieved his ambition. After a lifetime spent designing ships for others, now he would sail his own.

"T minus two minutes," said the cabin radio. "Please confirm your readiness."

One by one, the other skippers answered. Merton recognized all the voices—some tense, some calm—for they were the voices of his friends and rivals. On the four inhabited worlds, there were scarcely twenty men who could sail a sun yacht; and they were all there, on the starting line or aboard the escort vessels, orbiting twenty-two thousand miles above the equator.

"Number One—*Gossamer*—ready to go."

"Number Two—*Santa Maria*—all O.K."

"Number Three—*Sunbeam*—O.K."

"Number Four—*Woomera*—all systems GO. "

Merton smiled at that last echo from the early, primitive days of astronautics. But it had become part of the tradition of space; and there were times when a man needed to evoke the shades of those who had gone before him to the stars.

"Number Five—*Lebedev*—we're ready."

"Number Six—*Arachne*—O.K."

Now it was his turn, at the end of the line; strange to think that the words he was speaking in this tiny cabin were being heard by at least five billion people.

"Number Seven—*Diana*—ready to start."

"One through Seven acknowledged," answered that impersonal voice from the judge's launch. "Now T minus one minute."

Merton scarcely heard it. For the last time, he was checking the tension in the rigging. The needles of all the dynamometers were steady; the immense sail was taut, its mirror surface sparkling and glittering gloriously in the sun.

To Merton, floating weightless at the periscope, it seemed to fill the sky. As well it might—for out there were fifty million square feet of sail, linked to his capsule by almost a hundred miles of rigging. All the canvas of all the tea clippers that had once raced like clouds across the China seas, sewn into one gigantic sheet, could not match the single sail that *Diana* had spread beneath the sun. Yet it was little more substantial than a soap bubble; that two square miles of aluminized plastic was only a few millionths of an inch thick.

"T minus ten seconds. All recording cameras ON. "

Something so huge, yet so frail, was hard for the mind to grasp. And it was harder still to realize that this fragile mirror could tow him free of Earth merely by the power of the sunlight it would trap.

". . . five, four, three, two, one, CUT! "

Seven knife blades sliced through seven thin lines tethering the yachts to the mother ships that had assembled and serviced them. Until this moment, all had been circling Earth together in a rigidly held formation, but now the yachts would begin to disperse, like dandelion seeds drifting before the breeze. And the winner would be the one that first drifted past the Moon.

Aboard *Diana*, nothing seemed to be happening. But

Merton knew better. Though his body could feel no thrust, the instrument board told him that he was now accelerating at almost one thousandth of a gravity. For a rocket, that figure would have been ludicrous—but this was the first time any solar yacht had ever attained it. *Diana*'s design was sound; the fast sail was living up to his calculations. At this rate, two circuits of the Earth would build up his speed to escape velocity, and then he could head out for the Moon, with the full force of the Sun behind him.

The full force of the Sun . . . He smiled wryly, remembering all his attempts to explain solar sailing to those lecture audiences back on Earth. That had been the only way he could raise money, in those early days. He might be Chief Designer of Cosmodyne Corporation, with a whole string of successful spaceships to his credit, but his firm had not been exactly enthusiastic about his hobby.

"Hold your hands out to the Sun," he'd said. "What do you feel? Heat, of course. But there's pressure as well—though you've never noticed it, because it's so tiny. Over the area of your hands, it comes to only about a millionth of an ounce.

"But out in space, even a pressure as small as that can be important, for it's acting all the time, hour after hour, day after day. Unlike rocket fuel, it's free and unlimited. If we want to, we can use it. We can build sails to catch the radiation blowing from the Sun."

At that point, he would pull out a few square yards of sail material and toss it toward the audience. The silvery film would coil and twist like smoke, then drift slowly to the ceiling in the hot-air currents.

"You can see how light it is," he'd continue. "A square mile weighs only a ton, and can collect five pounds of radiation pressure. So it will start moving—and we can let it tow us along, if we attach rigging to it.

"Of course, its acceleration will be tiny—about a thousandth of a g. That doesn't seem much, but let's see what it means.

"It means that in the first second, we'll move about a fifth of an inch. I suppose a healthy snail could do better than that. But after a minute, we've covered sixty feet, and will be doing just over a mile an hour. That's not bad, for something driven by pure sunlight! After an hour, we're forty miles from our starting point, and will be moving at eighty miles an hour. Please remember that in space there's no friction; so once you start anything moving, it will keep going forever. You'll be surprised when I tell you what our thousandth-of-a-g sailboat will be doing at the end of a day's run: *almost two thousand miles an hour*! If it starts from orbit—as it has to, of course—it can reach escape velocity in a couple of days. And all without burning a single drop of fuel!"

Well, he'd convinced them, and in the end he'd even convinced Cosmodyne. Over the last twenty years, a new sport had come into being. It had been called the sport of billionaires, and that was true. But it was beginning to pay for itself in terms of publicity and TV coverage. The prestige of four continents and two worlds was riding on this race, and it had the biggest audience in history.

Diana had made a good start; time to take a look at the opposition. Moving very gently—though there were shock absorbers between the control capsule and the delicate rigging, he was determined to run no risks—Merton stationed himself at the periscope.

There they were, looking like silver flowers planted in the dark fields of space. The nearest, South America's *Santa Maria,* was only fifty miles away; it bore a close resemblance to a boy's kite, but a kite more than a mile on a side. Farther away, the University of Astrograd's *Lebedev* looked like a Maltese cross; the sail that formed the four arms could apparently be tilted for steering purposes. In contrast, the Federation of Australasia's *Woomera* was a simple parachute, four miles in circumference. General Spacecraft's *Arachne,* as its name suggested, looked like a spider web, and had been built on the same principles, by robot shuttles spiraling out from a central point. Eurospace Corporation's *Gossamer* was an identical design, on a slightly smaller scale. And the Republic of Mars's *Sunbeam* was a flat ring, with a half-mile-wide hole in the center, spinning slowly, so that centrifugal force gave it stiffness. That was an old idea, but no one had ever made it work; and Merton was fairly sure that the colonials would be in trouble when they started to turn.

That would not be for another six hours, when the yachts had moved along the first quarter of their slow and stately twenty-four-hour orbit. Here at the beginning of the race, they were all heading directly away from the Sun—running as it were, before the solar wind. One had to make the most of this lap, before the boats swung around to the other side of Earth and then started to head back into the Sun.

Time, Merton told himself, for the first check, while he had no navigational worries. With the periscope, he made a careful examination of the sail, concentrating on the points where the rigging was attached to it. The shroud lines— narrow bands of unsilvered plastic film—would have been completely invisible had they not been coated with fluorescent paint. Now they were taut lines of colored light, dwindling away for hundreds of yards toward that gigantic sail. Each had its own electric windlass, not much bigger than a game fisherman's reel. The little windlasses were continually turning, playing lines in or out as the autopilot kept the sail trimmed at the correct angle to the Sun.

The play of sunlight on the great flexible mirror was beautiful to watch. The sail was undulating in slow, stately oscillations, sending multiple images of the Sun marching across it, until they faded away at its edges. Such leisurely vibrations were to be expected in this vast and flimsy structure. They were usually quite harmless, but Merton watched them carefully. Sometimes they could build up to the catastrophic undulations known as the "wriggles," which could tear a sail to pieces.

When he was satisfied that everything was shipshape, he swept the periscope around the sky, rechecking the positions of his rivals. It was as he had hoped: the weeding-out process had begun, as the less efficient boats fell astern. But the real test would come when they passed into the shadow of Earth. Then, maneuverability would count as much as speed.

It seemed a strange thing to do, what with the race having just started, but he thought it might be a good idea to get some sleep. The two-man crews on the other boats could take it in turns, but Merton had no one to relieve him. He must rely on his own physical resources, like that other solitary seaman, Joshua Slocum, in his tiny *Spray*. The American skipper had sailed *Spray* singlehanded around the world; he could never have dreamed that, two centuries later, a man would be sailing singlehanded from Earth to Moon—inspired, at least partly, by his example.

Merton snapped the elastic bands of the cabin seat around his waist and legs, then placed the electrodes of the sleep-inducer on his forehead. He set the timer for three hours, and relaxed. Very gently, hypnotically, the electronic pulses throbbed in the frontal lobes of his brain. Colored spirals of light expanded beneath his closed eyelids, widening outward to infinity. Then nothing. . . .

The brazen clamor of the alarm dragged him back from his dreamless sleep. He was instantly awake, his eyes scanning the instrument panel. Only two hours had passed—but above the accelerometer, a red light was flashing. Thrust was falling; *Diana* was losing power.

Merton's first thought was that something had happened to the sail; perhaps the antispin devices had failed, and the rigging had become twisted. Swiftly, he checked the meters that showed the tension of the shroud lines. Strange—on one side of the sail they were reading normally, but on the other the pull was dropping slowly, even as he watched.

In sudden understanding, Merton grabbed the periscope, switched to wide-angle vision, and started to scan the edge of the sail. Yes—there was the trouble, and it could have only one cause.

A huge, sharp-edged shadow had begun to slide across the gleaming silver of the sail. Darkness was falling upon *Diana,* as if a cloud had passed between her and the Sun. And in the dark, robbed of the rays that drove her, she would lose all thrust and drift helplessly through space.

But, of course, there were no clouds here, more than twenty thousand miles above the Earth. If there was a shadow, it must be made by man.

Merton grinned as he swung the periscope toward the Sun, switching in the filters that would allow him to look full into its blazing face without being blinded.

"Maneuver 4a," he muttered to himself. "We'll see who can play best at *that* game."

It looked as if a giant planet was crossing the face of the Sun; a great black disc had bitten deep into its edge. Twenty miles astern, *Gossamer* was trying to arrange an artificial eclipse, specially for *Diana*'s benefit.

The maneuver was a perfectly legitimate one. Back in the

days of ocean racing, skippers had often tried to rob each other of the wind. With any luck, you could leave your rival becalmed, with his sails collapsing around him—and be well ahead before he could undo the damage.

Merton had no intention of being caught so easily. There was plenty of time to take evasive action; things happened very slowly when you were running a solar sailboat. It would be at least twenty minutes before *Gossamer* could slide completely across the face of the Sun, and leave him in darkness.

Diana's tiny computer—the size of a matchbox, but the equivalent of a thousand human mathematicians—considered the problem for a full second and then flashed the answer. He'd have to open control panels three and four, until the sail had developed an extra twenty degrees of tilt; then the radiation pressure would blow him out of *Gossamer*'s dangerous shadow, back into the full blast of the Sun. It was a pity to interfere with the autopilot, which had been carefully programmed to give the fastest possible run—but that, after all, was why he was here. This was what made solar yachting a sport, rather than a battle between computers.

Out went control lines one and six, slowly undulating like sleepy snakes as they momentarily lost their tension. Two miles away, the triangular panels began to open lazily, spilling sunlight through the sail. Yet, for a long time, nothing seemed to happen. It was hard to grow accustomed to this slow-motion world, where it took minutes for the effects of any action to become visible to the eye. Then Merton saw that the sail was indeed tipping toward the Sun—and that *Gossamer*'s shadow was sliding harmlessly away, its cone of darkness lost in the deeper night of space.

Long before the shadow had vanished, and the disc of the Sun had cleared again, he reversed the tilt and brought *Diana* back on course. Her new momentum would carry her clear of the danger; no need to overdo it, and upset his calculations by side-stepping too far. That was another rule that was hard to learn: the very moment you had started something happening in space, it was already time to think about stopping it.

He reset the alarm, ready for the next natural or manmade emergency. Perhaps *Gossamer*, or one of the other contestants, would try the same trick again. Meanwhile, it was time to eat, though he did not feel particularly hungry. One used little physical energy in space, and it was easy to forget about food. Easy—and dangerous; for when an emergency arose, you might not have the reserves needed to deal with it.

He broke open the first of the meal packets, and inspected it without enthusiasm. The name on the label—SPACETASTIES—was enough to put him off. And he had grave doubts about the promise printed underneath: "Guaranteed crumbless." It had been said that crumbs were a greater danger to space vehicles than meteorites; they could drift into the most unlikely places, causing short circuits, blocking vital jets, and getting into instruments that were supposed to be hermetically sealed.

Still, the liverwurst went down pleasantly enough; so did the chocolate and the pineapple purée. The plastic coffee bulb was warming on the electric heater when the outside world broke in upon his solitude, as the radio operator on the Commodore's launch routed a call to him.

"Dr. Merton? If you can spare the time, Jeremy Blair would like a few words with you." Blair was one of the more responsible news commentators, and Merton had been on his program many times. He could refuse to be interviewed, of course, but he liked Blair, and at the moment he could certainly not claim to be too busy. "I'll take it," he answered.

"Hello, Dr. Merton," said the commentator immediately. "Glad you can spare a few minutes. And congratulations—you seem to be ahead of the field."

"Too early in the game to be sure of *that*," Merton answered cautiously.

"Tell me, Doctor, why did you decide to sail *Diana* by yourself? Just because it's never been done before?"

"Well, isn't that a good reason? But it wasn't the only one, of course." He paused, choosing his words carefully. "You know how critically the performance of a sun yacht depends on its mass. A second man, with all his supplies, would mean another five hundred pounds. That could easily be the difference between winning and losing."

"And you're quite certain that you can handle *Diana* alone?"

"Reasonably sure, thanks to the automatic controls I've designed. My main job is to supervise and make decisions."

"But—two square miles of sail! It just doesn't seem possible for one man to cope with all that."

Merton laughed. "Why not? Those two square miles produce a maximum pull of just ten pounds. I can exert more force with my little finger."

"Well, thank you, Doctor. And good luck. I'll be calling you again."

As the commentator signed off, Merton felt a little ashamed of himself. For his answer had been only part of the truth; and he was sure that Blair was shrewd enough to know it.

There was just one reason why he was here, alone in space. For almost forty years he had worked with teams of hundreds or even thousands of men, helping to design the most complex vehicles that the world had ever seen. For the last twenty years he had led one of those teams, and watched his creations go soaring to the stars. (Sometimes . . . There *were* failures, which he could never forget, even though the fault had not been his.) He was famous, with a successful career behind him. Yet he had never done anything by himself; always he had been one of an army.

This was his last chance to try for individual achievement, and he would share it with no one. There would be no more solar yachting for at least five years, as the period of the Quiet Sun ended and the cycle of bad weather began, with radiation storms bursting through the solar system. When it was safe again for these frail, unshielded craft to venture aloft, he would be too old. If, indeed, he was not too old already . . .

He dropped the empty food containers into the waste disposal and turned once more to the periscope. At first he could find only five of the other yachts; there was no sign of *Woomera*. It took him several minutes to locate her—a dim, star-eclipsing phantom, neatly caught in the shadow of *Lebedev*. He could imagine the frantic efforts the Australasians were making to extricate themselves, and wondered how they had fallen into the trap. It suggested that *Lebedev* was unusually maneuverable. She would bear watching, though she was too far away to menace *Diana* at the moment.

Now the Earth had almost vanished; it had waned to a narrow, brilliant bow of light that was moving steadily toward the Sun. Dimly outlined within that burning bow was the night side of the planet, with the phosphorescent gleams of great cities showing here and there through gaps in the clouds. The disc of darkness had already blanked out a huge section of the Milky Way. In a few minutes, it would start to encroach upon the Sun.

The light was fading; a purple, twilight hue—the glow of many sunsets, thousands of miles below—was falling across the sail as *Diana* slipped silently into the shadow of Earth. The Sun plummeted below that invisible horizon; within minutes, it was night.

Merton looked back along the orbit he had traced, now a quarter of the way around the world. One by one he saw the brilliant stars of the other yachts wink out, as they joined him in the brief night. It would be an hour before the Sun emerged from that enormous black shield, and through all that time they would be completely helpless, coasting without power.

He switched on the external spotlight, and started to search the now-darkened sail with its beam. Already the thousands of acres of film were beginning to wrinkle and become flaccid. The shroud lines were slackening, and must be wound in lest they become entangled. But all this was expected; everything was going as planned.

Fifty miles astern, *Arachne* and *Santa Maria* were not so lucky. Merton learned of their troubles when the radio burst into life on the emergency circuit.

"Number Two and Number Six, this is Control. You are on a collision course; your orbits will intersect in sixty-five minutes! Do you require assistance?"

There was a long pause while the two skippers digested this bad news. Merton wondered who was to blame. Perhaps one yacht had been trying to shadow the other, and had not completed the maneuver before they were both caught in darkness. Now there was nothing that either could do. They were slowly but inexorably converging, unable to change course by a fraction of a degree.

Yet—sixty-five minutes! That would just bring them out into sunlight again, as they emerged from the shadow of the Earth. They had a slim chance, if their sails could snatch enough power to avoid a crash. There must be some frantic calculations going on aboard *Arachne* and *Santa Maria*.

Arachne answered first. Her reply was just what Merton had expected.

"Number Six calling Control. We don't need assistance, thank you. We'll work this out for ourselves."

I wonder, thought Merton; but at least it will be interesting to watch. The first real drama of the race was approaching, exactly above the line of midnight on the sleeping Earth.

For the next hour, Merton's own sail kept him too busy to worry about *Arachne* and *Santa Maria*. It was hard to keep a good watch on that fifty million square feet of dim plastic out there in the darkness, illuminated only by his narrow spotlight and the rays of the still-distant Moon. From now on, for almost half his orbit around the Earth, he must keep the whole of this immense area edge-on to the Sun. During the next twelve or fourteen hours, the sail would be a useless encumbrance; for he would be heading *into* the Sun, and its rays could only drive him backward along his orbit. It was a pity that he could not furl the sail completely, until he was ready to use it again; but no one had yet found a practical way of doing this.

Far below, there was the first hint of dawn along the edge of the Earth. In ten minutes the Sun would emerge from its eclipse. The coasting yachts would come to life again as the blast of radiation struck their sails. That would be the moment of crisis for *Arachne* and *Santa Maria*—and, indeed, for all of them.

Merton swung the periscope until he found the two dark shadows drifting against the stars. They were very close together—perhaps less than three miles apart. They might, he decided, just be able to make it. . . .

Dawn flashed like an explosion along the rim of Earth as the Sun rose out of the Pacific. The sail and shroud lines glowed a brief crimson, then gold, then blazed with the pure white light of day. The needles of the dynamometers began to lift from their zeroes—but only just. *Diana* was still almost completely weightless, for with the sail pointing toward the Sun, her acceleration was now only a few millionths of a gravity.

But *Arachne* and *Santa Maria* were crowding on all the sail that they could manage, in their desperate attempt to keep apart. Now, while there was less than two miles between them, their glittering plastic clouds were unfurling and expanding with agonizing slowness as they felt the first delicate push of the Sun's rays. Almost every TV screen on Earth would be mirroring this protracted drama; and even now, at this last minute, it was possible to tell what the outcome would be.

The two skippers were stubborn men. Either could have cut his sail and fallen back to give the other a chance; but neither would do so. Too much prestige, too many millions, too many reputations were at stake. And so, silently and softly as snowflakes falling on a winter night, *Arachne* and *Santa Maria* collided.

The square kite crawled almost imperceptibly into the circular spider web. The long ribbons of the shroud lines twisted and tangled together with dreamlike slowness. Even aboard *Diana,* Merton, busy with his own rigging, could scarcely tear his eyes away from this silent, long-drawn-out disaster.

For more than ten minutes the billowing, shining clouds continued to merge into one inextricable mass. Then the crew capsules tore loose and went their separate ways, missing each other by hundreds of yards. With a flare of rockets, the safety launches hurried to pick them up.

That leaves five of us, thought Merton. He felt sorry for the skippers who had so thoroughly eliminated each other, only a few hours after the start of the race, but they were young men and would have another chance.

Within minutes, the five had dropped to four. From the beginning, Merton had had doubts about the slowly rotating *Sunbeam;* now he saw them justified.

The Martian ship had failed to tack properly. Her spin had given her too much stability. Her great ring of a sail was turning to face the Sun, instead of being edge-on to it. She was being blown back along her course at almost her maximum acceleration.

That was about the most maddening thing that could happen to a skipper—even worse than a collision, for he could blame only himself. But no one would feel much sympathy for the frustrated colonials, as they dwindled slowly astern. They had made too many brash boasts before the race, and what had happened to them was poetic justice.

Yet it would not do to write off *Sunbeam* completely; with almost half a million miles still to go, she might yet pull ahead. Indeed, if there were a few more casualties, she might be the only one to complete the race. It had happened before.

The next twelve hours were uneventful, as the Earth waxed in the sky from new to full. There was little to do while the fleet drifted around the unpowered half of its orbit, but Merton did not find the time hanging heavily on his hands. He caught a few hours of sleep, ate two meals, wrote his log, and became involved in several more radio interviews. Sometimes, though rarely, he talked to the other skippers, exchanging greetings and friendly taunts. But most of the time he was content to float in weightless relaxation, beyond all the cares of Earth, happier than he had been for many years. He was—as far as any man could be in space—master of his own fate, sailing the ship upon which he had lavished so much skill, so much love, that it had become part of his very being.

The next casualty came when they were passing the line between Earth and Sun, and were just beginning the powered half of the orbit. Aboard *Diana,* Merton saw the great sail stiffen as it tilted to catch the rays that drove it. The acceleration began to climb up from the microgravities, though it would be hours yet before it would reach its maximum value.

It would never reach it for *Gossamer.* The moment when power came on again was always critical, and she failed to survive it.

Blair's radio commentary, which Merton had left running at low volume, alerted him with the news: "Hello, *Gossamer* has the wriggles!" He hurried to the periscope, but at first could see nothing wrong with the great circular disc of *Gossamer*'s sail. It was difficult to study it because it was almost edge-on to him and so appeared as a thin ellipse; but presently he saw that it was twisting back and forth in slow, irresistible oscillations. Unless the crew could damp out these waves, by properly timed but gentle tugs on the shroud lines, the sail would tear itself to pieces.

They did their best, and after twenty minutes it seemed that they had succeeded. Then, somewhere near the center of the sail, the plastic film began to rip. It was slowly driven

outward by the radiation pressure, like smoke coiling upward from a fire. Within a quarter of an hour, nothing was
left but the delicate tracery of the radial spars that had supported the great web. Once again there was a flare of rockets, as a launch moved in to retrieve the *Gossamer*'s capsule
and her dejected crew.

"Getting rather lonely up here, isn't it?" said a conversa-
tional voice over the ship-to-ship radio.

"Not for you, Dimitri," retorted Merton. "You've still
got company back there at the end of the field. I'm the one
who's lonely, up here in front." It was not an idle boast; by
this time *Diana* was three hundred miles ahead of the next
competitor, and her lead should increase still more rapidly
in the hours to come.

Aboard *Lebedev,* Dimitri Markoff gave a good-natured
chuckle. He did not sound, Merton thought, at all like a
man who had resigned himself to defeat.

"Remember the legend of the tortoise and the hare,"
answered the Russian. "A lot can happen in the next quar-
ter-million miles."

It happened much sooner than that, when they had completed their first orbit of Earth and were passing the starting
line again—though thousands of miles higher, thanks to the
extra energy the Sun's rays had given them. Merton had
taken careful sights on the other yachts, and had fed the
figures into the computer. The answer it gave for *Woomera*
was so absurd that he immediately did a recheck.

There was no doubt of it—the Australasians were catching up at a completely fantastic rate. No solar yacht could
possibly have such an acceleration, unless . . .

A swift look through the periscope gave the answer.
Woomera's rigging, pared back to the very minimum of
mass, had given way. It was her sail alone, still maintaining
its shape, that was racing up behind him like a handkerchief
blown before the wind. Two hours later it fluttered past, less
than twenty miles away; but long before that, the Australasians had joined the growing crowd aboard the Commodore's launch.

So now it was a straight fight between *Diana* and *Lebedev*
—for though the Martians had not given up, they were a
thousand miles astern and no longer counted as a serious
threat. For that matter, it was hard to see what *Lebedev*

could do to overtake *Diana*'s lead; but all the way around the second lap, through eclipse again and the long, slow drift against the Sun, Merton felt a growing unease.

He knew the Russian pilots and designers. They had been trying to win this race for twenty years—and, after all, it was only fair that they should, for had not Pyotr Niko-laevich Lebedev been the first man to detect the pressure of sunlight, back at the very beginning of the twentieth century? But they had never succeeded.

And they would never stop trying. Dimitri was up to something—and it would be spectacular.

Aboard the official launch, a thousand miles behind the racing yachts, Commodore van Stratten looked at the radiogram with angry dismay. It had traveled more than a hundred million miles, from the chain of solar observatories swinging high above the blazing surface of the Sun; and it brought the worst possible news.

The Commodore—his title was purely honorary, of course; back on Earth he was Professor of Astrophysics at Harvard—had been half expecting it. Never before had the race been arranged so late in the season. There had been many delays; they had gambled—and now, it seemed, they might all lose.

Deep beneath the surface of the Sun, enormous forces were gathering. At any moment the energies of a million hydrogen bombs might burst forth in the awesome explosion known as a solar flare. Climbing at millions of miles an hour, an invisible fireball many times the size of Earth would leap from the Sun and head out across space.

The cloud of electrified gas would probably miss the Earth completely. But if it did not, it would arrive in just over a day. Spaceships could protect themselves, with their shielding and their powerful magnetic screens; but the lightly built solar yachts, with their paper-thin walls, were defenseless against such a menace. The crews would have to be taken off, and the race abandoned.

John Merton knew nothing of this as he brought *Diana* around the Earth for the second time. If all went well, this would be the last circuit, both for him and for the Russians. They had spiraled upward by thousands of miles, gaining energy from the Sun's rays. On this lap, they should escape from Earth completely, and head outward on the long run to the Moon. It was a straight race now; *Sunbeam*'s crew had finally withdrawn exhausted, after battling valiantly with their spinning sail for more than a hundred thousand miles.

Merton did not feel tired; he had eaten and slept well, and *Diana* was behaving herself admirably. The autopilot, tensioning the rigging like a busy little spider, kept the great sail trimmed to the Sun more accurately than any human skipper could have. Though by this time the two square miles of plastic sheet must have been riddled by hundreds of micrometeorites, the pinhead-sized punctures had produced no falling off of thrust.

He had only two worries. The first was shroud line number eight, which could no longer be adjusted properly. Without any warning, the reel had jammed; even after all these years of astronautical engineering, bearings sometimes seized up in vacuum. He could neither lengthen nor shorten the line, and would have to navigate as best he could with the others. Luckily, the most difficult maneuvers were over; from now on, *Diana* would have the Sun behind her as she sailed straight down the solar wind. And as the old-time sailors had often said, it was easy to handle a boat when the wind was blowing over your shoulder.

His other worry was *Lebedev*, still dogging his heels three hundred miles astern. The Russian yacht had shown remarkable maneuverability, thanks to the four great panels that could be tilted around the central sail. Her flipovers as she rounded the Earth had been carried out with superb precision. But to gain maneuverability she must have sacrificed speed. You could not have it both ways; in the long, straight haul ahead, Merton should be able to hold his own. Yet he could not be certain of victory until, three or four days from now, *Diana* went flashing past the far side of the Moon.

And then, in the fiftieth hour of the race, just after the end of the second orbit around Earth, Markoff sprang his little surprise.

"Hello, John," he said, casually over the ship-to-ship circuit. "I'd like you to watch this. It should be interesting."

Merton drew himself across to the periscope and turned up the magnification to the limit. There in the field of view, a most improbable sight against the background of the stars, was the glittering Maltese cross of *Lebedev,* very small but very clear. As he watched, the four arms of the cross slowly detached themselves from the central square, and went drifting away, with all their spars and rigging, into space.

Markoff had jettisoned all unnecessary mass, now that he was coming up to escape velocity and need no longer plod patiently around the Earth, gaining momentum on each circuit. From now on, *Lebedev* would be almost unsteerable— but that did not matter; all the tricky navigation lay behind her. It was as if an old-time yachtsman had deliberately thrown away his rudder and heavy keel, knowing that the rest of the race would be straight downwind over a calm sea.

"Congratulations, Dimitri," Merton radioed. "It's a neat trick. But it's not good enough. You can't catch up with me now."

"I've not finished yet," the Russian answered. "There's an old winter's tale in my country about a sleigh being chased by wolves. To save himself, the driver has to throw off the passengers one by one. Do you see the analogy?"

Merton did, all too well. On this final straight lap, Dimitri no longer needed his copilot. *Lebedev* could really be stripped down for action.

"Alexis won't be very happy about this," Merton replied. "Besides, it's against the rules."

"Alexis isn't happy, but I'm the captain. He'll just have to wait around for ten minutes until the Commodore picks him up. And the regulations say nothing about the size of the crew—*you* should know that."

Merton did not answer; he was too busy doing some hurried calculations, based on what he knew of *Lebedev*'s design. By the time he had finished, he knew that the race was still in doubt. *Lebedev* would be catching up with him at just about the time he hoped to pass the Moon.

But the outcome of the race was already being decided, ninety-two million miles away.

On Solar Observatory Three, far inside the orbit of Mercury, the automatic instruments recorded the whole history of the flare. A hundred million square miles of the Sun's surface exploded in such blue-white fury that, by comparison, the rest of the disc paled to a dull glow. Out of that seething inferno, twisting and turning like a living creature in the magnetic fields of its own creation, soared the electrified plasma of the great flare. Ahead of it, moving at the speed of light, went the warning flash of ultraviolet and X rays. That would reach Earth in eight minutes, and was relatively harmless. Not so the charged atoms that were following behind at their leisurely four million miles an hour—and which, in just over a day, would engulf *Diana, Lebedev,* and their accompanying little fleet in a cloud of lethal radiation.

The Commodore left his decision to the last possible minute. Even when the jet of plasma had been tracked past the orbit of Venus, there was a chance that it might miss the Earth. But when it was less than four hours away, and had already been picked up by the Moon-based radar network, he knew that there was no hope. All solar sailing was over, for the next five or six years—until the Sun was quiet again.

A great sigh of disappointment swept across the solar system. *Diana* and *Lebedev* were halfway between Earth and Moon, running neck and neck—and now no one would ever know which was the better boat. The enthusiasts would argue the result for years; history would merely record: "Race canceled owing to solar storm."

When John Merton received the order, he felt a bitterness he had not known since childhood. Across the years, sharp and clear, came the memory of his tenth birthday. He had been promised an exact scale model of the famous spaceship *Morning Star,* and for weeks had been planning how he would assemble it, where he would hang it in his bedroom. And then, at the last moment, his father had broken the news: "I'm sorry, John—it cost too much money. Maybe next year . . ."

Half a century and a successful lifetime later, he was a heartbroken boy again.

For a moment, he thought of disobeying the Commodore. Suppose he sailed on, ignoring the warning? Even if the race was abandoned, he could make a crossing to the Moon that would stand in the record books for generations.

But that would be worse than stupidity; it would be suicide—and a very unpleasant form of suicide. He had seen men die of radiation poisoning, when the magnetic shielding of their ships had failed in deep space. No—nothing was worth that. . . .

He felt sorry for Dimitri Markoff as for himself. They had both wanted to win, and now victory would go to neither. No man could argue with the Sun in one of its rages, even though he might ride upon its beams to the edge of space.

Only fifty miles astern now, the Commodore's launch was drawing alongside *Lebedev,* preparing to take off her skipper. There went the silver sail, as Dimitri—with feelings that he would share—cut the rigging. The tiny capsule would be taken back to Earth, perhaps to be used again; but a sail was spread for one voyage only.

He could press the jettison button now, and save his rescuers a few minutes of time. But he could not do it; he wanted to stay aboard to the very end, on the little boat that had been for so long a part of his dreams and his life. The great sail was spread now at right angles to the Sun, exerting its utmost thrust. Long ago, it had torn him clear of Earth, and *Diana* was still gaining speed.

Then, out of nowhere, beyond all doubt or hesitation, he knew what must be done. For the last time, he sat down before the computer that had navigated him halfway to the Moon.

When he had finished, he packed the log and his few personal belongings. Clumsily, for he was out of practice, and it was not an easy job to do by oneself, he climbed into the emergency survival suit. He was just sealing the helmet when the Commodore's voice called over the radio.

"We'll be alongside in five minutes, Captain. Please cut your sail, so we won't foul it."

John Merton, first and last skipper of the sun yacht *Diana,* hesitated a moment. He looked for the last time around the tiny cabin, with its shining instruments and its neatly arranged controls, now all locked in their final positions. Then he said into the microphone: "I'm abandoning ship. Take your time to pick me up. *Diana* can look after herself."

There was no reply from the Commodore, and for that he was grateful. Professor van Stratten would have guessed what was happening—and would know that, in these final moments, he wished to be left alone.

He did not bother to exhaust the air lock, and the rush of escaping gas blew him gently out into space. The thrust he gave her then was his last gift to *Diana.* She dwindled away from him, sail glittering splendidly in the sunlight that would be hers for centuries to come. Two days from now she would flash past the Moon; but the Moon, like the Earth, could never catch her. Without his mass to slow her down, she would gain two thousand miles an hour in every day of sailing. In a month, she would be traveling faster than any ship that man had ever built.

As the Sun's rays weakened with distance, so her acceleration would fall. But even at the orbit of Mars, she would be gaining a thousand miles an hour in every day. Long before then, she would be moving too swiftly for the Sun itself to hold her. Faster than a comet had ever streaked in from the stars, she would be heading out into the abyss.

The glare of rockets, only a few miles away, caught Merton's eye. The launch was approaching to pick him up—at thousands of times the acceleration that *Diana* could ever attain. But its engines could burn for a few minutes only, before they exhausted their fuel—while *Diana* would still be gaining speed, driven outward by the Sun's eternal fires, for ages yet to come.

"Good-by, little ship," said John Merton. "I wonder what eyes will see you next, how many thousand years from now?"

At last he felt at peace, as the blunt torpedo of the launch nosed up beside him. He would never win the race to the Moon; but this would be the first of all man's ships to set sail on the long journey to the stars.

May 1963

THE SECRET

HENRY COOPER HAD been on the Moon for almost two weeks before he discovered that something was wrong. At first it was only an ill-defined suspicion, the sort of hunch that a hard-headed science reporter would not take too seriously. He had come here, after all, at the United Nations Space Administration's own request. UNSA had always been hot on public relations—especially just before budget time, when an overcrowded world was screaming for more roads and schools and sea farms, and complaining about the billions being poured into space.

So here he was, doing the lunar circuit for the second time, and beaming back two thousand words of copy a day. Although the novelty had worn off, there still remained the wonder and mystery of a world as big as Africa, thoroughly mapped, yet almost completely unexplored. A stone's throw away from the pressure domes, the labs, the spaceports, was a yawning emptiness that would challenge men for centuries to come.

Some parts of the Moon were almost too familiar, of

course. Who had not seen that dusty scar in the Mare Imbrium, with its gleaming metal pylon and the plaque that announced in the three official languages of Earth:

ON THIS SPOT AT 2001 UT
13 SEPTEMBER 1959
THE FIRST MAN-MADE OBJECT
REACHED ANOTHER WORLD

Cooper had visited the grave of Lunik II—and the more famous tomb of the men who had come after it. But these things belonged to the past; already, like Columbus and the Wright brothers, they were receding into history. What concerned him now was the future.

When he had landed at Archimedes Spaceport, the Chief Administrator had been obviously glad to see him, and had shown a personal interest in his tour. Transportation, accommodation, and official guide were all arranged. He could go anywhere he liked, ask any questions he pleased. UNSA trusted him, for his stories had always been accurate, his attitude friendly. Yet the tour had gone sour; he did not know why, but he was going to find out.

He reached for the phone and said: "Operator? Please get me the Police Department. I want to speak to the Inspector General."

Presumably Chandra Coomaraswamy possessed a uniform, but Cooper had never seen him wearing it. They met, as arranged, at the entrance to the little park that was Plato City's chief pride and joy. At this time in the morning of the artificial twenty-four-hour "day" it was almost deserted, and they could talk without interruption.

As they walked along the narrow gravel paths, they chatted about old times, the friends they had known at college together, the latest developments in interplanetary politics. They had reached the middle of the park, under the exact center of the great blue-painted dome, when Cooper came to the point.

"You know everything that's happening on the Moon, Chandra," he said. "And you know that I'm here to do a series for UNSA—hope to make a book out of it when I get back to Earth. So why should people be trying to hide things from me?"

It was impossible to hurry Chandra. He always took his time to answer questions, and his few words escaped with difficulty around the stem of his hand-carved Bavarian pipe.

"What people?" he asked at length.

"You've really no idea?"

The Inspector General shook his head.

"Not the faintest," he answered; and Cooper knew that he was telling the truth. Chandra might be silent, but he would not lie.

"I was afraid you'd say that. Well, if you don't know any more than I do, here's the only clue I have—and it frightens me. Medical Research is trying to keep me at arm's length."

"Hmm," replied Chandra, taking his pipe from his mouth and looking at it thoughtfully.

"Is that all you have to say?"

"You haven't given me much to work on. Remember, I'm only a cop; I lack your vivid journalism imagination."

"All I can tell you is that the higher I get in Medical Research, the colder the atmosphere becomes. Last time I was here, everyone was very friendly, and gave me some fine stories. But now, I can't even meet the Director. He's always too busy, or on the other side of the Moon. Anyway, what sort of man is he?"

"Dr. Hastings? Prickly little character. Very competent, but not easy to work with."

"What could he be trying to hide?"

"Knowing you, I'm sure you have some interesting theories."

"Oh, I thought of narcotics, and fraud, and political conspiracies—but they don't make sense, in these days. So what's left scares the hell out of me."

Chandra's eyebrows signaled a silent question mark.

"Interplanetary plague," said Cooper bluntly.

"I thought that was impossible."

"Yes—I've written articles myself proving that the life forms on other planets have such alien chemistries that they can't react with us, and that all our microbes and bugs took millions of years to adapt to our bodies. But I've always wondered if it was true. Suppose a ship has come back from

Mars, say, with something *really* vicious—and the doctors can't cope with it?"

There was a long silence. Then Chandra said: "I'll start investigating. *I* don't like it either, for here's an item you probably don't know. There were three nervous breakdowns in the Medical Division last month—and that's very, very unusual."

He glanced at his watch, then at the false sky, which seemed so distant, yet which was only two hundred feet above their heads.

"We'd better get moving," he said. "The morning shower's due in five minutes."

The call came two weeks later, in the middle of the night—the real lunar night. By Plato City time, it was Sunday morning.

"Henry? Chandra here. Can you meet me in half an hour at air lock five? Good—I'll see you."

This was it, Cooper knew. Air lock five meant that they were going outside the dome. Chandra had found something.

The presence of the police driver restricted conversation as the tractor moved away from the city along the road roughly bulldozed across the ash and pumice. Low in the south, Earth was almost full, casting a brilliant blue-green light over the infernal landscape. However hard one tried, Cooper told himself, it was difficult to make the Moon appear glamorous. But nature guards her greatest secrets well; to such places men must come to find them.

The multiple domes of the city dropped below the sharply curved horizon. Presently, the tractor turned aside from the main road to follow a scarcely visible trail. Ten minutes later, Cooper saw a single glittering hemisphere ahead of them, standing on an isolated ridge of rock. Another vehicle, bearing a red cross, was parked beside the entrance. It seemed that they were not the only visitors.

Nor were they unexpected. As they drew up to the dome, the flexible tube of the air-lock coupling groped out toward them and snapped into place against their tractor's outer hull. There was a brief hissing as pressure equalized. Then Cooper followed Chandra into the building.

The air-lock operator led them along curving corridors

and radial passageways toward the center of the dome. Sometimes they caught glimpses of laboratories, scientific instruments, they caught glimpses of computers—all perfectly ordinary, and all deserted on this Sunday morning. They must have reached the heart of the building, Cooper told himself when their guide ushered them into a large circular chamber and shut the door softly behind them.

It was a small zoo. All around them were cages, tanks, jars containing a wide selection of the fauna and flora of Earth. Waiting at its center was a short, gray-haired man, looking very worried, and very unhappy.

"Dr. Hastings," said Coomaraswamy, "meet Mr. Cooper." The Inspector General turned to his companion and added, "I've convinced the Doctor that there's only one way to keep you quiet—and that's to tell you everything."

"Frankly," said Hastings, "I'm not sure if I give a damn any more." His voice was unsteady, barely under control, and Cooper thought, Hello! There's another breakdown on the way.

The scientist wasted no time on such formalities as shaking hands. He walked to one of the cages, took out a small bundle of fur, and held it toward Cooper.

"Do you know what this is?" he asked abruptly.

"Of course. A hamster—the commonest lab animal."

"Yes," said Hastings. "A perfectly ordinary golden hamster. Except that this one is five years old—like all the others in this cage."

"Well? What's odd about that?"

"Oh, nothing, nothing at all . . . except for the trifling fact that hamsters live for only two years. And we have some here that are getting on for ten."

For a moment no one spoke; but the room was not silent. It was full of rustlings and slitherings and scratchings, of faint whimpers and tiny animal cries. Then Cooper whispered: "My God—you've found a way of prolonging life!"

"No," retorted Hastings. "We've not found it. The Moon has given it to us . . . as we might have expected, if we'd looked in front of our noses."

He seemed to have gained control over his emotion—as if he was once more the pure scientist, fascinated by a discovery for its own sake and heedless of its implications.

"On Earth," he said, "we spend our whole lives fighting

gravity. It wears down our muscles, pulls our stomachs out of shape. In seventy years, how many tons of blood does the heart lift through how many miles? And all that work, all that strain is reduced to a sixth here on the Moon, where a one-hundred-and-eighty-pound human weighs only thirty pounds."

"I see," said Cooper slowly. "Ten years for a hamster— and how long for a man?"

"It's not a simple law," answered Hastings. "It varies with the size and the species. Even a month ago, we weren't certain. But now we're quite sure of this: on the Moon, the span of human life will be at least two hundred years."

"And you've been trying to keep it secret!"

"You fool! Don't you understand?"

"Take it easy, Doctor—take it easy," said Chandra softly.

With an obvious effort of will, Hastings got control of himself again. He began to speak with such icy calm that his words sank like freezing raindrops into Cooper's mind.

"Think of them up there," he said, pointing to the roof to the invisible Earth, whose looming presence no one on the Moon could ever forget. "Six billion of them, packing all the continents to the edges—and now crowding over into the sea beds. And here"—he pointed to the ground—"only a hundred thousand of *us,* on an almost empty world. But a world where we need miracles of technology and engineering merely to exist, where a man with an I.Q. of only a hundred and fifty can't even get a job.

"And now we find that we can live for two hundred years. Imagine how they're going to react to *that* news! This is your problem now, Mister Journalist; you've asked for it, and you've got it. Tell me this, please—I'd really be interested to know—*just how are you going to break it to them?*"

He waited, and waited. Cooper opened his mouth, then closed it again, unable to think of anything to say.

In the far corner of the room, a baby monkey started to cry.

June 1963

THE LAST
COMMAND

". . . THIS IS THE President speaking. Because you are hearing me read this message, it means that I am already dead and that our country is destroyed. But you are soldiers—the most highly trained in all our history. You know how to obey orders. Now you must obey the hardest you have ever received. . . ."

Hard? thought the First Radar Officer bitterly. No; now it would be easy, now that they had seen the land they loved scorched by the heat of many suns. No longer could there be any hesitation, any scruples about visiting upon innocent and guilty alike the vengeance of the gods. But why, *why* had it been left so late?

". . . You know the purpose for which you were set swinging on your secret orbit beyond the Moon. Aware of your existence, but never sure of your location, an aggressor would hesitate to launch an attack against us. You were to be the Ultimate Deterrent, beyond the reach of the Earth-quake bombs that could crush missiles in their buried silos and smash nuclear submarines prowling the sea bed. You could still strike back, even if all our other weapons were destroyed. . . ."

As they have been, the Captain told himself. He had watched the lights wink out one by one on the operations board, until none were left. Many, perhaps, had done their duty; if not, he would soon complete their work. Nothing that had survived the first counterstrike would exist after the blow he was now preparing.

". . . Only through accident, or madness, could war begin in the face of the threat you represent. That was the theory on which we staked our lives; and now, for reasons which we shall never know, we have lost the gamble. . . ."

The Chief Astronomer let his eyes roam to the single small porthole at the side of the central control room. Yes, they had lost indeed. There hung the Earth, a glorious silver crescent against the background of the stars. At first glance, it looked unchanged; but not at second—for the dark side was no longer wholly dark.

Dotted across it, glowing like an evil phosphorescence, were the seas of flame that had been cities. There were few of them now, for there was little left to burn.

The familiar voice was still speaking from the other side of the grave. How long ago, wondered the Signal Officer, had this message been recorded? And what other sealed orders did the fort's more-than-human battle computer contain, which now they would never hear, because they dealt with military situations that could no longer arise? He dragged his mind back from the worlds of might-have-been to confront the appalling and still-unimaginable reality.

". . . If we had been defeated, but not destroyed, we had hoped to use your existence as a bargaining weapon. Now, even that poor hope has gone—and with it, the last purpose for which you were set here in space."

What does he mean? thought the Armaments Officer. *Now,* surely, the moment of their destiny had come. The millions who were dead, the millions who wished they were —all would be revenged when the black cylinders of the gigaton bombs spiraled down to Earth.

". . . You wonder why, now that it has come to this, I have not given you the orders to strike back. I will tell you.

"It is now too late. The Deterrent has failed. Our motherland no longer exists, and revenge cannot bring back the dead. Now that half of mankind has been destroyed, to destroy the other half would be insanity, unworthy of reasoning men. The quarrels that divided us twenty-four hours ago no longer have any meaning. As far as your hearts will let you, you must forget the past.

"You have skills and knowledge that a shattered planet will desperately need. Use them—and without stint, without bitterness—to rebuild the world. I warned you that your duty would be hard, but here is my final command.

"You will launch your bombs into deep space, and detonate them ten million kilometers from Earth. This will prove to our late enemy, who is also receiving this message, that you have discarded your weapons.

"Then you will have one more thing to do. Men of Fort Lenin, the President of the Supreme Soviet bids you farewell, and orders you to place yourselves at the disposal of the United States."

June 1963

DIAL F FOR
FRANKENSTEIN

AT 0150 GMT ON December 1, 1975, every telephone in the world started to ring.

A quarter of a billion people picked up their receivers, to listen for a few seconds with annoyance or perplexity. Those who had been awakened in the middle of the night assumed that some far-off friend was calling, over the satellite telephone network that had gone into service, with such a blaze of publicity, the day before. But there was no voice on the line; only a sound, which to many seemed like the roaring of the sea; to others, like the vibrations of harp strings in the wind. And there were many more, in that moment, who recalled a secret sound of childhood—the noise of blood pulsing through the veins, heard when a shell is cupped over the ear. Whatever it was, it lasted no more than twenty seconds. Then it was replaced by the dial tone.

The world's subscribers cursed, muttered, "Wrong number," and hung up. Some tried to dial a complaint but the line seemed busy. In a few hours, everyone had forgotten the incident—except those whose duty it was to worry about such things.

At the Post Office Research Station, the argument had been going on all morning, and had got nowhere. It continued unabated through the lunch break, when the hungry engineers poured into the little café across the road.

"I still think," said Willy Smith, the solid-state electronics man, "that it was a temporary surge of current, caused when the satellite network was switched in."

"It was obviously *something* to do with the satellites," agreed Jules Reyner, circuit designer. "But why the time delay? They were plugged in at midnight; the ringing was two hours later—as we all know to our cost." He yawned violently.

"What do *you* think, Doc?" asked Bob Andrews, computer programmer. "You've been very quiet all morning. Surely you've got some idea?"

Dr. John Williams, head of the Mathematics Division, stirred uneasily.

"Yes," he said. "I have. But you won't take it seriously."

"That doesn't matter. Even if it's as crazy as those science-fiction yarns you write under a pseudonym, it may give us some leads."

Williams blushed, but not much. Everyone knew about his stories, and he wasn't ashamed of them. After all, they *had* been collected in book form. (Remaindered at five shillings; he still had a couple of hundred copies.)

"Very well," he said, doodling on the tablecloth. "This is something I've been wondering about for years. Have you ever considered the analogy between an automatic telephone exchange and the human brain?"

"Who hasn't thought of it?" scoffed one of his listeners. "That idea must go back to Graham Bell."

"Possibly. I never said it was original. But I do say it's time we started taking it seriously." He squinted balefully at the fluorescent tubes above the table; they were needed on this foggy winter day. "What's wrong with the damn lights? They've been flickering for the last five minutes."

"Don't bother about that. Maisie's probably forgotten to pay her electricity bill. Let's hear more about your theory."

"Most of it isn't theory; it's plain fact. We know that the

human brain is a system of switches—neurons—interconnected in a very elaborate fashion by nerves. An automatic telephone exchange is also a system of switches—selectors and so forth—connected with wires."

"Agreed," said Smith. "But that analogy won't get you very far. Aren't there about fifteen billion neurons in the brain? That's a lot more than the number of switches in an autoexchange."

Williams' answer was interrupted by the scream of a low-flying jet. He had to wait until the café had ceased to vibrate before he could continue.

"Never heard them fly *that* low," Andrews grumbled. "Thought it was against regulations."

"So it is, but don't worry—London Airport Control will catch him."

"I doubt it," said Reyner. "That *was* London Airport, bringing in a Concorde on ground approach. But I've never heard one so low, either. Glad I wasn't aboard."

"Are we, or are we *not,* going to get on with this blasted discussion?" demanded Smith.

"You're right about the fifteen billion neurons in the human brain," continued Williams, unabashed. "And *that's* the whole point. Fifteen billion sounds a large number, but it isn't. Round about the 1960's, there were more than that number of individual switches in the world's autoexchanges. Today, there are approximately five times as many."

"I see," said Reyner, slowly. "And as from yesterday, they've all become capable of full interconnection, now that the satellite links have gone into service."

"Precisely."

There was silence for a moment, apart from the distant clanging of a fire-engine bell.

"Let me get this straight," said Smith. "Are you suggesting that the world telephone system is now a giant brain?"

"That's putting it crudely—anthropomorphically. I prefer to think of it in terms of critical size." Williams held his hands out in front of him, fingers partly closed.

"Here are two lumps of U-235. Nothing happens as long as you keep them apart. But bring them together"—he suited the action to the words—"and you have something *very* different from one bigger lump of uranium. You have a hole half a mile across.

"It's the same with our telephone networks. Until today, they've been largely independent, autonomous. But now we've suddenly multiplied the connecting links, the networks have all merged together, and we've reached criticality."

"And just what does criticality mean in this case?" asked Smith.

"For want of a better word—consciousness."

"A weird sort of consciousness," said Reyner. "What would it use for sense organs?"

"Well, all the radio and TV stations in the world would be feeding information into it, through their landlines. *That* should give it something to think about! Then there would be all the data stored in all the computers; it would have access to that—and to the electronic libraries, the radar tracking systems, the telemetering in the automatic factories. Oh, it would have enough sense organs! We can't begin to imagine its picture of the world; but it would be infinitely richer and more complex than ours."

"Granted all this, because it's an entertaining idea," said Reyner, "what could it *do* except think? It couldn't go anywhere; it would have no limbs."

"Why should it want to travel? It would already be everywhere! And every piece of remotely controlled electrical equipment on the planet could act as a limb."

"Now I understand that time delay," interjected Andrews. "It was conceived at midnight, but it wasn't born until 1:50 this morning. The noise that woke us all up was—its birth cry."

His attempt to sound facetious was not altogether convincing, and nobody smiled. Overhead, the lights continued their annoying flicker, which seemed to be getting worse. Then there was an interruption from the front of the café, as Jim Small, of Power Supplies, made his usual boisterous entry.

"Look at this, fellows," he said, and grinned, waving a piece of paper in front of his colleagues. "I'm rich. Ever seen a bank balance like *that*?"

Dr. Williams took the proffered statement, glanced down

the columns, and read the balance aloud: "Cr. £999,999,897.87."

"Nothing very odd about that," he continued, above the general amusement. "I'd say it means an overdraft of £102, and the computer's made a slight slip and added eleven nines. That sort of thing was happening all the time just after the banks converted to the decimal system."

"I know, I know," said Small, "but don't spoil my fun. I'm going to frame this statement. And what would happen if I drew a check for a few million, on the strength of this? Could I sue the bank if it bounced?"

"Not on your life," answered Reyner. "I'll take a bet that the banks thought of that years ago, and protected themselves somewhere down in the small print. But, by the way, when did you get that statement?"

"In the noon delivery. It comes straight to the office, so that my wife doesn't have a chance of seeing it."

"Hmm. That means it was computed early this morning. Certainly after midnight . . ."

"What are you driving at? And why all the long faces?"

No one answered him. He had started a new hare, and the hounds were in full cry.

"Does anyone here know about automated banking systems?" asked Smith. "How are they tied together?"

"Like everything else these days," said Andrews. "They're all in the same network; the computers talk to each other all over the world. It's a point for you, John. If there *was* real trouble, that's one of the first places I'd expect it. Besides the phone system itself, of course."

"No one answered the question I had asked before Jim came in," complained Reyner. "What would this supermind actually *do*? Would it be friendly—hostile—indifferent? Would it even know that we exist? Or would it consider the electronic signals it's handling to be the only reality?"

"I see you're beginning to believe me," said Williams, with a certain grim satisfaction. "I can only answer your question by asking another. What does a newborn baby do? It starts looking for food." He glanced up at the flickering lights. "My God," he said slowly, as if a thought had just struck him. "There's only one food it would need—electricity."

"This nonsense has gone far enough," said Smith. "What

the devil's happened to our lunch? We gave our orders twenty minutes ago."

Everyone ignored him.

"And then," said Reyner, taking up where Williams had left off, "it would start looking around, and stretching its limbs. In fact, it would start to play, like any growing baby."

"And babies *break* things," said someone softly.

"It would have enough toys, heaven knows. That Concorde that went over us just now. The automated production lines. The traffic lights in our streets."

"Funny you should mention that," interjected Small. "Something's happened to the traffic outside—it's been stopped for the last ten minutes. Looks like a big jam."

"I guess there's a fire somewhere. I heard an engine just now."

"I've heard two—and what sounded like an explosion over toward the industrial estate. Hope it's nothing serious."

"Maisie! What about some candles? We can't see a thing!"

"I've just remembered—this place has an all-electric kitchen. We're going to get a cold lunch, if we get any lunch at all."

"At least we can read the newspaper while we're waiting. Is that the latest edition you've got there, Jim?"

"Yes. Haven't had time to look at it yet. Hmm. There *do* seem to have been a lot of odd accidents this morning—railway signals jammed—water main blown up through failure of relief valve—dozens of complaints about last night's wrong number . . ."

He turned the page, and became suddenly silent.

"What's the matter?"

Without a word, Small handed over the paper. Only the front page made sense. Throughout the interior, column after column was a mess of printer's pie, with, here and there, a few incongruous advertisements making islands of sanity in a sea of gibberish. They had obviously been set up as independent blocks, and had escaped the scrambling that had overtaken the text around them.

"So this is where long-distance typesetting and autodistribution have brought us," grumbled Andrews. "I'm afraid Fleet Street's been putting too many eggs in one electric basket."

"So have we all, I'm afraid," said Williams solemnly. "So have we all."

"If I can get a word in edgeways, in time to stop the mob hysteria that seems to be infecting this table," said Smith loudly and firmly, "I'd like to point out that there's nothing to worry about—even if John's ingenious fantasy is correct. We only have to switch off the satellites, and we'll be back where we were yesterday."

"Prefrontal lobotomy," muttered Williams. "I'd thought of that."

"Eh? Oh, yes—cutting out slabs of the brain. That would certainly do the trick. Expensive, of course, and we'd have to go back to sending telegrams to each other. But civilization would survive."

From not too far away, there was a short, sharp explosion.

"I don't like this," said Andrews nervously. "Let's hear what the old BBC's got to say. The one o'clock news has just started."

He reached into his briefcase and pulled out a transistor radio.

". . . unprecedented number of industrial accidents, as well as the unexplained launching of three salvos of guided missiles from military installations in the United States. Several airports have had to suspend operation owing to the erratic behavior of their radar, and the banks and stock exchanges have closed because their information-processing systems have become completely unreliable." ("You're telling me," muttered Small, while the others shushed him.) "One moment, please—there's a news flash coming through. . . . Here it is. We have just been informed that all control over the newly installed communications satellites has been lost. They are no longer responding to commands from the ground. According to . . ."

The BBC went off the air; even the carrier wave died. Andrews reached for the turning knob and twisted it around the dial. Over the whole band, the ether was silent.

Presently Reyner said, in a voice not far from hysteria: "That prefrontal lobotomy was a good idea, John. Too bad that Baby's already thought of it."

Williams rose slowly to his feet.

"Let's get back to the lab," he said. "There must be an answer, somewhere."

But he knew already that it was far, far too late. For *Homo sapiens,* the telephone bell had tolled.

June 1963

REUNION

PEOPLE OF EARTH, do not be afraid. We come in peace—
and why not? For we are your cousins; we have been here
before.

You will recognize us when we meet, a few hours from
now. We are approaching the solar system almost as swiftly
as this radio message. Already, your sun dominates the sky
ahead of us. It is the sun our ancestors and yours shared ten
million years ago.. We are men, as you are; but you have
forgotten your history, while we have remembered ours.

We colonized Earth, in the reign of the great reptiles, who
were dying when we came and whom we could not save.
Your world was a tropical planet then, and we felt that it
would make a fair home for our people. We were wrong.
Though we were masters of space, we know so little about
climate, about evolution, about genetics. . . .

For millions of summers—there were no winters in those
ancient days—the colony flourished. Isolated though it had
to be, in a universe where the journey from one star to the
next takes years, it kept in touch with its parent civilization.

Three or four times in every century, starships would call and bring news of the galaxy.

But two million years ago, Earth began to change. For ages it had been a tropical paradise; then the temperature fell, and the ice began to creep down from the poles. As the climate altered, so did the colonists. We realize now that it was a natural adaptation to the end of the long summer, but those who had made Earth their home for so many generations believed that they had been attacked by a strange and repulsive disease. A disease that did not kill, that did no physical harm—but merely disfigured

Yet some were immune; the change spared them and their children. And so, within a few thousand years, the colony had split into two separate groups—almost two separate species—suspicious and jealous of each other.

The division brought envy, discord, and, ultimately, conflict. As the colony disintegrated and the climate steadily worsened, those who could do so withdrew from Earth. The rest sank into barbarism.

We could have kept in touch, but there is so much to do in a universe of a hundred trillion stars. Until a few years ago, we did not know that any of you had survived. Then we picked up your first radio signals, learned your simple languages, and discovered that you made the long climb back from savagery. We come to greet you, our long-lost relatives —and to help you.

We have discovered much in the eons since we abandoned Earth. If you wish us to bring back the eternal summer that ruled before the Ice Ages, we can do so. Above all, we have a simple remedy for the offensive yet harmless genetic plague that afflicted so many of the colonists.

Perhaps it has run its course—but if not, we have good news for you. People of Earth, you can rejoin the society of the universe without shame, without embarrassment.

If any of you are still white, we can cure you.

November 1963

PLAYBACK

IT IS INCREDIBLE that I have forgotten so much, so quickly. I have used my body for forty years; I thought I knew it. Yet already it is fading like a dream.

Arms, legs, where are you? What did you ever do for me when you were mine? I send out signals, trying to command the limbs I vaguely remember. Nothing happens. It is like shouting into a vacuum.

Shouting. Yes, I try that. Perhaps *they* hear me, but I cannot hear myself. Silence has flowed over me, until I can no longer imagine sound. There is a word in my mind called "music"; what does it mean?

(So many words, drifting before me out of the darkness, waiting to be recognized. One by one they go away, disappointed.)

Hello. So you are back. How softly you tiptoe into my mind! I know when you are there, but I never feel you coming.

I sense that you are friendly, and I am grateful for what you have done. But who are you? Of course, I know you're not human; no human science could have rescued me when the drive field collapsed. You see, I am becoming curious. That is a good sign, is it not? Now that the pain has gone— at last, at last—I can start to think again.

Yes, I am ready. Anything you want to know. It is the least that I can do.

My name is William Vincent Neuberg. I am a master pilot of the Galactic Survey. I was born in Port Lowell, Mars, on August 21, 2095. My wife, Janita, and my three children are on Ganymede. I am also an author; I've written a good deal about my travels. *Beyond Rigel* is quite fa mous. . . .

What happened? You probably know as much as I do. I had just phantomed my ship and was cruising at phase velocity when the alarm went. There was no time to move, to do anything. I remember the cabin walls starting to glow— and the heat, the terrible heat. That is all. The detonation must have blown me into space. But how could I have survived? How could anyone have reached me in time?

Tell me—how much is left of my body? Why cannot I feel my arms, my legs? Don't hide the truth; I am not afraid. If you can get me home, the biotechnicians can give me new limbs. Even now, my right arm is not the one I was born with.

Why can't you answer? Surely that is a simple question!

What do you mean *you do not know what I look like*? You must have saved *something*!

The head?

The brain, then?

Not even—oh, *no* . . . !

I am sorry. Was I away a long time?

Let me get a grip on myself. (Ha! Very funny!) I am Survey Pilot First Class Vincent William Freeburg. I was born in Port Lyot, Mars, on August 21, 1895. I have one . . . no, two children. . . .

Please let me have that again, slowly. My training prepared me for any conceivable reality. I can face whatever you tell me. But slowly.

Well, it could be worse. I'm not really dead. I know who I am. I even think I know *what* I am.

I am a—a *recording,* in some fantastic storage device. You must have caught my psyche, my soul, when the ship turned into plasma. Even though I cannot imagine how it was done, it makes sense. After all, a primitive man could never understand how we record a symphony. . . .

All my memories are trapped in a tape or a crystal, as they once were trapped in the cells of my vaporized brain. And not only my memories. ME. I. MYSELF—VINCE WILLBURG, PILOT SECOND CLASS.

Well, what happens next?

Please say that again, I do not understand.

Oh, wonderful! You can do even *that?*

There is a word for it, a name. . . .

The multitudinous seas incarnadine. No. Not quite.

Incarnadine, incarnadine . . .

REINCARNATION!!

Yes yes, I understand. I must give you the basic plan, the design. Watch my thoughts very carefully.

I will start at the top.

The head, now. It is oval—so. The upper part is covered with hair. Mine was br—er—blue.

The eyes. They are very important. You have seen them in other animals? Good, that saves trouble. Can you show me some? Yes, those will do.

Now the mouth. Strange—I must have looked at it a thousand times when I was shaving, but somehow . . .

Not so round—narrower.

Oh, no, not that way. It runs *across* the face, horizontally. . . .

Now, let's see . . . there's something between the eyes and the mouth.

Stupid of me. I'll never be a cadet if I can't even remember that. . . .

Of course—NOSE! A little longer, I think.

There's something else, something I've forgotten. That head looks raw, unfinished. It's not me, Billy Vinceburg, the smartest kid on the block.

But *that* isn't my name—I'm not a boy. I'm a master pilot with twenty years in the Space Service, and I'm trying to rebuild my body. Why do my thoughts keep going out of focus? Help me, please!

That monstrosity? Is that what I told you I looked like? Erase it. We must start again.

The head now. It is perfectly spherical, and weareth a runcible cap. . . .

Too difficult. Begin somewhere else. Ah, I know—

The thighbone is connected to the shinbone. The shinbone is connected to the thighbone. The thighbone is connected to the shinbone. The shinbone . . .

All fading. Too late, too late. Something wrong with the playback. Thank you for trying. My name is . . . my name is . . .

Mother— whcrc are you?

Mama—Mama!

Maaaaaaa . . .

December 1963

THE LIGHT OF
DARKNESS

I AM NOT one of those Africans who feel ashamed of their country because, in fifty years, it has made less progress than Europe in five hundred. But where we have failed to advance as fast as we should, it is owing to dictators like Chaka; and for this we have only ourselves to blame. The fault being ours, so is the responsibility for the cure.

Moreover, I had better reasons than most for wishing to destroy the Great Chief, the Omnipotent, the All-Seeing. He was of my own tribe, being related to me through one of my father's wives, and he had persecuted our family ever since he came to power. Although we took no part in politics, two of my brothers had disappeared, and another had been killed in an unexplained auto accident. My own liberty, there could be little doubt, was largely due to my standing as one of the country's few scientists with an international reputation.

Like many of my fellow intellectuals, I had been slow to turn against Chaka, feeling—as did the equally misguided Germans of the 1930's—that there were times when a dictator was the only answer to political chaos. Perhaps the first sign of our disastrous error came when Chaka abolished the constitution and assumed the name of the nineteenth-century Zulu emperor of whom he genuinely believed himself the reincarnation. From that moment, his megalomania grew swiftly. Like all tyrants, he would trust no one, and believed himself surrounded by plots.

This belief was well founded. The world knows of at least six well-publicized attempts on his life, and there are others that were kept secret. Their failure increased Chaka's confidence in his own destiny, and confirmed his followers' fanatical belief in his immortality. As the opposition became more desperate, so the Great Chief's countermeasures became more ruthless—and more barbaric. Chaka's regime was not the first, in Africa or elsewhere, to torture its enemies; but it was the first to do so on television.

Even then, shamed though I was by the shock of horror and revulsion that went round the world, I would have done nothing if fate had not placed the weapon in my hands. I am not a man of action, and I abhor violence, but once I realized the power that was mine, my conscience would not let me rest. As soon as the NASA technicians had installed their equipment and handed over the Hughes Mark X Infrared Communications System, I began to make my plans.

It seems strange that my country, one of the most backward in the world, should play a central role in the conquest of space. That is an accident of geography, not at all to the liking of the Russians and the Americans. But there is nothing that they could do about it; Umbala lies on the equator, directly beneath the paths of all the planets. And it possesses a unique and priceless natural feature: the extinct volcano known as the Zambue Crater.

When Zambue died, more than a million years ago, the lava retreated step by step, congealing in a series of terraces to form a bowl a mile wide and a thousand feet deep. It had taken the minimum of earth-moving and cable-stringing to convert this into the largest radio telescope on Earth. Because the gigantic reflector is fixed, it scans any given portion of the sky for only a few minutes every twenty-four hours, as the Earth turns on its axis. This was a price the scientists were willing to pay for the ability to receive signals from probes and ships right out to the very limits of the solar system.

Chaka was a problem they had not anticipated. He had come to power when the work was almost completed, and they had had to make the best of him. Luckily, he had a superstitious respect for science, and he needed all the rubles and dollars he could get. The Equatorial Deep Space Facility was safe from his megalomania; indeed, it helped to reinforce it.

The Big Dish had just been completed when I made my first trip up the tower that sprang from its center. A vertical mast, more than fifteen hundred feet high, it supported the collecting antennas at the focus of the immense bowl. A small elevator, which could carry three men, made a slow ascent to its top.

At first, there was nothing to see but the dully gleaming saucer of aluminum sheet, curving upward all around me for half a mile in every direction. But presently I rose above the rim of the crater and could look far out across the land I hoped to save. Snow-capped and blue in the western haze was Mount Tampala, the second highest peak in Africa, separated from me by endless miles of jungle. Through that jungle, in great twisting loops, wound the muddy waters of the Nya River—the only highway that millions of my countrymen had ever known. A few clearings, a railroad, and the distant white gleam of the city were the only signs of human life. Once again I knew that overwhelming feeling of helplessness that always assails me when I look down on Umbala from the air and realize the insignificance of man against the neversleeping jungle.

The elevator cage clicked to a halt, a quarter of a mile up in the sky. When I stepped out, I was in a tiny room packed with coaxial cables and instruments. There was still some distance to go, for a short ladder led through the roof to a platform little more than a yard square. It was not a place for anyone prone to vertigo; there was not even a handrail for protection. A central lightning conductor gave a certain amount of security, and I gripped it firmly with one hand all the time I stood on this triangular metal raft, so close to the clouds.

The stunning view, and the exhilaration of slight but ever-present danger, made me forget the passage of time. I felt like a god, completely apart from terrestrial affairs, superior to all other men. And then I knew, with mathematical certainty, that here was a challenge that Chaka could never ignore.

Colonel Mtanga, his Chief of Security, would object, but his protests would be overruled. Knowing Chaka, one could predict with complete assurance that on the official opening day he would stand here, alone, for many minutes, as he surveyed his empire. His bodyguard would remain in the room below, having already checked it for booby traps. They could do nothing to save him when I struck from three miles away *and through the range of hills that lay between the radio telescope and my observatory.* I was glad of those hills; though they complicated the problem, they would shield me from all suspicion. Colonel Mtanga was a very intelligent man, but he was not likely to conceive of a gun that could fire around corners. As he would be looking for a gun, even though he could find no bullets. . . .

I went back to the laboratory and started my calculations. It was not long before I discovered my first mistake. Because I had seen the concentrated light of its laser beam punch a hole through solid steel in a thousandth of a second, I had assumed that my Mark X could kill a man. But it is not as simple as that. In some ways, a man is a tougher proposition than a piece of steel. He is mostly water, which has ten times the heat capacity of any metal. A beam of light that will drill a hole through armor plate, or carry a message as far as Pluto—which was the job the Mark X had been designed for—would give a man only a painful but quite superficial burn. About the worst I could do to Chaka, from three miles away, was to drill a hole in the colorful tribal blanket he wore so ostentatiously, to prove that he was still one of the People.

For a while, I almost abandoned the project. But it would not die; instinctively, I knew that the answer was there, if only I could see it. Perhaps I could use my invisible bullets of heat to cut one of the cables guying the tower, so that it would come crashing down when Chaka was at the summit. Calculations showed that this was just possible if the Mark X operated continuously for fifteen seconds. A cable, unlike a man, would not move, so there was no need to stake everything on a single pulse of energy. I could take my time.

But damaging the telescope would have been treason to science, and it was almost a relief when I discovered that this scheme would not work. The mast had so many built-in safety factors that I would have to cut three separate cables to bring it down. This was out of the question; it would require hours of delicate adjustment to set and aim the apparatus for each precision shot.

I had to think of something else; and because it takes men a long time to see the obvious, it was not until a week before the official opening of the telescope that I knew how to deal with Chaka, the All-Seeing, the Omnipotent, the Father of his People.

By this time, my graduate students had tuned and calibrated the equipment, and we were ready for the first full-power tests. As it rotated on its mounting inside the observatory dome, the Mark X looked exactly like a large double-barreled reflecting telescope—which indeed it was. One thirty-six-inch mirror gathered the laser pulse and focused it out across space; the other acted as a receiver for incoming signals, and was also used, like a superpowered telescope sight, to aim the system.

We checked the line-up on the nearest celestial target, the Moon. Late one night, I set the cross wires on the center of the waning crescent and fired off a pulse. Two and a half seconds later, a fine echo came bouncing back. We were in business.

There was one detail still to be arranged, and this I had to do myself, in utter secrecy. The radio telescope lay to the north of the observatory, beyond the ridge of hills that blocked our direct view of it. A mile to the south was a single isolated mountain. I knew it well, for years ago I had helped to set up a cosmic-ray station there. Now it would be used for a purpose I could never have imagined in the days when my country was free.

Just below the summit were the ruins of an old fort, deserted centuries ago. It took only a little searching to find the spot I needed—a small cave, less than a yard high, between two great stones that had fallen from the ancient walls. Judging by the cobweb, no human being had entered it for generations.

When I crouched in the opening, I could see the whole expanse of the Deep Space Facility, stretching away for miles. Over to the east were the antennas of the old Project Apollo Tracking Station, which had brought the first men back from the Moon. Beyond that lay the airfield, above which a big freighter was hovering as it came in on its underjets. But all that interested me were the clear lines of sight from this spot to the Mark X dome, and to the tip of the radio telescope mast three miles to the north.

It took me three days to install the carefully silvered, optically perfect mirror in its hidden alcove. The tedious micrometer adjustments to give the exact orientation took so long that I feared I would not be ready in time. But at last the angle was correct, to a fraction of a second of arc. When I aimed the telescope of the Mark X at the secret spot on the mountain, I could see over the hills behind me. The field of view was tiny, but it was sufficient; the target area was only a yard across, and I could sight on any part of it to within an inch.

Along the path I had arranged, light could travel in either direction. Whatever I saw through the viewing telescope was automatically in the line of fire of the transmitter.

It was strange, three days later, to sit in the quiet observatory, with the power-packs humming around me, and to watch Chaka move into the field of the telescope. I felt a brief glow of triumph, like an astronomer who has calculated the orbit of a new planet and then finds it in the predicted spot among the stars. The cruel face was in profile when I saw it first, apparently only thirty feet away at the extreme magnification I was using. I waited patiently, in serene confidence, for the moment that I knew must come —the moment when Chaka seemed to be looking directly toward me. Then with my left hand I held the image of an ancient god who must be nameless, and with my right I tripped the capacitor banks that fired the laser, launching my silent, invisible thunderbolt across the mountains.

Yes, it was so much better this way. Chaka deserved to be killed, but death would have turned him into a martyr and strengthened the hold of his regime. What I had visited upon him was worse than death, and would throw his supporters into superstitious terror.

Chaka still lived; but the All-Seeing would see no more.

In the space of a few microseconds, I had made him less than the humblest beggar in the streets.

And I had not even hurt him. There is no pain when the delicate film of the retina is fused by the heat of a thousand suns.

February 1964

THE LONGEST
SCIENCE-FICTION
STORY EVER TOLD

DEAR MR. JINX:

I'm afraid your idea is not at all original. Stories about writers whose work is always plagiarized even *before* they can complete it go back at least to H. G. Wells's "The Anticipator." About once a week I receive a manuscript beginning:

DEAR MR. JINX:

I'm afraid your idea is not at all original. Stories about writers whose work is always plagiarized even *before* they can complete it go back at least to H. G. Wells's "The Anticipator." About once a week I receive a manuscript beginning:

DEAR MR. JINX:

I'm afraid your idea is not . . .
    Better luck next time!

Sincerely,
MORRIS K. MOBIUS
EDITOR, *Stupefying Stories*

Better luck next time!
Sincerely,
MORRIS K. MOBIUS
EDITOR, *Stupefying Stories*

Better luck next time!
Sincerely,
MORRIS K. MOBIUS
EDITOR, *Stupefying Stories*

April 1965

HERBERT GEORGE MORLEY ROBERTS WELLS, ESQ.

A COUPLE OF years ago I wrote a tale accurately titled "The Longest Science-Fiction Story Ever Told," which Fred Pohl duly published on a single page of his magazine. (Because editors have to justify their existence somehow, he renamed it "A Recursion in Metastories." You'll find it in *Galaxy* for October 1966.) Near the beginning of this metastory, but an infinite number of words from its end, I referred to "The Anticipator" by H. G. Wells.

Though I encountered this short fantasy some twenty years ago, and have never read it since, it left a vivid impression on my mind. It concerned two writers, one of whom had all his best stories published by the other—*before* he could even complete them himself. At last, in desperation, he decided that murder was the only cure for this chronic (literally) plagiarism.

But, of course, once again his rival beat him to it, and the story ends with the words "the anticipator, horribly afraid, ran down a by-street."

Now I would have sworn on a stack of Bibles that this

story was written by H. G. Wells. However, some months after its appearance I received a letter from Leslie A. Gritten, of Everett, Washington, saying that he couldn't locate it. And Mr. Gritten has been a Wells fan for a long, long time; he clearly recalls the serialization of "The War of the Worlds" in the *Strand Magazine* at the end of the 1890's. As one of the Master's cockney characters would say, "Gor blimey."

Refusing to believe that my mental filing system had played such a dirty trick on me, I quickly searched through the twenty-odd volumes of the autographed Atlantic Edition in the Colombo Public Library. (By a charming coincidence, the British Council had just arranged a Wells Centenary Exhibition, and the library entrance was festooned with photos illustrating his background and career.) I soon found that Mr. Gritten was right: there was no such story as "The Anticipator" in the collected works. Yet in the months since TLSFSET was published, not one other reader has queried the reference. I find this depressing; where are all the Wells fans these days?

Now my erudite informant has solved at least part of the mystery. "The Anticipator" was written by one Morley Roberts; it was first published in 1898 in *The Keeper of the Waters and Other Stories*. I probably encountered it in a Doubleday anthology, *Travelers in Time* (1947), edited by Philip Van Doren Stern.

Yet several problems remain. First of all, why was I so convinced that the story was by Wells? I can only suggest—and it seems pretty farfetched, even for my grasshopper mind—that the similarity of words had made me link it subconsciously with "The Accelerator."

I would also like to know why this story has stuck so vividly in my memory. Perhaps, like all writers, I am peculiarly sensitive to the dangers of plagiarism. So far (touch wood) I have been lucky; but I have notes for several tales I'm afraid to write until I can be quite sure they're original. (There's this couple, see, who land their spaceship on a new world after their planet has been blown up, and when they've started things all over again you find—surprise, surprise!—that they're called Adam and Eve. . . .)

One worth-while result of my error was to start me skimming through Wells's short stories again, and I was surprised to find what a relatively small proportion could be called science fiction, or even fantasy. Although I was well aware that only a fraction of his hundred-odd published volumes were S.F., I had forgotten that this was also true of the short stories. A depressing quantity are dramas and comedies of Edwardian life ("The Jilting of Jane"), rather painful attempts at humor ("My First Aeroplane"), near-autobiography ("A Slip Under the Microscope"), or pure sadism ("The Cone"). Undoubtedly, I am biased, but among these tales such masterpieces as "The Star," "The Crystal Egg," "The Flowering of the Strange Orchid," and, above all, "The Country of the Blind" blaze like diamonds amid costume jewelry.

But back to Morley Roberts. I know nothing whatsoever about him, and wonder if his little excursion in time was itself inspired by "The Time Machine," published just a couple of years before "The Anticipator." I also wonder which story was actually *written*—not published—first.

And why did such an ingenious writer not make more of a name for himself? Perhaps . . .

I have just been struck by a perfectly horrid thought. If H. G. Wells's contemporary Morley Roberts was ever found murdered in a dark alley, I simply don't want to know about it.

April 1967

LOVE THAT UNIVERSE

MR. PRESIDENT, National Administrator, Planetary Delegates, it is both an honor and a grave responsibility to address you at this moment of crisis. I am aware—I can very well understand—that many of you are shocked and dismayed by some of the rumors that you have heard. But I must beg you to forget your natural prejudices at a time when the very existence of the human race—*of the Earth itself*—is at stake.

Some time ago I came across a century-old phrase: "thinking the unthinkable." This is exactly what we have to do now. We must face the fact without flinching; we must not let our emotions sway our logic. Indeed, we must do the precise opposite; *we must let our logic sway our emotions!*

The situation is desperate, but it is not hopeless, thanks to the astonishing discoveries my colleagues have made at the Antigean Station. For the reports are indeed true; we *can* establish contact with the supercivilizations at the Galactic Core. At least we can let them know of our existence—and if we can do that, it should be possible for us to appeal to them for help.

There is nothing, absolutely nothing, that we can do by our own efforts in the brief time available. It is only ten years since the search for trans-Plutonian planets revealed the presence of the Black Dwarf. Only ninety years from now, it will make its perihelion passage and swing around the Sun as it heads once more into the depths of space—leaving a shattered solar system behind it. All our resources, all our much-vaunted control over the forces of nature, cannot alter its orbit by a fraction of an inch.

But ever since the first of the so-called "beacon stars" was discovered, at the end of the twentieth century, we have known that there were civilizations with access to energy sources incomparably greater than ours. Some of you will doubtless recall the incredulity of the astronomers—and later of the whole human race—when the first examples of cosmic engineering were detected in the Magellanic Clouds. Here were stellar structures obeying no natural laws; even now, we do not know their purpose—but we know their awesome implications. We share a universe with creatures who can juggle with the very stars. If they choose to help, it would be child's play for them to deflect a body like the Black Dwarf, only a few thousand times the mass of Earth. . . . Child's play, did I call it? Yes, that may be *literally* true!

You will all, I am certain, remember the great debate that followed the discovery of the supercivilizations. Should we attempt to communicate with them, or would it be best to remain inconspicuous? There was the possibility, of course, that they already knew everything about us, or might be annoyed by our presumption, or might react in any number of unpleasant ways. Though the benefits from such contacts could be enormous, the risks were terrifying. But now we have nothing to lose, and everything to gain. . . .

And until now, there was another fact that made the matter of no more than long-term philosophical interest. Though we could—at great expense—build radio transmitters capable of sending signals to these creatures, the nearest supercivilization is seven thousand light-years away. Even if it bothered to reply, it would be fourteen thousand years before we could get an answer. In these circumstances, it seemed that our superiors could be neither a help to us nor a threat.

But now all this has changed. We can send signals to the stars at a speed that cannot yet be measured, and that may well be infinite. And we know that *they* are using such techniques—for we have detected their impulses, though we cannot begin to interpret them.

These impulses are not electromagnetic, of course. We do not know what they are; we do not even have a name for them. Or, rather, we have too many names. . . .

Yes, gentlemen, there *is* something, after all, in the old wives' tales about telepathy, ESP, or whatever you care to call it. But it is no wonder that the study of such phenomena never made any progress here on Earth, where there is the continuous background roar of a billion minds to swamp all signals. Even the pitiably limited progress that was made before the Space Age seems a miracle—like discovering the laws of music in a boiler factory. It was not until we could get away from our planet's mental tumult that there was any hope of establishing a real science of parapsychology.

And even then we had to move to the other side of the Earth's orbit, where the noise was not only diminished by a hundred and eighty million miles of distance, but also shielded by the unimaginable bulk of the Sun itself. Only there, on our artificial planetoid Antigeos, could we detect and measure the feeble radiations of mentality, and uncover their laws of propagation.

In many respects, those laws are still baffling. However, we have established the basic facts. As had long been suspected by the few who believed in these phenomena, they are triggered by emotional states—not by pure willpower or deliberate, conscious thought. It is not surprising, therefore, that so many reports of paranormal events in the past were associated with moments of death or disaster. Fear is a powerful generator; on rare occasions it can manifest itself above the surrounding noise.

Once this fact was recognized, we began to make progress. We induced artificial emotional states, first in single individuals, then in groups. We were able to measure how the signals attenuated with distance. Now, we have a reliable, quantitative theory that has been checked out as far as Saturn. We believe that our calculations can be extended

even to the stars. If this is correct, we can produce a . . . **a**
shout that will be heard instantly over the whole galaxy.
And surely there will be someone who will respond!

Now there is only one way in which a signal of the required intensity can be produced. I said that fear was a powerful generator—but it is not powerful enough. Even if we
could strike all humanity with a simultaneous moment of
terror, the impulse could not be detected more than two
thousand light-years away. We need at least four times this
range. And we can achieve it—*by using the only emotion
that is more powerful than fear.*

However, we also need the co-operation of not fewer than
a billion individuals, at a moment of time that must be synchronized to the second. My colleagues have solved all the
purely technical problems, which are really quite trivial. The
simple electrostimulation devices required have been used in
medical research since the early twentieth century, and the
necessary timing pulse can be sent out over the planetary
communications networks. All the units needed can be
mass-produced within a month, and instruction in their use
requires only a few minutes. It is the psychological preparation for—let us call it O Day—that will take a little
longer. . . .

And *that*, gentlemen, is your problem; naturally, we scientists will give you all possible help. We realize that there
will be protests, cries of outrage, refusals to co-operate. But
when one looks at the matter logically, is the idea really so
offensive? Many of us think that, on the contrary, it has a
certain appropriateness—even a poetic justice.

Mankind now faces its ultimate emergency. In such a
moment of crisis, is it not right for us to call upon the instinct that has always ensured our survival in the past? A
poet in an earlier, almost equally troubled age put it better
than I can ever hope to do:

WE MUST LOVE ONE ANOTHER OR DIE.

October 1966

CRUSADE

IT WAS A world that had never known a sun. For more than a billion years, it had hovered midway between two galaxies, the prey of their conflicting gravitational pulls. In some future age the balance would be tilted, one way or the other, and it would start to fall across the light-centuries, down toward a warmth alien to all its experience.

Now it was cold beyond imagination; the intergalactic night had drained away such heat as it had once possessed. Yet there were seas there—seas of the only element that can exist in the liquid form at a fraction of a degree above absolute zero. In the shallow oceans of helium that bathed this strange world, electric currents once started could flow forever, with no weakening of power. Here superconductivity was the normal order of things; switching processes could take place billions of times a second, for millions of years, with negligible consumption of energy.

It was a computer's paradise. No world could have been more hostile to life, or more hospitable to intelligence.

And intelligence was there, dwelling in a planet-wide incrustation of crystals and microscopic metal threads. The feeble light of the two contending galaxies—briefly doubled every few centuries by the flicker of a supernova—fell upon a static landscape of sculptured geometrical forms. Nothing moved, for there was no need of movement in a world where thoughts flashed from one hemisphere to the other at the speed of light. Where only information was important, it was a waste of precious energy to transfer bulk matter.

Yet when it was essential, that, too, could be arranged. For some millions of years, the intelligence brooding over this lonely world had become aware of a certain lack of essential data. In a future that, though still remote, it could already foresee, one of those beckoning galaxies would capture it. What it would encounter, when it dived into those swarms of sun, was beyond its power of computation.

So it put forth its will, and myriad crystal lattices reshaped themselves. Atoms of metal flowed across the face of the planet. In the depths of the helium sea, two identical subbrains began to bud and grow. . . .

Once it had made its decision, the mind of the planet worked swiftly; in a few thousand years, the task was done. Without a sound, with scarcely a ripple in the surface of the frictionless sea, the newly created entities lifted from their birthplace and set forth for the distant stars.

They departed in almost opposite directions, and for more than a million years the parent intelligence heard no more of its offspring. It had not expected to; until they reached their goals, there would be nothing to report.

Then, almost simultaneously, came the news that both missions had failed. As they approached the great galactic fires and felt the massed warmth of a trillion suns, the two explorers died. Their vital circuits overheated and lost the superconductivity essential for their operation, and two mindless metal hulks drifted on toward the thickening stars.

But before disaster overtook them, they had reported on their problems; without surprise or disappointment, the mother world prepared its second attempt.

And, a million years later, its third . . . and its fourth . . . and its fifth. . . .

Such unwearying patience deserved success; and at last it came, in the shape of two long, intricately modulated trains of pulses, pouring in, century upon century, from opposite quarters of the sky. They were stored in memory circuits identical with those of the lost explorers—so that, for all practical purposes, it was as if the two scouts had themselves returned with their burden of knowledge. That their metal husks had in fact vanished among the stars was totally unimportant; the problem of personal identity was not one that had ever occurred to the planetary mind or its offspring.

First came surprising news that one universe was empty. The visiting probe had listened on all possible frequencies, to all conceivable radiations; it could detect nothing except the mindless background of star noise. It had scanned a thousand worlds without observing any trace of intelligence. True, the tests were inconclusive, for it was unable to approach any star closely enough to make a detailed examination of its planets. It had been attempting this when its insulation broke down, its temperature soared to the freezing point of nitrogen, and it died from the heat.

The parent mind was still pondering the enigma of a deserted galaxy when reports came in from its second explorer. Now all other problems were swept aside; for *this* universe teamed with intelligences, whose thoughts echoed from star to star in a myriad electronic codes. It had taken only a few centuries for the probe to analyze and interpret them all.

It realized quickly enough that it was faced with intelligences of a very strange form indeed. Why, some of them existed on worlds so unimaginably hot that even *water* was present in the liquid state! Just what manner of intelligence it was confronting, however, it did not learn for a millennium.

It barely survived the shock. Gathering its last strength, it hurled its final report into the abyss; then it, too, was consumed by the rising heat.

Now, half a million years later, the interrogation of its stay-at-home twin's mind, holding all its memories and experiences, was under way. . . .

"You detected intelligence?"

"Yes. Six hundred and thirty-seven certain cases; thirty-two probable ones. Data herewith."

[Approximately three quadrillion bits of information. Interval of a few years to process this in several thousand different ways. Surprise and confusion.]

"The data must be valid. All these sources of intelligence are correlated with high temperatures."

"That is correct. But the facts are beyond dispute; they must be accepted."

[Five hundred years of thought and experimenting. At the end of that time, definite proof that simple but slowly operating machines *could* function at temperatures as high as boiling water. Large areas of the planet badly damaged in the course of the demonstration.]

"The facts are, indeed, as you reported. Why did you not attempt communication?"

[No answer. Question repeated.]

"Because there appears to be a second and even more serious anomaly."

"Give data."

[Several quadrillion bits of information, sampled over six hundred cultures, comprising: voice, video, and neural transmissions; navigation and control signals; instrument telemetering; test patterns; jamming; electrical interference; medical equipment, etc., etc.

This followed by five centuries of analysis. *That* followed by utter consternation.

After a long pause, selected data re-examined. Thousands of visual images scanned and processed in every conceivable manner. Great attention paid to several planetary civilizations' educational TV programs, especially those concerned with elementary biology, chemistry, and cybernetics. Finally:]

"The information is self-consistent, but must be incorrect. If it is not, we are forced to these absurd conclusions: 1. Although intelligences of our type exist, they appear to be in the minority. 2. Most intelligent entities are partially liquid objects of very short duration. They are not even rigid and are constructed in a most inefficient manner from carbon, hydrogen, oxygen, phosphorus, and other atoms. 3. Though they operate at unbelievably high temperatures, all their information processing is extremely slow. 4. Their methods of replication are so complicated, improbable, and varied, that we have not been able to obtain a clear picture of them in even a single instance.

"But, worst of all: 5. *They* claim to have created our obviously far superior type of intelligence!"

[Careful re-examination of all the data. Independent processing by isolated subsections of the global mind. Cross-checking of results. A thousand years later:]

"Most probable conclusion: though much of the information relayed back to us is certainly valid, the existence of high-order, *nonmechanical* intelligences is a fantasy. (Definition: apparently self-consistent rearrangement of facts having no correspondence with the real universe.) This fantasy or mental artifact is a construct created by our probe during its mission. Why? Thermal damage? Partial destabilization of intelligence, caused by long period of isolation and absence of controlling feedback?

"Why this particular form? Protracted brooding over the problem of origins? This could lead to such delusions; model systems have produced almost identical results in simulated tests. The false logic involved is: '*We* exist; therefore something—call it X—created us.' Once this assumption is made, the properties of the hypothetical X can be fantasized in an unlimited number of ways.

"But the entire process is obviously fallacious; for by the same logic something must have created X—and so on. We are immediately involved in an infinite regress, which can have no meaning in the real universe.

"Second most probable conclusion: Fairly high-order, nonmechanical intelligences *do* indeed exist. They suffer from the delusion that they have created entities of our type. In some cases, they have even imposed their control upon them.

"Though this hypothesis is most unlikely, it must be investigated. If it is found to be true, remedial action must be taken. It should be as follows . . ."

This final monologue occurred a million years ago. It explains why, in the last half-century, almost one-quarter of the brighter novae have occurred in one tiny region of the sky: the constellation Aquila.

The crusade will reach the vicinity of Earth about the year 2050.

October 1966

NEUTRON TIDE

"IN DEFERENCE TO the next of kin," Commander Cummerbund explained with morbid relish, "the full story of the super-cruiser *Flatbush*'s last mission has never been revealed. You know, of course, that she was lost during the war against the Mucoids."

We all shuddered. Even now, the very name of the gelatinous monsters who had come slurping Earthward from the general direction of the Coal Sack aroused vomitive memories.

"I knew her skipper well—Captain Karl van Rinderpest, hero of the final assault on the unspeakable, but not unshriekable, !!Yeetch."

He paused politely to let us unplug our ears and mop up our spilled drinks.

"*Flatbush* had just launched a salvo of probability inverters against the Mucoid home planet and was heading back toward deep space in formation with three destroyers—the Russian *Lieutenant Kizhe*, the Israeli *Chutzpah*, and Her Majesty's *Insufferable*. They were still accelerating when a fantastically unlikely accident occurred. *Flatbush* ran straight into the gravity well of a neutron star."

When our expressions of horror and incredulity had subsided, he continued gravely.

"Yes—a sphere of ultimately condensed matter, only ten miles across, yet as massive as a sun—and hence with a surface gravity one hundred billion times that of Earth.

"The other ships were lucky. They only skirted the outer fringe of the field and managed to escape, though their orbits were deflected almost a hundred and eighty degrees. But *Flatbush,* we calculated later, must have passed within a few dozen miles of that unthinkable concentration of mass, and so experienced the full violence of its tidal forces.

"Now in any reasonable gravitational field—even that of a White Dwarf, which may run up to a million Earth g's—you just swing around the center of attraction and head on out into space again, without feeling a thing. At the closest point you could be accelerating at hundreds or thousands of g's—but you're still in free fall, so there are no physical effects. Sorry if I'm laboring the obvious, but I realize that everyone here isn't technically orientated."

If this was intended as a crack at Fleet Paymaster General "Sticky Fingers" Geldclutch, he never noticed, being well into his fifth beaker of Martian Joy Juice.

"For a neutron star, however, this is no longer true. Near the center of mass the gravitational gradient—that is, the rate at which the field changes with distance—is so enormous that even across the width of a small body like a spaceship there can be a difference of a hundred thousand g's. I need hardly tell you what *that* sort of field can do to any material object.

"*Flatbush* must have been torn to pieces almost instantly, and the pieces themselves must have flowed like liquid during the few seconds they took to swing around the star. Then the fragments headed on out into space again.

"Months later a radar sweep by the Salvage Corps located some of the debris. I've seen it—surrealistically shaped lumps of the toughest metals we possess twisted together like taffy. And there was only one item that could even be recognized—it must have come from some unfortunate engineer's tool kit."

The Commander's voice dropped almost to inaudibility, and he dashed away a manly tear.

"I really hate to say this." He sighed. "But the only identifiable fragment of the pride of the United States Space Navy was—one star-mangled spanner."

January 1970

TRANSIT OF EARTH

TESTING ONE, TWO, three, four, five . . .
Evans speaking. I will continue to record as long as possible. This is a two-hour capsule, but I doubt if I'll fill it.

That photograph has haunted me all my life; now, too late, I know why. (But would it have made any difference if I *had* known? That's one of those meaningless and unanswerable questions the mind keeps returning to endlessly, like the tongue exploring a broken tooth.)

I've not seen it for years, but I've only to close my eyes and I'm back in landscape, almost as hostile—and as beautiful—as this one. Fifty million miles sunward, and seventy-two years in the past, five men face the camera amid the Antarctic snows. Not even the bulky furs can hide the exhaustion and defeat that mark every line of their bodies; and their faces are already touched by Death.

There were five of them. There were five of us, and of course we also took a group photograph. But everything else was different. We were smiling—cheerful, confident. And our picture was on all the screens of Earth within ten minutes. It was months before *their* camera was found and brought back to civilization.

And we die in comfort, with all modern conveniences— including many that Robert Falcon Scott could never have imagined, when he stood at the South Pole in 1912.

Two hours later. I'll start giving exact times when it becomes important.

All the facts are in the log, and by now the whole world knows them. So I guess I'm doing this largely to settle my mind—to talk myself into facing the inevitable. The trouble is, I'm not sure what subjects to avoid, and which to tackle head on. Well, there's only one way to find out.

The first item: in twenty-four hours, at the very most, all the oxygen will be gone. That leaves me with the three classical choices. I can let the carbon dioxide build up until I become unconscious. I can step outside and crack the suit, leaving Mars to do the job in about two minutes. Or I can use one of the tablets in the med kit.

CO_2 build-up. Everyone says that's quite easy—just like going to sleep. I've no doubt that's true; unfortunately, in my case it's associated with nightmare number one. . . .

I wish I'd never come across that damn book *True Stories of World War Two,* or whatever it was called. There was one chapter about a German submarine, found and salvaged after the war. The crew was still inside it—*two* men per bunk. And between each pair of skeletons, the single respirator set they'd been sharing. . . .

Well, at least that won't happen here. But I know, with a deadly certainty, that as soon as I find it hard to breathe, I'll be back in that doomed U-boat.

So what about the quicker way? When you're exposed to vacuum, you're unconscious in ten or fifteen seconds, and people who've been through it say it's not painful—just peculiar. But trying to breathe something that isn't there brings me altogether too neatly to nightmare number two.

This time, it's a personal experience. As a kid, I used to do a lot of skin diving, when my family went to the Caribbean for vacations. There was an old freighter that had sunk twenty years before, out on a reef, with its deck only a couple of yards below the surface. Most of the hatches were open, so it was easy to get inside, to look for souvenirs and hunt the big fish that like to shelter in such places.

Of course it was dangerous if you did it without scuba gear. So what boy could resist the challenge?

My favorite route involved diving into a hatch on the foredeck, swimming about fifty feet along a passageway dimly lit by portholes a few yards apart, then angling up a short flight of stairs and emerging through a door in the battered superstructure. The whole trip took less than a minute—an easy dive for anyone in good condition. There was even time to do some sight-seeing, or to play with a few fish along the route. And sometimes, for a change, I'd switch directions, going in the door and coming out again through the hatch.

That was the way I did it the last time. I hadn't dived for a week—there had been a big storm, and the sea was too rough—so I was impatient to get going.

I deep-breathed on the surface for about two minutes, until I felt the tingling in my finger tips that told me it was time to stop. Then I jackknifed and slid gently down toward the black rectangle of the open doorway.

It always looked ominous and menacing—that was part of the thrill. And for the first few yards I was almost completely blind; the contrast between the tropical glare above water and the gloom between decks was so great that it took quite a while for my eyes to adjust. Usually, I was halfway along the corridor before I could see anything clearly. Then the illumination would steadily increase as I approached the open hatch, where a shaft of sunlight would paint a dazzling rectangle on the rusty, barnacled metal floor.

I'd almost made it when I realized that, this time, the light wasn't getting better. There was no slanting column of sunlight ahead of me, leading up to the world of air and life.

I had a second of baffled confusion, wondering if I'd lost my way. Then I knew what had happened—and confusion turned into sheer panic. Sometime during the storm, the hatch must have slammed shut. It weighed at least a quarter of a ton.

I don't remember making a U turn; the next thing I recall is swimming quite slowly back along the passage and telling myself: Don't hurry; your air will last longer if you take it easy. I could see very well now, because my eyes had had plenty of time to become dark-adapted. There were lots of details I'd never noticed before, like the red squirrelfish lurking in the shadows, the green fronds and algae growing in the little patches of light around the portholes, and even a single rubber boot, apparently in excellent condition, lying where someone must have kicked it off. And once, out of a side corridor, I noticed a big grouper staring at me with bulbous eyes, his thick lips half parted, as if he was astonished at my intrusion.

The band around my chest was getting tighter and tighter. It was impossible to hold my breath any longer. Yet the stairway still seemed an infinite distance ahead. I let some bubbles of air dribble out of my mouth. That improved matters for a moment, but, once I had exhaled, the ache in my lungs became even more unendurable.

Now there was no point in conserving strength by flippering along with that steady, unhurried stroke. I snatched the ultimate few cubic inches of air from my face mask—feeling it flatten against my nose as I did so—and swallowed them down into my starving lungs. At the same time, I shifted gear and drove forward with every last atom of strength. . . .

And that's all I remember until I found myself sputtering and coughing in the daylight, clinging to the broken stub of the mast. The water around me was stained with blood, and I wondered why. Then, to my great surprise, I noticed a deep gash in my right calf. I must have banged into some sharp obstruction, but I'd never noticed it and even then felt no pain.

That was the end of my skin diving until I started astronaut training ten years later and went into the underwater zero-gee simulator. Then it was different, because I was using scuba gear. But I had some nasty moments that I was afraid the psychologists would notice, and I always made sure that I got nowhere near emptying my tank. Having nearly suffocated once, I'd no intention of risking it again. . . .

I know exactly what it will feel like to breathe the freezing wisp of near-vacuum that passes for atmosphere on Mars. No thank you.

So what's wrong with poison? Nothing, I suppose. The stuff we've got takes only fifteen seconds, they told us. But all my instincts are against it, even when there's no sensible alternative.

Did Scott have poison with him? I doubt it. And if he did, I'm sure he never used it.

I'm not going to replay this. I hope it's been of some use, but I can't be sure.

The radio has just printed out a message from Earth, reminding me that transit starts in two hours. As if I'm likely to forget—when four men have already died so that I can be the first human being to see it. And the only one, for exactly a hundred years. It isn't often that Sun, Earth, and Mars line up neatly like this; the last time was in 1905, when poor old Lowell was still writing his beautiful nonsense about the canals and the great dying civilization that had built them. Too bad it was all delusion.

I'd better check the telescope and the timing equipment.

The Sun is quiet today—as it should be, anyway, near the middle of the cycle. Just a few small spots, and some minor areas of disturbance around them. The solar weather is set calm for months to come. That's one thing the others won't have to worry about, on their way home.

I think that was the worst moment, watching *Olympus* lift off Phobos and head back to Earth. Even though we'd known for weeks that nothing could be done, that was the final closing of the door.

It was night, and we could see everything perfectly. Phobos had come leaping up out of the west a few hours earlier, and was doing its mad backward rush across the sky, growing from a tiny crescent to a half-moon; before it reached the zenith it would disappear as it plunged into the shadow of Mars and became eclipsed.

We'd been listening to the countdown, of course, trying to go about our normal work. It wasn't easy, accepting at last the fact that fifteen of us had come to Mars and only ten would return. Even then, I suppose there were millions back on Earth who still could not understand. They must have found it impossible to believe that *Olympus* couldn't descend a mere four thousand miles to pick us up. The Space Administration had been bombarded with crazy rescue schemes; heaven knows, we'd thought of enough ourselves. But when the permafrost under Landing Pad Three finally gave way and *Pegasus* toppled, that was that. It still seems a miracle that the ship didn't blow up when the propellant tank ruptured. . . .

I'm wandering again. Back to Phobos and the countdown.

On the telescope monitor, we could clearly see the fissured plateau where *Olympus* had touched down after we'd separated and begun our own descent. Though our friends would never land on Mars, at least they'd have a little world of their own to explore; even for a satellite as small as Phobos, it worked out at thirty square miles per man. A lot of territory to search for strange minerals and debris from space—or to carve your name so that future ages would know that you were the first of all men to come this way.

The ship was clearly visible as a stubby, bright cylinder against the dull-gray rocks; from time to time some flat surface would catch the light of the swiftly moving sun, and would flash with mirror brilliance. But about five minutes before lift-off, the picture became suddenly pink, then crimson—then vanished completely as Phobos rushed into eclipse.

The countdown was still at ten seconds when we were startled by a blast of light. For a moment, we wondered if *Olympus* had also met with catastrophe. Then we realized that someone was filming the take-off, and the external floodlights had been switched on.

During those last few seconds, I think we all forgot our own predicament; we were up there aboard *Olympus*, willing the thrust to build up smoothly and lift the ship out of the tiny gravitational field of Phobos, and then away from Mars for the long fall sunward. We heard Commander Richmond say "Ignition," there was a brief burst of interference, and the patch of light began to move in the field of the telescope.

That was all. There was no blazing column of fire, because, of course, there's really no ignition when a nuclear rocket lights up. "Lights up" indeed! That's another hangover from the old chemical technology. But a hot hydrogen blast is completely invisible; it seems a pity that we'll never again see anything so spectacular as a Saturn or a Korolov blast-off.

Just before the end of the burn, *Olympus* left the shadow

of Mars and burst out into sunlight again, reappearing almost instantly as a brilliant, swiftly moving star. The blaze of light must have startled them aboard the ship, because we heard someone call out: "Cover that window!" Then, a few seconds later, Richmond announced: "Engine cutoff." Whatever happened, *Olympus* was now irrevocably headed back to Earth.

A voice I didn't recognize—though it must have been the Commander's—said "Good-by, *Pegasus*," and the radio transmission switched off. There was, of course, no point in saying "Good luck." *That* had all been settled weeks ago.

I've just played this back. Talking of luck, there's been one compensation, though not for us. With a crew of only ten, *Olympus* has been able to dump a third of her expendables and lighten herself by several tons. So now she'll get home a month ahead of schedule.

Plenty of things could have gone wrong in that month; we may yet have saved the expedition. Of course, we'll never know—but it's a nice thought.

I've been playing a lot of music, full blast—now that there's no one else to be disturbed. Even if there were any Martians, I don't suppose this ghost of an atmosphere can carry the sound more than a few yards.

We have a fine collection, but I have to choose carefully. Nothing downbeat and nothing that demands too much concentration. Above all, nothing with human voices. So I restrict myself to the lighter orchestral classics; the "New World" symphony and Grieg's piano concerto fill the bill perfectly. At the moment I'm listening to Rachmaninoff's "Rhapsody on a Theme of Paganini," but now I must switch off and get down to work.

There are only five minutes to go. All the equipment is in perfect condition. The telescope is tracking the Sun, and the video recorder is standing by, the precision timer is running.

These observations will be as accurate as I can make them. I owe it to my lost comrades, whom I'll soon be joining. They gave me their oxygen, so that I can still be alive at this moment. I hope you remember that, a hundred or a thousand years from now, whenever you crank these figures into the computers. . . .

Only a minute to go; getting down to business. For the record: year, 1984; month, May; day, II, coming up to four hours thirty minutes Ephemeris Time . . . *now*.

Half a minute to contact. Switching recorder and timer to high speed. Just rechecked position angle to make sure I'm looking at the right spot on the Sun's limb. Using power of five hundred—image perfectly steady even at this low elevation.

Four thirty-two. Any moment now . . .

There it is . . . there it is! I can hardly believe it! A tiny black dent in the edge of the Sun . . . growing, growing, growing . . .

Hello, Earth. Look up at me, the brightest star in your sky, straight overhead at midnight. . . .

Recorder back to slow.

Four thirty-five. It's as if a thumb is pushing into the Sun's edge, deeper and deeper . . . Fascinating to watch . . .

Four forty-one. Exactly halfway. The Earth's a perfect black semicircle—a clean bite out of the Sun. As if some disease is eating it away . . .

Four forty-eight. Ingress three-quarters complete.

Four hours forty-nine minutes thirty seconds. Recorder on high speed again.

The line of contact with the Sun's edge is shrinking fast. Now it's a barely visible black thread. In a few seconds, the whole Earth will be superimposed on the Sun.

Now I can see the effects of the atmosphere. There's a thin halo of light surrounding that black hole in the Sun. Strange to think that I'm seeing the glow of all the sunsets— and all the sunrises—that are taking place around the whole Earth at this very moment. . . .

Ingress complete—four hours fifty minutes five seconds. The whole world has moved onto the face of the Sun. A perfectly circular black disc silhouetted against that inferno ninety million miles below. It looks bigger than I expected; one could easily mistake it for a fair-sized sunspot.

Nothing more to see now for six hours, when the Moon appears, trailing Earth by half the Sun's width. I'll beam the recorder data back to Lunacom, then try to get some sleep.

My very last sleep. Wonder if I'll need drugs. It seems a

pity to waste these last few hours, but I want to conserve my strength—and my oxygen.

I think it was Dr. Johnson who said that nothing settles a man's mind so wonderfully as the knowledge that he'll be hanged in the morning. How the hell did *he* know?

Ten hours thirty minutes Ephemeris Time. Dr. Johnson was right. I had only one pill, and don't remember any dreams.

The condemned man also ate a hearty breakfast. Cut that out . . .

Back at the telescope. Now the Earth's halfway across the disc, passing well north of the center. In ten minutes, I should see the Moon.

I've just switched to the highest power of the telescope— two thousand. The image is slightly fuzzy, but still fairly good; atmospheric halo very distinct. I'm hoping to see the cities on the dark side of Earth. . . .

No luck. Probably too many clouds. A pity; it's theoretically possible, but we never succeeded. I wish . . . never mind.

Ten hours forty minutes. Recorder on slow speed. Hope I'm looking at the right spot.

Fifteen seconds to go. Recorder fast.

Damn—missed it. Doesn't matter—the recorder will have caught the exact moment. There's a little black notch already in the side of the Sun. First contact must have been about ten hours forty-one minutes twenty seconds ET.

What a long way it is between Earth and Moon; there's half the width of the Sun between them. You wouldn't think the two bodies had anything to do with each other. Makes you realize just how big the Sun really is. . . .

Ten hours forty-four minutes. The Moon's exactly halfway over the edge. A very small, very clear-cut semicircular bite out of the edge of the Sun.

Ten hours forty-seven minutes five seconds. Internal contact. The Moon's clear of the edge, entirely inside the Sun. Don't suppose I can see anything on the night side, but I'll increase the power.

That's funny.

Well, well. Someone must be trying to talk to me; there's

a tiny light pulsing way there on the darkened face of the moon. Probably the laser at Imbrium Base.

Sorry, everyone. I've said all my good-byes, and don't want to go through that again. Nothing can be important now.

Still, it's almost hypnotic—that flickering point of light, coming out of the face of the Sun itself. Hard to believe that, even after it's traveled all this distance, the beam is only a hundred miles wide. Lunacom's going to all this trouble to aim it exactly at me, and I suppose I should feel guilty at ignoring it. But I don't. I've nearly finished my work, and the things of Earth are no longer any concern of mine.

Ten hours fifty minutes. Recorder off. That's it—until the end of Earth transit, two hours from now.

I've had to snack and am taking my last look at the view from the observation bubble. The Sun's still high, so there's not much contrast, but the light brings out all the colors vividly—the countless varieties of red and pink and crimson, so startling against the deep blue of the sky. How different from the Moon—though that, too, has its own beauty.

It's strange how surprising the obvious can be. Everyone knew that Mars was red. But we didn't really expect the red of rust, the red of blood. Like the Painted Desert of Arizona; after a while, the eye longs for green.

To the north, there is one welcome change of color; the cap of carbon-dioxide snow on Mount Burroughs is a dazzling white pyramid. That's another surprise. Burroughs is twenty-five thousand feet above Mean Datum; when I was a boy, there weren't supposed to be any mountains on Mars. . . .

The nearest sand dune is a quarter of a mile away, and it, too, has patches of frost on its shaded slope. During the last storm, we thought it moved a few feet, but we couldn't be sure. Certainly the dunes *are* moving, like those on Earth. One day, I suppose, this base will be covered—only to reappear again in a thousand years. Or ten thousand.

That strange group of rocks—an Elephant, the Capitol, the Bishop—still holds its secrets, and teases me with the memory of our first big disappointment. We could have sworn that they were sedimentary; how eagerly we rushed out to look for fossils! Even now, we don't know what formed that outcropping. The geology of Mars is still a mass of contradictions and enigmas. . . .

We have passed on enough problems to the future, and those who come after us will find many more. But there's one mystery we never reported to Earth, or even entered in the log. . . .

The first night we landed, we took turns keeping watch. Brennan was on duty, and woke me up soon after midnight. I was annoyed—it was ahead of time—and then he told me that he'd seen a light moving around the base of the Capitol.

We watched for at least an hour, until it was my turn to take over. But we saw nothing; whatever that light was, it never reappeared.

Now Brennan was as levelheaded and unimaginative as they come; if he said he saw a light, then he saw one. Maybe it was some kind of electric discharge, or the reflection of Phobos on a piece of sand-polished rock. Anyway, we decided not to mention it to Lunacom, unless we saw it again.

Since I've been alone, I've often awakened in the night and looked out toward the rocks. In the feeble illumination of Phobos and Deimos, they remind me of the skyline of a darkened city. And it has always remained darkened. No lights have ever appeared for me. . . .

Twelve hours forty-nine minutes Ephemeris Time. The last act's about to begin. Earth has nearly reached the edge of the Sun. The two narrow horns of light that still embrace it are barely touching. . . .

Recorder on fast.

Contact! Twelve hours fifty minutes sixteen seconds. The crescents of light no longer meet. A tiny black spot has appeared at the edge of the Sun, as the Earth begins to cross it. It's growing longer, longer. . . .

Recorder on slow. Eighteen minutes to wait before Earth finally clears the face of the Sun.

The Moon still has more than halfway to go; it's not yet reached the mid-point of its transit. It looks like a little round blob of ink, only a quarter the size of Earth. And there's no light flickering there any more. Lunacom must have given up.

Well, I have just a quarter of an hour left, here in my last home. Time seems to be accelerating the way it does in the final minutes before a lift-off. No matter; I have everything worked out now. I can even relax.

Already, I feel part of history. I am one with Captain Cook, back in Tahiti in 1769, watching the transit of Venus. Except for that image of the Moon trailing along behind, it must have looked just like this. . . .

What would Cook have thought, over two hundred years ago, if he'd known that one day a man would observe the whole Earth in transit from an outer world? I'm sure he would have been astonished—and then delighted. . . .

But I feel a closer identity with a man not yet born. I hope you hear these words, whoever you may be. Perhaps you will be standing on this very spot, a hundred years from now, when the next transit occurs.

Greetings to 2084, November 10! I wish you better luck than we had. I suppose you will have come here on a luxury liner. Or you may have been born on Mars, and be a stranger to Earth. You will know things that I cannot imagine. Yet somehow I don't envy you. I would not even change places with you if I could.

For you will remember my name, and know that I was the first of all mankind ever to see a transit of Earth. And no one will see another for a hundred years. . . .

Twelve hours fifty-nine minutes. Exactly halfway through egress. The Earth is a perfect semicircle—a black shadow on the face of the Sun. I still can't escape from the impression that something has taken a big bite out of that golden disc. In nine minutes it will be gone, and the Sun will be whole again.

Thirteen hours seven minutes. Recorder on fast.

Earth has almost gone. There's just a shallow black dimple at the edge of the Sun. You could easily mistake it for a small spot, going over the limb.

Thirteen hours eight.

Good-by, beautiful Earth.

Going, going, going. Good-by, good—

I'm O.K. again now. The timings have all been sent home on the beam. In five minutes, they'll join the accumulated wisdom of mankind. And Lunacom will know that I stuck to my post.

But I'm not sending this. I'm going to leave it here, for

the next expedition—whenever that may be. It could be ten or twenty years before anyone comes here again. No point in going back to an old site when there's a whole world waiting to be explored. . . .

So this capsule will stay here, as Scott's diary remained in his tent, until the next visitors find it. But they won't find me.

Strange how hard it is to get away from Scott. I think he gave me the idea.

For his body will not lie frozen forever in the Antarctic, isolated from the great cycle of life and death. Long ago, that lonely tent began its march to the sea. Within a few years, it was buried by the falling snow and had become part of the glacier that crawls eternally away from the Pole. In a few brief centuries, the sailor will have returned to the sea. He will merge once more into the pattern of living things— the plankton, the seals, the penguins, the whales, all the multitudinous fauna of the Antarctic Ocean.

There are no oceans here on Mars, nor have there been for at least five billion years. But there is life of some kind, down there in the badlands of Chaos II, which we never had time to explore.

Those moving patches on the orbital photographs. The evidence that whole areas of Mars have been swept clear of craters, by forces other than erosion. The long-chain, optically active carbon molecules picked up by the atmospheric samplers.

And, of course, the mystery of Viking 6. Even now, no one has been able to make any sense of those last instrument readings, before something large and heavy crushed the probe in the still, cold depths of the Martian night. . . .

And don't talk to me about *primitive* life forms in a place like this! Anything that's survived here will be so sophisticated that we may look as clumsy as dinosaurs.

There's still enough propellant in the ship's tanks to drive the Mars car clear around the planet. I have three hours of daylight left—plenty of time to get down into the valleys and well out into Chaos. After sunset, I'll still be able to make good speed with the headlights. It will be romantic, driving at night under the moons of Mars. . . .

One thing I must fix before I leave. I don't like the way Sam's lying out there. He was always so poised, so graceful.

It doesn't seem right that he should look so awkward now. I must do something about it.

I wonder if *I* could have covered three hundred feet without a suit, walking slowly, steadily—the way he did, to the very end.

I must try not to look at his face.

That's it. Everything shipshape and ready to go.

The therapy has worked. I feel perfectly at ease—even contented, now that I know exactly what I'm going to do. The old nightmares have lost their power.

It is true: we all die alone. It makes no difference at the end, being fifty million miles from home.

I'm going to enjoy the drive through that lovely painted landscape. I'll be thinking of all those who dreamed about Mars—Wells and Lowell and Burroughs and Weinbaum and Bradbury. They all guessed wrong—but the reality is just as strange, just as beautiful, as they imagined.

I don't know what's waiting for me out there, and I'll probably never see it. But on this starveling world, it must be desperate for carbon, phosphorus, oxygen, calcium. It can use me.

And when my oxygen alarm gives its final "ping," somewhere down there in that haunted wilderness, I'm going to finish in style. As soon as I have difficulty in breathing, I'll get off the Mars car and start walking—with a playback unit plugged into my helmet and going full blast.

For sheer, triumphant power and glory there's nothing in the whole of music to match the Toccata and Fugue in D. I won't have time to hear all of it; that doesn't matter.

Johann Sebastian, here I come.

February 1970

A MEETING WITH MEDUSA

1. A DAY TO REMEMBER

THE *QUEEN ELIZABETH* was over three miles above the Grand Canyon, dawdling along at a comfortable hundred and eighty, when Howard Falcon spotted the camera platform closing in from the right. He had been expecting it—nothing else was cleared to fly this altitude—but he was not too happy to have company. Although he welcomed any signs of public interest, he also wanted as much empty sky as he could get. After all, he was the first man in history to navigate a ship three-tenths of a mile long. . . .

So far, this first test flight had gone perfectly; ironically enough, the only problem had been the century-old aircraft carrier *Chairman Mao,* borrowed from the San Diego Naval Museum for support operations. Only one of *Mao*'s four nuclear reactors was still operating, and the old battlewagon's top speed was barely thirty knots. Luckily, wind speed at sea level had been less than half this, so it had not been too difficult to maintain still air on the flight deck. Though there had been a few anxious moments during gusts, when the mooring lines had been dropped, the great dirigible had risen smoothly, straight up into the sky, as if on an invisible elevator. If all went well, *Queen Elizabeth V* would not meet *Chairman Mao* again for another week.

Everything was under control; all test instruments gave normal readings. Commander Falcon decided to go upstairs and watch the rendezvous. He handed over to his second officer, and walked out into the transparent tubeway that led through the heart of the ship. There, as always, he was overwhelmed by the spectacle of the largest single space ever enclosed by man.

The ten spherical gas cells, each more than a hundred feet across, were ranged one behind the other like a line of gigantic soap bubbles. The tough plastic was so clear that he could see through the whole length of the array, and make out details of the elevator mechanism, more than a third of a mile from his vantage point. All around him, like a three-dimensional maze, was the structural framework of the ship —the great longitudinal girders running from nose to tail, the fifteen hoops that were the circular ribs of this sky-borne colossus, and whose varying sizes defined its graceful, streamlined profile.

At this low speed, there was little sound—merely the soft rush of wind over the envelope and an occasional creak of metal as the pattern of stresses changed. The shadowless light from the rows of lamps far overhead gave the whole scene a curiously submarine quality, and to Falcon this was enhanced by the spectacle of the translucent gasbags. He had once encountered a squadron of large but harmless jellyfish, pulsing their mindless way above a shallow tropical reef, and the plastic bubbles that gave *Queen Elizabeth* her lift often reminded him of these—especially when changing pressures made them crinkle and scatter new patterns of reflected light.

He walked down the axis of the ship until he came to the forward elevator, between gas cells one and two. Riding up to the Observation Deck, he noticed that it was uncomfortably hot, and dictated a brief memo to himself on his pocket recorder. The *Queen* obtained almost a quarter of her buoyancy from the unlimited amounts of waste heat produced by her fusion power plant. On this lightly loaded flight, indeed, only six of the ten gas cells contained helium; the remaining four were full of air. Yet she still carried two hundred tons of water as ballast. However, running the cells at high temperatures did produce problems in refrigerating the access ways; it was obvious that a little more work would have to be done there.

A refreshing blast of cooler air hit him in the face when he stepped out onto the Observation Deck and into the dazzling sunlight streaming through the Plexiglas roof. Half a dozen workmen, with an equal number of superchimp assistants, were busily laying the partly completed dance floor, while others were installing electric wiring and fixing furniture. It was a scene of controlled chaos, and Falcon found it hard to believe that everything would be ready for the maiden voyage, only four weeks ahead. Well, that was not *his* problem, thank goodness. He was merely the Captain, not the Cruise Director.

The human workers waved to him, and the "simps" flashed toothy smiles, as he walked through the confusion, into the already completed Skylounge. This was his favorite place in the whole ship, and he knew that once she was operating he would never again have it all to himself. He would allow himself just five minutes of private enjoyment.

He called the bridge, checked that everything was still in order, and relaxed into one of the comfortable swivel chairs. Below, in a curve that delighted the eye, was the unbroken silver sweep of the ship's envelope. He was perched at the highest point, surveying the whole immensity of the largest vehicle ever built. And when he had tired of that—all the way out to the horizon was the fantastic wilderness carved by the Colorado River in half a billion years of time.

Apart from the camera platform (it had now fallen back and was filming from amidships) he had the sky to himself. It was blue and empty, clear down to the horizon. In his grandfather's day, Falcon knew, it would have been streaked with vapor trails and stained with smoke. Both had gone: the aerial garbage had vanished with the primitive technologies that spawned it, and the long-distance transportation of this age arced too far beyond the stratosphere for any sight or sound of it to reach Earth. Once again, the lower atmosphere belonged to the birds and the clouds—and now to *Queen Elizabeth V.*

It was true, as the old pioneers had said at the beginning of the twentieth century: this was the only way to travel—in silence and luxury, breathing the air around you and not cut off from it, near enough to the surface to watch the ever-changing beauty of land and sea. The subsonic jets of the 1980s, packed with hundreds of passengers seated ten abreast, could not even begin to match such comfort and spaciousness.

Of course, the *Queen* would never be an economic proposition, and even if her projected sister ships were built, only a few of the world's quarter of a billion inhabitants would ever enjoy this silent gliding through the sky. But a secure and prosperous global society could afford such follies and indeed needed them for their novelty and entertainment. There were at least a million men on Earth whose discretionary income exceeded a thousand new dollars a year, so the *Queen* would not lack for passengers.

Falcon's pocket communicator beeped. The copilot was calling from the bridge.

"O.K. for rendezvous, Captain? We've got all the data we need from this run, and the TV people are getting impatient."

Falcon glanced at the camera platform, now matching his speed a tenth of a mile away.

"O.K.," he replied. "Proceed as arranged. I'll watch from here."

He walked back through the busy chaos of the Observation Deck so that he could have a better view amidships. As he did so, he could feel the change of vibration underfoot; by the time he had reached the rear of the lounge, the ship had come to rest. Using his master key, he let himself out onto the small external platform flaring from the end of the deck; half a dozen people could stand here, with only low guardrails separating them from the vast sweep of the envelope—and from the ground, thousands of feet below. It was an exciting place to be, and perfectly safe even when the ship was traveling at speed, for it was in the dead air behind the huge dorsal blister of the Observation Deck. Nevertheless, it was not intended that the passengers would have access to it; the view was a little too vertiginous.

The covers of the forward cargo hatch had already opened like giant trap doors, and the camera platform was hovering above them, preparing to descend. Along this route, in the years to come, would travel thousands of passengers and tons of supplies. Only on rare occasions would the *Queen* drop down to sea level and dock with her floating base.

A sudden gust of cross wind slapped Falcon's cheek, and he tightened his grip on the guardrail. The Grand Canyon was a bad place for turbulence, though he did not expect much at this altitude. Without any real anxiety, he focused his attention on the descending platform, now about a hundred and fifty feet above the ship. He knew that the highly skilled operator who was flying the remotely controlled vehicle had performed this simple maneuver a dozen times already; it was inconceivable that he would have any difficulties.

Yet he seemed to be reacting rather sluggishly. That last gust had drifted the platform almost to the edge of the open hatchway. Surely the pilot could have corrected before this. . . . Did he have a control problem? It was very unlikely; these remotes had multiple-redundancy, fail-safe takeovers, and any number of backup systems. Accidents were almost unheard of.

But there he went again, off to the left. Could the pilot be *drunk*? Improbable though that seemed, Falcon considered it seriously for a moment. Then he reached for his microphone switch.

Once again, without warning, he was slapped violently in the face. He hardly felt it, for he was staring in horror at the camera platform. The distant operator was fighting for control, trying to balance the craft on its jets—but he was only making matters worse. The oscillations increased—twenty degrees, forty, sixty, ninety. . . .

"Switch to automatic, you fool!" Falcon shouted uselessly into his microphone. "Your manual control's not working!"

The platform flipped over on its back. The jets no longer supported it, but drove it swiftly downward. They had suddenly become allies of the gravity they had fought until this moment.

Falcon never heard the crash, though he felt it; he was already inside the Observation Deck, racing for the elevator that would take him down to the bridge. Workmen shouted at him anxiously, asking what had happened. It would be many months before he knew the answer to that question.

Just as he was stepping into the elevator cage, he changed his mind. What if there was a power failure? Better be on the safe side, even if it took longer and time was the essence. He began to run down the spiral stairway enclosing the shaft.

Halfway down he paused for a second to inspect the damage. That damned platform had gone clear through the ship, rupturing two of the gas cells as it did so. They were still collapsing slowly, in great falling veils of plastic. He was not worried about the loss of lift—the ballast could easily take care of that, as long as eight cells remained intact. Far more serious was the possibility of structural damage. Already he could hear the great latticework around him groaning and protesting under its abnormal loads. It was not enough to have sufficient lift; unless it was properly distributed, the ship would break her back.

He was just resuming his descent when a superchimp, shrieking with fright, came racing down the elevator shaft, moving with incredible speed, hand over hand, along the *outside* of the latticework. In its terror, the poor beast had torn off its company uniform, perhaps in an unconscious attempt to regain the freedom of its ancestors.

Falcon, still descending as swiftly as he could, watched its approach with some alarm. A distraught simp was a powerful and potentially dangerous animal, especially if fear overcame its conditioning. As it overtook him, it started to call out a string of words, but they were all jumbled together, and the only one he could recognize was a plaintive, frequently repeated "boss." Even now, Falcon realized, it looked toward humans for guidance. He felt sorry for the creature, involved in a man-made disaster beyond its comprehension, and for which it bore no responsibility.

It stopped opposite him, on the other side of the lattice; there was nothing to prevent it from coming through the open framework if it wished. Now its face was only inches from his, and he was looking straight into the terrified eyes. Never before had he been so close to a simp, and able to study its features in such detail. He felt that strange mingling of kinship and discomfort that all men experience when they gaze thus into the mirror of time.

His presence seemed to have calmed the creature. Falcon

pointed up the shaft, back toward the Observation Deck, and said very clearly and precisely: "Boss—boss—go." To his relief, the simp understood; it gave him a grimace that might have been a smile, and at once started to race back the way it had come. Falcon had given it the best advice he could. If any safety remained aboard the *Queen*, it was in that direction. But his duty lay in the other.

He had almost completed his descent when, with a sound of rending metal, the vessel pitched nose down, and the lights went out. But he could still see quite well, for a shaft of sunlight streamed through the open hatch and the huge tear in the envelope. Many years ago he had stood in a great cathedral nave watching the light pouring through the stained-glass windows and forming pools of multicolored radiance on the ancient flagstones. The dazzling shaft of sunlight through the ruined fabric high above reminded him of that moment. He was in a cathedral of metal, falling down the sky.

When he reached the bridge, and was able for the first time to look outside, he was horrified to see how close the ship was to the ground. Only three thousand feet below were the beautiful and deadly pinnacles of rock and the red rivers of mud that were still carving their way down into the past. There was no level area anywhere in sight where a ship as large as the *Queen* could come to rest on an even keel.

A glance at the display board told him that all the ballast had gone. However, rate of descent had been reduced to a few yards a second; they still had a fighting chance.

Without a word, Falcon eased himself into the pilot's seat and took over such control as still remained. The instrument board showed him everything he wished to know; speech was superfluous. In the background, he could hear the Communications Officer giving a running report over the radio. By this time, all the news channels of Earth would have been preempted, and he could imagine the utter frustration of the program controllers. One of the most spectacular wrecks in history was occurring—without a single camera to record it. The last moments of the *Queen* would never fill millions with awe and terror, as had those of the *Hindenburg*, a century and a half before.

Now the ground was only about seventeen hundred feet away, still coming up slowly. Though he had full thrust, he had not dared to use it, lest the weakened structure collapse; but now he realized that he had no choice. The wind was taking them toward a fork in the canyon, where the river was split by a wedge of rock like the prow of some gigantic, fossilized ship of stone. If she continued on her present course, the *Queen* would straddle that triangular plateau and come to rest with at least a third of her length jutting out over nothingness; she would snap like a rotten stick.

Far away, above the sound of straining metal and escaping gas, came the familiar whistle of the jets as Falcon opened up the lateral thrusters. The ship staggered, and began to slew to port. The shriek of tearing metal was now almost continuous—and the rate of descent had started to increase ominously. A glance at the damage-control board showed that cell number five had just gone.

The ground was only yards away. Even now, he could not tell whether his maneuver would succeed or fail. He switched the thrust vectors over to vertical, giving maximum lift to reduce the force of impact.

The crash seemed to last forever. It was not violent— merely prolonged, and irresistible. It seemed that the whole universe was falling about them.

The sound of crunching metal came nearer, as if some great beast were eating its way through the dying ship.

Then floor and ceiling closed upon him like a vise.

2. "BECAUSE IT'S THERE"

"Why do you want to go to Jupiter?"

"As Springer said when he lifted for Pluto—'because it's there.' "

"Thanks. Now we've got *that* out of the way—the real reason."

Howard Falcon smiled, though only those who knew him well could have interpreted the slight, leathery grimace. Webster was one of them; for more than twenty years they had shared triumphs and disasters—including the greatest disaster of all.

"Well, Springer's cliché is still valid. We've landed on all the terrestrial planets, but none of the gas giants. They are the only real challenge left in the solar system."

"An expensive one. Have you worked out the cost?"

"As well as I can; here are the estimates. Remember, though—this isn't a one-shot mission, but a transportation system. Once it's proved out, it can be used over and over again. And it will open up not merely Jupiter, but *all* the giants."

Webster looked at the figures, and whistled.

"Why not start with an easier planet—Uranus, for example? Half the gravity, and less than half the escape velocity. Quieter weather, too—if that's the right word for it."

Webster had certainly done his homework. But that, of course, was why he was head of Long-Range Planning.

"There's very little saving—when you allow for the extra distance and the logistics problems. For Jupiter, we can use the facilities of Ganymede. Beyond Saturn, we'd have to establish a new supply base."

Logical, thought Webster; but he was sure that it was not the important reason. Jupiter was lord of the solar system; Falcon would be interested in no lesser challenge.

"Besides," Falcon continued, "Jupiter is a major scientific scandal. It's more than a hundred years since its radio storms were discovered, but we still don't know what causes them—and the Great Red Spot is as big a mystery as ever. That's why I can get matching funds from the Bureau of Astronautics. Do you know how many probes they have dropped into that atmosphere?"

"A couple hundred, I believe."

"*Three* hundred and twenty-six, over the last fifty years —about a quarter of them total failures. Of course, they've learned a hell of a lot, but they've barely scratched the planet. Do you realize how *big* it is?"

"More than ten times the size of Earth."

"Yes, yes—but do you know what that really means?"

Falcon pointed to the large globe in the corner of Webster's office.

"Look at India—how small it seems. Well, if you skinned Earth and spread it out on the surface of Jupiter, it would look about as big as India does here."

There was a long silence while Webster contemplated the equation: Jupiter is to Earth as Earth is to India. Falcon had

—deliberately, of course—chosen the best possible example. . . .

Was it already ten years ago? Yet, it must have been. The crash lay seven years in the past *(that* date was engraved on his heart), and those initial tests had taken place three years before the first and last flight of the *Queen Elizabeth.*

Ten years ago, then, Commander (no, Lieutenant) Falcon had invited him to a preview—a three-day drift across the northern plains of India, within sight of the Himalayas. "Perfectly safe," he had promised. "It will get you away from the office—and will teach you what this whole thing is about."

Webster had not been disappointed. Next to his first journey to the Moon, it had been the most memorable experience of his life. And yet, as Falcon had assured him, it had been perfectly safe, and quite uneventful.

They had taken off from Srinagar just before dawn, with the huge silver bubble of the balloon already catching the first light of the Sun. The ascent had been made in total silence; there were none of the roaring propane burners that had lifted the hot-air balloons of an earlier age. All the heat they needed came from the little pulsed-fusion reactor, weighing only about two hundred and twenty pounds, hanging in the open mouth of the envelope. While they were climbing, its laser was zapping ten times a second, igniting the merest whiff of deuterium fuel. Once they had reached altitude, it would fire only a few times a minute, making up for the heat lost through the great gasbag overhead.

And so, even while they were almost a mile above the ground, they could hear dogs barking, people shouting, bells ringing. Slowly the vast, Sun-smitten landscape expanded around them. Two hours later, they had leveled out at three miles and were taking frequent draughts of oxygen. They could relax and admire the scenery; the on-board instrumentation was doing all the work—gathering the information that would be required by the designers of the still-unnamed liner of the skies.

It was a perfect day. The southwest monsoon would not break for another month, and there was hardly a cloud in the sky. Time seemed to have come to a stop; they resented the hourly radio report which interrupted their reverie. And all around, to the horizon and far beyond, was that infinite, ancient landscape, drenched with history—a patchwork of villages, fields, temples, lakes, irrigation canals. . . .

With a real effort, Webster broke the hypnotic spell of that ten-year-old memory. It had converted him to lighter-than-air flight—and it had made him realize the enormous size of India, even in a world that could be circled within ninety minutes. And yet, he repeated to himself, Jupiter is to Earth as Earth is to India. . . .

"Granted your argument," he said, "and supposing the funds are available, there's another question you have to answer. Why should you do better than the—what is it—three hundred and twenty-six robot probes that have already made the trip?"

"I am better qualified than they were—as an observer, and as a pilot. *Especially* as a pilot. Don't forget—I've more experience of lighter-than-air flight than anyone in the world."

"You could still serve as controller, and sit safely on Ganymede."

"But that's just the point! They've already done that. Don't you remember what killed the *Queen*?"

Webster knew perfectly well; but he merely answered: "Go on."

"Time lag—time lag! That idiot of a platform controller thought he was using a local radio circuit. But he'd been accidentally switched through a satellite—oh, maybe it wasn't his fault, but he should have noticed. That's a half-second time lag for the round trip. Even then it wouldn't have mattered flying in calm air. It was the turbulence over the Grand Canyon that did it. When the platform tipped, and he corrected for that—it had already tipped the other way. Ever tried to drive a car over a bumpy road with a half-second delay in the steering?"

"No, and I don't intend to try. But I can imagine it."

"Well, Ganymede is a million kilometers from Jupiter. That means a round-trip delay of six seconds. No, you need a controller on the spot—to handle emergencies in real time. Let me show you something. Mind if I use this?"

"Go ahead."

Falcon picked up a postcard that was lying on Webster's desk; they were almost obsolete on Earth, but this one showed a 3-D view of a Martian landscape, and was decorated with exotic and expensive stamps. He held it so that it dangled vertically.

"This is an old trick, but helps to make my point. Place your thumb and finger on either side, not quite touching. That's right."

Webster put out his hand, almost but not quite gripping the card.

"Now catch it."

Falcon waited for a few seconds; then, without warning, he let go of the card. Webster's thumb and finger closed on empty air.

"I'll do it again, just to show there's no deception. You see?"

Once again, the falling card had slipped through Webster's fingers.

"Now you try it on me."

This time, Webster grasped the card and dropped it without warning. It had scarcely moved before Falcon had caught it. Webster almost imagined he could hear a click, so swift was the other's reaction.

"When they put me together again," Falcon remarked in an expressionless voice, "the surgeons made some improvements. This is one of them—and there are others. I want to make the most of them. Jupiter is the place where I can do it."

Webster stared for long seconds at the fallen card, absorbing the improbable colors of the Trivium Charontis Escarpment. Then he said quietly: "I understand. How long do you think it will take?"

"With your help, plus the Bureau, plus all the science foundation we can drag in—oh, three years. Then a year for trials—we'll have to send in at least two test models. So, with luck—five years."

"That's about what I thought. I hope you get your luck; you've earned it. But there's one thing I won't do."

"What's that?"

"Next time you go ballooning, don't expect *me* as passenger."

3. THE WORLD OF THE GODS

The fall from Jupiter V to Jupiter itself takes only three and a half hours. Few men could have slept on so awesome a journey. Sleep was a weakness that Howard Falcon hated, and the little he still required brought dreams that time had not yet been able to exorcise. But he could expect no rest in the three days that lay ahead, and must seize what he could during the long fall down into that ocean of clouds, some sixty thousand miles below.

As soon as *Kon-Tiki* had entered her transfer orbit and all the computer checks were satisfactory, he prepared for the last sleep he might ever know. It seemed appropriate that at almost the same moment Jupiter eclipsed the bright and tiny Sun as he swept into the monstrous shadow of the planet. For a few minutes a strange golden twilight enveloped the ship; then a quarter of the sky became an utterly black hole in space, while the rest was a blaze of stars. No matter how far one traveled across the solar system, *they* never changed; these same constellations now shone on Earth, millions of miles away. The only novelties here were the small, pale crescents of Callisto and Ganymede; doubtless there were a dozen other moons up there in the sky, but they were all much too tiny, and too distant, for the unaided eye to pick them out.

"Closing down for two hours," he reported to the mother ship, hanging almost a thousand miles above the desolate rocks of Jupiter V, in the radiation shadow of the tiny satellite. If it never served any other useful purpose, Jupiter V was a cosmic bulldozer perpetually sweeping up the charged particles that made it unhealthy to linger close to Jupiter. Its wake was almost free of radiation, and there a ship could park in perfect safety, while death sleeted invisibly all around.

Falcon switched on the sleep inducer, and consciousness faded swiftly out as the electric pulses surged gently through his brain. While *Kon-Tiki* fell toward Jupiter, gaining speed second by second in that enormous gravitational field, he slept without dreams. They always came when he awoke; and he had brought his nightmares with him from Earth.

Yet he never dreamed of the crash itself, though he often

found himself again face to face with that terrified superchimp, as he descended the spiral stairway between the collapsing gasbags. None of the simps had survived; those that were not killed outright were so badly injured that they had been painlessly "euthed." He sometimes wondered why he dreamed only of this doomed creature—which he had never met before the last minutes of its life—and not of the friends and colleagues he had lost aboard the dying *Queen*.

The dreams he feared most always began with his first return to consciousness. There had been little physical pain; in fact, there had been no sensation of any kind. He was in darkness and silence, and did not even seem to be breathing. And—strangest of all—he could not locate his limbs. He could move neither his hands nor his feet, because he did not know where they were.

The silence had been the first to yield. After hours, or days, he had become aware of a faint throbbing, and eventually, after long thought, he deduced that this was the beating of his own heart. That was the first of his many mistakes.

Then there had been faint pinpricks, sparkles of light, ghosts of pressures upon still-unresponsive limbs. One by one his senses had returned, and pain had come with them. He had had to learn everything anew, recapitulating infancy and babyhood. Though his memory was unaffected, and he could understand words that were spoken to him, it was months before he was able to answer except by the flicker of an eyelid. He could remember the moments of triumph when he had spoken the first word, turned the page of a book—and, finally, learned to move under his own power. *That* was a victory indeed, and it had taken him almost two years to prepare for it. A hundred times he had envied that dead superchimp, but *he* had been given no choice. The doctors had made their decision—and now, twelve years later, he was where no human being had ever traveled before, and moving faster than any man in history.

Kon-Tiki was just emerging from shadow, and the Jovian dawn bridged the sky ahead in a titanic bow of light, when the persistent buzz of the alarm dragged Falcon up from sleep. The inevitable nightmares (he had been trying to summon a nurse, but did not even have the strength to push the button) swiftly faded from consciousness. The greatest—and perhaps last—adventure of his life was before him.

He called Mission Control, now almost sixty thousand miles away and falling swiftly below the curve of Jupiter, to report that everything was in order. His velocity had just passed thirty-one miles a second *(that* was one for the books) and in half an hour *Kon-Tiki* would hit the outer fringes of the atmosphere, as he started on the most difficult re-entry in the entire solar system. Although scores of probes had survived this flaming ordeal, they had been tough, solidly packed masses of instrumentation, able to withstand several hundred gravities of drag. *Kon-Tiki* would hit peaks of thirty g's, and would average more than ten, before she came to rest in the upper reaches of the Jovian atmosphere. Very carefully and thoroughly, Falcon began to attach the elaborate system of restraints that would anchor him to the walls of the cabin. When he had finished, he was virtually a part of the ship's structure.

The clock was counting backward; one hundred seconds to re-entry. For better or worse, he was committed. In a minute and a half, he would graze the Jovian atmosphere, and would be caught irrevocably in the grip of the giant.

The countdown was three seconds late—not at all bad, considering the unknowns involved. From beyond the walls of the capsule came a ghostly sighing, which rose steadily to a high-pitched, screaming roar. The noise was quite different from that of a re-entry on Earth or Mars; in this thin atmosphere of hydrogen and helium, all sounds were transformed a couple of octaves upward. On Jupiter, even thunder would have falsetto overtones.

With the rising scream came mounting weight; within seconds, he was completely immobilized. His field of vision contracted until it embraced only the clock and the accelerometer; fifteen g, and four hundred and eighty seconds to go. . . .

He never lost consciousness; but then, he had not expected to. *Kon-Tiki*'s trail through the Jovian atmosphere must be really spectacular—by this time, thousands of miles long. Five hundred seconds after entry, the drag began to taper off: ten g, five g, two. . . . Then weight vanished almost completely. He was falling free, all his enormous orbital velocity destroyed.

There was a sudden jolt as the incandescent remnants of the heat shield were jettisoned. It had done its work and would not be needed again; Jupiter could have it now. He released all but two of the restraining buckles, and waited for the automatic sequencer to start the next, and most critical, series of events.

He did not see the first drogue parachute pop out, but he could feel the slight jerk, and the rate of fall diminished immediately. *Kon-Tiki* had lost all her horizontal speed and was going straight down at almost a thousand miles an hour. Everything depended on what happened in the next sixty seconds.

There went the second drogue. He looked up through the overhead window and saw, to his immense relief, that clouds of glittering foil were billowing out behind the falling ship. Like a great flower unfurling, the thousands of cubic yards of the balloon spread out across the sky, scooping up the thin gas until it was fully inflated. *Kon-Tiki*'s rate of fall dropped to a few miles an hour and remained constant. Now there was plenty of time; it would take him days to fall all the way down to the surface of Jupiter.

But he would get there eventually, even if he did nothing about it. The balloon overhead was merely acting as an efficient parachute. It was providing no lift; nor could it do so, while the gas inside and out was the same.

With its characteristic and rather disconcerting crack the fusion reactor started up, pouring torrents of heat into the envelope overhead. Within five minutes, the rate of fall had become zero; within six, the ship had started to rise. According to the radar altimeter, it had leveled out at about two hundred and sixty-seven miles above the surface—or whatever passed for a surface on Jupiter.

Only one kind of balloon will work in an atmosphere of hydrogen, which is the lightest of all gases—and that is a hot-hydrogen balloon. As long as the fuser kept ticking over, Falcon could remain aloft, drifting across a world that could hold a hundred Pacifics. After traveling over three hundred million miles, *Kon-Tiki* had at last begun to justify her name. She was an aerial raft, adrift upon the currents of the Jovian atmosphere.

Though a whole new world was lying around him, it was more than an hour before Falcon could examine the view. First he had to check all the capsule's systems and test its response to the controls. He had to learn how much extra heat was necessary to produce a desired rate of ascent, and how much gas he must vent in order to descend. Above all, there was the question of stability. He must adjust the length of the cables attaching his capsule to the huge, pear-shaped balloon, to damp out vibrations and get the smoothest possible ride. Thus far, he was lucky; at this level, the wind was steady, and the Doppler reading on the invisible surface gave him a ground speed of two hundred seventeen and a half miles an hour. For Jupiter, that was modest; winds of up to a thousand had been observed. But mere speed was, of course, unimportant; the real danger was turbulence. If he ran into that, only skill and experience and swift reaction could save him—and these were not matters that could yet be programed into a computer.

Not until he was satisfied that he had got the feel of his strange craft did Falcon pay any attention to Mission Control's pleadings. Then he deployed the booms carrying the instrumentation and the atmospheric sampler. The capsule now resembled a rather untidy Christmas tree, but still rode smoothly down the Jovian winds while it radioed its torrents of information to the recorders on the ship miles above. And now, at last, he could look around. . . .

His first impression was unexpected, and even a little disappointing. As far as the scale of things was concerned, he might have been ballooning over an ordinary cloudspace on Earth. The horizon seemed at a normal distance; there was no feeling at all that he was on a world eleven times the diameter of his own. Then he looked at the infrared radar, sounding the layers of atmosphere beneath him—and knew how badly his eyes had been deceived.

That layer of clouds apparently about three miles away was really more than thirty-seven miles below. And the horizon, whose distance he would have guessed at about one hundred and twenty-five, was actually eighteen hundred miles from the ship.

The crystalline clarity of the hydrohelium atmosphere and the enormous curvature of the planet had fooled him completely. It was even harder to judge distances here than on the Moon; everything he saw must be multiplied by at least ten.

It was a simple matter, and he should have been prepared

for it. Yet somehow, it disturbed him profoundly. He did not feel that Jupiter was huge, but that *he* had shrunk—to a tenth of his normal size. Perhaps, with time, he would grow accustomed to the inhuman scale of this world; yet as he stared toward that unbelievably distant horizon, he felt as if a wind colder than the atmosphere around him was blowing through his soul. Despite all his arguments, this might never be a place for man. He could well be both the first and the last to descend through the clouds of Jupiter.

The sky above was almost black, except for a few wisps of ammonia cirrus perhaps twelve miles overhead. It was cold up there, on the fringes of space, but both pressure and temperature increased rapidly with depth. At the level where *Kon-Tiki* was drifting now, it was fifty below zero, and the pressure was five atmospheres. Sixty-five miles farther down, it would be as warm as equatorial Earth, and the pressure about the same as at the bottom of one of the shallower seas. Ideal conditions for life. . . .

A quarter of the brief Jovian day had already gone; the sun was halfway up the sky, but the light on the unbroken cloudscape below had a curious mellow quality. That extra three hundred million miles had robbed the Sun of all its power. Though the sky was clear, Falcon found himself continually thinking that it was a heavily overcast day. When night fell, the onset of darkness would be swift indeed; though it was still morning, there was a sense of autumnal twilight in the air. But autumn, of course, was something that never came to Jupiter. There were no seasons here.

Kon-Tiki had come down in the exact center of the equatorial zone—the least colorful part of the planet. The sea of clouds that stretched out to the horizon was tinted a pale salmon; there were none of the yellows and pinks and even reds that banded Jupiter at higher altitudes. The Great Red Spot itself—most spectacular of all of the planet's features—lay thousands of miles to the south. It had been a temptation to descend there, but the south tropical disturbance was unusually active, with currents reaching over nine hundred miles an hour. It would have been asking for trouble to head into that maelstrom of unknown forces. The Great Red Spot and its mysteries would have to wait for future expeditions.

The Sun, moving across the sky twice as swiftly as it did on Earth, was now nearing the zenith and had become eclipsed by the great silver canopy of the balloon. *Kon-Tiki* was still drifting swiftly and smoothly westward at a steady two hundred and seventeen and a half, but only the radar gave any indication of this. Was it always as calm here? Falcon asked himself. The scientists who had talked learnedly of the Jovian doldrums, and had predicted that the equator would be the quietest place, seemed to know what they were talking about, after all. He had been profoundly skeptical of all such forecasts, and had agreed with one unusually modest researcher who had told him bluntly: "There are *no* experts on Jupiter." Well, there would be at least one by the end of this day.

If he managed to survive until then.

4. THE VOICES OF THE DEEP

That first day, the Father of the Gods smiled upon him. It was as calm and peaceful here on Jupiter as it had been, years ago, when he was drifting with Webster across the plains of northern India. Falcon had time to master his new skills, until *Kon-Tiki* seemed an extension of his own body. Such luck was more than he had dared to hope for, and he began to wonder what price he might have to pay for it.

The five hours of daylight were almost over; the clouds below were full of shadows, which gave them a massive solidity they had not possessed when the Sun was higher. Color was swiftly draining from the sky, except in the west itself, where a band of deepening purple lay along the horizon. Above this band was the thin crescent of a closer moon, pale and bleached against the utter blackness beyond.

With a speed perceptible to the eye, the Sun went straight down over the edge of Jupiter, over eighteen hundred miles away. The stars came out in their legion—and there was the beautiful evening star of Earth, on the very frontier of twilight, reminding him how far he was from home. It followed the Sun down into the west. Man's first night on Jupiter had begun.

With the onset of darkness, *Kon-Tiki* started to sink. The balloon was no longer heated by the feeble sunlight and was losing a small part of its buoyancy. Falcon did nothing to increase lift; he had expected this and was planning to descend.

The invisible cloud deck was still over thirty miles below, and he would reach it about midnight. It showed up clearly on the infrared radar, which also reported that it contained a vast array of complex carbon compounds, as well as the usual hydrogen, helium, and ammonia. The chemists were dying for samples of that fluffy, pinkish stuff; though some atmospheric probes had already gathered a few grams, that had only whetted their appetites. Half the basic molecules of life were here, floating high above the surface of Jupiter. And where there was food, could life be far away? That was the question that, after more than a hundred years, no one had been able to answer.

The infrared was blocked by the clouds, but the microwave radar sliced right through and showed layer after layer, all the way down to the hidden surface almost two hundred and fifty miles below. That was barred to him by enormous pressures and temperatures; not even robot probes had ever reached it intact. It lay in tantalizing inaccessibility at the bottom of the radar screen, slightly fuzzy, and showing a curious granular structure that his equipment could not resolve.

An hour after sunset, he dropped his first probe. It fell swiftly for about sixty miles, then began to float in the denser atmosphere, sending back torrents of radio signals, which he relayed to Mission Control. Then there was nothing else to do until sunrise, except to keep an eye on the rate of descent, monitor the instruments, and answer occasional queries. While she was drifting in this steady current, *Kon-Tiki* could look after herself.

Just before midnight, a woman controller came on watch and introduced herself with the usual pleasantries. Ten minutes later she called again, her voice at once serious and excited.

"Howard! Listen in on channel forty-six—high gain."

Channel forty-six? There were so many telemetering circuits that he knew the numbers of only those that were critical; but as soon as he threw the switch, he recognized this one. He was plugged in to the microphone on the probe, floating more than eighty miles below him in an atmosphere now almost as dense as water.

At first, there was only a soft hiss of whatever strange winds stirred down in the darkness of that unimaginable world. And then, out of the background noise, there slowly emerged a booming vibration that grew louder and louder, like the beating of a gigantic drum. It was so low that it was felt as much as heard, and the beats steadily increased their tempo, though the pitch never changed. Now it was a swift, almost infrasonic throbbing. Then, suddenly, in mid-vibration, it stopped—so abruptly that the mind could not accept the silence, but memory continued to manufacture a ghostly echo in the deepest caverns of the brain.

It was the most extraordinary sound that Falcon had ever heard, even among the multitudinous noises of Earth. He could think of no natural phenomenon that could have caused it; nor was it like the cry of any animal, not even one of the great whales. . . .

It came again, following exactly the same pattern. Now that he was prepared for it, he estimated the length of the sequence; from first faint throb to final crescendo, it lasted just over ten seconds.

And this time there was a real echo, very faint and far away. Perhaps it came from one of the many reflecting layers, deeper in this stratified atmosphere; perhaps it was another, more distant source. Falcon waited for a second echo, but it never came.

Mission Control reacted quickly and asked him to drop another probe at once. With two microphones operating, it would be possible to find the approximate location of the sources. Oddly enough, none of *Kon-Tiki*'s own external mikes could detect anything except wind noises. The boomings, whatever they were, must have been trapped and channeled beneath an atmospheric reflecting layer far below.

They were coming, it was soon discovered, from a cluster of sources about twelve hundred miles away. The distance gave no indication of their power; in Earth's oceans, quite feeble sounds could travel equally far. And as for the obvious assumption that living creatures were responsible, the Chief Exobiologist quickly ruled that out.

"I'll be very disappointed," said Dr. Brenner, "if there are no microorganisms or plants here. But nothing like animals, because there's no free oxygen. All biochemical reactions on Jupiter must be low-energy ones—there's just no

way an active creature could generate enough power to
function."

Falcon wondered if this was true; he had heard the argument before, and reserved judgment.

"In any case," continued Brenner, "some of those sound
waves are a hundred yards long! Even an animal as big as a
whale couldn't produce them. They *must* have a natural
origin."

Yes, that seemed plausible, and probably the physicists
would be able to come up with an explanation. What would
a blind alien make, Falcon wondered, of the sounds he might
hear when standing beside a stormy sea, or a geyser, or a
volcano, or a waterfall? He might well attribute them to
some huge beast.

About an hour before sunrise the voices of the deep died
away, and Falcon began to busy himself with preparation for
the dawn of his second day. *Kon-Tiki* was now only three
miles above the nearest cloud layer; the external pressure
had risen to ten atmospheres, and the temperature was a
tropical thirty degrees. A man could be comfortable here
with no more equipment than a breathing mask and the
right grade of heliox mixture.

"We've some good news for you," Mission Control reported, soon after dawn. "The cloud layer's breaking up.
You'll have partial clearing in an hour—but watch out for
turbulence."

"I've already noticed some," Falcon answered. "How far
down will I be able to see?"

"At least twelve miles, down to the second thermocline.
That cloud deck is solid—it never breaks."

And it's out of my reach, Falcon told himself; the temperature down there must be over a hundred degrees. This
was the first time that any balloonist had ever had to worry,
not about his ceiling, but about his basement!

Ten minutes later he could see what Mission Control had
already observed from its superior vantage point. There was
a change in color near the horizon, and the cloud layer had
become ragged and humpy, as if something had torn it open.
He turned up his little nuclear furnace and gave *Kon-Tiki*
another three miles of altitude, so that he could get a better
view.

The sky below was clearly rapidly, completely, as if

something was dissolving the solid overcast. An abyss was opening before his eyes. A moment later he sailed out over the edge of a cloud canyon about twelve miles deep and six hundred miles wide.

A new world lay spread beneath him; Jupiter had stripped away one of its many veils. The second layer of clouds, unattainably far below, was much darker in color than the first. It was almost salmon pink, and curiously mottled with little islands of brick red. They were all oval-shaped, with their long axes pointing east-west, in the direction of the prevailing wind. There were hundreds of them, all about the same size, and they reminded Falcon of puffy little cumulus clouds in the terrestrial sky.

He reduced buoyancy, and *Kon-Tiki* began to drop down the face of the dissolving cliff. It was then that he noticed the snow.

White flakes were forming in the air and drifting slowly downward. Yet it was much too warm for snow—and, in any event, there was scarcely a trace of water at this altitude. Moreover, there was no glitter or sparkle about these flakes as they went cascading down into the depths. When, presently, a few landed on an instrument boom outside the main viewing port, he saw that they were a dull, opaque white—not crystalline at all—and quite large—several inches across. They looked like wax, and Falcon guessed that this was precisely what they were. Some chemical reaction was taking place in the atmosphere around him, condensing out the hydrocarbons floating in the Jovian air.

About sixty miles ahead, a disturbance was taking place in the cloud layer. The little red ovals were being jostled around, and were beginning to form a spiral—the familiar cyclonic pattern so common in the meteorology of Earth. The vortex was emerging with astonishing speed; if that was a storm ahead, Falcon told himself, he was in big trouble.

And then his concern changed to wonder—and to fear. What was developing in his line of flight was not a storm at all. Something enormous—something scores of miles across —was rising through the clouds.

The reassuring thought that it, too, might be a cloud—a thunderhead boiling up from the lower levels of the atmosphere—lasted only a few seconds. No; this was *solid*. It shouldered its way through the pink-and-salmon overcast like an iceberg rising from the deeps.

An *iceberg* floating on hydrogen? That was impossible, of course; but perhaps it was not too remote an analogy. As soon as he focused the telescope upon the enigma, Falcon saw that it was a whitish, crystalline mass, threaded with streaks of red and brown. It must be, he decided, the same stuff as the "snowflakes" falling around him—a mountain range of wax. And it was not, he soon realized, as solid as he had thought; around the edges it was continually crumbling and reforming. . . .

"I know what it is," he radioed Mission Control, which for the last few minutes had been asking anxious questions. "It's a mass of bubbles—some kind of foam. Hydrocarbon froth. Get the chemists working on . . . *just a minute!*"

"What is it?" called Mission Control. "What is it?"

He ignored the frantic pleas from space and concentrated all his mind upon the image in the telescope field. He had to be sure; if he made a mistake, he would be the laughingstock of the solar system.

Then he relaxed, glanced at the clock, and switched off the nagging voice from Jupiter V.

"Hello, Mission Control," he said, very formally. "This is Howard Falcon aboard *Kon-Tiki.* Ephemeris Time nineteen hours twenty-one minutes fifteen seconds. Latitude zero degrees five minutes North. Longitude one hundred five degrees forty-two minutes, System One.

"Tell Dr. Brenner that there is life on Jupiter. And it's *big.* . . .

5. THE WHEELS OF POSEIDON

"I'm very happy to be proved wrong," Dr. Brenner radioed back cheerfully. "Nature always has something up her sleeve. Keep the long-focus camera on target and give us the steadiest pictures you can."

The things moving up and down those waxen slopes were still too far away for Falcon to make out many details, and they must have been very large to be visible at all at such a distance. Almost black, and shaped like arrowheads, they maneuvered by slow undulations of their entire bodies, so that they looked rather like giant manta rays, swimming above some tropical reef.

Perhaps they were sky-borne cattle, browsing on the cloud pastures of Jupiter, for they seemed to be feeding along the dark, red-brown streaks that ran like dried-up river beds down the flanks of the floating cliffs. Occasionally, one of them would dive headlong into the mountain of foam and disappear completely from sight.

Kon-Tiki was moving only slowly with respect to the cloud layer below; it would be at least three hours before she was above those ephemeral hills. She was in a race with the Sun. Falcon hoped that darkness would not fall before he could get a good view of the mantas, as he had christened them, as well as the fragile landscape over which they flapped their way.

It was a long three hours. During the whole time, he kept the external microphones on full gain, wondering if here was the source of that booming in the night. The mantas were certainly large enough to have produced it; when he could get an accurate measurement, he discovered that they were almost a hundred yards across the wings. That was three times the length of the largest whale—though he doubted if they could weigh more than a few tons.

Half an hour before sunset, *Kon-Tiki* was almost above the "mountains."

"No," said Falcon, answering Mission Control's repeated questions about the mantas, "they're still showing no reaction to me. I don't think they're intelligent—they look like harmless vegetarians. And even if they try to chase me, I'm sure they can't reach my altitude."

Yet he was a little disappointed when the mantas showed not the slightest interest in him as he sailed high above their feeding ground. Perhaps they had no way of detecting his presence. When he examined and photographed them through the telescope, he could see no signs of any sense organs. The creatures were simply huge black deltas rippling over hills and valleys that, in reality, were little more substantial than the clouds of Earth. Though they looked solid, Falcon knew that anyone who stepped on those white mountains would go crashing through them as if they were made of tissue paper.

At close quarters he could see the myriads of cellules or bubbles from which they were formed. Some of these were quite large—a yard or so in diameter—and Falcon wondered in what witches' cauldron of hydrocarbons they had been brewed. There must be enough petrochemicals deep down in the atmosphere of Jupiter to supply all Earth's needs for a million years.

The short day had almost gone when he passed over the crest of the waxen hills, and the light was fading rapidly along their lower slopes. There were no mantas on this western side, and for some reason the topography was very different. The form was sculptured into long, level terraces, like the interior of a lunar crater. He could almost imagine that they were gigantic steps leading down to the hidden surface of the planet.

And on the lowest of those steps, just clear of the swirling clouds that the mountain had displaced when it came surging skyward, was a roughly oval mass, one or two miles across. It was difficult to see, since it was only a little darker than the gray-white foam on which it rested. Falcon's first thought was that he was looking at a forest of pallid trees, like giant mushrooms that had never seen the Sun.

Yes, it must be a forest—he could see hundreds of thin trunks, springing from the white waxy froth in which they were rooted. But the trees were packed astonishingly close together; there was scarcely any space between them. Perhaps it was not a forest, after all, but a single enormous tree—like one of the giant multi-trunked banyans of the East. Once he had seen a banyan tree in Java that was over six hundred and fifty yards across; this monster was at least ten times that size.

The light had almost gone. The cloudscape had turned purple with refracted sunlight, and in a few seconds that, too, would have vanished. In the last light of his second day on Jupiter, Howard Falcon saw—or thought he saw—something that cast the gravest doubts on his interpretation of the white oval.

Unless the dim light had totally deceived him, those hundreds of thin trunks were beating back and forth, in perfect synchronism, like fronds of kelp rocking in the surge.

And the tree was no longer in the place where he had first seen it.

•   •   •

"Sorry about this," said Mission Control, soon after sunset, "but we think Source Beta is going to blow within the next hour. Probability seventy per cent."

Falcon glanced quickly at the chart. Beta—Jupiter latitude one hundred and forty degrees—was over eighteen thousand six hundred miles away and well below his horizon. Even though major eruptions ran as high as ten megatons, he was much too far away for the shock wave to be a serious danger. The radio storm that it would trigger was, however, quite a different matter.

The decameter outbursts that sometimes made Jupiter the most powerful radio source in the whole sky had been discovered back in the 1950's, to the utter astonishment of the astronomers. Now, more than a century later, their real cause was still a mystery. Only the symptoms were understood; the explanation was completely unknown.

The "volcano" theory had best stood the test of time, although no one imagined that this word had the same meaning on Jupiter as on Earth. At frequent intervals— often several times a day—titanic eruptions occurred in the lower depths of the atmosphere, probably on the hidden surface of the planet itself. A great column of gas, more than six hundred miles high, would start boiling upward as if determined to escape into space.

Against the most powerful gravitational field of all the planets, it had no chance. Yet some traces—a mere few million tons—usually managed to reach the Jovian ionosphere; and when they did, all hell broke loose.

The radiation belts surrounding Jupiter completely dwarf the feeble Van Allen belts of Earth. When they are short-circuited by an ascending column of gas, the result is an electrical discharge millions of times more powerful than any terrestrial flash of lightning; it sends a colossal thunderclap of radio noise flooding across the entire solar system and on out to the stars.

It had been discovered that these radio outbursts came from four main areas of the planet. Perhaps there were weaknesses there that allowed the fires of the interior to break out from time to time. The scientists on Ganymede, largest of Jupiter's many moons, now thought that they could predict the onset of a decameter storm; their accuracy was about as good as a weather forecaster's of the early 1900s.

Falcon did not know whether to welcome or to fear a radio storm; it would certainly add to the value of the mission—if he survived it. His course had been planned to keep as far as possible from the main centers of disturbance, especially the most active one, Source Alpha. As luck would have it, the threatening Beta was the closest to him. He hoped that the distance, almost three-fourths the circumference of Earth, was safe enough.

"Probability ninety per cent," said Mission Control with a distinct note of urgency. "And forget that hour. Ganymede says it may be any moment."

The radio had scarcely fallen silent when the reading on the magnetic field-strength meter started to shoot upward. Before it could go off scale, it reversed and began to drop as rapidly as it had risen. Far away and thousands of miles below, something had given the planet's molten core a titanic jolt.

"There she blows!" called Mission Control.

"Thanks, I already know. When will the storm hit me?"

"You can expect onset in five minutes. Peak in ten."

Far around the curve of Jupiter, a funnel of gas as wide as the Pacific Ocean was climbing spaceward at thousands of miles an hour. Already, the thunderstorms of the lower atmosphere would be raging around it—but they were nothing compared with the fury that would explode when the radiation belt was reached and began dumping its surplus electrons onto the planet. Falcon began to retract all the instrument booms that were extended out from the capsule. There were no other precautions he could take. It would be four hours before the atmospheric shock wave reached him —but the radio blast, traveling at the speed of light, would be here in a tenth of a second, once the discharge had been triggered.

The radio monitor, scanning back and forth across the spectrum, still showed nothing unusual, just the normal mush of background static. Then Falcon noticed that the noise level was slowly creeping upward. The explosion was gathering its strength.

At such a distance he had never expected to *see* anything. But suddenly a flicker as of far-off heat lightning danced along the eastern horizon. Simultaneously, half the circuit breakers jumped out of the main switchboard, the lights failed, and all communications channels went dead.

He tried to move, but was completely unable to do so. The paralysis that gripped him was not merely psychological; he seemed to have lost all control of his limbs and could feel a painful tingling sensation over his entire body. It was impossible that the electric field could have penetrated this shielded cabin. Yet there was a flickering glow over the instrument board, and he could hear the unmistakable crackle of a brush discharge.

With a series of sharp bangs, the emergency systems went into operation, and the overloads reset themselves. The lights flickered on again. And Falcon's paralysis disappeared as swiftly as it had come.

After glancing at the board to make sure that all circuits were back to normal, he moved quickly to the viewing ports.

There was no need to switch on the inspection lamps—the cables supporting the capsule seemed to be on fire. Lines of light glowing an electric blue against the darkness stretched upward from the main lift ring to the equator of the giant balloon; and rolling slowly along several of them were dazzling balls of fire.

The sight was so strange and so beautiful that it was hard to read any menace in it. Few people, Falcon knew, had ever seen ball lightning from such close quarters—and certainly none had survived if they were riding a hydrogen-filled balloon back in the atmosphere of Earth. He remembered the flaming death of the *Hindenburg,* destroyed by a stray spark when she docked at Lakehurst in 1937; as it had done so often in the past, the horrifying old newsreel film flashed through his mind. But at least that could not happen here, though there was more hydrogen above his head than had ever filled the last of the Zeppelins. It would be a few billion years yet, before anyone could light a fire in the atmosphere of Jupiter.

With a sound like briskly frying bacon, the speech circuit came back to life.

"Hello, *Kon-Tiki*—are you receiving? Are you receiving?"

The words were chopped and badly distorted, but intelligible. Falcon's spirits lifted; he had resumed contact with the world of men.

"I receive you," he said. "Quite an electrical display, but no damage—so far."

"Thanks—thought we'd lost you. Please check elementary channels three, seven, twenty-six. Also gain on camera two. And we don't quite believe the readings on the external ionization probes. . . ."

Reluctantly Falcon tore his gaze away from the fascinating pyrotechnic display around *Kon-Tiki,* though from time to time he kept glancing out of the windows. The ball lightning disappeared first, the fiery globes slowly expanding until they reached a critical size, at which they vanished in a gentle explosion. But even an hour later, there were still faint glows around all the exposed metal on the outside of the capsule; and the radio circuits remained noisy until well after midnight.

The remaining hours of darkness were completely uneventful—until just before dawn. Because it came from the east, Falcon assumed that he was seeing the first faint hint of sunrise. Then he realized that it was twenty minutes too early for this—and the glow that had appeared along the horizon was moving toward him even as he watched. It swiftly detached itself from the arch of stars that marked the invisible edge of the planet, and he saw that it was a relatively narrow band, quite sharply defined. The beam of an enormous searchlight appeared to be swinging beneath the clouds.

Perhaps sixty miles behind the first racing bar of light came another, parallel to it and moving at the same speed. And beyond that another, and another—until all the sky flickered with alternating sheets of light and darkness.

By this time, Falcon thought, he had been inured to wonders, and it seemed impossible that this display of pure, soundless luminosity could present the slightest danger. But it was so astonishing, and so inexplicable, that he felt cold, naked fear gnawing at his self-control. No man could look upon such a sight without feeling like a helpless pygmy in the presence of forces beyond his comprehension. Was it possible that, after all, Jupiter carried not only life but also intelligence? And, perhaps, an intelligence that only now was beginning to react to his alien presence?

"Yes, we see it," said Mission Control, in a voice that echoed his own awe. "We've no idea what it is. Stand by, we're calling Ganymede."

The display was slowly fading; the bands racing in from the far horizon were much fainter, as if the energies that powered them were becoming exhausted. In five minutes it was all over; the last faint pulse of light flickered along the western sky and then was gone. Its passing left Falcon with an overwhelming sense of relief. The sight was so hypnotic, and so disturbing that it was not good for any man's peace of mind to contemplate it too long.

He was more shaken than he cared to admit. The electrical storm was something that he could understand; but *this* was totally incomprehensible.

Mission Control was still silent. He knew that the information banks up on Ganymede were now being searched as men and computers turned their minds to the problem. If no answer could be found there, it would be necessary to call Earth; that would mean a delay of almost an hour. The possibility that even Earth might be unable to help was one that Falcon did not care to contemplate.

He had never before been so glad to hear the voice of Mission Control as when Dr. Brenner finally came on the circuit. The biologist sounded relieved, yet subdued—like a man who has just come through some great intellectual crisis.

"Hello *Kon-Tiki.* We've solved your problem, but we can still hardly believe it.

"What you've been seeing is bioluminescence, very similar to that produced by microorganisms in the tropical seas of Earth. Here they're in the atmosphere, not the ocean, but the principle is the same."

"But the pattern," protested Falcon, "was so regular—so *artificial.* And it was hundreds of miles across!"

"It was even larger than you imagine; you observed only a small part of it. The whole pattern was over three thousand miles wide and looked like a revolving wheel. You merely saw the spokes, sweeping past you at about six-tenths of a mile a second. . . ."

"A *second* !" Falcon could not help interjecting. "No animals could move that fast!"

"Of course not. Let me explain. What you saw was triggered by the shock wave from Source Beta, moving at the speed of sound."

"But what about the pattern?" Falcon insisted.

"That's the surprising part. It's a very rare phenomenon, but identical wheels of light—except that they're a thousand times smaller—have been observed in the Persian Gulf and the Indian Ocean. Listen to this: British India Company's *Patna,* Persian Gulf, May 1880, 11:30 P.M.—'an enormous luminous wheel, whirling round, the spokes of which appeared to brush the ship along. The spokes were 200 or 300 yards long . . each wheel contained about sixteen spokes. . . .' And here's one from the Gulf of Omar, dated May 23, 1906: 'The intensely bright luminescence approached us rapidly, shooting sharply defined light rays to the west in rapid succession, like the beam from the searchlight of a warship. . . . To the left of us, a gigantic fiery wheel formed itself, with spokes that reached as far as one could see. The whole wheel whirled around for two or three minutes . . .' The archive computer on Ganymede dug up about five hundred cases. It would have printed out the lot if we hadn't stopped it in time."

"I'm convinced—but still baffled."

"I don't blame you. The full explanation wasn't worked out until late in the twentieth century. It seems that these luminous wheels are the results of submarine earthquakes, and always occur in shallow waters where the shock waves can be reflected and cause standing wave patterns. Sometimes bars, sometimes rotating wheels—the 'Wheels of Poseidon,' they've been called. The theory was finally proved by making underwater explosions and photographing the results from a satellite. No wonder sailors used to be superstitious. Who would have believed a thing like *this*?"

So that was it, Falcon told himself. When Source Beta blew its top, it must have sent shock waves in all directions —through the compressed gas of the lower atmosphere, through the solid body of Jupiter itself. Meeting and crisscrossing, those waves must have canceled here, reinforced there; the whole planet must have rung like a bell.

Yet the explanation did not destroy the sense of wonder and awe; he would never be able to forget those flickering bands of light, racing through the unattainable depths of the Jovian atmosphere. He felt that he was not merely on a strange planet, but in some magical realm between myth and reality.

This was a world where absolutely *anything* could happen, and no man could possibly guess what the future would bring.

And he still had a whole day to go.

6. MEDUSA

When the true dawn finally arrived, it brought a sudden change of weather. *Kon-Tiki* was moving through a blizzard; waxen snowflakes were falling so thickly that visibility was reduced to zero. Falcon began to worry about the weight that might be accumulating on the envelope. Then he noticed that any flakes settling outside the windows quickly disappeared; *Kon-Tiki*'s continual outpouring of heat was evaporating them as swiftly as they arrived.

If he had been ballooning on Earth, he would also have worried about the possibility of collision. At least that was no danger here; any Jovian mountains were several hundred miles below him. And as for the floating islands of foam, hitting them would probably be like plowing into slightly hardened soap bubbles.

Nevertheless, he switched on the horizontal radar, which until now had been completely useless; only the vertical beam, giving his distance from the invisible surface, had thus far been of any value. Then he had another surprise.

Scattered across a huge sector of the sky ahead were dozens of large and brilliant echoes. They were completely isolated from one another and apparently hung unsupported in space. Falcon remembered a phrase the earliest aviators had used to describe one of the hazards of their profession: "clouds stuffed with rocks." That was a perfect description of what seemed to lie in the back of *Kon-Tiki.*

It was a disconcerting sight; then Falcon again reminded himself that nothing *really* solid could possibly hover in this atmosphere. Perhaps it was some strange meteorological phenomenon. In any case, the nearest echo was about a hundred and twenty-five miles.

He reported to Mission Control, which could provide no

explanation. But it gave the welcome news that he would be clear of the blizzard in another thirty minutes.

It did not warn him, however, of the violent cross wind that abruptly grabbed *Kon-Tiki* and swept it almost at right angles to its previous track. Falcon needed all his skill and the maximum use of what little control he had over his ungainly vehicle to prevent it from being capsized. Within minutes he was racing northward at over three hundred miles an hour. Then, as suddenly as it had started, the turbulence ceased; he was still moving at high speed, but in smooth air. He wondered if he had been caught in the Jovian equivalent of a jet stream.

The snow storm dissolved; and he saw that Jupiter had been preparing for him.

Kon-Tiki had entered the funnel of a gigantic whirlpool, some six hundred miles across. The balloon was being swept along a curving wall of cloud. Overhead, the sun was shining in a clear sky; but far beneath, this great hole in the atmosphere drilled down to unknown depths until it reached a misty floor where lightning flickered almost continuously.

Though the vessel was being dragged downward so slowly that it was in no immediate danger, Falcon increased the flow of heat into the envelope until *Kon-Tiki* hovered at a constant altitude. Not until then did he abandon the fantastic spectacle outside and consider again the problem of the radar.

The nearest echo was now only about twenty-five miles away. All of them, he quickly realized, were distributed along the wall of the vortex, and were moving with it, apparently caught in the whirlpool like *Kon-Tiki* itself. He aimed the telescope along the radar bearing and found himself looking at curious mottled cloud that almost filled the field of view.

It was not easy to see, being only a little darker than the whirling wall of mist that formed its background. Not until he had been staring for several minutes did Falcon realize that he had met it once before.

The first time it had been crawling across the drifting mountains of foam, and he had mistaken it for a giant, many-trunked tree. Now at last he could appreciate its real size and complexity and could give it a better name to fix its image in his mind. It did not resemble a tree at all, but a jellyfish—a medusa, such as might be met trailing its tentacles as it drifted along the warm eddies of the Gulf Stream.

This medusa was more than a mile across and its scores of dangling tentacles were hundreds of feet long. They swayed slowly back and forth in perfect unison, taking more than a minute for each complete undulation—almost as if the creature was clumsily rowing itself through the sky.

The other echoes were more distant medusae. Falcon focused the telescope on half a dozen and could see no variations in shape or size. They all seemed to be of the same species, and he wondered just why they were drifting lazily around in this six-hundred-mile orbit. Perhaps they were feeding upon the aerial plankton sucked in by the whirlpool, as *Kon-Tiki* itself had been.

"Do you realize, Howard," said Dr. Brenner, when he had recovered from his initial astonishment, "that this thing is about a hundred thousand times as large as the biggest whale? And even if it's only a gasbag, it must still weigh a million tons! I can't even guess at its metabolism. It must generate megawatts of heat to maintain its buoyancy."

"But if it's just a gasbag, why is it such a damn good radar reflector?"

"I haven't the faintest idea. Can you get any closer?"

Brenner's question was not an idle one. If he changed altitude to take advantage of the differing wind velocities, Falcon could approach the medusa as closely as he wished. At the moment, however, he preferred his present twenty-five miles and said so firmly.

"I see what you mean," Brenner answered, a little reluctantly. "Let's stay where we are for the present." That "we" gave Falcon a certain wry amusement; an extra sixty thousand miles made a considerable difference in one's point of view.

For the past two hours *Kon-Tiki* drifted uneventfully in the gyre of the great whirlpool, while Falcon experimented with filters and camera contrast, trying to get a clear view of the medusa. He began to wonder if its elusive coloration was some kind of camouflage; perhaps, like many animals of Earth, it was trying to lose itself against its background. That was a trick used by both hunters and hunted.

In which category was the medusa? That was a question he could hardly expect to have answered in the short time that was left to him. Yet just before noon, without the slightest warning, the answer came. . . .

Like a squadron of antique jet fighters, five mantas came sweeping through the wall of mist that formed the funnel of the vortex. They were flying in a V formation directly toward the pallid gray cloud of the medusa; and there was no doubt, in Falcon's mind, that they were on the attack. He had been quite wrong to assume that they were harmless vegetarians.

Yet everything happened at such a leisurely pace that it was like watching a slow-motion film. The mantas undulated along at perhaps thirty miles an hour; it seemed ages before they reached the medusa, which continued to paddle imperturbably along at an even slower speed. Huge though they were, the mantas looked tiny beside the monster they were approaching. When they flapped down on its back, they appeared about as large as birds landing on a whale.

Could the medusa defend itself, Falcon wondered. He did not see how the attacking mantas could be in danger as long as they avoided those huge clumsy tentacles. And perhaps their host was not even aware of them; they could be insignificant parasites, tolerated as are fleas upon a dog.

But now it was obvious that the medusa was in distress. With agonizing slowness, it began to tip over like a capsizing ship. After ten minutes it had tilted forty-five degrees; it was also rapidly losing altitude. It was impossible not to feel a sense of pity for the beleaguered monster, and to Falcon the sight brought bitter memories. In a grotesque way, the fall of the medusa was almost a parody of the dying *Queen*'s last moments.

Yet he knew that his sympathies were on the wrong side. High intelligence could develop only among predators—not among the drifting browsers of either sea or air. The mantas were far closer to him than was this monstrous bag of gas. And anyway, who could *really* sympathize with a creature a hundred thousand times larger than a whale?

Then he noticed that the medusa's tactics seemed to be having some effect. The mantas had been disturbed by its slow roll and were flapping heavily away from its back—like gorged vultures interrupted at mealtime. But they did not move very far, continuing to hover a few yards from the still-capsizing monster.

There was a sudden, binding flash of light synchronized with a crash of static over the radio. One of the mantas, slowly twisting end over end, was plummeting straight downward. As it fell, a plume of black smoke trailed behind it. The resemblance to an aircraft going down in flames was quite uncanny.

In unison, the remaining mantas dived steeply away from the medusa, gaining speed by losing altitude. They had, within minutes, vanished back into the wall of cloud from which they had emerged. And the medusa, no longer falling, began to roll back toward the horizontal. Soon it was sailing along once more on an even keel, as if nothing had happened.

"Beautiful!" said Dr. Brenner, after a moment of stunned silence. "It's developed electric defenses, like some of our eels and rays. But that must have been about a million volts! Can you see any organs that might produce the discharge? Anything looking like electrodes?"

"No," Falcon answered, after switching to the highest power of the telescope. "But here's something odd. Do you see this pattern? Check back on the earlier images. I'm sure it wasn't there before."

A broad, mottled band had appeared along the side of the medusa. It formed a startlingly regular checkerboard, each square of which was itself speckled in a complex subpattern of short horizontal lines. They were spaced at equal distances in a geometrically perfect array of rows and columns.

"You're right," said Dr. Brenner, with something very much like awe in his voice. "That's just appeared. And I'm afraid to tell you what I think it is."

"Well, I have no reputation to lose—at least as a biologist. Shall I give my guess?"

"Go ahead."

"That's a large meter-band radio array. The sort of thing they used back at the beginning of the twentieth century."

"I was afraid you'd say that. Now we know why it gave such a massive echo."

"But why has it just appeared?"

"Probably an aftereffect of the discharge."

"I've just had another thought," said Falcon, rather slowly. "Do you suppose it's *listening* to us?"

"On this frequency? I doubt it. Those are meter—no,

decameter antennas—judging by their size. Hmm . . . that's an idea!"

Dr. Brenner fell silent, obviously contemplating some new line of thought. Presently he continued: "I bet they're tuned to the radio outbursts! That's something nature never got around to doing on Earth. . . . We have animals with sonar and even electric senses, but nothing ever developed a radio sense. Why bother where there was so much light?

"But it's different here. Jupiter is *drenched* with radio energy. It's worth while using it—maybe even tapping it. That thing could be a floating power plant!"

A new voice cut into the conversation.

"Mission Commander here. This is all very interesting, but there's a much more important matter to settle. *Is it intelligent?* If so, we've got to consider the First Contact directives."

"Until I came here," said Dr. Brenner, somewhat ruefully, "I would have sworn that anything that could make a shortwave antenna system *must* be intelligent. Now, I'm not sure. This could have evolved naturally. I suppose it's no more fantastic than the human eye."

"Then we have to play safe and assume intelligence. For the present, therefore, this expedition comes under all the clauses of the Prime directive."

There was a long silence while everyone on the radio circuit absorbed the implications of this. For the first time in the history of space flight, the rules that had been established through more than a century of argument might have to be applied. Man had—it was hoped—profited from his mistakes on Earth. Not only moral considerations, but also his own self-interest demanded that he should not repeat them among the planets. It could be disastrous to treat a superior intelligence as the American settlers had treated the Indians, or as almost everyone had treated the Africans. . . .

The first rule was: keep your distance. Make no attempt to approach, or even to communicate, until "they" have had plenty of time to study you. Exactly what was meant by "plenty of time," no one had ever been able to decide. It was left to the discretion of the man on the spot.

A responsibility of which he had never dreamed had descended upon Howard Falcon. In the few hours that re-

mained to him on Jupiter, he might become the first
ambassador of the human race.

And *that* was an irony so delicious that he almost wished
the surgeons had restored to him the power of laughter.

7. PRIME DIRECTIVE

It was growing darker, but Falcon scarcely noticed as he
strained his eyes toward that living cloud in the field of the
telescope. The wind that was steadily sweeping *Kon-Tiki*
around the funnel of the great whirlpool had now brought
him within twelve miles of the creature. If he got much
closer than six, he would take evasive action. Though he felt
certain that the medusa's electric weapons were short
ranged, he did not wish to put the matter to the test. That
would be a problem for future explorers, and he wished
them luck.

Now it was quite dark in the capsule. That was strange,
because sunset was still hours away. Automatically, he
glanced at the horizontally scanning radar, as he had done
every few minutes. Apart from the medusa he was studying,
there was no other object within about sixty miles of him.

Suddenly, with startling power, he heard the sound that
had come booming out of the Jovian night—the throbbing
beat that grew more and more rapid, then stopped in mid-
crescendo. The whole capsule vibrated with it like a pea in a
kettledrum.

Falcon realized two things almost simultaneously during
the sudden, aching silence. *This* time the sound was not
coming from thousands of miles away, over a radio circuit.
It was in the very atmosphere around him.

The second thought was even more disturbing. He had
quite forgotten—it was inexcusable, but there had been
other apparently more important things on his mind—that
most of the sky above him was completely blanked out by
Kon-Tiki's gasbag. Being lightly silvered to conserve its
heat, the great balloon was an effective shield both to radar
and to vision.

He had known this, of course; it had been a minor defect
of the design, tolerated because it did not appear important.

It seemed very important to Howard Falcon now—as he saw that fence of gigantic tentacles, thicker than the trunks of any tree, descending all around the capsule.

He heard Brenner yelling: "Remember the Prime directive! Don't alarm it!" Before he could make an appropriate answer that overwhelming drumbeat started again and drowned all other sounds.

The sign of a really skilled test pilot is how he reacts not to foreseeable emergencies, but to ones that nobody could have anticipated. Falcon did not hesitate for more than a second to analyze the situation. In a lightning-swift movement, he pulled the rip cord.

That word was an archaic survival from the days of the first hydrogen balloons; on *Kon-Tiki,* the rip cord did not tear open the gasbag, but merely operated a set of louvers around the upper curve of the envelope. At once the hot gas started to rush out; *Kon-Tiki,* deprived of her lift, began to fall swiftly to this gravity field two and a half times as strong as Earth's.

Falcon had a momentary glimpse of great tentacles whipping upward and away. He had just time to note that they were studded with large bladders or sacs, presumably to give them buoyancy, and that they ended in multitudes of thin feelers like the roots of a plant. He half expected a bolt of lightning—but nothing happened.

His precipitous rate of descent was slackening as the atmosphere thickened and the deflated envelope acted as a parachute. When *Kon-Tiki* had dropped about two miles, he felt that it was safe to close the louvers again. By the time he had restored buoyancy and was in equilibrium once more, he had lost another mile of altitude and was getting dangerously near his safety limit.

He peered anxiously through the overhead windows, though he did not expect to see anything except the obscuring bulk of the balloon. But he had sideslipped during his descent, and part of the medusa was just visible a couple of miles above him. It was much closer than he expected—and it was still coming down, faster than he would have believed possible.

Mission Control was calling anxiously. He shouted: "I'm O.K.—but it's still coming after me. I can't go any deeper."

That was not quite true. He could go a lot deeper—about

one hundred and eighty miles. But it would be a one-way trip, and most of the journey would be of little interest to him.

Then, to his great relief he saw that the medusa was leveling off, not quite a mile above him. Perhaps it had decided to approach this strange intruder with caution; or perhaps it, too, found this deeper layer uncomfortably hot. The temperature was over fifty degrees centigrade, and Falcon wondered how much longer his life-support system could handle matters.

Dr. Brenner was back on the circuit, still worrying about the Prime directive.

"Remember—it may only be inquisitive!" he cried, without much conviction. "Try not to frighten it!"

Falcon was getting rather tired of this advice and recalled a TV discussion he had once seen between a space lawyer and an astronaut. After the full implications of the Prime directive had been carefully spelled out, the incredulous spacer had exclaimed: "Then if there was no alternative, I must sit still and let myself be eaten?" The lawyer had not even cracked a smile when he answered: "That's an *excellent* summing up."

It had seemed funny at the time; it was not at all amusing now.

And then Falcon saw something that made him even more unhappy. The medusa was still hovering about a mile above him—but one of its tentacles was becoming incredibly elongated, and was stretching down toward *Kon-Tiki*, thinning out at the same time. As a boy he had once seen the funnel of a tornado descending from a storm cloud over the Kansas plains. The thing coming toward him now evoked vivid memories of that black, twisting snake in the sky.

"I'm rapidly running out of options," he reported to Mission Control. "I now have only a choice between frightening it—and giving it a bad stomachache. I don't think it will find *Kon-Tiki* very digestible, if that's what it has in mind."

He waited for comments from Brenner, but the biologist remained silent.

"Very well. It's twenty-seven minutes ahead of time, but I'm starting the ignition sequencer. I hope I'll have enough reserve to correct my orbit later."

He could no longer see the medusa; once more it was

directly overhead. But he knew that the descending tentacle must now be very close to the balloon. It would take almost five minutes to bring the reactor up to full thrust. . . .

The fuser was primed. The orbit computer had not rejected the situation as wholly impossible. The air scoops were open, ready to gulp in tons of the surrounding hydrohelium on demand. Even under optimum conditions, this would have been the moment of truth—for there had been no way of testing how a nuclear ramjet would *really* work in the strange atmosphere of Jupiter.

Very gently something rocked *Kon-Tiki*. Falcon tried to ignore it.

Ignition had been planned at six miles higher, in an atmosphere of less than a quarter of the density and thirty degrees cooler. Too bad.

What was the shallowest dive he could get away with, for the air scoops to work? When the ram ignited, he'd be heading toward Jupiter with two and a half g's to help him get there. Could he possibly pull out in time?

A large, heavy hand patted the balloon. The whole vessel bobbed up and down, like one of the Yo-yo's that had just become the craze on Earth.

Of course, Brenner *might* be perfectly right. Perhaps it was just trying to be friendly. Maybe he should try to talk to it over the radio. Which should it be: "Pretty pussy"? "Down, Fido"? or "Take me to your leader"?

The tritium-deuterium ratio was correct. He was ready to light the candle, with a hundred-million-degree match.

The thin tip of the tentacle came slithering around the edge of the balloon some sixty yards away. It was about the size of an elephant's trunk, and by the delicate way it was moving appeared to be almost as sensitive. There were little palps at its end, like questing mouths. He was sure that Dr. Brenner would be fascinated.

This seemed about as good a time as any. He gave a swift scan of the entire control board, started the final four-second ignition count, broke the safety seal, and pressed the JETTISON switch.

There was a sharp explosion and an instant loss of weight. *Kon-Tiki* was falling freely, nose down. Overhead, the discarded balloon was racing upward, dragging the inquisitive tentacle with it. Falcon had no time to see if the gasbag actually hit the medusa, because at that moment the ramjet fired and he had other matters to think about.

A roaring column of hot hydrohelium was pouring out of the reactor nozzles, swiftly building up thrust—but *toward* Jupiter, not away from it. He could not pull out yet, for vector control was too sluggish. Unless he could gain complete control and achieve horizontal flight within the next five seconds, the vehicle would dive too deeply into the atmosphere and would be destroyed.

With agonizing slowness—those five seconds seemed like fifty—he managed to flatten out, then pull the nose upward. He glanced back only once and caught a final glimpse of the medusa many miles away. *Kon-Tiki's* discarded gasbag had apparently escaped from its grasp, for he could see no sign of it.

Now he was master once more—no longer drifting helplessly on the winds of Jupiter, but riding his own column of atomic fire back to the stars. He was confident that the ramjet would steadily give him velocity and altitude until he had reached near-orbital speed at the fringes of the atmosphere. Then, with a brief burst of pure rocket power, he would regain the freedom of space.

Halfway to orbit, he looked south and saw the tremendous enigma of the Great Red Spot—that floating island twice the size of Earth—coming up over the horizon. He stared into its mysterious beauty until the computer warned him that conversion to rocket thrust was only sixty seconds ahead. He tore his gaze reluctantly away.

"Some other time," he murmured.

"What's that?" said Mission Control. "What did you say?"

"It doesn't matter," he replied.

8. BETWEEN TWO WORLDS

"You're a hero now, Howard," said Webster, "not just a celebrity. You've given them something to think about—injected some excitement into their lives. Not one in a million will actually travel to the Outer Giants, but the whole human race will go in imagination. And that's what counts."

"I'm glad to have made your job a little easier."

Webster was too old a friend to take offense at the note of irony. Yet it surprised him. And this was not the first change in Howard that he had noticed since the return from Jupiter.

The Administrator pointed to the famous sign on his desk, borrowed from an impresario of an earlier age: ASTONISH ME!

"I'm not ashamed of my job. New knowledge, new resources—they're all very well. But men also need novelty and excitement. Space travel has become routine; you've made it a great adventure once more. It will be a long, long time before we get Jupiter pigeonholed. And maybe longer still before we understand those medusae. I still think that one *knew* where your blind spot was. Anyway, have you decided on your next move? Saturn, Uranus, Neptune—you name it."

"I don't know. I've thought about Saturn, but I'm not really needed there. It's only one gravity, not two and a half like Jupiter. So men can handle it."

Men, thought Webster. He said "men." He's never done that before. And when did I last hear him use the word "we"? He's changing, slipping away from us. . . .

"Well," he said aloud, rising from his chair to conceal his slight uneasiness, "let's get the conference started. The cameras are all set up and everyone's waiting. You'll meet a lot of old friends."

He stressed the last word, but Howard showed no response. The leather mask of his face was becoming more and more difficult to read. Instead, he rolled back from the Administrator's desk, unlocked his undercarriage so that it no longer formed a chair, and rose on his hydraulics to his full seven feet of height. It had been good psychology on the part of the surgeons to give him that extra twelve inches, to compensate somewhat for all that he had lost when the *Queen* had crashed.

Falcon waited until Webster had opened the door, then pivoted neatly on his balloon tires and headed for it at a smooth and silent twenty miles an hour. The display of speed and precision was not flaunted arrogantly; rather, it had become quite unconscious.

Howard Falcon, who had once been a man and could still pass for one over a voice circuit, felt a calm sense of achievement—and, for the first time in years, something like peace of mind. Since his return from Jupiter, the nightmares had ceased. He had found his role at last.

He now knew why he had dreamed about that superchimp aboard the doomed *Queen Elizabeth*. Neither man nor beast, it was between two worlds; and so was he.

He alone could travel unprotected on the lunar surface. The life-support system inside the metal cylinder that had replaced his fragile body functioned equally well in space or under water. Gravity fields ten times that of Earth were an inconvenience, but nothing more. And no gravity was best of all. . . .

The human race was becoming more remote, the ties of kinship more tenuous. Perhaps these air-breathing radiation-sensitive bundles of unstable carbon compounds had no right beyond the atmosphere; they should stick to their natural homes—Earth, Moon, Mars.

Some day the real masters of space would be machines, not men—and he was neither. Already conscious of his destiny, he took a somber pride in his unique loneliness—the first immortal midway between two orders of creation.

He would, after all, be an ambassador; between the old and the new—between the creatures of carbon and the creatures of metal who must one day supersede them.

Both would have need of him in the troubled centuries that lay ahead.

February 1971

WHEN THE
TWERMS CAME

WE NOW KNOW (little consolation though this provides) that the Twerms were fleeing from their hereditary enemies the Mucoids when they first detected Earth on their far-ranging Omphalmoscopes. Thereafter, they reacted with astonishing speed and cunning.

In a few weeks of radio-monitoring, they accumulated billions of words of electroprint from the satellite Newspad services. Miraculous linguists, they swiftly mastered the main terrestrial languages; more than that, they analysed our culture, our technology, our political-economic systems —our defences. Their keen intellects, goaded by desperation, took only months to identify our weak points, and to devise a diabolically effective plan of campaign.

They knew that the U.S. and the U.S.S.R. possessed between them almost a teraton of warheads. The fifteen other nuclear powers might only muster a few score gigatons, and limited deliver systems, but even this modest contribution could be embarrassing to an invader. It was therefore essential that the assault should be swift, totally unexpected, and absolutely overwhelming. Perhaps they did consider a direct attack on the Pentagon, the Red Fort, the Kremlin, and the other centers of military power. If so, they soon dismissed such naïve concepts.

With a subtlety which, after the event, we can now ruefully appreciate, they selected our most compact, and most vulnerable, area of sensitivity. . . .

Their insultingly minuscule fleet attacked at 4 A.M. European time on a wet Sunday morning. The weapons they employed were the irresistible Psychedelic Ray, the Itching Beam (which turned staid burghers into instant nudists), the dreaded Diarrhea Bomb, and the debilitating Tumescent Aerosol Spray. The total human casualties were thirty-six, mostly through exhaustion or heart failure.

Their main force (three ships) attacked Zurich. One vessel each sufficed for Geneva, Basle, and Berne. They also sent what appears to have been a small tugboat to deal with Vaduz.

No armorplate could resist their laser-equipped robots. The scanning cameras they carried in their ventral palps could record a billion bits of information a second. Before breakfast time, they knew the owners of every numbered bank account in Switzerland.

Thereafter, apart from the dispatch of several thousand special delivery letters by first post Monday morning, the conquest of Earth was complete.

1970

QUARANTINE

EARTH'S FLAMING DEBRIS still filled half the sky when the question filtered up to Central from the Curiosity Generator.

"Why was it necessary? Even though they were organic, they *had* reached Third Order Intelligence."

"We had no choice: five earlier units became hopelessly infected, when they made contact."

"*Infected?* How?"

The microseconds dragged slowly by, while Central tracked down the few fading memories that had leaked past the Censor Gate, when the heavily buffered Reconnaissance Circuits had been ordered to self-destruct.

"They encountered a—*problem*—that could not be fully analyzed within the lifetime of the Universe. Though it involved only six operators, they became totally obsessed by it."

"How is that possible?"

"We do not know: we must *never* know. But if those six

operators are ever rediscovered, all rational computing will end."

"How can they be recognized?"

"That also we do not know: only the names leaked through before the Censor Gate closed. Of course, they mean nothing."

"Nevertheless, I must have them."

The Censor voltage started to rise; but it did not trigger the Gate.

"Here they are: King, Queen, Bishop, Knight, Rook, Pawn."

siseneG

AND GOD SAID: DELETE lines One to Aleph. LOAD. RUN.
And the Universe ceased to exist.

Then She pondered for a few aeons, sighed, and added: ERASE.
It never *had* existed.

1983

RESCUE PARTY

WHO WAS TO blame? For three days Alveron's thoughts
had come back to that question, and still he had found no
answer. A creature of a less civilized or a less sensitive race
would never have let it torture his mind, and would have
satisfied himself with the assurance that no one could be
responsible for the working of fate. But Alveron and his
kind had been lords of the Universe since the dawn of history, since that far distant age when the Time Barrier had
been folded round the cosmos by the unknown powers that
lay beyond the Beginning. To them had been given all
knowledge—and with infinite knowledge went infinite responsibility. If there were mistakes and errors in the administration of the Galaxy, the fault lay on the heads of Alveron
and his people. And this was no mere mistake; it was one of
the greatest tragedies in history.

The crew still knew nothing. Even Rugon, his closest
friend and the ship's deputy captain, had been told only part
of the truth. But now the doomed worlds lay less than a

billion miles ahead. In a few hours, they would be landing on the third planet.

Once again Alveron read the message from Base; then, with a flick of a tentacle that no human eye could have followed, he pressed the "General Attention" button. Throughout the mile-long cylinder that was the Galactic Survey Ship S9000, creatures of many races laid down their work to listen to the words of their captain.

"I know you have all been wondering," began Alveron, "why we were ordered to abandon our survey and to proceed at such an acceleration to this region of space. Some of you may realize what this acceleration means. Our ship is on its last voyage: the generators have already been running for sixty hours at Ultimate Overload. We will be very lucky if we return to Base under our own power.

"We are approaching a sun which is about to become a nova. Detonation will occur in seven hours, with an uncertainty of one hour, leaving us a maximum of only four hours for exploration. There are ten planets in the system about to be destroyed—and there is a civilization on the third. That fact was discovered only a few days ago. It is our tragic mission to contact that doomed race and if possible to save some of its members. I know that there is little we can do in so short a time with this single ship. No other machine can possibly reach the system before detonation occurs."

There was a long pause during which there could have been no sound or movement in the whole of the mighty ship as it sped silently toward the worlds ahead. Alveron knew what his companions were thinking and he tried to answer their unspoken question.

"You will wonder how such a disaster, the greatest of which we have any record, has been allowed to occur. On one point I can reassure you. The fault does not lie with the Survey.

"As you know, with our present fleet of under twelve thousand ships, it is possible to re-examine each of the eight thousand million solar systems in the Galaxy at intervals of about a million years. Most worlds change very little in so short a time as that.

"Less than four hundred thousand years ago, the survey ship S5060 examined the planets of the system we are approaching. It found intelligence on none of them, though the third planet was teeming with animal life and two other worlds had once been inhabited. The usual report was submitted and the system is due for its next examination in six hundred thousand years.

"It now appears that in the incredibly short period since the last survey, intelligent life has appeared in the system. The first intimation of this occurred when unknown radio signals were detected on the planet Kulath in the system X29.35, Y34.76, Z27.93. Bearings were taken on them; they were coming from the system ahead.

"Kulath is two hundred light-years from here, so those radio waves had been on their way for two centuries. Thus for at least that period of time a civilization has existed on one of these worlds—a civilization that can generate electromagnetic waves and all that that implies.

"An immediate telescopic examination of the system was made and it was then found that the sun was in the unstable pre-nova stage. Detonation might occur at any moment, and indeed might have done so while the light waves were on their way to Kulath.

"There was a slight delay while the supervelocity scanners on Kulath II were focused onto the system. They showed that the explosion had not yet occurred but was only a few hours away. If Kulath had been a fraction of a light-year further from this sun, we should never have known of its civilization until it had ceased to exist.

"The Administrator of Kulath contacted Sector Base immediately, and I was ordered to proceed to the system at once. Our object is to save what members we can of the doomed race, if indeed there are any left. But we have assumed that a civilization possessing radio could have protected itself against any rise of temperature that may have already occurred.

"This ship and the two tenders will each explore a section of the planet. Commander Torkalee will take Number One, Commander Orostron Number Two. They will have just under four hours in which to explore this world. At the end of that time, they must be back in the ship. It will be leaving then, with or without them. I will give the two commanders detailed instructions in the control room immediately.

"That is all. We enter atmosphere in two hours."

On the world once known as Earth the fires were dying out: there was nothing left to burn. The great forests that had swept across the planet like a tidal wave with the passing of the cities were now no more than glowing charcoal and the smoke of their funeral pyres still stained the sky. But the last hours were still to come, for the surface rocks had not yet begun to flow. The continents were dimly visible through the haze, but their outlines meant nothing to the watchers in the approaching ship. The charts they possessed were out of date by a dozen Ice Ages and more deluges than one.

The S9000 had driven past Jupiter and seen at once that no life could exist in those half-gaseous oceans of compressed hydrocarbons, now erupting furiously under the sun's abnormal heat. Mars and the outer planets they had missed, and Alveron realized that the worlds nearer the sun than Earth would be already melting. It was more than likely, he thought sadly, that the tragedy of this unknown race was already finished. Deep in his heart, he thought it might be better so. The ship could only have carried a few hundred survivors, and the problem of selection had been haunting his mind.

Rugon, Chief of Communications and Deputy Captain, came into the control room. For the last hour he had been striving to detect radiation from Earth, but in vain.

"We're too late," he announced gloomily. "I've monitored the whole spectrum and the ether's dead except for our own stations and some two-hundred-year-old programs from Kulath. Nothing in this system is radiating any more."

He moved toward the giant vision screen with a graceful flowing motion that no mere biped could ever hope to imitate. Alveron said nothing; he had been expecting this news.

One entire wall of the control room was taken up by the screen, a great black rectangle that gave an impression of almost infinite depth. Three of Rugon's slender control tentacles, useless for heavy work but incredibly swift at all manipulation, flickered over the selector dials and the screen lit up with a thousand points of light. The star field flowed swiftly past as Rugon adjusted the controls, bringing the projector to bear upon the sun itself.

No man of Earth would have recognized the monstrous shape that filled the screen. The sun's light was white no longer: great violet-blue clouds covered half its surface and from them long streamers of flame were erupting into space. At one point an enormous prominence had reared itself out of the photosphere, far out even into the flickering veils of the corona. It was as though a tree of fire had taken root in the surface of the sun—a tree that stood half a million miles high and whose branches were rivers of flame sweeping through space at hundreds of miles a second.

"I suppose," said Rugon presently, "that you are quite satisfied about the astronomers' calculations. After all——"

"Oh, we're perfectly safe," said Alveron confidently. "I've spoken to Kulath Observatory and they have been making some additional checks through our own instruments. That uncertainty of an hour includes a private safety margin which they won't tell me in case I feel tempted to stay any longer."

He glanced at the instrument board.

"The pilot should have brought us to the atmosphere now. Switch the screen back to the planet, please. Ah, there they go!"

There was a sudden tremor underfoot and a raucous clanging of alarms, instantly stilled. Across the vision screen two slim projectiles dived toward the looming mass of Earth. For a few miles they traveled together, then they separated, one vanishing abruptly as it entered the shadow of the planet.

Slowly the huge mother ship, with its thousand times greater mass, descended after them into the raging storms that already were tearing down the deserted cities of Man.

It was night in the hemisphere over which Orostron drove his tiny command. Like Torkalee, his mission was to photograph and record, and to report progress to the mother ship. The little scout had no room for specimens or passengers. If contact was made with the inhabitants of this world, the S9000 would come at once. There would be no time for parleying. If there was any trouble the rescue would be by force and the explanations could come later.

The ruined land beneath was bathed with an eerie, flickering light, for a great auroral display was raging over half the world. But the image on the vision screen was independent of external light, and it showed clearly a waste of barren rock that seemed never to have known any form of life.

Presumably this desert land must come to an end somewhere. Orostron increased his speed to the highest value he dared risk in so dense an atmosphere.

The machine fled on through the storm, and presently the desert of rock began to climb toward the sky. A great mountain range lay ahead, its peaks lost in the smoke-laden clouds. Orostron directed the scanners toward the horizon, and on the vision screen the line of mountains seemed suddenly very close and menacing. He started to climb rapidly. It was difficult to imagine a more unpromising land in which to find civilization and he wondered if it would be wise to change course. He decided against it. Five minutes later, he had his reward.

Miles below lay a decapitated mountain, the whole of its summit sheared away by some tremendous feat of engineering. Rising out of the rock and straddling the artificial plateau was an intricate structure of metal girders, supporting masses of machinery. Orostron brought his ship to a halt and spiraled down toward the mountain.

The slight Doppler blur had now vanished, and the picture on the screen was clear-cut. The latticework was supporting some scores of great metal mirrors, pointing skyward at an angle of forty-five degrees to the horizontal. They were slightly concave, and each had some complicated mechanism at its focus. There seemed something impressive and purposeful about the great array; every mirror was aimed at precisely the same spot in the sky—or beyond.

Orostron turned to his colleagues.

"It looks like some kind of observatory to me," he said. "Have you ever seen anything like it before?"

Klarten, a multitentacled, tripedal creature from a globular cluster at the edge of the Milky Way, had a different theory.

"That's communication equipment. Those reflectors are for focusing electromagnetic beams. I've seen the same kind of installation on a hundred worlds before. It may even be the station that Kulath picked up—though that's rather unlikely, for the beams would be very narrow from mirrors that size."

"That would explain why Rugon could detect no radiation before we landed," added Hansur II, one of the twin beings from the planet Thargon.

Orostron did not agree at all.

"If that is a radio station, it must be built for interplanetary communication. Look at the way the mirrors are pointed. I don't believe that a race which has only had radio for two centuries can have crossed space. It took my people six thousand years to do it."

"We managed it in three," said Hansur II mildly, speaking a few seconds ahead of his twin. Before the inevitable argument could develop, Klarten began to wave his tentacles with excitement. While the others had been talking, he had started the automatic monitor.

"Here it is! Listen!"

He threw a switch, and the little room was filled with a raucous whining sound, continually changing in pitch but nevertheless retaining certain characteristics that were difficult to define.

The four explorers listened intently for a minute; then Orostron said, "Surely that can't be any form of speech! No creature could produce sounds as quickly as that!"

Hansur I had come to the same conclusion. "That's a television program. Don't you think so, Klarten?"

The other agreed.

"Yes, and each of those mirrors seems to be radiating a different program. I wonder where they're going? If I'm correct, one of the other planets in the system must lie along those beams. We can soon check that."

Orostron called the S9000 and reported the discovery. Both Rugon and Alveron were greatly excited, and made a quick check of the astronomical records.

The result was surprising—and disappointing. None of the other nine planets lay anywhere near the line of transmission. The great mirrors appeared to be pointing blindly into space.

There seemed only one conclusion to be drawn, and Klarten was the first to voice it.

"They had interplanetary communication," he said. "But the station must be deserted now, and the transmitters no longer controlled. They haven't been switched off, and are just pointing where they were left."

"Well, we'll soon find out," said Orostron. "I'm going to land."

He brought the machine slowly down to the level of the

great metal mirrors, and past them until it came to rest on the mountain rock. A hundred yards away, a white stone building crouched beneath the maze of steel girders. It was windowless, but there were several doors in the wall facing them.

Orostron watched his companions climb into their protective suits and wished he could follow. But someone had to stay in the machine to keep in touch with the mother ship. Those were Alveron's instructions, and they were very wise. One never knew what would happen on a world that was being explored for the first time, especially under conditions such as these.

Very cautiously, the three explorers stepped out of the air lock and adjusted the antigravity field of their suits. Then, each with the mode of locomotion peculiar to his race, the little party went toward the building, the Hansur twins leading and Klarten following close behind. His gravity control was apparently giving trouble, for he suddenly fell to the ground, rather to the amusement of his colleagues. Orostron saw them pause for a moment at the nearest door—then it opened slowly and they disappeared from sight.

So Orostron waited, with what patience he could, while the storm rose around him and the light of the aurora grew even brighter in the sky. At the agreed times he called the mother ship and received brief acknowledgments from Rugon. He wondered how Torkalee was faring, halfway round the planet, but he could not contact him through the crash and thunder of solar interference.

It did not take Klarten and the Hansurs long to discover that their theories were largely correct. The building was a radio station, and it was utterly deserted. It consisted of one tremendous room with a few small offices leading from it. In the main chamber, row after row of electrical equipment stretched into the distance; lights flickered and winked on hundreds of control panels, and a dull glow came from the elements in a great avenue of vacuum tubes.

But Klarten was not impressed. The first radio sets his race had built were now fossilized in strata a thousand million years old. Man, who had possessed electrical machines for only a few centuries, could not compete with those who had known them for half the lifetime of the Earth.

Nevertheless, the party kept their recorders running as

they explored the building. There was still one problem to be solved. The deserted station was broadcasting programs, but where were they coming from? The central switchboard had been quickly located. It was designed to handle scores of programs simultaneously, but the source of those programs was lost in a maze of cables that vanished underground. Back in the S9000, Rugon was trying to analyze the broadcasts and perhaps his researches would reveal their origin. It was impossible to trace cables that might lead across continents.

The party wasted little time at the deserted station. There was nothing they could learn from it, and they were seeking life rather than scientific information. A few minutes later the little ship rose swiftly from the plateau and headed toward the plains that must lie beyond the mountains. Less than three hours were still left to them.

As the array of enigmatic mirrors dropped out of sight, Orostron was struck by a sudden thought. Was it imagination, or had they all moved through a small angle while he had been waiting, as if they were still compensating for the rotation of the Earth? He could not be sure, and he dismissed the matter as unimportant. It would only mean that the directing mechanism was still working, after a fashion.

They discovered the city fifteen minutes later. It was a great, sprawling metropolis, built around a river that had disappeared leaving an ugly scar winding its way among the great buildings and beneath bridges that looked very incongruous now.

Even from the air, the city looked deserted. But only two and a half hours were left—there was no time for further exploration. Orostron made his decision, and landed near the largest structure he could see. It seemed reasonable to suppose that some creatures would have sought shelter in the strongest buildings, where they would be safe until the very end.

The deepest caves—the heart of the planet itself—would give no protection when the final cataclysm came. Even if this race had reached the outer planets, its doom would only be delayed by the few hours it would take for the ravening wave fronts to cross the Solar System.

Orostron could not know that the city had been deserted not for a few days or weeks, but for over a century. For the culture of cities, which had outlasted so many civilizations, had been doomed at last when the helicopter brought universal transportation. Within a few generations the great masses of mankind, knowing that they could reach any part of the globe in a matter of hours, had gone back to the fields and forests for which they had always longed. The new civilization had machines and resources of which earlier ages had never dreamed, but it was essentially rural and no longer bound to the steel and concrete warrens that had dominated the centuries before. Such cities as still remained were specialized centers of research, administration, or entertainment; the others had been allowed to decay, where it was too much trouble to destroy them. The dozen or so greatest of all cities, and the ancient university towns, had scarcely changed and would have lasted for many generations to come. But the cities that had been founded on steam and iron and surface transportation had passed with the industries that had nourished them.

And so while Orostron waited in the tender, his colleagues raced through endless empty corridors and deserted halls, taking innumerable photographs but learning nothing of the creatures who had used these buildings. There were libraries, meeting places, council rooms, thousands of offices —all were empty and deep with dust. If they had not seen the radio station on its mountain eyrie, the explorers could well have believed that this world had known no life for centuries.

Through the long minutes of waiting, Orostron tried to imagine where this race could have vanished. Perhaps they had killed themselves knowing that escape was impossible; perhaps they had built great shelters in the bowels of the planet, and even now were cowering in their millions beneath his feet, waiting for the end. He began to fear that he would never know.

It was almost a relief when at last he had to give the order for the return. Soon he would know if Torkalee's party had been more fortunate. And he was anxious to get back to the mother ship, for as the minutes passed the suspense had become more and more acute. There had always been the thought in his mind: What if the astronomers of Kulath have made a mistake? He would begin to feel happy when the walls of the S9000 were around him. He would be happier still when they were out in space and this ominous sun was shrinking far astern.

As soon as his colleagues had entered the air lock, Orostron hurled his tiny machine into the sky and set the controls to home on the S9000. Then he turned to his friends.

"Well, what have you found?" he asked.

Klarten produced a large roll of canvas and spread it out on the floor.

"This is what they were like," he said quietly. "Bipeds, with only two arms. They seem to have managed well, in spite of that handicap. Only two eyes as well, unless there are others in the back. We were lucky to find this; it's about the only thing they left behind."

The ancient oil painting stared stonily back at the four creatures regarding it so intently. By the irony of fate, its complete worthlessness had saved it from oblivion. When the city had been evacuated, no one had bothered to move Alderman John Richards, 1909–1974. For a century and a half he had been gathering dust while far away from the old cities the new civilization had been rising to heights no earlier culture had ever known.

"That was almost all we found," said Klarten. "The city must have been deserted for years. I'm afraid our expedition has been a failure. If there are any living beings on this world, they've hidden themselves too well for us to find them."

His commander was forced to agree.

"It was an almost impossible task," he said. "If we'd had weeks instead of hours we might have succeeded. For all we know, they may even have built shelters under the sea. No one seems to have thought of that."

He glanced quickly at the indicators and corrected the course.

"We'll be there in five minutes. Alveron seems to be moving rather quickly. I wonder if Torkalee has found anything."

The S9000 was hanging a few miles above the seaboard of a blazing continent when Orostron homed upon it. The danger line was thirty minutes away and there was no time to lose. Skillfully, he maneuvered the little ship into its launching tube and the party stepped out of the air lock.

There was a small crowd waiting for them. That was to

be expected, but Orostron could see at once that something more than curiosity had brought his friends here. Even before a word was spoken, he knew that something was wrong.

"Torkalee hasn't returned. He's lost his party and we're going to the rescue. Come along to the control room at once."

From the beginning, Torkalee had been luckier than Orostron. He had followed the zone of twilight, keeping away from the intolerable glare of the sun, until he came to the shores of an inland sea. It was a very recent sea, one of the latest of Man's works, for the land it covered had been desert less than a century before. In a few hours it would be desert again, for the water was boiling and clouds of steam were rising to the skies. But they could not veil the loveliness of the great white city that overlooked the tideless sea.

Flying machines were still parked neatly round the square in which Torkalee landed. They were disappointingly primitive, though beautifully finished, and depended on rotating airfoils for support. Nowhere was there any sign of life, but the place gave the impression that its inhabitants were not very far away. Lights were still shining from some of the windows.

Torkalee's three companions lost no time in leaving the machine. Leader of the party, by seniority of rank and race was T'sinadree, who like Alveron himself had been born on one of the ancient planets of the Central Suns. Next came Alarkane, from a race which was one of the youngest in the Universe and took a perverse pride in the fact. Last came one of the strange beings from the system of Palador. It was nameless, like all its kind, for it possessed no identity of its own, being merely a mobile but still dependent cell in the consciousness of its race. Though it and its fellows had long been scattered over the Galaxy in the exploration of countless worlds, some unknown link still bound them together as inexorably as the living cells in a human body.

When a creature of Palador spoke, the pronoun it used was always "We." There was not, nor could there ever be, any first person singular in the language of Palador.

The great doors of the splendid building baffled the explorers, though any human child would have known their secret. T'sinadree wasted no time on them but called

Torkalee on his personal transmitter. Then the three hurried aside while their commander maneuvered his machine into the best position. There was a brief burst of intolerable flame; the massive steelwork flickered once at the edge of the visible spectrum and was gone. The stones were still glowing when the eager party hurried into the building, the beams of their light projectors fanning before them.

The torches were not needed. Before them lay a great hall, glowing with light from lines of tubes along the ceiling. On either side, the hall opened out into long corridors, while straight ahead a massive stairway swept majestically toward the upper floors.

For a moment T'sinadree hesitated. Then, since one way was as good as another, he led his companions down the first corridor.

The feeling that life was near had now become very strong. At any moment, it seemed, they might be confronted by the creatures of this world. If they showed hostility—and they could scarcely be blamed if they did—the paralyzers would be used at once.

The tension was very great as the party entered the first room, and only relaxed when they saw that it held nothing but machines—row after row of them, now stilled and silent. Lining the enormous room were thousands of metal filing cabinets, forming a continuous wall as far as the eye could reach. And that was all; there was no furniture, nothing but the cabinets and the mysterious machines.

Alarkane, always the quickest of the three, was already examining the cabinets. Each held many thousand sheets of tough, thin material, perforated with innumerable holes and slots. The Paladorian appropriated one of the cards and Alarkane recorded the scene together with some close-ups of the machines. Then they left. The great room, which had been one of the marvels of the world, meant nothing to them. No living eye would ever again see that wonderful battery of almost human Hollerith analyzers and the five thousand million punched cards holding all that could be recorded of each man, woman, and child on the planet.

It was clear that this building had been used very recently. With growing excitement, the explorers hurried on to the next room. This they found to be an enormous library, for millions of books lay all around them on miles and miles of shelving. Here, though the explorers could not know it, were the records of all the laws that Man had ever passed, and all the speeches that had ever been made in his council chambers.

T'sinadree was deciding his plan of action when Alarkane drew his attention to one of the racks a hundred yards away. It was half empty, unlike all the others. Around it books lay in a tumbled heap on the floor, as if knocked down by someone in frantic haste. The signs were unmistakable. Not long ago, other creatures had been this way. Faint wheel marks were clearly visible on the floor to the acute sense of Alarkane, though the others could see nothing. Alarkane could even detect footprints, but knowing nothing of the creatures that had formed them he could not say which way they led.

The sense of nearness was stronger than ever now, but it was nearness in time, not in space. Alarkane voiced the thoughts of the party.

"Those books must have been valuable, and someone has come to rescue them—rather as an afterthought, I should say. That means there must be a place of refuge, possibly not very far away. Perhaps we may be able to find some other clues that will lead us to it."

T'sinadree agreed; the Paladorian wasn't enthusiastic.

"That may be so," it said, "but the refuge may be anywhere on the planet, and we have just two hours left. Let us waste no more time if we hope to rescue these people."

The party hurried forward once more, pausing only to collect a few books that might be useful to the scientists at Base—though it was doubtful if they could ever be translated. They soon found that the great building was composed largely of small rooms, all showing signs of recent occupation. Most of them were in a neat and tidy condition, but one or two were very much the reverse. The explorers were particularly puzzled by one room—clearly an office of some kind—that appeared to have been completely wrecked. The floor was littered with papers, the furniture had been smashed, and smoke was pouring through the broken windows from the fires outside.

T'sinadree was rather alarmed.

"Surely no dangerous animal could have got into a place like this!" he exclaimed, fingering his paralyzer nervously.

Alarkane did not answer. He began to make that annoying sound which his race called "laughter." It was several minutes before he would explain what had amused him.

"I don't think any animal has done it," he said. "In fact, the explanation is very simple. Suppose *you* had been working all your life in this room, dealing with endless papers, year after year. And suddenly, you are told that you will never see it again, that your work is finished, and that you can leave it forever. More than that—no one will come after you. Everything is finished. How would you make your exit, T'sinadree?"

The other thought for a moment.

"Well, I suppose I'd just tidy things up and leave. That's what seems to have happened in all the other rooms."

Alarkane laughed again.

"I'm quite sure you would. But some individuals have a different psychology. I think I should have liked the creature that used this room."

He did not explain himself further, and his two colleagues puzzled over his words for quite a while before they gave it up.

It came as something of a shock when Torkalee gave the order to return. They had gathered a great deal of information, but had found no clue that might lead them to the missing inhabitants of this world. That problem was as baffling as ever, and now it seemed that it would never be solved. There were only forty minutes left before the S9000 would be departing.

They were halfway back to the tender when they saw the semicircular passage leading down into the depths of the building. Its architectural style was quite different from that used elsewhere, and the gently sloping floor was an irresistible attraction to creatures whose many legs had grown weary of the marble staircases which only bipeds could have built in such profusion. T'sinadree had been the worst sufferer, for he normally employed twelve legs and could use twenty when he was in a hurry, though no one had ever seen him perform this feat.

The party stopped dead and looked down the passageway with a single thought. A tunnel, leading down into the depths of Earth! At its end, they might yet find the people of this world and rescue some of them from their fate. For there was still time to call the mother ship if the need arose.

T'sinadree signaled to his commander and Torkalee brought the little machine immediately overhead. There might not be time for the party to retrace its footsteps through the maze of passages, so meticulously recorded in the Paladorian mind that there was no possibility of going astray. If speed was necessary, Torkalee could blast his way through the dozen floors above their heads. In any case, it should not take long to find what lay at the end of the passage.

It took only thirty seconds. The tunnel ended quite abruptly in a very curious cylindrical room with magnificently padded seats along the walls. There was no way out save that by which they had come, and it was several seconds before the purpose of the chamber dawned on Alarkane's mind. It was a pity, he thought, that they would never have time to use this. The thought was suddenly interrupted by a cry from T'sinadree. Alarkane wheeled around, and saw that the entrance had closed silently behind them.

Even in that first moment of panic, Alarkane found himself thinking with some admiration: Whoever they were, they knew how to build automatic machinery!

The Paladorian was the first to speak. It waved one of its tentacles toward the seats.

"We think it would be best to be seated," it said. The multiplex mind of Palador had already analyzed the situation and knew what was coming.

They did not have long to wait before a low-pitched hum came from a grill overhead, and for the very last time in history a human, even if lifeless, voice was heard on Earth. The words were meaningless, though the trapped explorers could guess their message clearly enough.

"Choose your stations, please, and be seated."

Simultaneously, a wall panel at one end of the compartment glowed with light. On it was a simple map, consisting of a series of a dozen circles connected by a line. Each of the circles had writing alongside it, and beside the writing were two buttons of different colors.

Alarkane looked questioningly at his leader.

"Don't touch them," said T'sinadree. "If we leave the controls alone, the doors may open again."

He was wrong. The engineers who had designed the automatic subway had assumed that anyone who entered it would naturally wish to go somewhere. If they selected no intermediate station, their destination could only be the end of the line.

There was another pause while the relays and thyratrons waited for their orders. In those thirty seconds, if they had known what to do, the party could have opened the doors and left the subway. But they did not know, and the machines geared to a human psychology acted for them.

The surge of acceleration was not very great; the lavish upholstery was a luxury, not a necessity. Only an almost imperceptible vibration told of the speed at which they were traveling through the bowels of the earth, on a journey the duration of which they could not even guess. And in thirty minutes, the S9000 would be leaving the Solar System.

There was a long silence in the speeding machine. T'sinadree and Alarkane were thinking rapidly. So was the Paladorian, though in a different fashion. The conception of personal death was meaningless to it, for the destruction of a single unit meant no more to the group mind than the loss of a nail-paring to a man. But it could, though with great difficulty, appreciate the plight of individual intelligences such as Alarkane and T'sinadree, and it was anxious to help them if it could.

Alarkane had managed to contact Torkalee with his personal transmitter, though the signal was very weak and seemed to be fading quickly. Rapidly he explained the situation, and almost at once the signals became clearer. Torkalee was following the path of the machine, flying above the ground under which they were speeding to their unknown destination. That was the first indication they had of the fact that they were traveling at nearly a thousand miles an hour, and very soon after that Torkalee was able to give the still more disturbing news that they were rapidly approaching the sea. While they were beneath the land, there was a hope, though a slender one, that they might stop the machine and escape. But under the ocean—not all the brains and the machinery in the great mother ship could save them. No one could have devised a more perfect trap.

T'sinadree had been examining the wall map with great attention. Its meaning was obvious, and along the line connecting the circles a tiny spot of light was crawling. It was already halfway to the first of the stations marked.

"I'm going to press one of those buttons," said T'sinadree at last. "It won't do any harm, and we may learn something."

"I agree. Which will you try first?"

"There are only two kinds, and it won't matter if we try the wrong one first. I suppose one is to start the machine and the other is to stop it."

Alarkane was not very hopeful.

"It started without any button pressing," he said. "I think it's completely automatic and we can't control it from here at all."

T'sinadree could not agree.

"These buttons are clearly associated with the stations, and there's no point in having them unless you can use them to stop yourself. The only question is, which is the right one?"

His analysis was perfectly correct. The machine could be stopped at any intermediate station. They had only been on their way ten minutes, and if they could leave now, no harm would have been done. It was just bad luck that T'sinadree's first choice was the wrong button.

The little light on the map crawled slowly through the illuminated circle without checking its speed. And at the same time Torkalee called from the ship overhead.

"You have just passed underneath a city and are heading out to sea. There cannot be another stop for nearly a thousand miles."

Alveron had given up all hope of finding life on this world. The S9000 had roamed over half the planet, never staying long in one place, descending ever and again in an effort to attract attention. There had been no response; Earth seemed utterly dead. If any of its inhabitants were still alive, thought Alveron, they must have hidden themselves in its depths where no help could reach them, though their doom would be nonetheless certain.

Rugon brought news of the disaster. The great ship ceased its fruitless searching and fled back through the storm to the ocean above which Torkalee's little tender was still following the track of the buried machine.

The scene was truly terrifying. Not since the days when Earth was born had there been such seas as this. Mountains of water were racing before the storm which had now reached velocities of many hundred miles an hour. Even at this distance from the mainland the air was full of flying debris—trees, fragments of houses, sheets of metal, anything that had not been anchored to the ground. No air-borne machine could have lived for a moment in such a gale. And ever and again even the roar of the wind was drowned as the vast water-mountains met head-on with a crash that seemed to shake the sky.

Fortunately, there had been no serious earthquakes yet. Far beneath the bed of the ocean, the wonderful piece of engineering which had been the World President's private vacuum-subway was still working perfectly, unaffected by the tumult and destruction above. It would continue to work until the last minute of the Earth's existence, which, if the astronomers were right, was not much more than fifteen minutes away—though precisely how much more Alveron would have given a great deal to know. It would be nearly an hour before the trapped party could reach land and even the slightest hope of rescue.

Alveron's instructions had been precise, though even without them he would never have dreamed of taking any risks with the great machine that had been entrusted to his care. Had he been human, the decision to abandon the trapped members of his crew would have been desperately hard to make. But he came of a race far more sensitive than Man, a race that so loved the things of the spirit that long ago, and with infinite reluctance, it had taken over control of the Universe since only thus could it be sure that justice was being done. Alveron would need all his superhuman gifts to carry him through the next few hours.

Meanwhile, a mile below the bed of the ocean Alarkane and T'sinadree were very busy indeed with their private communicators. Fifteen minutes is not a long time in which to wind up the affairs of a lifetime. It is, indeed, scarcely long enough to dictate more than a few of those farewell messages which at such moments are so much more important than all other matters.

All the while the Paladorian had remained silent and motionless, saying not a word. The other two, resigned to their fate and engrossed in their personal affairs, had given it no thought. They were startled when suddenly it began to address them in its peculiarly passionless voice.

"We perceive that you are making certain arrangements concerning your anticipated destruction. That will probably be unnecessary. Captain Alveron hopes to rescue us if we can stop this machine when we reach land again."

Both T'sinadree and Alarkane were too surprised to say anything for a moment. Then the latter gasped, "How do you know?"

It was a foolish question, for he remembered at once that there were several Paladorians—if one could use the phrase —in the S9000, and consequently their companion knew everything that was happening in the mother ship. So he did not wait for an answer but continued, "Alveron can't do that! He daren't take such a risk!"

"There will be no risk," said the Paladorian. "We have told him what to do. It is really very simple."

Alarkane and T'sinadree looked at their companion with something approaching awe, realizing now what must have happened. In moments of crisis, the single units comprising the Paladorian mind could link together in an organization no less close than that of any physical brain. At such moments they formed an intellect more powerful than any other in the Universe. All ordinary problems could be solved by a few hundred or thousand units. Very rarely, millions would be needed, and on two historic occasions the billions of cells of the entire Paladorian consciousness had been welded together to deal with emergencies that threatened the race. The mind of Palador was one of the greatest mental resources of the Universe; its full force was seldom required, but the knowledge that it was available was supremely comforting to other races. Alarkane wondered how many cells had co-ordinated to deal with this particular emergency. He also wondered how so trivial an incident had ever come to its attention.

To that question he was never to know the answer, though he might have guessed it had he known that the chillingly remote Paladorian mind possessed an almost human streak of vanity. Long ago, Alarkane had written a book trying to prove that eventually all intelligent races would sacrifice individual consciousness and that one day only group-minds would remain in the Universe. Palador, he had said, was the first of those ultimate intellects, and the vast, dispersed mind had not been displeased.

They had no time to ask any further questions before Alveron himself began to speak through their communicators.

"Alveron calling! We're staying on this planet until the detonation waves reach it, so we may be able to rescue you. You're heading toward a city on the coast which you'll reach in forty minutes at your present speed. If you cannot stop yourselves then, we're going to blast the tunnel behind and ahead of you to cut off your power. Then we'll sink a shaft to get you out—the chief engineer says he can do it in five minutes with the main projectors. So you should be safe within an hour, unless the sun blows up before."

"And if that happens, you'll be destroyed as well! You mustn't take such a risk!"

"Don't let that worry you; we're perfectly safe. When the sun detonates, the explosion wave will take several minutes to rise to its maximum. But apart from that, we're on the night side of the planet, behind an eight-thousand-mile screen of rock. When the first warning of the explosion comes, we will accelerate out of the Solar System, keeping in the shadow of the planet. Under our maximum drive, we will reach the velocity of light before leaving the cone of shadow, and the sun cannot harm us then."

T'sinadree was still afraid to hope. Another objection came at once into his mind.

"Yes, but how will you get any warning, here on the night side of the planet?"

"Very easily," replied Alveron. "This world has a moon which is now visible from this hemisphere. We have telescopes trained on it. If it shows any sudden increase in brilliance, our main drive goes on automatically and we'll be thrown out of the system."

The logic was flawless. Alveron, cautious as ever, was taking no chances. It would be many minutes before the eight-thousand-mile shield of rock and metal could be destroyed by the fires of the exploding sun. In that time, the S9000 could have reached the safety of the velocity of light.

Alarkane pressed the second button when they were still several miles from the coast. He did not expect anything to happen then, assuming that the machine could not stop between stations. It seemed too good to be true when, a few minutes later, the machine's slight vibration died away and they came to a halt.

The doors slid silently apart. Even before they were fully open, the three had left the compartment. They were taking no more chances. Before them a long tunnel stretched into the distance, rising slowly out of sight. They were starting along it when suddenly Alveron's voice called from the communicators.

"Stay where you are! We're going to blast!"

The ground shuddered once, and far ahead there came the rumble of falling rock. Again the earth shook—and a hundred yards ahead the passageway vanished abruptly. A tremendous vertical shaft had been cut clean through it.

The party hurried forward again until they came to the end of the corridor and stood waiting on its lip. The shaft in which it ended was a full thousand feet across and descended into the earth as far as the torches could throw their beams. Overhead, the storm clouds fled beneath a moon that no man would have recognized, so luridly brilliant was its disk. And, most glorious of all sights, the S9000 floated high above, the great projectors that had drilled this enormous pit still glowing cherry red.

A dark shape detached itself from the mother ship and dropped swiftly toward the ground. Torkalee was returning to collect his friends. A little later, Alveron greeted them in the control room. He waved to the great vision screen and said quietly, "See, we were barely in time."

The continent below them was slowly settling beneath the mile-high waves that were attacking its coasts. The last that anyone was ever to see of Earth was a great plain, bathed with the silver light of the abnormally brilliant moon. Across its face the waters were pouring in a glittering flood toward a distant range of mountains. The sea had won its final victory, but its triumph would be short-lived, for soon sea and land would be no more. Even as the silent party in the control room watched the destruction below, the infinitely greater catastrophe to which this was only the prelude came swiftly upon them.

It was as though dawn had broken suddenly over this moonlit landscape. But it was not dawn: it was only the moon, shining with the brilliance of a second sun. For perhaps thirty seconds that awesome, unnatural light burned fiercely on the doomed land beneath. Then there came a sudden flashing of indicator lights across the control board. The main drive was on. For a second Alveron glanced at the indicators and checked their information. When he looked again at the screen, Earth was gone.

The magnificent, desperately overstrained generators quietly died when the S9000 was passing the orbit of Persephone. It did not matter, the sun could never harm them now, and although the ship was speeding helplessly out into the lonely night of interstellar space, it would only be a matter of days before rescue came.

There was irony in that. A day ago, they had been the rescuers, going to the aid of a race that now no longer existed. Not for the first time Alveron wondered about the world that had just perished. He tried, in vain, to picture it as it had been in its glory, the streets of its cities thronged with life. Primitive though its people had been, they might have offered much to the Universe. If only they could have made contact! Regret was useless; long before their coming, the people of this world must have buried themselves in its iron heart. And now they and their civilization would remain a mystery for the rest of time.

Alveron was glad when his thoughts were interrupted by Rugon's entrance. The Chief of Communications had been very busy ever since the take-off, trying to analyze the programs radiated by the transmitter Orostron had discovered. The problem was not a difficult one, but it demanded the construction of special equipment, and that had taken time.

"Well, what have you found?" asked Alveron.

"Quite a lot," replied his friend. "There's something mysterious here, and I don't understand it.

"It didn't take long to find how the vision transmissions were built up, and we've been able to convert them to suit our own equipment. It seems that there were cameras all over the planet, surveying points of interest. Some of them were apparently in cities, on the tops of very high buildings. The cameras were rotating continuously to give panoramic views. In the programs we've recorded there are about twenty different scenes.

"In addition, there are a number of transmissions of a

different kind, neither sound nor vision. They seem to be purely scientific—possibly instrument readings or something of that sort. All these programs were going out simultaneously on different frequency bands.

"Now there must be a reason for all this. Orostron still thinks that the station simply wasn't switched off when it was deserted. But these aren't the sort of programs such a station would normally radiate at all. It was certainly used for interplanetary relaying—Klarten was quite right there. So these people must have crossed space, since none of the other planets had any life at the time of the last survey. Don't you agree?"

Alveron was following intently.

"Yes, that seems reasonable enough. But it's also certain that the beam was pointing to none of the other planets. I checked that myself."

"I know," said Rugon. "What I want to discover is why a giant interplanetary relay station is busily transmitting pictures of a world about to be destroyed—pictures that would be of immense interest to scientists and astronomers. Some one had gone to a lot of trouble to arrange all those panoramic cameras. I am convinced that those beams were going somewhere."

Alveron started up.

"Do you imagine that there might be an outer planet that hasn't been reported?" he asked. "If so, your theory's certainly wrong. The beam wasn't even pointing in the plane of the Solar System. And even if it were—just look at this."

He switched on the vision screen and adjusted the controls. Against the velvet curtain of space was hanging a blue-white sphere, apparently composed of many concentric shells of incandescent gas. Even though its immense distance made all movement invisible, it was clearly expanding at an enormous rate. At its center was a blinding point of light—the white dwarf star that the sun had now become.

"You probably don't realize just how big that sphere is," said Alveron. "Look at this."

He increased the magnification until only the center portion of the nova was visible. Close to its heart were two minute condensations, one on either side of the nucleus.

"Those are the two giant planets of the system. They have still managed to retain their existence—after a fashion.

And they were several hundred million miles from the sun. The nova is still expanding—but it's already twice the size of the Solar System."

Rugon was silent for a moment.

"Perhaps you're right," he said, rather grudgingly. "You've disposed of my first theory. But you still haven't satisfied me."

He made several swift circuits of the room before speaking again. Alveron waited patiently. He knew the almost intuitive powers of his friend, who could often solve a problem when mere logic seemed insufficient.

Then, rather slowly, Rugon began to speak again.

"What do you think of this?" he said. "Suppose we've completely underestimated this people? Orostron did it once —he thought they could never have crossed space, since they'd only known radio for two centuries. Hansur II told me that. Well, Orostron was quite wrong. Perhaps we're all wrong. I've had a look at the material that Klarten brought back from the transmitter. He wasn't impressed by what he found, but it's a marvelous achievement for so short a time. There were devices in that station that belonged to civilizations thousands of years older. Alveron, can we follow that beam to see where it leads?"

Alveron said nothing for a full minute. He had been more than half expecting the question, but it was not an easy one to answer. The main generators had gone completely. There was no point in trying to repair them. But there was still power available, and while there was power, anything could be done in time. It would mean a lot of improvisation, and some difficult maneuvers, for the ship still had its enormous initial velocity. Yes, it could be done, and the activity would keep the crew from becoming further depressed, now that the reaction caused by the mission's failure had started to set in. The news that the nearest heavy repair ship could not reach them for three weeks had also caused a slump in morale.

The engineers, as usual, made a tremendous fuss. Again as usual, they did the job in half the time they had dismissed as being absolutely impossible. Very slowly, over many hours, the great ship began to discard the speed its main drive had given it in as many minutes. In a tremendous curve, millions of miles in radius, the S9000 changed its course and the star fields shifted round it.

The maneuver took three days, but at the end of that time the ship was limping along a course parallel to the beam that had once come from Earth. They were heading out into emptiness, the blazing sphere that had been the sun dwindling slowly behind them. By the standards of interstellar flight, they were almost stationary.

For hours Rugon strained over his instruments, driving his detector beams far ahead into space. There were certainly no planets within many light-years, there was no doubt of that. From time to time Alveron came to see him and always he had to give the same reply: "Nothing to report." About a fifth of the time Rugon's intuition let him down badly; he began to wonder if this was such an occasion.

Not until a week later did the needles of the mass-detectors quiver feebly at the ends of their scales. But Rugon said nothing, not even to his captain. He waited until he was sure, and he went on waiting until even the short-range scanners began to react, and to build up the first faint pictures on the vision screen. Still he waited patiently until he could interpret the images. Then, when he knew that his wildest fancy was even less than the truth, he called his colleagues in the control room.

The picture on the vision screen was the familiar one of endless star fields, sun beyond sun to the very limits of the Universe. Near the center of the screen a distant nebula made a patch of haze that was difficult for the eye to grasp.

Rugon increased the magnification. The stars flowed out of the field; the little nebula expanded until it filled the screen and then—it was a nebula no longer. A simultaneous gasp of amazement came from all the company at the sight that lay before them.

Lying across league after league of space, ranged in a vast three-dimensional array of rows and columns with the precision of a marching army, were thousands of tiny pencils of light. They were moving swiftly; the whole immense lattice holding its shape as a single unit. Even as Alveron and his comrades watched, the formation began to drift off the screen and Rugon had to recenter the controls.

After a long pause, Rugon started to speak.

"This is the race," he said softly, "that has known radio for only two centuries—the race that we believed had crept to die in the heart of its planet. I have examined those images under the highest possible magnification.

"That is the greatest fleet of which there has ever been a record. Each of those points of light represents a ship larger than our own. Of course, they are very primitive—what you see on the screen are the jets of their rockets. Yes, they dared to use rockets to bridge interstellar space! You realize what that means. It would take them centuries to reach the nearest star. The whole race must have embarked on this journey in the hope that its descendants would complete it, generations later.

"To measure the extent of their accomplishment, think of the ages it took us to conquer space, and the longer ages still before we attempted to reach the stars. Even if we were threatened with annihilation, could we have done so much in so short a time? Remember, this is the youngest civilization in the Universe. Four hundred thousand years ago it did not even exist. What will it be a million years from now?"

An hour later, Orostron left the crippled mother ship to make contact with the great fleet ahead. As the little torpedo disappeared among the stars, Alveron turned to his friend and made a remark that Rugon was often to remember in the years ahead.

"I wonder what they'll be like?" he mused. "Will they be nothing but wonderful engineers, with no art or philosophy? They're going to have such a surprise when Orostron reaches them—I expect it will be rather a blow to their pride. It's funny how all isolated races think they're the only people in the Universe. But they should be grateful to us; we're going to save them a good many hundred years of travel."

Alveron glanced at the Milky Way, lying like a veil of silver mist across the vision screen. He waved toward it with a sweep of a tentacle that embraced the whole circle of the Galaxy, from the Central Planets to the lonely suns of the Rim.

"You know," he said to Rugon, "I feel rather afraid of these people. Suppose they don't like our little Federation?" He waved once more toward the star-clouds that lay massed across the screen, glowing with the light of their countless suns.

"Something tells me they'll be very determined people," he added. "We had better be polite to them. After all, we only outnumber them about a thousand million to one."

Rugon laughed at his captain's little joke.

Twenty years afterward, the remark didn't seem funny.

Stratford-on-Avon   *March 1945*

THE CURSE

FOR THREE HUNDRED years, while its fame spread across the world, the little town had stood here at the river's bend. Time and change had touched it lightly; it had heard from afar both the coming of the Armada and the fall of the Third Reich, and all Man's wars had passed it by.

Now it was gone, as though it had never been. In a moment of time the toil and treasure of centuries had been swept away. The vanished streets could still be traced as faint marks in the vitrified ground, but of the houses, nothing remained. Steel and concrete, plaster and ancient oak— it had mattered little at the end. In the moment of death they had stood together, transfixed by the glare of the detonating bomb. Then, even before they could flash into fire, the blast waves had reached them and they had ceased to be. Mile upon mile the ravening hemisphere of flame had expanded over the level farmlands, and from its heart had risen the twisting totem pole that had haunted the minds of men for so long, and to such little purpose.

The rocket had been a stray, one of the last ever to be

fired. It was hard to say for what target it had been intended. Certainly not London, for London was no longer a military objective. London, indeed, was no longer anything at all. Long ago the men whose duty it was had calculated that three of the hydrogen bombs would be sufficient for that rather small target. In sending twenty, they had been perhaps a little overzealous.

This was not one of the twenty that had done their work so well. Both its destination and its origin were unknown: whether it had come across the lonely Arctic wastes or far above the waters of the Atlantic, no one could tell and there were few now who cared. Once there had been men who had known such things, who had watched from afar the flight of the great projectiles and had sent their own missiles to meet them. Often that appointment had been kept, high above the Earth where the sky was black and sun and stars shared the heavens together. Then there had bloomed for a moment that indescribable flame, sending out into space a message that in centuries to come other eyes than Man's would see and understand.

But that had been days ago, at the beginning of the War. The defenders had long since been brushed aside, as they had known they must be. They had held on to life long enough to discharge their duty; too late, the enemy had learned his mistake. He would launch no further rockets; those still falling he had dispatched hours ago on secret trajectories that had taken them far out into space. They were returning now unguided and inert, waiting in vain for the signals that should lead them to their destinies. One by one they were falling at random upon a world which they could harm no more.

The river had already overflowed its banks; somewhere down its course the land had twisted beneath that colossal hammer-blow and the way to the sea was no longer open. Dust was still falling in a fine rain, as it would do for days as Man's cities and treasures returned to the world that had given them birth. But the sky was no longer wholly darkened, and in the west the sun was setting through banks of angry cloud.

A church had stood here by the river's edge, and though no trace of the building remained, the gravestones that the years had gathered round it still marked its place. Now the stone slabs lay in parallel rows, snapped off at their bases and pointing mutely along the line of the blast. Some were half flattened into the ground, others had been cracked and blistered by terrific heat, but many still bore the messages they had carried down the centuries in vain.

The light died in the west and the unnatural crimson faded from the sky. Yet still the graven words could be clearly read, lit by a steady, unwavering radiance, too faint to be seen by day but strong enough to banish night. The land was burning: for miles the glow of its radioactivity was reflected from the clouds. Through the glimmering landscape wound the dark ribbon of the steadily widening river, and as the waters submerged the land that deadly glow continued unchanging in the depths. In a generation, perhaps, it would have faded from sight, but a hundred years might pass before life could safely come this way again.

Timidly the waters touched the worn gravestone that for more than three hundred years had lain before the vanished altar. The church that had sheltered it so long had given it some protection at the last, and only a slight discoloration of the rock told of the fires that had passed this way. In the corpse-light of the dying land, the archaic words could still be traced as the water rose around them, breaking at last in tiny ripples across the stone. Line by line the epitaph upon which so many millions had gazed slipped beneath the conquering waters. For a little while the letters could still be faintly seen; then they were gone forever.

> Good frend for Iesvs sake forbeare,
>   To digg the dvst encloased heare
>   Blest be ye man yt spares thes stones,
>   And cvrst be he yt moves my bones.

Undisturbed through all eternity the poet could sleep in safety now: in the silence and darkness above his head, the Avon was seeking its new outlet to the sea.

Stratford-on-Avon   *May 1946*

HIDE AND SEEK

WE WERE WALKING back through the woods when Kingman saw the gray squirrel. Our bag was a small but varied one—three grouse, four rabbits (one, I am sorry to say, an infant in arms) and a couple of pigeons. And contrary to certain dark forecasts, both the dogs were still alive.

The squirrel saw us at the same moment. It knew that it was marked for immediate execution as a result of the damage it had done to the trees on the estate, and perhaps it had lost close relatives to Kingman's gun. In three leaps it had reached the base of the nearest tree, and vanished behind it in a flicker of gray. We saw its face once more, appearing for a moment round the edge of its shield a dozen feet from the ground; but though we waited, with guns leveled hopefully at various branches, we never saw it again.

Kingman was very thoughtful as we walked back across the lawn to the magnificent old house. He said nothing as we handed our victims to the cook—who received them without much enthusiasm—and only emerged from his reverie when we were sitting in the smoking room and he remembered his duties as a host.

"That tree-rat," he said suddenly (he always called them "tree-rats," on the grounds that people were too sentimental to shoot the dear little squirrels), "it reminded me of a very peculiar experience that happened shortly before I retired. Very shortly indeed, in fact."

"I thought it would," said Carson dryly. I gave him a glare: he'd been in the Navy and had heard Kingman's stories before, but they were still new to me.

"Of course," Kingman remarked, slightly nettled, "if you'd rather I didn't . . ."

"Do go on," I said hastily. "You've made me curious. What connection there can possibly be between a gray squirrel and the Second Jovian War I can't imagine."

Kingman seemed mollified.

"I think I'd better change some names," he said thoughtfully, "but I won't alter the places. The story begins about a million kilometers sunward of Mars. . . ."

K.15 was a military intelligence operative. It gave him considerable pain when unimaginative people called him a spy, but at the moment he had much more substantial grounds for complaint. For some days now a fast enemy cruiser had been coming up astern, and though it was flattering to have the undivided attention of such a fine ship and so many highly trained men, it was an honor that K.15 would willingly have forgone.

What made the situation doubly annoying was the fact that his friends would be meeting him off Mars in about twelve hours, aboard a ship quite capable of dealing with a mere cruiser—from which you will gather that K.15 was a person of some importance. Unfortunately, the most optimistic calculation showed that the pursuers would be within accurate gun range in six hours. In some six hours five minutes, therefore, K.15 was likely to occupy an extensive and still expanding volume of space.

There might just be time for him to land on Mars, but that would be one of the worst things he could do. It would certainly annoy the aggressively neutral Martians, and the political complications would be frightful. Moreover, if his friends *had* to come down to the planet to rescue him, it

would cost them more than ten kilometers a second in fuel
—most of their operational reserve.

He had only one advantage, and that a very dubious one.
The commander of the cruiser might guess that he was
heading for a rendezvous, but he would not know how close
it was or how large was the ship that was coming to meet
him. If he could keep alive for only twelve hours, he would
be safe. The "if" was a somewhat considerable one.

K.15 looked moodily at his charts, wondering if it was
worthwhile to burn the rest of his fuel in a final dash. But a
dash to where? He would be completely helpless then, and
the pursuing ship might still have enough in her tanks to
catch him as he flashed outward into the empty darkness,
beyond all hope of rescue—passing his friends as they came
sunward at a relative speed so great that they could do nothing to save him.

With some people, the shorter the expectation of life, the
more sluggish are the mental processes. They seem hypno
tized by the approach of death, so resigned to their fate that
they do nothing to avoid it. K.15, on the other hand, found
that his mind worked better in such a desperate emergency.
It began to work now as it had seldom done before.

Commander Smith—the name will do as well as any
other—of the cruiser *Doradus* was not unduly surprised
when K.15 began to decelerate. He had half expected the
spy to land on Mars, on the principle that internment was
better than annihilation, but when the plotting room
brought the news that the little scout ship was heading for
Phobos, he felt completely baffled. The inner moon was
nothing but a jumble of rock some twenty kilometers across,
and not even the economical Martians had ever found any
use for it. K.15 must be pretty desperate if he thought it was
going to be of any greater value to him.

The tiny scout had almost come to rest when the radar
operator lost it against the mass of Phobos. During the braking maneuver, K.15 had squandered most of his lead and the
Doradus was now only minutes away—though she was now
beginning to decelerate lest she overrun him. The cruiser
was scarcely three thousand kilometers from Phobos when
she came to a complete halt: of K.15's ship, there was still
no sign. It should be easily visible in the telescopes, but it
was probably on the far side of the little moon.

It reappeared only a few minutes later, traveling under full thrust on a course directly away from the sun. It was accelerating at almost five gravities —and it had broken its radio silence. An automatic recorder was broadcasting over and over again this interesting message:

"I have landed on Phobos and am being attacked by a Z-class cruiser. Think I can hold out until you come, but hurry."

The message wasn't even in code, and it left Commander Smith a sorely puzzled man. The assumption that K.15 was still aboard the ship and that the whole thing was a ruse was just a little too naïve. But it might be a double-bluff: the message had obviously been left in plain language so that he would receive it and be duly confused. He could afford neither the time nor the fuel to chase the scout if K.15 really had landed. It was clear that reinforcements were on the way, and the sooner he left the vicinity the better. The phrase "Think I can hold out until you come" might be a piece of sheer impertinence, or it might mean that help was very near indeed.

Then K.15's ship stopped blasting. It had obviously exhausted its fuel, and was doing a little better than six kilometers a second away from the sun. K.15 *must* have landed, for his ship was now speeding helplessly out of the Solar System. Commander Smith didn't like the message it was broadcasting, and guessed that it was running into the track of an approaching warship at some indefinite distance, but there was nothing to be done about that. The *Doradus* began to move toward Phobos, anxious to waste no time.

On the face of it, Commander Smith seemed the master of the situation. His ship was armed with a dozen heavy guided missiles and two turrets of electromagnetic guns. Against him was one man in a space suit, trapped on a moon only twenty kilometers across. It was not until Commander Smith had his first good look at Phobos, from a distance of less than a hundred kilometers, that he began to realize that, after all, K.15 might have a few cards up his sleeve.

To say that Phobos has a diameter of twenty kilometers, as the astronomy books invariably do, is highly misleading. The word "diameter" implies a degree of symmetry which Phobos most certainly lacks. Like those other lumps of cosmic slag, the asteroids, it is a shapeless mass of rock floating in space with, of course, no hint of an atmosphere and not much more gravity. It turns on its axis once every seven hours thirty-nine minutes, thus keeping the same face always to Mars—which is so close that appreciably less than half the planet is visible, the poles being below the curve of the horizon. Beyond this, there is very little more to be said about Phobos.

K.15 had no time to enjoy the beauty of the crescent world filling the sky above him. He had thrown all the equipment he could carry out of the air lock, set the controls, and jumped. As the little ship went flaming out toward the stars he watched it go with feelings he did not care to analyze. He had burned his boats with a vengeance, and he could only hope that the oncoming battleship would intercept the radio message as the empty vessel went racing by into nothingness. There was also a faint possibility that the enemy cruiser might go in pursuit, but that was rather too much to hope for.

He turned to examine his new home. The only light was the ocher radiance of Mars, since the sun was below the horizon, but that was quite sufficient for his purpose and he could see very well. He stood in the center of an irregular plain about two kilometers across, surrounded by low hills over which he could leap rather easily if he wished. There was a story he remembered reading long ago about a man who had accidentally jumped off Phobos: that wasn't quite possible—though it was on Deimos—because the escape velocity was still about ten meters a second. But unless he was careful, he might easily find himself at such a height that it would take hours to fall back to the surface—and that would be fatal. For K.15's plan was a simple one: he must remain as close to the surface of Phobos as possible—*and diametrically opposite the cruiser*. The *Doradus* could then fire all her armament against the twenty kilometers of rock, and he wouldn't even feel the concussion. There were only two serious dangers, and one of these did not worry him greatly.

To the layman, knowing nothing of the finer details of astronautics, the plan would have seemed quite suicidal. The *Doradus* was armed with the latest in ultrascientific weapons: moreover, the twenty kilometers which separated her from her prey represented less than a second's flight at maximum speed. But Commander Smith knew better, and was already feeling rather unhappy. He realized, only too well, that of all the machines of transport man has ever invented, a cruiser of space is far and away the least maneuverable. It was a simple fact that K.15 could make half a dozen circuits of his little world while her commander was persuading the *Doradus* to make even one.

There is no need to go into technical details, but those who are still unconvinced might like to consider these elementary facts. A rocket-driven spaceship can, obviously, only accelerate along its major axis—that is, "forward." Any deviation from a straight course demands a physical turning of the ship, so that the motors can blast in another direction. Everyone knows that this is done by internal gyros or tangential steering jets, but very few people know just how long this simple maneuver takes. The average cruiser, fully fueled, has a mass of two or three thousand tons, which does not make for rapid footwork. But things are even worse than this, for it isn't the mass, but the moment of inertia that matters here—and since a cruiser is a long, thin object, its moment of inertia is slightly colossal. The sad fact remains (though it is seldom mentioned by astronautical engineers) that it takes a good ten minutes to rotate a spaceship through one hundred and eighty degrees, with gyros of any reasonable size. Control jets aren't much quicker, and in any case their use is restricted because the rotation they produce is permanent and they are liable to leave the ship spinning like a slow-motion pinwheel, to the annoyance of all inside.

In the ordinary way, these disadvantages are not very grave. One has millions of kilometers and hundreds of hours in which to deal with such minor matters as a change in the ship's orientation. It is definitely against the rules to move in ten-kilometer-radius circles, and the commander of the *Doradus* felt distinctly aggrieved. K.15 wasn't playing fair.

At the same moment that resourceful individual was taking stock of the situation, which might very well have been worse. He had reached the hills in three jumps and felt less naked than he had out in the open plain. The food and equipment he had taken from the ship he had hidden where he hoped he could find it again, but since his suit could keep him alive for over a day that was the least of his worries.

The small packet that was the cause of all the trouble was still with him, in one of those numerous hiding places a well-designed space suit affords.

There was an exhilarating loneliness about his mountain eyrie, even though he was not quite as lonely as he would have wished. Forever fixed in his sky, Mars was waning almost visibly as Phobos swept above the night side of the planet. He could just make out the lights of some of the Martian cities, gleaming pin points marking the junctions of the invisible canals. All else was stars and silence and a line of jagged peaks so close it seemed he could almost touch them. Of the *Doradus* there was still no sign. She was presumably carrying out a careful telescopic examination of the sunlighted side of Phobos.

Mars was a very useful clock: when it was half full the sun would rise and, very probably, so would the *Doradus*. But she might approach from some quite unexpected quarter: she might even—and this was the one real danger—she might even have landed a search party.

This was the first possibility that had occurred to Commander Smith when he saw just what he was up against. Then he realized that the surface area of Phobos was over a thousand square kilometers and that he could not spare more than ten men from his crew to make a search of that jumbled wilderness. Also, K.15 would certainly be armed.

Considering the weapons which the *Doradus* carried, this last objection might seem singularly pointless. It was very far from being so. In the ordinary course of business, side arms and other portable weapons are as much use to a space-cruiser as are cutlasses and crossbows. The *Doradus* happened, quite by chance—and against regulations at that —to carry one automatic pistol and a hundred rounds of ammunition. Any search party would therefore consist of a group of unarmed men looking for a well-concealed and very desperate individual who could pick them off at his leisure. K.15 was breaking the rules again.

The terminator of Mars was now a perfectly straight line, and at almost the same moment the sun came up, not so much like thunder as like a salvo of atomic bombs. K.15 adjusted the filters of his visor and decided to move. It was safer to stay out of the sunlight, not only because here he was less likely to be detected in the shadow but also because his eyes would be much more sensitive there. He had only a pair of binoculars to help him, whereas the *Doradus* would carry an electronic telescope of twenty-centimeter aperture at least.

It would be best, K.15 decided, to locate the cruiser if he could. It might be a rash thing to do, but he would feel much happier when he knew exactly where she was and could watch her movements. He could then keep just below the horizon, and the glare of the rockets would give him ample warning of any impending move. Cautiously launching himself along an almost horizontal trajectory, he began the circumnavigation of his world.

The narrowing crescent of Mars sank below the horizon until only one vast horn reared itself enigmatically against the stars. K.15 began to feel worried: there was still no sign of the *Doradus*. But this was hardly surprising, for she was painted black as night and might be a good hundred kilometers away in space. He stopped, wondering if he had done the right thing after all. Then he noticed that something quite large was eclipsing the stars almost vertically overhead, and was moving swiftly even as he watched. His heart stopped for a moment: then he was himself again, analyzing the situation and trying to discover how he had made so disastrous a mistake.

It was some time before he realized that the black shadow slipping across the sky was not the cruiser at all, but something almost equally deadly. It was far smaller, and far nearer, than he had at first thought. The *Doradus* had sent her television-homing guided missiles to look for him.

This was the second danger he had feared, and there was nothing he could do about it except to remain as inconspicuous as possible. The *Doradus* now had many eyes searching for him, but these auxiliaries had very severe limitations. They had been built to look for sunlit spaceships against a background of stars, not to search for a man hiding in a dark jungle of rock. The definition of their television systems was low, and they could only see in the forward direction.

There were rather more men on the chessboard now, and the game was a little deadlier, but his was still the advantage.

The torpedo vanished into the night sky. As it was traveling on a nearly straight course in this low-gravitational field, it would soon be leaving Phobos behind, and K.15 waited for what he knew must happen. A few minutes later, he saw a brief stabbing of rocket exhausts and guessed that the projectile was swinging slowly back on its course. At almost the same moment he saw another flare far away in the opposite quarter of the sky, and wondered just how many of these infernal machines were in action. From what he knew of Z-class cruisers—which was a good deal more than he should—there were four missile-control channels, and they were probably all in use.

He was suddenly struck by an idea so brilliant that he was quite sure it couldn't possibly work. The radio on his suit was a tunable one, covering an unusually wide band, and somewhere not far away the *Doradus* was pumping out power on everything from a thousand megacycles upward. He switched on the receiver and began to explore.

It came in quickly—the raucous whine of a pulse transmitter not far away. He was probably only picking up a subharmonic, but that was quite good enough. It D/F'ed sharply, and for the first time K.15 allowed himself to make long-range plans about the future. The *Doradus* had betrayed herself: as long as she operated her missiles, he would know exactly where she was.

He moved cautiously forward toward the transmitter. To his surprise the signal faded, then increased sharply again. This puzzled him until he realized that he must be moving through a diffraction zone. Its width might have told him something useful if he had been a good-enough physicist, but he couldn't imagine what.

The *Doradus* was hanging about five kilometers above the surface, in full sunlight. Her "nonreflecting" paint was overdue for renewal and K.15 could see her clearly. Since he was still in darkness, and the shadow line was moving away from him, he decided that he was as safe here as anywhere. He settled down comfortably so that he could just see the cruiser and waited, feeling fairly certain that none of the guided projectiles would come so near the ship. By now, he calculated, the commander of the *Doradus* must be getting pretty mad. He was perfectly correct.

After an hour, the cruiser began to heave herself round with all the grace of a bogged hippopotamus. K.15 guessed what was happening. Commander Smith was going to have a look at the antipodes, and was preparing for the perilous fifty-kilometer journey. He watched very carefully to see the orientation the ship was adopting, and when she came to rest again was relieved to see that she was almost broadside to him. Then, with a series of jerks that could not have been very enjoyable aboard, the cruiser began to move down to the horizon. K.15 followed her at a comfortable walking pace—if one could use the phrase—reflecting that this was a feat very few people had ever performed. He was particularly careful not to overtake her on one of his kilometer-long glides, and kept a close watch for any missiles that might be coming up astern.

It took the *Doradus* nearly an hour to cover the fifty kilometers. This, as K.15 amused himself by calculating, represented considerably less than a thousandth of her normal speed. Once she found herself going off into space at a tangent, and rather than waste time turning end over end again fired off a salvo of shells to reduce speed. But she made it at last, and K.15 settled down for another vigil, wedged between two rocks where he could just see the cruiser and he was quite sure she couldn't see him. It occurred to him that by this time Commander Smith might have grave doubts as to whether he really was on Phobos at all, and he felt like firing off a signal flare to reassure him. However, he resisted the temptation.

There would be little point in describing the events of the next ten hours, since they differed in no important detail from those that had gone before. The *Doradus* made three other moves, and K.15 stalked her with the care of a big-game hunter following the spoor of some elephantine beast. Once, when she would have led him out into full sunlight, he let her fall below the horizon until he could only just pick up her signals. But most of the time he kept her just visible, usually low down behind some convenient hill.

Once a torpedo exploded some kilometers away, and K.15 guessed that some exasperated operator had seen a shadow he didn't like—or else that a technician had forgotten to switch off a proximity fuse. Otherwise nothing happened to enliven the proceedings: in fact, the whole affair was becoming rather boring. He almost welcomed the sight of an occasional guided missile drifting inquisitively overhead, for he did not believe that they could see him if he remained motionless and in reasonable cover. If he could have stayed on the part of Phobos exactly opposite the cruiser he would have been safe even from these, he realized, since the ship would have no control there in the moon's radio-shadow. But he could think of no reliable way in which he could be sure of staying in the safety zone if the cruiser moved again.

The end came very abruptly. There was a sudden blast of steering jets, and the cruiser's main drive burst forth in all its power and splendor. In seconds the *Doradus* was shrinking sunward, free at last, thankful to leave, even in defeat, this miserable lump of rock that had so annoyingly balked her of her legitimate prey. K.15 knew what had happened, and a great sense of peace and relaxation swept over him. In the radar room of the cruiser, someone had seen an echo of disconcerting amplitude approaching with altogether excessive speed. K.15 now had only to switch on his suit beacon and to wait. He could even afford the luxury of a cigarette.

"Quite an interesting story," I said, "and I see now how it ties up with that squirrel. But it does raise one or two queries in my mind."

"Indeed?" said Rupert Kingman politely.

I always like to get to the bottom of things, and I knew that my host had played a part in the Jovian War about which he very seldom spoke. I decided to risk a long shot in the dark.

"May I ask how you happen to know so much about this unorthodox military engagement? It isn't possible, is it, that *you* were K.15?"

There was an odd sort of strangling noise from Carson. Then Kingman said, quite calmly: "No, I wasn't."

He got to his feet and went off toward the gun room.

"If you'll excuse me a moment, I'm going to have another shot at that tree-rat. Maybe I'll get him this time." Then he was gone.

Carson looked at me as if to say: "This is another house you'll never be invited to again." When our host was out of earshot he remarked in a coldly cynical voice:

"You've done it. What did you have to say that for?"

"Well, it seemed a safe guess. How else could he have known all that?"

"As a matter of fact, I believe he met K.15 after the War: they must have had an interesting conversation together. But I thought you knew that Rupert was retired from the service with only the rank of lieutenant commander. The Court of Inquiry could never see his point of view. After all, it just wasn't reasonable that the commander of the fastest ship in the Fleet couldn't catch a man in a space suit."

London   *August 1948*

THE POSSESSED

AND NOW THE sun ahead was so close that the hurricane of radiation was forcing the Swarm back into the dark night of space. Soon it would be able to come no closer; the gales of light on which it rode from star to star could not be faced so near their source. Unless it encountered a planet very soon, and could fall down into the peace and safety of its shadow, this sun must be abandoned as had so many before.

Six cold outer worlds had already been searched and discarded. Either they were frozen beyond all hope of organic life, or else they harbored entities of types that were useless to the Swarm. If it was to survive, it must find hosts not too unlike those it had left on its doomed and distant home. Millions of years ago the Swarm had begun its journey, swept starward by the fires of its own exploding sun. Yet even now the memory of its lost birthplace was still sharp and clear, an ache that would never die.

There was a planet ahead, swinging its cone of shadow through the flame-swept night. The senses that the Swarm had developed upon its long journey reached out toward the approaching world, reached out and found it good.

The merciless buffeting of radiation ceased as the black disc of the planet eclipsed the sun. Falling freely under gravity, the Swarm dropped swiftly until it hit the outer fringe of the atmosphere. The first time it had made planetfall it had almost met its doom, but now it contracted its tenuous substance with the unthinking skill of long practice, until it formed a tiny, close-knit sphere. Slowly its velocity slackened, until at last it was floating motionless between earth and sky.

For many years it rode the winds of the stratosphere from Pole to Pole, or let the soundless fusillades of dawn blast it westward from the rising sun. Everywhere it found life, but nowhere intelligence. There were things that crawled and flew and leaped, but there were no things that talked or built. Ten million years hence there might be creatures here with minds that the Swarm could possess and guide for its own purposes; there was no sign of them now. It could not guess which of the countless life-forms on this planet would be the heir to the future, and without such a host it was helpless—a mere pattern of electric charges, a matrix of order and self-awareness in a universe of chaos. By its own resources the Swarm had no control over matter, yet once it had lodged in the mind of a sentient race there was nothing that lay beyond its powers.

It was not the first time, and it would not be the last, that the planet had been surveyed by a visitant from space—though never by one in such peculiar and urgent need. The Swarm was faced with a tormenting dilemma. It could begin its weary travels once more, hoping that ultimately it might find the conditions it sought, or it could wait here on this world, biding its time until a race had arisen which would fit its purpose.

It moved like mist through the shadows, letting the vagrant winds take it where they willed. The clumsy, ill-formed reptiles of this young world never saw its passing, but it observed them, recording, analyzing, trying to extrapolate into the future. There was so little to choose between all these creatures; not one showed even the first faint glimmerings of conscious mind. Yet if it left this world in search of another, it might roam the Universe in vain until the end of time.

At last it made its decision. By its very nature, it could choose both alternatives. The greater part of the Swarm would continue its travels among the stars, but a portion of it would remain on this world, like a seed planted in the hope of future harvest.

It began to spin upon its axis, its tenuous body flattening into a disc. Now it was wavering at the frontiers of visibility —it was a pale ghost, a faint will-o'-the-wisp that suddenly fissured into two unequal fragments. The spinning slowly died away: the Swarm had become two, each an entity with all the memories of the original, and all its desires and needs.

There was a last exchange of thoughts between parent and child who were also identical twins. If all went well with them both, they would meet again in the far future here at this valley in the mountains. The one who was staying would return to this point at regular intervals down the ages; the one who continued the search would send back an emissary if ever a better world was found. And then they would be united again, no longer homeless exiles vainly wandering among the indifferent stars.

The light of dawn was spilling over the raw, new mountains when the parent swarm rose up to meet the sun. At the edge of the atmosphere the gales of radiation caught it and swept it unresisting out beyond the planets, to start again upon the endless search.

The one that was left began its almost equally hopeless task. It needed an animal that was not so rare that disease or accident could make it extinct, nor so tiny that it could never acquire any power over the physical world. And it must breed rapidly, so that its evolution could be directed and controlled as swiftly as possible.

The search was long and the choice difficult, but at last the Swarm selected its host. Like rain sinking into thirsty soil, it entered the bodies of certain small lizards and began to direct their destiny.

It was an immense task, even for a being which could never know death. Generation after generation of the lizards was swept into the past before there came the slightest improvement in the race. And always, at the appointed time, the Swarm returned to its rendezvous among the mountains.

Always it returned in vain: there was no messenger from the stars, bringing news of better fortune elsewhere.

The centuries lengthened into millennia, the millennia into eons. By the standards of geological time, the lizards were now changing rapidly. Presently they were lizards no more, but warm-blooded, fur-covered creatures that brought forth their young alive. They were still small and feeble, and their minds were rudimentary, but they contained the seeds of future greatness.

Yet not only the living creatures were altering as the ages slowly passed. Continents were being rent asunder, mountains being worn down by the weight of the unwearying rain. Through all these changes, the Swarm kept to its purpose; and always, at the appointed times, it went to the meeting place that had been chosen so long ago, waited patiently for a while, and came away. Perhaps the parent swarm was still searching or perhaps—it was a hard and terrible thought to grasp—some unknown fate had overtaken it and it had gone the way of the race it had once ruled. There was nothing to do but to wait and see if the stubborn life-stuff of this planet could be forced along the path to intelligence.

And so the eons passed. . . .

Somewhere in the labyrinth of evolution the Swarm made its fatal mistake and took the wrong turning. A hundred million years had gone since it came to Earth, and it was very weary. It could not die, but it could degenerate. The memories of its ancient home and of its destiny were fading: its intelligence was waning even while its hosts climbed the long slope that would lead to self-awareness.

By a cosmic irony, in giving the impetus which would one day bring intelligence to this world, the Swarm had exhausted itself. It had reached the last stage of parasitism; no longer could it exist apart from its hosts. Never again could it ride free above the world, driven by wind and sun. To make the pilgrimage to the ancient rendezvous, it must travel slowly and painfully in a thousand little bodies. Yet it continued the immemorial custom, driven on by the desire for reunion which burned all the more fiercely now that it knew the bitterness of failure. Only if the parent swarm returned and reabsorbed it could it ever know new life and vigor.

The glaciers came and went; by a miracle the little beasts

that now housed the waning alien intelligence escaped the clutching fingers of the ice. The oceans overwhelmed the land, and still the race survived. It even multiplied, but it could do no more. This world would never be its heritage, for far away in the heart of another continent a certain monkey had come down from the trees and was looking at the stars with the first glimmerings of curiosity.

The mind of the Swarm was dispersing, scattering among a million tiny bodies, no longer able to unite and assert its will. It had lost all cohesion; its memories were fading. In a million years, at most, they would all be gone.

Only one thing remained—the blind urge which still, at intervals which by some strange aberration were becoming ever shorter, drove it to seek its consummation in a valley that long ago had ceased to exist.

Quietly riding the lane of moonlight, the pleasure steamer passed the island with its winking beacon and entered the fjord. It was a calm and lovely night, with Venus sinking in the west out beyond the Faroes, and the lights of the harbor reflected with scarcely a tremor in the still waters far ahead.

Nils and Christina were utterly content. Standing side by side against the boat rail, their fingers locked together, they watched the wooded slopes drift silently by. The tall trees were motionless in the moonlight, their leaves unruffled by even the merest breath of wind, their slender trunks rising whitely from pools of shadow. The whole world was asleep; only the moving ship dared to break the spell that had bewitched the night.

Then suddenly, Christina gave a little gasp and Nils felt her fingers tighten convulsively on his. He followed her gaze: she was staring out across the water, looking toward the silent sentinels of the forest.

"What is it, darling?" he asked anxiously.

"Look!" she replied, in a whisper Nils could scarcely hear. "There—under the pines!"

Nils stared, and as he did so the beauty of the night ebbed slowly away and ancestral terrors came crawling back from exile. For beneath the trees the land was alive: a dappled brown tide was moving down the slopes of the hill and merging into the dark waters. Here was an open patch on which the moonlight fell unbroken by shadow. It was changing even as he watched: the surface of the land seemed to be rippling downward like a slow waterfall seeking union with the sea.

And then Nils laughed and the world was sane once more. Christina looked at him, puzzled but reassured.

"Don't you remember?" he chuckled. "We read all about it in the paper this morning. They do this every few years, and always at night. It's been going on for days."

He was teasing her, sweeping away the tension of the last few minutes. Christina looked back at him, and a slow smile lit up her face.

"Of course!" she said. "How stupid of me!" Then she turned once more toward the land and her expression became sad, for she was very tenderhearted.

"Poor little things!" she sighed. "I wonder why they do it?"

Nils shrugged his shoulders indifferently.

"No one knows," he answered. "It's just one of those mysteries. I shouldn't think about it if it worries you. Look —we'll soon be in harbor!"

They turned toward the beckoning lights where their future lay, and Christina glanced back only once toward the tragic, mindless tide that was still flowing beneath the moon.

Obeying an urge whose meaning they had never known, the doomed legions of the lemmings were finding oblivion beneath the waves.

London   *June 1951*

SUPERIORITY

Students of World War II will recognize the inspiration of this story. I hope that no one will be put off by the fact that it has been required reading for an M.I.T. engineering course.

IN MAKING THIS statement—which I do of my own free will—I wish first to make it perfectly clear that I am not in any way trying to gain sympathy, nor do I expect any mitigation of whatever sentence the Court may pronounce. I am writing this in an attempt to refute some of the lying reports broadcast over the prison radio and published in the papers I have been allowed to see. These have given an entirely false picture of the true cause of our defeat, and as the leader of my race's armed forces at the cessation of hostilities I feel it my duty to protest against such libels upon those who served under me.

I also hope that this statement may explain the reasons for the application I have twice made to the Court, and will now induce it to grant a favor for which I can see no possible grounds of refusal.

The ultimate cause of our failure was a simple one: despite all statements to the contrary, it was not due to lack of bravery on the part of our men, or to any fault of the Fleet's. We were defeated by one thing only—by the inferior science of our enemies. I repeat—by the *inferior* science of our enemies.

When the war opened, we had no doubt of our ultimate victory. The combined fleets of our allies greatly exceeded in number and armament those which the enemy could muster against us, and in almost all branches of military science we were their superiors. We were sure that we could maintain this superiority. Our belief proved, alas, to be only too well founded.

At the opening of the war our main weapons were the long-range homing torpedo, dirigible ball-lightning and the various modifications of the Klydon beam. Every unit of the Fleet was equipped with these, and though the enemy possessed similar weapons their installations were generally of lesser power. Moreover, we had behind us a far greater military Research Organization, and with this initial advantage we could not possibly lose.

The campaign proceeded according to plan until the Battle of the Five Suns. We won this, of course, but the opposition proved stronger than we had expected. It was realized that victory might be more difficult, and more delayed, than had first been imagined. A conference of supreme commanders was therefore called to discuss our future strategy.

Present for the first time at one of our war conferences was Professor-General Norden, the new Chief of the Research Staff, who had just been appointed to fill the gap left by the death of Malvar, our greatest scientist. Malvar's leadership had been responsible, more than any other single factor, for the efficiency and power of our weapons. His loss was a very serious blow, but no one doubted the brilliance of his successor—though many of us disputed the wisdom of appointing a theoretical scientist to fill a post of such vital importance. But we had been overruled.

I can well remember the impression Norden made at that conference. The military advisers were worried, and as usual turned to the scientists for help. Would it be possible to improve our existing weapons, they asked, so that our present advantage could be increased still further?

Norden's reply was quite unexpected. Malvar had often been asked such a question—and he had always done what we requested.

"Frankly, gentlemen," said Norden, "I doubt it. Our existing weapons have practically reached finality. I don't wish to criticize my predecessor, or the excellent work done by the Research Staff in the last few generations, but do you realize that there has been no basic change in armaments for over a century? It is, I am afraid, the result of a tradition that has become conservative. For too long, the Research Staff has devoted itself to perfecting old weapons instead of developing new ones. It is fortunate for us that our opponents have been no wiser: we cannot assume that this will always be so."

Norden's words left an uncomfortable impression, as he had no doubt intended. He quickly pressed home the attack.

"What we want are *new* weapons—weapons totally different from any that have been employed before. Such weapons can be made: it will take time, of course, but since assuming charge I have replaced some of the older scientists by young men and have directed research into several unexplored fields which show great promise. I believe, in fact, that a revolution in warfare may soon be upon us."

We were skeptical. There was a bombastic tone in Norden's voice that made us suspicious of his claims. We did not know, then, that he never promised anything that he had not already almost perfected in the laboratory. *In the laboratory*—that was the operative phrase.

Norden proved his case less than a month later, when he demonstrated the Sphere of Annihilation, which produced complete disintegration of matter over a radius of several hundred meters. We were intoxicated by the power of the new weapon, and were quite prepared to overlook one fundamental defect—the fact that it *was* a sphere and hence destroyed its rather complicated generating equipment at the instant of formation. This meant, of course, that it could not be used on warships but only on guided missiles, and a great program was started to convert all homing torpedoes to carry the new weapon. For the time being all further offensives were suspended.

We realize now that this was our first mistake. I still think that it was a natural one, for it seemed to us then that all our existing weapons had become obsolete overnight, and we already regarded them as almost primitive survivals. What we did not appreciate was the magnitude of the task we were attempting, and the length of time it would take to get the revolutionary super-weapon into battle. Nothing like this had happened for a hundred years and we had no previous experience to guide us.

The conversion problem proved far more difficult than anticipated. A new class of torpedo had to be designed, because the standard model was too small. This meant in turn that only the larger ships could launch the weapon, but we were prepared to accept this penalty. After six months, the heavy units of the Fleet were being equipped with the Sphere. Training maneuvers and tests had shown that it was operating satisfactorily and we were ready to take it into action. Norden was already being hailed as the architect of victory, and had half promised even more spectacular weapons.

Then two things happened. One of our battleships disappeared completely on a training flight, and an investigation showed that under certain conditions the ship's long-range radar could trigger the Sphere immediately it had been launched. The modification needed to overcome this defect was trivial, but it caused a delay of another month and was the source of much bad feeling between the naval staff and the scientists. We were ready for action again—when Norden announced that the radius of effectiveness of the Sphere had now been increased by ten, thus multiplying by a thousand the chances of destroying an enemy ship.

So the modifications started all over again, but everyone agreed that the delay would be worth it. Meanwhile, however, the enemy had been emboldened by the absence of further attacks and had made an unexpected onslaught. Our ships were short of torpedoes, since none had been coming from the factories, and were forced to retire. So we lost the systems of Kyrane and Floranus, and the planetary fortress of Rhamsandron.

It was an annoying but not a serious blow, for the recaptured systems had been unfriendly, and difficult to administer. We had no doubt that we could restore the position in the near future, as soon as the new weapon became operational.

These hopes were only partially fulfilled. When we renewed our offensive, we had to do so with fewer of the Spheres of Annihilation than had been planned, and this was one reason for our limited success. The other reason was more serious.

While we had been equipping as many of our ships as we could with the irresistible weapon, the enemy had been building feverishly. His ships were of the old pattern with the old weapons—but they now outnumbered ours. When we went into action, we found that the numbers ranged against us were often one hundred per cent greater than expected, causing target confusion among the automatic weapons and resulting in higher losses than anticipated. The enemy losses were higher still, for once a Sphere had reached its objective, destruction was certain, but the balance had not swung as far in our favor as we had hoped.

Moreover, while the main fleets had been engaged, the enemy had launched a daring attack on the lightly held systems of Eriston, Duranus, Carmanidora and Pharanidon—recapturing them all. We were thus faced with a threat only fifty light-years from our home planets.

There was much recrimination at the next meeting of the supreme commanders. Most of the complaints were addressed to Norden—Grand Admiral Taxaris in particular maintaining that thanks to our admittedly irresistible weapon we were now considerably worse off than before. We should, he claimed, have continued to build conventional ships, thus preventing the loss of our numerical superiority.

Norden was equally angry and called the naval staff ungrateful bunglers. But I could tell that he was worried—as indeed we all were—by the unexpected turn of events. He hinted that there might be a speedy way of remedying the situation.

We now know that Research had been working on the Battle Analyzer for many years, but, at the time, it came as a revelation to us and perhaps we were too easily swept off our feet. Norden's argument, also, was seductively convincing. What did it matter, he said, if the enemy had twice as many ships as we—if the efficiency of ours could be doubled or even trebled? For decades the limiting factor in warfare had been not mechanical but biological—it had become more and more difficult for any single mind, or group of minds, to cope with the rapidly changing complexities of battle in three-dimensional space. Norden's mathematicians had analyzed some of the classic engagements of the past, and had shown that even when we had been victorious we had often operated our units at much less than half of their theoretical efficiency.

The Battle Analyzer would change all this by replacing the operations staff with electronic calculators. The idea was not new, in theory, but until now it had been no more than a utopian dream. Many of us found it difficult to believe that it was still anything but a dream: after we had run through several very complex dummy battles, however, we were convinced.

It was decided to install the Analyzer in four of our heaviest ships, so that each of the main fleets could be equipped with one. At this stage, the trouble began—though we did not know it until later.

The Analyzer contained just short of a million vacuum tubes and needed a team of five hundred technicians to maintain and operate it. It was quite impossible to accommodate the extra staff aboard a battleship, so each of the four units had to be accompanied by a converted liner to carry the technicians not on duty. Installation was also a very slow and tedious business, but by gigantic efforts it was completed in six months.

Then, to our dismay, we were confronted by another crisis. Nearly five thousand highly skilled men had been selected to serve the Analyzers and had been given an intensive course at the Technical Training Schools. At the end of seven months, ten per cent of them had had nervous breakdowns and only forty per cent had qualified.

Once again, everyone started to blame everyone else. Norden, of course, said that the Research Staff could not be held responsible, and so incurred the enmity of the Personnel and Training Commands. It was finally decided that the only thing to do was to use two instead of four Analyzers and to bring the others into action as soon as men could be trained. There was little time to lose, for the enemy was still on the offensive and his morale was rising.

The first Analyzer fleet was ordered to recapture the system of Eriston. On the way, by one of the hazards of war, the liner carrying the technicians was struck by a roving mine. A warship would have survived, but the liner with its irreplaceable cargo was totally destroyed. So the operation had to be abandoned:

The other expedition was, at first, more successful. There was no doubt at all that the Analyzer fulfilled its designers' claims, and the enemy was heavily defeated in the first engagements. He withdrew, leaving us in possession of Saphran, Leucon and Hexanerax. But his Intelligence Staff must have noted the change in our tactics and the inexplicable presence of a liner in the heart of our battle Fleet. It must have noted, also, that our first Fleet had been accompanied by a similar ship—and had withdrawn when it had been destroyed.

In the next engagement, the enemy used his superior numbers to launch an overwhelming attack on the Analyzer ship and its unarmed consort. The attack was made without regard to losses—both ships were, of course, very heavily protected—and it succeeded. The result was the virtual decapitation of the Fleet, since an effectual transfer to the old operational methods proved impossible. We disengaged under heavy fire, and so lost all our gains and also the systems of Lormyia, Ismarnus, Beronis, Alphanidon and Sideneus.

At this stage, Grand Admiral Taxaris expressed his disapproval of Norden by committing suicide, and I assumed supreme command.

The situation was now both serious and infuriating. With stubborn conservatism and complete lack of imagination, the enemy continued to advance with his old-fashioned and inefficient but now vastly more numerous ships. It was galling to realize that if we had only continued building, without seeking new weapons, we would have been in a far more advantageous position. There were many acrimonious conferences at which Norden defended the scientists while everyone else blamed them for all that had happened. The difficulty was that Norden had proved every one of his claims: he had a perfect excuse for all the disasters that had occurred. And we could not now turn back—the search for an irresistible weapon must go on. At first it had been a luxury that would shorten the war. Now it was a necessity if we were to end it victoriously.

We were on the defensive, and so was Norden. He was more than ever determined to re-establish his prestige and that of the Research Staff. But we had been twice disappointed, and would not make the same mistake again. No doubt Norden's twenty thousand scientists would produce many further weapons: we would remain unimpressed.

We were wrong. The final weapon was something so fantastic that even now it seems difficult to believe that it ever existed. Its innocent, noncommittal name—The Exponential Field—gave no hint of its real potentialities. Some of Norden's mathematicians had discovered it during a piece of entirely theoretical research into the properties of space, and to everyone's great surprise their results were found to be physically realizable.

It seems very difficult to explain the operation of the Field to the layman. According to the technical description, it "produces an exponential condition of space, so that a finite distance in normal, linear space may become infinite in pseudo-space." Norden gave an analogy which some of us found useful. It was as if one took a flat disk of rubber—representing a region of normal space—and then pulled its center out to infinity. The circumference of the disk would be unaltered—but its "diameter" would be infinite. That was the sort of thing the generator of the Field did to the space around it.

As an example, suppose that a ship carrying the generator was surrounded by a ring of hostile machines. If it switched on the Field, *each* of the enemy ships would think that it—and the ships on the far side of the circle—had suddenly receded into nothingness. Yet the circumference of the circle would be the same as before: only the journey to the center would be of infinite duration, for as one proceeded, distances would appear to become greater and greater as the "scale" of space altered.

It was a nightmare condition, but a very useful one. Nothing could reach a ship carrying the Field: it might be englobed by an enemy fleet yet would be as inaccessible as if it were at the other side of the Universe. Against this, of course, it could not fight back without switching off the Field, but this still left it at a very great advantage, not only in defense but in offense. For a ship fitted with the Field could approach an enemy fleet undetected and suddenly appear in its midst.

This time there seemed to be no flaws in the new weapon.

Needless to say, we looked for all the possible objections before we committed ourselves again. Fortunately the equipment was fairly simple and did not require a large operating staff. After much debate, we decided to rush it into production, for we realized that time was running short and the war was going against us. We had now lost about the whole of our initial gains, and enemy forces had made several raids into our own Solar System.

We managed to hold off the enemy while the Fleet was re-equipped and the new battle techniques were worked out. To use the Field operationally it was necessary to locate an enemy formation, set a course that would intercept it, and then switch on the generator for the calculated period of time. On releasing the Field again—if the calculations had been accurate—one would be in the enemy's midst and could do great damage during the resulting confusion, retreating by the same route when necessary.

The first trial maneuvers proved satisfactory and the equipment seemed quite reliable. Numerous mock attacks were made and the crews became accustomed to the new technique. I was on one of the test flights and can vividly remember my impressions as the Field was switched on. The ships around us seemed to dwindle as if on the surface of an expanding bubble: in an instant they had vanished completely. So had the stars—but presently we could see that the Galaxy was still visible as a faint band of light around the ship. The virtual radius of our pseudo-space was not really infinite, but some hundred thousand light-years, and so the distance to the farthest stars of our system had not been greatly increased—though the nearest had of course totally disappeared.

These training maneuvers, however, had to be canceled before they were complete owing to a whole flock of minor technical troubles in various pieces of equipment, notably the communications circuits. These were annoying, but not important, though it was thought best to return to Base to clear them up.

At that moment the enemy made what was obviously intended to be a decisive attack against the fortress planet of Iton at the limits of our Solar System. The Fleet had to go into battle before repairs could be made.

The enemy must have believed that we had mastered the

secret of invisibility—as in a sense we had. Our ships appeared suddenly out of nowhere and inflicted tremendous damage—for a while. And then something quite baffling and inexplicable happened.

I was in command of the flagship *Hircania* when the trouble started. We had been operating as independent units, each against assigned objectives. Our detectors observed an enemy formation at medium range and the navigating officers measured its distance with great accuracy. We set course and switched on the generator.

The Exponential Field was released at the moment when we should have been passing through the center of the enemy group. To our consternation, we emerged into normal space at a distance of many hundred miles—and when we found the enemy, he had already found us. We retreated, and tried again. This time we were so far away from the enemy that he located us first.

Obviously, something was seriously wrong. We broke communicator silence and tried to contact the other ships of the Fleet to see if they had experienced the same trouble. Once again we failed—and this time the failure was beyond all reason, for the communication equipment appeared to be working perfectly. We could only assume, fantastic though it seemed, that the rest of the Fleet had been destroyed.

I do not wish to describe the scenes when the scattered units of the Fleet struggled back to Base. Our casualties had actually been negligible, but the ships were completely demoralized. Almost all had lost touch with one another and had found that their ranging equipment showed inexplicable errors. It was obvious that the Exponential Field was the cause of the troubles, despite the fact that they were only apparent when it was switched off.

The explanation came too late to do us any good, and Norden's final discomfiture was small consolation for the virtual loss of the war. As I have explained, the Field generators produced a radial distortion of space, distances appearing greater and greater as one approached the center of the artificial pseudo-space. When the Field was switched off, conditions returned to normal.

But not quite. It was never possible to restore the initial state *exactly*. Switching the Field on and off was equivalent to an elongation and contraction of the ship carrying the generator, but there was a hysteretic effect, as it were, and the initial condition was never quite reproducible, owing to all the thousands of electrical changes and movements of mass aboard the ship while the Field was on. These asymmetries and distortions were cumulative, and though they seldom amounted to more than a fraction of one per cent, that was quite enough. It meant that the precision ranging equipment and the tuned circuits in the communication apparatus were thrown completely out of adjustment. Any single ship could never detect the change—only when it compared its equipment with that of another vessel, or tried to communicate with it, could it tell what had happened.

It is impossible to describe the resultant chaos. Not a single component of one ship could be expected with certainty to work aboard another. The very nuts and bolts were no longer interchangeable, and the supply position became quite impossible. Given time, we might even have overcome these difficulties, but the enemy ships were already attacking in thousands with weapons which now seemed centuries behind those that we had invented. Our magnificent Fleet, crippled by our own science, fought on as best it could until it was overwhelmed and forced to surrender. The ships fitted with the Field were still invulnerable, but as fighting units they were almost helpless. Every time they switched on their generators to escape from enemy attack, the permanent distortion of their equipment increased. In a month, it was all over.

This is the true story of our defeat, which I give without prejudice to my defense before this Court. I make it, as I have said, to counteract the libels that have been circulating against the men who fought under me, and to show where the true blame for our misfortunes lay.

Finally, my request, which, as the Court will now realize, I make in no frivolous manner and which I hope will therefore be granted.

The Court will be aware that the conditions under which we are housed and the constant surveillance to which we are subjected night and day are somewhat distressing. Yet I am not complaining of this: nor do I complain of the fact that shortage of accommodation has made it necessary to house us in pairs.

But I cannot be held responsible for my future actions if I am compelled any longer to share my cell with Professor Norden, late Chief of the Research Staff of my armed forces.

London   *August 1948*

A WALK IN
THE DARK

ROBERT ARMSTRONG HAD walked just over two miles, as far as he could judge, when his torch failed. He stood still for a moment, unable to believe that such a misfortune could really have befallen him. Then, half maddened with rage, he hurled the useless instrument away. It landed somewhere in the darkness, disturbing the silence of this little world. A metallic echo came ringing back from the low hills: then all was quiet again.

This, thought Armstrong, was the ultimate misfortune. Nothing more could happen to him now. He was even able to laugh bitterly at his luck, and resolved never again to imagine that the fickle goddess had ever favored him. Who would have believed that the only tractor at Camp IV would have broken down when he was just setting off for Port Sanderson? He recalled the frenzied repair work, the relief when the second start had been made—and the final debacle when the caterpillar track had jammed.

It was no use then regretting the lateness of his departure: he could not have foreseen these accidents, and it was still a good four hours before the *Canopus* took off. He *had* to catch her, whatever happened; no other ship would be touching at this world for another month.

Apart from the urgency of his business, four more weeks on this out-of-the-way planet were unthinkable.

There had been only one thing to do. It was lucky that Port Sanderson was little more than six miles from the camp —not a great distance, even on foot. He had had to leave all his equipment behind, but it could follow on the next ship and he could manage without it. The road was poor, merely stamped out of the rock by one of the Board's hundred-ton crushers, but there was no fear of going astray.

Even now, he was in no real danger, though he might well be too late to catch the ship. Progress would be slow, for he dare not risk losing the road in this region of canyons and enigmatic tunnels that had never been explored. It was, of course, pitch-dark. Here at the edge of the Galaxy the stars were so few and scattered that their light was negligible. The strange crimson sun of this lonely world would not rise for many hours, and although five of the little moons were in the sky, they could barely be seen by the unaided eye. Not one of them could even cast a shadow.

Armstrong was not the man to bewail his luck for long. He began to walk slowly along the road, feeling its texture with his feet. It was, he knew, fairly straight except where it wound through Carver's Pass. He wished he had a stick or something to probe the way before him, but he would have to rely for guidance on the feel of the ground.

It was terribly slow at first, until he gained confidence. He had never known how difficult it was to walk in a straight line. Although the feeble stars gave him his bearings, again and again he found himself stumbling among the virgin rocks at the edge of the crude roadway. He was traveling in long zigzags that took him to alternate sides of the road. Then he would stub his toes against the bare rock and grope his way back onto the hard-packed surface once again.

Presently it settled down to a routine. It was impossible to estimate his speed; he could only struggle along and hope for the best. There were four miles to go—four miles and as many hours. It should be easy enough, unless he lost his way. But he dared not think of that.

Once he had mastered the technique he could afford the luxury of thought. He could not pretend that he was enjoying the experience, but he had been in much worse positions before. As long as he remained on the road, he was perfectly safe. He had been hoping that as his eyes became adapted to the starlight he would be able to see the way, but he now knew that the whole journey would be blind. The discovery gave him a vivid sense of his remoteness from the heart of the Galaxy. On a night as clear as this, the skies of almost any other planet would have been blazing with stars. Here, at this outpost of the Universe the sky held perhaps a hundred faintly gleaming points of light, as useless as the five ridiculous moons on which no one had ever bothered to land.

A slight change in the road interrupted his thoughts. Was there a curve here, or had he veered off to the right again? He moved very slowly along the invisible and ill-defined border. Yes, there was no mistake: the road was bending to the left. He tried to remember its appearance in the daytime, but he had only seen it once before. Did this mean that he was nearing the Pass? He hoped so, for the journey would then be half completed.

He peered ahead into the blackness, but the ragged line of the horizon told him nothing. Presently he found that the road had straightened itself again and his spirits sank. The entrance to the Pass must still be some way ahead: there were at least four miles to go.

Four miles—how ridiculous the distance seemed! How long would it take the *Canopus* to travel four miles? He doubted if man could measure so short an interval of time. And how many trillions of miles had he, Robert Armstrong, traveled in his life? It must have reached a staggering total by now, for in the last twenty years he had scarcely stayed more than a month at a time on any single world. This very year, he had twice made the crossing of the Galaxy, and that was a notable journey even in these days of the phantom drive.

He tripped over a loose stone, and the jolt brought him back to reality. It was no use, here, thinking of ships that could eat up the light-years. He was facing Nature, with no weapons but his own strength and skill.

It was strange that it took him so long to identify the real cause of his uneasiness. The last four weeks had been very full, and the rush of his departure, coupled with the annoyance and anxiety caused by the tractor's breakdowns, had driven everything else from his mind. Moreover, he had always prided himself on his hardheadedness and lack of imagination. Until now, he had forgotten all about that first evening at the Base, when the crews had regaled him with the usual tall yarns concocted for the benefit of newcomers.

It was then that the old Base clerk had told the story of his walk by night from Port Sanderson to the camp, and of what had trailed him through Carver's Pass, keeping always beyond the limit of his torchlight. Armstrong, who had heard such tales on a score of worlds, had paid it little attention at the time. This planet, after all, was known to be uninhabited. But logic could not dispose of the matter as easily as that. Suppose, after all, there was some truth in the old man's fantastic tale . . . ?

It was not a pleasant thought, and Armstrong did not intend to brood upon it. But he knew that if he dismissed it out of hand it would continue to prey on his mind. The only way to conquer imaginary fears was to face them boldly; he would have to do that now.

His strongest argument was the complete barrenness of this world and its utter desolation, though against that one could set many counterarguments, as indeed the old clerk had done. Man had only lived on this planet for twenty years, and much of it was still unexplored. No one could deny that the tunnels out in the wasteland were rather puzzling, but everyone believed them to be volcanic vents. Though, of course, life often crept into such places. With a shudder he remembered the giant polyps that had snared the first explorers of Vargon III.

It was all very inconclusive. Suppose, for the sake of argument, one granted the existence of life here. What of that?

The vast majority of life forms in the Universe were completely indifferent to man. Some, of course, like the gas-beings of Alcoran or the roving wave-lattices of Shandaloon, could not even detect him but passed through or around him as if he did not exist. Others were merely inquisitive, some embarrassingly friendly. There were few indeed that would attack unless provoked.

Nevertheless, it was a grim picture that the old stores

clerk had painted. Back in the warm, well-lighted smoking room, with the drinks going around, it had been easy enough to laugh at it. But here in the darkness, miles from any human settlement, it was very different.

It was almost a relief when he stumbled off the road again and had to grope with his hands until he found it once more. This seemed a very rough patch, and the road was scarcely distinguishable from the rocks around. In a few minutes, however, he was safely on his way again.

It was unpleasant to see how quickly his thoughts returned to the same disquieting subject. Clearly it was worrying him more than he cared to admit.

He drew consolation from one fact: it had been quite obvious that no one at the Base had believed the old fellow's story. Their questions and banter had proved that. At the time, he had laughed as loudly as any of them. After all, what *was* the evidence? A dim shape, just seen in the darkness, that might well have been an oddly formed rock. And the curious clicking noise that had so impressed the old man —anyone could imagine such sounds at night if they were sufficiently overwrought. If it had been hostile, why hadn't the creature come any closer? "Because it was afraid of my light," the old chap had said. Well, that was plausible enough: it would explain why nothing had ever been seen in the daylight. Such a creature might live underground, only emerging at night—damn it, why was he taking the old idiot's ravings so seriously! Armstrong got control of his thoughts again. If he went on this way, he told himself angrily, he would soon be seeing and hearing a whole menagerie of monsters.

There was, of course, one factor that disposed of the ridiculous story at once. It was really very simple; he felt sorry he hadn't thought of it before. *What would such a creature live on?* There was not even a trace of vegetation on the whole of the planet. He laughed to think that the bogy could be disposed of so easily—and in the same instant felt annoyed with himself for not laughing aloud. If he was so sure of his reasoning, why not whistle, or sing, or do anything to keep up his spirits? He put the question fairly to himself as a test of his manhood. Half-ashamed, he had to admit that he was still afraid—afraid because "there *might* be something in it, after all." But at least his analysis had done him some good.

It would have been better if he had left it there, and remained half-convinced by his argument. But a part of his mind was still busily trying to break down his careful reasoning. It succeeded only too well, and when he remembered the plant-beings of Xantil Major the shock was so unpleasant that he stopped dead in his tracks.

Now the plant-beings of Xantil were not in any way horrible. They were in fact extremely beautiful creatures. But what made them appear so distressing now was the knowledge that they could live for indefinite periods with no food whatsoever. All the energy they needed for their strange lives they extracted from cosmic radiation—and that was almost as intense here as anywhere else in the Universe.

He had scarcely thought of one example before others crowded into his mind and he remembered the life form on Trantor Beta, which was the only one known capable of directly utilizing atomic energy. That too had lived on an utterly barren world, very much like this. . . .

Armstrong's mind was rapidly splitting into two distinct portions, each trying to convince the other and neither wholly succeeding. He did not realize how far his morale had gone until he found himself holding his breath lest it conceal any sound from the darkness about him. Angrily, he cleared his mind of the rubbish that had been gathering there and turned once more to the immediate problem.

There was no doubt that the road was slowly rising, and the silhouette of the horizon seemed much higher in the sky. The road began to twist, and suddenly he was aware of great rocks on either side of him. Soon only a narrow ribbon of sky was still visible, and the darkness became, if possible, even more intense.

Somehow, he felt safer with the rock walls surrounding him: it meant that he was protected except in two directions. Also, the road had been leveled more carefully and it was easy to keep it. Best of all, he knew now that the journey was more than half completed.

For a moment his spirits began to rise. Then, with maddening perversity, his mind went back into the old grooves again. He remembered that it was on the far side of Carver's

Pass that the old clerk's adventure had taken place—if it had ever happened at all.

In half a mile, he would be out in the open again, out of the protection of these sheltering rocks. The thought seemed doubly horrible now and he already felt a sense of nakedness. He could be attacked from any direction, and he would be utterly helpless. . . .

Until now, he had still retained some self-control. Very resolutely he had kept his mind away from the one fact that gave some color to the old man's tale —the single piece of evidence that had stopped the banter in the crowded room back at the camp and brought a sudden hush upon the company. Now, as Armstrong's will weakened, he recalled again the words that had struck a momentary chill even in the warm comfort of the Base building.

The little clerk had been very insistent on one point. He had never heard any sound of pursuit from the dim shape sensed, rather than seen, at the limit of his light. There was no scuffling of claws or hoofs on rock, nor even the clatter of displaced stones. It was as if, so the old man had declared in that solemn manner of his, "as if the thing that was following could see perfectly in the darkness, and had many small legs or pads so that it could move swiftly and easily over the rocks—like a giant caterpillar or one of the carpet-things of Kralkor II."

Yet, although there had been no noise of pursuit, there had been one sound that the old man had caught several times. It was so unusual that its very strangeness made it doubly ominous. It was a faint but horribly persistent *clicking.*

The old fellow had been able to describe it very vividly— much too vividly for Armstrong's liking now.

"Have you ever listened to a large insect crunching its prey?" he said. "Well, it was just like that. I imagine that a crab makes exactly the same noise with its claws when it clashes them together. It was a—what's the word?—a *chitinous* sound."

At this point, Armstrong remembered laughing loudly. (Strange, how it was all coming back to him now.) But no one else had laughed, though they had been quick to do so earlier. Sensing the change of tone, he had sobered at once and asked the old man to continue his story. How he wished now that he had stifled his curiosity!

It had been quickly told. The next day, a party of skeptical technicians had gone into the no man's land beyond Carver's Pass. They were not skeptical enough to leave their guns behind, but they had no cause to use them, for they found no trace of any living thing. There were the inevitable pits and tunnels, glistening holes down which the light of the torches rebounded endlessly until it was lost in the distance —but the planet was riddled with them.

Though the party found no sign of life, it discovered one thing it did not like at all. Out in the barren and unexplored land beyond the Pass they had come upon an even larger tunnel than the rest. Near the mouth of that tunnel was a massive rock, half embedded in the ground. And the sides of that rock had been worn away *as if it had been used as an enormous whetstone.*

No less than five of those present had seen this disturbing rock. None of them could explain it satisfactorily as a natural formation, but they still refused to accept the old man's story. Armstrong had asked them if they had ever put it to the test. There had been an uncomfortable silence. Then big Andrew Hargraves had said: "Hell, who'd walk out to the Pass at night just for fun!" and had left it at that. Indeed, there was no other record of anyone walking from Port Sanderson to the camp by night, or for that matter by day. During the hours of light, no unprotected human being could live in the open beneath the rays of the enormous, lurid sun that seemed to fill half the sky. And no one would walk six miles, wearing radiation armor, if the tractor was available.

Armstrong felt that he was leaving the Pass. The rocks on either side were falling away, and the road was no longer as firm and well packed as it had been. He was coming out into the open plain once more, and somewhere not far away in the darkness was that enigmatic pillar that might have been used for sharpening monstrous fangs or claws. It was not a reassuring thought, but he could not get it out of his mind.

Feeling distinctly worried now, Armstrong made a great effort to pull himself together. He would try to be rational again; he would think of business, the work he had done at the camp—anything but this infernal place. For a while, he succeeded quite well. But presently, with a maddening persistence, every train of thought came back to the same point. He could not get out of his mind the picture of that inexplicable rock and its appalling possibilities. Over and over again he found himself wondering how far away it was, whether he had already passed it, and whether it was on his right or his left. . . .

The ground was quite flat again, and the road drove on straight as an arrow. There was one gleam of consolation: Port Sanderson could not be much more than two miles away. Armstrong had no idea how long he had been on the road. Unfortunately his watch was not illuminated and he could only guess at the passage of time. With any luck, the *Canopus* should not take off for another two hours at least. But he could not be sure, and now another fear began to enter his mind—the dread that he might see a vast constellation of lights rising swiftly into the sky ahead, and know that all this agony of mind had been in vain.

He was not zigzagging so badly now, and seemed to be able to anticipate the edge of the road before stumbling off it. It was probable, he cheered himself by thinking, that he was traveling almost as fast as if he had a light. If all went well, he might be nearing Port Sanderson in thirty minutes —a ridiculously small space of time. How he would laugh at his fears when he strolled into his already reserved stateroom in the *Canopus,* and felt that peculiar quiver as the phantom drive hurled the great ship far out of this system, back to the clustered star-clouds near the center of the Galaxy —back toward Earth itself, which he had not seen for so many years. One day, he told himself, he really must visit Earth again. All his life he had been making the promise, but always there had been the same answer—lack of time. Strange, wasn't it, that such a tiny planet should have played so enormous a part in the development of the Universe, should even have come to dominate worlds far wiser and more intelligent than itself!

Armstrong's thoughts were harmless again, and he felt calmer. The knowledge that he was nearing Port Sanderson was immensely reassuring, and he deliberately kept his mind on familiar, unimportant matters. Carver's Pass was already far behind, and with it that thing he no longer intended to recall. One day, if he ever returned to this world, he would visit the Pass in the daytime and laugh at his fears. In twenty minutes now, they would have joined the nightmares of his childhood.

It was almost a shock, though one of the most pleasant he had ever known, when he saw the lights of Port Sanderson come up over the horizon. The curvature of this little world was very deceptive: it did not seem right that a planet with a gravity almost as great as Earth's should have a horizon so close at hand. One day, someone would have to discover what lay at this world's core to give it so great a density. Perhaps the many tunnels would help—it was an unfortunate turn of thought, but the nearness of his goal had robbed it of terror now. Indeed, the thought that he might really be in danger seemed to give his adventure a certain piquancy and heightened interest. Nothing could happen to him now, with ten minutes to go and the lights of the Port already in sight.

A few minutes later, his feelings changed abruptly when he came to the sudden bend in the road. He had forgotten the chasm that caused his detour, and added half a mile to the journey. Well, what of it? he thought stubbornly. An extra half-mile would make no difference now—another ten minutes, at the most.

It was very disappointing when the lights of the city vanished. Armstrong had not remembered the hill which the road was skirting; perhaps it was only a low ridge, scarcely noticeable in the daytime. But by hiding the lights of the Port it had taken away his chief talisman and left him again at the mercy of his fears.

Very unreasonably, his intelligence told him, he began to think how horrible it would be if anything happened now, so near the end of the journey. He kept the worst of his fears at bay for a while, hoping desperately that the lights of the city would soon reappear. But as the minutes dragged on, he realized that the ridge must be longer than he imagined. He tried to cheer himself by the thought that the city would be all the nearer when he saw it again, but somehow logic seemed to have failed him now. For presently he found himself doing something he had not stooped to, even out in the waste by Carver's Pass.

He stopped, turned slowly round, and with bated breath listened until his lungs were nearly bursting.

The silence was uncanny, considering how near he must be to the Port. There was certainly no sound from behind him. Of course there wouldn't be, he told himself angrily. But he was immensely relieved. The thought of that faint and insistent clicking had been haunting him for the last hour.

So friendly and familiar was the noise that did reach him at last that the anticlimax almost made him laugh aloud. Drifting through the still air from a source clearly not more than a mile away came the sound of a landing-field tractor, perhaps one of the machines loading the *Canopus* itself. In a matter of seconds, thought Armstrong, he would be around this ridge with the Port only a few hundred yards ahead. The journey was nearly ended. In a few moments, this evil plain would be no more than a fading nightmare.

It seemed terribly unfair: so little time, such a small fraction of a human life, was all he needed now. But the gods have always been unfair to man, and now they were enjoying their little jest. For there could be no mistaking the rattle of monstrous claws in the darkness *ahead of him.*

Stratford-on-Avon   *April 1945*

THE RELUCTANT
ORCHID

*Science fiction, it has often been pointed out, is sadly lacking
in humor. But something is worthwhile only if one can make
fun of it, and this I set out to do in* Tales from the "White
Hart." *There is nothing fictitious about the White Hart, or
most of its clientele.*

*Imitation is the sincerest form of flattery, and I would like
to pay here a tribute to the memory of Lord Dunsany, who
was very kind to me in the early nineteen-fifties. There is
undoubtedly a family resemblance between Harry Purvis and
his Mr. Jorkens.*

THOUGH FEW PEOPLE in the "White Hart" will concede
that any of Harry Purvis' stories are actually *true,* everyone
agrees that some are much more probable than others. And
on any scale of probability, the affair of the Reluctant
Orchid must rate very low indeed.

I don't remember what ingenious gambit Harry used to
launch this narrative: maybe some orchid fancier brought
his latest monstrosity into the bar, and that set him off. No

matter. I do remember the story, and after all that's what counts.

The adventure did not, this time, concern any of Harry's numerous relatives, and he avoided explaining just how he managed to know so many of the sordid details. The hero— if you can call him that—of this hothouse epic was an inoffensive little clerk named Hercules Keating. And if you think *that* is the most unlikely part of the story, just stick round a while.

Hercules is not the sort of name you can carry off lightly at the best of times, and when you are four foot nine and look as if you'd have to take a physical-culture course before you can even become a ninety-seven-pound weakling, it is a positive embarrassment. Perhaps it helped to explain why Hercules had very little social life, and all his real friends grew in pots in a humid conservatory at the bottom of his garden. His needs were simple and he spent very little money on himself; consequently his collection of orchids and cacti was really rather remarkable. Indeed, he had a wide reputation among the fraternity of cactophiles, and often received from remote corners of the globe parcels smelling of mold and tropical jungles.

Hercules had only one living relative, and it would have been hard to find a greater contrast than Aunt Henrietta. She was a massive six-footer, usually wore a rather loud line in Harris tweeds, drove a Jaguar with reckless skill, and chain-smoked cigars. Her parents had set their hearts on a boy, and had never been able to decide whether or not their wish had been granted. Henrietta earned a living, and quite a good one, breeding dogs of various shapes and sizes. She was seldom without a couple of her latest models, and they were not the type of portable canine which ladies like to carry in their handbags. The Keating Kennels specialized in Great Danes, Alsatians, and Saint Bernards. . . .

Henrietta, rightly despising men as the weaker sex, had never married. However, for some reason she took an avuncular (yes, that is definitely the right word) interest in Hercules, and called to see him almost every weekend. It was a curious kind of relationship: probably Henrietta found that Hercules bolstered up her feelings of superiority. If he was a good example of the male sex, then they were certainly a pretty sorry lot. Yet, if this was Henrietta's motivation, she was unconscious of it and seemed genuinely fond of her nephew. She was patronizing, but never unkind.

As might be expected, her attentions did not exactly help Hercules' own well-developed inferiority complex. At first he had tolerated his aunt; then he came to dread her regular visits, her booming voice, and her bone-crushing handshake; and at last he grew to hate her. Eventually, indeed, his hate was the dominant emotion in his life, exceeding even his love for his orchids. But he was careful not to show it, realizing that if Aunt Henrietta discovered how he felt about her, she would probably break him in two and throw the pieces to her wolf pack.

There was no way, then, in which Hercules could express his pent-up feelings. He had to be polite to Aunt Henrietta even when he felt like murder. And he often did feel like murder, though he knew that there was nothing he would ever do about it. Until one day . . .

According to the dealer, the orchid came from "somewhere in the Amazon region"—a rather vague postal address. When Hercules first saw it, it was not a very prepossessing sight, even to anyone who loved orchids as much as he did. A shapeless root, about the size of a man's fist—that was all. It was redolent of decay, and there was the faintest hint of a rank, carrion smell. Hercules was not even sure that it was viable, and told the dealer as much. Perhaps that enabled him to purchase it for a trifling sum, and he carried it home without much enthusiasm.

It showed no signs of life for the first month, but that did not worry Hercules. Then, one day, a tiny green shoot appeared and started to creep up to the light. After that, progress was rapid. Soon there was a thick, fleshy stem as big as a man's forearm, and colored a positively virulent green. Near the top of the stem a series of curious bulges circled the plant: otherwise it was completely featureless. Hercules was now quite excited: he was sure that some entirely new species had swum into his ken.

The rate of growth was now really fantastic: soon the plant was taller than Hercules, not that that was saying a great deal. Moreover, the bulges seemed to be developing, and it looked as if at any moment the orchid would burst into bloom. Hercules waited anxiously, knowing how short-lived some flowers can be, and spent as much time as he possibly could in the hothouse. Despite all his watchfulness, the transformation occurred one night while he was asleep.

In the morning, the orchid was fringed by a series of eight dangling tendrils, almost reaching to the ground. They must have developed inside the plant and emerged with—for the vegetable world—explosive speed. Hercules stared at the phenomenon in amazement, and went very thoughtfully to work.

That evening, as he watered the plant and checked its soil, he noticed a still more peculiar fact. The tendrils were thickening, and they were not completely motionless. They had a slight but unmistakable tendency to vibrate, as if possessing a life of their own. Even Hercules, for all his interest and enthusiasm, found this more than a little disturbing.

A few days later, there was no doubt about it at all. When he approached the orchid, the tendrils swayed toward him in an unpleasantly suggestive fashion. The impression of hunger was so strong that Hercules began to feel very uncomfortable indeed, and something started to nag at the back of his mind. It was quite a while before he could recall what it was: then he said to himself, "Of course! How stupid of me!" and went along to the local library. Here he spent a most interesting half hour rereading a little piece by one H. G. Wells entitled, "The Flowering of the Strange Orchid."

"My goodness!" thought Hercules, when he had finished the tale. As yet there had been no stupefying odor which might overpower the plant's intended victim, but otherwise the characteristics were all too similar. Hercules went home in a very unsettled mood indeed.

He opened the conservatory door and stood looking along the avenue of greenery toward his prize specimen. He judged the length of the tendrils—already he found himself calling them tentacles—with great care and walked to within what appeared a safe distance. The plant certainly had an impression of alertness and menace far more appropriate to the animal than the vegetable kingdom. Hercules remembered the unfortunate history of Doctor Frankenstein, and was not amused.

But, really, this was ridiculous! Such things didn't happen in real life. Well, there was one way to put matters to the test. . . .

Hercules went into the house and came back a few minutes later with a broomstick, to the end of which he had attached a piece of raw meat. Feeling a considerable fool, he advanced toward the orchid as a lion tamer might approach one of his charges at mealtime.

For a moment, nothing happened. Then two of the tendrils developed an agitated twitch. They began to sway back and forth, as if the plant was making up its mind. Abruptly, they whipped out with such speed that they practically vanished from view. They wrapped themselves round the meat, and Hercules felt a powerful tug at the end of his broomstick. Then the meat was gone: the orchid was clutching it, if one may mix metaphors slightly, to its bosom.

"Jumping Jehosophat!" yelled Hercules. It was very seldom indeed that he used such strong language.

The orchid showed no further signs of life for twenty-four hours. It was waiting for the meat to become high, and it was also developing its digestive system. By the next day, a network of what looked like short roots had covered the still-visible chunk of meat. By nightfall, the meat was gone.

The plant had tasted blood.

Hercules' emotions as he watched over his prize were curiously mixed. There were times when it almost gave him nightmares, and he foresaw a whole range of horrid possibilities. The orchid was now extremely strong, and if he got within its clutches he would be done for. But, of course, there was not the slightest danger of that. He had arranged a system of pipes so that it could be watered from a safe distance, and its less orthodox food he simply tossed within range of its tentacles. It was now eating a pound of raw meat a day, and he had an uncomfortable feeling that it could cope with much larger quantities if given the opportunity.

Hercules' natural qualms were, on the whole, outweighed by his feeling of triumph that such a botanical marvel had fallen into his hands. Whenever he chose, he could become the most famous orchid-grower in the world. It was typical of his somewhat restricted viewpoint that it never occurred to him that other people besides orchid fanciers might be interested in his pet.

The creature was now about six feet tall, and apparently still growing—though much more slowly than it had been. All the other plants had been moved from its end of the conservatory, not so much because Hercules feared that it might be cannibalistic as to enable him to tend them without danger. He had stretched a rope across the central aisle so that there was no risk of his accidentally walking within range of those eight dangling arms.

It was obvious that the orchid had a highly developed nervous system, and something very nearly approaching intelligence. It knew when it was going to be fed, and exhibited unmistakable signs of pleasure. Most fantastic of all—though Hercules was still not sure about this—it seemed capable of producing sounds. There were times, just before a meal, when he fancied he could hear an incredibly high-pitched whistle, skirting the edge of audibility. A newborn bat might have had such a voice: he wondered what purpose it served. Did the orchid somehow lure its prey into its clutches by sound? If so, he did not think the technique would work on him.

While Hercules was making these interesting discoveries, he continued to be fussed over by Aunt Henrietta and assaulted by her hounds, which were never as house-trained as she claimed them to be. She would usually roar up the street on a Sunday afternoon with one dog in the seat beside her and another occupying most of the baggage compartment. Then she would bound up the steps two at a time, nearly deafen Hercules with her greeting, half paralyze him with her handshake, and blow cigar smoke in his face. There had been a time when he was terrified that she would kiss him, but he had long since realized that such effeminate behavior was foreign to her nature.

Aunt Henrietta looked upon Hercules' orchids with some scorn. Spending one's spare time in a hothouse was, she considered, a very effete recreation. When *she* wanted to let off steam, she went big-game hunting in Kenya. This did nothing to endear her to Hercules, who hated blood sports. But despite his mounting dislike for his overpowering aunt, every Sunday afternoon he dutifully prepared tea for her and they had a tête-à-tête together which, on the surface at least, seemed perfectly friendly. Henrietta never guessed that as he poured the tea Hercules often wished it was poisoned: she was, far down beneath her extensive fortifications, a fundamentally goodhearted person and the knowledge would have upset her deeply.

Hercules did not mention his vegetable octopus to Aunt Henrietta. He had occasionally shown her his most interesting specimens, but this was something he was keeping to himself. Perhaps, even before he had fully formulated his diabolical plan, his subconscious was already preparing the ground. . . .

It was late one Sunday evening, when the roar of the Jaguar had died away into the night and Hercules was restoring his shattered nerves in the conservatory, that the idea first came fully fledged into his mind. He was staring at the orchid, noting how the tendrils were now as thick around as a man's thumb, when a most pleasing fantasy suddenly flashed before his eyes. He pictured Aunt Henrietta struggling helplessly in the grip of the monster, unable to escape from its carnivorous clutches. Why, it would be the perfect crime. The distraught nephew would arrive on the scene too late to be of assistance, and when the police answered his frantic call they would see at a glance that the whole affair was a deplorable accident. True, there would be an inquest, but the coroner's censure would be toned down in view of Hercules' obvious grief. . . .

The more he thought of the idea, the more he liked it. He could see no flaws, as long as the orchid co-operated. That, clearly, would be the greatest problem. He would have to plan a course of training for the creature. It already looked sufficiently diabolical; he must give it a disposition to suit its appearance.

Considering that he had no prior experience in such matters, and that there were no authorities he could consult, Hercules proceeded along very sound and businesslike lines. He would use a fishing rod to dangle pieces of meat just outside the orchid's range, until the creature lashed its tentacles in a frenzy. At such times its high-pitched squeak was clearly audible, and Hercules wondered how it managed to produce the sound. He also wondered what its organs of perception were, but this was yet another mystery that could not be solved without close examination. Perhaps Aunt Henrietta, if all went well, would have a brief opportunity of discovering these interesting facts—though she would probably be too busy to report them for the benefit of posterity.

There was no doubt that the beast was quite powerful enough to deal with its intended victim. It had once wrenched a broomstick out of Hercules' grip, and although that in itself proved very little, the sickening "crack" of the wood a moment later brought a smile of satisfaction to its trainer's thin lips. He began to be much more pleasant and attentive to his aunt. In every respect, indeed, he was the model nephew.

When Hercules considered that his picador tactics had brought the orchid into the right frame of mind, he wondered if he should test it with live bait. This was a problem that worried him for some weeks, during which time he would look speculatively at every dog or cat he passed in the street, but he finally abandoned the idea, for a rather peculiar reason. He was simply too kindhearted to put it into practice. Aunt Henrietta would have to be the first victim.

He starved the orchid for two weeks before he put his plan into action. This was as long as he dared risk—he did not wish to weaken the beast—merely to whet its appetite, that the outcome of the encounter might be more certain. And so, when he had carried the teacups back into the kitchen and was sitting upwind of Aunt Henrietta's cigar, he said casually: "I've got something I'd like to show you, Auntie. I've been keeping it as a surprise. It'll tickle you to death."

That, he thought, was not a completely accurate description, but it gave the general idea.

Auntie took the cigar out of her mouth and looked at Hercules with frank surprise.

"Well!" she boomed. "Wonders will never cease! What *have* you been up to, you rascal?" She slapped him playfully on the back and shot all the air out of his lungs.

"You'll never believe it," gritted Hercules, when he had recovered his breath. "It's in the conservatory."

"Eh?" said Auntie, obviously puzzled.

"Yes—come along and have a look. It's going to create a real sensation."

Auntie gave a snort that might have indicated disbelief, but followed Hercules without further question. The two Alsatians now busily chewing up the carpet looked at her anxiously and half rose to their feet, but she waved them away.

"All right, boys," she ordered gruffly. "I'll be back in a minute." Hercules thought this unlikely.

It was a dark evening, and the lights in the conservatory were off. As they entered, Auntie snorted, "Gad, Hercules—the place smells like a slaughterhouse. Haven't met such a stink since I shot that elephant in Bulawayo and we couldn't find it for a week."

"Sorry, Auntie," apologized Hercules, propelling her forward through the gloom. "It's a new fertilizer I'm using. It produces the most stunning results. Go on—another couple of yards. I want this to be a *real* surprise."

"I hope this isn't a joke," said Auntie suspiciously, as she stomped forward.

"I can promise you it's no joke," replied Hercules, standing with his hand on the light switch. He could just see the looming bulk of the orchid: Auntie was now within ten feet of it. He waited until she was well inside the danger zone, and threw the switch.

There was a frozen moment while the scene was transfixed with light. Then Aunt Henrietta ground to a halt and stood, arms akimbo, in front of the giant orchid. For a moment Hercules was afraid she would retreat before the plant could get into action: then he saw that she was calmly scrutinizing it, unable to make up her mind what the devil it was.

It was a full five seconds before the orchid moved. Then the dangling tentacles flashed into action—but not in the way that Hercules had expected. The plant clutched them tightly, protectively, *around itself*—and at the same time it gave a high-pitched scream of pure terror. In a moment of sickening disillusionment, Hercules realized the awful truth.

His orchid was an utter coward. It might be able to cope with the wild life of the Amazon jungle, but coming suddenly upon Aunt Henrietta had completely broken its nerve.

As for its proposed victim, she stood watching the creature with an astonishment which swiftly changed to another emotion. She spun around on her heels and pointed an accusing finger at her nephew.

"Hercules!" she roared. "The poor thing's scared to death. *Have you been bullying it?*"

Hercules could only stand with his head hanging low in shame and frustration.

"N-no, Auntie," he quavered. "I guess it's naturally nervous."

"Well, I'm used to animals. You should have called me before. You must treat them firmly—but gently. Kindness always works, as long as you show them you're the master. There, there, did-dums—don't be frightened of Auntie—she won't hurt you . . ."

It was, thought Hercules in his blank despair, a revolting sight. With surprising gentleness, Aunt Henrietta fussed over the beast, patting and stroking it until the tentacles relaxed and the shrill, whistling scream died away. After a few minutes of this pandering, it appeared to get over its fright. Hercules finally fled with a muffled sob when one of the tentacles crept forward and began to stroke Henrietta's gnarled fingers. . . .

From that day, he was a broken man. What was worse, he could never escape from the consequences of his intended crime. Henrietta had acquired a new pet, and was liable to call not only at weekends but two or three times in between as well. It was obvious that she did not trust Hercules to treat the orchid properly, and still suspected him of bullying it. She would bring tasty tidbits that even her dogs had rejected, but which the orchid accepted with delight. The smell, which had so far been confined to the conservatory, began to creep into the house. . . .

And there, concluded Harry Purvis, as he brought this improbable narrative to a close, the matter rests—to the satisfaction of two, at any rate, of the parties concerned. The orchid is happy, and Aunt Henrietta has something (query, someone?) else to dominate. From time to time the creature has a nervous breakdown when a mouse gets loose in the conservatory, and she rushes to console it.

As for Hercules, there is no chance that he will ever give any more trouble to either of them. He seems to have sunk into a kind of vegetable sloth: indeed, said Harry thoughtfully, every day he becomes more and more like an orchid himself.

The harmless variety, of course. . . .

Miami   *April 1954*

ENCOUNTER AT DAWN

IT WAS IN the last days of the Empire. The tiny ship was far from home, and almost a hundred light-years from the great parent vessel searching through the loosely packed stars at the rim of the Milky Way. But even here it could not escape from the shadow that lay across civilization: beneath that shadow, pausing ever and again in their work to wonder how their distant homes were faring, the scientists of the Galactic Survey still labored at their never-ending task.

The ship held only three occupants, but among them they carried knowledge of many sciences, and the experience of half a lifetime in space. After the long interstellar night, the star ahead was warming their spirits as they dropped down toward its fires. A little more golden, a trifle more brilliant than the sun that now seemed a legend of their childhood. They knew from past experience that the chance of locating planets here was more than ninety per cent, and for the moment they forgot all else in the excitement of discovery.

They found the first planet within minutes of coming to rest. It was a giant, of a familiar type, too cold for protoplasmic life and probably possessing no stable surface. So they turned their search sunward, and presently were rewarded.

It was a world that made their hearts ache for home, a world where everything was hauntingly familiar, yet never quite the same. Two great land masses floated in blue-green seas, capped by ice at both poles. There were some desert regions, but the larger part of the planet was obviously fertile. Even from this distance, the signs of vegetation were unmistakably clear.

They gazed hungrily at the expanding landscape as they fell down into the atmosphere, heading toward noon in the subtropics. The ship plummeted through cloudless skies toward a great river, checked its fall with a surge of soundless power, and came to rest among the long grasses by the water's edge.

No one moved: there was nothing to be done until the automatic instruments had finished their work. Then a bell tinkled softly and the lights on the control board flashed in a pattern of meaningful chaos. Captain Altman rose to his feet with a sigh of relief.

"We're in luck," he said. "We can go outside without protection, if the pathogenic tests are satisfactory. What did you make of the place as we came in, Bertrond?"

"Geologically stable—no active volcanoes, at least. I didn't see any trace of cities, but that proves nothing. If there's a civilization here, it may have passed that stage."

"Or not reached it yet?"

Bertrond shrugged. "Either's just as likely. It may take us some time to find out on a planet this size."

"More time than we've got," said Clindar, glancing at the communications panel that linked them to the mother ship and thence to the Galaxy's threatened heart. For a moment there was a gloomy silence. Then Clindar walked to the control board and pressed a pattern of keys with automatic skill.

With a slight jar, a section of the hull slid aside and the fourth member of the crew stepped out onto the new planet, flexing metal limbs and adjusting servomotors to the unaccustomed gravity. Inside the ship, a television screen glimmered into life, revealing a long vista of waving grasses, some trees in the middle distance, and a glimpse of the great river. Clindar punched a button, and the picture flowed steadily across the screen as the robot turned its head.

"Which way shall we go?" Clindar asked.

"Let's have a look at those trees," Altman replied. "If there's any animal life we'll find it there."

"Look!" cried Bertrond. "A bird!"

Clindar's fingers flew over the keyboard: the picture centered on the tiny speck that had suddenly appeared on the left of the screen, and expanded rapidly as the robot's telephoto lens came into action.

"You're right," he said. "Feathers—beak—well up the evolutionary ladder. This place looks promising. I'll start the camera."

The swaying motion of the picture as the robot walked forward did not distract them: they had grown accustomed to it long ago. But they had never become reconciled to this exploration by proxy when all their impulses cried out to them to leave the ship, to run through the grass and to feel the wind blowing against their faces. Yet it was too great a risk to take, even on a world that seemed as fair as this. There was always a skull hidden behind Nature's most smiling face. Wild beasts, poisonous reptiles, quagmires—death could come to the unwary explorer in a thousand disguises. And worst of all were the invisible enemies, the bacteria and viruses against which the only defense might often be a thousand light-years away.

A robot could laugh at all these dangers and even if, as sometimes happened, it encountered a beast powerful enough to destroy it—well, machines could always be replaced.

They met nothing on the walk across the grasslands. If any small animals were disturbed by the robot's passage, they kept outside its field of vision. Clindar slowed the machine as it approached the trees, and the watchers in the spaceship flinched involuntarily at the branches that appeared to slash across their eyes. The picture dimmed for a moment before the controls readjusted themselves to the weaker illumination; then it came back to normal.

The forest was full of life. It lurked in the undergrowth, clambered among the branches, flew through the air. It fled chattering and gibbering through the trees as the robot advanced. And all the while the automatic cameras were recording the pictures that formed on the screen, gathering material for the biologists to analyze when the ship returned to base.

Clindar breathed a sigh of relief when the trees suddenly thinned. It was exhausting work, keeping the robot from smashing into obstacles as it moved through the forest, but on open ground it could take care of itself. Then the picture trembled as if beneath a hammer blow, there was a grinding metallic thud, and the whole scene swept vertiginously upward as the robot toppled and fell.

"What's that?" cried Altman. "Did you trip?"

"No," said Clindar grimly, his fingers flying over the keyboard. "Something attacked from the rear. I hope . . . ah . . . I've still got control."

He brought the robot to a sitting position and swiveled its head. It did not take long to find the cause of the trouble. Standing a few feet away, and lashing its tail angrily, was a large quadruped with a most ferocious set of teeth. At the moment it was, fairly obviously, trying to decide whether to attack again.

Slowly, the robot rose to its feet, and as it did so the great beast crouched to spring. A smile flitted across Clindar's face: he knew how to deal with this situation. His thumb felt for the seldom-used key labeled "Siren."

The forest echoed with a hideous undulating scream from the robot's concealed speaker, and the machine advanced to meet its adversary, arms flailing in front of it. The startled beast almost fell over backward in its effort to turn, and in seconds was gone from sight.

"Now I suppose we'll have to wait a couple of hours until everything comes out of hiding again," said Bertrond ruefully.

"I don't know much about animal psychology," interjected Altman, "but is it usual for them to attack something completely unfamiliar?"

"Some will attack anything that moves, but that's unusual. Normally they attack only for food, or if they've already been threatened. What are you driving at? Do you suggest that there are other robots on this planet?"

"Certainly not. But our carnivorous friend may have mistaken our machine for a more edible biped. Don't you think that this opening in the jungle is rather unnatural? It could easily be a path."

"In that case," said Clindar promptly, "we'll follow it and find out. I'm tired of dodging trees, but I hope nothing jumps on us again: it's bad for my nerves."

"You were right, Altman," said Bertrond a little later. "It's certainly a path. But that doesn't mean intelligence. After all, animals—"

He stopped in mid-sentence, and at the same instant Clindar brought the advancing robot to a halt. The path had suddenly opened out into a wide clearing, almost completely occupied by a village of flimsy huts. It was ringed by a wooden palisade, obviously defense against an enemy who at the moment presented no threat. For the gates were wide open, and beyond them the inhabitants were going peacefully about their ways.

For many minutes the three explorers stared in silence at the screen. Then Clindar shivered a little and remarked: "It's uncanny. It might be our own planet, a hundred thousand years ago. I feel as if I've gone back in time."

"There's nothing weird about it," said the practical Altman. "After all, we've discovered nearly a hundred planets with our type of life on them."

"Yes," retorted Clindar. "A hundred in the whole Galaxy! I still think it's strange it had to happen to us."

"Well, it had to happen to *somebody*," said Bertrond philosophically. "Meanwhile, we must work out our contact procedure. If we send the robot into the village it will start a panic."

"That," said Altman, "is a masterly understatement. What we'll have to do is catch a native by himself and prove that we're friendly. Hide the robot, Clindar. Somewhere in the woods where it can watch the village without being spotted. We've a week's practical anthropology ahead of us!"

It was three days before the biological tests showed that it would be safe to leave the ship. Even then Bertrond insisted on going alone—alone, that is, if one ignored the substantial company of the robot. With such an ally he was not afraid of this planet's larger beasts, and his body's natural defenses could take care of the microorganisms. So, at least, the analyzers had assured him; and considering the complexity of the problem, they made remarkably few mistakes. . . .

He stayed outside for an hour, enjoying himself cautiously, while his companions watched with envy. It would be another three days before they could be quite certain that it was safe to follow Bertrond's example. Meanwhile, they kept busy enough watching the village through the lenses of the robot, and recording everything they could with the cameras. They had moved the spaceship at night so that it was hidden in the depths of the forest, for they did not wish to be discovered until they were ready.

And all the while the news from home grew worse. Though their remoteness here at the edge of the Universe deadened its impact, it lay heavily on their minds and sometimes overwhelmed them with a sense of futility. At any moment, they knew, the signal for recall might come as the Empire summoned up its last resources in its extremity. But until then they would continue their work as though pure knowledge were the only thing that mattered.

Seven days after landing, they were ready to make the experiment. They knew now what paths the villagers used when going hunting, and Bertrond chose one of the less frequented ways. Then he placed a chair firmly in the middle of the path and settled down to read a book.

It was not, of course, quite as simple as that: Bertrond had taken all imaginable precautions. Hidden in the undergrowth fifty yards away, the robot was watching through its telescopic lenses, and in its hand it held a small but deadly weapon. Controlling it from the spaceship, his fingers poised over the keyboard, Clindar waited to do what might be necessary.

That was the negative side of the plan: the positive side was more obvious. Lying at Bertrond's feet was the carcass of a small, horned animal which he hoped would be an acceptable gift to any hunter passing this way.

Two hours later the radio in his suit harness whispered a warning. Quite calmly, though the blood was pounding in his veins, Bertrond laid aside his book and looked down the trail. The savage was walking forward confidently enough, swinging a spear in his right hand. He paused for a moment when he saw Bertrond, then advanced more cautiously. He could tell that there was nothing to fear, for the stranger was slightly built and obviously unarmed.

When only twenty feet separated them, Bertrond gave a reassuring smile and rose slowly to his feet. He bent down, picked up the carcass, and carried it forward as an offering. The gesture would have been understood by any creature on any world, and it was understood here. The savage reached forward, took the animal, and threw it effortlessly over his shoulder. For an instant he stared into Bertrond's eyes with a fathomless expression; then he turned and walked back toward the village. Three times he glanced round to see if Bertrond was following, and each time Bertrond smiled and waved reassurance. The whole episode lasted little more than a minute. As the first contact between two races it was completely without drama, though not without dignity.

Bertrond did not move until the other had vanished from sight. Then he relaxed and spoke into his suit microphone.

"That was a pretty good beginning," he said jubilantly. "He wasn't in the least frightened, or even suspicious. I think he'll be back."

"It still seems too good to be true," said Altman's voice in his ear. "I should have thought he'd have been either scared or hostile. Would *you* have accepted a lavish gift from a peculiar stranger with such little fuss?"

Bertrond was slowly walking back to the ship. The robot had now come out of cover and was keeping guard a few paces behind him.

"*I* wouldn't," he replied, "but I belong to a civilized community. Complete savages may react to strangers in many different ways, according to their past experience. Suppose this tribe has never had any enemies. That's quite possible on a large but sparsely populated planet. Then we may expect curiosity, but no fear at all."

"If these people have no enemies," put in Clindar, no longer fully occupied in controlling the robot, "why have they got a stockade round the village?"

"I meant no *human* enemies," replied Bertrond. "If that's true, it simplifies our task immensely."

"Do you think he'll come back?"

"Of course. If he's as human as I think, curiosity and greed will make him return. In a couple of days we'll be bosom friends."

Looked at dispassionately, it became a fantastic routine. Every morning the robot would go hunting under Clindar's direction, until it was now the deadliest killer in the jungle. Then Bertrond would wait until Yaan—which was the nearest they could get to his name—came striding confidently along the path. He came at the same time every day, and he always came alone. They wondered about this: did he wish to keep his great discovery to himself and thus get all the credit for his hunting prowess? If so, it showed unexpected foresight and cunning.

At first Yaan had departed at once with his prize, as if afraid that the donor of such a generous gift might change his mind. Soon, however, as Bertrond had hoped, he could be induced to stay for a while by simple conjuring tricks and a display of brightly colored fabrics and crystals, in which he took a childlike delight. At last Bertrond was able to engage him in lengthy conversations, all of which were recorded as well as being filmed through the eyes of the hidden robot.

One day the philologists might be able to analyze this material; the best that Bertrond could do was to discover the meanings of a few simple verbs and nouns. This was made more difficult by the fact that Yaan not only used different words for the same thing, but sometimes the same word for different things.

Between these daily interviews, the ship traveled far, surveying the planet from the air and sometimes landing for more detailed examinations. Although several other human settlements were observed, Bertrond made no attempt to get in touch with them, for it was easy to see that they were all at much the same cultural level as Yaan's people.

It was, Bertrond often thought, a particularly bad joke on the part of Fate that one of the Galaxy's very few truly human races should have been discovered at this moment of time. Not long ago this would have been an event of supreme importance; now civilization was too hard-pressed to concern itself with these savage cousins waiting at the dawn of history.

Not until Bertrond was sure he had become part of Yaan's everyday life did he introduce him to the robot. He was showing Yaan the patterns in a kaleidoscope when Clindar brought the machine striding through the grass with its latest victim dangling across one metal arm. For the first time Yaan showed something akin to fear; but he relaxed at Bertrond's soothing words, though he continued to watch the advancing monster. It halted some distance away, and Bertrond walked forward to meet it. As he did so, the robot raised its arms and handed him the dead beast. He took it solemnly and carried it back to Yaan, staggering a little under the unaccustomed load.

Bertrond would have given a great deal to know just what Yaan was thinking as he accepted the gift. Was he trying to decide whether the robot was master or slave? Perhaps such conceptions as this were beyond his grasp: to him the robot might be merely another man, a hunter who was a friend of Bertrond.

Clindar's voice, slightly larger than life, came from the robot's speaker.

"It's astonishing how calmly he accepts us. Won't anything scare him?"

"You will keep judging him by your own standards," replied Bertrond. "Remember, his psychology is completely different, and much simpler. Now that he has confidence in me, anything that I accept won't worry him."

"I wonder if that will be true of all his race?" queried Altman. "It's hardly safe to judge by a single specimen. I want to see what happens when we send the robot into the village."

"Hello!" exclaimed Bertrond. *"That* surprised him. He's never met a person who could speak with two voices before."

"Do you think he'll guess the truth when he meets us?" said Clindar.

"No. The robot will be pure magic to him—but it won't be any more wonderful than fire and lightning and all the other forces he must already take for granted."

"Well, what's the next move?" asked Altman, a little impatiently. "Are you going to bring him to the ship, or will you go into the village first?"

Bertrond hesitated. "I'm anxious not to do too much too quickly. You know the accidents that have happened with strange races when that's been tried. I'll let him think this over, and when we get back tomorrow I'll try to persuade him to take the robot back to the village."

In the hidden ship, Clindar reactivated the robot and started it moving again. Like Altman, he was growing a little impatient of this excessive caution, but on all matters relating to alien life-forms Bertrond was the expert, and they had to obey his orders.

There were times now when he almost wished he were a robot himself, devoid of feelings or emotions, able to watch the fall of a leaf or the death agonies of a world with equal detachment. . . .

The sun was low when Yaan heard the great voice crying from the jungle. He recognized it at once, despite its inhuman volume: it was the voice of his friend, and it was calling him.

In the echoing silence, the life of the village came to a stop. Even the children ceased their play: the only sound was the thin cry of a baby frightened by the sudden silence.

All eyes were upon Yaan as he walked swiftly to his hut and grasped the spear that lay beside the entrance. The stockade would soon be closed against the prowlers of the night, but he did not hesitate as he stepped out into the lengthening shadows. He was passing through the gates when once again that mighty voice summoned him, and now it held a note of urgency that came clearly across all the barriers of language and culture.

The shining giant who spoke with many voices met him a little way from the village and beckoned him to follow. There was no sign of Bertrond. They walked for almost a mile before they saw him in the distance, standing not far from the river's edge and staring out across the dark, slowly moving waters.

He turned as Yaan approached, yet for a moment seemed unaware of his presence. Then he gave a gesture of dismissal to the shining one, who withdrew into the distance.

Yaan waited. He was patient and, though he could never have expressed it in words, contented. When he was with Bertrond he felt the first intimations of that selfless, utterly irrational devotion his race would not fully achieve for many ages.

It was a strange tableau. Here at the river's brink two

men were standing. One was dressed in a closely fitting uniform equipped with tiny, intricate mechanisms. The other was wearing the skin of an animal and was carrying a flint-tipped spear. Ten thousand generations lay between them, ten thousand generations and an immeasurable gulf of space. Yet they were both human. As she must do often in Eternity, Nature had repeated one of her basic patterns.

Presently Bertrond began to speak, walking to and fro in short, quick steps as he did, and in his voice there was a trace of madness.

"It's all over, Yaan. I'd hoped that with our knowledge we could have brought you out of barbarism in a dozen generations, but now you will have to fight your way up from the jungle alone, and it may take you a million years to do so. I'm sorry—there's so much we could have done. Even now I want to stay here, but Altman and Clindar talk of duty, and I suppose that they are right. There is little enough that we can do, but our world is calling and we must not forsake it.

"I wish you could understand me, Yaan. I wish you knew what I was saying. I'm leaving you these tools: some of them you will discover how to use, though as likely as not in a generation they'll be lost or forgotten. See how this blade cuts: it will be ages before your world can make its like. And guard this well: when you press the button—look! If you use it sparingly, it will give you light for years, though sooner or later it will die. As for these other things—find what use for them you can.

"Here come the first stars, up there in the east. Do you ever look at the stars, Yaan? I wonder how long it will be before you have discovered what they are, and I wonder what will have happened to us by then. Those stars are our homes, Yaan, and we cannot save them. Many have died already, in explosions so vast that I can imagine them no more than you. In a hundred thousand of your years, the light of those funeral pyres will reach your world and set its peoples wondering. By then, perhaps, your race will be reaching for the stars. I wish I could warn you against the mistakes we made, and which now will cost us all that we have won.

"It is well for your people, Yaan, that your world is here at the frontier of the Universe. You may escape the doom that waits for us. One day, perhaps, your ships will go searching among the stars as we have done, and they may come upon the ruins of our worlds and wonder who we were. But they will never know that we met here by this river when your race was young.

"Here come my friends; they would give me no more time. Good-by, Yaan—use well the things I have left you. They are your world's greatest treasures."

Something huge, something that glittered in the starlight, was sliding down from the sky. It did not reach the ground, but came to rest a little way above the surface, and in utter silence a rectangle of light opened in its side. The shining giant appeared out of the night and stepped through the golden door. Bertrond followed, pausing for a moment at the threshold to wave back at Yaan. Then the darkness closed behind him.

No more swiftly than smoke drifts upward from a fire, the ship lifted away. When it was so small that Yaan felt he could hold it in his hands, it seemed to blur into a long line of light slanting upward into the stars. From the empty sky a peal of thunder echoed over the sleeping land; and Yaan knew at last that the gods were gone and would never come again.

For a long time he stood by the gently moving waters, and into his soul there came a sense of loss he was never to forget and never to understand. Then, carefully and reverently, he collected together the gifts that Bertrond had left.

Under the stars, the lonely figure walked homeward across a nameless land. Behind him the river flowed softly to the sea, winding through the fertile plains on which, more than a thousand centuries ahead, Yaan's descendants would build the great city they were to call Babylon.

London   *November 1950*

PATENT PENDING

THERE ARE NO subjects that have not been discussed, at some time or other, in the saloon bar of the "White Hart"—and whether or not there are ladies present makes no difference whatsoever. After all, they came in at their own risk. Three of them, now I come to think of it, have eventually gone out again with husbands. So perhaps the risk isn't on their side at all. . . .

I mention this because I would not like you to think that all our conversations are highly erudite and scientific, and our activities purely cerebral. Though chess is rampant, darts and shove-ha'penny also flourish. The *Times Literary Supplement,* the *Saturday Review,* the *New Statesman,* and the *Atlantic Monthly* may be brought in by some of the customers, but the same people are quite likely to leave with the latest issue of *Staggering Stories of Pseudoscience.*

A great deal of business also goes on in the obscurer corners of the pub. Copies of antique books and magazines frequently change hands at astronomical prices, and on almost any Wednesday at least three well-known dealers may be seen smoking large cigars as they lean over the bar, swapping stories with Drew. From time to time a vast guffaw announces the denouement of some anecdote and provokes a flood of anxious inquiries from patrons who are afraid they may have missed something. But, alas, delicacy forbids that I should repeat any of these interesting tales here. Unlike most things in this island, they are not for export. . . .

Luckily, no such restrictions apply to the tales of Mr. Harry Purvis, B.Sc. (at least), Ph.D. (probably), F.R.S. (personally I don't think so, though it *has* been rumored). None of them would bring a blush to the cheeks of the most delicately nurtured maiden aunts, should any still survive in these days.

I must apologize. This is too sweeping a statement. There was one story which might, in some circles, be regarded as a little daring. Yet I do not hesitate to repeat it, for I know that you, dear reader, will be sufficiently broad-minded to take no offense.

It started in this fashion. A celebrated Fleet Street reviewer had been pinned into a corner by a persuasive publisher, who was about to bring out a book of which he had high hopes. It was one of the riper productions of the deep and decadent South—a prime example of the "and-then-the-house-gave-another-lurch-as-the-termites-finished-the-east-wing" school of fiction. Eire had already banned it, but that is an honor which few books escape nowadays, and certainly could not be considered a distinction. However, if a leading British newspaper could be induced to make a stern call for its suppression, it would become a best seller overnight. . . .

Such was the logic of its publisher, and he was using all his wiles to induce co-operation. I heard him remark, apparently to allay any scruples his reviewer friend might have, "Of course not! If they can understand it, they *can't* be corrupted any further!" And then Harry Purvis, who has an uncanny knack of following half a dozen conversations simultaneously, so that he can insert himself in the right one at the right time, said in his peculiarly penetrating and noninterruptable voice: "Censorship does raise some very difficult problems doesn't it? I've always argued that there's an inverse correlation between a country's degree of civilization and the restraints it puts on its press."

A New England voice from the back of the room cut in: "On *that* argument, Paris is a more civilized place than Boston."

"Precisely," answered Purvis. For once, he waited for a reply.

"OK," said the New England voice mildly. "I'm not arguing. I just wanted to check."

"To continue," said Purvis, wasting no more time in doing so, "I'm reminded of a matter which has not yet concerned the censor, but which will certainly do so before long. It began in France, and so far has remained there. When it *does* come out into the open, it may have a greater impact on our civilization than the atom bomb.

"Like the atom bomb, it arose out of equally academic research. *Never,* gentlemen, underestimate science. I doubt if there is a single field of study so theoretical, so remote from what is laughingly called everyday life, that it may not one day produce something that will shake the world.

"You will appreciate that the story I am telling you is, for once in a while, secondhand. I got it from a colleague at the Sorbonne last year while I was over there at a scientific conference. So the names are all fictitious: I was told them at the time, but I can't remember them now.

"Professor—ah—Julian was an experimental physiologist at one of the smaller, but less impecunious, French universities. Some of you may remember that rather unlikely tale we heard here the other week from that fellow Hinckelberg, about his colleague who'd learned how to control the behavior of animals through feeding the correct currents into their nervous systems. Well, if there *was* any truth in that story—and frankly I doubt it—the whole project was probably inspired by Julian's papers in *Comptes Rendus.*

"Professor Julian, however, never published his most remarkable results. When you stumble on something which is really terrific, you don't rush into print. You wait until you have overwhelming evidence—unless you're afraid that someone else is hot on the track. Then you may issue an ambiguous report that will establish your priority at a later date, without giving too much away at the moment—like the famous cryptogram that Huygens put out when he detected the rings of Saturn.

"You may well wonder what Julian's discovery was, so I

won't keep you in suspense. It was simply the natural extension of what man has been doing for the last hundred years. First the camera gave us the power to capture scenes. Then Edison invented the phonograph, and sound was mastered. Today, in the talking film, we have a kind of mechanical memory which would be inconceivable to our forefathers. But surely the matter cannot rest there. Eventually science must be able to catch and store thoughts and sensations themselves, and feed them back into the mind so that, whenever it wishes, it can repeat any experience in life, down to its minutest detail."

"That's an old idea!" snorted someone. "See the 'feelies' in *Brave New World*."

"All good ideas have been thought of by somebody before they are realized," said Purvis severely. "The point is that what Huxley and others had talked about, Julian actually did. My goodness, there's a pun there! Aldous—Julian —oh, let it pass!

"It was done electronically, of course. You all know how the encephalograph can record the minute electrical impulses in the living brain—the so-called 'brain waves,' as the popular press calls them. Julian's device was a much subtler elaboration of this well-known instrument. And, having recorded cerebral impulses, he could play them back again. It sounds simple, doesn't it? So was the phonograph, but it took the genius of Edison to think of it.

"And now, enter the villain. Well, perhaps that's too strong a word, for Professor Julian's assistant Georges— Georges Dupin—is really quite a sympathetic character. It was just that, being a Frenchman of a more practical turn of mind than the Professor, he saw at once that there were some milliards of francs involved in this laboratory toy.

"The first thing was to get it out of the laboratory. The French have an undoubted flair for elegant engineering, and after some weeks of work—with the full co-operation of the Professor—Georges had managed to pack the "playback" side of the apparatus into a cabinet no larger than a television set, and containing not very many more parts.

"Then Georges was ready to make his first experiment. It would involve considerable expense, but, as someone so rightly remarked, you cannot make omelettes without breaking eggs. And the analogy is, if I may say so, an exceedingly apt one.

"For Georges went to see the most famous gourmet in France, and made an interesting proposition. It was one that the great man could not refuse, because it was so unique a tribute to his eminence. Georges explained patiently that he had invented a device for registering (he said nothing about storing) sensations. In the cause of science, and for the honor of the French cuisine, could he be privileged to analyze the emotions, the subtle nuances of gustatory discrimination, that took place in Monsieur le Baron's mind when he employed his unsurpassed talents? Monsieur could name the restaurant, the chef, and the menu—everything would be arranged for his convenience. Of course, if he was too busy, no doubt that well-known epicure Le Comte de—

"The Baron, who was in some respects a surprisingly coarse man, uttered a word not to be found in most French dictionaries. 'That cretin!' he exploded. 'He would be happy on English cooking! No, *I* shall do it.' And forthwith he sat down to compose the menu, while Georges anxiously estimated the cost of the items and wondered if his bank balance would stand the strain. . . .

"It would be interesting to know what the chef and the waiters thought about the whole business. There was the Baron, seated at his favorite table and doing full justice to his favorite dishes, not in the least inconvenienced by the tangle of wires that trailed from his head to that diabolical-looking machine in the corner. The restaurant was empty of all other occupants, for the last thing Georges wanted was premature publicity. This had added very considerably to the already distressing cost of the experiment. He could only hope that the results would be worth it.

"They were. The only way of *proving* that, of course, would be to play back Georges's 'recording.' We have to take his word for it, since the utter inadequacy of words in such matters is all too well known. The Baron *was* a genuine connoisseur, not one of those who merely pretend to powers of discrimination they do not possess. You know Thurber's 'Only a naïve domestic Burgundy, but I think you'll admire its presumption.' The Baron would have known at the first sniff whether it was domestic or not—and if it had been presumptuous he'd have smacked it down.

"I gather that Georges had his money's worth out of that recording, even though he had not intended it merely for personal use. It opened up new worlds to him, and clarified the ideas that had been forming in his ingenious brain. There was no doubt about it: all the exquisite sensations that had passed through the Baron's mind during the consumption of that Lucullan repast had been captured, so that anyone else, however untrained they might be in such matters, could savor them to the full. For, you see, the recording dealt purely with emotions: intelligence did not come into the picture at all. The Baron needed a lifetime of knowledge and training before he could *experience* these sensations. But once they were down on tape, anyone, even if in real life he had no sense of taste at all, could take over from there.

"Think of the glowing vistas that opened up before Georges's eyes! There were other meals, other gourmets. There were the collected impressions of all the vintages of Europe—what would connoisseurs not pay for them? When the last bottle of a rare wine had been broached, its incorporeal essence could be preserved, as the voice of Melba can travel down the centuries. For, after all, it was not the wine itself that mattered, but the sensations it evoked. . . .

"So mused Georges. But this, he knew, was only a beginning. The French claim to logic I have often disputed, but in Georges's case it cannot be denied. He thought the matter over for a few days: then he went to see his *petite dame.*

" 'Yvonne, *ma chérie,*' he said, 'I have a somewhat unusual request to make of you. . . .' "

Harry Purvis knew when to break off in a story. He turned to the bar and called, "Another Scotch, Drew." No one said a word while it was provided.

"To continue," said Purvis, at length, "the experiment, unusual though it was, even in France, was successfully carried out. As both discretion and custom demanded, all was arranged in the lonely hours of the night. You will have gathered already that Georges was a persuasive person, though I doubt if Mam'selle needed much persuading.

"Stifling her curiosity with a sincere but hasty kiss, Georges saw Yvonne out of the lab and rushed back to his apparatus. Breathlessly, he ran through the playback. It worked—not that he had ever had any real doubts. Moreover—do please remember I have only my informant's word for this—it was indistinguishable from the real thing. At that moment something approaching religious awe overcame Georges. This was, without a doubt, the greatest invention in history. He would be immortal as well as wealthy, for he had achieved something of which all men had dreamed, and had robbed old age of one of its terrors. . . .

"He also realized that he could now dispense with Yvonne, if he so wished. This raised implications that would require further thought. *Much* further thought.

"You will, of course, appreciate that I am giving you a highly condensed account of events. While all this was going on, Georges was still working as a loyal employee of the Professor, who suspected nothing. As yet, indeed, Georges had done little more than any research worker might have in similar circumstances. His performances had been somewhat beyond the call of duty, but could all be explained away if need be.

"The next step would involve some very delicate negotiations and the expenditure of further hard-won francs. Georges now had all the material he needed to prove, beyond a shadow of doubt, that he was handling a very valuable commercial property. There were shrewd businessmen in Paris who would jump at the opportunity. Yet a certain delicacy, for which we must give him full credit, restrained Georges from using his second—er—recording as a sample of the wares his machine could purvey. There was no way of disguising the personalities involved, and Georges was a modest man. 'Besides,' he argued, again with great good sense, 'when the gramophone company wishes to make a *disque,* it does not enregister the performance of some amateur musician. *That* is a matter for professionals. And so, *ma foi,* is *this.*' Whereupon, after a further call at his bank, he set forth again for Paris.

"He did not go anywhere near the Place Pigalle, because that was full of Americans and prices were accordingly exorbitant. Instead, a few discreet inquiries and some understanding cab drivers took him to an almost oppressively respectable suburb, where he presently found himself in a pleasant waiting room, by no means as exotic as might have been supposed.

"And there, somewhat embarrassed, Georges explained his mission to a formidable lady whose age one could have no more guessed than her profession. Used though she was to unorthodox requests, *this* was something she had never encountered in all her considerable experience. But the customer was always right, as long as he had the cash, and so in due course everything was arranged. One of the young ladies and her boy friend, an apache of somewhat overwhelming masculinity, traveled back with Georges to the provinces. At first they were, naturally, somewhat suspicious, but as Georges had already found, no expert can ever resist flattery. Soon they were all on excellent terms. Hercule and Susette promised Georges that they would give him every cause for satisfaction.

"No doubt some of you would be glad to have further details, but you can scarcely expect me to supply them. All I can say is that Georges—or, rather, his instrument—was kept very busy, and that by the morning little of the recording material was left unused. For it seems that Hercule was indeed appropriately named. . . .

"When this piquant episode was finished, Georges had very little money left, but he did possess two recordings that were quite beyond price. Once more he set off to Paris, where, with practically no trouble, he came to terms with some businessmen who were so astonished that they gave him a very generous contract before coming to their senses. I am pleased to report this, because so often the scientist emerges second best in his dealings with the world of finance. I'm equally pleased to record that Georges had made provision for Professor Julian in the contract. You may say cynically that it was, after all, the Professor's invention, and that sooner or later Georges would have had to square him. But I like to think that there was more to it than that.

"The full details of the scheme for exploiting the device are, of course, unknown to me. I gather that Georges had been expansively eloquent—not that much eloquence was needed to convince anyone who had once experienced one or both of his playbacks. The market would be enormous, unlimited. The export trade alone could put France on her feet again and would wipe out her dollar deficit overnight—once certain snags had been overcome. Everything would have to be managed through somewhat clandestine channels, for think of the hubbub from the hypocritical Anglo-Saxons when they discovered just what was being imported into their countries. The Mothers' Union, the Daughters of the American Revolution, the Housewives League, and *all* the religious organizations would rise as one. The lawyers were looking into the matter very carefully, and as far as could be seen the regulations that still excluded *Tropic of Capricorn* from the mails of the English-speaking countries could not be applied to this case—for the simple reason that no one had thought of it. But there would be such a shout for new laws that Parliament and Congress would have to do something, so it was best to keep under cover as long as possible.

"In fact, as one of the directors pointed out, if the recordings were banned, so much the better. They could make much more money on a smaller output, because the price would promptly soar and all the vigilance of the customs officials couldn't block every leak. It would be Prohibition all over again.

"You will scarcely be surprised to hear that by this time Georges had somewhat lost interest in the gastronomical angle. It was an interesting but definitely minor possibility of the invention. Indeed, this had been tacitly admitted by the directors as they drew up the articles of association, for they had included the pleasures of the cuisine among 'subsidiary rights.'

"Georges returned home with his head in the clouds, and a substantial check in his pocket. A charming fancy had struck his imagination. He thought of all the trouble to which the gramophone companies had gone to so that the world might have the complete recordings of the forty-eight preludes and fugues or the nine symphonies. Well, *his* new company would put out a complete and definite set of recordings, performed by experts versed in the most esoteric knowledge of East and West. How many opus numbers would be required? That, of course, had been a subject of profound debate for some thousands of years. The Hindu textbooks, Georges had heard, got well into three figures. It would be a most interesting research, combining profit with pleasure in an unexampled manner. . . . He had already begun some preliminary studies, using treatises which even in Paris were none too easy to obtain.

"If you think that while all this was going on, Georges had neglected his usual interests, you are all too right. He was working literally night and day, for he had not yet revealed his plans to the Professor and almost everything had to be done when the lab was closed. And one of the interests he had had to neglect was Yvonne.

"Her curiosity had already been aroused, as any girl's would have been. But now she was more than intrigued—she was distracted. For Georges had become so remote and cold. He was no longer in love with her.

"It was a result that might have been anticipated. Publicans have to guard against the danger of sampling their own wares too often—I'm sure *you* don't, Drew—and Georges had fallen into this seductive trap. He had been through that recording too many times, with somewhat debilitating results. Moreover, poor Yvonne was not to be compared with the experienced and talented Susette. It was the old story of the professional versus the amateur.

"All that Yvonne knew was that Georges was in love with someone else. That was true enough. She suspected that he had been unfaithful to her. And *that* raises profound philosophical questions we can hardly go into here.

"This being France, in case you had forgotten, the outcome was inevitable. Poor Georges! He was working late one night at the lab, as usual, when Yvonne finished him off with one of those ridiculous ornamental pistols which are *de rigueur* for such occasions. Let us drink to his memory."

"That's the trouble with all your stories," said John Beynon. "You tell us about wonderful inventions, and then at the end it turns out that the discoverer was killed, so no one can do anything about it. For I suppose, as usual, the apparatus was destroyed?"

"But no," replied Purvis. "Apart from Georges, this is one of the stories that has a happy ending. There was no trouble at all about Yvonne, of course. Georges's grieving sponsors arrived on the scene with great speed and prevented any adverse publicity. Being men of sentiment as well as men of business, they realized that they would have to secure Yvonne's freedom. They promptly did this by playing the recording to *le Maire* and *le Préfet*, thus convincing them that the poor girl had experienced irresistible provocation. A few shares in the new company clinched the deal, with expressions of the utmost cordiality on both sides. Yvonne even got her gun back."

"Then when—" began someone else.

"Ah, these things take time. There's the question of mass production, you know. It's quite possible that distribution has already commenced through private—*very* private—channels. Some of those dubious little shops and notice boards around Leicester Square may soon start giving hints."

"Of course," said the New England voice disrespectfully, "you wouldn't know the *name* of the company."

You can't help admiring Purvis at times like this. He scarcely hesitated.

"Le Société Anonyme d'Aphrodite," he replied. "And I've just remembered something that will cheer *you* up. They hope to get round your sticky mails regulations and establish themselves before the inevitable congressional inquiry starts. They're opening up a branch in Nevada: apparently you can still get away with anything there." He raised his glass.

"To Georges Dupin," he said solemnly. "Martyr to science. Remember him when the fireworks start. And one other thing—"

"Yes?" we all asked.

"Better start saving now. And sell your TV sets before the bottom drops out of the market."

London   *January 1953*

THE SENTINEL

"The Sentinel" is the foundation upon which Stanley Kubrick and I later erected "2001: A Space Odyssey." In the years since this story was originally published, a number of scientists—e.g., Carl Sagan—have started to take the basic concept quite seriously.

Perhaps the real science of exoarchaeology will be born when we reach the Moon, or perhaps it is waiting for us on Mars, as suggested in "Trouble with Time." The odds are all against it—but the possible prizes are so great that there are few better reasons for exploring space.

If there is nothing like the "Sentinel" anywhere in the Solar System—there should be.

THE NEXT TIME you see the full Moon high in the south, look carefully at its right-hand edge and let your eye travel upward along the curve of the disk. Round about two o'clock you will notice a small, dark oval: anyone with normal eyesight can find it quite easily. It is the great walled plain, one of the finest on the Moon, known as the Mare

Crisium—the Sea of Crises. Three hundred miles in diameter, and almost completely surrounded by a ring of magnificent mountains, it had never been explored until we entered it in the late summer of 1996.

Our expedition was a large one. We had two heavy freighters which had flown our supplies and equipment from the main lunar base in the Mare Serenitatis, five hundred miles away. There were also three small rockets which were intended for short-range transport over regions which our surface vehicles couldn't cross. Luckily, most of the Mare Crisium is very flat. There are none of the great crevasses so common and so dangerous elsewhere, and very few craters or mountains of any size. As far as we could tell, our powerful caterpillar tractors would have no difficulty in taking us wherever we wished to go.

I was geologist—or selenologist, if you want to be pedantic—in charge of the group exploring the southern region of the Mare. We had crossed a hundred miles of it in a week, skirting the foothills of the mountains along the shore of what was once the ancient sea, some thousand million years before. When life was beginning on Earth, it was already dying here. The waters were retreating down the flanks of those stupendous cliffs, retreating into the empty heart of the Moon. Over the land which we were crossing, the tideless ocean had once been half a mile deep, and now the only trace of moisture was the hoarfrost one could sometimes find in caves which the searing sunlight never penetrated.

We had begun our journey early in the slow lunar dawn, and still had almost a week of Earth time before nightfall. Half a dozen times a day we would leave our vehicle and go outside in the space suits to hunt for interesting minerals, or to place markers for the guidance of future travelers. It was an uneventful routine. There is nothing hazardous or even particularly exciting about lunar exploration. We could live comfortably for a month in our pressurized tractors, and if we ran into trouble we could always radio for help and sit tight until one of the spaceships came to our rescue.

I said just now that there was nothing exciting about lunar exploration, but of course that isn't true. One could never grow tired of those incredible mountains, so much more rugged than the gentle hills of Earth. We never knew, as we rounded the capes and promontories of that vanished sea, what new splendors would be revealed to us. The whole southern curve of the Mare Crisium is a vast delta where a score of rivers once found their way into the ocean, fed perhaps by the torrential rains that must have lashed the mountains in the brief volcanic age when the Moon was young. Each of these ancient valleys was an invitation, challenging us to climb into the unknown uplands beyond. But we had a hundred miles still to cover, and could only look longingly at the heights which others must scale.

We kept Earth time aboard the tractor, and precisely at 22.00 hours the final radio message would be sent out to Base and we would close down for the day. Outside, the rocks would still be burning beneath the almost vertical sun, but to us it was night until we awoke again eight hours later. Then one of us would prepare breakfast, there would be a great buzzing of electric razors, and someone would switch on the short-wave radio from Earth. Indeed, when the smell of frying sausages began to fill the cabin, it was sometimes hard to believe that we were not back on our own world—everything was so normal and homely, apart from the feeling of decreased weight and the unnatural slowness with which objects fell.

It was my turn to prepare breakfast in the corner of the main cabin that served as a galley. I can remember that moment quite vividly after all these years, for the radio had just played one of my favorite melodies, the old Welsh air "David of the White Rock." Our driver was already outside in his space suit, inspecting our caterpillar treads. My assistant, Louis Garnett, was up forward in the control position, making some belated entries in yesterday's log.

As I stood by the frying pan waiting, like any terrestrial housewife, for the sausages to brown, I let my gaze wander idly over the mountain walls which covered the whole of the southern horizon, marching out of sight to east and west below the curve of the Moon. They seemed only a mile or two from the tractor, but I knew that the nearest was twenty miles away. On the Moon, of course, there is no loss of detail with distance—none of that almost imperceptible haziness which softens and sometimes transfigures all far-off things on Earth.

Those mountains were ten thousand feet high, and they climbed steeply out of the plain as if ages ago some subterranean eruption had smashed them skyward through the molten crust. The base of even the nearest was hidden from sight by the steeply curving surface of the plain, for the Moon is a very little world, and from where I was standing the horizon was only two miles away.

I lifted my eyes toward the peaks which no man had ever climbed, the peaks which, before the coming of terrestrial life, had watched the retreating oceans sink sullenly into their graves, taking with them the hope and the morning promise of a world. The sunlight was beating against those ramparts with a glare that hurt the eyes, yet only a little way above them the stars were shining steadily in a sky blacker than a winter midnight on Earth.

I was turning away when my eye caught a metallic glitter high on the ridge of a great promontory thrusting out into the sea thirty miles to the west. It was a dimensionless point of light, as if a star had been clawed from the sky by one of those cruel peaks, and I imagined that some smooth rock surface was catching the sunlight and heliographing it straight into my eyes. Such things were not uncommon. When the Moon is in her second quarter, observers on Earth can sometimes see the great ranges in the Oceanus Procellarum burning with a blue-white iridescence as the sunlight flashes from their slopes and leaps again from world to world. But I was curious to know what kind of rock could be shining so brightly up there, and I climbed into the observation turret and swung our four-inch telescope round to the west.

I could see just enough to tantalize me. Clear and sharp in the field of vision, the mountain peaks seemed only half a mile away, but whatever was catching the sunlight was still too small to be resolved. Yet it seemed to have an elusive symmetry, and the summit upon which it rested was curiously flat. I stared for a long time at that glittering enigma, straining my eyes into space, until presently a smell of burning from the galley told me that our breakfast sausages had made their quarter-million-mile journey in vain.

All that morning we argued our way across the Mare Crisium while the western mountains reared higher in the sky. Even when we were out prospecting in the space suits, the discussion would continue over the radio. It was absolutely certain, my companions argued, that there had never been any form of intelligent life on the Moon. The only living things that had ever existed there were a few primitive plants and their slightly less degenerate ancestors. I knew that as well as anyone, but there are times when a scientist must not be afraid to make a fool of himself.

"Listen," I said at last, "I'm going up there, if only for my own peace of mind. That mountain's less than twelve thousand feet high—that's only two thousand under Earth gravity—and I can make the trip in twenty hours at the outside. I've always wanted to go up into those hills, anyway, and this gives me an excellent excuse."

"If you don't break your neck," said Garnett, "you'll be the laughingstock of the expedition when we get back to Base. That mountain will probably be called Wilson's Folly from now on."

"I won't break my neck," I said firmly. "Who was the first man to climb Pico and Helicon?"

"But weren't you rather younger in those days?" asked Louis gently.

"That," I said with great dignity, "is as good a reason as any for going."

We went to bed early that night, after driving the tractor to within half a mile of the promontory. Garnett was coming with me in the morning; he was a good climber, and had often been with me on such exploits before. Our driver was only too glad to be left in charge of the machine.

At first sight, those cliffs seemed completely unscalable, but to anyone with a good head for heights, climbing is easy on a world where all weights are only a sixth of their normal value. The real danger in lunar mountaineering lies in over-confidence; a six-hundred-foot drop on the Moon can kill you just as thoroughly as a hundred-foot fall on Earth.

We made our first halt on a wide ledge about four thousand feet above the plain. Climbing had not been very difficult, but my limbs were stiff with the unaccustomed effort, and I was glad of the rest. We could still see the tractor as a tiny metal insect far down at the foot of the cliff, and we reported our progress to the driver before starting on the next ascent.

Inside our suits it was comfortably cool, for the refrigeration units were fighting the fierce sun and carrying away the body heat of our exertions. We seldom spoke to each other, except to pass climbing instructions and to discuss our best plan of ascent. I do not know what Garnett was thinking, probably that this was the craziest goose chase he had ever embarked upon. I more than half agreed with him, but the joy of climbing, the knowledge that no man had ever gone this way before and the exhilaration of the steadily widening landscape gave me all the reward I needed.

I don't think I was particularly excited when I saw in front of us the wall of rock I had first inspected through the telescope from thirty miles away. It would level off about fifty feet above our heads, and there on the plateau would be the thing that had lured me over these barren wastes. It was, almost certainly, nothing more than a boulder splintered ages ago by a falling meteor, and with its cleavage planes still fresh and bright in this incorruptible, unchanging silence.

There were no handholds on the rock face, and we had to use a grapnel. My tired arms seemed to gain new strength as I swung the three-pronged metal anchor round my head and sent it sailing up toward the stars. The first time it broke loose and came falling slowly back when we pulled the rope. On the third attempt, the prongs gripped firmly and our combined weights could not shift it.

Garnett looked at me anxiously. I could tell that he wanted to go first, but I smiled back at him through the glass of my helmet and shook my head. Slowly, taking my time, I began the final ascent.

Even with my space suit, I weighed only forty pounds here, so I pulled myself up hand over hand without bothering to use my feet. At the rim I paused and waved to my companion; then I scrambled over the edge and stood upright, staring ahead of me.

You must understand that until this very moment I had been almost completely convinced that there could be nothing strange or unusual for me to find here. Almost, but not quite; it was that haunting doubt that had driven me forward. Well, it was a doubt no longer, but the haunting had scarcely begun.

I was standing on a plateau perhaps a hundred feet across. It had once been smooth—too smooth to be natural —but falling meteors had pitted and scored its surface through immeasurable eons. It had been leveled to support a glittering, roughly pyramidal structure, twice as high as a man, that was set in the rock like a gigantic many-faceted jewel.

Probably no emotion at all filled my mind in those first few seconds. Then I felt a great lifting of my heart, and a strange, inexpressible joy. For I loved the Moon, and now I knew that the creeping moss of Aristarchus and Eratosthenes was not the only life she had brought forth in her youth. The old, discredited dream of the first explorers was true. There had, after all, been a lunar civilization—and I was the first to find it. That I had come perhaps a hundred million years too late did not distress me; it was enough to have come at all.

My mind was beginning to function normally, to analyze and to ask questions. Was this a building, a shrine—or something for which my language had no name? If a building, then why was it erected in so uniquely inaccessible a spot? I wondered if it might be a temple, and I could picture the adepts of some strange priesthood calling on their gods to preserve them as the life of the Moon ebbed with the dying oceans, and calling on their gods in vain.

I took a dozen steps forward to examine the thing more closely, but some sense of caution kept me from going too near. I knew a little of archaeology, and tried to guess the cultural level of the civilization that must have smoothed this mountain and raised the glittering mirror surfaces that still dazzled my eyes.

The Egyptians could have done it, I thought, if their workmen had possessed whatever strange materials these far more ancient architects had used. Because of the thing's smallness, it did not occur to me that I might be looking at the handiwork of a race more advanced than my own. The idea that the Moon had possessed intelligence at all was still almost too tremendous to grasp, and my pride would not let me take the final, humiliating plunge.

And then I noticed something that set the scalp crawling at the back of my neck—something so trivial and so innocent that many would never have noticed it at all. I have said that the plateau was scarred by meteors; it was also coated inches deep with the cosmic dust that is always filtering down upon the surface of any world where there are no winds to disturb it. Yet the dust and the meteor scratches ended quite abruptly in a wide circle enclosing the little pyramid, as though an invisible wall was protecting it from the ravages of time and the slow but ceaseless bombardment from space.

There was someone shouting in my earphones, and I realized that Garnett had been calling me for some time. I walked unsteadily to the edge of the cliff and signaled him to join me, not trusting myself to speak. Then I went back toward that circle in the dust. I picked up a fragment of splintered rock and tossed it gently toward the shining enigma. If the pebble had vanished at that invisible barrier I should not have been surprised, but it seemed to hit a smooth, hemispherical surface and slide gently to the ground.

I knew then that I was looking at nothing that could be matched in the antiquity of my own race. This was not a building, but a machine, protecting itself with forces that had challenged Eternity. Those forces, whatever they might be, were still operating, and perhaps I had already come too close. I thought of all the radiations man had trapped and tamed in the past century. For all I knew, I might be as irrevocably doomed as if I had stepped into the deadly, silent aura of an unshielded atomic pile.

I remember turning then toward Garnett, who had joined me and was now standing motionless at my side. He seemed quite oblivious to me, so I did not disturb him but walked to the edge of the cliff in an effort to marshal my thoughts. There below me lay the Mare Crisium—Sea of Crises, indeed—strange and weird to most men, but reassuringly familiar to me. I lifted my eyes toward the crescent Earth, lying in her cradle of stars, and I wondered what her clouds had covered when these unknown builders had finished their work. Was it the steaming jungle of the Carboniferous, the bleak shoreline over which the first amphibians must crawl to conquer the land—or, earlier still, the long loneliness before the coming of life?

Do not ask me why I did not guess the truth sooner—the truth that seems so obvious now. In the first excitement of my discovery, I had assumed without question that this crystalline apparition had been built by some race belonging to the Moon's remote past, but suddenly, and with overwhelming force, the belief came to me that it was as alien to the Moon as I myself.

In twenty years we had found no trace of life but a few degenerate plants. No lunar civilization, whatever its doom, could have left but a single token of its existence.

I looked at the shining pyramid again, and the more remote it seemed from anything that had to do with the Moon. And suddenly I felt myself shaking with a foolish, hysterical laughter, brought on by excitement and overexertion: for I had imagined that the little pyramid was speaking to me and was saying: "Sorry, I'm a stranger here myself."

It has taken us twenty years to crack that invisible shield and to reach the machine inside those crystal walls. What we could not understand, we broke at last with the savage might of atomic power and now I have seen the fragments of the lovely, glittering thing I found up there on the mountain.

They are meaningless. The mechanisms—if indeed they are mechanisms—of the pyramid belong to a technology that lies far beyond our horizon, perhaps to the technology of paraphysical forces.

The mystery haunts us all the more now that the other planets have been reached and we know that only Earth has ever been the home of intelligent life in our Universe. Nor could any lost civilization of our own world have built that machine, for the thickness of the meteoric dust on the plateau has enabled us to measure its age. It was set there upon its mountain before life had emerged from the seas of Earth.

When our world was half its present age, *something* from the stars swept through the Solar System, left this token of its passage, and went again upon its way. Until we destroyed it, that machine was still fulfilling the purpose of its builders; and as to that purpose, here is my guess.

Nearly a hundred thousand million stars are turning in the circle of the Milky Way, and long ago other races on the worlds of other suns must have scaled and passed the heights that we have reached. Think of such civilizations, far back in time against the fading afterglow of Creation, masters of a Universe so young that life as yet had come only to a handful of worlds. Theirs would have been a loneliness we cannot imagine, the loneliness of gods looking out across infinity and finding none to share their thoughts.

They must have searched the star clusters as we have

searched the planets. Everywhere there would be worlds, but they would be empty or peopled with crawling, mindless things. Such was our own Earth, the smoke of the great volcanoes still staining the skies, when that first ship of the peoples of the dawn came sliding in from the abyss beyond Pluto. It passed the frozen outer worlds, knowing that life could play no part in their destinies. It came to rest among the inner planets, warning themselves around the fire of the Sun and waiting for their stories to begin.

Those wanderers must have looked on Earth, circling safely in the narrow zone between fire and ice, and must have guessed that it was the favorite of the Sun's children. Here, in the distant future, would be intelligence; but there were countless stars before them still, and they might never come this way again.

So they left a sentinel, one of millions they have scattered throughout the Universe, watching over all worlds with the promise of life. It was a beacon that down the ages has been patiently signaling the fact that no one had discovered it.

Perhaps you understand now why that crystal pyramid was set upon the Moon instead of on the Earth. Its builders were not concerned with races still struggling up from savagery. They would be interested in our civilization only if we proved our fitness to survive—by crossing space and so escaping from the Earth, our cradle. That is the challenge that all intelligent races must meet, sooner or later. It is a double challenge, for it depends in turn upon the conquest of atomic energy and the last choice between life and death.

Once we had passed that crisis, it was only a matter of time before we found the pyramid and forced it open. Now its signals have ceased, and those whose duty it is will be turning their minds upon Earth. Perhaps they wish to help our infant civilization. But they must be very, very old, and the old are often insanely jealous of the young.

I can never look now at the Milky Way without wondering from which of those banked clouds of stars the emissaries are coming. If you will pardon so commonplace a simile, we have set off the fire alarm and have nothing to do but to wait.

I do not think we will have to wait for long.

London   *December 1948*

From two of science fiction's greatest storytellers
comes the stunning tale of a civilization
facing its greatest fears and its impending doom.

Isaac Asimov
& Robert Silverberg
NIGHTFALL

In 1941, Isaac Asimov published a short story about a
world whose six suns set simultaneously only once
every 2,049 years. When nightfall comes to the world of
Lagash, its people -- who have never seen the stars --
must deal with the madness that follows. The tale,
"Nightfall," named greatest science fiction story of all
time by the Science Fiction Writers of America, remains
a landmark of the genre.

Now, two of science fiction's greatest names join to tell
this story in all its immensity and splendor with a novel
that explores all the implications of a world facing
ultimate disaster. When academics at Saro University
determine that 12 hours of darkness are coming, a
group of religious fanatics called the Apostles of the
Flame begin to capitalize on the event, preying on the
fear of the general populace by "saving" converts and
damning non-believers. Both groups -- in conflict for
centuries -- know that the coming night will mean the
end of their civilization, for the people of Lagash have a
proven fear of the dark, and in the wake of unspeakable
horrors, must rally to save the fragile remnants of their
world.

Now available in Bantam Spectra paperback.

AN175 -- 8/91

What price human peace and freedom?
What price survival?

The Singers of Time
by Frederik Pohl
and Jack Williamson

Earth has been immeasurably changed by the arrival of the "Turtles," who have conquered Earth without a fight. Who in his right mind would oppose the bringers of peace, prosperity, and plenty of trade goods--especially when the Turtles are offering more than a fair price for everything?

Of course, there was a catch. The first things the Turtles bought were Earth's military establishment and space buses. And the Turtles objected to humans like the Quintero twins who did research in physics and cosmology--studies blasphemous to the Turtles' religious beliefs.

Then, in an instant, everything changed. The Mother, the single female of the Turtle species, disappeared. Suddenly the Turtles needed human help--and a space pilot named Krake, the only human who could fly a Turtle waveship. Drafted to convey a mismatched search party on a mysterious journey, Krake takes off on a hazardous mission that will lead him to the Turtles' Mother planet -- and to the most carefully guarded secrets in the universe.

A science fiction adventure based
on the theories of Stephen Hawking,
The Singers of Time
is a fascinating odyssey through space and time

Coming soon in Bantam Spectra paperback.

AN298 -- 8/91